Published by GeorgeThomasClark.com

ISBN: Trade Paperback – 978-0-9910623-8-6
ISBN: E-Book – 978-0-9883627-0-3

Drawing on the cover: Nina Landgraff

GeorgeThomasClark.com
Bakersfield, CA

Books by
George Thomas Clark

In Other Hands
The Bold Investor
Paint it Blue
Death in the Ring
Obama on Edge
Echoes from Saddam Hussein
Hitler Here
Tales of Romance

Praise for George Thomas Clark and *Hitler Here*

Hitler Here is cleverly constructed using short first-person narratives by the major historical players and personalities of the period. This unique combination of multiple perspectives dynamically brings the period to life; the frustrations and fears of Germany between 1914 and 1945 are made urgent and real to the reader. The novel is painstakingly and excellently researched, but it avoids reading like a textbook by portraying the characters in a human manner and focusing on the mental illnesses, social stigmas, physical defects, and addictions that shaped them. This is not to say that Clark is sympathetic, but rather that he illustrates with precision their frightening madness, cunning, and brutality. Hitler comes alive in a chillingly believable way that makes him even more disturbing. In short, this book answers the question of how an atrocity like the rule of Hitler could happen.

— Historical Novels Review Online

Hitler Here documents Clark's ability to carry an extended and complex plot focused upon Adolf Hitler, his friends and his subordinates. The novel is expertly researched and, instead of a traditional unbroken narrative, offers a collection of first-person reports and views from a variety of figures who piece together a dark, unfolding story of the atrocities of World War II. A compelling tale, all the more horrific for its grounding in truth.

— The Midwest Book Review

An excellent look into Hitler's mind as well as the minds of those around him. Each detail of his life is brought to paper like never before, giving the reader a penetrating view of the man.

— Book Review Café

George Thomas Clark offers a unique synopsis of conversations between Hitler, his cohorts, and his opponents, and brings the reader into their thoughts and feelings. This book is most interesting throughout.

— Lt. Col. Arne Christiansen (retired)

Gripping…The characters come alive…A must read for lovers of history.

— Dr. M. Gautham Machaiah

Hitler Here is one of the best…No, it is the best book about Hitler that I've ever read, and I'm proud to have it in my library.

— The Midnight Bookworm

HITLER HERE

A Biographical Novel

By

George Thomas Clark

CONTENTS

Acknowledgements

I would like to thank the many historians, biographers, politicians, generals, and eyewitnesses who have established a historical record that is both clear and compelling. In particular, I want to emphasize how much I learned from the works of William Shirer, John Toland, Richard Hanser, Max Gallo, Dr. Walter C. Langer, Robert G.L. Waite, Albert Speer, General Heinz Guderian, and General Erich von Manstein. I must, as well, acknowledge that Adolf Hitler — in speeches, private conversations, and in his book, *Mein Kampf* — was startlingly candid, even when trying to deceive, and was therefore the most informative of all. Whenever helpful, I have quoted those who made history; and, in recognition, I offer a list of references at the end of this book. Also, credit Nina Landgraff for a striking cover illustration.

1

PROLOGUE

CONCEPTION
By A Historian

How did this happen? It's really quite logical to begin in the backwoods of Austria with Maria Ana Schiklgruber, a plump and childless peasant already in her forties, and Georg Heidler, a shiftless and unstable moron. No one wants either of them so they end up together, and their sad union produces a child, Alois Shicklgruber, who they naturally are unable to take care of and who is raised by Georg's younger brother.

Alois, by a not small genetic miracle, proves to be made of better stuff and grows into a fine looking and formidable customs agent, and has enough status to summon his sixteen-year old second cousin to serve as his live-in maid. Klara is rather simple and plain but not without a certain ripeness and sexual heat. Picture, if you will, her dallying with Alois in the room next to where his sick wife lies in bed. And why, we should ask, has Alois married a woman fourteen years older? He wants her patrimony. That's rather greedy for a fellow who already has a good salary. But don't judge Alois harshly. Nay, I say we should commend him for vigor and ambition. Almost every day he leaves his apartment at the Pommer Inn in Brannau and strides downstairs to the room of Fanni, a maid who so pleases him that he sends Klara home.

Soon Alois ostensibly has an ideal life. His ugly old wife moves out and dutifully dies, and he marries the pregnant Fanni, and they have two children in a marriage that's going to last, and Klara's probably going to be stuck with a dunce or in spinsterhood. But she gets lucky. Fanni contracts tuberculosis, and Alois summons Klara to care for his wife. And, though I'm uncomfortable admitting it, I still admire Alois' spirit. Right away he's back in bed with Klara, and she gets pregnant just before Fanni dies.

The first, second, and third children of Alois and Klara Hitler also die, and when Adolf arrives his mother nurses and scrubs him with uncommon dedication, and worriedly checks his little scrotum every day, hoping a second testicle will soon descend. That doesn't help, and neither does this — one evening Alois comes home drunk and in a hurry, and as he pounds Klara little Adolf runs in and she frantically waves get away, she's got no time for him now. But she usually does. He's her special surviving boy and not going to die.

"Alois also has important plans for the boy, especially after he decks Adolf's thirteen-year old half-brother, Alois, Jr., and sends the boy scuffing away down the road toward a couple of stints in prison. Now Adolf is the oldest male to survive, and it's his duty to uphold the status of the Hitler name, which Alois has selected as a stronger version of Heidler. Regrettably, the boy is unmotivated, and Alois slaps his face for flunking his first year at the Realschule. A few months later, Adolf is certainly obedient enough, albeit glum, as his father takes him on a tour of the customs station where he served his highest rank and final duty. The old man, in fact, continues to control him until the instant he falls out of his chair, dead from a stroke in his favorite tavern.

Adolf, then only thirteen and the unrivalled man of the house, intensifies his disregard for authority and withdraws further inside a suffering self. Indeed, the disconsolate boy can't help being what he is. And it's certainly his right — even his destiny — to scowl and feel bad and be unable to interact in a normal way. There'll always be lots of people like him, quitting school at age sixteen, getting drunk for the first (and only) time, and losing his certificate for that year's work. That's understandable. But this next part is rather unusual. He's in the school director's office to seek a duplicate for his mother. And he waits and waits, terribly hung-over and nervous, until the frowning director marches out and hands him his original certificate torn into four pieces and used for toilet paper. It's easy to imagine how ashamed he is, but incomprehensible why so many times he tells people about it.

He's a strange and lethargic lad, daily sleeping until noon in the only bedroom; his mother and little sister, Paula, who's a half-wit, have to sleep in the living room. They're gone now, and Adolf's struggling to get up, and he looks so tired and bored as he fiddles with a sketch then writes a few lines before he paints a bit then reads a book soon shoved under the bed so he can scan the newspapers. He has so many hobbies he has no task. Up two hours and he's already out on the couch, staring at the ceiling, and there's his mother walking in to say, "Adolf, listen to me, do you hear me? Look at my hand. My hand is pointing at your father's pipes. Your father's pipes are on the shelf. Do you see them? I've placed them there for an important reason. They're living representatives of your father and represent what he said. Look at them. You will obey him and go to work. His picture on the wall is looking at you now. Don't think your father is dead in every way. He isn't. He's here and so are his pipes."

Luckily for Adolf, the old gentleman is thoroughly dead or he'd have kicked him out into the mundane world of daily work, and Adolf wouldn't have been spending his mother's dwindling cash to buy tweed suits and broad brimmed hats and black gloves and go to the opera so often. He's fortunate his only friend, Gustl Kubizek, not merely tolerates but is enchanted by his loud and impromptu speeches about tearing down the hideous old buildings of Linz to clear space for spectacular new structures he'll design and that will soar beyond anything ever. If he really believes he's so great, why is he following that pretty blond Stefanie walking down the street? He's virtually stalking her, and every day tells Gustl he loves her; but he's much too scared to speak to her or even let her see him. That's unfortunate.

In 1907, at age eighteen, Adolf is confronted by an even more painful problem: a surgeon has to amputate his mother's cancerous breast. Klara is certainly brave and selfless as she suffers. Her hunchback sister, Johanna, despite those schizophrenic symptoms, is there to help. Adolf also has a hunchback cousin. But I digress. Some months later, just before Christmas, a shriveled Klara tells Gustl Kubizek to keep being her son's good friend because he has no one else.

I suppose it's better his mother didn't know the Academy of Fine Art in Vienna has already rejected him. That would've only worried her more. So would this scene in his cramped apartment in Vienna. His friend Gustl is up early and out at music school and work, and Adolf is still staggering out of bed at noon, and walking in a haze and loafing in the usual ways until he starts composing an opera despite not having any musical training. That's troubling, but not as much as his reading racist pamphlets — those Aryan clarions — with such passion. Look at him. He's outraged by what he's told. The Jews are lazy. Lazy? Well, my goodness, the dear boy is setting the standard in that regard. And he's reading that the Jews are sexual deviates of a particularly uncouth sort. Isn't that ironic?

At this stage, however, Adolf is incapable of any sort of intimacy. He can't even tell Gustl when the Academy of Fine Arts rejects him again. He undoubtedly hurts, walking into that huge and ornate building and looking at those lists and not seeing his name in the good column and, finally, having to read that his drawings were "done with insufficient success." Hell, name a medium and an artist and you'll see a wave of rejections. He doesn't have to hide from Kubizek and everyone else and scurry into a rat hole to wait until his modest inheritance runs out.

It's 1909, he's twenty years old, and black clouds are swirling, and the first raindrop hammers him, and he can only lean forward to keep walking into a park to look for the biggest and bushiest trees. Some of them have broad branches with plenty of leaves. Nevertheless, the rain is penetrating him and his knapsack, and beyond the trees he sees shiny, fast racing rain that's much wetter and faster than the rain where he is. All night he cringes under a downpour loud in the leaves, and in the morning he stands there skinny white and naked, and everything's wet, and his paintings and sketches are destroyed, and he begins roaming for weeks, sleeping on and under benches until it gets very cold and he scurries into a cavernous pipe and curls up with his back to the other bums.

It's sad to see anyone have to beg. Can you image? There is Adolf Hitler asking cultured Viennese for handouts. Most tell him to get away. That humiliates him, but he hears when the other bums talk about, the Hostel for the Homeless, owned by Jews. They take him in and provide his first shower and decent meal in three months. And he meets Reinhold Hanisch. What a character he is, full of hot air but an experienced man of the road who soon takes him across town to more permanent quarters in the Home for Men.

Now Adolf's got a cubicle to sleep in and almost every morning he's down by the big window in the reading room, sketching forms from photographs of Viennese scenes and filling them in with watercolors. And Hanisch easily sells his paintings until Adolf stops working regularly. Then he claims Hanisch cheats him and he lies right there in court about the worth of his work, but Hanisch produces receipts. Yes, that's troubling. So is his ranting in the reading room that Germany — his Germany, where he's never been — will need to absorb Austria and a lot of Poland as well as northern Italy and Switzerland and Bohemia. That, incidentally, is a prominent view of the time.

Adolf isn't going to change anything. He's merely a bigmouth calling a muscular deliveryman a political imbecile and filthy dog, and the fellow charges him and — boom — belts him with a right straight to the mouth, knocking him back into a wall, and puts a fist in front of his nose and says no more shit.

Most people, we should emphasize, definitely want to help him. There's Jakob Altenburg saying, "Good morning, Herr Hitler," as Adolf enters his art gallery, and as usual he buys everything Adolf brings him. So do most of Altenburg's colleagues. That's pretty good for a painter in his early twenties. Many artists never go as far as he already has. He still needs to improve, of course. He needs to grow. And I certainly endorse his plan to go to Munich. But before that journey, we learn something else that, frankly, is troubling.

There Adolf is at the bedside of his dying hunchback Aunt Johanna, and he's telling her he's the best student in art school but can only survive if he gets a modest loan. A loan? Hell, he bilks her out of her entire estate. At least he doesn't get everything until she dies.

Well, on to Munich. What a beautiful city. Munich. What a beautiful sound. Look at him headed there on the train. He's glowing, absolutely glowing. I've never seen him so happy. Let's listen to his thoughts: "Tormented since childhood by a secret desire for a secret love, I at last open my arms and venture forth to the beckoning bosom of my mother country. This special reunion begins on a vivid spring day as the train brings me into Munich where architectural delights at once proclaim this city the absolute creative center of the world. Also, for the first time in my life, I hear people speaking good clear German, and am thrilled to be surrounded by the music of real Germans instead of the garbled grunts of a mad mix of Austrian mongrels. In this new and special setting, I am naturally drawn to the Schwabing District, the celebrated home of artistic souls. And after an extraordinary day of exploration, I rent a furnished room and sleep with the warmest feelings I've had since childhood.

"In Munich my whole life soon becomes infused with a new spirit of belonging, and every morning I'm so inspired I bound to my easel, which is perched ready with a canvas held high and also ready. Now I paint larger pictures of pretty scenes, and am nauseated by the new Expressionist paintings slobbered on canvases by lunatics who burn their time blabbering in sidewalk cafes. Unlike those pretentious artists, I'm very productive and can't stand even to look at them. Walking by I invariably keep my face pointed straight ahead and bear no expression."

The young man, even allowing for the subjectivity of personal taste, is limited. He doesn't realize how good the Expressionists are, and that their powerful work foretells chaos. He can only see the literal and envisions nothing. He needs to try to create his own world instead of cranking out rather pretty but otherwise undistinguished city scenes and landscapes. He claims he would've been a great artist if political events hadn't intervened. I don't think so, but he might've tried.

DISCOVERY
1914-1924

THE GREAT WAR
By Adolf Hitler

I heard crowds rumbling in the Munich streets below my room and ran downstairs to discover that the heir to the Austro-Hungarian throne, Archduke Francis Ferdinand, had been murdered. At first I was silent with regret, fearing the bullets were fired by German patriots aghast at Ferdinand's ceaseless Slavization of what should have been a German empire. But when precise news arrived it was a delight, for it was a Serb who had just killed the greatest friend of the Serbs.

Now senile Austria had to act. In the southeastern section of the empire there lurked a morbid and hostile foe whose manifest intent was to chop itself free of the monarchy and form a Slavic state. An enraged Germanic population would have revolted against the Hapsburg monarchy had it not declared war on Serbia in late July 1914. Russia then mobilized against Austria, and Germany gave Russia an ultimatum to demobilize by high noon the next day. When the hour arrived with no response, Kaiser Wilhelm signed the instrument of attack. Germany was at war, and I stood trembling with a huge happy throng outside the Hall of Field Marshals. That afternoon I wrote a personal petition to King Ludwig of Bavaria and beseeched him to let me join one of his regiments. Due to the overwhelming events I expected a delay in response to my simple request but had to wait only overnight for the letter telling me I was assigned to a Bavarian regiment. As I carefully folded my cherished document, I was struck by deep throbbing fear the war might end before I arrived.

I begged authorities to let me start training at once, and every day for the next two weeks I marched, ran, crawled, and climbed until my lungs burned and sweat oozed all over my face and body, turning dirt into mud. Like everyone else, I was so happy when the time came to go to the war. We took a nice train and saw our Rhine River for the first time and all sang "Die Wacht Am Rhine," and we were very excited. We knew victory was assured and were anxious to meet the French. Soon we engaged them often, and I served as a daring and dependable dispatch carrier, and learned much about modern war, and so did we all. Many could not deal with the eternal wait to be menaced in tall trenches deep-watered filthy and stinking with death. But I could handle it, and I liked it. I was also blessed by Providence. Everyone remarked about a shot ripping off my sleeve without hurting me. And one night a voice in my head told me to get up and move just before a shell blew up everyone where I had been sitting. I did not have to be afraid, not even the day our artillery in the rear was booming, and the shells were exploding short and killing front line Germans. I, too, was in a bunker near the front, and French machinegun fire crisscrossed all around, ricocheting threats among exploding death.

"We need volunteers to take a message," said the commander.

Most of the men averted their eyes, but right away I stepped forward and said, "I'll do it."

Eventually a few others agreed also to try.

"Maybe one of you can get through," said the commander.

Grim and determined I sprang into hell, crouching on the run as bullets ripped by, and I kept churning, even as others fell, until I delivered the message. Everyone was so impressed. I was awarded the Iron Cross First Class for valor, and proudly I wore my medal.

I loved duty and never wanted to leave, especially for Christmas, and did not want to receive any letters or packages, or go into infected places, either. I had to concentrate always on the threat and hated anyone who spoke of pain or surrender or defeat. I did not even want to leave when I was wounded in the thigh. I asked to stay but they put me on a train heading east out of France and back into Germany where I was shocked by congregations of greasy bearded faces that complained about the rigors of a war they were not fighting. They were fomenting, and Germany was being ravaged within. I had to get back to war as soon as possible.

COMMANDER
By Hugo Gutmann

Adolf Hitler followed my orders and transported messages faithfully under perilous conditions. Everyone knew he was worthy of the Iron Cross First Class because I said so. I said give Corporal Hitler his due. But he sometimes acted arrogantly and even ignored his obligation to salute me as his superior.

WAR ART
By Adolf Hitler

When I could not find duty I sat on anything available and opened my pack to withdraw sketching and painting materials. There was much original material now, and I was better and more mature. I loved my Sunken Lane. I painted it soon after the day scores of German soldiers were slaughtered there. My painting was a dark muddy Sunken Lane with many dead bare trees standing stark on each side and represented well the corpses even though they were no longer there.

I loved to draw the ruins of war. There was something heroic about charred and shattered buildings. They had stood and taken it and were in part still standing. It was easy for any shrewd observer to see that my scenes of destruction, though placid and gray, automatically implied the horror that befell the people who had built and existed in what was no longer there.

I was good at spontaneous drawings of soldiers and did not think while doing them. I worked rapidly, and the sketches came out jaunty and crisp. My best was On the Road to Cannes. I depicted our platoon during a tired but spirited journey on foot. Spiked caps crowned our uplifted heads, and we were happy to be leaving what was no longer there.

STABBED IN THE BACK
By Adolf Hitler

We were in a slithering trench on a small hill in western Belgium, and as big shells whistled at us we stuck our faces in the mud. For hours the shells shredded earth and flesh, but we did not leave. We were determined and we stayed. When it got dark they started shooting shells of gas that our masks did not stop, and they shot at us all night. I could not keep my eyes open long because there were so many tears and they felt like acid in my eyes.

In the morning everything was dim and distorted, and I had trouble seeing some of my comrades who had inhaled too much gas and gone crazy breathing out blood. I was still alive, and said I could take a message to battalion headquarters. I must have been able to get the message there. Definitely, I was soon on a train bound east for a hospital in East Prussia, our cradle of militarism. Even if I could have risen as high as the window, I would not have seen a thing.

I was blind and mute in bed, and I was tired and disheveled and distraught. With my eyes on fire I thought I would never see to paint again. I still held hope, trapped in my darkened abyss, that our enemies could yet be defeated. And in a few weeks, as my vision and voice gradually returned, I was ready for duty. But by the fall of 1918 the nation had been gravely weakened by treachery, and then the November Criminals surrendered her. When I received word of the armistice, my eyes again began to burn and my voice disappeared, and I had to stagger blindly back to my bed where I submerged my face under the covers and tried to withstand the horror of the bloody rape taking place. I was as betrayed as our nation, and after many black days I once again was contacted by eternal Providence and told of my mission: someday, I had to act.

Now, back in my barracks in Bavaria, I could only watch in anguish as Jews and communists rioted and ruined us here and all over Germany, crushing us under the bloody Star of David. And when the wretched new government in Berlin signed the shameful Treaty of Versailles, even the dead surely realized we had been stabbed in the back.

THE MEETING WAS MINE
By Adolf Hitler

A few weeks ago I uncovered some traitors in the barracks, and they got shot. Since then the Army had ordered me to monitor the schemers in dozens of political organizations around Munich. My assignment for this 1919 night was the German Workers Party. It had a meeting pigeonholed in the dank back room of a small old beer hall. Perhaps three dozen lower class men were present, and their boring speaker would have forced me instantly out the door had I not been required to stay long enough to get a report. A discussion followed the speech, and everything said was shallow and insignificant. To me it was obvious the German Workers Party could never be anything but a small congregation of bumblers. I was thoroughly embarrassed to be among them and standing to leave when an impertinent little man got up and spouted, "Jews aren't the problem. Bavaria needs to separate from militaristic Prussia and form a union with peace loving Austria."

Firing to my feet I said, "You're a liar and an idiot. Jews are the ultimate problem. First, they ensnare the masses with high interest loans. Then they conspire to rig the stock market and swindle German workers before loaning the money back to those who've already earned what they're now borrowing. And Austria, for God's sake. Austria's absolutely infested with the same garbage that's ruined our Germany and put us where we are. And this lout wants us to suffer more."

An astonished audience watched as the man scampered away like a wet poodle with water flying. Again I tried to leave, but just before I reached the door someone grabbed my arm, and I was pulled around facing the tall silly-faced man who had sat at the front table during the meeting. Behind his smile loomed the pasty wan look of not having been well in a while, and he shoved a slender pink pamphlet into my hand, closed my fist and urged, "Please read this and come back again."

I turned away, and not until walking back to the barracks did I glance at the title, My Political Awakening, which did not intrigue me, nor did the author, Anton Drexler, whoever he was. I was thinking about mice and walking faster now as I concentrated on the fun I'd have. Right after arriving in my room I put crumbs on the floor, then lay quietly in bed, hunched happily on my side. When those droll little creatures started making that soft scratching little sound, I felt very good and was proud to help them avoid some of the devouring hunger I'd suffered in my youth.

Later that night I could not sleep. It seemed I never really slept. I wished I could. I needed to escape. Instead, I groped for the light and sat up wondering what to do. Each minute chewed on me until I noticed the pink pamphlet on top of my paper pile. I picked it up and decided to give Drexler a chance. Soon, with mounting pleasure, I realized he understood the threat posed by the Jew, and was shrewd putting two words together: National Socialism. I did not know if I had put those together before Drexler, but the pamphlet was good, and I reviewed it twice during the week before putting it back on the pile. In a few days, to my surprise and consternation, I received a presumptuous postcard congratulating me for being a new member of the German Workers Party. I had not asked and was not interested. Only curiosity prompted me to accept their invitation to the next meeting. Regret hammered me the instant I saw the dilapidated restaurant. Moving in tentatively on my toes, wishing to be elsewhere, I passed through the deserted dining room to a small back room where four men sat at a table in front of a not much larger group of grubby men. Within a second of entering, the pusher of pink pamphlets scooted over and double pumped my hand and irritated me with the loud exhortation: "Here's the bigmouth Austrian who's going to spread our word."

I was given a seat up front facing the committee. Soon a seedy shrimp of a fellow limped in, and the pamphleteer, Anton Drexler, came over and took both our arms and introduced me to Karl Harrer, national chairman of the German Workers Party. Drexler was the Munich chairman.

For an excruciating period the members read and discussed in earnest a letter they had received from Nuremberg, and did the same with their letter in response to Nuremberg, and they just sat up there congratulating each other as if a single missive represented a national groundswell. This whole thing was dreadful. No real political party would be like this. They had nothing: no leadership, no organization, not even a rubber stamp. This was the group beseeching me to join it.

* * *

The typing was very boring, but I could not avoid it. We had dull every-Wednesday-night committee meetings with the same six stupid faces staring at me in the corner of a small cafe, and all they ever did was act like tea drinkers, and there could never be any action unless I borrowed an Army typewriter and sat down to pound out hundreds of slips announcing the German Workers Party's first public meeting. My next task was worse. I had always viewed people who hand out notices as sycophantic boobs too shallow for important work. That's what they looked like, with faces so simple they seemed almost begging passersby to stop and take one. When passing out my slips, I maintained firmness, and surely no one mistook me for a stupid handyman.

On the night of the meeting, as we sat and waited, some committee members groaned: "We shouldn't be doing this. There might be disagreements, even violence."

"So what?" I said. "We have to open up and grow."

Only several people came. The committeemen gloated and Karl Harrer snorted, "Well, Hitler, this is most impressive."

Glancing at his clubfoot, I said, "The meeting in two weeks will be much better."

To the few faithful in attendance I spoke as if to a multitude, and finished by asking them to help the cause by bringing three people each to the next meeting.

In a few days, overwhelmed by urgency, I faced fellow committee members and said, "You have, gentlemen, repeatedly forgotten or failed to absorb the most essential maxim of political growth, that of embracing the heart of the masses and skillfully manipulating it with propaganda. It is therefore mandatory for the health of the party that I become our official propagandist, effective immediately."

A few grumbled but I ignored them and began to spend savings from my still active Army salary to have our red announcements and posters mimeographed in bulk and distributed in town as well as the barracks. At subsequent meetings I stationed a man to examine everyone, and he counted eleven then thirteen and soon three dozen new listeners. After my speeches, which were always well received, we asked for donations in the name of a party ready to forsake half measures and do what must be done.

Now, unmistakably, was the moment to leave dingy cafes and project our ideas before large audiences in significant places. For that I lobbied loudly and also pointed a lot. A few insolent souls agreed with our crippled and ill-spoken national chairman who said, "The party'll be committing suicide if we hold a meeting in a large hall, and few show up."

"There's no reason to fear that. This time we'll also advertise in the Volkischer Beobachter."

Out into Munich I went to seek a site just right for speaking. I entered taverns and restaurants and even a few warehouses, and everywhere I stood listening to my echo, trying to determine which place was conducive to success of this first major test. My first stride into a magnificent beer hall built me way up. I felt the air lift me up to the high open ceiling, and I floated high over the long room, feeling vibrations of what it would be like to fill this hall with people roaring

Heil. An employee of the Hofbrauhaus stepped toward me, his voice resounding into empty space as he said, "I see you haven't been here before."

"I've come to rent the place for a night. How much will it cost?"

His response drilled me.

"Oh yes," he said. "This is the biggest beer hall in all the world. It is a very good price for that."

At first I certainly was insulted by his suggestion I rent the cellar. No offense remained after I walked down to see a place impressive enough to reserve for an October 1919 night. That meeting commenced with a forgettable speaker who left a hundred people in silence. I then stepped behind a wobbly lectern, straightened it with two outstretched hands, and thanked the men for coming and told them they were witnessing the birth of a movement. I explained the need for a vigorous new voice in politics and patiently enumerated the horrors that had befallen Germany. Then I thundered: "We need good, brave, patriotic men like you to help end the misery. We can again be strong and free and dominant. I know that's what you really want. You should. That's your birthright. But you will have none of your rights so long as they're being stolen from within. Germany can only be revived if you, in the mightiest Teutonic tradition, pick up your broadswords and smite those who are hurting you."

While this modest room beneath the world's biggest beer hall shook with approval, hypocritical Harrer limped to the lectern and asked for donations. I acted like I did not notice money taken out of pockets. The rest of the night was a dream. Three hundred marks were slapped into our coffers.

Funds gleaned from our first mass meeting were plied to preparations for the second. Advertising was increased and we rented a slightly larger beer cellar where more than one-hundred sixty were seated as I stated: "The lie you have all heard a thousand times. The lie states that Germany should not complain about having to live with the terms of the Treaty of Versailles because Germany had done far worse to Russia in March 1918 by making it sign the Treaty of Brest-Litovsk. That is scandalous nonsense, for the two are as different as dark and light. At Brest-Litovsk we merely wanted to absorb free floating states that had often been gateways of invasion into our homeland. Russia certainly had no intrinsic claim on those areas. We'd earned them with overwhelming victories on the battlefields of the Great War.

"Our enemies, by contrast, didn't win anything in battle. German troops still occupied foreign soil when we were stabbed in the back. This unparalleled treachery has emboldened the Versailles bandits not only to strip us of war winnings but also to tear mortal flesh from our nation and give it to Belgium and France and Poland and Denmark. Our colonies have also been stolen. And that bloody pillage isn't nearly enough to satisfy those who hate us. While we starve here in Germany, they're preparing to drain us of billions of gold marks annually. And why are we to be punished with such high reparations? According to our enemies, it's because Germany is solely responsible for the war and must accordingly bear all guilt.

"Gentlemen, I must tell you tonight: there is more outrage still. Our enemies have limited our Army, the finest in the world, to one hundred thousand men and no panzers. Our incomparable German General Staff has also been abolished, and the Navy reduced to insignificance. Versailles has taken our land, our traditions, and our hope. We must rise and resist the way things are going. Germany misery can only be broken by German iron."

* * *

Catapulted by thunderous approval, I soon held forth before a crowd of two hundred, and within weeks my words shot off the roof over four hundred loud and lively souls. Now no sane individual could doubt my worth and rectitude. And I hoped Munich's countless self-proclaimed Volkisch experts would stop arguing that only they understood nature's plan of vigorous growth for the Aryan race. If these Volkisch Methuselahs really had so much insight, why were they still in the same dank back rooms where they'd always been? And why were the German folk so thoroughly in the yoke of other races?

"I'm not for an instant going to stand flat with my hands in my pockets watching people cling to yesterday and all its horrors," I told committee members early in 1920. "Those who still don't have the basic gall to stand up and do something decisive are no longer going to have a voice in this party. We have a mission to carry out. In only four months we've risen from a humble and ineffectual kettle club to become a movement genuinely on the eve of major emergence. Now we can make our next move. Herr Drexler and I will formulate and write out our official party program in points to be presented later to our biggest audience yet."

Despite reservations, I decided to let Drexler put some of his socialist ideas into the program. I drew up the main points, twenty-five in all. We showed them to the committee at the next private meeting. Most members seemed enthusiastic, and before anyone could distract me I bounded up and said, "Gentlemen, this occasion calls for the boldest possible step. That step, appropriately enough, is to unveil the official party program before a vibrant crowd in the huge hall of the Hofbrauhaus, in whose very cellar we launched our first big public meeting."

"At least we could afford the cellar," said Karl Harrer. "We can't realistically afford the hall."

"I keep wondering about you, Harrer. You've criticized every little setback and ignored all our big gains. Now you want to hold the party back from its greatest opportunity. What are your motives? They must be personal. Let me finish. Shut up. Exactly what I said was true. Everyone can see it's true. It is palpably true. I can scream too. Everybody here knows the party must grow."

The night of February twenty-fourth was cold, and a little snow drifted down sideways onto the ground. In my trench coat, outside the Hofbrauhaus, I shivered as I wondered if publicity had been adequate to entice people out of warm homes into the brisk Bavarian night. What if Harrer is right, I thought? What if only a few scraggly souls come, and everywhere there are only echoes and uncertainties? What if the party does go broke?

UPROAR
By A Police Reporter

My contacts tipped me the communists were going to stomp the new group of radical nationalists on their big night. Accordingly, I stationed myself a little further from the podium than usual. You didn't need to be close to hear Hitler shriek, "We demand," as he introduced each of twenty-five points. After explaining, he jammed his fists into his hips and stared at a capacity audience before he pronounced: "Do you understand the point and agree?"

Dozens of big beer mugs hurled toward Hitler tailed off short and cracked heads where I would have been. Flying froth still dampened my ears. I was baffled by the uproar. The German Workers Party platform offered something for almost everyone: trust busting and profit sharing, maternity welfare and old age pensions, and a promise of vigorous militarism. At numerous political meetings I had seen similar points received with ennui.

Several speakers followed Hitler, who, sitting on stage, was uncomfortable with their dull talk and kept shifting in his chair, rumpling an already frazzled blue suit whose cuffs clung to his shins. I was impressed, however, that he had worked so hard sweat soaked through his coat and formed a big circle under each arm.

I QUIT
By Karl Harrer

I was not there. I did not care about any twenty-five points. A few days before, I had told party members that was enough. Hitler was alienating the workers, the very people our party was founded to protect. And I was appalled to see how people reacted to his speeches. I knew his lunatic speaking style would soon shock all the common people away.

I was also very much opposed to the intensity of Hitler's anti-Semitism. I was anti-Semitic, too, and opposed economic exploitation by Jews, but I did not like the way Hitler cursed and gestured about them. That was the same way he did about me.

FARSIGHTED ME
By Dietrich Eckart

I liked the strongest of beers because I stood tall and thick with a very big gut and only a lot of any strong beer could get me like I wanted to be. My favorites were brewed very dark brown and ominous, and I drank big mugs fast lest the mounds of food I downed weaken the brew. At home I often had several snorts of whiskey before going to taverns, and when I stepped inside I boomed hearty hellos to partisans who awaited me, and felt the focused force of the shots burning my big ulcer before the booze did its job and provided sedation with appropriate disorientation.

My table on this convivial night was lined long and full on both sides, as usual, and I was raucous with suggestions about what fate should befall the plundering enemies of Germany. "For the Jews," I said, "should come forced cramming into boxcars for a quick trip to the bottom of the Red Sea. They wouldn't be agitating among us then, would they?"

Cheers and clinks from toasted mugs greeted my statement. I loved to smile wide, and my broad mouth was big open, but my mirth was soon ruptured by the sad open faces that looked hopefully at me. Their supplication was clear.

"What kind of man would it take to become the great Fuehrer who can liberate Germany?" said one, speaking for all.

That was perhaps my favorite of all questions, and I had already assimilated talents, characteristics and subtleties into an image of Germany's most ideal man. I put down my mug hard, as a gavel, and drew a long breath into my round robust frame before I declared: "The man who will liberate Germany must be a brave one who can flourish despite the sound of machine-gun bullets whirring around him. He can't be a long-tailed priggish politician, and he can't be an officer. No one respects them anymore. The right Fuehrer should come not from the aristocracy that has failed us but from the solid core of the working class. That'll bring support from the masses, and if he's a bachelor, as he should be, then he can get the women, too. He really doesn't have to be very bright because politics isn't a game of intellect. Our man just needs to be able to talk, talk, talk."

Of course I was ecstatic to soon hear Hitler. Right after the speech I charged around people heading up front and clasped his slender right hand with both of my ham hands. He looked shyly up at me and said, "I enjoyed so much your great translation of Peer Gynt."

"My friend," I said, "your artistry with words has given me pleasure and reason to believe the fate of Germany is every day improving."

I could see I'd have to scrub some of the backwoods off Hitler. His scruffy clothes were all right with me but not good enough to deal with the kings of money and industry. In a few days, leaving a restaurant, I saw there in a store window the trench coat I'd hoped to find. Rushing over, I held it next to my body and sensed it would fit right on Hitler's slim shoulders and taper in dashing fashion.

Despite his improved appearance, Hitler was often stiff as a scolded schoolboy during our forays through Munich's prestigious points of food and drink, and I'd say, "Come on and have a beer. That'll loosen your belly up."

He always refused alcohol but sometimes relaxed a little when I introduced him as Germany's Messiah. Wealthy patrons could tell he was an unusual guy, and they gave generously to our best hope for resurgence. We certainly needed that. In March 1920 the Allied Control Commission thrashed our faces again, ordering nine hundred esteemed military leaders to be betrayed and turned over for trial as war criminals. This outrage was exacerbated by the gross demand that sixty thousand men be immediately removed from the armed forces. Many of these men were in the Ehrhardt Brigade, which had liberated Munich from the communists a year before, and battered the Poles and Russians in and out of the Reich to save everyone from a burial in red. Now the same shameless Social Democratic government the Ehrhardt Brigade had protected was trying to make everyone go home jobless.

A few high ranking officers in the Berlin military district conferred with nationalist bureaucrats and decided not only not to disband the Ehrhardt Brigade but to send President Friedrich Ebert and his charlatans an ultimatum demanding new elections, suppression of strikes, censorship of the press, and in general a set of principles in tune with Teutonic greatness. When the ultimatum was rejected,

Commander Ehrhardt and his Free Corps stalwarts goose-stepped toward Berlin from their suburban barracks.

The sun had just risen cold and unseen behind gray clouds as the Ehrhardt Brigade strode straight-legged and brisk into unguarded Berlin. General von Seeckt, the Chief of the General Staff, refused to stop the invasion and proclaimed: "Our troops do not fire on our troops." President Ebert and his timid cabinet had already deserted Berlin before dawn, and the most authoritative figure in town was the champion of the right himself, General Erich Ludendorff, who had recently returned from exile in Sweden. Joining Ludendorff near Brandenburg Gate was the man just named Chancellor of Germany — Dr. Wolfgang Kapp.

In Munich, contacts told Hitler and me that military officials were delighted by the Kapp Putsch. In fact, on the night of the same day, March thirteenth, Army officers in Bavaria ousted the Social Democratic government and installed Gustav von Kahr as dictator. Kahr, long an official of the now-abolished Bavarian monarchy, knew how to behave.

The Army planned to send a liaison officer to Berlin to coordinate communication between the respective military regimes. Hitler, an enlisted man, volunteered for the mission. His new commander, a forceful captain named Ernst Roehm, gave him permission to go and allowed me to accompany.

We had a very damp and windy cold flight in an open little airplane, and Hitler kept looking down at obscure gray ground, then glancing at me, horrified.

"Don't worry," I said. "Our pilot won the pour le mérite."

I jostled in the turbulence no less than Hitler, but it was he who heaved. The first time, he didn't turn his head, and the wind wetted his face. Later, he did turn, and streaked the side of the plane all the way back to the tail.

Lamenting he was lost, our pilot began to descend to the nearest airfield, and we could see scores of men in civilian clothes running around like midgets with toy rifles in hand. Just before we landed, Hitler stuck on a goatee.

"Who are you?" a traitor asked, fingering his trigger.

"He's my accountant, and I'm a merchant," I said. "We've business in Berlin."

"Political business?"

"Certainly not. I sell clothes."

"That's fortunate."

LESSONS LEARNED
By Adolf Hitler

Cold gray Berlin lay in disarray, and we had to hold our noses every time we passed a pile of rotting garbage.

"What the hell's happening, and where's the Free Corps?" Eckart shouted to an empty street masked by boarded windows.

We wandered, and aggravated our confusion. Eventually, a citizen with an old wooden wagon and two skinny horses offered a ride. Around the debris he maneuvered a hideous trail to the Chancellery. Few people were there, and most scurried in and out of offices, hurrying to leave.

"Where's Chancellor Kapp?" I shouted.

My query hastened the pace of departure, and Eckart and I pivoted and false-started before dashing down several vacant halls, looking for something but finding nothing until up to us ran a very big and presumptuous looking Jew.

"I'm Trebitsch Lincoln, press secretary for Chancellor Kapp," he said.

Eckart looked away, disgusted, ready to leave.

"Where is Kapp?" I said.

"He's en route to Sweden. The Putsch is over. You men are the ones from Munich? Well, thank you for coming anyway. There's nothing for you to do here. Don't let them find out who you are."

Lincoln gave us a sly half-smile and turned and walked hastily away. Eckart and I locked eyes in unstated revulsion: only a debacle could account for an elephant-nose Jew dealing with the public.

Soon enough, from gracious aristocrats, we learned a few details. For more thorough information we conferred with a bevy of nationalists and also had the thrill of meeting the illustrious General Ludendorff. He and other patriots characterized Kapp as a jowly, agricultural bureaucrat who wound up leading a revolution solely because he had always stridently supported German expansion. Those who installed him should have realized they needed a Fuehrer, not a

Volkisch fat ass.

Kapp was so contemptible that most people had ignored his orders, and the State Bank even refused to pay the new government's bills. Meanwhile, the exiled President Ebert was scheming to prepare the ultimate paralysis: a general strike. Twelve million workers honored his wanton call, and the current state of chaos began to envelop Berlin. Despite Commander Ehrhardt's repeated warnings to shoot strike leaders, Kapp had delayed. Finally, he agreed but soon backed down. The Ehrhardt Brigade had then begun a silent and slack-kneed march out of town. As the men filed by a crowd, they were cursed by an outrageous boy. Two troopers leaped from the line and pounced on the wretch with rifle butts to the head. He was dead under jackboots before his wailing father could interfere. Numerous do-gooders screamed obscenities at the Free Corps and did not shut up when so ordered. An officer instructed his men to ready rifles and machine guns, then bellowed: "Fire."

Righteous force was indisputably needed. Sixty thousand traitorous workers, calling themselves a Red Army, were ransacking the Ruhr while an obscene Soviet Republic in Saxony held cities hostage and made dire threats. The cycle of festering decay was in fact entirely unavoidable. Every time I took a walk in Berlin, I was accosted.

"Come on, there's nothing worthwhile here," I urged Dietrich Eckart.

He fanned kisses from beefy paws, waving and laughing. "Don't frown so much. Life is comprised of more than politics, lad, be sure of that."

"This is the opposite of life," I said. "Look around."

The once saintly status of German motherhood was being shattered by middle-aged women who roamed back and forth along the gutters, trying to convince men to defile them. And what would the future be with girls now ten or so stalking around in painted faces and dresses that bared skinny legs up to the crotch? I could not long stand to watch this lustful abomination of decency. No one approached these misguided girls while I was there, but by the grace of righteous German womanhood, I swear I would have attacked anyone who did. Eckart agreed about that.

We also had to pass several ultimate havens of degeneracy, the homosexual fleshpots. I refused to enter any Babylonian abyss but peeped through doors and windows and saw men hugging and kissing each other with all the ardor of slobbering lunatics. And out of these joints they came, arm in arm, strolling toward home to do you know what. I assuredly was moved to regurgitate more than once at the sight of so many clinging pederasts.

We returned to Munich at the end of March. And on April third all patriots were delighted by news that Free Corps brigades had reassembled and rushed to the Ruhr to slaughter communist thugs and liberate the citizenry. President Ebert, still terrified by communist insurrections that followed his general strike, had beseeched General von Seeckt to rescind his resignation and take charge of all military units. Then the very troops Ebert had called renegades were paid the same bonus they were supposed to have received from a Kapp regime that could not pay because of Ebert's strike.

CARICATURES
By George Grosz

Waiting until rage overloaded my sensitivity circuits and blazed through my brain, I grabbed a pencil and on beckoning empty white paper launched dexterous assaults on the callous, the pompous and the inane, whoever was most overcharging my overwrought system. That distinction was often earned by those straight-backed practitioners of dueling and defense, Prussian officers of the German General Staff. These monocle-wearing warriors, raised on the precept that military might always resolves everything, considered themselves supreme despite losing a war that precipitated post-war terror in a nation they were born and trained to defend. Bureaucrats were almost as loathsome. I drew them with faces of pained conceit that signaled the world not to question their inflexibility. Industrialists also made me sick. They had backed the Great War because it made them money, and now, while their victims scrounged, they kept getting fatter of face and wallet.

GREAT SYMBOL
By Adolf Hitler

When I resigned from the Army, it wasn't a divorce but a simple change of status and a brand new address. With my fifty-mark demobilization pay in pocket, and the able aid of a strong party comrade, I removed my few belongings from the barracks and transported them to two small rooms reached by wooden stairs. Apartments like mine stood on stores and shadowed the streets.

Up there in my place, at a worn wooden table, I conceived a new party name: National Socialist German Workers Party. Then I began making numerous sketches. Our party needed a symbol and a flag that could instantly seize the eye and emblazon forever our image in the retentive minds of millions.

Hundreds of ideas were delivered to our tiny party headquarters in a creaky Munich tavern, and I was chagrined by suggestions that our flag bear the same black, red and gold as the Weimar Republic that today embraces Marxists and Jews and spits on those who strive for national unity. Also, I could not accept recommendations to revive the black, white and red flag flown by Imperial Germany prior to the crime that ended the Great War. I am still inspired by that flag and the might it represented, but it would be folly for us as a new movement to hoist a flag that, frankly, represents defeat and all the mistakes that permitted deceit to defeat us.

The one good idea was submitted by a dentist whose sketch, by coincidence, looked much like my final rendition. I placed our sketches side by side and admired them before making some alterations and sending specifications to a seamstress in the party. When the new flag arrived, I was humbled by its profound simplicity. Red warned potential transgressors; white formed a pure circle of unity; and in the circle blared a black swastika, ancient symbol of Aryan might.

BETRAYED
By An Archaeologist

The swastika has been betrayed. Its misrepresentation is a rage. For thousands of years it has been drawn, displayed and worn with pride in Europe, Asia, America and the Middle East. Archaeology has proved that Jews in ancient Palestine decorated pottery and synagogue walls with the swastika. The spirit represented was the wheel of the sun and the cycle of life.

SPEECHES
By The Munich Post

At a glance no single abnormality leaped from Hitler unless I counted as one the whole glaring assimilation of abnormalities that he was. Only after each startling introduction could I look for specific absurdities. His mustache had to be the capper. It was a cut-very-narrow patch of fur that only partially plugged very wicked nostrils. Light always reflected harsh white off Hitler's pallid nose and face, and his complexion reminded me of the ultra-white underside of a big fish pulled in cold and stiff. I would have expected a powerful body to generate Hitler's commanding voice, but you could see through his coat that he was frail and sunken of chest, and somewhat round and matronly in the hips. To me, this guy with the blue eyes roasting red looked like a professional fanatic of unknown persuasion who in a more balanced society would have been confined to a cage.

This does not imply I was bored waiting in huge halls jammed with buzzing, beer drinking activists. Repeatedly I rotated my neck to check every conceivable entrance, always guessing: which way, this way, that way, or over there, and with whom?

"Here he comes, here he comes," oafs would utter when shoulders shuffled over there. No, not now. That's just them, not him. You really did know it when Hitler arrived. He came late from nowhere all in an instant walking fast, surrounded by scowling roughnecks waving to move, and he stalked up a crowded path to the front looking stern nowhere except straight ahead.

Once on stage Hitler gazed at his audience with fatherly aplomb, and waited until everyone tightened before beginning to speak like an entirely reasonable man. He often sputtered and halted before gradually warming up, and then he became one of the men. They had all served at the front and suffered together, and in the war this mere corporal had been as common as anyone. Now he was more, though, and I dutifully reported this brash young politician was every week or two attracting crowds as large as four thousand.

At times, sitting cramped, I was irritated by the rousing turnouts for this guy. I knew he didn't deserve all this. And I wasn't excited like everyone else. They jumped and clapped and yelled as problems dissolved and spirits soared. But Adolf Hitler is only a demagogue, I reminded myself.

PROTOCOLS OF THE ELDERS OF ZION
By Alfred Rosenburg

Born from good Germanic folk in the Baltic territory of Estonia, I had grown up always having to flinch beneath the totalitarian hand of our ignoble Russian protector, the czar. Lots of Germans lived in the Baltic, and we, along with most others, did not want to be Russian and all that implied. Certain dogs nevertheless asserted I must have been a Russian since I had studied architecture at Moscow University. Others accused me of joining the communists during the Bolshevik revolution.

All that was absurd, and during the Great War I returned to Estonia and tried to join the German Army that had just conquered many Eastern territories. But the Germans said I was not a real German and would not take me. Very disappointed, I remained in Estonia to study philosophy, foreign affairs and race. And at underground meetings in 1920 some important people were intrigued that I planned to go to Germany.

"Where in Germany?"

"Munich," I said.

"In that case, Herr Rosenberg, we have a special task for you."

In Munich on the streets I readily ascertained, even before Russian émigrés told me, that Dietrich Eckart was the man to see. I arrived at his house one early morning.

"Yes, he's there. Just keep knocking," his old lady landlord said, smiling at me and staying to look.

I knocked harder, and heard a rumble toward the door.

"What the hell's wrong with you?" Eckart grumbled. "You better have a good reason for this intrusion."

A brown towel was wrapped way around a waist submerged by his belly.

"I'm ready to show you irrefutable documentation that Jewry is bent on international control. Are you interested?"

"Of course," Eckart said, pulling me inside with a strong arm.

He soon introduced me to Hitler, and I certainly was let down to see a little man with a sloped forehead frowning at me. A lot of uncouth party members in the room also frowned. Later, Hitler and Eckart and I privately discussed the *Protocols of the Elders of Zion*, and Hitler became more enthusiastic as he realized how much new information I had.

In no time I was writing articles and being consulted about the scope of Jewish treachery. That is why Nazi goons hated me. Daily they groped around Hitler like ninnies, but when I came over he'd always go into the other room to listen to my views. Later, at his speeches, I was thrilled by the voice of a man who said things I said and wanted me and my philosophy in his party of forward advance.

THOSE PROTOCOLS
By Henry Ford

I was shocked by the *Protocols of the Elders of Zion*, and ordered my company to publish them as part of a book called *The International Jew: The World's Foremost Problem*. I was so worried I printed three million copies and sent them free to schools and public libraries and sold the rest. Those Protocols definitely were not bunk.

MUSCLE
By General Erich Ludendorff

Righteous and proud, I lived in my donated villa in Munich, guarded by armed and ready patriots from the Ehrhardt Brigade. I had stationed myself in this hotbed to help Germany surmount the array of rifles leveled at us from within and without. As my support increased, I sensed I was surging back to a position of influence and potential paramountcy. Young corporal Hitler could certainly help me, so often I hosted this duly deferential lad for vital discussions. With me wielding armed might, our cause could succeed. We simply needed more might.

I ordered intermediaries to arrange a meeting between Hitler and me, and Gregor Strasser, an annoyed socialist in Landshut with the demonstrated energy to assemble and train a private army, and equip it with machine guns and artillery. This Strasser was an Iron Cross winner and had to be a damn good man.

After my limousine pulled up in front of his chemical store, a burly and smiling Strasser greeted me and then shook hands with a rather glum Hitler. Strasser then introduced his brother, Otto, and Hitler and Otto glared at each other until Gregor led us into an office littered with disassembled weapons. I did not wait long before I straightened and said, "There is a singular goal that supersedes all others, and that is to unite all nationalists. Anything short of that and we're too diffuse to help each other and sometimes we're even against each other. I ask you, Herr Strasser, to subordinate yourself and your storm troops under my military leadership and under the political guidance of Herr Hitler and his National Socialists."

I nodded at Hitler, who said, "Herr Strasser, if you'll provide your nationalist and socialist instincts and talents, I'll put you in charge of the Lower Bavarian political district. Your clout would then be greatly increased."

"A moment, please, Herr Hitler," said Otto Strasser. "You're talking blindly about political clout and territory you don't even possess. You hold no office."

"I don't need an office. I have political power by virtue of my extraordinary rapport with the people."

"What is the National Socialist program?" Otto demanded.

"The program, like the office, is not necessary. All that matters is power. Pure power means control."

"Ridiculous," said Otto. "Power is only a means to generate the greatest social good. What is your program?"

"I won't share my program with any leftist traitor who fought against the Kapp Putsch."

"Kapp is a withering reactionary. Your supporting him makes a mockery of your titular claims of socialism."

I uplifted both hands and said, "The distinction now, gentlemen, is that our new nationalist politics can't be communistic and neither can they be capitalistic. Those are imbalances of the past."

Gregor Strasser seemed enthusiastic.

"We already have three thousand members in the party," Hitler told him.

"I'll need a little time to consider," said Strasser.

"That's appropriate," I said.

On the way home I concluded Strasser and his storm troops probably would join us, and that old feeling of growing authority made me feel good sitting erect in my uniform on a plush seat next to Hitler.

THE VOLKISCHER BEOBACHTER
By Adolf Hitler

Late on a December night getting cold toward Christmas, as I sat in the bare-walled basement of our beer hall headquarters, two fellow nationalists rushed down in and told me the financially struggling Volkischer Beobachter had just been placed on sale, and someone from another party planned to buy it.

Angrily I jumped up and said, "The Volkischer Beobachter just ran a front page article demanding the 'most ruthless measures to sweep out Jewish vermin with an iron broom.' That's a paper already spiritually our own. I won't permit anyone else to buy it."

At two a.m. I dashed to Dietrich Eckart's apartment, knowing he'd be reclining awake on the couch.

"We've got to raise funds before the opposition," I said. "It's urgent. Get up."

"You can't roust anyone at this hour and expect a cheerful reply in cash," he said. "In the morning's soon enough."

In the morning I did not feel well. Eeriness scraped through my head and stomach, and I sensed some blue bloods out there would laugh under their long noses about my asking for more money. Eckart could act for me this morning. And I'd send Anton Drexler to help. He'd be happy I finally gave him something to do. As a founder of the party, though in no way an architect of its current success, he was entitled to this bone of contribution.

I tried to recover in bed but was overwhelmed by wretched thoughts about how all the big, powerful Jewish organs trumpeted their ideas profitably and how all the Volkisch papers seemed swallowed by insolvency. For this I could not blame the Jews. No, the main problem with Volkisch organs was incompetent owners who depended on kindly contributors instead of hard work. Under these circumstances I'd never be able to sleep or even lie still. Pulling myself out of bed, I marched to party headquarters and began to think. What if I didn't get my paper? What if my voice was again stifled? I was miserable and couldn't stand it anymore, and jumped up ready to tell Eckart and Drexler as they walked in.

"Here it is," Eckart pronounced, thrusting a document in the air and shaking it. "The Volkischer Beobachter is forevermore in the right hands."

We party members cheered and embraced the two men, and I said, "This paper will always be not only an ideological springboard but a business of solvent intent."

"It'd better be that at the least. My personal note guarantees payment of all debts this publication now has, as well as those it might in the future incur."

Later, at his apartment, Eckart revealed that some high-ranking officers had arranged for thousands of marks in secret Army funds to be applied to the purchase. What a sensation. In little more than a year, I had earned thousands of enchanted followers, an expanding party organization, and now my own battle paper.

BITES
By Adolf Hitler

The Versailles bandits began 1921 by taking more big bites out of us. In London they decided that reparations in excess of a hundred million gold marks must be bestowed upon them as righteous victors. And soon, in Paris, they raised their sabers and said pay soon or they, the French, with allied collusion, would storm in and occupy a Ruhr basin already frozen around starving people. The shaking hands of our foundation-quaking Social Democratic government thus signed the first of numerous dark checks drawn against our insolvent national body. Everyone in Germany was likewise lightened in the wallet and burdened anew.

IS HE A TRAITOR?
By Anton Drexler

In the summer we on the executive committee summoned Hitler, and I told him, "The rest of us want a voice in matters. You're not the only one who should determine everything. Please think about these things. We'd like to know when we can talk again."

Hitler just gave us that jaw-grinding glare, held it there, and walked out.

In a week or so we heard he was in Berlin, making speeches before nationalist groups and meeting with all sorts of influential people on the right. We did not know what to think but assumed he was forging alliances. Hoping to prevent him from becoming even more preponderant, we too looked for allies.

Hitler learned what we were doing and scurried back to Munich where he presented himself regally and announced he was resigning. He said little more, and left. It certainly was not my desire for him to leave the party. I just wanted him to quit treating everyone like oxen yoked in his behalf.

Circumventing the committee, Hitler sent printed ultimatums to everyone in the party. He wrote: "I demand to be first chairman, with absolute dictatorial power. This is necessary not because of any love of power on my part but because foreign elements are burrowing in on the party foundation and threatening to topple Germany's best hope for freedom. In the name of expediency, I also demand the executive committee either be abolished or emasculated."

We told him he could wait forever on his eight-day limit. When that expired I was sure he'd return. Instead, Hitler reissued his demands.

Around a table we cursed while discussing phrases and charges to use against him in three thousand copies of a pamphlet called "Adolf Hitler: Is He a Traitor?" We naturally accused him of unbridled ambition in pursuit of dictatorial power and of shunning anyone who would not help him attain his selfish goals. Though I contributed some observations in that vein, I did not think it appropriate for others to write that Hitler was bribed by Jews, and even acted like a Jew who wasted unearned money on a wide selection of women. After the Munich Post reprinted the pamphlet, Hitler sued and won.

Dietrich Eckart came as an emissary and stated: "Gentlemen of the committee, I understand your sore feelings and the inflexibility of your heartfelt principles. You are men of honor and important columns in this vital movement. I must, therefore, beseech you to consider the nature of your personal duty to our cause, and to embrace the leadership of the only man gifted enough to be our eternal shepherd. In the most profound sense, I'm not asking you to pledge allegiance to Adolf Hitler. I'm asking you to unite and pledge allegiance to the man who is somehow supernaturally harnessed for the good of the great German folk."

"He's rude and doesn't even pretend to be restrained," I said.

"Yes, I know he can be coarse. We all recognize that. But that's hardly the issue. Our issue is efficacy, and for that this party can have no one save Hitler. Remember, I too am a party member and am thus willing to subordinate myself in pursuit of greater good.

"If you don't soon act, you may be entirely too late. Hitler, with his talents and contacts, could start another party any day. He's talking about it now. If he does, you'll be back to fifty souls at meetings, and his voice will elsewhere command attention. I ask you not to stifle yourselves in a futile effort to stifle Hitler. Sign this party charter, and all our voices will be heard."

YOUR MANDATE
By Adolf Hitler

Only with great caring and self-restraint could I be so gracious as to accept the impassioned call, from comrades in a full hall, to step forward and acknowledge their greatest need.

"I have always been committed to building this party, your party, into a movement of national and historical prowess," I stated. "Therefore, from the beginning, I undertook important action that would generate a real chance at major success. I could not tolerate anyone who was less committed to national salvation than I, and that is why we are here. Several sneaky cowards quite selfishly distributed a pamphlet that slanders me with insults and lies while claiming great urgency. I say, if these pamphleteering phonies really are righteous, why then are they so gutless they didn't even sign their names? There's no mystery in that. They dared not sign and publicly reveal themselves as deceivers.

"Now, thankfully, all that is over."

Unsmiling but pleased, I stepped back to let the whoops and claps clear, and I looked all around the room, looking right at the men, feeling them happy on my eyes.

"Yes, these matters have been resolved, and our strength and resolve have greatly increased by virtue of simplification. Now no one will ever have to wonder who the Fuehrer really is."

LEFTIST ASSAULTS
By Adolf Hitler

Most opposition clowns delivered speeches in the pseudo witty style of academicians too white-livered to say anything of worth. The result, inevitably, was that most in the audience snored, and those not fortunate enough to fall asleep usually fled. My enemies also attempted to inundate everyone with mounds of syrupy written matter. I snickered at that because I absolutely knew the spoken word was an infinitely superior means of mass communication. The written word is always prey, in its printed and inflexible form, to the preconceived prejudices of whoever happens to pick it up. If a person is already hostile to the unchangeable thoughts expressed, then he certainly will not bother to read more than a little. I, on the contrary, am never abandoned since I can divine the mood of any audience and ring its ears like well-rung bells.

Lacking any skills to compete with me, my enemies resorted to the vilest acts of abject desperation: lies, treachery, and violence. The leader of the Social Democrats in Munich, Erhard Auer, claimed that one night on a stroll he was several times fired upon, and only saved his life with improvisational bravery that shocked his attackers into shivering retreat. Though not one of these purported attackers was apprehended, or even tentatively identified, the Social Democrats unlimbered their putrid party organ and launched a profusion of scurrilous attacks against our movement. Among other imminent unpleasantness, they stated our influence would thenceforth be on the wane, their fists being the primary impetus of our demise.

I assumed the threats were serious, in a blustery way, but did not expect noteworthy action soon. Consequently, I summoned only fifty or so monitor troops for a November 1921 meeting at the Hofbrauhaus. Around six that evening, however, we learned that several hundred workers from communist-infested factories had vowed to disrupt us.

Entering the hall, I saw a big beer table — my stage — shoved against a wall in a corner up front. Packed in close, husky factory workers turned and snapped at me and ostentatiously chugged beers before putting their empty mugs under tables. I stared at the heathens before walking into a small side room where my monitor troops awaited.

"Achtung, line up at once," I said. "Tonight, men, for the first time in the party's history, there awaits us a threat of sufficient size and malice to threaten the life of our movement as well as our actual existence as living human beings. I order all of you to bravely deliver your utmost, despite our outnumbered predicament. Not a man is permitted to leave this hall unless he's a corpse being carried out. I myself will obviously remain as well. Though I can't fathom it happening — beware. If I see any man displaying cowardice, I'll personally tear off his swastika armband and terminate his party membership. Make sure you attack at the first inkling of trouble, or problems will spread."

"Heil. Heil. Heil," they exploded, and we marched into the big banquet room, and I mounted my table and began to speak. For more than an hour no one interrupted, except for an occasional ignorant shout or an inept attempt at humor, and I thought the leftists might understand the futility of trying to disrupt a master communicator. Then I relearned a valuable tenet: never decrease vigilance. I did, and instantly an obscene comment stunned me into a half second of silence. Quickly a communist poltroon pounced on a nearby table and yelled: "Freiheit," the querulous Red call of liberation.

Before me the men started thrashing each other with fists, chair legs and mugs, and the shrieks and howls became so intense I remained tall and intent on the table, not worried at all by volleys of heavy glass heaved at my head. Gathering in tight groups of eight to ten, my boys walloped specific targets before moving on, and within twenty minutes most of the several hundred slobs had been beaten raw and red down the stairs out of the building. With peace restored, a comrade leaped onto a chair and shouted, "This meeting goes on. Herr Hitler still holds the stage."

A special announcement was now mandatory, and I stated: "Tonight you have seen and participated in noble acts of sacrifice and bravery, and at the same time initiated our own official arm of party protection. Henceforth, that muscular arm will be called our Storm Detachments and will be designated by the initials SA. May no one cross any boundary dictated by the SA."

THUGS
By Otto Ballerstedt

The mouth of Adolf Hitler always twisted when my name, Otto Ballerstedt, was mentioned. Numerous people told me so, and I knew anyway since Hitler had occasionally tried to interrupt me at some of my Bavarian League meetings as well as at general political rallies. One time he ended an outburst by asserting: "The Jews have woven an international spider web to trap vital resources for themselves and to ensnare anyone who wants to stop them."

I at once opened my eyes and mouth so very wide, and said, "Well,

Herr Hitler, my goodness, indeed. That sounds like an awfully fearsome predicament we're in. I've seen some rather unsightly spider webs, but none so gruesome as that conjured by you. And during numerous forays for facts, I've discussed many matters, international and political, with many men of note, and not one has ever reported a sighting such as yours, even in the metaphorical sense. I tell you, Herr Hitler, to those who worldwide number but several million, you attribute the most pervasive and astounding feats of financial and physical might. You must think each Jew possesses the capabilities of ten Aryans, or else how could you be so convinced they have the power to ruin us all?"

Slurs and snickers flew at Hitler, and his mouth twisted even more shouting back something no one remembered. We only recalled his rage and exasperation as he spun and departed, followed by frowning goons.

Though the Treaty of Versailles prohibited any extracurricular military activity, it was known by anyone who wanted that on various obscure and dusty roads Hitler's men were being marched and drilled like a group getting ready for battle. I sent two men on scouting trips, and the first time they came back hooting that the Nazis, while being screeched at by a former Free Corps officer, proudly propped on their shoulders a motley set of gnarled sticks. The only thing uniform about their slovenly uniforms was a swastika armband. Later, I heard what I had already expected: the Army granted the Nazis access to its training facilities, and officers like Captain Ernst Roehm helped in training. I know damn well the Army also gave them weapons.

In cities the Nazis occasionally grabbed dissenters or elderly Jews and beat them up. To hell with that. They weren't going to intimidate me. At the Lowenbrau, I stood on stage ready to tell followers about Hitler's recent accidental compliment: "Ballerstedt is my most dangerous rival." Certainly I was. My tongue tied his in knots every time we tangled.

I had not examined the crowd beforehand and was startled, just as I spoke, when several hundred men, most seated near me, jumped up and turned around hollering for Hitler, who quite uninvited had just lunged through the door. He moved morosely toward me, as rapidly as possible through jammed aisles, and his men chanted: "Step aside. Give Hitler the floor."

"I will not," I said. "This is our meeting. We organized it, and we paid for the hall. Shut up or get out. That's a better alternative than your visitors receive."

Next, beyond comprehension, Hitler charged and mounted the stage, followed by a swarm. Right at me he sprinted, snarling and yelling as he punched my face, aided by others who kicked me and rapped me with sticks. At first, I protested on my back. Then I could only cover up in a hall full of roars. After the Nazis finished pounding our small security group and me, I was picked up and tossed off stage and landed on a wooden chair.

Hitler would have given one of his delightful addresses right there, but the police arrived and arrested him and several other thugs. The next day authorities assured me he would be brought to trial. After being so informed in his cell, Hitler said, "That's quite all right. Ballerstedt didn't get to speak."

PARTIES
By Wilhelm Frick

People with cracked heads and swollen blue faces came in all the time saying they had rented halls but Nazis rushed in and ruined their meetings. They came in complaining that gangs had insulted them from roving trucks covered red in banners, then stopped and clobbered them when they objected to the insults. I listened carefully and nodded, and often nodded more, and looked concerned as I rubbed my hand over my short salty hair.

"I'll try to do something about this," I said. "Remember, we're in a state of war, even after the war, and sometimes even trying to improve causes problems. I'll still try to help you."

These people did not understand, and I did not have time to explain since they had never understood and never would. My boss, the Police President of Munich, did understand, and we often discussed the problem of misplaced complaints.

DEFENSE OF LIBERTY
By Erhard Auer

As a schoolboy I independently read about the American and French revolutions, and developed a belief, unusual in my country, that people deserve to be free. By adulthood I viewed monarchs and dictators as arrogant enemies of liberty, and consequently based my burgeoning political career on democratic principles. Naturally, Adolf Hitler considered me a most heinous enemy.

I still did not publicly claim the Nazis had tried to shoot me in late 1921. Our Social Democratic party paper did say the Nazis were dangerous and objectionable, but we knew who had been targeting non-reactionary politicians all over Germany. It was the Organization Consul, phrased in succinct and sepulchral tones as the O.C., a band of butchers. The more humane their target, the more vicious their attack. But Hitler was not pinned to them, not directly.

Hitler was in trouble with the Bavarian parliament because of his threats to overthrow the state, his illegal organizing, and persistent use of violence, albeit non-lethal violence to date. The parliament in unison condemned him for those transgressions, and further censured him for his recent conviction for attacking Otto Ballerstedt, as well as for the fact he was not even a German but an Austrian.

In parliament sentiment grew to deport Hitler at once. That step would certainly be damaging to his political career. Austria was neither large enough nor distraught enough to accommodate a movement like his. At a final meeting on his residency, in March 1922, leaders of key parties argued that Bavaria should no longer have to tolerate the alien Hitler and his agitators. Every party boss felt that way, except me.

I stood at our table, the fingertips of both hands playing softly on top, as I stated: "I'm no supporter of Hitler. You all know that. He's immersed in all that is vile and repressive, and he's a loud and dangerous foe of the democratic principles framed at the heart of our Weimar Republic. But that should not matter. The ignorance and enmity of Hitler are not at issue. We're here to determine whether or not our constitutional declaration of liberty and free speech means anything. If it does not mean anything, then surely there is no inherent contradiction in booting Hitler back to Austria because his free speech was never really free, and he disagreed with us, so he must go. But who must go next? Certainly we will not all of us forever agree. Then who will have to leave? I need the protection of free speech. We all need the same protection. Adolf Hitler deserves the same democratic rights as any man. Objectionable as he is, he should be allowed to stay. And don't worry. He's only a comical figure. His absurdity will certainly be fleeting."

ELIMINATION
By Commander Ehrhardt

After the betrayal of all I fought for, I had made sacred vows to cleanse the Fatherland. First I had formed the Ehrhardt Brigade and trained my men to be the toughest and most brutal of all Free Corps fighters. Then we destroyed many foes, some pretending to be unarmed, and liberated much of Germany. Unsurprisingly, the bogus Social Democratic government had not appreciated my patriotism and forced me into exile in Hungary. But that did not stifle me. I maintained a variety of furtive contacts before police officials arranged documents with a new name so I could return to my task in Germany.

Our primary enemies were no longer marauding communists, who had already been crushed, but the more subtle and insidious leftist leaders who agitated legislatively and thereby perpetuated trouble. For the time being, I did not need legions of Free Corps troops, only the talent and dedication of a few fanatical men from the Organization Consul. We had first struck big a year ago when bullets from the dark executed a hostile socialist. This act was so popular that patriotic students sang about a "hero brave whose shot brought deliverance again to all."

Soon we concentrated on Matthias Erzberger. Though he'd become a private citizen, this intolerable dastard had sat on his cowardly ass in the notorious railroad compartment in Compiegne and signed the armistice that gave Germany away in the Great War. Erzberger subsequently compounded his crimes by insisting in the Reichstag that Germany acquiesce to the outrages of Versailles. He also stated that advocates of German expansion — not the Weimar Republic — were responsible for Germany's treatment by other nations.

On a fresh summer morning, as Matthias Erzberger had loafed on the soft ground beneath high pines in the Black Forest, two O.C. men shot him in the gut. He staggered away before being felled from twenty paces, then terminated by a double coup de grâce to the skull. Police soon identified the patriots, but more redoubtable documents were arranged, and the men scooted across the Hungarian border.

Our action was again celebrated in nationalist lyrics "thanking God for this most splendid murder," and by rightist elements in the press who'd realized Erzberger should long ago have been dead. There were some protests, however, and in Berlin the Reichstag declared a state of emergency and forbade the press to incite attacks on leaders of the Weimar Republic. Despite these governmental moans, the O.C. continued to operate.

The assignment in June 1922 was Philipp Scheidemann, criminal first Chancellor of the Weimar Republic, who had contrived to get rich while Germany got poor. Now, as Lord Mayor of Kassel, he was sauntering through a nature area near his home. When his daughter and granddaughter wandered into the flowers, one of my two men sprang at the startled swine and squeezed a big red rubber bulb. Prussic acid shot through a syringe onto Scheidemann's pompous face, but his thick goatee and mustache prevented much penetration, and he was able to grab his revolver and, while staggering, shoot a couple of times to force a retreat. Both of my men were promptly apprehended and sentenced to a few years in prison.

"Why the hell did this happen?" I said during a secret meeting. "At least we have a much bigger enemy. You all know his name. I want him dead. And don't try any goddamn gimmicks."

JUSTICE RIGHT AND LEFT
By Walther Rathenau

I was thoroughly aggrieved by the tragedy and sheer idiocy that everywhere enveloped the country. The German mark continued to plummet, along with our national wealth, and we were ever saddled with the quite unfair and unrealistic Versailles reparations assessed us not on the basis of sound international principle but on the base instinct of shortsighted revenge. These complex problems demanded profound insight and rare experience, and I well knew that my controversial talents made me a glaring target for the band of Neanderthals on the right who tried to kill anyone not sharing their zest for stupidity and brutality. Underneath my coat, not far from my heart, I kept a pistol always loaded and ready.

I realized some Germans never would recognize who I was as a man. They looked at me only as a Jew. I was proud to be a Jew, but I was even prouder to be a German. My family had charged to prominence in a great Germany that permitted my father to launch the German Edison Company and provide the magic of incandescent light. I voraciously studied science, economics and the arts, and soared to company president with such efficiency that respect was rarely denied.

During our nation's struggle for survival, I had served as Chief of the War Materials Division. Combining an administrative flair with my ability to extract pure nitrogen from the air, I generated a supply of explosives well beyond what otherwise could have been possible. The prominence of the War Materials Division increased as our strategic predicament worsened, and I exerted influence over vast economic resources, as a means to improve war efforts.

The worst lies about the war concerned the final days, when traditional military means clearly would not save the Reich. I had tried to rouse the nation to arm and resist the encroaching enemy. But when this plan was discussed with the illustrious General Ludendorff, that defeatist was so febrile with fear he lacked the ability to do his job as a soldier, and could only say no, then desert the Fatherland.

Years later, as Foreign Minister of Germany, I recently journeyed to Genoa for an economic conference. After several amiable conversations with the Russian commissar of foreign affairs, we decided to drive east along the blue Riviera coast to Rapallo where we discussed how our nations could extricate themselves from defeat and economic devastation. Readily we agreed to renew diplomatic relations, expand trade and renounce reparations affecting each other. And most stunning: Russia and Germany pledged to interact militarily. We planned, with support from Lenin, to send German officers to Russia to train Soviet troops in exchange for the Russians manufacturing tanks and munitions prohibited us by Versailles. I should note that the head of the German Army, General Hans von Seeckt, was delighted with this treaty, which doubled or trebled his theretofore limited logistical options.

Though the informed majority in Germany applauded the Rapallo Treaty, reactionaries could not comprehend the breakthrough. They called me a Bolshevik bedfellow and an even worse than typical Jew. I also outraged a number of factions by advocating we comply with the ludicrous Versailles demand for a hundred-thirty billion gold marks in reparations. I had clearly explained in the Reichstag, and elsewhere, that paying a few exorbitant bills now would prove, by sheer economic logic, that we were unable to continue.

I hated our vulnerability as much as anyone, and often thought about when Germany would be great again. Ours was a nation of ambition and vigor. Right now I could see those qualities in several road workers we drove by just after leaving my Berlin estate. On this promising June morning, sitting straight up in the back seat of my open limousine, I knew what had to come. Nearby, as we slowed at a series of sharp turns, I heard a roar just before a long car lunged alongside, then shot just ahead and jerked over, forcing my car off the road. As I prepared to stand and ask the meaning of such idiocy, I saw for the first time a luminous leather jacket. I did not see a face in the leather, only a gun held straight and level and bursting now with fire that ripped me in the chest and knocked me bloody back at an angle in the back seat. Another nice leather jacket stood and threw an egg grenade that buffeted my inert body before returning it against the seat. The chauffeur immediately sped to look for a doctor.

Soon I received spiritual vindication in several public protests. During the largest, seven hundred thousand Berliners gathered on the streets and denounced not only my murder but also the bestiality of an increasing number of Germans. In the three and a half years preceding my death, approximately three hundred fifty political assassinations were committed by rightists, and but twenty-three by leftists. Yet, due to the complicity of police, judges and soldiers, the average leftist received a fifteen-year prison sentence while the average rightist got four months. The police did hunt down my killers, and shot one. The other shouted a tribute to Commander Ehrhardt, then shot himself.

PROTECTION OF THE REPUBLIC
By Adolf Hitler

To a large group huddled in our headquarters, I pronounced: "Today is much like the day two thousand years ago when another man of vision and courage was dragged away by the gang of Jerusalem and nailed to a cross. That, in principle, is being done to me because I had the conviction to silence the disease-stricken voice of Otto Ballerstedt. Now I too must suffer."

In Stadelheim Prison I hated the cramped solitude and frequently had to use my private bathroom before I resumed pacing the stark gray cell, abruptly turning at the end of each short swipe. This sickening regimen, which took so long to eat up any time, made me focus and keep focusing, and all over inside I knew my pain, that inextinguishable flame, was caused by atrocities directed right at me.

A couple of weeks into imprisonment, the jailer brought me two newspapers with headlines announcing the Reichstag's new decree: Law For the Protection of the Republic. Despite its pious cries for law and order, this decree was really something very different, and I was broiling to explain.

The night of my release, I stood before a crowd at the Burgerbrau and stared a long time before starting.

"You are aware, I am sure, where I have been," I said. "I have been in jail more than a month because I sought to defend our right to free speech. That right was taken away here in the Free State of Bavaria, and now, as everyone including even the insane must surely know, the November Criminals in Berlin have slapped all of our lives into straitjackets for the obvious purpose of halting our national progress and continuing their devastation of our political parties, our press, and our Volkisch nation. They have called this emergency decree the Law for the Protection of the Republic. Considering that it was enacted after the death of a Hebrew power broker, I think it would be much more appropriate to call it the Law for the Protection of Jews. And that, of course, is the very point. It is we who need protection, not the Jews."

KING OF MUNICH
By A Waiter

At certain late night hours people often began to ask, with not altogether complimentary inflection, "Where is the king of Munich?"

"I'm sure the King and his esteemed entourage will enter shortly," I'd say, eager as ever to tend to the needs of an emerging celebrity.

With grinding regularity, there he came through the door held open by a flunky, and everyone in Cafe Heck could see him strut, bullwhip in hand, toward his regular table in the rear. He always wore a baggy and ruffled trench coat, and his hat looked as if someone just sat on it. A few times customers remarked quietly that he looked like a clown or a tramp who wanted very much to look like neither.

At his table he sat with his back to the rear wall. And when he wasn't talking to someone, and sometimes when he was, he stared at the entrance or other tables.

"I think that bourgeois pimp over there doesn't like us," I once heard him remark to Ulrich Graf.

"I'll crush him if you say."

"That we cannot do right now, Graf. This is a place of distinction and our muscle must be saved for proper occasions."

Ulrich Graf was the primary bodyguard, and his blockish frame, honed as an amateur wrestler, always lurked near Hitler. The Fuehrer sometimes patted Graf's chunky hands and said, "Now, being here with me is a lot better than being an apprentice butcher with bloody entrails all over yourself, isn't it, Graf?"

Everyone around the table laughed. Graf enjoyed the joke, too. He was proud to be close to the Fuehrer.

Emil Maurice also sat near Hitler most of the time. He was a former convict, but no one said what he had done. Now he was a good chauffeur and quite adept at signaling me to make sure his Fuehrer had plenty of pastry. I also brought lots of beer to the table, and with a stein of water Hitler toasted his growing entourage. The most striking member was Captain Ernst Roehm, who had a big bullet hole in his cheek and a nose that had been partly blasted away. Alfred Rosenburg often came, too, and after replacing the dissipated Dietrich Eckart as editor of the Volkischer Beobachter, he got to sit closer to Hitler.

Many customers turned their necks toward the rear and ogled the king and his court, and some ventured back to introduce themselves. Sometimes socialites stopped by and flirted while Hitler blushed. Until recently, this elegant cafe society had been unavailable to him, and some said he did not like it when closing time came. That meant he had to trudge to two tiny rooms for another night of solitude and insomnia.

LOST ACE
By Hermann Goering

On this gray and chill November 1922 day in Munich, I was almost thirty years old and standing uninspired at a political rally with my fiancée, who had been supporting me with an allowance from her husband. Never had Carin said or even intimated that I was in any way negligent. She was always divine and delicate, and told me she knew what was really in me. Still, I had daily been sitting in university classes with students a decade my junior, and I hated sitting and school and the condition Germany was in, and especially I hated taking from Carin. I knew my life could not possibly always be this way but did not know how it would change, and I sensed if I did not soon develop the options of a man, I would somehow lose her.

The rally this day offered only sporadic noise, and the crowd became so restive it began shouting for Hitler, who by coincidence was standing nearby. He frowned and shook his head, then departed with his entourage.

Having heard so much about this new political force, I decided to attend the next Nazi meeting. Inconspicuously, I sat to one side in the rear.

"I didn't speak to that tame group of bourgeoisie because they had nothing in their arsenal but popcorn," Hitler bellowed. "There's no use trying to remove heathens from our backs by spewing more words, be they sweet or venomous. What we need are soldiers and arms and the will to strike the oppressors. That's what I'm seeking. That's what I'm going to get. And that's what is going to liberate Germany."

Flying from my seat, I stood clapping with gusto and vowed to meet this kindred spirit.

Soon, one afternoon, I entered the rather austere Nazi headquarters, announced my name, and said I would like to have a word with Hitler. The clerical helper left lethargically and returned with enthusiasm. The Fuehrer wanted to see me immediately. And when I walked in his little office, he was beaming and stepped forward to shake my hand.

"You know, it's an extraordinary coincidence you've come here this instant," he said. "There you stand, a great fighter pilot who won the pour le mérite, and I can think of no one who'd inspire me more. You're a patriot and a hero."

"Thank you very much," I said. "I've come to tell you I'd be honored to serve in your movement. You're the only man I've seen who knows what to do."

Hitler clasped my hand again and said, "Your grasp of the picture is accurate. And your presence today is especially opportune since I've resolved to put the most professional man possible at the head of the SA. These storm troops have been loyal and quite effective, but our opposition can only grow stronger and better organized. It's essential to upgrade ourselves to the fullest. So to you, Herr Goering, I offer command of the SA, and thus the responsibility for protecting and promoting the movement we both know means everything for Germany."

Stunned and delighted, I accepted. Now I knew I could again become the man I'd been during the war. Adolf Hitler had given me that chance.

AMERICA INVESTIGATES
By Captain Truman Smith

Not long after being trained at Yale and educated at West Point, I was stationed in Berlin as an assistant military attaché in the American Embassy. This certainly was a riveting time and place, and everyone said Bavaria rumbled with even more political action. The nationwide implications so concerned Ambassador Houghton that he sent me to investigate the possibility of Bavaria breaking away from Germany, and to determine the intentions and potential of the young radical, Adolf Hitler.

I began my assignment in Munich by interviewing General

Ludendorff, the deposed Crown Prince Rupprecht, and numerous journalists and politicians. They were nearly unanimous in saying Hitler energized the masses and promoted his party better than anyone in the region. No one believed he had any immediate prospect of gaining power in Bavaria, or of forcing it to secede from Germany, but many Bavarians obviously wanted to disassociate from Berlin and the Weimar Republic.

Informed of my inquiries, Hitler invited me to attend a demonstration of storm troops outside the new party headquarters. Twenty four hundred methodically stomping black boots overwhelmed several blocks in each direction, and when the boots stopped, Hitler started talking, and soon his threatening voice boomed off buildings on both sides of the street. His men, who were very different from the fellows I'd known at Yale, shot right arms straight out and yelled, "Heil Hitler, Heil Hitler," the words rumbling in my ears. This was all quite unforgettable.

In a few days, climbing worn wooden steps at the appointed address, I was perplexed. Could this really be where Bavaria's lion of politics lived? I didn't find out until a bodyguard opened the door and invited me in to an almost entirely barren apartment. Hitler stepped up to shake my hand, then motioned to a small table where we sat and talked.

"The Germany you've been witnessing can only be righted by a dictatorship," he said. "That's what the German people want. Democracy hasn't worked. It's a disaster. And so are the reparations. If you want Germany to keep paying, you'll have to help us. Only a strong Germany can prevent the Marxists from taking over. If that happens, Marxist expansionist logic would compel a joint Russian-German attack on the West. I don't want that. I prefer friendship with the West."

"What about your threats against the Jews?"

"I just want them to be denied citizenship and access to public affairs. European history proves that a moderate position. Don't forget, at various times the British, French, and Spanish have thrown the Jews entirely out of their countries."

I did not leave agreeing with Hitler. Instead, I departed with the (duly reported) conviction that he was an uncommonly intense and skillful demagogue who would continue to be a force in regional politics, and whenever possible would try to take over Bavaria, and

Germany. His speeches made that clear to anyone with ears. He himself had told me the German people awaited the arousal and return of the ancient, sword-wielding Barbarossa to slay the enslavers of Germany.

INFLATION
By An Economist

I hated to shop. Before leaving home, I had to pile trillions of marks into my wheelbarrow. Today it was especially hard pushing down the street. I left the wheelbarrow in front of my colleague's apartment just a minute while I went inside to rest. And when I returned some swine had dumped the money and taken my wheelbarrow.

PROPER PROTESTS
By Adolf Hitler

Many things disturbed me in January 1923, and France's cowardly occupation of the Ruhr was but one, and certainly not the most important. I was responding to all the evils when I began to organize a massive First Party Day for late that month in Munich. After arrangements were announced, the new Police President of Munich claimed I was threatening the Bavarian government, and he severely cut my plans. I demanded to see this ridiculous police puppet, and standing hot in his office I pointed at his nose and said, "Our plans will proceed regardless. And if you try to stop our movement of national betterment, then you can shoot me first because I'll be conspicuously in the lead, and two hours later the government will be finished."

"In that case, Herr Hitler, I'm banning all your political activities for First Party Day. But don't worry. I'll also ban the Social Democratic rally."

These outrageous abrogations of liberty devastated me. How could I allow my voice to be stuffed at this critical instant? I appealed to Captain Ernst Roehm, whose distinguished war record enabled him to get me an audience with General von Lossow, Chief of the National Army in Bavaria.

I told him: "Excellency, if you will only permit our National Socialist movement, which has always supported the Army and in fact has many adherents in the Army, to continue to speak out in order to help Germany, I will with haste report to you following Party Day activities. I haven't the minutest intention of staging a Putsch."

Lossow agreed to remove the ban. But the Police President, trying not to appear a completely impotent bureaucrat, insisted we limit ourselves to six meetings, and keep our storm troops away from the open drilling spaces on Field of Mars and instead cram into Circus Krone, which was not suited for large marches.

Naturally, I implemented my plans unchanged from conception. At each of a dozen halls, I was received by serious men ready to follow a Fuehrer who stepped to the fore and offered strength they found nowhere else. The next day, as I arrived on a smooth, snow-carpeted Field of Mars, six thousand storm troops were lined up in perfect rows, staring at me.

Within days I decreed that National Socialists would not be supporting Germany's passive resistance in the Ruhr. The French certainly wouldn't worried about our workers loafing while our factories rotted. Since Germany was too disarmed and weak to crush the French militarily, the best alternative would be to destroy the coal mines and factories and leave their blackened remains as jagged tombstones commemorating the resistance of a great people.

MAY DAY
By Adolf Hitler

I conferred with several armed and semi-organized nationalist groups, and we agreed not to permit communists and other leftists to openly stage May Day demonstrations that, after all, would express contempt for the misery they had already inflicted on Germany. Roehm and I then visited General von Lossow, and I told him, "It's mandatory the Army intervene against the leftists, and further that you turn over to us the weapons belonging to nationalist groups previously under your temporary care."

"Protecting the health of the state is my foremost duty," said the general. "Anyone making threats will be shot."

"The health of the state is already imperiled," I insisted.

"I hope my position is clear, Herr Hitler."

The Chief of Bavarian State Police, Colonel von Seisser, was comparably uncooperative, even when I said, "Any Red rallies will proceed only if they surmount my body, alive or dead."

A few days later I ordered Roehm and a few SA elite to go to the Army barracks and offer guards what their commanders surely wanted: Nazi assistance in quelling the inevitable leftist outrages on May first. The guards helped us load numerous rifles and machine guns onto a transport truck, one of several recently purchased.

Early on May Day various patriotic leagues took positions at important locations in Munich, and I deployed my men and others, fully equipped, at a military training site. While most of the men drilled and tended to their weapons, some hounded me to hurry and attack.

"At this point there's nothing realistic to attack," I told them. "The police have cordoned off access to the communists. And we can't attack the police since they've been so helpful. We've got to wait. Patience is mandatory in every battle."

Around noon, I thought I saw... no, probably not. Not that. That would be absolutely it. But it was — Ernst Roehm being driven onto the grounds by units from the Army and police. Fifteen hundred armed comrades stared right at me as I clutched my helmet by the strap twisting in my hand. When Roehm stepped out, he said, "I've just come from General von Lossow. He's never talked to me like that, and I've never seen him like that. Believe me, those weapons must be returned immediately."

"Just a minute, Roehm," said Gregor Strasser, leader of a group. "If we attack now, the National Army'll come over to us immediately. They won't defend something not worth defending."

"We're not prepared for a Putsch," I said. "That's not our purpose today. Besides, Captain Roehm, I'm sure, can arrange for us to return the weapons to the barracks ourselves. We can do that, can't we, Captain?"

That is what we did. We did not hand anything over under gunpoint. And on the way to the barracks, we clobbered some communists and burned their flags and banners, and at the fleeing bastards I shouted, "If we hadn't been betrayed, your fate would be much more severe."

That night at a rally in Circus Krone, I said, "I should remind you that we're now so powerful the Army and police have to combine to deal with us. That is a victory. And we still have plenty of weapons. Our goals remain unchanged, and our young movement will soon be ready."

It did not matter some SA units called me a coward for not launching a suicidal attack, or that some newspapers said I was in eclipse en route to oblivion. That summer I simply vacationed at a magnificent place in the Bavarian Alps. This was not oblivion even if not the political apex. It was the top of the world, and from there I could see far beyond those who belittled me.

ON THE OBERSALZBERG
By Dietrich Eckart

Never had I seen Adolf so peaked as when I met him at the train station
in Berchtesgaden. His eyes were as darkly encircled as those of an abandoned raccoon, and he carried as his burden the shy and diffident expression of one who had several times been kicked in delicate places.

"The May Day demonstration wasn't so damaging as that," I said. "I know your mood'll improve in this Alpine paradise. You'll mend here just like me."

I still liked and supported Adolf as much as ever and had already said I did not resent his removing me as editor of the Volkischer Beobachter. Several times I had passed out on my desk, and was anyway tired of the regimen and more interested in the relaxed status of a convivial ideologue.

During the summer I wanted to give Adolf a few ideas to aid his continued ascendancy in Bavarian, and German, politics. When I tried to speak to him, however, he just turned his head and looked out our boarding house window at the mountains. Maybe Adolf wasn't intentionally rude, but he certainly was not the same. Once, from the next room, unknown to him, I saw and heard him in front of the manager's wife.

"I can't stand the perversion and decay of Berlin," he pronounced, waving his whip like an intoxicated conductor. "I tell you, I was so disgusted I nearly imagined myself to be Jesus Christ as he found his father's temple occupied by Hebrew money-changers and was moved to seize his whip and thrash the heathens out. I too shall someday descend on Berlin for a similar process of eviction."

I think the lady was impressed. She definitely was attentive. I was disgusted. Often I had called Hitler Germany's Messiah, but that was meant as a realistic assessment of earthly powers. When a man starts saying he really is Christ-like, it's time for a trip to the insane asylum. I was not actually proposing to have Adolf committed. I had been committed, but for drugs, not for attributing divine powers to myself. Adolf just needed to settle down.

GERMAN DAYS
By General Erich Ludendorff

Organizers of the German Days celebration urged me to be the most honored guest and said my presence would ensure the biggest display of patriotism since the outbreak of the Great War. I agreed, and on September first I stood in Nuremberg as legions of old comrade officers marched by with the pride of imminent commitment. Countless uniformed veterans and paramilitary members also joined the procession while hundreds of thousands of cheering Germans covered us with lilacs and roses. Following two hours of martial revelry, we principles gathered on a huge stage, and I let Hitler stand next to me, as he requested. I knew he had been in a bit of a fall and was too good a fellow for that. So he stood right by me as I received cheers and adulation. We still had plans, Hitler and I, and I knew he'd be a damn good aide if I decided to stage an armed and dictatorial takeover of Bavaria.

During the second day of celebration, I made a few dignified statements about the predicament of the country, and others spoke with comparable restraint. But Hitler played the agitator and said, "In a few weeks the dice will roll. What we are preparing today will be greater than the Great War, and it will be fought on German soil for the whole world."

THE BATTLE LEAGUE
By Ernst Roehm

For three weeks I encouraged, lectured, threatened and sometimes even pleaded with various paramilitary leaders to stifle their egos and embrace altruism by giving full political control of the Battle League to Adolf Hitler. Colonel Kriebel, the military commander, and others objected because they did not want to enter dangerous situations unless they deemed it mandatory. This position seemed unchangeable until September twenty-sixth, when the new Chancellor of Germany, Gustav Streseman, called off passive resistance in the Ruhr and resumed paying reparations. The following day Hitler met with the paramilitary leaders. They debated for two hours, but no one would yield to him. Ultimately, he clenched both fists in front of his chest and said, "Do you expect me to stand limp with no mandate while the French claw the flesh right out of our starving mouths? Is that what you really want? And do you want the communists to continue burrowing under our skin while we sit here and discuss who should have leadership? You're all capable men. That's not in doubt. You are, however, far more astute in matters of the sword. And, as the tenets of Clauswitz have surely instructed all of us, the sword must always be guided by the unwavering hand of political expertise. I ask you in the name of righteous salvation to give me political command of the Battle League."

Several strong men, shaking with emotion, stepped up to take Hitler's hand and pledge their efforts to his control.

OUR ORDER
By Gustav von Kahr

"Now that I've regained considerable influence, as State Commissar, I can certainly use your help, and that of your German Battle League," I told Hitler. "But you're not to do anything rash."

"I have fourteen demonstrations planned tomorrow, and I'll be addressing all of them," he said.

"You will not. Anything of a revolutionary nature will be carefully planned and orchestrated. I won't permit you to unilaterally foment trouble that could besmirch all of us. You've done ample speechmaking for the moment."

Hitler ejected from his chair and with both hands thrashed the air above his head, bouncing up and down as he screamed, "You're betraying the country and flushing away rights and stifling free speech and liberty."

I tried to respond but he continued his regrettable antics until wilting back in the chair, his arms limp at his sides. Before dismissing him, I called for my secretary to bring some water.

I had bigger worries in Berlin where Chancellor Gustav Stresemann declared the Emergency Act giving General von Seeckt absolute power over the Army. When the general smashed leftist revolts in Saxony and Hamburg and a few other pockets, that was good work. But then Seeckt got so intoxicated he commanded General von Lossow to force the Volkischer Beobachter to cease publication. The newspaper had been running articles that called Seeckt a democratic lackey, and asserted the general was a pawn for Jewish interests, and his wife a scheming Jewess. Chancellor Stresemann was also attacked, quite correctly, for being as tainted as Seeckt.

I summoned Lossow to my office, and we agreed the order was inappropriate and against the national interests of Bavaria. A letter to that effect was sent to Berlin. Seeckt responded that Lossow had to be sacked immediately. I countered that General von Lossow would under any and all circumstances remain in command of Bavarian forces. And my next step was the most stunning: I ordered the Bavarian troops of the National Army to take a special oath to Bavaria. In German history, that had never happened.

CLOSING IN
By Erwin von Scheubner-Richter

Throughout October 1923, as all factions readied to act, we Nazis gathered weapons for a march on Berlin. The Bavarian leaders — Kahr, Lossow and Seisser — also wanted to take the capital. But after they did not invite Hitler to one of their meetings, he trembled the triumvirate with a bewitching speech at Circus Krone that called for us to keep advancing until the swastika rested atop Berlin Palace. Hitler thought the ecstatic response would provide leverage in a meeting with Colonel von Seisser two days later.

"Kahr is a monarchist moron whose main goal is to put royalty back on top of Bavaria," Hitler said. "I propose you and General von Lossow join me in supreme leadership, not only in Bavaria, but all of Germany."

"I've always been sickened by Ludendorff's contempt for Bavarians," said Seisser. "I refuse to be associated with him."

In a subsequent meeting, Lossow again warned Hitler against unauthorized initiatives.

My friend Alfred Rosenburg and I then suggested we kidnap Kahr at a November fourth commemoration of German Memorial Day. But this option was rejected because a few party cowards convinced Hitler to "quit listening to Baltics who'll ruin the movement." Nevertheless, on November seventh, I was able to assemble various SA and Battle League members at my apartment, and they told Hitler, "The men can't hold back much longer. If action doesn't come soon, they'll go home or join the Army. They need regular paychecks. Some are starting to believe you might be flimsy as the rest."

Slapping the coffee table, Hitler burst to attention and said, "Don't worry. At last the instant has arrived for me to lead Germany out of the morass of betrayal and into the sweet state of redemption. Tomorrow night we take over."

Several men protested.

"I thought you wanted action. Well, here it is, now. I don't want to hear any more complaints from any of you. We can't make our plans so long range and safe that any nun would approve. This is a Putsch, not a church service. Tomorrow night we strike."

PUTSCH
By Adolf Hitler

Due to the essentials of secrecy, I only told a few people about the operative decision last night. Now, by phone and messenger, I was ordering SA and Battle League leaders to assemble their storm troops and be at the Burgerbrau, or the nearby Lowenbrau, at eight tonight. Some men asked what was up, and I told them not to ask, and others knew by my tone not to ask.

In early afternoon I left party headquarters and went to Cafe Heck. I had to relax, and it was important I appear relaxed to others. I sat and ate and sipped quite congenially with my official photographer, Heinrich Hoffmann, and I then asked him to accompany me on some errands. After I insisted he wait for me outside a couple of places, he made the ridiculous statement: "You're acting funny. What's going on?"

"Hoffmann," I said, "I simply have urgent business, and my head and my tooth are one in pain, and there should be nothing easier to understand than that, and I must go."

I returned to party headquarters. There was nothing to do but wait with Rosenburg, Graf and Drexler. As the minutes scraped toward eight, I repeatedly parted the curtains to look outside at my red Mercedes, which was fueled and ready to plunge us toward confrontation. I certainly was not frightened. I knew what to do. At the right moment I signaled to march outside and we climbed in my car and I ordered Graf to drive fast. Soon we pulled up to the Burgerbrau, a massive hall in the center of gardens and restaurants. Lots of unidentified armed men were already walking around outside, and everyone looked at me as I led our group out of the car.

"What's this?" said Drexler. "You said we were going to a political meeting outside town."

I put my hand on his shoulder, pulled him close and said, "Tonight is the night of the National Socialist revolution."

"I wish you all the best, but I'm not giving my unequivocal support to something like this," Drexler said.

I did not care. The rest of us walked into the lobby. I simply stared aside police posted at the entry and gathered with comrades who watched me point into the crammed assemblage and say, "There's Gustav von Kahr up there sputtering about what Germany needs, has always needed, and always will if he, or someone like him, retains primary power."

I glanced at a few watches near me before peeking inside again. General von Lossow and Colonel von Seisser sat on stage behind Kahr. They were all ridiculous and intolerable, and every minute pained me until strong engines and big tires finally creased the night. In an instant Hermann Goering, steel helmet pulled down tight and machine pistol in hand, charged through the door, followed by about twenty of his best shock troops.

Just inside the auditorium a group of police stood without conviction in my path. I ordered them to march outside immediately, and they did. Then I undid the snug belt around my trench coat, threw the coat to an assistant and drew my pistol from a pocket inside my cutaway coat.

"All right, now, to the stage," I shouted.

"Heil Hitler."

As I bulled toward the buffoons, panic and commotion erupted in the hall, and blue bloods spilled into the aisles and riddled the air with hoots and squeals. I grabbed a chair, placed it in my path and stood on it, and directed my pistol straight up at the high ceiling and fired a loud shot that quieted everyone well before the echo had ceased.

"There will be silence," I roared. "A machine gun is poised at the door, and its presence is an ongoing reminder to all of you that the long-delayed national revolution has begun and is progressing with remarkable rapidity. Hundreds of armed and dedicated troops have surrounded this building and no one is permitted to leave. We've already taken over District Military Headquarters and the Police Ministry, and we've deposed the Bavarian government as well as the Reich government, and the forces that count in Germany are at this moment advancing under the swastika."

Springing from the chair, pistol poised in my right hand, I used my left to pry through people and tables, and after overcoming final obstacles I mounted the stage and glared at Kahr, Lossow and Seisser and commanded they follow me at once into a side room for essential discussions. At first they were reluctant to comply, stepping back and standing rigid, so I waved my pistol in their faces.

"Leave them alone, you lout," came one of countless barbs. Still absolutely undaunted, I wheeled toward the nervous gathering of three thousand upper crusts and assured them: "Our three distinguished Bavarian Leaders will not be harmed, and we'll only need to talk ten minutes or so before concluding our business of state."

Graf and I and some storm troops followed the trio into a small room, and I began to explain the triumvirate's exciting opportunities. When my throat became dry I ordered a beer and took several gulps.

"You're a swine," said Seisser.

"You must forgive me, but what I do, I do for the love and survival of Germany. I couldn't wait and let the communists again strike first."

Kahr leaned his lips toward an ear of Seisser. I aimed my pistol and said, "No talking unless I say so."

"You can shoot me if you want," said Kahr, "but I won't be coerced into this."

"You misunderstand," I said. "The object of our presence here is really quite simple. And though I very much regret having to offer you splendid opportunities under such compelling circumstances, I must tell you there are ample bullets in my gun for all three of you, whether you want to be shot or not. I'll also shoot myself if you don't at once offer your cooperation to our patriotic tour de force that can only make you, and Germany, more powerful. Ritter von Kahr, you will be the state administrator. General von Lossow, you will be the Reich Army Minister. Colonel von Seisser, you will be the Reich Police Minister. I, who will serve as president, am promoting you gentlemen well beyond anything you could have dreamed of, yet you stand there resistant and glum. I must remind you that you will either join me, and succeed with me, or you will cease to exist."

"What is General Ludendorff's place in all of this? Where is he?" said Kahr.

"The general will lead our new Army in its victories over Berlin, and elsewhere," I said.

"Where is he?" Kahr persisted.

"He is en route and certainly almost here."

UNSIGHTLY
By Professor von Mueller

Our proud group of rich and titled Germans was increasingly indignant about being detained and threatened and seeing ladies pinched by a bunch of common baboons, and we kept pounding tables and stomping feet until SA leader Hermann Goering, in a delightful emulation of his Fuehrer, climbed a chair and fired a pistol shot through the roof. That elicited the desired calm, but harsh sounds had resumed when Hitler, ridiculous in a floppy coat and tails and too big trousers, reappeared and pushed a path to the podium. His face was very pale and wet, and he ground his teeth before shouting, "The machine gun will be activated if there is not silence."

Penetrating like a shriek from the wild, his voice (more than the gun) earned him the floor.

"I don't know why you're acting this way," he entreated. "Tonight is indisputably one of the most important nights in all of German history, and signals the end of the reign of the November Criminals and the start of a nationalist government fully committed to restoring the things we treasure most. Right now our distinguished Bavarian leaders are in the other room grappling with their souls about how they can help make a better Germany. As they strain in this most crucial instant of their lives, may I tell them you'll support them?"

Torrents of Ja and Heil erupted.

"This is an overwhelming mandate for a free Germany," Hitler pronounced. "I assure every one of you that the German revolution will either be a success or all of us will soon be dead."

OUTRAGEOUSLY UNINFORMED
By General Erich Ludendorff

I did not even have my uniform on, and was still wearing a hunting jacket, when from out of the dark fog came a rap on the villa door. Standing in front, the small and normally sedate Erwin von Scheubner-Richter was almost in a pant as he said, "Hitler has just launched the national revolution and success is impossible without your immediate intervention."

"The hell, what? I'm the Quartermaster General, the national hero. Why was I not informed of this? For what conceivable reason was I left out? I hope you're aware, Scheubner-Richter, that without my help and prestige Hitler wouldn't have a fraction of the martial backing he currently has, nor would he be in a position to even sneakily start something he obviously can't proceed with without me."

"Will you please, Herr Quartermaster General, in the spirit of a true nationalist Germany, come with me at once to the Burgerbrau?" said Scheubner-Richter, motioning to Hitler's pretentious car.

"I will go for a united Germany," I said.

After traveling at high speeds in bad visibility with a shaken

Scheubner-Richter at the wheel, I marched into the Burgerbrau and ignited applause and roaring heils. Hitler came out a side room, walking rapidly toward me, smiling, hand extended, head bowing, and said, "Excellency, Excellency, thankfully you are here."

I did not reply but looked toward the little room, and Hitler said, "Yes, this way, follow me."

Kahr, Lossow and Seisser were impressed by my presence, and I assured them I had not known anything, either, but was willing to improvise and join the cause.

"Of course you know, Herr General, that Hitler's going to be dictator of Germany," said Kahr. "As head of the National Army, you'd be under his command."

That was another insult, certainly, but I did not plan to remain in that position long. On I plunged in behalf of the Putsch, first addressing my two colleagues in a soldierly fashion.

"General von Lossow," I concluded, "you are a gentleman and an officer, and I need your hand to seal the promise of cooperation in pursuit of a decent Germany."

Lossow approached me, watery eyed, and clasped my hand and said, "Excellency, it would be an honor for me, and for Germany, to again have the opportunity to follow your commands." Colonel von Seisser also readily extended his hand and, after some coaxing, Kahr too sealed his word with a handshake. Then Hitler, sporting a too wide grin, almost pranced leading us out in front of the impatient audience. On stage we took turns affirming our dedication to the new national government, and hundreds burst into an especially rousing rendition of Deutschland Uber Alles.

Soon after the happy audience was dismissed, we received reports that troops at the Army Engineer barracks were resisting our overtures. Hitler announced he was going to the scene and asked me — perhaps he thought he told me — to assume command at the Burgerbrau.

GONE
By Adolf Hitler

Action was inconclusive at the Army Engineer barracks and the outcome would not anyway be of immediate import. I hustled back to my car, sensing that Roehm had by now received the order to lead his men from their rally at the Lowenbrau to capture District Military Headquarters. I had also called the Police Ministry. Wilhelm Frick was assuring worried officers there that the Putsch was positive and to relax and do nothing until he advised.

As we sped up to the Burgerbrau, my bodyguards looked at me in awe. They knew I was now as good as dictator of Germany. That's what I felt like, popping out of my car and marching into the big hall.

Immediately I noticed Ludendorff — tall, gray, and grim — and I said: "Excellency, I don't see our three compatriots. Where are they?"

"I've excused them for duties elsewhere."

"You can't possibly have turned loose the very men who can help us most when they're here, and hurt us most when they're elsewhere."

"I won't permit you to question the word of honor of German officers," said Ludendorff.

"Your integrity isn't in question, Herr General. But you've blundered, and I'm extremely worried what they might be doing in these critical hours without our supervision."

I sank onto a stool and slumped over a hard beer table, and was preparing another riposte when singing and marching lured us out the door and to abrupt attention as with glee we received one thousand elite cadets from the Infantry School. We ordered them to march with their swastika banners to Kahr's administrative offices and take over.

Ludendorff and I were then driven to District Military Headquarters for a conference with Roehm. He told us a brass band had signaled his arrival as people in the street cheered. Inside, several soldiers had opened the gate, and he entered alone, out-stared anyone hostile, and demanded access for all his men.

"The soldiers know General von Lossow is with us," said Roehm. "Where is he, by the way?"

"We're attempting to locate him now," said Ludendorff.

Roehm's face wrenched.

"Well, what other key installations have we taken over so far?" he asked, looking at Ludendorff, who did not answer, then at me.

"The infantry cadets have probably already seized Kahr's offices," I said. "That task should be well under way."

"What else?" said Roehm. "There are lots of facilities, and we have plenty of men."

"I cannot be precisely sure, given the complexities of operations, just what we currently have under control," I said. "Our main imperative now is to reestablish contact with Kahr, Lossow and Seisser. We've been sending messages, in the Quartermaster General's name, instructing Lossow and Seisser to report here. I hope they haven't been arrested by anti-Putsch elements."

"I'm disappointed we didn't capture more when opportunities were open," said Roehm, swiveling his eyes between Ludendorff and me.

"Don't concern yourself with disappointments, Captain," said Ludendorff. "You have more immediate duties."

FOOLS
By The Duty Officer

At District Military Headquarters they came into the telephone room from time to time: Hitler, Ludendorff and Roehm.

"Keep trying to get General von Lossow, and don't stop," said Ludendorff, leaning over to emphasize the gravity of his order. I hadn't realized his jaw receded so much.

Roehm, decorated with war medals that bounced on his chest as he paced, told me I was also to place every possible call for Kahr and Seisser. Hitler primarily stared at me. Then these revolutionaries ignored me, discussing tactics before going into the next room.

Soon a call came from the Infantry Barracks, and I was given orders. With great vigor but considerable circumspection, I obeyed.

When the three intrepid men reentered, I said, "Herr General, there has been no contact whatever from General von Lossow. Shall I keep trying?"

"You can't keep trying except when I'm here to oversee," Roehm said. "Otherwise, stay off the phones.

"We have a report, Herr General, that a National Army unit is en route here from the south. We're about to be attacked, but we still haven't determined the whereabouts of our supposed allies. With due deference to your automatic assumption of an officer integrity, I think we've been duped, Herr General."

"We still mustn't presuppose the dishonor of a German officer, Captain Roehm."

"Perhaps not, Herr General, but you must forgive me for surmising the dishonor of this German telephone duty officer. Sir, you're under arrest, and if circumstances were any more critical, I'd order you shot. That's if I could restrain myself from the honor of pulling the trigger."

PUTSCH PRINCIPLES
By Erhard Auer

Getting ready for bed I heard harsh knocks, and before I reached the door it smashed in from boot blasts that propelled into my living room the snarling faces of men wearing swastikas. They grabbed my wife and jerked her against a wall, and the way she looked at me, though in many respects easily understood, was also in part inscrutable. Was she angry with me because, as Bavaria's Social Democratic leader, I had spoken out to protect Hitler's right to freedom of speech? Was she angry because I had argued that Hitler should not be deported? Was her look of pain and terror a message that I would in some way be to blame if these heathens killed her?

Maybe these were not so much my wife's expressions as impressions in my mind, a mind now fraught with guilt about defending a man who was, as if by his own hand, invading our home. We were taken to some obscure building and held with a number of prominent politicians. Later we were joined by quite a few Jews who had been torn from their homes. For all of us the night was cold, rough and uncertain. I definitely hoped the Hitler revolution would not succeed, and did not think it could. That would be too much for Germany, and for me. I told my wife that my defending Adolf Hitler as a matter of principle was no longer morally defensible.

SUPPRESSION
By Gustav von Kahr

I was dizzy and nauseated and having trouble keeping my car straight on dark residential streets. Yes, I had publicly promised to support an illegal Germany. But that was forced on me. And I had said, right there on stage, that I would be an agent of the monarchy. So I had not done anything wrong. I knew I had done right once I thought about it. That buoyed me enough to keep driving.

I went to my administrative offices and helped calm renegades before driving to the Infantry Barracks. There, just after three on the cool snow-damp morning of November ninth, General von Lossow strode to me, shook my hand and presented a copy of the message he had just ordered transmitted over all German wireless stations. The message stated all three of us repudiated the Hitler Putsch because "expressions of support extracted at gunpoint are invalid." There was also a warning not to misuse our names for nefarious purposes. Regrettably, Munich had already been plastered with posters that trumpeted the successful Putsch and stressed Lossow and I were involved.

Though just as upset as the others, I really did not want to refute anything right away. I was very sleepy and reclined on a couch and would have slept, but they insisted I compose something now. The sentences did not form rapidly, but I was able to state the Putsch was illegal and so were its methods. In the name of Bavaria, I abolished the National Socialist party and other right wing groups as well as their Battle Leagues and paramilitary organizations. All that rabble would be gone, and Hitler and the others punished to the fullest for this reprehensible betrayal not only of Bavaria, but of the trust we gave them. I ordered this dictate posted all over Munich on the spaces vacated by Putsch posters torn down and destroyed.

We were also committed to silencing, and keeping far away, those Prussian-infested troublemakers from the Chancellery in Berlin. General von Seeckt had threatened that if we in Bavaria did not stop the Putsch, he would send his (non-Bavarian) national troops to do the job, probably in a most unsavory manner. We did not want Prussians and Weimar stooges in Bavaria. We already had enough refuse.

WRETCHED
By Adolf Hitler

At District Military Headquarters it was already five a.m., a horrible time that split my stomach, and everything worsened the instant we talked to a morose colonel who had just been to the Infantry Barracks.

"Never," said Ludendorff. "Never will I trust anyone in the Army. They're unworthy of honor and trust. Never again will I wear the putrid uniform of the German General Staff. It's encrusted with lies and defeat."

"We still have much hope, Herr General," I said.

"Quite correct," Ludendorff responded. "I know the rank and file of the National Army can still be convinced to follow me. Why should soldiers follow traitors instead of a supreme wartime commander?"

I jumped up and started walking while I talked. "Those swine don't understand the power embodied in my voice, Herr General. No later than this very evening they'll be crawling because I'm going to hold fourteen mass rallies, and I shall deliver the most passionate speeches of my career, and I'll whip every person in every audience into a state of patriotic fervor, and they'll be ready to march with us against anyone in opposition."

Ludendorff and I and our staffs were then driven back to the Burgerbrau. Darkness encased the big building, and before entering I pulled my trench coat tight and pounded cold ground with big boots.

ERRANDS
By An Assistant

Hitler was curled up on a cot when I hurried over and asked if he wanted to give me dictation for that evening's rally posters.

"Oh," he said. "Well, not now. We have plenty of time for that. But do go at once and call the Police Ministry. I must find out how we're doing there."

Upon returning, I hesitated to speak.

"Don't stand there with your tongue clamped in interruption of my nap," Hitler snapped.

"I'm sorry. But they were very unfriendly and wouldn't answer any questions. And just before hanging up on me they said Frick wouldn't be home for breakfast."

With each hand Hitler grabbed the side of his cot and shook it, and said, not so much to me standing rigid before him, but to something: "You idiots. You absolute scum sucking morons. Don't you understand what this has been all about? Don't you understand I've forever acted with restraint and good faith? Aren't you aware I could have killed Kahr, Lossow and Seisser? Don't you know I could have shot up and taken over Kahr's administrative offices? Hasn't it occurred to your putrid brains that I could have destroyed telephone and telegraph installations? I could have done all of those things, and more. But I didn't. I love Bavaria so much, yet I've been betrayed again. I'm sick of having my sacrifices rammed back in me. I'm sick of being told of evermore treachery. Maybe we can still overcome all of this, but if not, fine, then we can all hang ourselves. Now get out of here."

AROUSAL
By Julius Streicher

Since arriving from home in Nuremberg, I had been dashing around Munich to examine our prospects. Now, as light crept into gray sky, I rushed into the Burgerbrau, shaking my whip overhead.

"Where's Hitler?" I asked a storm trooper.

"He's in there but he can't talk."

"Stick your head in a sack of manure," I said, and pushed into the room.

"Fuehrer, you must lift yourself at once and overwhelm the masses. They're waiting for you in the streets."

Lying down, Hitler raised his head a little. I looked into empty eyes and said, "Herr Hitler, get up. Thousands of storm troops and armed men just told me they're ready to thrash our enemies. Swastikas are flying from windows and balconies. It's time to inspire these patriots to wreak bloody victory. What's the matter?"

"Streicher, you must not bother me," said Hitler. "I'm ruminating on matters of greater importance. Here, hand me that pen and paper. I'll place you in charge of all speaking and the organization thereof. You're a fine speaker. Go do the job."

THE NEWS
By A Nazi

It wasn't necessary to pay eight billion marks. I had been given a copy of the Volkischer Beobachter, and read about our devastatingly successful Putsch. We would soon be marching on a vulnerable Berlin. That was great. But some posters, just brought in and passed around, had big black letters that claimed: "The Prussian Ludendorff Is Guilty of High Treason." I did not understand that even when I stared at the general.

WE SHALL MARCH
By General Erich Ludendorff

The floor of the Burgerbrau was muddy and wet, the condition of the men the same, and there was an overwhelming smell. I nevertheless knew this stink was far better still than the wrenching odor of betrayal emitted from the living carcasses of Kahr, Lossow and Seisser. Those Germans had grievously damaged a great patriotic cause, and were threatening all of us in this cauldron of a beer cellar. I rapped the table with my fist, shooting up to shout, "If we continue to sit and gaggle, we'll soon be surrounded and face the alternative of being crushed or surrendering ignominiously. We shall march!"

I ordered Colonel Kreibel to assemble our men out front, and immediately those who had been sitting around damp and disheartened, and in danger of further decline, began to move with the resoluteness of soldiers preparing for immediate operation. The men may not have had standard uniforms, but I knew inside their patch-covered garments beat the common hearts of patriotic Germans. In front of the procession now stood the color guard, holding the Imperial German Flag and a swastika banner. Our leadership lined up next, with Hitler and me in the center. Behind us formed the Shock Troop Hitler. Each of eighty men was armed with a carbine and two potato masher grenades. Then came two thousand followers, carrying guns and bayonets, and filling the street side to side.

"This will show the traitors how most of Munich really feels," Hitler said.

"That's why I planned it. The National Army would never fire on me."

A little before noon I nodded, and my directive was issued: "Forward March."

In ten minutes we reached Ludwig Bridge, where a small group of Green Police poised to prevent us from crossing the Isar River. Some of the police shouted "Heil" while others pointed guns at us.

The police commander ordered, "Stop or we'll shoot."

One of our men said, "We're your comrades. Don't ..."

A trumpet blast from the rear shot into my open mouth, and at least forty men charged the police and socked them with rifle butts and pistol handles, then denounced their traitorous behavior. I vetoed cries to shoot the police, and instead ordered my men to quit slapping and spitting on the prisoners and to simply take them back to the Burgerbrau.

ON WE MARCHED
By Adolf Hitler

Our patriotic songs pulled shopkeepers, clerks and students away from meaningless daily obligations and into long broad columns that now moved with pace toward St. Mary's Plaza, the heart of Munich. Before me I could soon see rising the beautiful Gothic arches upholding Town Hall, and there our Nazi flags hung already high.

The instant we entered the plaza I heard Julius Streicher tell a throng: "The enemies of Hitler and Ludendorff are oozing scabs that must be torn away right now."

While our columns slowed to move through, we began to sing "O Germany, High in Honor," and everyone applauded so hard it pushed us on.

WHERE NOW?
By Colonel Hermann Kreibel

Behind us and everywhere else so many excited people were compressed into tight spaces that I wondered how we were going to turn around and march back to the Burgerbrau. When we pressed beyond St. Mary's Plaza and headed toward the Hall of the Field Marshals, I was quite surprised. I did not know why we were going that way, but it did not matter because that was the way General Ludendorff was going.

A FEELING
By Erwin von Scheubner-Richter

As we passed the Hall of the Field Marshals, me trudging next to a silent Hitler, I recalled how many times he had told me the happiest moment in his life occurred at this noble venue in 1914 when the Great War arrived and gave him the opportunity to defend Germany. Today, almost a decade later, he had infinitely more prestige but clearly was not happy, and he shared my foreboding. I could tell. Next to me he walked.

I had expressed my misgivings at the start of this march; Hitler hadn't replied, but his expression concurred. Now, finally, we saw what we'd sensed and feared: a platoon of Green Police running fast out from one side of the Hall of the Field Marshals onto and across Residenz Street where in tight formations the men blocked our way and activated rifles, pistols and truncheons. Many in our column must have sensed a devastating roadblock, and those near the front stopped singing. Graf, Hitler's bodyguard, waved an arm and shouted, "Don't shoot. General Ludendorff is coming."

Like an electrical shock, it stunned me when Hitler suddenly interlocked his arm with mine, and jerked. His terror surged into me and added to mine. Some of our men started thrusting bayonets at the police, who thrust back, and as the shouting and confusion increased, an inevitable first shot was fired, unknown in source but clear, startling and unmistakably not the last. After a brief delay, cracks sounded aplenty, and I was blasted in the chest and certainly dead before, or not long after, my falling body yanked Hitler to the pavement.

GREEN POLICE
By Lieutenant Michel von Godin

Only after one in the mob had first shot at me, and hit an officer just behind, did my Green Police spontaneously begin a torrent of fire. Everywhere the traitors began to fall, or dive for protection, or simply run, throwing their rifles away before scattering through buildings and alleys. In less than a minute, at least a hundred of them lay dead or wounded.

I'd expected a much tougher battle from so many armed men. But most of them hadn't even shot back. Despicable cowards, I thought. When my officers and I began to examine their abandoned rifles, lonesome implements of war littering the streets, we were more than startled. The traitors had come at us in great numbers, with grim faces and bayonets on their rifles, and most had done so with unloaded weapons.

I ALONE
By General Erich Ludendorff

Tall and dignified, I strode in contempt of those so thoroughly debauched they'd actually fired near me, former Quartermaster General of the German Imperial Army and symbol incarnate of Teutonic victory and well being. No one around merited acknowledgment. So, with one hand formally in my coat pocket and the other at my side, I kept walking like a lone sentinel through the cordon of Green Police and on over into the Hall of the Field Marshals, where at least I could commune with the spirit and memory of great men.

A few police officers came, trying to be solicitous, and offered to notify my family that I was all right.

"It would insult my family to receive any news from traitors like you," I said.

"Oh, Excellency," they entreated.

"Don't call me Excellency. From your tainted mouths the term is obscene. You call me Herr Ludendorff. And don't ever call me General again, either. I don't want to be associated with an Army that didn't keep its word."

"Excellency, I am sorry, but we must take you to the police station for a few questions," said a police officer, bowing crisply.

"Since I'm now a civilian in spirit, as well as fact, it doesn't bother me to follow the orders of a subordinate like you. My duty here today has been completed."

TOO QUICK
By Adolf Hitler

My bodyguard had buried me with his big body until shooting ceased, and I thought he was dead. Almost everyone looked dead. And my left shoulder dangled on fire. Bullets must have destroyed it. I held my left arm in my right hand as I wobbled to my feet and began to run in a daze. Even after I pinned the bad arm to my chest, each stride on the rocky surface jarred my shoulder and head. Everything was a horror. The whole world was infested with liars and murderers, and I could never get away. How would I? No. That won't work. Will it? It might. No. It's impossible. The Green Police will get me before. I impulsively shot my right arm up and waved, dropping my wounded left as if onto hot knives. Then the yellow fiat turned and accelerated and angled next to me.

"Good God, what all has happened?" said the SA's chief doctor, bounding out of the car.

"The Green Police are trying to kill me. They've already killed the others."

"What's the matter? Where do you hurt? Your shoulder. Take off your coat."

"Not now, you idiot. They're after me. They're after you, too. Get me into the car."

The yellow car rolled off, driven by an aide.

"We'll be back at the Burgerbrau in minutes," said the doctor. "Lots of men and prisoners are still there."

"No," I said. "It would be suicidal to go back. Drive me into the mountains."

The ride in back was miserable, but the voices in front were only a nuisance because I did not care.

TERMINATED
By General von Lossow

By mid-afternoon on November ninth, less than twenty-four hours after the beginning of the cowardly attempt at armed takeover, the combined military and police forces of Bavaria were able to destroy the ignoble and enfeebled Putsch of Ludendorff and Hitler. With enormous pride I reported to Commissar von Kahr not only that the Putsch had been popped but that my bailiwick, District Military Headquarters, had been liberated, along with the Burgerbrau, and that Ernst Roehm had been arrested. Many other troublemakers were already in custody, and we were confident about soon finding Hitler. Hermann Goering was also loose but our reports indicated a bullet had forced him to crawl away from the debacle. We also wanted Rudolf Hess, Hitler's all-purpose ruffian, and did not consider him smart enough to elude us for long. Obviously, none of them had been smart enough to deal with the real authorities in Bavaria.

UNEXPECTED GUEST
By Helene Hanfstaengl

A voice cut my mother-in-law off the phone and warned her against further speaking. Then the voice announced that my house would be searched in a few minutes. By the time I hung up, Hitler had clomped half way down the stairs and was looking big-eyed at me as I came around the corner. When I told him the nature of the call, he actually yelped, and wheeled and darted up the stairs into his room, his urgency pulling me along.

"I won't give a pack of lizards the opportunity to execute me, " he said in high pitch, then snatched his pistol from a table and started to aim at his head before I grabbed his right hand with both of mine and easily twisted the weapon away.

"You really disappoint me, trying to surrender everything so meekly after an initial setback," I said. "Is this the type of man, as you've been telling everyone, who can and should lead Germany back to greatness? Are you showing any concern for the thousands who've already followed you and those millions who will if they have a chance? I think it's time for you to act as a proper Fuehrer and deal bravely with this temporary problem."

Hitler's head flopped down. Several times he tried to raise both hands to his face, but only his right could be lifted that high, and he put that hand over his face and sat there shaking quietly. I went to hide his gun and returned to tell him: "Hold your head up, and take you hand off your face so you can uphold your duty to decide what everyone should do while you're gone. I'll safe keep the papers."

"You're a saint. Thank you."

"I'll write down what you say. You sign the papers."

Just after finishing our task, we heard barking outside and loud orders issued. I rushed to hide the party papers and ran downstairs, answering the door after the first knock. Three State Police officers stared at me. A lieutenant said he wanted to search the house and hoped it would not be an inconvenience. I nodded and led them toward the stairs, thinking they would probably have to carry an inert Hitler away. Instead, he was standing at the top of the stairs.

"I've been waiting for you," he screamed at the police. "I've been anticipating the arrival of yet more who desire to trample the future of Germany. You have a fine job, yes you do, the very best. Your job is to continue the betrayal of your country. Unless you're complete naive imbeciles, you're aware of the mad, unending array of problems crippling your country. Those problems were caused, were forced on all of us, by the very people I was trying to liberate you from. Yes, I'm glad you're here. Do something more to hurt your country. Take me away. Do it quickly. You'll be heroes and no more of my time will be squandered talking to hateful traitors."

The police were stunned and hesitant. Hitler walked down the stairs and shook hands with the lieutenant, who seemed to enjoy the gesture.

"Young man, I'm ready to leave," Hitler said. "Helene, will you please drape my trench coat over me and, with the lieutenant's permission, pin my Iron Cross on the outside?"

The lieutenant nodded, and I complied. Then, as Hitler was shaking my hand, and those of the maids, my little son, Egon, ran down the stairs, yelling at the mean men to stop hurting Onkel Dolf. Hitler leaned over and hugged the boy hard.

One of the officers opened the front door, and Hitler stepped out into a dark wind that fluttered his coat like a sail on the high seas. The cars were loud when they started, and they moved away.

SAVED
By Franz Hemmrich

The police drove Hitler into Landesburg and gave him to me to put in a cell just gotten ready. He was hunched under a soiled coat, his left arm wavering in a sling, and though the cell door was open, I had to guide him in. I hung his coat on one of two chairs at a small table and helped him onto a cot.

"You need a good meal," I said, "and here's a fellow bringing you one now. Just put the tray on the table, thank you."

Hitler waved off the food and almost collapsed back onto the cot. As his eyes glazed off the white ceiling, the only response to my words was the chill rain whipping wet and smooth off two glass windows covered by bars.

If Hitler looked out his windows in the morning, he saw a detachment of Army troops setting up camp. They had many weapons and strong orders to stop rescue attempts. This was all exciting and absolutely fitting. To us this place was not merely a prison: it was Fortress Landesberg, our bastion of big walls and watchtowers with a long ago legacy of repulsed invasions. Finally we had a potential conflict matching the purpose of the place, but we thought problems unlikely.

When I brought Hitler his nice breakfast, he was stretched on the cot and staring at the ceiling. I wondered if his eyes had been open all night. From the looks of them, they might have.

"I'll leave this on the table. You should eat something."

He only muttered, "I'll never eat again," but I was delighted and went around telling my friends Hitler had spoken to me. When I returned to pick up the tray, I saw he hadn't eaten anything.

In subsequent days Hitler had plenty of visitors. I listened to conversations from outside the door and often heard him vow he'd never take another bite of nourishment because he was the terrible man who caused the fiasco that killed so many noble men. Every time someone assured him of his worthiness, he said, "No, no, no. Here, look at these papers from New York, Paris, Berlin, all over the world. They're calling me ridiculous, inconsequential, comical, and saying I'll probably be executed. My conscience won't permit me to eat."

While Hitler daily became more bony and drawn, I twice did chance to inspect the contents of his soup bowl and dish of rice. Since it was unlikely the Fuehrer's guests would beg him to eat, then snatch a little of his food, I knew he'd been nibbling.

ADRIFT
By Dietrich Eckart

Often, after I had lectured about politics until quite late, and guests left my apartment, I knew I would be foolish to keep drinking since that would only incur a massive hangover.

"No more of this rot gut," I'd thought. "It's time for something more penetrating and powerful, something less bloating than a voluminous concoction offering alcohol and nothing more. Here is the stuff, looking small in my hand, that turns all crap into gold and transforms every headache into an intellectual orgasm. It's this mere water-looking wet stuff in the bottle that's so sweet when sucked out and pushed long and smooth into my soul."

I'd picked up a syringe and put the long needle, shiny and sharp, into the still, clear liquid. Then, always, the morphine hit me instantly in the arm and the brain, and made me warm all over as I floated high and happy so close to heaven that almost nothing could ever hurt again, and anything that could did not matter, not here now floating warm through life, leaning back, lying low on the couch with my head on a pillow propped up, looking hazily at the meteoric future of Adolf Hitler, and very sad that I, though only fifty-five, would not be present.

TRAINING
By Adolf Hitler

Since my enemies would be trying to kill me at my trial, I trained like an intellectual warrior, studying history and philosophy and economics, and also took on the most hellish exercise imaginable: I reread Marx. If necessary, I wanted to be able to present to the court, in scholarly fashion, the variety of ills posed by that philosophy, and as well I viewed my study as long-term preparation for our inevitable day of collision with Marxism.

While my mind and spirit were being honed, I added physical strength, aided by countless kind Germans who sent a delectable variety of cakes and pastries and other goodies that piqued my appetite much more than the prison diet, which itself had begun to seem at least tolerable. As I chewed on sweets, I paced my cell and launched many invectives against upcoming courtroom foes. And when I became angrier at their arrogance and stupidity, I intensified my rhetoric and walked very fast back and across my cell, chewing up adversaries just as fast as candy.

OPENING STATEMENT
By Adolf Hitler

Determined to prove myself a man of stature and worthy of the best in Germany, I opened with a cannonade to the court: "Yes, I was responsible for the Putsch. I alone bore responsibility for the deed intended to liberate Germany. But such an act obviously did not make me a criminal because it would be impossible to commit a treasonous act against a government so fundamentally traitorous as that established in shame in 1918. No, I was neither a criminal nor a traitor but a tireless worker who transformed a small, struggling party into a movement of significance and energy that inspired hope throughout Bavaria. And that very popularity, ladies and gentlemen, has led us to the most ironic and unfair situation that today exists in this courtroom. I want you to know that my primary accusers — Commissar von Kahr, General von Lossow, and Colonel von Seisser — were very supportive of my party and me, and they actually discussed and conspired with us about various means of overthrowing the criminal government in Berlin. I certainly do not criticize them for that. I merely ask why they too are not sitting in the dock, for I only did what they themselves so often contemplated and hoped for."

OUTRAGEOUS UNDERLING
By General von Lossow

That infuriating little peasant kept lurching from his seat and assaulting authorities with insults and accusations delivered in a tone loud enough to get him shot if he had still officially been the undeniable nothing he had been in the Army during the war. Now he was an inferior little troublemaker, unemployed and unemployable, who was nevertheless permitted to rant without end about his superiority.

Kahr and Seisser certainly did nothing to shut him up. They were utterly overwhelmed by Hitler's tirades and just sat there taking it like stuffed turkeys. Not me. When Hitler pounded me with barrages of bullshit, I counterattacked, and once told the court: "Hitler is both brutal and sentimental, a dangerous combination. His brutality can't be controlled in his insatiable quest to become dictator of Germany. And his sentimentality is a dubious gift that permits him to tickle emotions and trick the masses into following his call. He's fit to be a drummer, an abrasive one, but not a Fuehrer. We've got to be careful, just as the psychiatrist testified, because Hitler has this fantastic vision of himself as the German Mussolini."

Regardless of what Hitler said about me, about my well-documented opposition to the Weimar democracy, it was he who shoved his pistol in our faces to force us to take part in the Putsch. It was he who actually revolted. He should have to pay. But I was paying, too. My career in the Army was now over. I shouldn't have also had to take crap from the drummer boy. A gun in my hand could have solved that problem.

WORDS FOR FOREVER
By Adolf Hitler

This was my day, the last day of the trial, March twenty-seventh, 1924. This was my day to say final words to the court and forever emblazon myself on the psyche of the German nation and the pages of historical endeavor. Destiny beat strong in my chest as the presiding judge asked me to rise, and I was warmed by spectators who clearly had been moved by what I had already said and who, I could feel, would be transported much further by what then welled inside me, awaiting release.

"I have been indicted as one who sought to overthrow the government and assume a titled position for the purpose not only of exercising power, but for base self-aggrandizement," I stated. "That charge is absurd and insulting because it is absolutely unworthy of a great man to limit himself to the mere post of a minister. My task is clearly much larger and more essential. My mission is to be the destroyer of Marxism. I could not discharge this sacred duty if I allowed myself to be encumbered by rivals, purported equals, who might interfere with my vision of progress. I vow never to accept a title that carries any limitations. In that regard, I invoke my memory of standing at the grave of Richard Wagner, and being proud that this genius had refused to allow any of his titles to be etched on his gravestone. For posterity he willed the ultimate designation, his simple name of eminence."

The spectators, crammed close in their seats, looked at me with happy and serious expectation. They heard, and more importantly felt, what I said and what I meant, and there were nods of affirmation as I stated: "My desire to be the Fuehrer of a resurgent Germany is just as natural for me as flying is for a bird. Nothing Gustav von Kahr ever said indicated he was truly the stuff of a dictator. He said he had taken his post of commissar only because he was 'compelled.' That is an attitude so flimsy it makes its carrier unworthy of being a dictator. A worthy dictator is a man with the innate conviction and drive to propel himself forward through obstacles and opponents, and to ask, no, to demand that responsibility be placed on his strong shoulders. A dictator is a man who cannot exist without striving for the honor of elevating his people by the force of his uniqueness. I did not see these qualities anywhere else in Germany, so it fell on me to act. This was a responsibility I surely could not have ignored.

"As a result, all of us have been rewarded by the Putsch of November eighth. What might in an instant appear to be a setback clearly becomes a moral and strategic victory when it is considered that many thousands have since joined our ranks. No one has blamed me for those who have fallen. No mother has told me that I am responsible for the death of her son. No, there has only been an escalating level of enthusiasm. This means someday the masses who gathered behind our swastika banner will be united with the temporarily misguided opponents who shot them. I was relieved that the Green Police had perpetrated the act. It had not been my cherished National Army that besmirched its honor. The National Army will someday be at one with us."

"Herr Hitler, I cannot allow you to impugn the honor of the Green Police," said the presiding judge.

Without hesitation or even acknowledgment, I continued: "National Socialism will grow, and grow with the inevitability and resoluteness of a natural process. Then we on trial will be reconciled with the eternal court of history, which alone can rightfully decide the charges made against us. I already know what the verdict here will be, but that does not matter. The higher court, that of everlasting justice, will judge us as brave men who craved the best for Germany and who marched proudly into the abyss of bullets and death to sacrifice for the nation. I assure the court before me that it does not matter how many times it proclaims us guilty, the goddess of the higher court of history will surely someday tear up the verdict and embrace us warmly with acquittal."

Silence overwhelmed the room when I finished. After recovering, the judge meekly asked my fellow defendants if they too wanted to speak. They declined, of course. Their words could only have sounded frail and meaningless.

VERDICT
By Judge Georg Neithardt

To every judge it was clear Hitler remained a fine asset and should be sent back to his task of national salvation. The Bavarian Minister of Justice agreed. But he said Hitler could not be let go now. Otherwise, authorities in Berlin would demand another trial. And that would be taken from Bavaria and placed in Leipzig, much nearer Berlin, and the fate of Hitler would be in the grasp of his enemies.

On the day of the verdict, April first, an escort of guards wedged me through the large and eager crowd cordoning the courtroom. Inside, I immediately noticed a quite inordinate number of pretty women, many holding flowers and chattering how nice it would be to give the flowers to Hitler personally. There would not be time for that. I ordered everyone seated and we began reading the sentences. General Ludendorff was deemed innocent of all charges and released. Ernst Roehm and Wilhelm Frick and a few others received short sentences and were also set free because they promised to be law abiding. When Hitler was sentenced to a minimum of five years, the audience responded with appalling silence.

The court offered clarification: "Hitler acted out of the highest nationalistic motives and his fervor would not have led to the unfortunate circumstances if only Kahr, Lossow and Seisser had been more forthright and assertive in stating their opposition to a Putsch. Hitler will not be deported to Austria because he is so thoroughly and energetically a German in spirit and deed that ejecting him would be a travesty."

Raucous applause forced me to order restraint. Then I permitted Hitler to walk to the big window and make himself visible to his followers outside, and they smiled and waved and many shouted, "Heil."

This had been an exciting trial, and Hitler's authoritative demeanor made him famous in Germany and got him a lot of notice abroad. He certainly was correct. The Putsch had been a success.

PRISONER
By Franz Hemmerich

When a tired Adolf Hitler got back to Fortress Landesberg, I shook his hand with both of mine. We were all happy to see him, even though we didn't want him locked up, and hoped he would like his freshly painted cell with new shelves as well as two other cells now available to him.

Abiding always by the rules, Hitler arose early every day and bathed in his own tub. When I peeked in he seemed groggy and disoriented as he splashed water on himself, but we are all a little slow in the morning. The water woke him, and he was fastidious in all hygiene, which certainly befit a Fuehrer. He had his choice of breakfasting alone or with his closest high-ranking associates, who were also housed on the second floor. Less important prisoners were kept below.

At around eight o'clock, other personnel and I gathered along an observation point over a long narrow courtyard, and we were anxious to see Hitler do well in wrestling or boxing or a few games with balls. But he just observed or refereed, and sometimes retrieved errant balls. Whenever the men asked him to join, he would rub his left shoulder and say, "My injuries preclude participation." After athletics Hitler liked to stroll in the courtyard. Hands clasped on his tailbone and head cast down, he moved slowly down the compacted gravel path to one boundary wall, then returned the same way to the opposite wall, this way and that. Hitler had arranged to have his chauffeur, Emil Maurice, live with him in prison, and Maurice often got to take walks with him and share thoughts so important to all. Sometimes the Nazis serenaded Hitler with fight songs, and even though his pace did not change, his steps did seem stimulated.

At noon all ranking Nazis gathered in the common dining room and stood behind their chairs around the table, waiting for Hitler. He was greeted with "Achtung," and the men stood even straighter as he marched to the seat at the head of the table. Individual greetings sounded around, and when Hitler sat down, everyone else did, too. A prisoner then brought in a big pot, the main and only course, and served Hitler first and then the others. The men spoke a little to those nearby, but most conversation was dictated by the Fuehrer, who discoursed on a variety of artistic and social matters.

Returning to his cell after lunch, he did a lot of reading and writing, and everyone agreed he was a very intellectual man. I did not know anyone who studied so much. Later, he stayed at his desk and greeted distinguished visitors until it was time for tea and strolling then dinner and more exercise followed occasionally by group political discussions that I monitored from outside the dining room. The dedicated Hitler often did not come to the activities, staying instead in his cell to work. Prison rules said lights were to be out by ten, but that would have been inconvenient so we said sure when he asked for later light.

I controlled the parcel room, watching carefully as men opened gifts, and this was a fine duty. Packages for Hitler bulged from shelves. He received flowers and fruit and beer and books and about everything else, and without him having to tell us — guards and fellow prisoners — we helped him haul his presents back to his cell, and soon to his other cells. The Fuehrer gave me some flowers and chocolates for my wife, and as I presented them I told her she'd love to shop in a place as pretty and sweet as his cell.

STARTING A BOOK
By Adolf Hitler

With me jammed in prison, men that I had made politically began to gloat and potshot me, and then formed a coalition of Volkisch candidates who arrogantly planned to annex my movement. When I discovered that, only remarkable self-restraint prevented me from tearing apart my stuffed, over-sweet smelling cell number seven. I would subordinate myself and my movement to decidedly inferior followers under no circumstances that could exist on this earth.

That spring my displeasure burned from stomach to brain as the Volkisch bloc surprisingly received more votes than everyone but the Bavarian People's Party. Soon, national elections were held, and thirty-two Volkisch candidates won places in the odious parliamentary government. Ludendorff and many others flexed mightily after their essentially insignificant victories, and only the few shrewd among them knew their success was entirely due to my dynamic deeds before the Putsch and to my tour de force during the trial.

Rather than battle coattail clingers now free to move and conspire as they pleased, I announced I was stepping down from National Socialist leadership during imprisonment. Furthermore, I asked those of a political bent not to visit because I was far too engrossed writing a book, long in gestation, that offered a blueprint as profound as the title: *Four and a Half Years of Struggle Against Lies, Stupidity and Cowardice*. Dictating to Emil Maurice, I started with details of my modest upbringing and the subsequent years of squalor and hardship as a teenage orphan and young man without sustenance from family.

Then I began to identify critical problems, and asserted that the survival of a race always depends on having abundant living space. Every German therefore needed to know that nature has neither the ability nor the desire to arbitrarily award certain huge tracts of land to some people, and more limited parcels to others. No, what nature does with exquisite righteousness and brutality is float high above and watch the struggle among her children for riches so available to the special one with the energy and might to take what will then most naturally be his. Unfortunately, I often had to point out, in anguished shouts of dictation, that the advantages conferred on us as a birthright had not been heeded, and that culturally inferior but more ruthless races were acquiring gigantic tracts of land that did not truly belong to them and that should, by right and by necessity, belong to the German people.

Because of our inherent superiority, we could not fail to win the rewards necessary for survival unless we neglected to protect our bloodlines. With the utmost care I formulated the necessary precepts and policies to maintain racial purity. For help in this vital task, I arranged for the erudite Rudolf Hess to surrender and serve as my personal secretary. To him I dictated unbreakable laws from the wild, and stressed that just as a lion would never risk his survival and health with sexual or humanitarian gestures toward a zebra, we must not risk our uniqueness because of uncalled for empathy for lower species. Any time, for example, that prime Aryan specimens are crossbred with members of lower species, such as Negroes, Slavs or Jews, the Aryan race is inevitably bastardized and diminished. In North America today, the benefits of almost pure Germanic breeding are obvious as our brethren dominate a burgeoning continent. By contrast, the genetically inferior peoples of Central and South America have been incapable of rising to Aryan levels.

We Aryans must also acknowledge our natural right to utilize all lower human types for our betterment. History is rife with examples of higher cultures prospering with the domesticated aid of inferior peoples. This process of human enslavement was in effect long before widespread domestication of animals, not the other way around. Inferior races actually benefit from domination since they alone would be unable to quickly make complex decisions, regarding crises and survival, that can only be conceived by a mind unified by pure racial superiority. The rotten brood of bastards would therefore be subject to massive loss of life in the pinch, and perhaps extinction, and rightly so.

To ensure that chaos and destruction are avoided, I designated additional duties of a vigilant Volkisch state. Only the healthy should be allowed to produce children. A sick person who because of vanity begets a child, also likely to be sick, is a disgrace. But a sick person deserves great honor if he acknowledges his infirmity and does not beget a child, and instead adopts and raises a healthy baby for the nation. Even if disabled parents somehow produce a brilliant but crippled child, it would be unworthy of the Greek and Aryan ideal of great physical beauty combined with brilliance and nobility.

Those of sound health have an outright obligation to provide fine babies for the nation and should be compelled to propagate, even by financial means if that is what is lacking. The state, by encouraging those who should and by preventing those who should not, can in time create a population of unprecedented intelligence, power and pulchritude.

Deep in my pulsating soul I knew I was great enough to implement these exciting and transcendent principles. Still, I felt a sense of desolation since large walls and unjust laws prevented me from charging forth to do my desperately needed duties. For now I could only doggedly create my tract of principles, my bible, on which I would found things no one could imagine.

MODEL PRISONER
By Prison Governor Leyboldt

By the fall of 1924, the State Attorney's office requested I do something I had planned on and felt justified in doing for a long time: write a memorandum to the Ministry of Justice requesting the release from confinement of Adolf Hitler by October first.

This heartfelt step was nothing less than a reasonable freedom call for a repentant man of talent and virtue who would by October have been in overall detainment almost eleven months, ample time considering the quality of the individual. I noted that Hitler had been a most amenable and modest prisoner who never made exceptional demands, and who not only maintained personal self control at all times, but in friendly and subtle fashion encouraged his fellow inmates to do the same.

I also declared that Hitler had undoubtedly matured much during his months of confinement, and his inevitable return to political life would be characterized by a calm approach well within the boundaries of legal acceptability. He harbored no thoughts of malice and revenge, and would neither conspire against the government nor haggle unduly with political associates and adversaries. All this I knew from my conversations with him and the favorable reports of my personnel.

I closed my memo by commending Hitler's acute and versatile intelligence, and his prodigious will power, and noted the above facts merited an early release, which the patient Hitler, after seeing so many of his comrades free, was justifiably counting on. A short while after sending this letter, I was offended by news that Bavarian authorities, who did not have my close daily vantage point, had rejected my observations and claimed the "ruthless Hitler posed a permanent danger" to Bavaria, and if released should at least be deported.

The aforementioned authorities did have their way, and Hitler was not released in October or November. Though he never complained to me, his look of hurt and contrition, which he tried so hard to conceal, prompted me in early December to write again in his behalf. My overture augmented renewed efforts by Hitler's lawyers, and on the morning of December twentieth I walked to cell number seven and told its occupant: "You don't need to proceed with Christmas decorations. You'll be celebrating at home."

In warm holiday spirit Hitler presented all his money to the few comrades still there. And as tears dripped from our eyes, Hitler thanked Franz Hemmerich and me for understanding, and told us we would always be part of him.

RELEASE
By Heinrich Hoffmann

The blue of the sky had for days been deep hidden by dark clouds, and I shivered wet as I waited for this day to become great. Then, with a cold clang, the big iron prison gate shut behind Adolf Hitler, and he was free.

Since I had not been allowed to photograph him in prison, and only a couple of pictures were taken on the sly by someone else, I was ready when he said, "Hoffmann, for history, let's have one good shot of me now."

I focused on my favorite subject, his right hand clutching the side of party printer Adolf Mueller's fine touring car, and captured just right forever the etched-in-granite expression on a formidable face. We three then got in the car for the hour ride to Munich.

With admiration and affection Hitler stroked various parts of Mueller's car and said, "Oh, how I wish I could drive."

"You mean you can't?" said Mueller. "You used to have a Mercedes. Why can't you drive?"

"I just can't. My mind is everywhere. I know I would be good, very good, behind the wheel, but I choose not to confine my mind to the road. That would limit my creative options, now wouldn't it?"

Hitler braced his feet and back, grimaced a little, and said, "Mueller, let me have some excitement. Push the pedal to the floor."

"I'm sorry," said Mueller, "it's too wet. We might skid. My duty to you, and to myself, dictates a moderate pace."

During the final several miles into Munich, jubilant Nazis provided a motorcycle escort, and a just-informed crowd waved as we pulled in front of Herr Hitler's notoriously modest abode. Acting quickly, his friends had filled his apartment with gifts he could now enjoy in freedom.

As Hitler climbed the stairs, his old dog with a long memory leaped onto his chest, licking his face, and would have knocked him back down the steps if we hadn't propped him from behind. Inside, Hitler was soon encircled by an enthused and sympathetic group.

"Don't waste your sorrow on me," he said. "My recent experience has made me a much deeper and more discerning man. Before I was a babe, too soft and trusting. Now I promise you the insight of a veteran, the fearlessness of a fighter and the optimism of a Fuehrer."

RISE
1925-1933

NEW YEAR
By A Festive Lady

At this party everyone was laughing and drinking and bumping into each other, and the buzz increased as 1925 approached. A lot of us still felt this could be even better. We knew our host, Heinrich Hoffmann, was a friend of Adolf Hitler, and we urged him to get Hitler to come.

"I asked him twice," Hoffmann said, "and he didn't want to. Anyway, he's busy working at home."

"Oh, Herr Hoffmann," said one girl, drink in hand nuzzled to her chest, "he just got out of prison. Surely he'd appreciate some New Year's cheer. Please, give him a call."

Hoffmann shrugged all right and walked to the phone. Turning his back to us, he paused a bit, then started to talk. We could not understand what he said, but the smile we sensed from behind proved what Hoffmann revealed a few seconds later: "Herr Hitler has agreed to come. But only for a half hour."

Many pretty women were present, and I knew all of them would try, or want to try, to get close to Hitler and meet him. I finished my drink and got another and drank that too, and kept glancing toward the door, waiting, a little nervous about what to do.

When Hitler came in, natty in a cutaway suit, everyone enlivened and many stepped up to greet him. I waited half a room away, mingling with various people, discussing this and that, always really thinking how I could get to him. After a while he began excusing himself, whittling away hangers-on until he eventually presented himself standing alone on a dark spot, mistletoe overhead.

Down I put my drink, right on the floor, and with foxy steps moved fast from the side and stepped in front of him and took his hands and gave him a big hard kiss right on the mouth, his mustache so nice on my face, just as I had imagined.

Instantly, I dropped his hands and stepped back once, then twice. Hitler's face froze, and he surely appeared a man either kicked in the shins or grievously insulted. I had done neither but was scared he would yell and make everyone at the party not like me.

Hoffmann stepped up and patted his shoulder and said, "Herr Hitler, your allure for the ladies is remarkable. Millions of men in

Germany would love to be kissed by a woman like that."

I stumbled into a small group and tried, my heart still stinging, to be normal and gay. In a little while Hitler walked rigidly out the door, and Hoffman came over and said, "Don't worry. It's all right."

"I'm sorry," I said. "I didn't mean to be rude. I guess he didn't like me. Obviously he didn't like me at all."

UNBREAKABLE ME
By Adolf Hitler

Never was my will broken. Never did my spirit waver. Never was I anything but resolute and determined to save Germany from the abyss. No sacrifice was too great for that nor any degradation too severe: I held my burning gut and walked right into the office of Heinrich Held, a reactionary swine and the new Prime Minister of Bavaria.

"I've matured," I told him, "and I realize that strictly legal approaches are the only ways for National Socialism and me to proceed. It would be my honor to serve as your ally, and I could be more useful to you if my party, my paper and my voice are at once unfettered."

"I'm very concerned, Herr Hitler, about the anti-Catholic positions of the Nazis and other nationalist groups."

"General Ludendorff is increasingly unstable and primarily responsible for those indiscretions. I'm quite dubious about the general and will make sure his antipathy is minimized."

In a couple of weeks, Held told associates, "The Beast has been tamed and the chains can now be loosened."

Immediately I revived the Volkischer Beobachter, and the comeback edition trumpeted that I would speak the following February evening. My return to public oratory had been carefully delayed since my release, and Munich was now ready to be plucked like a tight violin string. While hundreds were being turned away from the Burgerbrau, two thousand activists simmered inside. The instant I entered, the huge hall erupted.

I knew that many prominent Nazis were present, and I also knew Ernst Roehm and Gregor Strasser, due to various disagreements, were not. They did not really matter. What counted was my being there and speaking. Soon after starting I settled down heating up, and sensed the instant to shout, "We must not assume the suffering that has descended like a shroud over seventy million Germans cannot go on. It can and it has, and you know you've been powerless to stop it. That is why I stand here today, to tell you that I accept responsibility for everything. I accept the responsibility to change your appalling lives and elevate you to a position of pride and joy. But I can't proceed when our ranks are riddled by selfish and disloyal swine. I won't tolerate interference from those bent on sabotaging the movement.

"Anyone who doesn't like that is free to get up right now and walk out forever. I know I can start again by myself and still very soon become the Fuehrer of a growing new movement. But why ruin the sense of inspired community we have here tonight? We should simply cast away our disagreements and hurt feelings, and rejoice that our enemies will never destroy us as long as we're together."

Everyone rumbled and rose, and some jumped on tables, and many rolled toward the stage, looking up as I with open hands embraced formerly disagreeable Nazis who not only proclaimed their loyalty but then turned to the crowd and shouted to form the vanguard behind Hitler. At the same time, countless wives took handkerchiefs from purses and unabashedly wiped watering eyes in happy expression of the spirit that was carrying all of us away.

My overwhelming return compelled me to schedule several mass meetings for March, but the cowards in government accused me of inflaming Bavaria and revoked my license to speak. I demanded to protest in person, and with unbridled candor I said, "Anyone wanting to have a fight with the Nazis can have one. And anyone attacking us will be stabbed from all sides. I will successfully lead the German people in their fight for freedom, if not peacefully, then with force."

Like the meek sheep they had become, most other German states then forbade me to speak publicly. If at first this seemed a fatal development, my enemies were delusional. In fact, I still addressed closed party meetings and gave private talks to influential groups gathered in opulent homes. I also organized the future by dividing the whole country — including Germanic entities Austria, the Sudetenland, and Danzig — into political districts that had a leader appointed by me. And each district was broken into a party circle, and each circle split into a local group. We also established departments of Economics, Justice, Foreign Affairs, and Race and Culture.

Very busy, I was chauffeured from task to task in my new high-powered Mercedes, and at home I polished the first edition of my newly renamed book, *Mein Kampf,* which would soon be coming out, and I began work on a second volume. Many new principals and insights still needed expression.

UNGRATEFUL COMRADE
By Ernst Roehm

From the beginning I had permitted Corporal Hitler to address me, a captain, in the familiar "Du" form. People perceived him very differently when they heard that, as well as when they saw the many veterans I recruited and the piles of arms and cash I procured. After the Putsch I'd continued to contribute to the nationalist cause, assimilating an otherwise displaced group of men into a paramilitary organization called the Frontliners — thirty thousand strong by April 1925.

Despite my efforts, Hitler, through intermediaries, had become increasingly hostile. I even had difficulty convincing this illustrious man to grant me an appointment. When we finally met, I told him, "Your distrust saddens and insults me. I'm the closest ally you've got. All I seek is to maintain control of something I've built up and to keep it clear of as many political quagmires as possible."

"You've built up nothing," Hitler stated, moving back and forth, nailing me with glares. "You have a following only because the men know you're associated with me, and it is with me that political power rests. I obviously need to remind you that military power is an impotent club unless it's wielded under strict civilian political control."

"I resent that. You know I've helped your career more than anyone. I've also been your best friend, yet now you seem anxious to degrade everything."

"I'm concerned your unbridled martial force will ruin and otherwise obstruct the very path I'm now designing for National Socialism," said Hitler. "I'm creating a movement along the lines of legal advancement. I can't allow any group associated with me, but not subordinate to me, to jeopardize my career and my movement."

"I'm offering to provide a military foundation for the movement, not to usurp your political power."

Hitler picked up the whip on his desk, hesitated a second, then slammed it and yelled: "You want me in the same compromising position I was in during the Putsch. You're trying to destroy me, the movement, all my progress, everything. Because of your outrageous disloyalty, and unmentionable desires, you're willing to betray me as a friend and rightful master of all aspects of this movement, over which I maintain personal responsibility. You disgust me."

"That will suffice, my friend," I said, staring at his boiling face. A few seconds later I walked out.

The following day I sent a letter of resignation from the SA — the Party's paramilitary arm — and requested written acknowledgment from the Fuehrer. I hoped he could still show some sign of appreciation. After two weeks and no reply, I ignored my pride and wrote again to thank him for his comradeship and to beg him not to forsake me as a personal friend. Again there was no response. This time I resigned all duties — including leadership of the Frontliners — to the man I had thought needed me.

Hitler was happy to have me gone, I slowly realized. He wanted ass-lickers in a world of bourgeois tranquility. What a bore. I always needed a scrap.

NEW RESPONSIBILITIES
By Gregor Strasser

The nationalist political successes I had helped engineer while Hitler was in prison not only worried him, they impressed him. He needed a man like me right now. Consequently, I was not surprised in early spring 1925 when he approached me and said, "You know, my friend, if National Socialism's to become a truly national movement, we've got to expand our Bavarian base and move into the north. You already have many contacts. It would please me so much if you'd organize the party there, and in western Germany."

Hitler clasped my shoulders and shook them.

"Your offer," I said, "is intriguing. If we can agree on the nature of my role, then I think we can proceed. I'd need a large measure of autonomy."

"You shall have it," said Hitler, thrusting an open hand. "I'm inundated here in the south."

I thereupon began to crisscross northern Germany, giving speeches and chairing meetings and raising funds, and within months party membership more than doubled. As my duties increased, so did my need for dedicated staff members. I wasn't particularly pleased with my secretary, Heinrich Himmler, who often complained about not having taken advantage of his experience as a chicken farmer. Fortunately, he soon resigned and returned to the farm, and that gave me the opportunity to hire Joseph Goebbels, a talented young zealot who right away designed clever posters, and wrote good speeches and letters for me, and even delivered his own fine speeches. When I'd met Goebbels, and watched this tiny man limp into my office on a shrunken leg, I hadn't perceived him as an orator. But he was. And he was also opposed to the "calcified big shots," in the Munich headquarters, who restricted the growth of the Fuehrer.

Goebbels agreed that an assertive campaign was necessary to change the national thrust of Nazism. Our north German coalition began to publish a fortnightly newsletter called National Socialist Letters. With Goebbels editing and my brother Otto contributing, we attacked the capitalist economic system and its outrageous waste of resources. In the fall we also formulated a program far more socialistic than the Twenty-Five Points offered by Hitler a few years ago. Among the key principles, we advocated taxes on corporate profits to redistribute revenue to workers and local governments. We also endorsed Russia's cooperative farm practices that had abolished large landholdings and benefited millions of peasants and small farmers.

Our new program was presented to the twenty-five district leaders from northern and western Germany in January 1926. Hitler had been invited to attend this conference but chose not to venture into dangerous territory, albeit of the same party. He remained in the south, doodling and such, and sent economist Gottfried Feder as proxy.

"No spies in our midst," Goebbels shouted at Feder. "Out. Out. No reactionaries. Maybe we'll let you stay, but you're going to be watched."

Almost everyone voted for our program. Then, as Feder defended Hitler's absurd position that princes should maintain their stolen properties and holdings, a grimacing Goebbels sprang up and verbally pole-axed the economist, and reactionaries in general, for a half hour.

With increasing volume and enthusiasm he closed his oration: "The Munich leadership is obviously bankrupt. It still embraces a wretched past and precludes a just future. Under the circumstances I must demand that the petit bourgeois Adolf Hitler be at once expelled from the party."

That evening I told Goebbels, "You sounded great, and were morally correct, but not everything you said should be meant literally."

"I know it was a little strong, but we can't let the Fuehrer degenerate any further into rightist horseshit."

SHOWDOWN
By Joseph Goebbels

Outside the hall in Bamberg, waiting for Hitler, we stood as a group at least twenty yards from southern district leaders and officials, and we, each of us from the north, looked around at lots of big posters and banners announcing the urgency of this meeting and the primacy of Hitler. The banners and posters were very red and covered whole walls and windows, and Gregor Strasser leaned over to me and said, "Those damn things look pretty good, even if they read like garbage."

This would be a private party meeting, but lots of strangers were standing on both sides of the street, talking to each other and grinning over at various southern scoundrels. Hitler must be coming soon. Everyone kept looking one way up the street. While waiting, I examined the posters and banners some more. We could have had them in the north but did not have enough money. Munich had a better organization but we had the ideology. Then, there came Hitler in that nice car. But that car was followed by another, and another, in long succession. Then the cars started coming two abreast, filling the street in wide columns moving past us up the street to make room for a shiny Mercedes that pulled in and parked in front of the hall. Hitler stepped out, and without looking at anyone he marched inside. Everyone followed and sat down.

Soon, glaring from the podium, Hitler pronounced: "Any question of changing the Nazis' original program of twenty-five points is not only an outrageous affront to those who have already fallen and died in its defense, but also an act of sacrilege. The program is the foundation of our religion, and any alteration would be tantamount to treason. This I cannot accept.

"You must all understand that private property is the basis for national wealth. Anyone who wants to take what belongs to the princes must be a Jew lover since no one is trying to expropriate properties the Jews have gained through deception.

"And anyone backing the Soviet Union is a despicable moron. That Jew-riddled morass of Bolsheviks poses an unending threat to the health of Germany. We've got to smash them. England and Italy are our natural allies."

My stomach twisted. Here, at the podium in Bamberg, the man I had revered was showing himself to be a reactionary like the goons who so foolishly applauded. Only to be polite did we, Strasser and I and some others, occasionally clap. My polite claps jarred a soul burning to refute Hitler. But when? He spoke for an excruciating four hours. This was perhaps the worst day of my life, horribly disillusioning. After Hitler finished, several northern comrades said, "Get up there. We need you."

I shook my head and waved them away. The depth of Hitler's corruption could not be changed by anyone, especially not by a weakened me. Strasser did rise and speak, but today he was even clumsier than Hitler and could not influence our adversaries. At least the Fuehrer was gracious enough to go over and embrace Strasser.

That was it. The meeting adjourned and Hitler's cronies surrounded him, sealing him off from reason, and Strasser and I and the others departed for the train station. Our dreams had disintegrated into a terrible future.

"We'll still fight for socialism," I told Gregor Strasser. But I didn't know how.

Two months later, still bedeviled by Hitler's betrayal, I almost tore up an envelope I received from him. What more reactionary twaddle might this contain? I opened it anyway and read the letter, and read again slowly, trying to hear the voice in my head over the pounding in my chest. Then I ran around my little office.

Hitler's chauffeur greeted me in Munich on April seventh. Lodging and fine meals were provided, and the next day, the big day, Hitler phoned and was so complimentary and kind. I grew ashamed of my attitude at Bamberg. He told me there would be a few thousand people in the Burgerbrau this afternoon and that he and they were anxious to hear me. Driven to the hall in a state of happy nervousness, I was afraid I might not be able to perform. What would happen if I let Hitler down after he had done so much for me? Entering the hall I was soothed to see him waiting. Then a roar from the crowd invigorated me. Soon I confidently took the podium and for more than two hours delivered a speech repeatedly punctuated by cheers and clapping. Just as I finished, Hitler rushed out and hugged me and told me I had been wonderful, and he kept his arm locked around my shoulder as he smiled at our National Socialist brothers.

Several times during my ten-day stay I had dinner with the Fuehrer, and he was unceasingly kind, brilliant and persuasive. He explained his positions with such insight and conviction that I realized how thoroughly he had formulated everything. His genius helped me open my mind and grow by questioning former misconceptions. When I saw him just before leaving Munich, he gave me a large bouquet of red roses and said, "You're destined to become increasingly important."

A few days later, for his thirty-seventh birthday, I mailed Hitler a card saying, "You are the ultimate man, and still so young." I was also young, only twenty-nine, and knew we would always be linked.

In a few weeks, after not much communication, I received an extraordinary invitation to visit him at his lodging high in the green Bavarian Alps. I was ensconced at an inn in nearby Berchtesgaden, and there I waited for the Fuehrer to summon me. I expected to see his Mercedes pull up very soon. I knew he was anxious to talk to me. He must be ready for me now. I was absolutely ready. Then I heard a car and looked outside. But that wasn't Hitler's. Nor was the next one. Where was the Mercedes? When was he going to send for me? I was in my room, waiting. There was nothing else to do. I could not go sightseeing, then not be there when Hitler beckoned. I stayed on alert the entire day but received no summons, not even word of postponement.

I did not sleep that night, and at dawn I was up pacing as I spoke about issues Hitler would surely want to discuss. His car had to arrive soon. I kept checking outside. Eventually, I picked up the phone. No. I could not call. That might make him mad. I put the phone down. I was very concerned. Maybe he was angry about something I had said. But what? Hadn't he promised a position of significance? Hadn't he asked me here? What was the matter? Where was his car? I looked out the window. It was starting to rain, and soon I could not see the mountains anymore, and I felt myself sinking back into the hole I had always been in. I hated life. It offered nothing but torture and isolation. I endured another night without peace, and in the morning I ached. My aches jumped at the knock on my door. The chauffeur had arrived.

"I've been here a long time," I said.

"The Fuehrer's anxious to see you," said Emil Maurice. "He's been very busy in conferences with Gregor Strasser."

Hitler greeted me with a firm, double-handed handshake and warmed me with a long gaze from strong blue eyes. We were together again at last, and immediately it became like before. Our empathy was extraordinary. I agreed with everything he said. And when the Fuehrer looked through the window and studied the Alpine panorama, I knew he was the most important man in Germany, and probably the world.

"You know, my friend, I must find the precise role for you in the party," he said. "There must be great challenges so you can rise and defeat them. I'm sure you know Berlin is falling apart. There's no effective leadership. Our party members are brawling with the SA. Everything's disorganized. Membership's also low. I don't know what I'm going to do. I'm quite busy here in Bavaria."

He did not mention Berlin again, and I did not ask. A month after my visit, the Fuehrer made it official: I was his new district leader of Berlin. Though very grateful, I was also hurt. He had just made Gregor Strasser the party's propaganda minister, even though I was a master of deception. At least the Fuehrer made it clear I had control over my propaganda and was autonomous from the Strasser brothers' daily socialist newspaper, Worksheet, and from the power base they had established in northern Germany.

My train pulled into Berlin on a portentous date, November ninth, 1926, the third anniversary of the Beer Hall Putsch. Cool and just now darkening, this sprawling capital of five million seethed with opportunity and motivated me to make every sacrifice. I had already told my girlfriend she could not come. The Fuehrer would not want his Berlin district leader frolicking with a half-Jew.

DATING
By Mimi Reiter

I was a blond sixteen-year old when I began working in my mother's dress shop in Berchtesgaden. Our shop occupied a room on the bottom floor of a building with a hotel on top, and many men stopped in and acted like they wanted dresses for their mothers or sisters. Then they would ask me out, but I had to say no because my mother was usually around until her sudden death, and now my older sister was the boss.

One man had been staying at the hotel a long time, and every time he came down he stared at me through the window. Whenever I sensed him I'd look up and he'd whip his eyes away and walk on out the door. I did not know much about politics but other people did and they told me that man was Adolf Hitler, the big politician. Then I started smiling when he looked in.

Hitler kept his German shepherd in a yard down the street and walked it a lot, holding his leash in one hand and whip in the other. I also had a German shepherd and began making sure to walk it at the same time. Our dogs always looked at each other and sometimes sniffed and Hitler usually glanced at me before he briskly moved on, giving his dog orders.

Once I steered my dog right into his and very quickly said, "Oh, excuse me, Herr Hitler. You have a beautiful dog and you're a fine politician."

"Thank you, thank you," he said. "You have a nice dog, too." He smiled at the ground and ordered his dog to be careful and move along.

The following afternoon Hitler's chauffeur came into our dress shop and asked if I would go with the Fuehrer to a concert the following day.

"Yes, I'd love to," I said.

"Fine," said Emil Maurice. "I'll pick you up..."

"I won't allow my sister to go out with a man twenty years older, at least, no matter who he is," said my sister, stepping up to Maurice. "My mother wouldn't have allowed it, either."

Maurice smiled at us and left. In a couple of days he returned and asked if my sister and I would do the Fuehrer the honor of attending an afternoon speech to party members. My sister couldn't say no to that. We went to a nearby hotel, and Hitler gave a speech like I'd never heard. The audience was really cheering, and at least two or three times a minute, it seemed, he paused to stare right at me, and people kept leaning to see who he was looking at. And after the speech he ignored everyone and rushed to my table, sitting next to me to say, "How did you like my speech? Was it good? I've done better many times, much better."

"Believe me, Herr Hitler, that was incredible."

"Oh, my little Mimi," he said. "I wanted so much for you to like it because I wanted this to be a special little gift for you. You're such a pretty child, just a beautiful blond doll. Here, let me cut this cake for you. Open up. There, wasn't that good. Have another bite."

I was very impressed by Hitler's attention, and the attention of my sister and others who watched him pat my hand and become quite solemn as he said, "I'm very sorry about your mother. I know too well the feeling of losing a beloved mother, and at the same age as you, too. Tonight I want us to walk our dogs to the cemetery."

By my mother's small graying headstone we stood as Hitler talked about our irreplaceable losses. Then, pausing to look carefully at the grave from end to end, he said, "I'm not like that yet."

Soon we left the cemetery, walking along the street, and Hitler gave his dog a command, and when it did not immediately respond he began lashing it with his whip. The dog howled and flinched, and Hitler grunted as he raised the whip higher each time. I was frightened and so was my cringing dog.

"You told me you couldn't live without your dog," I said.

"I had to do this. The dog needed it for discipline and he needed it for his guilt about not obeying my commands. He's a better dog now and he loves me more. See how he's licking my hand?"

Hitler settled down and we strolled back into the main part of Berchtesgaden, talking amiably, and eventually went around the side of my house, out of view, and he ordered both dogs to lie down, and they did. He then stood at attention, locking his hands behind his back and tightening his lips, before he leaned forward and said, "I would like for you to give me a goodnight kiss."

"I'm sorry, but I can't."

Straight up as a flagpole shot his head and body, and he glared at me and thrust out his right arm and said: "Heil Hitler."

He walked away, and I thought would not take me out again. I hoped he would, though. I just needed time. A girl needs time. And he did send Maurice to ask me again. Now we went for a ride in his Mercedes and sat very close in the big back seat while being driven over beautiful Alpine roads.

"Lean back," he said. "I want to look into your eyes. They're so much like my mother's."

He placed soft hands over my eyelids, pushed them closed and said, "I just want you to sleep and have beautiful fantasies, and I'll watch over you. Just lie there and sleep and dream."

Adolf and I started seeing each other a lot and often walked in the woods, holding hands and having lots of fun. But I had to be careful. One time he froze and said, "You must never laugh at me. You'll understand that someday."

Many times in the woods he kissed me all over my face and neck, grasping my back and waist, breathing hard all over, fondling me through my blouse. Once he was more excited than ever, and I felt it happening right there in the grass.

"Child, I could just squeeze and love you to bits right now."

"I want you to. I want you right now."

"Mimi, my child, we must be restrained."

"We have been. You wanted to kiss me first."

"Kisses are different. We can't go wild. You know I can't afford any indiscretions."

"The way you've been carrying on, you've got to want to. You can right now. What's wrong?"

CLEANING UP
By Joseph Goebbels

"No, there. That's right, right there," I told an assistant. "Make sure it's straight. I want everyone entering this office to see."

The picture frame, spanned by very clear polished glass, contained a letter to me signed big by Hitler and offered irrefutable documentation of my authority to purge a pig sty and build a National Socialist vanguard in Berlin.

First, I had moved local headquarters out of the smoke-saturated cellar that reeked like a ransacked opium den, and ordered unemployed party deadbeats who lounged around the old office to stay away from the new. And even though the Berlin portion of the party numbered only a thousand, I promptly jettisoned four hundred worthless members. I needed producers, not space-gobbling eyesores.

On January first, 1927 I began the year with a big speech.

"We are a party committed to growth," I told the remaining members, "and in order to expand, we need money. Henceforth, it will be necessary for each of you to contribute three marks per month in dues. Anyone here who cannot accept that is free to leave before being thrown out."

No one even flinched, and not because of fear. They were encouraged by my promise: "Your days of being vulnerable and isolated lambs, wandering meekly while packs of communists and Jews lurk in the ready to devour you, will not be allowed to continue. For the time being you're just a few hundred anonymous souls in a huge city. But I've come here committed to every form of publicity and agitation, and from now on our Nazi party name will be shouted, feared, and respected."

Since mass mailing and big newspaper advertisements were quite beyond our means, I began with an onslaught of posters that projected our version of truth in flaming white letters against crimson backgrounds. Most people either strongly agreed or disagreed. I preferred the latter, and insured more disharmony by scheduling our next meeting in Pharus Hall, which the communists considered their exclusive hallowed hall. Thousands of announcements were posted on pillars in numerous communist neighborhoods, and in bold print I mocked: "The Bourgeois State is approaching its end... Workers: the fate of the German nation is in your hands."

The communist press responded that Nazis would be thrashed for their temerity with sufficient severity to deter a return. I loved it. We'd see. Everyone would. All Berlin Nazis, wearing jackboots and swastika armbands, gathered outside our headquarters and began a high-stepping march through streets lined by thousands of citizens, many of whom cursed and threatened us. Every Nazi still moved unflinchingly all the way to Pharus Hall.

Right after local SA chief Kurt Daluege opened the meeting, a communist jumped up and made a crude remark. The dim but dedicated Daluege grabbed a water pitcher and fired it at the bigmouth, and instantly the hall was ignited by glass, wood and steel projectiles. For a good while I sat with arms crossed, next to where Daluege stood. Then I rose and shouted: "Coitus Interruptus." A half dozen storm troops, stationed at the rear, sprang and seized the instigator and beat him rapidly before tossing him outside. Simultaneously, our largest groups of storm troops, wielding blackjacks and knuckle-dusters, rushed in from each side and flattened dozens of Reds. Once we were secure, I ordered all our wounded men brought to the stage, and somberly I spoke about their sacrifice and suffering, and occasionally paused to pat or hug them as they writhed and groaned. One by one I excused them to be carried to the hospital, and each time I felt a roomful of angry and indignant faces. They were looking to me.

Most newspapers blasted us. Fantastic. We got twenty-six hundred applications for membership, five hundred with requests to be part of the aroused SA brotherhood. In March our Nazi bandwagon gained more horsepower as the speaking prohibition on Hitler was lifted. In Circus Krone, according to all reports, he was greeted by a roaring sellout crowd that rejoiced in his first public appearance in two years. News of the Fuehrer's return triumph spurred my speaking, and I preached to Berliners about the imminence of total collapse. Very few disagreed, but to those who did I promised that any current signs of improvement were nothing more than decorative harbingers of doom.

My dynamism attracted crowds of increasing size and intensity, and I could not tolerate insults. When a drunken old pastor bellowed that I did not look so good, I motioned for his removal. He ended up in the hospital, due primarily to his clumsiness. But Assistant Police Commissioner Bernhard Weiss vented his anti-Nazi paranoia and banned our party activities in Berlin. This was outrageous. The longest-nosed Jew I had ever seen, the most repulsive and decadent man imaginable, had arbitrarily taken away our National Socialist right to continued growth and free expression. That was his aim, but I merely emulated the Fuehrer and spoke at closed meetings. Also, I camouflaged party functions with names like "Hikers of 1923." The venomous Weiss then banned Nazi public activities throughout Prussia.

I countered by launching The Attack, my party newspaper that soon portrayed Bernhard Weiss, in words and caricatures, as a murderous Jew whose actions and appearance were alternately those of a spider, a reptile or a tramp. Weiss and others tried to suppress us with mounds of lawsuits and injunctions, but these efforts were not sustained. I cannot accept all the credit, or blame, for that. After all, I cannot be held responsible that one night while on a solitary stroll Weiss was grabbed and pummeled good by some policemen. These zealous defenders of the law had mistaken their boss for a criminal.

GHASTLY GOEBBELS
By Gregor Strasser

By the fall of 1927 I had begun to hear, from too many sources to ignore, that my dear friend Joseph Goebbels was telling everyone they should not bother reading my bourgeois rag, Worksheet, and should instead focus on his sparkling publication of venom, The Attack. After my many efforts to contact Goebbels were ignored, I went to his office and stepped in front of him as he was leaving.

"Listen," I said, "I want to talk to you about these outrageous betrayals."

"Get out of my way, you contemptible bastard," he said.

In the wake of such shameful behavior, Goebbels should have at least lessened the stridency of his rhetoric. Instead, he began ordering SA poltroons to belt our newspaper boys during deliveries, then scatter the stolen papers in muddy fields. I complained several times to the Fuehrer, who finally agreed to come to Berlin for a concerned attempt at mediation. Otto and I received him in our office, which someone had recently broken into and trashed.

"We've devoted well over a year and a lot of our own money to develop this newspaper," I told Hitler. "The Worksheet gets plenty of publicity for you and the party, and I resent anyone, especially a fellow party member and an erstwhile beneficiary, using criminal tactics to try to stop us from publishing. For your good as well as ours, I want you to order Goebbels to stop."

"I'm not sure it would be prudent for you to keep publishing, under these dangerous circumstances," said Hitler.

"We shall certainly continue to publish," I said. "We've earned every right to do so, and won't relinquish that right."

"It's not a moral question of right," Hitler said, "but a pragmatic question of who has superior might. You wouldn't have the means to deal with it if Goebbels ordered a group of his storm troops to attack."

Otto, staring at the Fuehrer, jerked his desk drawer open, grabbed a revolver and slammed it on the table. "I have eight shots in the chamber, Herr Hitler, and many bullets in reserve. There'll be lots of dead storm troops the next time they come."

"I don't doubt your bravery or resolve in defending yourself, but I can't permit you to murder my storm troops."

"Your storm troops, Herr Hitler?" said Otto. "I thought you said they were Herr Goebbels'. If the aggressors are yours, then, for the sake of their health, I advise you not to send them. If they're Herr Goebbels' men, then it's your duty as Fuehrer to prevent them from disturbing us further. Either way, I'll definitely shoot anyone who attacks me."

Hitler looked glumly at Otto, then looked down a second before stepping over to me and saying, "You and your brother have done so much for the party. You held it together and in many ways expanded it while I was in prison, and since then you've been vital in promoting our growth and influence. Without you the party might well have perished. Your friendship has also been incalculably important. That's why this tension between you and Goebbels tears at me so much. We can't permit personal differences to threaten our ultimate goals. Please don't ask me to choose between my beloved comrades. I consider each of you dear and essential, and want nothing more than for there to be peace among all of us."

Placing his hand on my shoulder, Hitler peered at me through moistened eyes, then tightened his grip before he turned and walked out the door.

"I told you the man's a scoundrel who wants domination and nothing else."

"That's not quite fair or accurate, Otto. I don't think you realize how good-natured and honest Hitler really is. He attaches great value to what I tell him."

"You're playing with a lion, Gregor, not a human being.

RETURN TO GERMANY
By Hermann Goering

I sent Hitler a telegram that I was coming home. I certainly wanted to see him again. Back in Germany I started calling right away but was always told: "The Fuehrer is very busy."

"This is Herr Hermann Goering, former commander of the SA, and winner of the pour le mérite. I'm sure the Fuehrer wants to talk to me."

After several days of painful delays, I was granted an audience.

"Very nice to see you," said Hitler.

"Mein Fuehrer, I wanted to return four years ago for the trial, but you told me to remain free and help the party. I've done that. Everywhere I've been, Austria, Sweden, Italy, I've told people, influential people, about the inevitable rise of National Socialism and its great leader. I even met with Mussolini."

"Yes, I heard. What did he offer you?"

"He didn't offer me anything, Mein Fuehrer. I was just establishing contacts for the party."

"What else have you been doing?"

"Well, in addition to my promotion of the party, I've been seeking a variety of business contacts in aviation and other fields."

"What was the nature of your employment?"

My face flushed.

"Frankly, Mein Fuehrer, my employment has been negligible. Conditions in Sweden have been absolutely horrendous. There must be five hundred applicants for every job, and only the most pliant are accepted. You know that's not my way.

"And so much of my time has been devoted to Carin. She's very weak and sick so often, but she loves you very much, Mein Fuehrer. She encouraged me to leave her and come to your side. She'll join me when she can, but she knows the party is paramount."

"You are aware, no doubt, that I already have an able SA commander?"

"Oh, yes, I realize I'd have to work for any significant position. I'm not asking for that now."

"Right now, I can't think of any appropriate openings. We have many fine men who've been here continuously."

"I just want to be involved in National Socialism again."

"Well, I'd certainly like for you to keep in touch. For now you need to go out and get a job, something to establish yourself, and then we shall see."

"I assure you, Mein Fuehrer, I'm still the man I was."

"I have many more meetings today," he said, patting my shoulder. "Let me know how things are going."

The way the Fuehrer looked at me was devastating. Didn't he understand? During the Putsch a bullet had ricocheted off cobblestones into my thigh and implanted not only steel but filthy stone slivers from the street. I'd escaped to Austria where a doctor failed to remove much of the debris. Soon the wound oozed, and I had to have an operation under chloroform. Afterward, throbbing in the groin, I was ripped by a fever so hot I yelled, "I wish I'd died and I will if something isn't done about the pain."

"My dearest, you're as white as the snow outside," said my wife.

I had convalesced for weeks before being able to travel to Italy with Carin. And though authorities had impounded my bank account in Munich, I stockpiled much morphine and tried to limit myself to two injections per day, one on arising and one at night. Even with increased doses, the sedation was dreadfully insufficient.

"Hermann, I know this has all been horrible for you," Carin said, "but it's also been terrible for me. Please try to stop your sudden rages. They hurt both of us."

I did my best. I wanted to be better. I wanted to be like before. But fat had steadily crept onto my body and misshaped my features around bloodshot eyes. By the time we'd returned to Sweden, Carin's health was worse even than my own. Her heart and lungs were weak and her blood pressure so unsteady she often fainted. This was an existence of torment, and every day when I checked the mail and saw that my letters to Hitler, my lifelines, had been unanswered, I realized if Carin were ever taken from me, my world would be worthless.

Of course I'd taken more morphine. Only as it entered my system did I regain some of the ebullience I'd always had. I needed morphine three times a day at least, usually four, then five, finally six, all I could get. The doctors had said my leg would never fully heal. When the sedation began to wear away, it was as if my nerves were being fried, and I absolutely could not sleep. Naturally, I screamed and threw things. But I wasn't throwing anything at Carin, not even close. Windows, walls, cabinets — those were the targets.

Carin's former husband had hired private detectives to confirm the rumors. Then he'd crushed her by vowing to invoke all legal and financial means to deprive us of custody of their son. Carin's doctor then told her parents that my behavior was applying a potentially fatal strain. The family decided — I had no say — that I would be taken to Aspudden Hospital for treatment. There I was informed my morphine intake would be gradually reduced until I was cured.

"I don't feel a thing from these shots," I told the doctors and nurses. "These are like water compared to what I've been taking. I've got to have more."

They usually hadn't even answered while shooting me with their cruelly diluted potions.

"I'm sweating, look at me, can't you see?" I said. "I've been like this since I got here. Don't you know how I feel?"

I had not believed they would continue this. If they knew, if for even a few seconds they could imagine, they certainly would give me a dose that wouldn't hurt them at all but would be for me a divine reprieve. That I certainly had to have. The pain was getting so bad I often broke down sobbing.

"I'm sick of your shameless whining," said one nurse, looking down at me on the floor. "You're obviously a coward who has far to go before becoming a man."

That would have been an intolerable insult from anyone, especially from some frowning frigid woman who had never been near, much less prevailed amid, the deadly whir of bullets. I shrieked and jumped up and pounced on her and slapped her face hard, knocking her against a wall, then grabbed her around the face and neck, shaking the cowardly trembling monster in my hands, and threw her on the floor and was going after her again when several attendants rushed in and jumped on me and held me down.

"Get the strait jacket, quick," someone shouted.

As I'd sat bound, struggling, crying, begging for more morphine, two doctors looked at me for a few minutes, certified me as insane and ordered that I be taken by the police forthwith to Langbro Asylum for the Insane where they tossed me into a padded cell, a maudlin madhouse, and did not let me out until I stopped screaming after several days that seemed like several tortured lifetimes. I was confined at Langbro for three months of enforced sobriety, and while there one of the psychiatrists told me he and his colleagues had concluded, and duly recorded, that I was a "sentimentalist lacking in basic moral courage."

Back home our dreary apartment had served as another detention center, and I could only sit and dream about my return to glory, and when that would be, and soon I was back at Langbro Asylum. This time I stayed two months before going home, and there I was until my return to Germany.

Late in 1927 I used a tiny Berlin hotel room for little but sleep. I was constantly out pursuing success and status. Without those things a man is nothing. That I had certainly learned. So I cajoled and convinced a wartime friend, for a modest sum, to chauffeur me around Berlin in his primary asset, a Mercedes Benz. I arrived in style at my appointments, and robust and jolly I certainly felt as I bounded out to greet executives from aircraft firms, most of whom soon signed contracts. I also reestablished my contacts from the war, and when these important people saw and sensed my success they were happy to let me host sales luncheons in their villas.

My life soared in the spring of 1928 when Carin was able to leave her hospital bed in Sweden and head for Berlin. Every day we had been writing letters, surrogate embraces with words dipped in ink and applied to paper as elicitations of love. Now Carin was with me again, and her delicate frame in my arms, her succulent face pressed to mine, made me feel, in my new world of regained dignity, like a man who simply could not be prevented from assuming a major role.

When Hitler called and asked me to meet him at the Sanssouci, his regular hotel in Berlin, it was an honor I had been anticipating. He shook my hand and stood examining me, then said, "My friend, there's absolutely no one with your combination of talents. No one. Thank God you're here at our time of greatest need. The ballot box is our only recourse for now, and we have to demonstrate our appeal by legal means that others have defined. That's why I need you so much. You will campaign and run as a National Socialist for me, won't you?"

My eyes watered right away, and a big salty tear rolled into the corner of my mouth. "Mein Fuehrer, you've honored me to the utmost. I'll campaign with vigor that'll terrify our opponents."

With just a few weeks to campaign, I mounted the speaking platforms of Berlin with fire and gusto, railing against enemies and exhorting the majority who cheered me. I could feel my future, and after the elections did not worry we only got eight hundred thousand votes, about two percent of the total. So what if we held but twelve Reichstag seats out of five hundred? So what if the Nazis had twice received more votes in 1924? I was in.

BERCHTESGADEN
By Mimi Reiter

I'd hated Adolf being away from Berchtesgaden. No one interested me but him, and I hoped I was at least part of why he came back after the elections. Right away he called and asked to see me, and we started spending lots of time alone. I wanted that, and always snuggled close and in many ways let him know what we needed. He usually got so excited I thought we were going to. I did not know how he could wait. And I did not understand why he instead wanted other things. They were very upsetting, but I thought if I agreed he would appreciate me more and someday love me the right way.

I was encouraged when he rented a house with a nice view and said he'd be around more. I assumed we'd become closer and happier. But after Adolf's half-sister Angela moved from Vienna to keep house for him, everything changed.

"Why don't you like me anymore?" I said. "There isn't anyone else, is there? Who is it? Why do you spend so much time with Geli, and not with me? You take her swimming and on drives and picnics all the time, and you just ignore me. Geli is just your niece. I love you. Why are you staying away from me? Why are you acting like this? You gave me the impression, you told me, that we were going to be together. I think we should get married right away."

"I won't be able to see you anymore, Mimi. We must never see each other again, and you're not to bother me."

I screamed and ran away. This had all been so abrupt and unfair, especially after what had happened. I rushed into my room, right past my sister and her husband, and tied one end of a clothesline around my neck and the other around my bedroom door, and slammed the door into darkness.

Later, my voice very weak, I told my brother-in-law he shouldn't have untied the rope. I was serious. I needed something. I had to have something, so I soon married a hotelkeeper. I did not like him much but he loved me the right way.

PEACE AND PROSPERITY
By Gustav Stresemann

In my quest for progress through pragmatism, I had long ago forsaken the aggressive approach that dominated German foreign policy before and during the Great War. Now, as Foreign Minister in the fall of 1928, I helped Germany obtain direly needed loans for industry in return for our cooperation in revised payment of reparations. My peaceful demeanor was also a factor in Germany, so recently a pariah, being accepted into the League of Nations, and I ensured our participation in the Treaty of Locarno, which quelled ancient territorial disputes between Germany, and France and Belgium, by promising to respect current borders, even though some German-speaking areas no longer belonged to us. This spirit of reconciliation permitted me, and thus Germany, to be a proud signatory of the Kellogg-Briand Pact that renounced war forever.

In this atmosphere of enlightened cooperation, Germany once again loomed as an economic bastion. Industrial production surpassed pre-war levels across the spectrum of smokestacks and national income rose about twelve percent. For the first time in years the number of unemployed fell below one million, and almost everyone felt we were prospering.

AWAITING ILLNESS
By Adolf Hitler

Many times I almost lashed fellow Nazis, my so called allies, after their incessant defeatist chatter had tired, bored and insulted me to the point of imminent outrage. Yet, I always retained control, and instead of lashing I edified them with explications of matters they could not perceive.

"Don't pay attention or otherwise lend significance to the election results of several months ago and our current meager representation in the Reichstag," I declared aloud and in writing. "And don't burden yourselves, or me, with worries about what liberal enemies are calling our insignificance and our demise. Of course, on the surface, where only the shallow and myopic can see, it appears we're a party in eclipse. But that is untrue. We are in fact a dynamic party on the verge of burgeoning.

"First, let me emphasize the positive points, from our perspective, of current German political trends. The elections, as I keep reminding you, showed substantial gains for our liberal enemies, the Social Democrats and the Communists. That's all right because the moderate parties, as well as other parties on the right, lost support. That means we're free to become the preeminent party on the right, and we'll be facing an ever-weakening center. Any gains by the left are bound to be as fleeting as this national illusion many call prosperity.

"I assure you nothing good can endure because there's so much sickness in our national body. Everyone but us is infected by the ultimate inducers of illness: the eternally conniving Jews. Their perversities and misdeeds are so vile and so vast that they defy comprehension. Nevertheless, you must all be aware that Jews are the systematic destroyers of young women. With the devil's horrid look of glee on their faces, dark-hearted Jewish men lurk ready to pounce on Aryan women and destroy their racial integrity by poisoning blood and committing various vile and unnatural sex acts. In this manner Jews target a race for subjugation, then set about to destroy it by ruining its women, whose fertile wombs should not be invaded by vermin.

"As shiftless as they are perverse, the Jews are a clan without a nation and without a culture. They survive only by usurping the economic resources of their superiors, and they celebrate by contaminating art and literature everywhere. Thus, instead of ennobling people, the Jews flush everyone into the dregs of their own base nature. This enables them to exterminate the national intelligentsia, and thereby make others vulnerable to their ultimate aim: permanent subjugation.

"We could have saved millions of German lives during the Great War if, early on, we had held fifteen thousand or so of the worst Hebrew corrupters under the very poison gas that later, on the fields of battle, took the sacred lives of so many brave young Germans who had been betrayed."

PARTY MANEUVERS
By Adolf Hitler

Early in 1929 I put Gregor Strasser in charge of the party's political organization, which had the immense responsibility to build my political base. And I promoted Joseph Goebbels to take Strasser's place as propaganda minister. Goebbels also retained his duties as district leader in Berlin. Both men were enormously important to me, and separately I told them so.

During this period the SA continued to expand and acquire vast military resources. Many local SA leaders were much too independent of me, however, and could be troublesome. I needed to nurture another group, the SS, and selected Heinrich Himmler, a young man in his late twenties, as my Reichsfuehrer SS. This incredible new title flabbergasted Himmler and inspired fanatical faith. He and his men understood I was utterly responsible for their existence and therefore wholly deserving of their fealty and protection.

In August, at our party rally in Nuremberg, we stunned the nation with energy, strength and organization. Dozens of specially decorated trains filled with Nazis roared into this beautiful and ancient city, and on the final day of celebration sixty thousand armed and uniformed SA men paraded beneath me for hours. As I proudly looked on, I hoped they would remember: we must always behave responsibly.

YOUNG PLAN
By Adolf Hitler

Now Germany's enemies made another dastardly move, concocting the Young Plan, which lowered reparations but mandated payments for the next sixty years. This "Plan," so gullibly lapped up by the Weimar democratic stooges, would obviously bankrupt the future of untold millions of innocent unborn German babies. We Nazis mobilized other Volkisch groups into a national committee to demand a plebiscite to reject the Young Plan. The committee was headed, in theory, by Alfred Hugenberg, a stumpy aristocrat with a butch haircut. He controlled a publishing empire as well as the Nationalist party, and our coalition proceeded to bombard and otherwise caress the German people with unprecedentedly sophisticated propaganda that assailed not only the Young Plan but other worthwhile targets.

NEW ADDRESS
By Geli Raubaul

Oh, I was excited. My mother, Angela Raubaul, and I had moved to Munich to live with her half-brother, Adolf Hitler, the famous politician. We had many servants in our apartment and a big reception room and a dining room and a library with lots of books where Onkel Alfi greeted many important people, and I know they had to be impressed by him and all the expensive antiques and paintings and other decorations. Some of Alfi's watercolors painted during the Great War also hung on the walls, and I thought they were quite good.

Onkel Alfi always made sure I had plenty of money to buy clothes and jewelry and lots of phonograph records, and he often escorted me to the theater and the opera and to his favorite restaurants, and proudly introduced me to many people. He held my arm and caressed my hand and talked sweet to me as all sorts of beautiful, well-dressed women watched. I knew how they felt. What woman wouldn't want that kind of attention from Adolf Hitler?

I was not really worried by some of the talk about Alfi and me. He explained to everyone I was in Munich to take singing lessons, and that's what I did. I wanted to sing, but the lessons and practice in between were very boring, and I just could not concentrate with so many other things to do.

I was certainly happy, and wanted Onkel Alfi to be happy, too. I told him it was O.K. his bedroom had a corridor connected to mine. He came in whenever he wanted. And one night after kissing me a long time, he panted, "My work's so difficult and nerve-wracking, Geli. You can't imagine. I've got to have a release. I want you to understand. I hope you do. I know you will, won't you? Please understand. Try to. I think you can. Please. You'll see. You can. Like this."

He stretched on the floor and groaned what he wanted.

"No, I just can't do that."

Jumping up, he stuck his finger in my face and said, "If I can't get what I need from you, then you'll certainly be replaced."

I covered my face, sobbing, and Alfi cupped his hands around my hands and cheeks and said, "Geli, please forgive me. It's just that I love you so much I can barely stand it. You're the only woman I could ever marry, and it kills me you won't make me feel better. Please, my little sweet, trust me and help me, and I'll help you."

I did what he asked, and hoped no one could hear.

GOOD JOB
By Eva Braun

I had just gotten a job with the prominent photographer, Heinrich Hoffmann, and begun work in his Munich studio as a clerk, bookkeeper and occasional darkroom assistant. Late on a Friday afternoon in October, when I climbed a ladder to reach some film on an upper shelf, someone came in and started talking to Herr Hoffmann. I had shortened my skirt the day before, and could feel myself being examined and was glad to get down.

"Eva, this is Herr Wolf."

"I am honored," said Herr Wolf, who glanced up from photos on the counter.

Herr Hoffmann sent me across the street to get some sausage and beer, and after I returned he asked me to join him and Herr Wolf. While we ate, Herr Wolf fidgeted with his worn felt hat, and I nearly laughed watching his skinny turtle's neck move around inside a too big collar.

"You are new here, Fraulein? Yes. So, how do you like it?"

"Oh, Herr Wolf," I said, smiling at both men. "I'm glad I was able to get down the ladder a lot better when you were here than I did this morning. This morning I was so clumsy I knocked a box off the top shelf, and at first I was worried about the box. But the box landed right on Herr Hoffmann's poor cat, and it screeched so loud I almost fell off the ladder, and the cat dashed toward the front door and, I couldn't believe it, crashed into the feet of the bakery clerk who'd just entered with an armful of bread. The fellow was so frightened he flew off his feet and smashed face first into a bunch of camera tripods and knocked them all over."

Both gentlemen really laughed, and Herr Hoffmann gave me a look of delight. Herr Wolf loosened up as we discussed our enthusiasm for American movies and German music and theater, and we all enjoyed ourselves and Herr Wolf had twinkling eyes when he left.

"Eva, don't you know who that man is?" said Herr Hoffmann.

"Why, Herr Wolf, of course."

"Eva, that's just a name he uses for privacy. I'm surprised you didn't recognize him. That's Adolf Hitler."

"Who is Adolf Hitler?"

Herr Hoffmann put his hands on his hips and glared at me. Then he walked away shaking his head. I couldn't imagine why he was so upset. I had no idea who Adolf Hitler was.

That night at dinner I said, "Daddy, who is Adolf Hitler?"

"Adolf Hitler!" he shouted. "The man is a disgusting fanatic. Germany doesn't need such scum."

I quickly turned to my mother and started talking about other things, and Daddy did not say more. Later that evening my mother explained: "Your father was recently considered for a promotion at school, but the officials are all Nazis, and they didn't give him a chance."

I knew Herr Hoffmann had many boxes of photos, so the next day at work, when I had a chance to be alone, I got out several huge files on Adolf Hitler and began to study the pictures. They were amazing. Now I definitely wanted him to come back. But waiting was no big deal. There were always plenty of younger men around. Still, it felt good the next time he walked in and stared at me. And on the way out, passing quickly, he nodded.

"Eva," said Herr Hoffmann. "Herr Hitler has asked that you join us at my house tonight."

This opportunity did not make me nervous. I sensed I was ready. Even at age seventeen I knew a lot about makeup and hair styling, and had dieted away a little plumpness, and felt I looked good enough to make Adolf Hitler keep looking. I certainly wanted a good man, and my mother wanted me to marry up, and both parents were enthused when I told them, "Important people will be there."

As I checked everything and added a little more perfume, I was happy I'd decided to leave convent school a few months earlier, after only one year instead of two. Everything was very strict and boring there, and I used to get into trouble for a lot of little things, like dancing, which I loved, and I just had to get away and have some fun. But back home I discovered Daddy was just as strict as Mother Superior. He checked all my mail and phone calls, and every night I had to be in bed, with lights out, by ten o'clock. Getting a job was the only way to escape.

Now, I was at Herr Hoffmann's, listening to my boss and Herr Hitler discuss photography and art. For a long time I could only smile but at the first pause I blurted, "Herr Hitler, I saw Herr Hoffmann's fine pictures of you. Your appeal to the German people is unbelievable, and women are so attracted to you."

Hitler smiled and said, "I suppose my many sacrifices do bring some compensation. But the pressures on me are enormous because my real bride is Germany."

"You could certainly have any woman," said Hoffmann.

Hitler did not reply. He simply hooked his arm through mine and walked me around the room, telling me more about the photographs and paintings on the walls.

At work Herr Hoffmann periodically told me that Hitler wanted to see me at the Hoffmann house or some discrete public place. Herr Hitler was always very polite, and I enjoyed being with him, and even when I did not see him for a while he sent me flowers and candy and other nice things.

BLESSED COLLAPSE
By Adolf Hitler

On Black Friday in October 1929 rich bankers and investors leaped from tall buildings and splattered on New York streets because all in an instant their fortunes were gone, swindled and otherwise stolen by an international clique of usurpers. In Berlin scores of businesses soon collapsed, and thousands of proud and industrious men had to take the debtor's oath. By now the treachery had become so absolutely manifest that the German people would soon be compelled to embrace their most ancient and essential need: a mighty Fuehrer.

Unfortunately, Foreign Minister Gustav Stresemann had died a few weeks before the crash. Though his death certainly was good news, I wished he could have lived just long enough to see the disintegration of his cowardly economic and foreign policies. I suspect Stresemann had still been naively happy, and that is quite unfair to the German people.

I did not fret in December when the Young Plan plebiscite received less than six million of the twenty-one million votes necessary to overturn Germany's obligation to pay reparations until the 1980's. My contribution to the campaign was, in fact, so well received that I immediately split from the publisher Alfred Hugenburg and other lazy capitalist lackeys who might encumber me during this time of promise.

BECOMING A HERO
By Horst Wessel

My father was a pastor who raised me to revere God and Fatherland. Those supreme German values were often spat on during the years I grew into a husky blond Aryan, so I began to attend Nazi meetings and beat hell out of many unruly communists, and always I tried to make Joseph Goebbels notice, and before long he promoted me to lead a platoon of storm troops. I became a valuable National Socialist, and that is why all patriots were outraged by the incident. There were many rumors about what happened, but none that said I was a pimp was true. I was not a pimp. I just fell in love with a lady named Erna who had one. I was only twenty-one and had never been with a woman until Erna took me home the night we met. I started getting all I wanted for free, and she soon asked me to move in.

There were many rumors about who her pimp was. Some said he was a National Socialist. Some said he was a communist. Even if he was a National Socialist on the surface, he had to be a communist at heart. I'll bet he was an infiltrator. He certainly was a lousy jealous pimp. He accused me of stealing Erna for business reasons. That is ridiculous. I tried to keep our apartment address secret because I loved Erna. But the pimp found out. I think the landlady gave us away. She was probably a communist, too, and angry about my patriotic Nazi poem called "Raise High The Flag," which immortalized brave comrades who had been "shot dead by Reds." The poem had so impressed Goebbels that he published it in The Attack.

The cowardly pimp rushed into our apartment with his thugs, completely surprising us, and glared at me before he hissed, "You know what this is for."

Then he shot me right in the mouth. Feeling my jaw and teeth shatter, I fell back on the floor and grabbed my face with both hands and held tight because at first I thought I was dead, and then thought I soon would be.

The pimp and his gang stole Erna and ran out. I could not see them leave but, floating in shock, I heard them as they pounded down the hall and then the stairs. I remember all that, and the police coming and saying to each other that I was not dead. Then they took me to the hospital.

Every day Goebbels came to visit me. I was in bad shape but very proud that such a brilliant man cared about me and told everyone in the room about my extraordinary value and bravery. The Attack was also running articles every day, and Goebbels stood by my bed, reading to me in his wonderful voice the things thousands of people all over Berlin were learning, that I was a "working class Jesus, a socialist Christ who lived in a tenement attic" among people I tried to help, only to be shot by communists.

I was getting weaker and had a lot of pain under the bandages where my face had been. But I still understood when Goebbels leaned down next to my ear and told me that my poem had been set to music and sung at the end of an important political meeting in the huge Sportpalast. Everyone stood, and tears flowed while they sang the "Horst Wessel Song," forevermore the Nazi anthem. This was an extraordinary honor for so young a man.

Following three weeks of hell, I died on February twenty-third, 1930 and was given a very big funeral. Hitler would have attended, too, but was too sick to come. Goebbels was there, along with hundreds of storm troops, my comrades. As my casket lay by the side of the open grave, Goebbels eulogized me in passionate terms. Then, solemnly, he called roll, one by one, and finally, after pausing, his rich voice sounded: "Horst Wessel?"

And every storm trooper roared: "Present."

At this moment some communists threw rocks over cemetery

fences, but they were run off because this occasion was much too sacred to permit any interruption. I also was too sacred and so was the Horst Wessel Song. The pimp and my landlord should have realized that. They were soon dead, and Erna, too.

TRUE SOCIALISTS
By Otto Strasser

Unlike my brother, Gregor, whose ideological ardor had been diluted by his affection for Hitler, I still believed we should nationalize industry and form an alliance with our socialist brothers in the Soviet Union. I also supported the strikes of people striving for fair treatment by employers. The workers were the ones who needed help from National Socialism, not wealthy individuals who fattened party coffers as well as Hitler's suddenly bulging wallet.

After his numerous phone calls and letters failed to control me, Hitler came to Berlin for a summit meeting in May. We met at the Hotel Sanssouci. Among others, Hitler was accompanied by his personal butt-shiner, Rudolf Hess. My brother came, too, as a quasi-moderator.

"Herr Strasser," said Hitler. "I've always been most impressed not only by your brains, but also your bravery and dedication. I want to bring you to Munich as my press chief. All you'd have to do is sell me your publishing outlets and become a more amenable member."

"Absolutely not," I said.

Hitler began to promenade around the room, periodically swatting his leg with a whip while he blabbered. A few hours later, as I still had not withered, he declared, "The great personality alone is responsible for all monumental changes in the world. No party members can challenge my conceptions because only I know the party's ultimate goals and how they can be achieved."

"You're too closely associated with major capitalists," I said.

"Your crude Marxism is a threat to the party's plan to forge an elite new master class motivated not by the morality of pity, but by the conviction they're entitled to rule because of superior race. If you don't step in line, I might proceed against you."

Frowning at me, Hitler left the room and returned to Munich.

Gregor said he would help, and announced to all the papers that Nazis had no arguments among themselves. Hitler publicly agreed. But privately I flinched when he started expelling my supporters from the party, a few here, a few there.

In June I renewed my criticism in a pamphlet called "Cushioned Ministerial Seats or Revolution." Hitler responded with written orders to Goebbels to expel me and the rest of my adherents, and accused us of "insubordination and advocacy of a policy that calls for the very things our Jewish-Marxist enemies desire." Further he decried, "The National Socialist Party will not become a debating club for rootless scribblers or unruly parlor Bolsheviks."

Goebbels convened a meeting for the Berlin district on June thirtieth, and as my faction tried to enter and debate our points, the SA threw us out. Gregor then stunned me by resigning as editor of our newspapers and publicly proclaiming me the "eternal dissident." He stated that he and other leftists were united behind the leadership of Adolf Hitler.

I soon struck at Hitler and the others by announcing in my papers that "the socialists are leaving the party."

Virtually no one came, and I had to wonder: where are all the socialists in the National Socialist party?

BIG CAMPAIGN
By Adolf Hitler

All of my opponents and even some supporters had been saying I was a garbage heap and that the Nazis, with but twelve seats in the Reichstag, would soon altogether sink. No one except me perceived the real situation, certainly not Chancellor Bruenig. When his lamentable economic measures hit legislative roadblocks, he asked President von Hindenburg to invoke the Emergency Powers articles of the constitution. The Reichstag countered with a demand to withdraw that dictatorial decree. Bruenig then convinced Hindenburg to dissolve the Reichstag, and new elections were called for September 1930. What idiots.

Unemployment had bloated to around three million, and so many of the sad and hopeless needed my embrace. To them I sped by car, rail and plane, crisscrossing the Reich to roar: "Since I hold no office, I cannot in any way be held responsible for the crises at hand. I am, however, absolutely confident I can change everything. And we must change, or even more disastrous events will soon surely follow."

Into the crowds I then surged, clasping hands and kissing faces, always striding and confident, the man on the move toward what was necessary and right and at the unified core of every righteous German.

Then, with elections just a few days away, a panicked Goebbels called and said, "Our district headquarters have just been raided and sacked by the SA."

I virtually crushed the phone in my hand as he added, "It was so bad I had to go to the police. They've been saying terrible things, Mein Fuehrer. Please, you've got to come right away."

His entreaty was at that point unnecessary. No one could have prevented my rushing to Berlin. Flanked by disciplined SS in black uniforms, I marched into beer halls where misguided men bombarded me with hisses and insults. Everything I had long cherished was about to collapse. This so aroused me that I was repeatedly able to declare, "I can't imagine why you feel you're unappreciated and being used as cannon fodder. I know very well how complete your sacrifices are, and I'm touched and grateful for them during every hour of every day. Most of you surely know that it is I who have lived the most abject life of all. For many years I resided alone in two tiny rooms, forsaking material comfort and the joys of family life, because of my full dedication to you, the German people.

"I know your wages aren't what you and I want them to be, but for the sake of the sacrifices you've already made, don't destroy our victories on the eve of fulfillment. I can at last guarantee that your immediate future will bring financial satisfaction and the even greater reward of being brave men in the vanguard of National Socialism."

Many times, overwhelmed by cheers and embraces that had so quickly replaced hostility, I just could not contain my tears. And soon, I announced that my storm troops would never again feel neglected. I was personally taking control of the SA.

Returning to the campaign in a flurry, I demanded all Nazis summon levels of energy and dedication heretofore unattained. I wanted to discover the most worthy and fanatical among them. It was like passing a magnet over a heap of dung and seeing how much iron clung to the magnet. The result was outstanding. During the final forty-eight hours before the elections, my men held at least two dozen large demonstrations in Berlin alone. And all over the Reich my words and my image were catapulted to the fore.

September fourteenth arrived with the scent of historical significance, and throughout the day I savored reports that many voters were turning out. They had surely been attracted by me. I could not imagine any other explanation. After midnight I went to our Munich election headquarters and was greeted by excited comrades who told me we might well win an extraordinary increase from twelve to perhaps sixty or seventy seats in the Reichstag.

"If Germans can think correctly, it'll be more than that," I said.

I thought, I certainly hoped, really I knew, that everything imaginable might go right and we could even approach a hundred seats. That's what I kept telling myself in those dark early-morning hours of enlightenment. Around five a.m., while I remained composed, party comrades pranced around the room, celebrating the unimaginable. We'd won a hundred-and-seven seats.

BORING CAMPAIGN
By Geli Raubaul

I was sick of all the campaigning and carrying on and told my uncle, "I don't want to be alone so much. I'm just as popular in my way as you are in yours."

"Don't talk like that, and don't think that."

"So many men are virtually begging to be with me."

"I won't let you do that. You're to be home every night by ten."

"That's ridiculous."

"It is not. Take that dress off. You're not going to wear anything that shows too much."

"I'll do what I want."

"No you won't. When you go out, someone from the Party's going to escort you."

Not everyone was willing to do things Adolf Hitler wouldn't like. Sometimes I still got to drink a lot of champagne, and felt really free and happy, and wanted to go right home and move out of my uncle's apartment. I only decided to wait because of the excitement.

FAMILY REUNION
By Alois Hitler, Jr.

I was a little uneasy Adolf summoned me to a family meeting late in 1930. I had not seen my half-brother in many years, since he was a boy, and knew he did not want to discuss our happy upbringing. My first wife, Brigid, and our son, William Patrick Hitler, would also be at the meeting, along with my sister, Angela.

I certainly did not want to see Brigid. After our marriage years ago when I lived in Liverpool, England, she'd started carping that I didn't earn enough as a waiter, and pressured me to open my own restaurant. I tried but soon went broke, and Brigid, who merely sat home with William Patrick sucking her breast, berated me for incompetence. Next I went into the boardinghouse business, which was also a bust, then the hotel business, which was likewise fruitless, and Brigid became nastier still. Of course I'd started seeing better women. And I didn't strain to keep secrets. I also gave William Patrick a few whacks if he cried too much or bothered me. When Brigid threatened to get the police, that was it. I got out, and without needless and unpleasant farewells. Back in Germany I had more fun and freedom, and found a new wife, and everything was all right until 1924 when I was jailed a few months for bigamy. I know Brigid traced me and notified the authorities. She was jealous, and angry I never sent William and her any money. That is true but no big deal. After all, she and William never sent me any money, either.

Today, Adolf was in a lather, an absolute rage, and those vicious hot eyes were so familiar as he barked, "William Patrick's been giving interviews to the Hearst newspapers, and they've published photos of him with the claim he's my nephew. That disgusts me. Don't any of you think I'll permit my talent and greatness to be traded on by family members. Further, if Alois' criminal record were made clear, it might ruin my career. It's critical no details of our family background become known."

Adolf glowered at me a few seconds before staring at William Patrick and telling the young man, "You couldn't possibly be related to me since your father was adopted by my father."

I did not say anything and neither did Angela.

"You must return to London and disclaim all relationship in the present and in the future," Adolf said to Brigid and William.

Adolf then handed me two thousand dollars to pay return passage and any other expenses Brigid and William might have. I assured them I'd take care of their bills and mail the remaining funds upon their arrival in England. Then Adolf told me to stay after the others left.

"All right, shithead," he said, "don't think you or that whore or that bastard are going to pull me into the gutter with you. I'm soon going to be in power in Germany, and this country will be intolerable for you unless you immediately do as I say."

I contacted the Hearst papers and offered to write a story about my brother's youth. Under my byline, I related what a kind and generous boy Adolf had been and told how he swept streets and scrubbed floors in order to support his little sister, Paula, after our saintly mother, Klara, had died. Adolf, I noted, was always a very hard worker who made countless sacrifices for his family.

BETTER SA
By Ernst Roehm

After Hitler forced me to relinquish command of the SA in 1925, I had tried to work as a civilian, but that was a sham. I was a military man to the core, and only the life of a soldier appealed to me. Since Bolivia was then the only place I could fight, I went.

What misery. Not only was Bolivia a country of brown-skinned ninnies with a putrid military tradition, it was a place so foreign to my instincts that my emotions were dying. I could not seem to find anyone in South America who understood my kind of love. About this I often wrote passionately to friends in Germany, and continued to yearn until Hitler sent me a telegram to return and take control of the SA and SS.

At our first meeting we discussed the nature of my role. Though the Fuehrer retained overall command, he did agree to let me arrange the hundred thousand men of the SA my way, under strict military guidelines. I began my task as chief of staff in January 1931, and at once purged numerous old SA leaders and replaced them with the right men for rapid growth. Soon I had one hundred seventy thousand storm troops who marched with the precision of soldiers or took to the streets and informally battered communists and Jews and anyone else in need.

As my influence proliferated, so did sordid and petty attacks by self-righteous hooligans who claimed I loaded upper echelons of the SA with cronies who'd gained favor for reasons other than merit. That was ridiculous, as Hitler well understood when he issued this decree: "The SA is not an institute for the moral education of genteel young ladies, but a formation of seasoned fighters. The sole purpose of any inquiry must be to ascertain whether or not the SA officer is performing his official duties within the SA. His private life cannot be an object of scrutiny unless it conflicts with basic principles of National Socialist ideology."

Goering, who wanted my job, and Himmler, the wretched Reichsfuehrer SS, and other genteel young ladies had to accept, if not acknowledge, that I was very effective. During this period of mounting unemployment and despair, my SA provided jobs, not to mention food, shelter and hope for thousands of young men who otherwise would have been hungry in the streets.

Despite my efficient command, Berlin SA leader Walter Stennes began causing trouble, and in the spring he arranged a secret conference of SA leaders who denounced Hitler and declared mutinous intentions. According to my sources, Goebbels was also there and in loud agreement.

Hitler generously offered to reassign Stennes to a desk job at the new and opulent party headquarters, the Brown House, in Munich. Stennes declined, so the Fuehrer empowered me to eradicate infected elements of the SA. My storm troops swiftly located the problems and smashed them to the point of hospitalization, or worse. Hitler then came to Berlin to convince other unruly storm troops to pledge allegiance, and I told him what I'm sure he already knew: Goebbels had been an instigator. Hitler responded the same way he did at a meeting of district leaders: "When a mother has many children and one of them goes astray, it is the wise mother who takes the child by the hand and holds on to him."

I was also disturbed by the major credit Himmler bestowed himself and the SS for squelching the Stennes revolt. My SA men had done most of the bone crushing. All Himmler's SS men did — and they were under my overall command anyway — was serve as Hitler's bodyguards as he went around weeping for loyalty. The Fuehrer surprised me by choosing an SS man to replace Stennes in Berlin. One of my men would have been better.

BIG MONEY
By Adolf Hitler

The beleaguered German people, staggering in 1931 with more than five million unemployed, would not have been able to comprehend the Nazis dealing with those we had so often said were partially to blame for the pitiful state of our nation. I therefore gave this order in strict confidence: expand in every way our relationships with the eminent men of industry.

While some National Socialists, at my direction, continued to publicly bemoan the excesses of money barons, I held clandestine meetings at private estates or beneath huge trees in dark German forests. There I told the capitalists, "I believe competition is essential to free-market productivity, and I promise to protect your assets. The country's got to have your talents. Only you can provide the jobs we need to avoid catastrophe. And only I can create the conditions you need for good business."

In the rotting Reichstag my delegates shouted at those who had unrelentingly, for thirteen straight years now, driven our nation right down into a cesspool. It would have been ludicrous to pretend democracy was working while the Hunger Chancellor, Bruenig, hid behind the malicious veil of the Emergency Powers article, and behaved as an incompetent dictator. By the fall of 1931 our movement faced increasingly brutal battles with a variety of anti-Germanic elements, and things were getting worse.

DECISION
By Geli Raubaul

Every time we were alone I wrapped Uncle Alf around my finger any way I wanted and was convinced he planned to marry me someday. That's why it hurt so much when he said Germany would always be his only bride. But at least he promised I'd forever be his only girlfriend. And I believed him. I just couldn't understand why he had recently been less enthusiastic and wasn't seeing me as much in Munich. Sometimes I told close friends how things really were, and they said I should move right out. I was tempted. It would have been easy. I think it would have. Actually, I was terrified to leave. And Alf wasn't going to force me. He wasn't going to fool me, either. I started looking through his desk, and my heart burst when I saw the picture of a girl. She had on a lot of make-up and wore long brown hair in a cheap, frilly way some people would be stupid enough to like. "To Adi with love, Eva," was written on back of the picture.

Once in a while I had gone out when Alf was out of town. Now I decided to do just what I wanted. I dated a ski instructor and a musician and also the chauffeur, Emil Maurice. One afternoon my uncle rushed in and caught Emil embracing me on the couch, and he shouted, "Get out of here. You're fired. Don't come back to this apartment or anywhere else Geli might be."

After Emil jumped up and left, I told Alf, "You can't tell me what to do while you're going with that dog of yours."

"I won't permit you to whore around as long as you're in this house. I have an obligation to protect you from ruthless men. And don't worry about Eva. She's just Hoffmann's secretary. It's important I keep him and all his employees satisfied."

I still went out with other men, and my uncle must have known something. He sensed enough to be in tears as he said, "From now on you can't go to Berchtesgaden or Vienna unless I go with you or give special permission. And I'm going to make sure you never get out any more without a chaperone."

"You have some very good chaperones, Uncle Alf."

"Just remember, Geli, if you leave me, you'll lose more money and status than you'll ever have anywhere else. I could replace you right away, you know."

In many ways he was very persuasive, but nothing could make up for the letter I found in September. That little tramp Eva wrote she enjoyed being with him so much she was counting the seconds until they could be together again. It was obvious she meant alone together.

"Fine," I snapped at my uncle as he packed his bags. "That's just fine. You expect me to stay home by myself for another damn weekend while you go off being famous and having your little meetings with Eva. Well, I have a boyfriend I'm going to see right after you leave."

Alf fired the pants in his hand onto the bed and yelled, "You're not going to leave this apartment while I'm gone."

"I'm leaving, and I'm going to have a good time. There's no reason to rot here alone when I can be out with a handsome young man."

"You're not doing that if you ever want to come back."

"Why would I want to come back to this horrible place?"

"You know you belong here."

"I hate it here."

"Shut up. Shut up. Right now, shut up." Alf jammed the rest of his clothes into his suitcase, closed it, and muttered goodbye without looking at me, then huffed out the bedroom. The repulsive Heinrich Hoffmann, who did everything he could to make my uncle like Eva, was waiting downstairs. Together they walked down the front steps and loaded the luggage into the big black Mercedes Benz.

I ran out onto the second floor balcony overlooking the street and the limousine my uncle was about to enter. I was going to yell everything was over. This time I was really going to tell him, firing my words down on his neck.

But he stunned me by spinning around and glaring up.

"For the last time, no. You're not going anywhere."

Then my uncle motioned for his chauffeur to drive off.

I left the balcony and walked downstairs and told our housekeeper, Frau Annie Winter, that I was going to be in my bedroom and did not want to be disturbed.

NO RESPONSE
By Frau Annie Winter

The Fuehrer tried so hard to be like a father to Geli, and I know he was exasperated as he left for a meeting. Geli had been yelling at him, and he had every right to yell back and make the girl understand what was for her own good. She was only twenty-three and could not possibly know as much about life as Adolf Hitler.

I thought it would be good for Geli to spend some time in her room so she could think about the things her uncle had been telling her. The staff and I left her alone the rest of the day. The next morning, Saturday around ten a.m., I took the newspaper to Geli's room and knocked. I knocked again but did not hear anything.

"Geli, are you in there?" I said. I really did not see how she could be anywhere else. But in case that flirt had somehow slipped out the window during the night, I called a few people, including her mother, Angela. No one had seen or heard from Geli. I became a little worried and got my husband. He tinkered with Geli's door and forced it open.

MESSAGE
By Heinrich Hoffmann

After our departure from Nuremberg a little while ago, we were having a pleasant Saturday morning drive north en route to party meetings in Hamburg. I was relaxed in the back seat and much enjoying the company of confidence of the Fuehrer, who rode in front, next to Julius Shreck. I was explaining which camera angles I felt flattered Hitler most when Shreck, after several increasingly alarmed glances into the rearview mirror, looked rapidly to his right and said, "Mein Fuehrer, we're being followed and the car's speeding to catch us."

Hitler wheeled around and looked back through the window, then ordered, "Better speed up. This could be an attempt to kill me."

While Shreck gunned the big Mercedes engine, I studied the vehicle behind us before saying, "Just a minute. That car's a taxi and the passenger's motioning for us to stop."

"You're right," said Hitler. "Pull over."

The passenger hopped out and ran to Hitler's side of the car. He was a uniformed employee of the Deutscher Hof Hotel where we stayed the previous night.

"Sir," the boy said to the Fuehrer, "Herr Rudolf Hess has a very urgent call from Munich."

"What is it? What's wrong?" said Hitler.

"I don't know. Herr Hess said he'll stay on the line until you get back to the hotel."

Hitler grimaced at me, then told Shreck, "Hurry up."

Shreck turned the limousine around and powered away. It was a quick trip back, and after several screeching turns through Nuremberg streets, Shreck braked hard in front of the Deutscher Hof Hotel, and Hitler sprinted inside, followed by Shreck and me. A hotel employee pointed at an open phone booth, and the Fuehrer threw his hat and whip onto the floor and grabbed the phone and said, "This is Hitler. What's the matter?

"No, God. I don't believe it. Hess, tell me the truth. Is Geli alive or is she dead?"

Hitler dropped the phone, staggered out of the booth, and in a barely audible voice said, "We must get back to Munich immediately."

Shreck concentrated like a race car driver as we blurred south along the highway, often swerving into oncoming lanes at terrifying speeds. Both of us were afraid to speak to the Fuehrer. I've never seen such agonized expressions. By the time we arrived at his apartment in Munich, he was so dazed that Shreck and I had to help him out of the car and steady him inside.

"Mein Fuehrer, I'm extraordinarily sorry," said Hess, rushing up. "Geli was a fantastic girl, and we all loved her very much."

Hitler wobbled, and Shreck took both shoulders and almost carried him to a couch where he slumped, nearly lifeless.

"I've got to die, too," Hitler muttered.

"No, Mein Fuehrer," Hess entreated, "Germany needs you too much."

"This has destroyed me."

"Don't worry," said Hess. "Justice officials have already been here and said this case is obviously a suicide. No official investigation will be necessary."

"I'll die if I have to look at Geli."

"We've already taken care of that," Hess said. "They ordered Geli be removed from here. Funeral arrangements are being made. Your sister has also been notified."

"I can't stand being here."

Hess eased over to me and whispered.

"We have the perfect place, Mein Fuehrer," I said. "Come on. Shreck and I will help you."

During the drive to Tegern Lake, Hitler sat slumped and silent until saying, "The only woman I ever could've married's dead, and so's my political career. I'm quitting public life and staying away from all women even if I decide to live. But I just want to die."

When we arrived, Shreck told me he'd hidden Hitler's revolver. We put him in a second floor bedroom and said to let us know if he wanted food, companionship, anything. My bedroom was directly underneath, and, on the thin, creaky floor between us, I began to hear countless haunted steps as Hitler walked across the room and back, back and forth, pacing the repetitive course of a tortured big cat in a small cage at the zoo. I could not sleep that night and was quite tired in the morning when I went upstairs and tapped on his door. Getting no response but still hearing footsteps, I gently opened the door and looked in. Hitler's hands were locked behind his back, and his head hung as he moved.

"Are you hungry?" I said.

He barely shook his head.

For three days at the house on Tegern Lake, Hitler was eternally on his feet, moving, moving, afraid to stop lest he become even more mired in misery. We received several distressing telephone calls from party lawyer Hans Frank, but at least there was the good news that Geli's body had been placed in a sealed lead coffin and promptly buried in Central Cemetery in Vienna. Though people who committed suicide weren't supposed to be buried in this consecrated ground, party officials had convinced the Father that Geli's death was due to her aberrant state of mind.

THE REAL WORLD
By Adolf Hitler

My beautiful young niece had just died so tragically, yet my ruthless enemies would not let the poor girl part in peace. Instead, they used her misfortune as a pretext to attack me. The Munich Post wrote that Geli was found with bruises all over her body and had suffered a broken nose. That was a lie according to everyone at the scene, including the police, many of whom hated me. The Post also insinuated I might be involved in my niece's death. I really felt this scurrilous campaign was choking the life out of me, and I wanted to disappear forever. But all I could do was issue, on September twenty-second, a public statement of the truth: "It is untrue that I and my niece had a quarrel. It is untrue that I was violently opposed to my niece going to Vienna. It is untrue that my niece was engaged to someone in Vienna and I forbade it."

The whole thing was untrue, but I could not let it destroy me. I needed to go to Vienna and be with Geli at her grave. Ernst Roehm and Heinrich Himmler, my loyal leaders of the SA and SS, had graciously represented me at Geli's funeral because I could not legally set foot in Austria. Soon a one-day waiver of my banishment was granted, and after being driven to the border in my Mercedes, I solemnly rode to Central Cemetery in a less conspicuous car driven by the local Nazi district leader.

With a big bouquet of flowers in my trembling hand, I walked slowly toward the freshly finished grave and looked down at words, etched in marble, that were soon covered with my tears:

Here Sleeps Our Beloved Child
Geli
She was Our Ray of Sunshine
Born 4 June 1908 — Died 18 September 1931
The Raubaul Family

I knew Geli was with me then, as she always would be. I knew that she knew how I felt. But I was afraid she was angry. Perhaps she did not really understand how I loved her, and why. It crushed me to think she might not appreciate my feelings. I put the pretty flowers on her grave, then, faintly at first, I began to hear her voice.

Oh God, Geli, don't do this. You must not say these things. I can hear you very clearly now, and it is not fair for you to talk to me like that. You know how very much I love you. I always will. I'll honor you just as much as my mother. I swear I'll display big pictures and busts of you at all of my residences. I promise to leave everything in your room just like it was, as if you were still here. I promise to carry your picture with me everywhere. That's how much I love you. So you must not say these things to me. Please don't say anymore. Geli, please rest quietly as I try to convey here what you mean. Geli...

ALF
By Geli Raubaul

No, no, Uncle Alf, I must speak candidly to you now that you are here so sad and tearful kneeling beside my grave. You know I could never really open up while I was alive. Now I feel much freer and more enlightened, and we can really talk. O.K?

I want you to know how it was when I, your beloved Geli, did slowly die. I want you to know I was conscious after I shot myself. I was not granted the grace of instantaneous death. No, I was very much awake for what seemed a very long time. I'm sure you're aware that during intensified moments of life — and death — a few minutes, or even a few seconds, can be an interminable drain.

Oh God, the blood came out, erupting, big gushes of it all over the beautiful bedroom you wanted me to have. And all I could do was just watch my life flow away in crimson, crimson all over the floor. It must have been at least one long second before I even weakened. And then I was down, down on the same floor where you used to grovel and make me undress and do those horrible things I could never forget.

Oh, Onkel Alf, I must be franker still, from here deep in this darkened morbid grave, and scream that you were not a real man. You know that. You wanted only the worst.

PERSEVERANCE
By Heinrich Hoffmann

Several days after his niece died, Adolf Hitler resumed his trip north to Hamburg to address the important Nazi meeting of district leaders and SA officials. A lesser man could not have regained control so soon. Projecting great strength, the Fuehrer announced that all rotten elements would have to be cashiered from the party, and obedience and faith in him were essential to the future.

During his private hours, away from the crowds, the Fuehrer was a little more subdued than usual. That was understandable. He had very many things to think about. Several times at the dinner table he remarked: "If I'm going to be able to persevere for the German nation, I have to protect my health. I can't eat any more meat. It's disgusting, like eating a corpse. No one should ever eat meat."

DUTY OF THE HEART
By Hermann Goering

Carin had been feverish and weakening, and her heart often beat faintly almost beyond detection. Many times, horrified, I thought she was gone and rushed to embrace her and kiss her pale beautiful face, and then was relieved to discover her life still lingered.

"I'm so tired," she said. "I often see a door for me in the sky."

"You're going to stay right here. I promise I'll always be with you."

"Having you here always makes me so happy."

Sometimes her luminous smile completely submerged her illness, and I began to believe the doctors had to be wrong. They did not understand how she was. She wanted me to love her and urged me to all the time. But that could be fatal. I had been warned. I just could not. I could not always stand being enflamed. Sometimes we had to. This was wonderful but strained Carin so much, and many times instead of complete physical love I simply kissed her and kissed her more and stroked her delicate brown hair until I felt my own heart might rupture.

In the fall, as Carin declined, her long-ill mother closed her eyes the final time, and Carin begged to attend the funeral in Stockholm.

"Dearest, I can't let you," I said. "The doctor said the trip would be the end."

Carin could not rest or relax, and after several days I was unable to refuse. "I'll go with you," I said. "But the funeral is already over."

"That's all right, darling. I want to be with my family, and I want to be with Mother."

In Stockholm I had to lift Carin gently off the train and down to the platform. Her son, Thomas, met us there, and despite the enduring beauty of his mother he looked at me with such concern I averted my eyes lest involuntary confirmation be noticed by my discerning wife.

That night, after but a few hours of shared grief with her father and four sisters, Carin fainted, falling straight over where she sat on the couch, and I carried her to the bedroom she had slept in as a youth. A doctor was summoned, and after examining Carin he privately told me, "I'm sorry. She probably won't survive the night."

No matter what, I could not accept that. For several days, with barely a break, I knelt beside Carin and held her hand and washed the feverish wetness off her forehead and mouth, and often I leaned down and whispered, trying not to sob, that she must not leave us. She must hold on. I ignored Hitler's urgent telegram telling me to return at once. I would never have deserted my wife when she was too sick to even open her eyes and talk.

Briefly I left her room one morning. When I returned, Thomas was standing beside her, and she was crying. Then she motioned for me.

"Thomas told me the Fuehrer needs you now," she whispered.

"I don't care."

"Please, sweetheart, listen to me. You have a duty to your country."

"My duty to you is more important. The Fuehrer can wait. They can all wait."

Carin put a warm hand on each side of my face and eased my head down on her chest, and breathed, "No, no Hermann. You must go. I won't let you stay. I'm better now. That you can see. Thomas will look after me."

One of Carin's sisters entered the room, and my wife said, "Fanny, the Fuehrer urgently needs Hermann back in Berlin. Please help him pack his things."

Carin raised my face from her chest and smiled at me.

"All right," I said. "Thomas will take care of you until I get back. Then I'll make sure you get well."

"Yes, darling," said Carin, "when you return everything will be much better."

INSOLENT CORPORAL
By President Paul von Hindenburg

At age eighty-four I was not quite sure about all the political details in Germany, but my shrewd and trustworthy advisor, General Kurt von Schleicher, kept me abreast of everything.

"No one can make any important political decisions without

including the Nazis," Schleicher had told me. "I've been in contact with Ernst Roehm, and I think it prudent for you to meet with him when you see Hitler."

"That's impossible. Granting some of my time to Corporal Hitler is bad enough, but I won't have my imperial offices degraded by that pervert. Hitler will have to come with someone else."

"Perhaps Hermann Goering would be acceptable to you, Herr President. He won the pour le mérite and comes from a diplomatic family."

"I suppose that would be all right. Let's be on with it."

I think Schleicher set the appointment for October tenth. The exact date didn't matter. Hitler mattered.

"Our troubled nation needs your cooperation," I told him.

"Herr President, my party has extraordinary patriotic aims, and we've already done so much for the survival of Germany. We represent the future, the very hope and soul of our nation..."

On he blubbered, and while I decided whether to at once dismiss this queer fellow, I stroked, and tapped, and tugged my bushy gray mustache. Then I held my hand up. "All right, all right, Herr Hitler," I said, rising. "I was doing patriotic deeds decades before your birth, and I'm much aware of what constitutes valuable service to the nation."

I stood tall, at well over six feet, and sternly I looked down on this fidgety Bohemian corporal in a cheap suit, and said, "Herr Hitler, I'm very unhappy with the violent and unruly, not to mention illegal, behavior of many of your men, your so called storm troops. A real commander keeps his men disciplined and orderly. This talent seems beyond you. How can you expect to hold an important role in government when you can't even maintain control over your own men?"

"My men are actually protecting good, decent Germans from wicked forces. In fact, we're doing what no one else can, Herr President, what no one else is committed to doing..."

I just frowned down on him, and rarely glanced at the silent Goering, who looked like a stupid stuffed pig. Both were strange fellows. This audience had proceeded long enough. I grimaced a few more times and that ended things.

After the two Nazis departed, I said to Schleicher, "As you surely witnessed, that Hitler just isn't right. I'd never tolerate him as my chancellor. Perhaps someday I'll appoint him postmaster so he can lick stamps with my face on them."

PARTING
By Hermann Goering

I could not get back to Sweden until Carin's birthday, the day of her funeral. Many people of nobility came to the ceremony, and all told me how kind Carin was and how sad they were. I was too sad to tell. As they carried Carin's coffin into the family tomb, Thomas walked to me and we embraced.

"My mother told me it would have destroyed her to leave while you were still here," he said.

REACQUAINTANCE
By Mimi Reiter

People in southern Bavaria were talking a lot about Hitler and his niece, and many knew he and I had been friendly a few years ago, and asked me all about him. I really did not know what to say. All that was over, until Rudolf Hess walked in one afternoon.

"The Fuehrer's been thinking about you all the time and wants to see you very much," he said.

I was still mad about how he had treated me, but after hesitating a little I hurried and packed some things and left a note for my hotelkeeper husband that I was going to Munich for awhile.

Greeting me in his lovely apartment, the Fuehrer kissed my hand several times and gave me candy and flowers. Right away we went into his quarters, and he told me how sad he was about Geli and how difficult his life was as a unique politician who had to deal with imbeciles while trying to save Germany from catastrophe. I could tell he wanted me to sit close to him on his big soft couch, and it was fun having this famous man tell me about such important things. I sat right next to the Fuehrer and put one arm around his shoulder and stroked his hands with my other hand, and said, "You're so much more than the man I married."

The Fuehrer embraced me and seemed very upset. I told him I understood, and we started kissing, and the more aroused I became the more I hoped things would be different. Quickly, I took my clothes off and said, "Now. This time. Please."

He got that look again, and I could tell he hadn't changed. Still, I was glad to see him and did everything he wanted.

Afterward, Adolf told me, "You're wonderful. I'll give you everything you want if you'll be my mistress."

"I want to be your wife."

"I can't marry you, Mimi. I can't marry anyone, not even you."

"If I was just your mistress, it would be too easy to drop me."

"I'm sorry, Mimi, but a great man like me must never get married. Besides, you already have a husband."

NEXT STEPS
By Adolf Hitler

The Weimar Constitution clearly stated that President von Hindenburg's seven-year term would end in 1932 and to continue in office he needed to run again and be reelected. Instead of obeying the laws he was sworn to protect, Chancellor Bruenig twice met me and cynically proposed I support an initiative to prolong Hindenburg's term. The old man didn't want to campaign again. That was outrageous. Everyone knew Hindenburg was antiquated to the point of incontinence, and allowing that doddering hulk to remain in office would automatically permit Bruenig to operate freely as chancellor and pursue the very inane policies that required evermore sacrifices while the German nation continued to degenerate.

I did not bother responding to Bruenig. He was unimportant. I waited awhile, then notified Hindenburg: "As a vitally concerned German, I cannot abrogate such a key element of the Weimar Constitution. That would be immoral and wrong."

Eventually, the old man decided he would run again after all. German reverence made him arrogant enough to want to hold onto power despite his abysmal performance. He had to be confronted, and I was the only one who might beat him. I knew I could. I was not afraid of any man. I just did not know when I should run. A big defeat now might ruin my career, and people would laugh. Maybe I would be stronger later. But maybe by then I would be weaker, swept from the forefront. I had made many comebacks, though, and could not imagine forever being denied leadership. This was my chance, if timing and circumstances were right.

If I did decide to run, I would need money. It absolutely nauseated me to even look at, much less make requests of, those hidebound industrialists with boundless pretensions and ridiculous top hats. But I knew I had to impress them soon. In January 1932 I got a nice, specially tailored pinstriped business suit and wore it to Dusseldorf for a big speech at the Industry Club where a cold and passive group of blue bloods stared at me as I stood before them.

"You don't have to accept Chancellor Bruenig's defeatist ideology that Germany's fate will be determined by its relations with foreign countries," I asserted. "On the contrary, foreign policy is determined by the inner condition of a people, and our inner condition, our health, is being gravely undermined by democracy. Majority rule principles are quite folly and ruinous because the brilliant, capable minds — the geniuses — of a nation are always in the minority. And if the majority — who are comprised primarily by the stupid, the weak, the cowardly and the inadequate — is allowed to govern, then the best elements in a society, those born for the task, will have their talents buried while those infinitely less capable are permitted to destroy the country."

Now the industrialists began to buzz. I stopped several seconds and adjusted my coat, looking out over them, harmoniously.

"Gentlemen, the solution to Germany's woes lies first in the recognition that economic systems in collapse are always preceded by the collapse of the state, and not vice versa. A vibrant economic life must always have at its foundation a flourishing and powerful state as protector. This we obviously do not have.

"Very soon Germany's destiny will be determined. If the present trends are permitted to continue, our nation will before long be enmeshed in Bolshevist chaos. Either we will succeed in again forging an iron hard national body out of the current disorganized mess, or our Germany of such inherent greatness will perish with ignominious finality. Only with fanatical faith and idealism can Germany again stand in the eyes of the world far more proudly than she stands today."

Pounding hands echoed in my chest, and I rubbed sweat from my right hand onto my damp coat and heartily shook hands with many who approached the podium. Maybe I really should run, I said to myself.

MY MAN
By Eva Braun

Nothing remotely compared to the joy of being with Adolf Hitler, and I was anxious to make this wonderful man my life's work. There were many obstacles, however. I didn't dare tell my parents I had been seeing him, and especially a lot since now I could go to his apartment. But I could not be out all night. My parents were mad enough about the late hours and asked a lot of questions. I know they would not have approved of the twenty-three year age difference. That did not matter to me or to Adolf. He often told me that was exactly the difference between his parents.

People always made it so difficult to do what I had to. Frau Annie Winter, the housekeeper, and Goering and Goebbels and others acted snobbishly and were very jealous. At first, I almost told Adolf about them not passing along my messages and calling me stupid. Instead, I decided never to be a burden.

INDECISION
By Joseph Goebbels

My shrewd slogans had become absolutely essential to the Fuehrer, and I also helped him and the party by dating Magda Quandt, who was once the wife of a very rich man. Now everyone in Germany knew this patrician blond had fallen in love with me, the Nazi propaganda minister. Magda wasn't merely beautiful. She thoroughly understood politics. I made sure. Meeting Hitler, she at once captivated him by quoting extensively from *Mein Kampf* and asking many astute questions. The Fuehrer became so animated he repeatedly kissed her hands, and later he insisted on being our best man.

After the wedding, I proudly moved into Magda's luxurious

apartment on the Reichkanzlerplatz. My old residence had not been good enough, but now Hitler and many others came to relax and be entertained. Magda was a great hostess and frequently served the Fuehrer lots of his favorite cakes and candies. He especially appreciated these favors since he was burdened by the very great decision about whether to run for president in the March elections.

"Six million Germans are unemployed, Mein Fuehrer," I said. "A party of our stature has to offer a candidate. We can't just sit back and watch the elections. Who else can stand up against Hindenburg?"

Instead of answering, Hitler merely paced and looked intently at the floor.

During subsequent meetings I reminded him, "Our storm troops are frustrated and angry and won't tolerate inaction. They need to see some indication they'll be rewarded for their sacrifices. Also, Mein Fuehrer, Hindenburg's advisers have been making plans. We need to counter with our own strategies."

By January twenty-first I had convinced Hitler to make his decision within two days. In two days he told me he was going to run but that no official public announcement could be made until we assessed what other parties were going to do. In a speech to district leaders the next day, Hitler again refused to commit. That night many party officials lamented he was squandering essential campaign time.

But it was not that the Fuehrer lacked confidence. In fact, he spent a lot of time showing party members sketches and models of what the new spectacular Berlin would look like after he assumed power and renovated the city. These were exciting plans, but we still wanted him to assure us, and the nation, that he would definitely be running. On February ninth and twelfth, he and I and other officials debated his candidacy at the Kaiserhof Hotel in Berlin.

"I just can't decide for certain, at least not publicly," said the Fuehrer. "I'm not sure about the voting projections."

"But we do have to take the risk," I said.

"We shall see."

Hindenburg announced his official decision to run on February fifteenth. Now we had been challenged. And I was ready to respond. I only needed official approval to unleash all my plans. But I had to keep waiting.

When I went to the Kaiserhof to see Hitler on February twenty-second, I was extremely nervous. That night I was scheduled to address thousands of party members at the Sportpalast.

"Mein Fuehrer, if I only offer them more indecision, they'll be very agitated."

And standing up there on stage, I'd be directly targeted for disapproval. I had to worry. I had to doubt, however slightly, the Fuehrer's resolve and toughness. I was looking hopefully at him as he got up and said, "Tonight it is your honor to pronounce my candidacy for president."

That night Nazis jumped and shouted and pounded for ten minutes. Following my speech, Hitler telephoned and then came over to visit Magda and me. We were all relieved he had showed himself to be our Fuehrer after all.

PRESIDENTIAL ELECTIONS
By Adolf Hitler

Well, I was running. I was running against Hindenburg and the old man would soon learn I was ready for an unprecedented campaign. But I was not yet an official German. I wasn't even a citizen of the country I was destined to save. That seemed shocking and unfair to many people, especially me. But it was no problem, not with my influence, and I gained German citizenship, officially, following my long spiritual union, when a state minister gladly appointed me as an attaché in Berlin. Now I could really run.

For the first eleven days in March I crisscrossed Germany by car, and to huge crowds I continually roared: "You have now been suffering for a decade and a half. First, your backs were stabbed to rob you of victory during the Great War, and since then a succession of treaties, travesties and emergency decrees has stolen your sacred national pride as well as your jobs and your homes. And what has the government offered to remedy your travails? I'll tell you: failure upon failure, collapse upon collapse, misery upon misery. Cowardice, apathy and hopelessness have undermined us everywhere, and I stand here guaranteeing you that my National Socialist comrades and I are not cowards, are not apathetic and are not hopeless. We are brave and we are dynamic, and we will forever bury the misery and incompetence of previous regimes. Our nation needs me to serve as your president. The alternative is more devastation. Germany Awake!"

Always my viewers erupted absolutely open-mouthed. And soon everyone else was listening to my speeches in theaters or on the radio or in the streets as loudspeakers roared from roving, swastika-swathed trucks. As usual, but far more pervasively, we decorated the nation's walls and telephone poles with bright political posters, and distributed millions of pamphlets and party newspapers. We all had to work feverishly because Bruenig, the Hunger Chancellor, was terrified by our burgeoning popularity and helped Hindenburg with countless dirty tricks, even banning us from radio stations controlled by the government.

The German people would nevertheless sense Hindenburg was a cadaver in waiting. He did not dare make any public appearances, and deigned to make but one radio address, a boring and pathetic pre-recorded sermon about how his reelection would protect the Fatherland "from serious disturbances whose outcome would be incalculable." He piously added he wasn't asking anyone to vote for him who didn't want to.

Compare that crap to me, my campaign, my statements. We were all very confident the German people would not opt for more senile incompetence, no matter how heroic the inert hulk may once have been. Goebbels was especially optimistic. On March twelfth in The Attack, he proclaimed: "Tomorrow Hitler will be President of the Reich." Logically, it had to be me. No one expected the other two candidates, the Communist and the Conservative, to get many votes.

During the night of March thirteenth, while votes were being tabulated, many party members became gloomy, and their pessimism angered me. So what if Hindenburg received about eighteen million votes and I got eleven million? That was really a victory for us. First, there would have to be another election: Hindenburg only got forty-nine percent of the vote. And my support signaled a huge increase of five million since 1930. I told Goebbels to do away with his maudlin musings about terrible defeats. I was not even slightly discouraged. In fact, that night I dictated a series of directives infused with tenacity and confidence. I began by saying, "The first election campaign has ended. The second has begun today. I shall lead it personally."

I did so with vigor and resolve and the aid of a passenger plane for flights of "Hitler Over Germany" that made my fervent campaign speeches even more omnipresent and accessible. Always I stressed that if elected, on April tenth, I could guarantee more jobs, more sales for business, more money for farmers, more soldiers, more international prestige, and a husband for every German woman. Such was my ambition, and I believed everything and so did my enraptured audiences. While this dynamic political and spiritual communion took place, a doubtless even more debauched Hindenburg sat fat on his fanny and offered no speeches, public or private.

Shockingly, many Germans still had not comprehended my clear and oft-repeated messages, and gave Hindenburg more than nineteen million votes, which represented fifty-three percent and a majority. At least I received almost thirteen and a half million votes, a bigger gain than Hindenburg's and a two-fold increase since 1930. I may have been a little exhausted, but I wasn't worried. Immediately I began planning to leapfrog campaign for legislative elections in several states. The trends were obvious and obviously in my favor. I simply had to grimace privately and remind myself what inevitably comes with unremitting effort.

BEHIND THE SCENES
By General Kurt von Schleicher

For years I'd been involved in nothing but General Staff paperwork and planning, and that would never have changed if I hadn't by chance met Oskar von Hindenburg, the president's son, and become friendly enough to convince him to urge his father to make General Wilhelm Groener the Minister of Defense. As Groener's primary adviser, I acquired a lot of influence about personnel and got close to the president and did not pay much attention, except to laugh, when people joked, in a not entirely jocular vein, about the dictionary defining my name as "intriguer" or "sneak."

"The SA has four hundred thousand storm troops, and many have surrounded Berlin," I'd told Groener and Chancellor Bruenig in early April. "We must assume the police's documents are accurate. The Nazis probably will try a Putsch if they win the election."

Groener and Bruenig had then assured Hindenburg the Nazis were vulnerable to suppression since the trade unions and Social Democrats were now supporting him against Hitler. After much vacillation, the president had signed an order executed the next day as police occupied scores of SA and SS facilities. The government's official decree stated: "It is exclusively the concern of the state to maintain an organized force. As soon as such a force is organized by private parties and the state tolerates this, a danger to law and order already exists."

Some of my informants said SA chief Ernst Roehm wanted to resist, but Hitler had insisted his party uphold the law. I helped the Fuehrer remain calm by conveying my outrage about the curtailment of his patriotic activities.

"The SA and SS have been banned, but the paramilitary organizations of other parties are untouched," I told Hindenburg. "Perhaps you could write a strong letter of complaint about this to Groener."

In the national interest, I revealed to newspaper reporters: "It seems General Groener has become a convert to pacifism and Marxism. Why else would he disband strong nationalist bodies like the SA and SS? You should also know he's much too ill with diabetes and old age to effectively discharge his duties. He's certainly unfit morally. His second wife gave birth to a child only five months after their marriage."

On May tenth General Groener made a pathetic attempt before the Reichstag to defend the SA and SS ban. Hermann Goering's devastating rhetoric scorched the weak-voiced and effete Minister of Defense, and as Groener slunk out of the Reichstag chamber I abruptly walked over and said, "You no longer have the support of the president or the Army, and you must resign immediately."

Two days later Groener appealed to Hindenburg on grounds he had long been loyal, especially at the end of the Great War when he did Hindenburg's dreaded duty and told the Kaiser he had to abdicate.

"Sentimentality is not the issue," said Hindenburg. "You'll have to resign."

Groener wrote me: "I'm hurt and furious that you, my old friend, disciple and adopted son, have deceived me." I really had not done that, certainly not for personal reasons.

It was difficult to determine what Hindenburg could remember, so I repeatedly reminded him that the once-helpful Bruenig thought the state should usurp unprofitable Prussian estates and resettle some of the many unemployed on them. Since Hindenburg spent most of the final two weeks in May at Neudeck, the Prussian estate given him by Junker landowners for his eightieth birthday, I figured he'd hear plenty.

On May thirtieth, shortly after Hindenburg returned to Berlin, he ordered Bruenig to see him. The chancellor was so politically naive he thought he was getting an opportunity to brag about his recent effort to lessen reparations and increase German armaments. Hindenburg did not have time for chitchat with a political liability like Bruenig. The president was anxious to attend a naval parade honoring veterans.

SURPRISE
By Franz von Papen

I was delighted General von Schleicher sent word he wanted to see me. As a member of the Prussian legislature, I had some significance but did not often get to have conferences with those who held national power. Certainly, I was not in any way in awe of such men. My background as an aristocrat and General Staff officer made me very proud. Still, Schleicher stunned me by saying, "Herr von Papen, I've discussed it with President von Hindenburg, and we believe you should become the next Chancellor of Germany."

I actually got dizzy a few seconds and paused to make sure I had understood. Then I dutifully stated, "I doubt very much if I'm the right man for the position."

General von Schleicher was very persuasive as he listed my attributes, and I agreed to at least go talk to Hindenburg. Though the towering president knew nothing about me, he said he needed my help.

"Herr President, I am honored. But I really don't have that kind of experience."

"My dear Papen, you've been a soldier and done your duty in the war. When the Fatherland calls, Prussia knows but one response, and that is obedience."

I then gracefully accepted my call to duty and vowed to serve Germany well.

General von Schleicher presented me a list of members for my cabinet, a distinguished group of noblemen and industrialists such as I'd always known. Schleicher himself would serve as the new Minister of Defense.

From the beginning my government was misunderstood by the thickheaded masses. Men like my cabinet members and me had ruled for decades, and average people should have deferred to our judgment. Instead, they made it clear they disapproved.

I had more important obligations to worry about. On June fourth, honoring Schleicher's agreement with Hitler, I dissolved the Reichstag and scheduled new elections for July thirty-first. And on June fifteenth, after some protests from impatient Nazis, I lifted the ban on the SA and SS. A variety of ruffians then began battling in the streets, and about a hundred died and more than a thousand were wounded. My administration was blamed, yet we had in no way been responsible.

ELECTORAL IMPLICATIONS
By Adolf Hitler

Buoyed by undeniable historical destiny, I embarked on our National Socialist campaign for the Reichstag elections. If my opponents expected me to be in any way disabled by the rigors of this, the third national election in five months, they were delusional. I revived "Hitler Over Germany" flights and gave at least fifty speeches during the final two weeks of the campaign. Delirious crowds grew often larger than one hundred thousand, and under my spell every kind of person became one unified German celebrating a national rebirth begotten by me. For this the Nazis were awarded a stunning and portentous victory. We received some fourteen million votes, more than the combined tallies of our least insignificant rivals, the Social Democrats and Communists. Now we would have two hundred thirty seats in the Reichstag, more than thirty-seven percent of the total. I soon met with General von Schleicher and issued entirely reasonable demands.

"Surely, my dear General," I said, "President von Hindenburg would never contend that that pipsqueak von Papen has even a fraction of my popular support."

"Yes, Herr Hitler, I'm sure you're correct. The president would not contend that at all."

"Naturally, General, you would remain as Minister of Defense in my government."

He politely nodded.

"General von Schleicher, this meeting has been productive,

delightful in many ways, and certainly one of great historical note," I said, patting him on the arm. "I suggest we order a plaque placed on the wall to commemorate this great day."

The general smiled at me, and I returned to my home on the Obersalzberg, feeling like the real Fuehrer. By August eleventh I sensed it was time to go to Berlin to await my summons from Hindenburg. After two days at the Hotel Kaiserhof and not being summoned, I demanded to see the president. Schleicher and Papen told me I would have to see them first. At noon we met. The meeting marked one of the most outrageous double crosses in German history.

"I'm not interested in being vice chancellor and receiving only a fraction of what I've earned over the years," I said.

"You must understand, this is not our decision," said Schleicher.

"I demand the full measure of power granted me by my popularity."

"Herr Hitler," said Papen. "I think you're underestimating my foresight and goodwill. If you'll cooperate with my government during these crucial times, I give you my word of honor, as a gentleman and former General Staff officer, that after a reasonable period of trusting and fruitful collaboration, I'll resign the chancellorship in your favor."

"I'm unalterably dedicated to destroying all of Germany's Marxists," I shouted, pinning both deceivers back in their ornate chairs. "That I can't do unless the government is run under my control. I'll never share power with do-nothings who haven't earned it."

Already I was stomping toward the door when Papen said, "Herr Hitler, the final decision in this matter will come from the president."

At three o'clock on that interminable afternoon, we received a call from the president's office. Goebbels, as instructed, informed Hindenburg's assistant: "There's no reason for the Fuehrer to come unless the decision has been made to appoint him chancellor."

"The president strongly urges you to come."

Hindenburg was standing, barely, propped by a cane under his great dead weight, as I entered his study. After brief formal greetings, I asserted, "Herr President, I'm the leader of by far the most influential party in Germany, and as such, I can't accept anything less than the chancellorship, various ministerial posts and an enabling act giving me the right to rule by decree."

"No, that's impossible," Hindenburg said. "I could never, in good conscience, transfer all the power of government to a new party that doesn't even enjoy a majority in the Reichstag. I won't forsake the

Weimar Republic so easily."

"Herr President, you've had two chancellors, Bruenig and Papen, who enjoyed but a fraction of my popularity and support. I'm merely demanding the prerogatives they enjoyed. How long can you persist in denying what I've earned?"

"Herr Hitler, I think it's clear to everyone the National Socialists are determined to wield absolute dictatorial power. If, however, you really are a man of good faith, you should be willing to cooperate with other parties and prove what positive things you can achieve. And if you were successful, you obviously would acquire growing influence in the coalition government."

"I cannot possibly accept such a deal," I said. "I have no choice but to proceed in opposition."

"In that case, Herr Hitler, I must remind you and everyone in your party to conduct yourselves in a chivalrous manner. I'll act very severely against any criminal acts of terror or force, like those so regrettably perpetrated by members of the SA."

I felt nauseated.

Hindenburg continued: "We're both old fellow soldiers and want to remain so since we may be dealing with each other again. Therefore, I extend my hand to you as a comrade-in-arms."

I accepted Hindenburg's large leathery hand and hoped he was perhaps not so bad at heart, just too senile to realize who alone could fulfill Germany's urgent needs.

After leaving, I went to Goebbels' apartment. I needed to relax, and I told my advisers not to talk to me. I did not feel good. The perpetrators of misery and incompetence were denying me again. I ruminated in silence interrupted two hours later by newspaper boys shouting outside. I sent someone down and discovered they were selling special editions with headlines blaring that I, like a little boy, had been reprimanded by Hindenburg. His deceitful "official communiqué" accused me of trying to grab full power for myself. And people who hadn't even talked to me claimed I was humiliated. That was ridiculous. I was simply livid at the betrayal. But I did not overreact. No, quite the opposite. That night, at a meeting with enraged SA leaders, I announced: Your desire to take over the country is quite natural and certainly justified — and very possible to achieve — but I have to insist that you march only in peace through the streets of Germany."

Later that night I was driven high to my home on the Obersalzberg. Despite the excruciating setbacks, I soon contemplated matters with confidence, soothed and stimulated by bright Bavarian peaks that climbed into clouds and coalesced with the sky. As I looked into heaven, I knew my lofty station: I was destined, and I could wait.

DEMOCRACY
By Adolf Hitler

Wanting the whole world to learn more about me, I graciously granted an August 1932 interview to two American correspondents. I was not obliged to treat these inferiors as equals, especially when the first ass asked, "Herr Hitler, why are you so hostile to the Jews, and do you differentiate between German Jews and Jews who come into Germany from other countries?"

"You have a Monroe Doctrine for America and we believe in a Monroe Doctrine for Germany. You exclude any would-be immigrants you don't care to admit. You regulate how many come in. You insist that they meet certain physical and political standards. We demand the same right. I assure you, I have no concern about Jews in other countries. But I'm passionately concerned about anti-German elements in our own country. For centuries Jews have undeniably been perpetrators of subversive movements. We must therefore deal with them as we see fit."

That quieted the first ninny. Then the second repeated the base rumor that I had demanded full dictatorial power.

"I certainly did not," I said. "I did demand power commensurate with my unparalleled political stature, but with due parliamentary safeguards. Rumors to the contrary are absolute ordure. But understand, I do in fact have the right to complete control. It's quite simple. The rules of democracy state that fifty-one percent constitutes a governing majority. Since I have thirty-seven percent of the total vote, I have seventy-five percent of the power necessary to govern. I am therefore entitled to three-quarters of the power and my opponents to the remaining quarter."

ALONE
By Eva Braun

For months I had only seen him two or three times, at Heinrich Hoffmann's house, and everything I said he either ignored or answered with a few gruff words. I could not imagine why he was acting so differently unless he had gotten tired of me. I wanted to tell my mother how I felt but knew my father would be furious. So I sat home, choking on secrets, and thought about Adolf having affairs with the fancy society women I saw him with in newspapers. He loved one of them now. I could feel it. Why else hadn't he contacted me or sent any gifts? Obviously, I no longer mattered. My dream of being his special woman was over, and by November first I decided I did not want any more. That night, alone in the family apartment, I wrote a letter saying goodbye and mailed it before going to my father's bedroom. In a drawer I found his pistol, then carried it into my bedroom and lay on my bed. Holding the gun pointing toward me with both hands, I looked up at a gray ceiling closing in, and shot myself in the neck.

Still awake I was lying there as blood oozed very thick and wet down the sides of my neck and shoulders onto the bedspread. I rolled over and groped for the phone, dropping and picking it up, coating it with blood, and called Dr. Plate, my boss' brother-in-law. Right away Dr. Plate came over and took me to a private clinic where he operated on me. I told my parents the whole thing had been an accident. And very soon — I couldn't believe it — there he was at my bedside, looking so concerned and holding a big bouquet of pretty flowers.

"You shouldn't have come. I know you're so busy," I whispered.

"Oh, my little one, I was horrified when I found out I almost lost you."

"I'm sorry about upsetting you."

"No, no, my little Eva. What you've done proves how serious you are. But you must never do it again. You're too important to me."

He came to see me regularly at the clinic and brought lots of presents, even after his party lost two million votes in another Reichstag election. Soon, I was released, with only a little scar on my neck, and we spent a lot of time together. He was always so nice to me, but he said, "I might have to kill myself if things keep going badly."

Then he put his head in my lap, and I stroked his hair and softly said, "Don't worry, my darling, the worst times always come just before victory. You can't think about giving up now. I know you'll soon have everything you want."

I leaned down and kissed his ear and cheek and forehead.

"Just wait. You'll see."

CONCILIATION
By Franz von Papen

Now, despite still having more Reichstag members than any other party, the Nazis would have to cooperate. I sent Hitler a letter imploring him to "put aside bitterness" and join me in forging all nationalist forces into a strong central government. I waited for his favorable reply, which I assumed was imminent, and then waited further before realizing he wasn't going to answer.

The ruffian apparently thought he was still strong enough to ignore the chancellor. I nevertheless managed to maintain my composure and send Hitler another nice letter. For several days I thought he wasn't going to respond this time, either, and when he did, I wished he hadn't. In his letter he claimed: "You have already betrayed me, and I am certainly not going to expose myself to more of your trickery."

None of the other nationalists wanted to cooperate, either, so on November seventeenth I met with Schleicher and discussed my desire, which many shared, to establish the president as an unassailable authority and to ban the Nazis and Communists and other troublemakers.

"The only reasonable thing for you to do," said Schleicher, "is resign your office and let President von Hindenburg use his immense prestige to establish a workable coalition of nationalists."

Shortly afterward, Hitler had two meetings with Hindenburg. The Nazi leader was audacious as ever, demanding the same kind of power I had exercised. The president turned him down and later told friends he could never "put a house painter in Bismarck's chair." Hindenburg was still too shrewd for that. When he summoned me for a meeting on December first, I was very encouraged.

156

POLITICAL ALTERNATIVE
By General Kurt von Schleicher

In Berlin the first evening of December was cold, and I shot frosty smoke from my mouth as I walked purposefully toward President von Hindenburg's office. This was the big meeting I had been angling for, Hindenburg, Papen and me — two chickens and a fox.

Also present, but irrelevant, were Hindenburg's son, Oskar, and State Secretary Otto Meissner. We four sat in chairs surrounding the front of the president's huge desk.

"What do you think we should do, Herr von Papen?" said Hindenburg.

"I believe, Herr President, that I should be reappointed chancellor and given the authority necessary to establish order. The Reichstag also needs to be suspended."

"That's absolutely outrageous, Herr President," I said. "Herr von Papen's plans are unconstitutional and would result in widespread opposition."

"The police can deal with the protesters," Papen huffed, "and any protesters they can't deal with, the Army surely can."

"You can do a lot with bayonets, but one thing you can't do is sit on them for a long time," I said, looking daggers at Papen before turning amiably toward the president. "I have a much more sensible, legal and constitutional plan, and one that Herr von Papen would be incapable of implementing. Given the groundwork I've established, I should be appointed chancellor. I've been in contact with Gregor Strasser and am confident I can convince him, and many other Nazis, to join my coalition government and form a viable majority in the Reichstag, which is something no one else can do."

"That would cause a stark deterioration in relations between the president and the Reichstag," Papen claimed.

"Obviously, the effect would be quite the opposite," said I. "Let me repeat, Herr von Papen. I'm talking about establishing a majority in the Reichstag that would be prepared to work with me as chancellor."

The debate continued, but in a short while Hindenburg had begun to so sag that he droned, "Herr von Papen, please undertake immediately the necessary discussions to form a government, to which

157

I shall entrust the carrying out of your plan."

"But Herr President," I said, "that would be an abrogation of your constitutional oath of office."

Hindenburg was already struggling to move, and the discussion ended. As Papen walked out he stopped and said, "I'm going to prevent your becoming chancellor. I guarantee that."

"See you at the cabinet meeting, Herr von Papen."

At the meeting, Papen recapitulated his ridiculous suggestions from the night before, then offered to let me speak, which he could not have stopped anyway.

I arose and stated, "In my duty as Minister of Defense, I not long ago directed the General Staff to study the feasibility of maintaining order if the Nazis and Communists were provoked into a civil war, as they surely would be if Herr von Papen's foundation-less government tried to rule by decree and emasculate the Reichstag. The results of the study are ominous. The General Staff unanimously concluded that the Army and the police, which are infiltrated by Nazis anyway, would be wholly incapable of maintaining peace in the event of such an uprising. And remember, the Nazis and Communists very recently joined forces during the paralyzing transport strike. Furthermore, under such chaotic conditions, the Army would be unable to deal with any incursions by the Poles on our eastern frontier. I see no reason to risk our national existence on the illegal and overly ambitious whims of an unpopular politician."

While the cabinet expressed due concern about my report, Papen scurried from the room to see Hindenburg, who had already been thoroughly briefed by the General Staff.

One never knew how this president might respond, even to overwhelming logic, so I was quite nervous until learning Papen had been denied the chancellorship and that I was summoned to see Hindenburg.

"Herr von Schleicher," said he, "since I'm an old man and unwilling to take responsibility for civil war, I ask you in God's name to try your luck in forming a government that will preserve the Fatherland."

"But Herr President, shouldn't I be kept in reserve, in case of an emergency, to serve you in other ways?"

"If you don't accept the chancellorship, I'll resign," he said.

POLITICAL OFFERING
By Gregor Strasser

By late 1932 more than eight million Germans were unemployed, and I thought I could help everyone, including the Fuehrer, by accepting the new chancellor's invitation to come to his house for a late-night political discussion.

"I'd like to make you Vice Chancellor of Germany as well as Premier of Prussia," Schleicher said. "I need support from the Nazis, and you can deliver."

"Naturally, I'd have to discuss any moves with the Fuehrer. I'm afraid I do have some reservations about his response."

With considerable trepidation, but also much hope, I entered the Kaiserhof Hotel on December fifth for a meeting with the Fuehrer and other key Nazis. The instant I suggested we cooperate with the Schleicher government, Goering and Goebbels began to sneer and make insulting objections. I ignored them and concentrated on Hitler, looking right at him, trying to break through the mounds of garbage strewn between himself and reason.

"Herr Hitler, you've been offered very important positions in government, and you keep turning them down with a fusillade of unfulfillable demands," I said. "If you don't start being more pragmatic, Schleicher can dissolve the Reichstag. We just don't have the money to run effective campaigns. Let's not throw away all the progress we've made, and all the promise we have, by insisting upon absolutism. We need to compromise."

"This movement was not founded, by me, for the purpose of infecting its principles by climbing into bed with other parties," Hitler stated. "I've always said, and will always insist, that the National Socialist movement will never compromise with any other party, and will in fact do everything possible to bring about the inevitable dissolution of all other political parties. I'll never bend my sacred principles."

With a curt turn to his cronies, the Fuehrer dismissed me.

Two days later I again went to the Kaiserhof. Everyone but Hitler was staring at me as I entered the conference room. He showed me his back. After a long pause he turned, arms across his chest, and he unlocked them and let both hands descend very slowly to his sides.

Then he pointed his right index finger at me and, from the first word, started screaming, "I'm surprised you didn't take advantage of this opportunity to stab me in the back. That's what you've been doing. You're the most disgusting traitor in the history of this party, in the entire history of this country."

I tried to speak but was inundated by Hitler's mouth.

"You've committed treason and been trying to gain power for yourself so you can destroy me and this movement. I couldn't have conceived that an old comrade like you would conspire with a slippery heathen like Schleicher. I can't find enough words to express my abhorrence of your vile treachery."

"Herr Hitler," I interjected, "my only goal has been to prevent you and this party from continuing on the path of ruination. I'm in no way a traitor. You certainly know that."

Hitler immediately resumed the abuse, and I walked right out, his words barking in my ears until I was some distance away. I returned to my room in another hotel and composed a letter summarizing our long and mutually beneficial association, and I reiterated, in much stronger terms than ever in person, the tragedy of the party's current course. That afternoon I sent the letter and went to a tavern with a friend.

"Now I'm a man sentenced to death," I said, shaking my mug so the little beer at the bottom rotated up and down frothy against the glass. "Remember what I'm telling you. If the Nazis do overcome their troubles and gain power, Germany will be in the clutches of an Austrian who's a congenital liar. And Roehm's a pervert, Goering's ruthless, and the clubfoot, Goebbels, is the worst of them, Satan in human form. I can't believe how things have worked out."

INTRIGUE
By Franz von Papen

Tired of always being the one dangled this way and that, like a puppet, I decided this time to attach the strings and pull. In that regard, I contacted Kurt von Schroeder, the influential banker, and arranged a secret meeting in his mansion on January fourth, 1933.

After we left our aides in another room and entered the library, Hitler said, "Someone took my picture coming in. Was it one of your men?"

"No," I said. "He took my picture, too. Who could it have been, Baron von Schroeder?"

"I don't know," said the banker. "But don't worry, Herr Hitler. We have good news."

"That's right," I said. "We've decided it would be good for the country if you and I, as coequals, formed a Papen-Hitler government, comprised of National Socialists and traditional nationalists, and replaced the corrupt Schleicher regime."

"Herr von Papen, the only government acceptable to me is one I head. Of course, there'd be prominent ministerial jobs for you and your allies, so long as all of you support essential changes I consider necessary. Specifically, I'm referring to the removal of un-Germanic elements from positions of influence. They certainly haven't been good for our country, or your business, have they, Baron von Schroeder?"

"No, they haven't," said the banker. "That's why my friends and I want to help. There's no reason for an opponent of communism to worry about money."

Hitler barely nodded.

In the morning I assumed Hitler and Schroeder were as displeased as I that Berlin newspapers featured front-page stories about the "treacherous Hitler-Papen meeting that sought to undermine Chancellor von Schleicher."

Hindenburg summoned me and said, "Schleicher told me you agreed with Hitler's demand that he become absolute head of government. That isn't true, is it?"

"Of course not."

"I certainly believe you, Herr von Papen. Schleicher insisted he always be present when you and I talk, but I can't agree to anything like that."

"What about Hitler?"

"I won't allow him to become chancellor."

I conveyed that to Hitler in mid-January at the villa of Joachim von Ribbentrop, a prominent champagne dealer and expert on foreign affairs.

"Then there's nothing more to discuss," Hitler said, and prepared to leave.

Ribbentrop, very genial and concerned, walked up to him and said, "Let's not break off these communications. I think it would be very helpful if you meet with Oskar von Hindenburg."

PRIVATE TALK
By Oskar von Hindenburg

Knowing that Schleicher had spies everywhere, State Secretary Meissner and I began the evening of January twenty-second with our wives in a special box at the opera, viewing an early work of Wagner. The opening act was quite noisy and boring, and I told Meissner it was appropriate Hitler loved messes like this. During intermission we were very social, and I must have shaken hands with twenty people. After the lights dimmed, we obtained a welcome Wagnerian reprieve and silently left our box, departing through an inconspicuous exit. We hustled to a taxi, and I ordered the driver to start driving. In a while I instructed we be taken in the direction of the Ribbentrop villa, though I did not specify the destination. A couple of blocks away I directed that we be let out, and Meissner and I, a harsh wind in our faces, began plowing loud steps deep in the snow.

Soon after arriving I was ungracefully greeted by Hitler, Goering and Wilhelm Frick, but cordially received by the more urbane Papen and Ribbentrop.

"Major von Hindenburg, I think you should join me privately in the other room," Hitler startled me.

I did not see any reason for a private conversation, but Ribbentrop opened a door adjoining the salon, and Hitler and I were alone.

"Major von Hindenburg, I have many appeals to make to your patriotic sensibilities this evening, and I'm confident that good common sense will also motivate you. I'm sure you're aware no government could possibly stand without the support of the National Socialists. We're the largest party by far. So there's no use in anyone pretending we deserve anything less than leadership, especially given this country's woeful economic situation and pathetic international standing. Germany needs someone to step boldly forward at this critical time, and there can be no doubt about which individual, quite uniquely, possesses the strength and will to save Germany from more bereavement. Germany can only be saved if I'm made chancellor."

"Herr Hitler, I don't think my father is prepared to appoint you chancellor at this time."

"Major von Hindenburg, I have much more of great importance to say. And please pass this along to your father. For a long time now, the Nazis have been quite concerned about the outright usurpation of Eastern Relief funds by your family and friends. Those emergency funds were meant to help Prussian landowners make their estates profitable and employ many Germans for the good of the Reich. We are appalled, quite frankly, that you and your father, and so many of your friends and associates, would become enmeshed in this flagrant criminal activity. Can you imagine the chagrin throughout Germany if the great Hindenburg name were dragged through a mire like that?"

"Surely you don't think my father and I have been involved."

"I want you to know, Major von Hindenburg, that I don't want this unpleasantness discussed in public. I simply want a little help in the Presidential Palace. That's quite reasonable, given my political accomplishments. I want to help you and your family, too. In fact, I think your family estate in Neudeck should have several thousand more acres. It certainly would if I were in power. And your rank of major is rather too low for a Hindenburg. I would much prefer you be a major general, something of that stature. You see what can happen?"

"These aren't things to even be discussed," I said.

"I believe we can rejoin the others now, Major von Hindenburg."

We all went into the dining room and were served beans, or something, from a pot. I didn't take more than a bite. I just drank the champagne everyone else had except Hitler. He drank mineral water.

As soon as possible I motioned Meissner it was time to leave. We summoned another taxi, and on the way back he kept asking how things had gone.

"Not much happened," I eventually said. "It just can't be helped."

UNPLEASANT DUTY
By President Paul von Hindenburg

I did not want any of this, and made sure the ceremony was short and unceremonial. I needed to go. I was about to when Hitler, looking ridiculous in his top hat, rushed up to me, much too close, and bowed so far I thought he was going to kiss my hand while he shook it. Then he started babbling about upholding the Weimar constitution and strengthening democracy and making Germany rich. Finally, he shut up and looked at me.

"And now, gentlemen, forward with God," I said, and left the room.

THIS GLORIOUS DAY
By Adolf Hitler

From the Presidential Palace I emerged, a little unbelieving but with unshakable belief. The throng outside became ecstatic the instant they realized what had happened, and I waved and nodded as my limousine eased across the square to our Nazi headquarters at the Kaiserhof Hotel. Upon entering, I strode fast with head high to the center of the room and raised both hands in triumph: "Gentlemen, we have done it. We have vanquished those who were against us and now we are there."

Comrades and hotel workers engulfed me, and to all I offered the warmth of my words and the friendship of my hand. Soon, with an unwavering sense of dedication to my people, I returned to matters of business. In an adjoining room I told Goebbels to arrange a spectacular parade for that evening.

"I know it won't be easy with such short notice," I said.

"Mein Fuehrer, I've been awaiting and ready for this moment for years."

Shortly after seven o'clock, destiny pounding in my heart, I stepped high to a window in the Chancellery and was immediately set aglow by the spotlight trained on me from below. In the dark distance I could hear first the drums and singing, and then the steps, hard and crisp and rhythmic, and becoming more intense. The men of the SA and SS were pouring through Brandenburg Gate as they marched toward me. Gradually, I began to see an ethereal gleam. Torches were illuminating the clear black winter sky, and before long the flames were firing very large and bright, and thousands of hard boots thundered into the sky. Then, as martial music exploded below me, the storm troops appeared — the arrival incarnate of a new era — marching, marching, marching through the Wilhelmstrasse, bordered on each side by countless pressed-together happy adherents who were experiencing their strongest ever sensation of hope. Everyone below was shouting, "Heil, Heil, Seig Heil," and I became more excited with each eruption, and the torches, so fiery bright, beacons of Germanic might, kept coming, coming, coming to ignite this night with significance so strong and thrilling it felt like my feet, my body, my soul were sizzling up and down, up and down, vibrating with the unmistakable energy of a force long beckoned and now inexorably on the scene, ready, ready, ready at last.

I waved to admirers. I bowed to them. I saluted. Impulsively I wheeled and yelled to Goering or Hess, Goebbels or Papen, who in the rear basked in my aura. Hindenburg was standing near all this, in his palace, and I wished he could comprehend.

Troops with torches held high marched by for hours and would not have stopped without Goebbels dismissing them. My colleagues and I continued the celebration at a dinner I could not eat. There was too much to talk about. And everyone was so fascinated to listen. I talked about changing politics and society and foreign relations, and building a new Chancellery to replace the cigar box that had sufficed for others, but not for me. There were many incredibly big plans, and as everyone looked attentively at me, I promised: "No power on earth will ever get me out of here alive."

POWER
1933-1937

START
By Adolf Hitler

After waiting so long I did not dally upon becoming chancellor — I pounced, and demanded new Reichstag elections, just as I'd promised, and the next day I liberated my voice from governmental restriction and to the nation broadcast themes of peace and international reconciliation. In complete candor, however, I did say: "Never again will the pernicious influence of Marxism, so undeniably responsible for our fourteen years of suffering, be permitted to wreak further damage on the German nation, which simply could not now survive even one year of Bolshevism."

Very soon, on February third, 1933, I privately addressed a group of the highest-ranking military leaders. Though the General Staff had produced many great military men in the nineteenth century, I sensed these aristocratic boobs did not measure up. They were also startlingly ignorant of who I really was. Some of them did at least rouse as I stated: "I shall increase your influence by radically strengthening the National Defense Force and designating it as the only body responsible for defense of the Reich. The new government will create, by authoritarian means, a domestic climate favorable to military growth. And when our domestic and martial might are sufficiently strong and cohesive, we'll eliminate the Versailles Treaty, and focus on the mandatory task to conquer new living space in the East and improve and control it with ruthless Germanization."

TRAITORS WITHIN
By Hermann Goering

The Fuehrer and I were appalled that average Germans still did not sense the threat. Thankfully, my new police organization — the Gestapo — invaded Karl Liebnecht House in Berlin and discovered documents detailing plans to destroy key facilities throughout the country and commit terroristic acts against the population. Some citizens wondered why the communists would leave incriminating papers at their abandoned headquarters. I announced that I would publish the evidence soon enough. But wasn't it clear? The communists couldn't compete at the polls, so now they were lurking underground. I worried about them all the time, and was startled by a frantic summons to the phone on February twenty-second.

"The Reichstag is on fire," a police officer howled.

I rumbled to my limousine and ordered my chauffeur to speed to our most venerated building. Jagged flames there were erupting through the dome and out windows, and everywhere I heard crackling and snapping as wood and glass broke and fell and smashed again. Up close the Reichstag was extraordinarily hot, despite windy cold weather, and I could feel what had happened. To the gathering crowd I shouted, "This is obviously the start of the communist uprising. They can't deny it anymore now."

Despite the danger I covered my mouth with a hand and charged into the inferno, desperate to save cherished tapestries and mementos. In my office, as smoke scorched my eyes, I began to cough and had to turn and turn again, lost, before I staggered back out, gagging and dizzy.

When my breath returned, I said to newsmen, "You see what'll happen to Europe if we Nazis don't strike back." I continued warning everyone until the Fuehrer arrived with Goebbels.

"Mein Fuehrer, this is the communist uprising. I've taken control and..."

Before I uttered another word, Hitler, with intensity and conviction greater even than my own, began to bellow, "We will show absolutely no mercy. None. The German people won't tolerate mercy anymore. We'll hang every communist in the country. We'll shoot those we don't hang. I want everyone in alliance with the communists arrested."

We had a ready list, and orders were issued immediately. Then we walked into a charred portion of the Reichstag where the fire had burned out. The Fuehrer stumbled on a hose but remained upright to say, "Good riddance to this shabby shack. I like the burning stink of it now better than a putrid parliament."

That night in the Reichstag, authorities caught one of the conspirators, a Dutch communist named Marinus van der Lubbe. Holding incendiaries and babbling about politics, the soot-covered swine insisted he had committed the crime alone. He was a high-grade moron at best. Possibly he thought he acted alone, but he couldn't have. I insisted the Prussian press service report that. Before I edited the release, it sounded like only one crazed arsonist was to blame. Nonsense. At least twenty men would have had to carry incendiaries enough to ignite such a quick conflagration. This was a conspiracy. The conspiracy had to be crushed. The Fuehrer worked all night on a special edition of the Volkischer Beobachter, and early next morning presided over a cabinet meeting.

"Gentlemen," he said, "you saw what happened last night and you know what was found at Karl Liebnecht House. Accordingly, some four thousand communist traitors have already been incarcerated. But we can't assume this measure is sufficient. We have to establish a legal basis for protecting ourselves and our nation. In a short while, Vice Chancellor von Papen and I will meet with President von Hindenburg to adjudicate this matter. You know we can all trust the president."

By divine coincidence, Hindenburg had been dining with Papen the previous evening at a fine restaurant near the Reichstag. From his table the esteemed president saw the dastardly glow, and was amenable when the Fuehrer placed on his desk two decrees, one For the Protection of the People and the State, and the other Against Betrayal of the German people and Treasonous Machinations. Hindenburg's large wavering hand thus signed into law essential measures that restricted treason-inducing constitutional flaws such as freedom of the press and sanctity of the home. We were further empowered to, in effect, proclaim a permanent state of emergency and intervene anywhere necessary for the health of the Reich. Also, any armed person causing a disturbance could be executed, hastily if necessary.

I was not at all bothered that Marinus van der Lubbe was the only one actually convicted at the trial. His shameful and moronic head was lopped off, and even though other communists were not executed, they were either in jail, in exile, or preparing to creep into exile. As to scurrilous charges, particularly in the foreign press, that Nazis were responsible for the fire: hogwash. The liberal do-gooders made too much of the fact that a formerly secret tunnel ran from my residence into the Reichstag. So what? I could have arrested the communists anyway.

ADVANTAGEOUS ELECTION
By Joseph Goebbels

It had been horrible living without an official position. People laughed and snickered and said I was nothing again and made insulting remarks about my foot. They were idiots. My foot did not matter as much anyway since Magda had urged me to get a special shoe built up a little to even things out.

What really counted now was the Fuehrer putting me in charge of the campaign for the Reichstag elections. This assignment stirred my creativity, and I quite readily conceived what our opponents were so abjectly unable to perceive: radio was the perfect means of projecting our message into every home. Now the airwaves of Germany began to sizzle with the sounds of our voices, which I enhanced with recordings of trumpets and loud-ringing bells. And for election eve I planned the ultimate communion, the Day of the Awakening Nation. In every city our supporters marched with countless glowing torches held high, and in the hills and mountains that night Freedom Fires were alight, signaling our might, and many times I said: "Tonight, our Germany is a single, enormous flaming banner showing people the way."

The Fuehrer was quite correct late the next day in describing election results as a "colossal victory." We won a stunning forty-four percent of the votes, far more than any other party, and acquired a clear mandate even if not the pedant's majority of fifty percent plus one.

Within days the Fuehrer declared that Bavaria and other unruly states must immediately be run primarily, if not exclusively, by Nazis. Storm troops began seizing state government offices, and on March eighth we announced the opening of concentration camps. All the while, however, the Fuehrer admonished the SA not to commit any excesses that would threaten our public progress. I told the Fuehrer I approved of his orders since many of the SA men were quite uncouth and incapable of proper behavior.

Now that my importance to the party was undeniably established, I received my reward. The Fuehrer named me Reich Propaganda Minister, and patiently explained to the cabinet that it was mandatory to establish one centralized ministry responsible for educating and propagandizing the nation. That meant everything reaching the eyes and ears of the public would be orchestrated by me. President von Hindenburg swore me into office on March fourteenth, and as he did so I forgave the doddering old fool for long referring to me as "the trumpeter."

Due to the essential nature of my task, the Fuehrer provided me with a palace, opposite the Reich Chancellery, for my ministry. This huge and ornately columned building was redecorated to my specifications, and so was an old mansion nearby. Now Magda and I could have our own bedrooms. She had agreed before marriage that a man of my inordinate virility and drive would need extra releases, and as I strolled through my new residence I was quite enthused.

DAY OF NATIONAL RISING
By Adolf Hitler

I sensed the nation was on the brink of trusting me absolutely, and knew if I actually obtained unequivocal trust I could forever save Germany from further mistreatment and degradation. This supreme and sacred goal inspired me what to do next.

"This is it," I told Goebbels.

"I can see how determined you are, Mein Fuehrer. What is it?"

"This is exactly what we need. Write this down. After I explain the key points, go to work immediately. Exclude everything else, then let me see your plans."

"What is it, Mein Fuehrer?"

"It is an act of consummation, Herr Reichminister."

The weather was quite bright and nice on March twenty-first, and everyone in Potsdam was dry and comfortable. That was very important. Many movie cameras in the streets recorded thousands of patriotic Germans as they waited for and then watched a procession of grandeur move toward Garrison Church for the ceremonial opening of the Reichstag. Enfeebled but venerated veterans of victorious Prussian wars last century marched to inspire the very best instincts, and so did an elegantly dressed throng of generals, admirals and diplomats. The foremost representative of German arms was, of course, President von Hindenburg, statuesque and awesome in spiked cap and medaled uniform as he staggered, cane in one hand, field marshal's baton in the other, toward Garrison Church. I too moved toward the church, accompanied by some ministers, and felt incredible pride and relief knowing that with each strong and somber step I neared the grave of the preeminent one, Frederick the Great of Prussia. This was consecrated territory, a shrine of kings, and once inside the church all of us were deeply touched when Hindenburg raised his baton to salute the bare and empty throne of Kaiser Wilhelm, who had been exiled in Holland since the betrayal of the Great War and was listening now to a broadcast of the ceremonies.

The choir began to sing Nun Dunket Alle Gott, and through high church tiers soared images of Frederick's great battlefield victories. Hindenburg then struggled to speak about national reconciliation and an end of "selfishness and party strife." In that spirit I spoke with hope and confidence about our National Rising and thanked President von Hindenburg for making possible "the union between the symbols of old greatness and new strength."

As I shook hands with the gallant old president, I bowed to hold a deferential pose, and realized right there what an important image this would be: I had pledged my support for our great president, and he accepted it.

Then Hindenburg solemnly, and with tears in his eyes, descended the steps to Frederick the Great's tomb and thereupon laid laurel wreaths carried down behind him by his son and an adjutant. This was an extraordinary moment in German history. Bugles blared as the choir erupted, and cannons exploded, shaking the church and seizing our souls. Soon, outside the church, Hindenburg and I shared the platform to receive thousands of high-stepping troops whose strength and precision were enhanced by rousing martial music. Then, on this spectacular day, I gave three loud cheers for Hindenburg.

ENABLING ACT
By Adolf Hitler

Outside Kroll Opera House in Berlin, before the official opening of the Reichstag, the SS stood strong in black uniforms. Inside, the SA congregated in stark brown shirts. I was also wearing a brown shirt, and tucked it in tight. After Goering introduced me, I marched to the podium in front of a huge Nazi banner and vowed to eliminate unemployment and assist the poor and middle class alike, even while respecting private property. I also promised to protect Germany by promoting peace with everyone.

In order to achieve these critical goals, which no one else had even remotely approached, I explained that the Law For Alleviating the Distress of People and Reich was vitally necessary. This bill was quite simple, including but five articles: the administration is responsible for legislation instead of the Reichstag; the administration has power to make constitutional changes; the right to draft laws is transferred from the president to the chancellor; the administration is empowered to make treaties with foreign states; and the legislation is restricted to only four years and the life of the current administration.

I assured the Reichstag: "Given the government's clear majority, there will be very few cases when it's necessary to invoke these emergency clauses. The parties in the Reichstag now have the chance for peaceful development and the reconciliation that should soon blossom. Therefore, passing this Enabling Act is paramount, and refusal to do so will be construed as opposition. You, the deputies, must decide for yourselves whether it is to be peace or war."

I could not hear for the roar as I stepped from the stage, and soon everyone was standing and singing Deutschland Uber Alles. The SA and SS became so enthused they loudly chanted, "An Enabling Act or hell to pay... An Enabling Act or hell to pay..."

During the three-hour recess before the vote, I told members of the Center Party: "Gentlemen, as I've already assured you, I'm going to guarantee civil and political liberties that might have been compromised by the decrees following the Reichstag fire. I'll write the letter within minutes and have it delivered to your offices during the vote. I guarantee it. We need your support. The Social Democrats are agitating."

I was very worried about the vote. Mathematically, we seemed assured of the two-thirds majority necessary. But maybe not. Germany's salvation had many times been denied, often by the Social Democrats. When the session reconvened, Otto Wels stood piously upon the platform, frowning his disapproval of the chants as well as the legislation. It was repulsive to think what this opposition leader might say. Then he began: "Our party is also patriotic and just as concerned as any about the future of Germany. The elections have given the National Socialist administration and its allies a majority, and thus the opportunity to govern constitutionally. They should not persecute those who criticize them because criticism is salutary. We German Democrats pledge ourselves solemnly in this historic hour to the principles of humanity and justice, of freedom and socialism. No enabling act can give you the power to destroy ideas which are eternal and indestructible."

I considered attacking Wels physically, as I had Otto Ballerstedt years ago, but now, as chancellor, I reminded myself to be more subdued, and merely ripped Vice Chancellor von Papen's cautioning arms off of my brown shirt and stormed on stage.

Like a righteous cannon, my right arm and index finger were leveled at the head of Wels. Then came the fusillade: "You come late, but still you come. The petty theories you have just proclaimed here, Mr. Deputy, are being communicated to world history just a bit too late. You have no right to speak to us about justice, be it personal or national. Your party has trounced Germany's national honor unrelentingly for fifteen years, and your policies have achieved nothing but the perpetuation of misery. And don't speak to us about persecutions. There are only a few of us here who did not suffer persecutions from your side in prison. We won't let you forget that for years the Social Democrats kept saying that I was a mere house painter who should be driven out of Germany with a dog whip. Well, my dear sir, the whip has quite righteously changed hands, and now you say that criticism is salutary. It is unfortunate, and indeed very ironic, that you didn't recognize the salutariness of criticism when we were in oppressed opposition. In those days our press was forbidden and forbidden again, our meetings were forbidden, and I was forbidden to speak, for years on end. Where was your love of liberty then?

"From now on, we National Socialists will be responsible for the liberation of the nation. We will provide the people more inalienable rights than you, at your present pace of regression, could have provided in a thousand years. You, gentlemen, are no longer needed. You may think that your star may rise again. Gentlemen, the star of Germany will rise and yours will sink. In the life of nations, what is rotten, old and feeble passes and does not come again."

Explosive approval indicated what would come: the Law For Alleviating the Stress of People and Reich passed almost five to one. My men celebrated by singing the "Horst Wessel Song."

CONSOLIDATION
By Adolf Hitler

To me it was quite clear indeed that the paramount need of every German was to be bound in significant ways to every other German. Since childhood I had so many times seen the destruction that inevitably occurs in the absence of protection and unity. That plight would never again effect a Germany that from metropolis to hamlet, and from national government to neighborhood committee, was being uniformly organized so everyone would have a place, a duty, a purpose. Imagine the pleasure of never really being alone, of always having something to be part of, to believe in, to guide you and make you happy.

BOYCOTT
By A Shopkeeper

When I had visited my brother in New York a few years ago, he played a joke on me and said: April Fool. Well, today in Germany was no joke.

"What are you doing in front of my store?" I said to three thugs in brown shirts.

"Get back inside. We're not bothering anyone."

Every time someone came toward the door, one of the thugs would say, "Sir, there are better places to shop than this. Why don't you try over there?"

Some of my customers came in anyway, but some did not.

"I want you guys out of here," I said early that afternoon.

"Oh, don't worry. We'll leave when the store closes."

"I'm calling the police."

No one came.

The brown shirts did not return the next day, but I had to wonder. Then we started to hear about the ban from civil service and limits on the numbers of lawyers and doctors.

"I've heard there's going to be a ban from the universities, too," said a friend.

LABOR DAY
By A Union Leader

I was in my union office when the invitation came. The Fuehrer was inviting all men of labor to a huge celebration at Tempelhof Airport in Berlin on May first. And he wanted us to wear the clothes of our trades.

Many big round spotlights, spaced just right, illuminated the Fuehrer as he arrived erect in a limousine, his arm thrust forward. Then several hundred thousand of us listened eagerly as he said: "To all of you I pledge honor and respect as well as a holiday with pay on this day for eternity. Germany is now strong again, free of shame, and you shall benefit."

Afterward, a number of the most important union leaders got to meet Hitler, and all of us told him how surprised and delighted we were.

Next morning in my office I was talking to several of my guys and we all agreed the holiday was a great gesture, especially with five million Germans still unemployed. We had big grins for the uniformed men walking in.

"Good morning, gentlemen," I said.

"This office is now the property of the state."

"What the hell do you mean?" I said.

"What the hell did it sound like?"

I charged them but they grabbed and took me to jail. Everything we had, everything any union in Germany had, was confiscated.

The Nazis immediately established the German Labor Front, led by Robert Ley, who promised that our rights were sacrosanct and on the verge of being expanded.

In a short while Ley declared: "Henceforth there will be no collective bargaining. The Fuehrer believes this divisive practice stifles economic growth. All labor issues will be regulated by labor trustees who understand the goals of the party."

Quite a few former union members said they were happy to finally have such an influential organization protecting their interests.

BOOKS
By A Librarian

In my library thousands of books I'd lovingly handled and placed on shelves were on this night grabbed and thrown into sacks and taken outside Berlin University where Goebbels said something about exorcising our past, and onto the bier my books went, they all went, burning up dark around the edges at first, then the whole page, pages at a time, the whole books, all of them consumed by raging heat at universities all over Germany, and, just before they turned to ashes, I wondered: how did Germany produce twice as many Nobel Prize winners as any other country?

BIG PARTY
By A Social Democrat

I was going to do something when they barged into headquarters of the Social Democratic Party. But before I budged they seized and threw me outside. There really wasn't anything I could do. What would you do?

Several weeks later, in June, the Nationalist Party got the same surprise, and on July fourth the German People's Party was also disbanded. The decree on July fourteenth clarified everything:

"The National Socialist German Workers Party constitutes the only political party in Germany. Anyone involved in maintaining the organizational structure of another political party, or in starting a new political party, will be punished with imprisonment, and perhaps an even greater penalty."

INDUSTRY
By Adolf Hitler

In a decisive move, I appointed Hjalmar Schacht President of the Reichsbank, a post he had held some years earlier, and unhesitatingly gave him the pervasive powers his genius warranted. He stressed that the Reichsbank must make billions of marks available to government and business in order to revive the economy. I had no need or desire to become enmeshed in the arcane complexities of economics, but I liked what Schacht promised and began to deliver: unlimited credit for a multitude of public programs and industrial developments.

Everyone enlivened as I scurried around the country, ceremoniously shoveling dirt and pounding hammers to launch the Battle of Work. Now factories really produced and buildings sprang into the sky and autobahns and dams started to form. Germany was absolutely robust, and I often praised the efforts being made by key financial personages. I also emphasized that the revolutionary zeal in the Reich was neither permanent nor a threat to those capable of promoting a prosperous Germany. When radical elements within my party cried for business positions, or the firing of someone simply because he was affluent, I could not comply. Instead, I explained: "In business, ability must be the only standard. An incompetent National Socialist can't expect to be promoted over a competent non-National Socialist, who at any rate will likely soon become a party member. Our historical standing won't be based on how many businessmen we jettisoned, but on how well we did in providing work."

REVOLUTION BETRAYED
By Ernst Roehm

Where the hell was the socialist wave sweeping the country? All I saw was Adolf very publicly snuggling with the cowardly bunch of philistines who had done nothing to advance National Socialism. My men in brown shirts were what got Adolf power. We were dedicated men toughened by sacrifice, yet Adolf was ignoring us more and more and acting like we were an embarrassment.

With three million men under my command, I did not have to tolerate slights, nor was I going to permit those pompous and ridiculous Prussian old fogies of the General Staff to be rewarded with unearned authority. The generals had already lost one war and certainly wouldn't be able to win the next.

"The Army should be subordinate to, if not absorbed by, the SA," I often proclaimed. "Then Germany would have a true National Socialist People's Army to really shake the world's foundation."

Adolf still continued to act like a rotten reactionary, and I kept hearing about his private insults that my men and I were morally and intellectually unfit to command. To hell with that. I guarantee we were a lot more than an effete political monitor, and my speech rang clear: "The SA is a permanent fact of political and military life. Our work is anything but complete, and we will continue our fight for a true revolution, a Second Revolution, to extirpate the old bureaucratic spirit of the petit bourgeoisie. We will be gentle if possible, and rough if necessary. We are, very essentially, the incorruptible guarantors of the fulfillment of the German revolution."

Adolf responded with inane excuses, telling me the SA worried and frightened many average Germans as well as the elite. That was fine, wasn't it? Wasn't that what he had always wanted us to do: to scare, bully and intimidate? Certainly. And I wasn't going to halt our momentum now. Aroused all the time, we staged huge demonstrations and parades with column after column of unsmiling brown shirts romping through the streets.

I knew Adolf would ultimately regain pride in his burgeoning storm troops. Goering and Himmler and Reinhard Heydrich, Himmler's young assistant, could whisper to Adolf all they wanted about my "indiscretions." Adolf had always known about them. So what? That was not what counted, and I knew Adolf still understood.

FOREIGN POLICY
By Adolf Hitler

Instead of attempting bold measures to eliminate the horrors raging around the Reich, my predecessors had piled capitulation upon capitulation to placate ancient and hostile foes whose appetite for German blood was merely whetted by each new concession of continued German weakness.

Who, after all, would ever fear and respect a timid nation that allowed itself to be limited to a mere one hundred thousand soldiers and tiny inventories of panzers, guns and ships? Certainly not England, which continued to loom large on the seas and at the same time insist that no continental nation, especially Germany, become strong enough to compete. France, an ally of England, remained our most threatening enemy and clearly desired an absolute end to any power at all called Germany. With sadistic thirst, the French had occupied the Ruhr during the twenties, murdering Germans and strangling the already constricted economy. Now this nation west of the Rhine was evermore infiltrated by Jews, who controlled the stock exchange and who shared with the chauvinist French a desire to dominate the Aryan people, and the world. This is hardly an amazement since France was becoming more and more negrified, and planned to spread the contamination of negro blood on the Rhine, in the heart of Europe.

These threats, regrettably, deal only with the West. We at all times had to be worried about the East, where a brutal Bolshevik Russia had already murdered millions of its best Germanic elements, and become so Slavified and Jewified that its belligerent and bastardizing intentions could not possibly be concealed or denied. Poland, of course, remained the barbaric nation that had devoured huge strips of mortal German flesh after the Great War, and isolated us from East Prussia and Danzig. Now Polish treachery intensified when bilious old Marshal Pilsudski talked to the French about an alliance to strike the Reich.

I was most encouraged by President Roosevelt's worldwide message urging nations to abolish offensive weapons and move toward everlasting world peace. I did not want war, and the very next day I said: "We are entirely ready to renounce all offensive weapons if the armed nations, on their side, will destroy their offensive weapons. We are even eager to disband our entire military establishment and destroy the small amount of arms remaining to us, if neighboring countries will do the same. However, if other nations persist in denying German equality, moral as well as military, then Germany will have to withdraw from the Disarmament Conference and the League of Nations."

Almost everywhere people called my overtures the Peace Speech and declared with relief that I had become a statesman. And they were correct. Separately, I expressed friendly intentions to England and Italy and Russia, and even to Poland and France. Germany wanted only security. But the French still did not want that, and they connived with the other "victors" to deny us adequate armaments until we served several more years of probation. That was what I had expected, but prayed would not happen. I had prayed the German nation would at last be unchained. For this I could wait no longer. On October nineteenth I broadcast my decision to abandon the Disarmament Conference and League of Nations.

Privately, to those who feared we might be attacked, I said: "The British have stated they understand our desire to be rid of unjust limitations that they themselves, according to former Prime Minister Lloyd George, would not have tolerated nearly as long and patiently as we. Furthermore, our opponents are a group of weak and irresolute blabbermouths who have neither the stomach nor mandate for aggressive action. For us this grand liberating act will extricate the German people from an entangling and obsolete network that has deprived us of freedom of purpose. Our people understand and support what we have done. That I shall prove with a national plebiscite."

On November twelfth, 1933, one day after the fifteenth anniversary of the armistice, our national shame, the German people made a thunderous pronouncement: ninety-five percent voted for withdrawal.

Despite the intransigence of those who encircled us, I made it known to England and France that I was still prepared to negotiate arms limitations. It was at the same time necessary to pronounce Germany's option to someday build a three-hundred thousand man defensive Army, which was entirely commensurate with forces already deployed by those we proposed to negotiate with. England probably would have discussed these principles with us, but the French, as I had sensed, would not. They babbled among themselves, concocting what threat I could not imagine, so I hastily continued negotiations, begun a couple of months earlier, with Poland. We assured this nation of Slavs that I was a simple soldier, born in Austria and nurtured in Bavaria, and did not share the hostile attitude of Prussian generals who had long lived near and among the Poles.

Germany and Poland definitely needed guarantees of peace so flagrantly absent elsewhere, and in January 1934 our interests coalesced when we signed a momentous ten-year nonaggression pact. Every German should have been elated: after fifteen years of cringing submissiveness, we were finally deemed fit to be allied with. Nevertheless, many parlor patriots and cafe politicians complained that I had officially approved and reinforced the theft of our land by the egregious Poles. My shortsighted domestic critics could damn well be displeased, but not too loudly. They, at any rate, did not understand the practical steps I was taking, and it would have been politically inexpedient, and absurd, to explain myself.

LETTER OF PRAISE
By Ernst Roehm

There was a crisp knock on my door, and an assistant entered to present a large envelope bearing the official seal of our chancellor, Adolf Hitler. I opened the envelope and read: "My Dear Chief of Staff, I want to express my gratitude that your assumption of leadership saved the SA at a time of serious crisis. Ultimately, the SA was responsible for assuring the victory of the National Socialist revolution on the domestic front, the existence of the National Socialist state, and the unity of our people. You, my dear Chief of Staff, have rendered inestimable services, and I thank destiny for permitting me to call a man like you my friend and comrade-in-arms."

This letter was published in all Nazi newspapers, and many others, early in 1934. While true that eleven other high ranking party officials received letters of commendation, I was the only one the Fuehrer addressed in a familiar way. A month earlier Adolf had appointed me to his cabinet, as minister without portfolio, and I was confident, despite some indications to the contrary, that he still really wanted the SA as his vanguard. Rather than waver while unscrupulous men undermined the movement, I issued to the Defense Ministry this memorandum: "The SA is responsible for the nation's security, and all military organizations, including the National Defense Force, should be forged into a People's Army under SA leadership."

The generals flinched. They wanted simply to continue as an organization of privileged slobs. All of them were contemptible, and the Minister of Defense, General von Blomberg, was the worst. Every time Hitler spoke, Blomberg either bowed, saluted or laughed. Then, squeezing his monocle over one arrogant eye, he lashed at me: "The General Staff is the only organization in Germany qualified to make complex decisions regarding rearmament and national defense. The SA's contributions and activities have been of quite another nature."

"The General Staff," I said, "showed itself to be incompetent during the Great War and cowardly and uncommitted afterward."

"Given the low caliber of men in the SA, and the questionable makeup of its leadership, I don't think there can be any consideration the Army will accept such a reorganization."

I looked at the Fuehrer, who was examining us in a noncommittal way.

"Can you explain to us, General von Blomberg, why you have at times loudly espoused democracy, and then Bolshevism? It seems your convictions have been contradictory, at best, and always against the interests of National Socialism."

Blomberg stiffened to attention, adjusted his monocle, then said, "It's true that I was once undecided about what course Germany needed to take to unify itself. But that was only until I met the Fuehrer. After that, I've had absolute conviction in the correctness and efficacy of National Socialism in forming a strong nationalist Germany."

Understandably, I did not scold my storm troops if they cuffed a few soldiers who neglected to salute them in the streets. Unruly citizens were likewise cuffed as a means of indoctrination. Either stand aside or salute or else. That had to be what Adolf really wanted. But in February, sources informed me he had recently told British diplomat Anthony Eden that he was going to reduce the SA by two-thirds and practically disarm us. I also knew that when Blomberg had threatened to resign because of my organizational proposals, the Fuehrer, instead of booting him, beseeched him to stay and refused his resignation.

Surely, Adolf would not long like the feel of his lips on the Army's ass.

I hoped his demeanor would improve on February twenty-eighth. In a meeting at the Defense Ministry, the vulgar high-columned bailiwick of Prussian generals, they were there, and so were my SA leaders and I, and my SS chiefs, headed by Himmler.

The Fuehrer began his speech by declaring: "The German people are moving toward a period of intense misery."

That heartened me.

"We cannot assume our economic improvement is permanent. It is not. Unless we obtain more living space in the East for the acquisition of natural resources, and for our expanding population, we will suffer an economic catastrophe. Our adversaries in the West will never yield to us the right to expand. That is why we must prepare to someday strike first in the West, and then in the East."

That was great. I could not stand life without opposition. The generals, cushion-seated in their pretty marble hall, were evidently startled by the notion of fighting. General Staff officers did not have time for war. Go on, I thought, tell them who really can fight.

Then the Fuehrer, who had been shouldered into power by the SA, glare-glanced at me while proclaiming: "The Army is the sole organization responsible for national defense. The SA is to be subordinate, and limited to political duties."

Even though their expressions did not change, I could feel the generals smirking. After the speech Hitler shook my hand as if in congratulation. Then he had me shake Blomberg's hand before we signed an agreement confirming the above. Amid all this harmony, Hitler looked very happy.

The celebratory feast had already been prepared in my mansion and was waiting to be devoured. The generals came, as I requested, along with my SA leaders, and we enjoyed fine food and champagne. Blomberg sat at the opposite end of the big table. There was not much to talk about. I didn't want to hear anything. The champagne was especially good. This was quite a reconciliation. Those generals certainly were gracious as they left. I appreciated their salutes and soldierly words.

When the door closed, I bellowed, "Hitler's a ridiculous liar and traitor, and he can wipe his ass with the agreement just signed."

Then I lifted my glass and said, "Come on and have some more champagne. Let's celebrate this new Treaty of Versailles."

By March I decided to compromise. I met with Adolf and said, "At least let's put several thousand SA officers into the Army. That'll strengthen the Army and help some of those who've done so much for you."

"That may be a good idea. I'll discuss it with the president."

In a few days Adolf called and told me that Hindenburg and the generals would never permit it. The SA had not received a proper military education.

To hell with those bastards. I wasn't going to sit on an organization that had burgeoned to four million angry men. I marched them in more big parades and reveled in the great strength churning before me.

In April, resolving to publicly defend the interests of a better Germany, I summoned foreign journalists and the entire diplomatic corps to a press conference where I stated: "The SA is responsible for consummating the gigantic struggle for the survival of the soul of the German people. The SA is composed of political soldiers, formed by the ideas of Adolf Hitler, and rejects the vomit-inducing influence of reactionaries and bourgeoisie. The SA is the heroic incarnation of National Socialism and the enemy of anyone who undermines those ideals. The SA is the National Socialist revolution."

DEAL AT SEA
By General Werner von Blomberg

We were in the northern German naval port of Kiel, on the misty April Baltic Sea. The cruiser Deutschland had just been painted, shined and scrutinized, and the guns primed, and the crew drilled and instructed, repeatedly. The Fuehrer was coming to take a cruise.

From an office at fleet headquarters, I stared out at the imposing gray hulk at rest in the dock and thought about how much larger it was than anything we had in the Army.

"That's a beautiful ship," I said to Admiral Raeder, Commander in Chief of the Navy. "That's a very nice ship."

"Thank you," Raeder replied. "The Fuehrer will enjoy his cruise. I know that."

"I know he will. It's important we all enjoy it."

"It's also important the Fuehrer do what we need," said General von Fritsch, Commander in Chief of the Army. "He really must do that. President von Hindenburg would like to be succeeded by a monarchial figure."

"The time for succession is imminent," I said. "The president is certainly going to die soon."

The Fuehrer's arrival was celebrated by his walk through a long two-column honor guard on the pier, and naval whistles pierced clear and pleasantly shrill as he stepped up the gangplank, followed by Raeder and Fritsch and me. The Fuehrer was very enthused about being on board, and several times, even during wet winds, he declined to go below, and stayed on deck to observe more operations. Admiral Raeder explained many things, and the Fuehrer concentrated intensely. In a short while he altogether astounded us with a textbook outpouring of worldwide naval statistics: the numbers of ships respective nations had, the kinds of ships, and the sizes of guns and engines.

"I didn't know those things, General von Fritsch. Did you?" I said.

"I certainly did not," he replied.

The Fuehrer smiled at Admiral Raeder.

We were on board three days as the Deutschland sailed north in the Baltic Sea past Denmark and into a couple of snowy Norwegian fjords before swinging south in the North Sea and returning to Germany. We had many conversations, sometimes as a quartet, and often, as Hitler requested, just us alone, conferring afloat darkened seas.

"Fritsch and Raeder, and every one of the generals, are very concerned," I said. "The SA is completely incapable of running a modern Army or Navy, and I can't fathom President von Hindenburg leaving the Fatherland vulnerable to SA influence."

"In complete frankness, General, you're correct," said the Fuehrer. "You're doubtless aware that I've repeatedly avowed the primacy, and the exclusivity, of the Army in matters of national defense. But Roehm doesn't understand the need for sophistication. He keeps agitating. I've warned him to stop."

"Mein Fuehrer, many of the generals — not me, but many of them — are afraid that your loyalty and indebtedness to Roehm and the SA will ultimately prompt you to act in their favor."

"I could never do that. I wouldn't. I've learned the absolute necessity of maintaining the support of the Army. I am from the Army. It wasn't I who betrayed the Army in 1918."

"Of course not."

"Listen carefully and always remember as I tell you that I want the Army and Navy, the traditional martial entities, to grow and become stronger, much stronger than they have ever been and much more powerful than any forces in the world. In order to survive, Germany must have forces of that caliber, and as you said, the SA could never provide that.

"I must emphasize, Herr Defense Minister, that a burgeoning National Defense Force would be much less than guaranteed, would in fact be virtually impossible, under a monarchial regime. The days of royal rule have now long since receded. The nation needs the kind of resolute and decisive leadership that I've provided, and must continue to provide, as president, when the great man dies."

"Many generals would probably like to see you president in the Germany you've described. But that seems impossible with the SA."

"Don't worry about the SA," the Fuehrer emphasized. "It won't be permitted to continue in anything approximating its current form. The SA won't be recognizable after I've altered it."

"It must not be recognizable, or relevant," I said.

"It won't be. I'm here giving you an absolute guarantee that the SA is outdated and will be emasculated to the point that the Army will never have to worry about it."

"This emasculation will be complete?"

"I assure you it will be complete enough to satisfy the Army. It is imperative for the country that I assume the presidency."

"I believe you shall."

"I need cooperation from the Army. That includes tangible expressions like the swastika you're wearing."

"I've encouraged other generals to wear the swastika, and now I think more of them will. We do have an understanding about the SA?"

"We have an ironclad deal," said the Fuehrer, "and I'd like to complete this Deutschland Pact with a handshake."

"Heil Hitler."

DEVELOPMENTS
By Heinrich Himmler

"Yes, of course I'll meet with you, Herr Minister President," I said when Goering called.

He sickened me. In particular, I detested his multicolored uniforms that made him look like a gorged peacock covered with unearned medals wiggling on his chest.

At the meeting, Goering was quite somber.

"Herr Reichsfuehrer, the SA is out of control," he said. "I tried to incorporate some of them into the Gestapo in Berlin, but the SA don't act like police. They act like criminals. As you know, they set up a number of private dungeons the Fuehrer wasn't consulted about. The atrocities there, the beatings, have been quite horrible, Herr Reichsfuehrer. People are tortured, starved, brutalized in every way. The lucky ones die right away."

"Yes, I've heard so," I replied, looking seriously at him, wondering what he thought about my SS sometimes helping the SA fire on his Gestapo when it tried to interfere. "I'm also worried about the SA. They've been very important, of course, but now they're a concern."

"I believe, Herr Reichsfuehrer, that you're far more qualified to be involved in police and security matters than anyone around. Germany needs you very much."

"Thank you very much, Herr Minister President."

Goering thrashed a fat hand in front of his chest and declared: "The SA is so large it could crush the SS at any time."

"I've thought of that."

"I don't think that would be good for either of us, Herr Reichsfuehrer. Roehm is bound to become concerned about, and jealous of, an SS organization that's so much more disciplined and military-like than the SA. Given his desire to control the entire National Defense Force, it's very unlikely he plans to tolerate the SS."

Goering studied me a few seconds before leaning forward and softly saying, "I must offer you some information I've obtained, and swear you to secrecy. I have your assurance? All right. I've been privy to numerous conversations between Roehm and his highest ranking SA officers, and they've repeatedly made remarks, actual threats, about killing me when they can. I must tell you, Herr Reichsfuehrer, that the same comments, the same threats, have been directed at you."

I did not change my impassive look, I'm sure of that.

"They're going to kill us unless we stop them," Goering continued.

"I don't have the means to control the SA, Herr Minister President. You've already emphasized that."

"I think you should have the means. I'd like you to become Inspector of the Gestapo, take over my duties. I don't have time for the Gestapo anymore."

"I'd be willing to do that, if that's what you want."

"It's imperative."

"You'd no longer oppose the SD expanding into Berlin?"

"Of course not. The SD is the finest security service in the Reich, and the SS can be proud of it."

"I'm proud you feel that way."

"I want you to expand. You've got the tools now."

"I certainly do, Herr Minister President, and I'm honored by your confidence."

"We need you to find out specifically how great a danger Roehm is to Hitler and the Reich. The Fuehrer needs to know."

"Roehm is a disgrace, but I'm not sure he's actually a danger to either Hitler or the Reich."

"I know that he is," Goering insisted. "Don't wait until he kills you."

"I'll go to work immediately."

Reinhard Heydrich and I celebrated with a long, very firm handshake when I informed him about the extraordinary increase in my status, and his. I told Heydrich that, in addition to being chief of the SD, he would be my executive head of the Gestapo. I would control it all as Reichsfuehrer SS.

My security organization sifted the Reich in regard to Roehm. He had talked to Schleicher, and Schleicher had talked to the French ambassador twice. We proved it. Heydrich's memo said that could indicate a French backed coup d' etat. The Fuehrer looked skeptical when I showed him the memo. But he was not happy then, or when we provided information that in one clique Roehm and Gregor Strasser would be respectively in charge of defense and economics.

"And on this list, was there any mention of me?" the Fuehrer asked.

"You were still listed as chancellor, but our sources indicated the new president will be Kaiser Wilhelm's son."

"Roehm hates royalty. The list doesn't add up."

"You might want to consider the SA arms caches we've uncovered," I said.

"I'm concerned about them, but they're relatively minor. The SA does need some weapons."

"Roehm should be disciplined because he didn't tell you."

"We shall see."

"I know you must be just as appalled as I am about the pimping, Mein Fuehrer. Roehm uses his SA men to procure sex."

"I'm aware of Ernst's proclivities."

"But these are just kids, Mein Fuehrer, teenagers."

"Ach, that really is disgusting. But not new."

"For many it's repugnant to think that a man like Roehm could take over the National Defense Force. What would he do then?"

"I've already defined the duties of the SA. Apparently I need to explain matters to him again."

SUMMONS
By Ernst Roehm

The message arrived by speeding motorcycle and was delivered with dispatch. The Fuehrer wanted to see me today, right away, very important. I wanted to see him, too. I really liked the man and respected his qualities, and was enthused late afternoon June fourth as I bounced into the Chancellery and received many salutes. Right away the Fuehrer came out of his big office, smiling at me, and took my hand in warm, comradely fashion, and patted my shoulder with his left hand, then invited me in and carefully closed the high double doors.

How was I, the Fuehrer wanted to know? Well, a little tired, a little sore, but I was fine. How was he? He was O.K., he said, but under extraordinary pressure, pressure from many sides.

"You know Hindenburg is going to die," he said.

"Yes."

"The question of succession is critical and still very much undecided."

"You know you have my backing and that of the SA."

"I'm not sure I do know that."

"After fifteen years of my unyielding support, you're doubting?"

"I'm not going to temporize with you. I never have."

"There's no need to," I said.

"There are a lot of indications you still don't understand that the Army — not the SA — is responsible for national defense."

"The SA was with you during the Putsch, and where was the Army? Against you."

"That's my point."

"That the SA was with you?"

"No, that the Army must be with me in order to achieve success."

"You became chancellor with the SA, not the Army."

"The Army didn't oppose me, as in the Putsch. The Army's nonintervention was critical."

"And so was the unrelenting support of the SA."

"I'm not minimizing your contributions."

"I think that you are."

"I am not," Adolf erupted. "But I'm telling you in straightforward fashion that rumors persist that the SA's activities are a danger to the stability of the nation."

"Rumors? Whose rumors?"

"Reports. Lots of them."

"Himmler's reports, I suppose."

"Many sources, my friend."

"We're your vanguard. Don't be influenced by anyone who tells you otherwise."

"I'm tired of your revolutionary rhetoric."

"Our task is not complete."

"Your task is what I say it is, and is complete when I say it is, and it is complete."

"Then," I said, "my reports about your dissolving the SA are correct."

"Of course not," Adolf said. "I'm simply telling you that the revolution is over. That doesn't mean the SA is unimportant. I have, in fact, guaranteed the SA's continued existence. However, I won't permit any individual, or any organization, to spread disorder. I'll strike at any such activity."

Hitler's hands squeezed fidgety on his desk. His desk was much too large. It looked like a stage. He sat behind his desk.

"I must have the cooperation and obedience of the SA," Adolf said.

He took his hands off the desk and wiped them, delicately, on his pants. His forehead was sweating. So was mine. My neck itched and so did my face. I had to scratch my neck. I wish I could have opened a button or two on my brown shirt, which was wet and sticking to my chest.

"The SA and I are your friends, and you know it, and I know that you're being influenced by those who are really your enemies and Germany's."

I continued to reiterate, until my jaw ached, that Adolf had my backing but his enemies did not. I believe he understood.

"The arms caches," Adolf said deliberately. "I want them turned over to the Army."

"What!"

"Immediately."

"Are we supposed to go around unarmed and vulnerable? That's ridiculous and you know it."

"At least turn over some of the weapons. Keep what you need, but be diplomatic, for once, and give the Army something to demonstrate your cooperation."

"You mean demonstrate my impotence?" I said bitterly.

"I mean your cooperation, goddamn it."

"Is there anything else, Mein Fuehrer?"

"Don't be arrogant with me, Ernst. And there are some other things. I've always tolerated your ways. I've always protected and respected your privacy. But now your personal excesses, and those of your men, especially a lot of the officers, are becoming a political embarrassment and hurting my chances of becoming president."

"My private life didn't prevent you from becoming chancellor."

"You're more of an issue now that we're in power. Our conduct must improve correspondingly."

"And your private conduct, Mein Fuehrer, has it improved?"

"My private life is absolutely circumspect and has never been an issue or cause of embarrassment."

"Oh, I see. I beg your pardon."

"I want you to get rid of the immoral elements in your command structure."

"And what do you mean by immoral, Mein Fuehrer?"

"The meaning is clear. I'm not going to tolerate any more perverse morality, and that includes drunkenness as well as the other thing. Get rid of those perverts. Get rid of them all."

"And you're ordering your Army and industrialist cronies to get rid of their prostitutes?"

"Don't forget who you're talking to."

"You're the Fuehrer. I've never questioned that."

"At least make things less obvious. You don't have to make such a spectacle, do you? It hurts me. And it damages our cause."

"That hasn't been my intention."

"That's been the result."

"All right. I'll do what you want. I can be more subtle."

"I hope, then, that I can count on your complete support and cooperation during this critical period, and in the future."

"You definitely have my support, Mein Fuehrer."

"I'm very relieved. You're my oldest and most important comrade, and it's vital that we agree in principle and approach."

"My task will always be to uphold the National Socialist principles personified in your leadership."

"I knew we could resolve this."

Adolf wearily arose, walked around his desk, and shook my hand before he escorted me out of his office. He did not look happy, and I know I did not, either. But things were better now, cleared up considerably. I saluted and trudged toward the exit. It was almost midnight.

Rheumatism had been hammering the hell out of my back for weeks, and I was irritable and needed a vacation in Bad Wiessee, a holiday hamlet nestled on Tegern Lake, my favorite place, a pretty blue lake backed by hills carpeted with thick green trees that made the lake a more vivid blue. There I could relax and bathe in mineral waters and enjoy my friends. The SA would be on leave throughout July. I decided to start early, and instructed my SA leaders to meet me in late June at Bad Wiessee so I could explain agreements Hitler and I had reached. On June seventh, shortly before leaving, I issued this bulletin: "A rested SA will return in August to the glorious mission it owes the people and the Fatherland. Adversaries of the SA should not think that we will not return, and all misguided people will receive an adequate reply, in whatever form necessity takes. Be assured that the SA is and remains the future of Germany."

MY GUEST
By Benito Mussolini

I did not want to. It was a nauseating notion, me hosting this political charlatan as if he were my equal. I really had to, though. I was determined to do a lot and had to make sure the Huns did not concern me. Hitler certainly needed me more. Russia and France had been talking about uniting against him. He had to have a powerful ally, and that could only be Italy. Hitler also knew he needed my expertise. I had been in power more than a decade and, as I waited at Lido airfield near Venice on June fourteenth, I knew I could control this guy. He had always shown who was paramount. In the early twenties, when he was as obscure as he was ridiculous, he sent a request for my autographed picture. I did not reply. Then his party asked me for a loan, since we were supposedly kindred movements, and this time I had replied and said no.

Now I was waiting for the German planes to arrive. Hitler had to come to see me. I certainly would not go to him. He had done everything he could to convince me to invite him. He sent his first overture with Hermann Goering, the blubbery, former lunatic asylum inmate. Then he sent his foreign press secretary, a tall gangly ass who attempted an impertinent combination of humor and diplomacy. Eventually I did deign to invite him. And as I first saw the German planes approaching, two dots growing larger in the sky, I was disgusted. In one of those, I thought, sits Hitler. I knew he was a babbler who seldom uttered a clear and meaningful phrase. He must have been a mere puppet, probably manipulated by the generals. Certainly he was a weak and passive figure who had not staged a dynamic revolution like mine. He was handed a modicum of power by a band of effete parliamentary democrats. Yet he had the effrontery to imply we were comparable. He would see.

I knew he was a hell of a weird fellow. He was not married and did not even have a mistress. That was extremely strange and disgusting. The man probably knew nothing about sex. I sure as hell did. When I wanted a woman, I grabbed her and made sure she moaned as I got her right there, hard and fast on the goddamn floor. I always did what I wanted. Even at age ten, I'd stabbed a schoolmate who crossed me. I was the Duce, and German planes were now on the ground.

Hitler minced down the steps like a shy maid with an over-laden tea tray. He was wearing a baggy bourgeois suit covered by a worn trench coat, and looked surprised to see so many troops lined up at attention. He had requested a mere informal greeting. Nonsense. I led him on an inspection of my men, who had to like the contrast. My jackboots overpowered his tawdry leather shoes. My black shirt and gold braids were striking and martial. My salutes were powerful and erect. Hitler saluted like a bent-armed sissy. This guy was in no way a Fuehrer.

We got into a torpedo boat that sped across the lagoon toward Venice. The men in my crew looked very sharp. Hitler kept eyeing their white uniforms, then looking down, then diffidently at me as he mumbled about the great artistic heritage of Venice and that Wagner had died here. Yes, yes, indeed, I said, we will talk more later today. Loud sirens signaled our arrival and so did the crowd's cheers for me.

"I have a lot of uniforms, Duce, but I didn't think I'd need them," Hitler said that afternoon.

"Oh, you look fine, fine," I said.

Then I began explaining foreign relations and leadership to Hitler, and I told him, "Your SA is far too disorderly. My Squadristi would never be permitted to act that way."

"I assure you the SA is extremely loyal to me, only very zealous in the pursuit of my revolution."

"In that case, fine. I just want stability in Austria. Chancellor Dollfuss is a good friend of Italy's and will continue to receive our political and military support. It's essential Austria remain independent."

Hitler squirmed and grasped his sweaty hair with his fingers and removed it from his odd forehead before the hair fell back down, and he kept repeating the repugnant ritual during my lecture. At the end, he stammered, "I must compliment you on your fine German, Duce. I didn't realize it was so good, and I had no idea you would hold our discussions without an interpreter. I know I could never negotiate in another language."

Hitler spoke such poor German that it was not easy to understand everything he said, which had not been much. He continued his submission that evening at a grand concert during which a raucous audience chanted "Duce, Duce, Duce." From the side of my eye, I saw Hitler's envy. It was also obvious next morning when eighty thousand whooping and idolatrous Italians honored me at the Plaza San Marco as I stood on a platform, as far away as possible from the awkward Hitler, who stood grim and overwhelmed with both hands and a hat covering his inactive groin.

That afternoon, at our final meeting, I began to elaborate my Austrian position.

"Duce," Hitler interrupted. "I want you to know that I'm superior to any politician who opposes me, in Germany or abroad. That's why we can be such valuable allies. It's proper and inevitable for you to expand your domain and for us to expand our German Reich. I'm not necessarily referring to an Anschluss with Austria. We might not need to annex it outright. Austria certainly is a Germanic state, though. And Dollfuss is a most unpopular figure. I think he should be deposed. He must be, Duce. He really has to be. There must be an Austrian government friendlier to its German mother. It's to your advantage if Germany feels comfortable about Austria. You and I are natural allies. We have goals and obligations...

"Some day, Duce, I'm going to attack France. That's what I have to do, and it's unavoidable. I'll overrun France before she can defend herself. And I'll do the same thing elsewhere. You can be part of this. Germany and Italy need each other as allies. We're an ideal ally, Duce. Germany is the most racially pure nation on earth, untainted, unlike all others, by negro blood. By pure racial logic, Germany would be guaranteed victory in any war. I know you understand race because of the glorious history of Rome."

I tried to glare Hitler's mouth shut, but he seemed to interpret that as my concentrated approval. So I tried to silence him by inattention. That did not work either. For more than two hours he rattled nonstop. This man was a half-mad, semi-hysterical buffoon, and I was delighted he finally flew away.

SPEAKING OUT
By Franz von Papen

"I've been saying plenty," I told my advisers, Edgar Jung and Herbert von Bose. "Don't imply I haven't."

"But Hitler hasn't responded," said Jung.

"I know that."

"That's why you must speak out," Jung said.

"I've told him Nazi excesses are wrong."

"Herr von Papen, you must speak out publicly," said Jung.

"That could be dangerous."

"You know you have to do it," Jung said.

"I've already indicated I will."

Jung wrote most of the speech, aided by Bose, and I agreed to deliver it at the University of Marburg on June seventeenth, 1934, the day after Hitler returned from Venice. President von Hindenburg was fast failing at his Prussian estate, but I hoped he was alive enough to protect me, even if only by the technicality he still breathed.

In the huge amphitheater at Marburg, a capacity crowd was standing to examine me as I entered. This was a bad spot, and I wanted to leave. I did not really have to be here. Someone else could give this speech. I felt like turning around, but that would have been impossible. A phalanx was easing me forward. Once onstage, I grabbed the lectern and peered out at the assemblage. The sight of some brown shirts jarred me, but I saw far more students and professors in gowns, and realized then that I really would go ahead. As soon as the audience was seated in silence, I began my speech, and built up to this point: "No nation can permit eternal revolution if that nation wishes to develop a sound social structure that can only be maintained by an incorruptible judiciary and an uncontested state authority. We must not allow Germany to become a train tearing nowhere except to inevitable derailment. The way to mobilize and gain the confidence of a nation is not by suppressing freedom, and therefore expressing contempt for the intelligence and integrity of our people."

A few groans were smothered by applause, and soon I could no longer see any brown shirts, for they were eclipsed by a wave of rising gowns.

Earlier I had wanted to omit the following part of my speech. Now I relished it. "The Propaganda Minister," I said with crisp inflection, "is enchanted by the docility of the press and the far too great control he has over communication in this country. He has forgotten that a press worthy of the name must point out injustices, errors and abuse. The government must lack confidence in its essential correctness and popularity since, like a weakling, it refuses to endure criticism and labels every dissenting patriot an enemy of the state."

There. I said it. No one comparable to me had done so. Now who could say I was a coward or opportunist? Certainly no one at Marburg. At Marburg they applauded and shook my hand.

Soon, in Berlin, Goebbels ordered my speech banned from its scheduled radio broadcast that evening. He also ordered journalists at Marburg not to file their stories. After the Frankfurt paper published part of my speech in its afternoon edition, Goebbels sent the Gestapo to find and destroy those issues. They did not get all of them. My staff also distributed several thousand copies printed on a private press.

Hitler was so worried he called me a pygmy and threatened to smash me and others with the fist he brandished during a vitriolic speech that afternoon. This whole response was outrageous. I went to the Chancellery on June twentieth and demanded to see Hitler immediately. Several hours later, tired and taut but still determined, I was permitted.

"Herr Vice Chancellor, please, come in," Hitler said.

"Thank you, Herr Chancellor."

"Please. Sit down."

"Thank you."

"It's very nice to see you. Much has been happening in our country."

"I'm afraid much has happened," I said. "It's unfortunate you didn't give more sincere consideration to what I said. My message was meant to be to your advantage as well as the nation's."

"Herr Vice Chancellor, I'm sorry about Goebbels. Perhaps he made a mistake. He did what he did only out of zealous regard for Germany."

"I'm not going to tolerate a junior minister burying an official speech by the Vice Chancellor of the Reich. Such a flagrant action undermines the whole structure of the government. Furthermore, I trust you're aware that at Marburg I was speaking with President von Hindenburg's unequivocal support. I'm afraid I must resign my office and report to the president immediately. He's not pleased with the state of affairs in the country, and I know he'll be outraged by this."

"I'm sorry, Herr Vice Chancellor, I cannot accept your resignation. You're far too valuable. The president certainly should be kept abreast of everything, however. I think you should go to Neudeck, and I'll go with you. Together we can explain everything, and the old gentleman can tell us what he wants us to do."

"My speech must be released."

"That we can discuss with the president."

"All right," I said. "We'll see Hindenburg together. When do you want to go?"

"Soon. Very soon. I'll let you know."

"Fine," I said.

QUICK TRIP
By Adolf Hitler

Hastily making quiet arrangements, I flew to Neudeck where many big trees cordoned the road leading long to Hindenburg's mansion. I wanted the final part of the drive to be slow. I was anxious to get there but I had to think. Then I was there, in front of the big eerie place, and the president's son, Oskar, and a few staff members received me respectfully.

"I'm sorry, but the president must rest for awhile and then be examined by his doctor before he can see you," Oskar told me. "Why don't you take a walk in the garden. General von Blomberg's there."

It was hot in the garden, and Blomberg was not smiling. I did not smile at him, either. We exchanged amenities and began to stroll silently.

"The president is very concerned," Blomberg eventually began.

"I am too."

"The president is ready to take action."

I stopped dead and looked straight at Blomberg.

"Action?" I said.

"Yes, action."

"I, too, am willing to take action, Herr General. I always have been."

"You have taken no action, Herr Chancellor."

"I certainly intend to."

"Neither Germany, the Army nor the president are prepared to wait any longer. We're not going to permit the Fatherland to be subverted by a gang of perverts and cutthroats. I must therefore ask you whether or not you're prepared to honor the Deutschland Pact. The Army must know. Yes or no?"

"I've always said the Army has my support."

"Are you prepared to honor the Deutschland Pact, Herr Reich Chancellor?"

"Of course I'll honor it. You've had my word on it and you have it now."

"The president and the generals want me to tell you that if the SA threat is not neutralized, the president will declare martial law, and the Army will enforce it. After such a scenario, I have no idea who would become next president, or who would be chancellor."

"I give you my unequivocal guarantee that the SA will be neutralized, just as you phrased it."

"And the nature of this neutralization?"

"General von Blomberg, I will thoroughly dismantle the SA in its current form. Absolutely."

"This must be done soon."

"It will be."

"You've been hesitating."

"I'm not hesitating, merely contemplating. I plan my operations thoroughly, Herr General, just as the Army."

"And Roehm?"

"He won't be part of the Army."

"He must not be."

Blomberg was present but in the background when Hindenburg received me. The old man had declined since our last meeting, and as he strained to rise it seemed he might break the cane he used to brace himself. He did not stand long, and each of us was seated by a servant.

"My trip to Italy was very successful, Herr President. The Duce and I got along splendidly, and we agreed that our nations have very much in common and will cooperate with each other in the future. We could be allies..."

"Herr Hitler," Hindenburg said, "the Fatherland must have order."

"Yes, it must," I said.

"If necessary, the Army will establish order. General von Blomberg has talked to you?"

"Yes. Yes he has."

"Then you understand that the present state of unrest, which threatens the Army and the country, cannot continue. If you prove unable to keep the Fatherland in a healthy, organized state, then I'll have to find someone who can. I've replaced all ineffective chancellors."

I looked at Blomberg, who did not look back.

That was it. An aide helped Hindenburg to his feet, and I rose too, and together we moved through the house. I had to walk at half my normal pace. I did not know what to say, and Hindenburg said nothing. At the front door we shook hands, and as I glimpsed his face, just before bowing, I saw wrinkles superimposed on wrinkles, and eyes that were deflated and distant, almost asleep. I saw an immense man propped on quicksand. I saw death.

LONG LISTS
By Reinhard Heydrich

Roehm offended everyone. His pudgy face and malicious pig eyes emphasized his nauseating habits. Only for expedience had I asked this man to be my child's godfather. That certainly did not matter now. My long and meticulous investigation proved that Roehm had ordered the SA to arm itself to rebel. The danger was underscored by continuous rattling from SA machine gun practice nearby. Still, some generals might try to convince Hitler to hold back. He probably wouldn't, though. He shouldn't. He really couldn't. We had to be ready. Himmler and I kept making lists on file cards. Goering had his own list. We compared lists. A lot of additions had to be made. The SA was not the only enemy. The lists were placed in envelopes and periodically amended.

PRESSING PUBLIC DUTIES
By Adolf Hitler

I was going to be very busy because I had many duties to perform. These were fine and important duties, and I was looking forward to them on June twenty-eighth when I flew to Essen, the metallurgical center of the world, to be the most honored guest at a wedding. This was the touching union of one of my fine young political leaders with a girl from far to the East who had decided to embrace our National Socialist cause as well as a Nazi husband. Throughout the day, I was protected and feted by SS and SA men who publicly and privately proclaimed their affection and respect for each other.

That Thursday afternoon, after the wedding, I went to the huge Krupp factory whose presence was heralded in all directions by a massive chimney more than twenty stories high. This extraordinary chimney, embellished by a swastika, poured out endless broad bursts of black smoke that bulged high into the sky and represented the revitalization of the economy and of German arms. In front of the chimney, I received a tribute. Then we toured the factory. Just before I left, Krupp asked to see me privately, and he said, "We keep hearing about a leftist revolution. That would wreck my company as well as Germany's rearmament."

"Don't worry," I told him. "Everything will soon be in order."

I was driven to the Hotel Kaiserhof in Essen, where Goering and others waited to tell me that Himmler had been calling all day, and at once I ordered he be contacted. Before the phone could be picked up, Himmler called again.

"This information, you're sure?" I said.

"Yes, for certain. SA units are arming, and it's clear they plan to attack the Army soon. Our corroboration is too widespread to be doubted."

"You're on alert?"

"Of course. Just as you ordered, Mein Fuehrer."

"Stay on alert and stay in touch."

Staggered by this growing treachery, I summoned Goering to a side of the room, along with Viktor Lutze, the only high ranking SA leader I could still trust.

"Gentlemen, is this possible?"

"Mein Fuehrer, I've been working with Himmler on this, and my alarm has only increased," said Goering.

"Lutze," I said, "do you swear Roehm called me a liar and a traitor, and made all those threats against me, after the generals left the party at his house?"

"I give you my word. He talks like that often. That's why I came to see you, because you weren't more alarmed."

"I thought it was rhetoric. Roehm's always been a bigmouth."

The phone rang again, one of Heydrich's agents.

"Who was the diplomat?" I said.

"We're not positive, but we know he was a foreign diplomat."

"What country was he from?"

"We're not sure about that, Mein Fuehrer. But we do have verification the SA just harassed a diplomat, and it could be damaging to the Reich."

I hammered the receiver down and directed that Roehm be called immediately at Bad Wiessee.

"Mein Fuehrer, I've been waiting to hear from you," he said.

"There are many highly disturbing matters I must speak to you about."

"Go ahead."

"Not now. In person. I need to meet with you and all top SA leaders."

"Good. We need to talk to you, too. When do you want to meet?"

"At eleven a.m. Saturday in Bad Wiessee."

"That's fine. We'll have special preparations for you, Mein Fuehrer."

"Make sure everyone's there."

"I certainly will. Good-bye."

I motioned for Goering with my right hand. Again I motioned, hurrying him up.

"Roehm's playing friendly," I said.

"It won't work. Not now," Goering replied.

"Go back to Berlin now and make sure everything's on utmost alert. I'll be in contact with you tomorrow from Bad Godesberg. Remember, 'Hummingbird.'"

"I'll never forget. Heil Hitler."

Early Friday morning the Volkischer Beobachter was rushed to me at the hotel. I clutched the newspaper and saw there on the front page, under a banner headline, the article I was so anxious to read. General von Blomberg, Defense Minister of the Reich and therefore its preeminent general, had pledged in writing: "The National Defense Force considers itself in close harmony with the Reich of Adolf Hitler. It stands behind the Fuehrer, who, coming from the ranks of the Army, is and always will be one of us."

Now my destiny was almost secured. Only treachery could stop it, but I was ready to overcome anything.

My entourage and I drove south into the Rhine Valley and visited a Labor Front camp. The sky was low and gray, and sometimes it rained, but the young men with strong bodies were still lined up and enthusiastic as I strode through and inspected them. Then I watched

them work and exercise, and listened to them sing. I could not visit all
the camps on the schedule, though. I whispered to aides. It was time to
go. I was hot despite the rain, and water mixed with my sweat, and I
felt dank and sticky and was tired of everyone staring at me. They did
not know what I might have to do. I definitely had to think about it.
Yes, Heil Hitler to you, too, I gestured while walking away.

In every town my black Mercedes passed through, citizens ran out
and shouted and waved, and occasionally I saluted back but kept
looking ahead. Early in the afternoon we arrived in Bad Godesberg,
and rapidly I walked up the steps of Hotel Dreesen while more people
cheered. At a meeting I spoke sternly for a long time. Then I went out
on the terrace for supper. I was not tense. Maybe I was a little tired,
but that was all. I was relaxed enough to talk quite a while to a waitress,
and she was thrilled by questions I asked about her simple life. But I
wanted to think alone. Everyone was dismissed. I looked out off the
terrace, and thought. The Rhine loomed luminous and long out of
sight two ways below me, and beautiful but impotent volcanic peaks
jutted high on the other side of the river. As the sun, partly masked by
clouds, crept behind the peaks, the Rhine grew dim and mysterious
and moved wide with dark currents of Teutonic history. My thoughts
were afloat on the Rhine. The Rhine flowed into me.

Goebbels arrived from Berlin. His smile was very large, and he kept
smiling, and he looked much too tense to be smiling. We sat and talked
about the crisis until lots of boys and girls from the Hitler Youth and
League of German Maidens appeared below the terrace, and I said they
could sing. Even after thunder cracked hard and loud across the sky,
and rain began to fall thick and fast and I went inside, they kept singing
and singing just for me. Not long after the raindrops and song had
ceased, a roaring motorcycle savaged the clear warm wet air. Goering's
courier ran up and handed me the alarm: "Berlin SA leader Karl Ernst
just called his mutinous storm troops to alert." Goering was recently
best man at Ernst's wedding, but I knew phone taps had revealed
Ernst often talked to Roehm about slicing the fat off Goering's ribs.
Now Karl Ernst expected me to believe he was going on his
honeymoon.

I summoned Viktor Lutze and grasped his hands and said, "Lutze,
it's definitely going to be necessary to remove Roehm as SA Chief of
Staff. He's a traitor. You already know that. I must ask you to swear
yourself to absolute secrecy and dedication to me."

"I long ago took an oath that dedicated my loyalty, even my life, to you, Mein Fuehrer."

"It will be your job to lead a more orderly SA. In the meantime, prepare yourself for the most critical hours of your life. These are my most difficult hours by far, Lutze, my most trying hours ever."

Another thundering motorcycle pounded my brain. Now Goering's courier warned that a great physician had been summoned in haste to the bedside of Hindenburg. The old man could be dying. He could even be dead. Maybe his reactionary cronies were trying to take over the country before Roehm attacked from the left. I swallowed bitter uncertainties. A little after midnight, Himmler called to report: "This afternoon at five o'clock the SA plan to occupy key buildings and installations in Berlin."

"Are you sure? I must know. I must know for sure."

"Our information is completely substantiated, Mein Fuehrer. They're going to eliminate you unless they're stopped. But we're prepared. I don't think they know how prepared we are."

I spun and stomped all over the room, shouting at Goebbels and others: "It's a Putsch. It's a Putsch. Those perverts are revolting. I can't believe this betrayal."

"Mein Fuehrer," said Goebbels, pacing near me, "you have every reason to believe. The Berlin SA tried to lynch me even though I was your district leader. You remember how damaging that was. Now, with Roehm, the SA is far more radical and dangerous."

Again the phone rang, each ring grating, a threat. The district leader of Bavaria revealed: "The SA have been marching in Munich's streets, protesting against you, Mein Fuehrer. They've been everywhere and they're shouting, 'The Fuehrer is no longer for us. The National Defense Force is against us.'"

"Who mobilized them?"

"We intercepted some pamphlets that ordered the men into the streets."

"Who authored the pamphlets?" I said.

"We don't know. But isn't it clear?"

"How many men are still in the streets?"

"Right now, very few. The SA ordered them to stop and go home."

"But they were in the streets?"

"Jawohl."

"Saying those things?"

"Jawohl."

"Stay at your post," I said.

Turning to my pilot, Hans Baur, I said, "We've got to go to Munich and then to Bad Wiessee right away, tonight."

"Several storms are between here and there," Baur said.

"I want regular calls to the weather bureau. Use the phone in the other room, and make sure we can leave as soon as possible. I've trusted Roehm too long."

A little after one a.m. Saturday, I learned we could fly. My staff at Hotel Dreesen mobilized rapidly and we drove to the airport near Bonn. By two o'clock we were airborne, and if the plane did not crash I knew I could do it. I could stop the rebellion. There was no reason to fear a crash. I sat in the cockpit next to the pilot and stared at a night now clear. Loud engines encased me in my essential thoughts and overwhelmed the banal chatter of Goebbels and Lutze and my adjutants.

The plane landed on a wet runway in Munich. Two armored cars were there and so was an Army detachment.

"I don't want the Army directly involved in this operation," I told the commander. "I'll handle this. I'm going to Bad Wiessee to settle accounts."

Several Nazi officials hustled up and saluted.

"Deploy the SS at the train station," I said. "Also around the Brown House. Let anyone in who wants in, but make sure no one leaves."

I was then driven to the Bavarian Ministry of the Interior. Within minutes of entering, I twice encountered SA officers I had entrusted with high rank, and both gave me an enthusiastic salute and Heil Hitler. Each time I ran right at them, running right into their startled phony faces, and ripped Nazi insignias off their brown shirts.

"You're a traitor."

"What, Mein Fuehrer? What's this?"

"You're a disgusting vile traitor and you're going to be shot dead."

"But, Mein Fuehrer ..."

"Shut your filthy lying mouth."

They and other implicated SA men, bad acting shock and hurt feelings, were taken to Stadelheim Prison. Teams of SS also began forays into Munich and environs. I knew — surely I could trust Goering, Himmler and Heydrich — that the same thing would happen in Berlin. Now I needed to get to the real stink hole, to Bad Wiesee.

But I could not, not yet. My stomach was on fire. Despite that, I kept trying to go. It was extremely difficult. Finally, I was able to. Then I washed my hands carefully. I was never too busy or pressured to wash my hands. I was very clean. I looked in the mirror. Right now, above all, I had to look like the Fuehrer. But this lighting was ridiculous, very distorted, the mirror, too. The mirror must have been curved. I did not really look like this. I was not that white. And my face could not possibly be so bloated. I did not have a bloated face or wretched black bags under my eyes. I was the Fuehrer rushing to Bad Wiessee, impelled by determination and rage.

In less than an hour we arrived at the Pension Hanselbauer, where Roehm and others were staying. Accompanied only by Lutze, Goebbels, and a small group, I walked to the front door and drew my revolver, put my whip in the left pocket of my belted leather coat, looked back at the men and nodded, then smashed the front door open with a kick.

"Where is Roehm?" I said to the landlady and an SA officer.

The traitor tried to draw his gun but we overpowered him. I dashed upstairs and started banging doors with either my fist or my gun.

"Open this door. This is the Fuehrer."

Some doors were opened voluntarily, others were demolished. Inside most of the rooms, I saw men involved in acts too vile to describe.

"You're a traitor and you're under arrest," I bellowed many times.

Edmund Heines, an influential SA officer, was nude with a cherubic, now defiled, boy.

"You'll be punished for your crimes," I said. "Get dressed."

"I'm not getting dressed until you explain these actions," Heines whined.

"Either get dressed now or be shot now."

He got up and put on his pants.

"Where is Roehm?"

Heines hesitated. I aimed. He pointed. I barged to Roehm's room and belted the door several times.

"Who is it?"

"This is Adolf Hitler. Open this door immediately."

The mattress squeaked, and there were footsteps before the door opened. I shoved Roehm back and entered.

"Ernst, you're under arrest for high treason. I've warned you many times about your sickening behavior."

He looked down, abject, speechless.

I turned and stormed up and down the hall, handling the operation. The SA were briefly kept in a cellar while Goebbels and I and the others conferred out front.

A large truck filled with about forty of Roehm's Headquarters Guards chugged up the road.

"What's happening here?" said one of the SA on the truck.

"Get back to Munich right now," snapped Wilhelm Brueckner, my adjutant.

"What's happening here? Why is the Fuehrer here at this hour? Where is Chief of Staff Roehm?"

"You're to return to Munich immediately," said Brueckner.

"We must see Chief of Staff Roehm before doing anything. He ordered us to be here today."

All the SA were armed. They might be part of the plot. How could they not be?

"Lieutenant, I am your Fuehrer, and I order you to return to Munich right now."

"Where is Chief of Staff Roehm?"

"If this truck isn't turned and headed back to Munich in ten seconds, you'll face my full wrath. All of you."

They obeyed.

"You've put yourself at too great a risk today, Mein Fuehrer," Lutze said. "But your brave conduct has enabled us to complete this critical operation."

"The operation is just beginning," I said.

GOOD MORNING
By Ernst Roehm

Daily I had been strolling the shores of Tegern Lake, talking with colleagues, and was so soothed to be surrounded by hills with trees, and hear the wind and then see the trees slightly sway, and then feel the wind rush down from the hills and cool my face and tickle my ears by rippling water near the shore where my bare feet tingled with water between the toes. Often I took everything off and submerged myself nearby in renowned sulfurous springs that penetrated my body in aromatic delight and massaged my bones and dissipated concerns.

At night our parties had been quite festive, and some nights the main feast was provided by charming young men recruited from all over Germany. I was not a stingy or jealous man and neither were most of my officers. We shared our visitors, often at the same time, in large, multi-limb mounds of flesh that moved all night. This time, though, I'd wanted to be well rested for the Fuehrer, so I retired fairly early. Only as an afterthought did I summon a young man to my room. This was just going to be a quick one, without variety or special effort. I stretched out on my stomach and rested my cheek on a pillow and just relaxed while the young man pleased his chief of staff. I was tired then, and wanted to sleep. "Well, all right, one more time if you want," I told him. He was very big and strong, and afterward I was so exhausted I said, "No, this time you can't spend the night, you'll have to go." And soon I was asleep.

Suddenly Saturday morning I'd wakened to a stampede. Throughout the Pension Hanselbauer, I heard things crashing, and people, too. Then the stairs were pounded by far more boots than I could account for, and my door was kicked open, splinters flying all over the room, and in rushed SS thug Sepp Dietrich, accompanied by at least twenty men who abruptly surrounded my bed.

"Roehm, you're under arrest," Dietrich shouted.

"What? What!"

"Get up and get dressed."

"The SS is subordinate to my SA command, Dietrich, and I want you the hell out of my room."

At once, several SS men grabbed and jerked me from bed, then slapped me, and someone pelted me in the face with my pants. The sounds of siege were still resounding through the building as I was dragged out of my room and down the stairs, and saw at least a hundred, maybe two hundred black shirts charging all around and manhandling and beating my SA men, cursing us, telling us we were under arrest.

When we'd all been collared, and corralled near the entrance, Dietrich waved toward the hole where the front door had been. Within seconds Hitler marched in, face contorted, and pointed his whip at me as he snarled, "You're under arrest for high treason."

"That's ridiculous."

"You've been preparing a Putsch for today."

"This is absurd, Mein Fuehrer. I've been preparing a special day for you."

"I know what you've been preparing."

"You think I'm planning to stage a Putsch in my underwear? Look around you. We've all been sleeping."

"I can barely stand the sight of what I see around me."

"I sent my guards home last night. We're having a vacation."

"You're a sickening pervert and you're under arrest."

"Good morning, Mein Fuehrer," I said while being jerked outside. "Good morning to you."

HUMMINGBIRD
By Adolf Hitler

After we shoved SA prisoners into an enclosed truck, I got in my car and we began to drive back to Munich. On the way we periodically encountered SA officers headed toward Bad Wiessee. Each time, I walked to their cars and told them they were under arrest, and instructed that they be put in the truck and taken to Stadelheim Prison with the rest of the rabble. Then I went to the train station and ensured that loudspeakers guided SA officers to convenient waiting areas.

Around ten a.m. I arrived at the Brown House, our beautiful new Nazi headquarters, and told Goebbels to immediately call Goering in Berlin. Into the phone Goebbels said one word — Hummingbird — and I nodded.

STATE OF EMERGENCY
By Reinhard Heydrich

Numerous Gestapo officers had been waiting in my anteroom for a long time. They did not know why. In key areas throughout the Reich, many somewhat more updated Gestapo and SS men clutched sealed envelopes that contained typewritten names. Everything had been meticulously prepared. I was waiting for the message. It was important to start. Operations should have commenced already. At a little after ten a.m., Himmler telephoned that Goebbels had called from the Fuehrer's side.

"That's what I've been waiting for," I said.

"We don't have to wait anymore," Himmler replied.

I hung up and began to shout, "Putsch by Roehm. Putsch by Roehm. State of emergency. State of emergency. The Fuehrer has ordered immediate action."

Running into the anteroom, I saw many startled faces.

"Roehm is staging a Putsch," I said. "The Fuehrer demands that we suppress it immediately. I'll soon talk to each of you individually in my office."

I called my switchboard operators, who had been drilled to process an unprecedented number of incoming and outgoing calls, and ordered operations activated throughout the Reich. Then the Gestapo entered my office one by one. Each was given a name, or names. Instructions were similar. Enemies of the Reich had to be stopped with certitude.

"Report back here to me when you're finished. I might have more instructions."

FROM THE PAST
By Gustav von Kahr

I was in my seventies and enjoying a long and peaceful retirement in Munich. I had rendered many services as a general, as Commissar of Bavaria with dictatorial powers and, most important, as the man who did not let Hitler's gun in my face in 1923 deter me from my duty. Only under duress had I told Hitler I would participate in his Putsch. As soon as I had a chance, I escaped. I escaped and organized Bavaria, and more than anyone else I put down Hitler's Putsch.

That was a long time ago. I was too old for politics and tired of the mess. I liked relaxing in my villa. It was a nice clear hot morning. My doorbell rang, and I slowly walked to greet whoever it was. Three men stood on the porch.

"Good morning," I obliged.

They converged, and one hit me in the stomach, bending me over, and they wrestled me toward their car. Inside, held low in the back seat, I gasped, "What's this? I'm Gustav von Kahr."

"That's the problem, old man."

I tried to sit up and wave to someone but only got my right arm up a little before the two in back beat me so bad I could not move. The man in front drove out somewhere, and the other two threw me out. Surely this is enough, I thought, whatever it is they are doing. I tried to get up but a kick to my face laid me flat, with eyes still open to see the ax come straight down and split my head. The man with the ax kept hitting my head and then he started chopping my body.

PROTEST
By Franz von Papen

Urgently, Goering had summoned me to his palace. Lots of armed police and SS patrolled in front, and men with machine guns lurked on the roof and aggravated my worries. When I entered, Goering was alternately conferring with Himmler, talking on the phone, and studying papers. I stood waiting. After long and pompous preoccupation, Goering, eyes on his papers, deigned to say: "Roehm is staging a rebellion in Munich and the Fuehrer has flown there to quash it. The Fuehrer has entrusted me with absolute power to crush the insurrection here in Berlin."

"He has no right to give you that authority. The law states that the vice chancellor is in charge when the chancellor is away."

"I am in charge," Goering said, looking at me the first time.

"Hindenburg should be alerted at once. He'll declare a state of emergency and empower the National Defense Force to do its duty."

"The president cannot be bothered now, Herr von Papen."

"I insist that the president be informed."

Goering had already resumed shuffling papers. I left his office briefly and returned to renew my demand.

"I recommend you concentrate on your personal security," he said. "Go home and remain there unless I give you permission to leave."

"I protest this. I'm not going to be placed under house arrest."

"Go home, Papen. Now."

Goering hadn't looked up again, and I soon melted out the door and headed toward the Vice Chancellery. I walked more slowly the closer I got. The SS were looking at me from rooftops.

Inside my offices, files crackled under foot as I tried to avoid stepping on drawers.

"Herr von Papen, dear God, it's Herbert von Bose," said one of my assistants, rushing up.

A few days ago the Nazis had arrested Edgar Jung, primary author of my Marburg speech, and now they had killed the other author, Herbert von Bose. Edgar Jung cut through my mind. Before I had only feared. Now I knew.

"Why has Herr von Bose been shot?" I demanded of the SS guard who stood in front of the door behind which Bose lay.

"He tried to escape."

A group of SS guards told me it was time I went home, and they took me there. Some guards stayed in front of my house. A police captain scrutinized me inside.

"You're a lucky man," the captain said.

"Lucky?"

"You're alive, aren't you?"

RELAXATION
By Kurt von Schleicher

I did not worry about rumors. They were ridiculous. I had not seen Roehm in months and did not anyway like or trust him. Warnings by friends that I should leave the country were unnecessary. As the chancellor who preceded Hitler, and a former General Staff officer, I was much too visible and powerful to conceivably be targeted for foul play.

I had not been politically active for more than a year, except to subtly, and in a primarily social context, let it be understood that I could be available if the country needed me, which it might. But I was really not concerned about power and all that. I had been having too much fun with my young wife and our child. We lived outside Berlin in a villa with a wide view of a pretty lake. From my study I could see my garden and the lake and many boats on the lake. I was in my study. It was a little before noon.

"This article makes me sick," I said to my wife, who was in the next room.

"What article, darling?"

"This obsequious one by General von Blomberg."

"Don't even think about that. You're much too good to think about things like that."

I received a phone call from a friend, and in a little while asked him to hold a minute because I heard the doorbell and my housekeeper open the door to a man asking to speak to me. I set the receiver on my desk.

Three men in big coats entered my study. It was a warm day for coats like that.

"Are you General von Schleicher?" said the one standing nearest my desk.

"Yes, I am."

Each man drew a pistol. I jumped up twisting away and began a quick step. They fired, and I collapsed with several bullets in the neck and back. One of the men hung up the phone. My wife ran screaming into the study and looked at me before staring at the men. Then, crying, she looked back down on me before looking up, and that is when they shot her. She fell not far from me. They did not shoot the housekeeper.

CLEAN MORALS
By Adolf Hitler

Everyone except me was overanxious about the SA at Stadelheim Prison.

"The prisoners will keep well enough where they are," I said. "We must first establish righteousness, in writing."

"Mein Fuehrer, I'd be honored if you grant me the privilege of executing Roehm," said Rudolf Hess. "I'll shoot him, beat him, anything you want."

"Shut up. All of you shut up.

"Lutze, as the new SA leader, it's your duty and honor to write down the new rules."

I demanded blind obedience and unquestioning discipline from SA leaders and men, and threatened to expel anyone who did not behave in an exemplary manner. There would be no more drunkenness, riding in limousines, or giving expensive dinners. Everyone also had to be loyal to and respectful toward the National Defense Force. And above all, it was mandatory SA leaders avoid behavior that might worry German mothers their sons would be violated if they joined the SA.

"Those are brilliant directives, Mein Fuehrer," said Hess.

"They are, indeed," said Martin Bormann, Hess' top aide. "And now, the prisoners at Stadelheim?"

"The prisoners will keep. Right now I want Lutze to read this charter back to me."

PARTY STALWART
By Gregor Strasser

I was having lunch at home with my family. It was a pleasant lunch because there was no discussion of politics. That was the rule. We were talking about our picnic the next day. When the doorbell rang, I said I'd be right back.

Out front, several big frowns startled me.

"Good afternoon," I stated.

"Gestapo."

As they engulfed me, I gasped for help but a glove grasped my mouth. Before they got me to the car, I heard my wife yelling, "Gregor, Gregor, Gregor."

The car accelerated.

"You'll be taken to your office to determine if you have subversive documents," I was told.

Afterward they drove straight to Gestapo headquarters and tossed me into a cell with several SA officers.

"Herr Strasser, thank God you're here. What's this madness? What's going on?"

"I have no idea."

"How could a man in your position not know?"

"I'm no longer involved," I said.

As I pondered those words, it was indeed difficult to comprehend no longer being in the Nazi party that had meant so much to me. How could I be merely the director of a chemical combine? Once I had been a prolific fund raiser and rousing speechmaker who expanded Nazi membership and influence tenfold in northern Germany when Hitler did not have the time or wherewithal. I had also employed and tutored Himmler and Goebbels, and both betrayed me. I never betrayed my principles, but Hitler could not tolerate real socialism in "his" National Socialist party. He forced me to quit, then excoriated me for being a traitor.

I was not a traitor then, and recently I had been amused by the rumor I was scheming with Schleicher. I also scoffed at whispers I had met with Hitler. His overtures were not meaningful, and I hadn't seen him for a long time.

"Strasser, you're to come with us right now for questioning," said a guard.

I was taken down the hall and put in a cell by myself. I knew Adolf was part of this, and my protégés Goebbels and Himmler, naturally. Who else would put me in jail? Who else feared me so much? Who else would order pistols stuck through bars and pointed at me?

I dived into the furthest corner of the cell before bullets stung me, and I kept jumping, dodging, diving, knowing this was it, yet struggling against it. When I had been shot enough to quit evading, and fall, someone came in, looked down on me, and fired a few more rounds. My chest heaved quite a while, considering.

DOGS
By Adolf Hitler

There were a lot of SA at the Brown House, and I was talking to them. I was yelling at them: "Roehm and others of your very highest leadership are traitors. They're sleazy, vile immoral traitors who've been arrested, and if any of you are like them, then you'll also be arrested and dealt with. The SA is going to change. Don't think this cesspool will continue."

The more I cursed and screeched, the more these SA men, who were of undetermined loyalty, looked like whipped dogs. Whipped dogs cause little trouble.

"Each of you is going to be thoroughly investigated," I warned, "and each of you is going to be thoroughly searched right now. Some of you might be released later, and if so you're to leave your weapons here and go straight home and take off your uniforms and stay home and hope that you're not implicated, and if you are, you'll be throttled, don't think you won't be."

"Heil Hitler, Heil Hitler, Sieg Heil, Sieg Heil."

I gave a final stare and walked out. Martin Bormann eased up to me in a vacuum in the otherwise crowded corridor, and whispered, "Mein Fuehrer, the SA mutineers at Stadelheim Prison, isn't it time we shot them?"

"There's much to do right now."

"Can we really wait?"

"I have urgent matters to deal with, Bormann. Don't bother me."

BRICKS
By An SS Officer

SA prisoners were brought out four at a time. Some protested, others pleaded through tears, a few walked in silence. All were placed right in front of the fading red brick wall in the courtyard of a cadet school near Berlin.

I don't know why we were positioned just several paces from the SA. Up so close our rifles blasted big holes from the backs of targets and splattered the fading red brick wall with flesh and blood. Sometimes the wall had to be splashed with a few buckets of water before shooting resumed.

I knew some of the men against the wall, quite a few, really, and even if I hadn't, it would have been a tough job.

NOW
By Adolf Hitler

"They'll be shot when everything else has been done," I said, "and you'll shut up in the meantime because you've all been interrupting my concentration, and besides it's now time to have them shot, so shut up.

Hand me the list of prisoners."

I read the list. These men were all traitors. I read the list again to make sure.

"Give me that pen," I said, and began to place an x, a neat, decisive x, by the name of each man. Except Roehm.

"I've decided to spare Roehm because of his importance to the movement."

"Roehm is a great danger to the movement, Mein Fuehrer," said Bormann.

"Shut up. Roehm is to be spared."

I handed the list to Sepp Dietrich and ordered him to carry out the x's.

ORDERS
By Sepp Dietrich

At Stadelheim Prison the warden said: "I need more confirmation than a list."

"Those x's are the Fuehrer's," I said.

"How do I know? That's not official procedure."

I called the Brown House and gave him the phone. Even with the receiver pressed to the warden's ear, I could hear Hitler screaming. The warden hung up and said to proceed. I instructed six SS men to go into the prison courtyard and ready their rifles. I went to the cell of the first marked man and, after a guard opened the door, announced: "You have been condemned to death by the Fuehrer for high treason. Heil Hitler."

The SA officer was taken without resistance into the courtyard and placed against a stone wall. An SS officer then barked, "By order of the Fuehrer. Ready. Aim. Fire."

Going back inside I passed Roehm's cell and hoped he was enjoying this. Then I got another SA officer, who said, "For God's sake, I'm your friend. And I've done nothing."

"You have been condemned to death by the Fuehrer for high treason. Heil Hitler."

I did not need to stay for the whole thing. My next in command could continue. I returned to the Brown House, clicked my heels in front of the Fuehrer and said, "The traitors have paid."

PRESS CONFERENCE
By Hermann Goering

I liked to change uniforms and sometimes did so several times a day, but this time I had to. I could not be sweaty during my five p.m. press conference at the Propaganda Ministry. Many German and foreign newsmen were waiting and very eager. I stepped forward and put my elbow on the podium and my chin in my palm, then looked around and paused before I mischievously rolled my eyes. There was no time for thorough explanation. I began pacing with delicate steps, and stated only essentials: "The SA has been increasingly disagreeable about adhering to the rules and the spirit of the movement. The SA has further compromised itself by indulging its perverse tastes. Upon discovering that the SA was allying itself with various reactionaries for the purpose of fomenting a second revolution, the Fuehrer ordered that the traitors be stopped. General von Schleicher was the key agent of the right who was scheming with the left."

I delivered a few more statements. Upon concluding, I folded my arms against my chest and stared at the newsmen. That was enough. I walked away.

"What, specifically, has been done with General von Schleicher?" a foreign newsman called to me.

I walked back to the podium.

"General von Schleicher violently resisted arrest and had to be shot. He is dead."

I walked away again and did not listen to questions.

RETURN TO BERLIN
By Adolf Hitler

The sun had recently gone down behind the plane, and as Goebbels kept remarking to Sepp Dietrich, the sky was a startling red. I could see that. I just did not want to talk about it. I wanted the plane to land. It was time I got back to Berlin. Gradually, the Saturday sunset did dim, but the sky was still not absolutely dark when we landed at Tempelhof

Airport.

Stepping from the plane I was aware of everything and right away picked out Goering and Himmler. They were standing below and looking at me proudly, and so was a crowd of officials from the SS and Gestapo, all of them here to protect and honor me. I grasped Goering's hand and Himmler's and lots of other hands, so many it was hard to concentrate. I was a little dizzy, though not too dizzy to take care of business. I was simply tired, as anyone would be without sleep, and as soon as possible I pried away and began to walk with Goering and Himmler. After several paces, I waved to stop.

"Let me see the list," I said to Himmler.

He pulled a long, rolled up paper from his sleeve. The list was soiled but names were legible. I could not read rapidly right now. I guided my eyes with an index finger. The names looked good but my eyes burned, and I had to rub them. That burned them more and irritated the skin underneath. I could still see the list was fine. I gave the list back to Himmler and moved toward a car.

"I'll see you at the Chancellery in a little while," I said.

My car door was opened, and as I bowed to step in I heard: "Bravo, Adolf. Bravo." I glanced at the maintenance men who had waited by a hangar to cheer their triumphant Fuehrer. Then I got in my car.

At the Chancellery, Goering and Himmler asked about Roehm.

"I've spared him because of his services. No, no more tonight. No, it isn't so pressing as that. I'll decide what's right. Tomorrow we'll look at the whole operation. That's all for tonight. Good night, gentlemen. Good night right now."

REASONING
By Hermann Goering

Himmler and I returned to the Chancellery late Sunday morning. The Fuehrer looked much better and said he felt fine.

"How do you feel?" he asked us, and motioned to sit down.

We both thanked him for inquiring and said we also felt fine on this glorious sunny day.

"Mein Fuehrer," I said, "none of us can ever rest peacefully as long as Roehm is alive."

"I've already told you my decision about Roehm."

"We felt, perhaps, that you were so busy, so preoccupied, that you might now, being well rested, change your mind," Himmler said.

"I haven't changed my mind. The SA's been struck. It's no longer a danger. And neither is Roehm."

"Mein Fuehrer," I said, "there are many things to consider."

"Are you suggesting I haven't considered them?"

"No, no, certainly not."

"I have considered everything."

"We need to be concerned about the Army," I said.

"I know a great deal more about the Army than either of you, and it was I who placated them."

"We must make sure the Army stays placated, Mein Fuehrer," said Himmler.

"The Army is now more loyal to me than ever and..."

"But Mein Fuehrer," I interjected, surprising Hitler, "the Army has acquiesced in our killing General von Schleicher. They've let us kill one of their own. They won't accept us then letting Roehm live. That's too much of a contradiction, and an insult to the Army. I can't imagine General von Blomberg would've sent out a proclamation of loyalty to every barracks in the Reich this morning if he'd known Roehm would be allowed to live. Can we really risk enraging the Army?"

"I didn't specifically promise the Army I'd kill Roehm."

"The Army interpreted it that you would," Himmler said.

"I believe in loyalty," Hitler asserted. "You, Himmler, are not being loyal to Roehm. He befriended you in the early twenties when nothing else was available, and he involved you in paramilitary activities and even permitted you to carry the Imperial flag during the Putsch."

"Mein Fuehrer, I don't think the Reichsfuehrer is discounting Roehm's contributions to our movement. What we're now doing, and what countless others have for months been doing, is to try to impress upon you the fact that Roehm cannot be controlled. He does not, in the sense the rest of us do, defer to you as the Fuehrer. He makes inflammatory statements he knows carry the threat of the brown shirts. I'm not sure Roehm could control the SA even if he desired to, which he clearly does not."

"I could keep him in jail."

"That wouldn't be effective," I said, reasoning with big hands open in front of my chest. "Roehm could rally tremendous support from prison. He'd be a martyr."

"We must also consider the confidentiality of the party," Himmler added. "Roehm knows a great deal about our activities, all of them. I also think he would be a threat to your confidentiality, Mein Fuehrer, especially if he were in prison. Imagine the things he might start saying — inventing, of course, but still saying loudly — now that his morals have been so thoroughly and publicly attacked. I'm sure he'd do everything he could to hurt the movement, and to hurt you, Mein Fuehrer, who he'd hold responsible for his imprisonment."

Hitler got up and walked away and put his hands on a table, leaning over. All we could see was his back. His head must have hung on his chest. He did not move for a long time. Himmler and I kept looking at each other when we weren't studying the Fuehrer's back.

"All right," Hitler finally said. He turned around. "I'll call Munich right away and give the order. I'll tell them to first offer Ernst the soldier's way out. I owe him that."

TEA PARTY
By Adolf Hitler

There was a large happy crowd in front of the Chancellery on Sunday afternoon. Mothers and fathers brought their children here so they could all see their Fuehrer on this important occasion. I went to the large window where I had stood above the torchlight parade the night I became chancellor, and I smiled at the cheering and saluting Germans below. Then I saluted them and they cheered louder.

I left the window and went to a tea party I was hosting for important officials and their wives and families. There was plenty of food and tea, and also a lot to drink, and everyone was in a fine mood. I certainly was. I joked with all the children and hugged as many as I could. The ladies at my party were particularly attentive, and I felt so good, so well rested and cleaned up, it was quite easy to fascinate and amuse them. Their husbands were pleased to see that. And everyone was delighted when servants said another large crowd had gathered outside. Again I marched to my favorite Chancellery window, and this time I waved before I smiled and saluted.

ALTERNATIVE
By Ernst Roehm

In my cell I was so hot my cot was soaked with sweat that fell continuously from my face and body. I tried to get comfortable by rolling around, but each spot was smelly and wet and worse. That would not matter for long. I was awaiting a future of fire. When a cold key clicked the lock to open my cell door, it was a terrifying relief. I sat up. Theodore Eicke walked in, staring at me. Two SS men followed. Eicke had once been in the SA, but the SS wanted him and soon promoted him to Commandant of Dachau and then put him in charge of reorganizing all concentration camps. His activities weakened me, and Eicke had known what I wanted to do. He placed a copy of the Volkischer Beobachter on a wood table by my cot. Then he reached into his pocket and put a revolver next to the newspaper.

"Roehm, we have some interesting reading for you. You also have one bullet and ten minutes to take advantage of the favor the Fuehrer has granted you."

I did not answer. They left.

I glanced at the paper and saw I had been replaced as SA Chief of Staff. I didn't read the rest. It was a lie. The Fuehrer had betrayed me, and a great opportunity for Germany was being destroyed.

Eicke and the two others came back.

"Roehm, you've been condemned to death by the Fuehrer for high treason. You should've died honorably."

"If Adolf wants to kill me, then he should do it himself."

"Stand up, Chief of Staff."

I stood at attention and scorched Eicke as well as I could.

Two SS men shakily pointed pistols and fired.

"Mein Fuehrer, Mein Fuehrer," I muttered before falling.

CONGRATULATIONS
By President Paul von Hindenburg

"What did you say happened? They killed the traitors? They killed the traitors. Good. That's what they should have done. Who did you say they killed? Roehm. Good. Other SA officers. Good. Schleicher? Schleicher! They killed General von Schleicher! That's outrageous. Investigate that. What? What do you mean they had to? For the country? All right. I suppose it's all right. They killed the traitors.

"What's this you want me to sign? A message. What does it say? Louder. I'm congratulating Hitler for gallant action and courage while crushing high treason? O.K. And my profound thanks. Who's this for? For Hitler and the newspapers. All right, I'll sign it. Where do I sign?"

FULL EXPLANATION
By Adolf Hitler

Hundreds of police, soldiers, and SS troops were armed almost everywhere in and around Kroll Opera House on July thirteenth, and numerous agents in civilian clothes dissolved into a crowd brightened by chandeliers. At eight o'clock, Goering introduced me. I had been in isolation for days, haunted by my obligation to somehow explain without causing undue pain.

"I must be blunt and frank," I told the officials and dignitaries. "Truth is best because these tragic events can also be instructive.

"There has been a crisis in the bosom of your young Reich, and the representatives of nihilism and permanent revolution were responsible for it. I could not tolerate this because I headed an administration that gained power by legal means and was the executor of the national will. Chief of Staff Roehm and other SA elements had still insisted upon being adventurers with the nation's health. These were irresponsible acts by undisciplined men born to conspiracy. They had nothing worthwhile to do so they spent their time criticizing everything and achieving nothing. Their purposeless lives isolated them from the real life of the nation and caused them anxieties they deluded themselves into thinking were the true concerns of the nation as a whole. These bacillus carriers of lies, fears and uncertainties conspired to spread their noxiousness for the purpose of staging a second revolution. My devastating realization was that only a ferocious and bloody repression could stop this revolt. My choice was to either annihilate a mere few dozen rebels or let tens of thousands of innocents on each side be killed."

Extended applause gave me time to clear my throat, which burned from speaking in an especially authoritative way.

"Why didn't I use the courts?" I continued. "It was because, at that moment, I alone was responsible for the German nation. I alone, during those critical twenty-four hours, was the supreme court of justice of the German people. I accepted complete responsibility for everything, and I ordered the leaders of the guilty shot. I ordered the abscesses caused by our internal and external poisons cauterized until the living flesh was burned. I also ordered that any rebels resisting arrest be shot immediately. The nation has to know its existence cannot be menaced with impunity by anyone, and whoever lifts his hand against the state will die for it."

Everyone roared. Then, with relief, I concluded: "We all deserve congratulations for preserving in blood what was acquired by the blood of our best friends."

A NEW SS
By Heinrich Himmler

Less than ten years ago my men often had to sell SA souvenirs. Now the Fuehrer proclaimed the SS an independent organization and directed it to maintain armed fighting units to protect the party. He knew that I, the Reichsfuehrer SS, was absolutely loyal and would energetically expand the organization for his good and the betterment of Aryan people. The Fuehrer also realized that the Army was not wholly trustworthy. Some generals complained about the death of Schleicher and wanted to severely limit Nazi influence. The Fuehrer, well informed by a vigilant SS, reminded General von Blomberg and others that the question of leadership had already been agreed upon and settled.

I was perfectly prepared to be the Reichsfuehrer of a large and loyal SS. My father, a professor, had insisted I keep a diary so I would learn the discipline of recording many details. From my start in the SS, I made sure proper records were kept and that the best procedures were identified and studied. I always understood how a job should be done and was exasperated whenever someone argued about what I was telling him (for his own good).

Even in my early twenties I had always been willing to take a strong stand. After my older brother became engaged, I found out about the woman, and I told him. He still hesitated. Though he had won an Iron Cross First Class during the Great War, I was more mature. I would have been in the war, too, but it ended before my officer training. I could not permit an immoral woman to disgrace my brother and our family. I wrote this woman and excoriated her for her behavior. When she responded arrogantly, I hired a private detective and also asked a friend to keep me informed. Then I wrote more letters to the girl and also wrote her family and friends, and friends of friends. Fortunately, the engagement was terminated.

I knew it was crucial to associate with the right kind of people. I had learned that from my father, who maintained up-to-date lists of the occupations held by fathers of my classmates. I always carefully decided which Nazis I needed to cultivate, and when. It was critical I do well in the party. I had studied a lot of agriculture in college, and worked on farms and for a company doing research on manure. But the pay was poor, and when my parents sent me money they insisted I account for every bit in writing. Meanwhile, I had tried to get jobs running farms in Russia and Turkey as well as in Germany, but the requirements were always pedantic. The Fuehrer wasn't like that at all. He gave me a great cause, and I vowed to reward him.

GARBAGE
By Benito Mussolini

I received reports and demanded confirmation. Austrian Nazis had supposedly just staged a Putsch and shot Chancellor Engelbert Dollfuss. This was an absolute betrayal by Hitler, especially since Dollfuss' wife and children were visiting me. They were out on the patio.

"Frau Dollfuss, I am sorry, but I have very distressing news from Austria," I said, and gave her the ominous but incomplete reports.

She of course became hysterical.

"Don't worry. I give you my word I'll immediately order my troops to mobilize on your southern border. I'll do everything possible to save your husband."

Hitler must have been terrified. He did nothing while the Austrian government crushed the Putsch and imprisoned the cutthroats. I soon went to Vienna and guaranteed Austria's independence, and also expressed my sincerest condolences to Frau Dollfuss. Our trauma worsened when we learned Nazi traitors had shot her husband in the neck and callously carried on while he lay at their feet, calling for help the four hours he bled to death.

"Hitler's obviously a threat," I began telling people. "He's also a horrible sexual degenerate. I could tell that when I talked to him. And he leads a nation of pederasts and murderers. The Germans have no historical basis for greatness. What is now Germany was nothing but a cauldron of illiterate savages when Rome flourished as the cultural and military center of the world. I tell you, the Germans mean war. If we let them, they'll overrun Europe, like the barbaric Germanic tribes of old. We've got to unite with other European nations right away."

A PASSING
By Adolf Hitler

The news came. I knew it had to happen. Still, it had been forever, and I could not actually feel it. I called a cabinet meeting immediately, as I had always planned, and we made a law to combine the offices of chancellor and president the instant the old man expired. I did not want to be called "President." Hindenburg, and others, had been called that. The law stipulated my official titles be Fuehrer and Reich Chancellor. I also dictated a new oath for the military. The oath would be exacted very soon.

I hurried to my plane and flew to Neudeck. On this hot summer day Hindenburg lay cold and gray on his old iron cot, and darkness spread wide beneath each eye. After being whispered to and gently prodded by his son, Hindenburg opened his stuporous eyes and mumbled before closing them, not having recognized me. I left.

The next day, August second, he died. This was the greatest moment of my life, and I put on a tuxedo, pranced onto the Chancellery balcony and saluted the crowds. While this was happening, the military — officers and men — swore "By God" personal allegiance to me, by name, vowing readiness to sacrifice lives. Never had there been a German oath like this.

In a few days, I presided at Hindenburg's funeral. There could be no thought of granting his request to be buried on his estate. He needed to be buried at Tannenberg, the site already memorialized for his Great War victory over the Russians. His casket looked quite imposing, draped in a big banner, and eight huge square towers six stories high, made higher by flames on top, surrounded the solemnity. I spoke and bade the departed warrior a place in Valhalla.

Before long, there was an outcry about Hindenburg's political testament. When I received the sealed envelope, I noted it was addressed to me personally and was therefore private. I published the contents soon enough. Hindenburg had wanted me to be the next president. His son verified that. Ninety percent of the voters also expressed approval in a plebiscite. Now absolutely in charge, I proclaimed my legacy would endure a thousand years.

PARTY RALLY
By Albert Speer

I, an architect still in his late twenties, could scarcely comprehend that the Fuehrer had designated me his architect, his special architect for eternity. I was going to design massive structures that would not only inspire us now but serve forever as beacons from a time of unparalleled greatness. I was also delighted the Fuehrer supported my dramatic plans for the 1934 Party Rally, permitting me to build a massive stone stage with a huge swastika emblazoned in front. In the background I placed three swastika banners towering ten stories high. I also readied thousands of flags. The Fuehrer shrewdly overruled Goering and enabled me to use almost every anti-aircraft searchlight in the nation. The result was spectacular. Spaced forty feet apart, columns of bright white shot five miles into the sky, illuminating the heavens, and we all felt like small unified creatures in a cathedral spanning the universe. When the Fuehrer strode the massive stone stage, he was alight on a stage already aglow.

HITLER IS
By Rudolf Hess

As the rally at Nuremberg was closing, I marched to the microphone but excitement was so overwhelming I had to step away and salute the Fuehrer. I was very proud and smiling as big as I could. In a moment I stepped back to the microphone, but everything was still so loud I again retreated to salute the Fuehrer. I did not want to wait too long, though. The Fuehrer might not like even this delay. So, quickly, I stepped to the microphone and, smiling big and very proud, I said: "The Party is Hitler. But Hitler is Germany just as Germany is Hitler."

STEPS TOWARD PEACE
By Adolf Hitler

We had to have peace but could not with Germany so weak. Ruthless nations would continue to ravage our defenseless land. That is why I had always called the Treaty of Versailles an abomination. Versailles insisted Germany be weak. I was not going to tolerate that anymore. Therefore, late in 1934, I privately gave orders to triple our Army to a more reasonable but still modest three hundred thousand men.

I was sure the British would understand. They were our racial and spiritual brothers, really, a clean very white and accomplished people who dominated much of the earth. I needed to tell them that. No conceivable alliance could better assure peace than a historical one between the greatest maritime power, England, and the greatest continental power, Germany. I did not want to include the French since they were bound by absurd treaties to aid Slavic Czechoslovakia,

Poland and Rumania, and remained hostile to a Germany that for her very survival needed to expand to the East. England certainly had no compelling interest in that sphere.

Right after I invited them, members of the British government anxiously agreed to come. My friendly intentions were most undiplomatically derailed, however, when England released a White Paper that decried Germany protecting itself and ignoring Versailles. The British further stated they considered it necessary to augment their air power. I sent word that I had a cold. It was a very bad cold, and I would not be talking. By March 1935 I had recovered sufficiently to announce to Britain's Daily Mail that the Luftwaffe was in fact Germany's official military arm in the air. The French then aggressively decided to prolong their period of military service.

Hostile forces gnawing around us needed a sharp signal. That I gave with the public order to expand our military forces to a half million men. The following day I announced military conscription would henceforth be universal. Then our nation celebrated with a massive martial parade down Unter Den Linden in Berlin. Everyone was ecstatic that we had forsworn shame and regained pride by heaping contempt upon the criminal strictures of our oppressors.

But what will the French and British do, many generals worried? They might belch a little, I said, but that's all. Soon we learned Foreign Secretary John Simon and Anthony Eden were asking if I still wanted to talk. Of course I did, and the British arrived on March twenty-fifth.

With earnestness I told my visitors: "Germany wants only the means to defend herself, which for a generation she has been denied. Then our nation will be strong enough to help England, and Western civilization, by blocking the festering Bolshevik threat to the East."

Only rarely was it necessary to speak sternly, only when they suggested Germany should be amenable to negotiations, in Lithuania, for example, that would legalize the persecution of German minorities. "Any cooperation between National Socialism and Bolshevism is forever an impossibility," I stated.

The general tone of the discussions was still absolutely cordial, and I knew we could establish a framework for generations of peace. I accepted the British offer to send an envoy to London in June to consummate naval talks about my magnanimous offer to guarantee them a three to one advantage on the seas. They certainly appreciated the implications for their vast empire. The empire was theirs. Germany only wanted security.

NEW LIFE
By Hermann Goering

I still loved my wife, Carin, as much as ever, and after her death a few years ago I had not really needed women, especially since I could not forget my final intimate moments with Carin. Though so very frail and pale and ill, she had still wanted me. She wanted me more than anything, and she beseeched me again and again, telling me that we must do so now, before she was gone, and she did not care about my worries, any worries, that we might hasten her end. We did what she wanted, but when I looked down on her pale grimacing face I would have to turn away. "This is so hard on you," I said. "We really shouldn't anymore. I just can't."

I had not been able to get interested again, even with lots of women trying to entice me. I could feel it was not right anymore. It would have reminded me of Carin. It would have been inferior. It would not have been possible. Then I met Emmy Sonnemann, a stage actress who was kind and gregarious and blonde and voluptuous, and just being with her, and laughing and telling her what I had done and dreamed of doing, was a great joy, a happy all over sensation that made me feel like a man again. This was incredible but also a great worry. Maybe I never could again. But I thought I could. Actually, I knew I could. I had to. I needed to. Emmy and I became so close. There was really never any question of our not doing so. I told Emmy that. We definitely will. We'll keep trying. And we did. We really did. God, we did. Emmy told me how glad she was. I didn't have to worry anymore. Now I knew I could. Emmy probably never doubted me. She understood I couldn't always because of my job. I went everywhere fast at all hours and was tired a lot. It was hard to do so many things. My stamina sometimes was not good. I was shorter than the Fuehrer but often weighed two hundred eighty pounds. Emmy did not mind, though. She said knowing me transformed her life.

Now I had so much, and so many outlets for my imagination. In addition to my renowned political and military duties, I became Master of the German Forests, and Master of the German Hunt, and my principal obligation, discharged with enthusiasm, was to expand German forests and ensure for generations a grand pristine environment inhabited by a variety of wildlife. One of my rewards was a huge tract of land a couple of hours northeast of Berlin. This vast and gorgeous place had big green trees high all over the horizon, and there were lakes in the hills, and into this splendor I imported bison and elk and deer, and I hunted and killed with the precision and skill of an ace.

Tucked into my bucolic heaven, I naturally found the perfect site, near a jewel of a little lake, on which to build my house. On this house I would spare nothing. This was to be the grandest house in Germany. This was to be Karinhall. I decorated Karinhall with the finest paintings and artifacts, and the elaborate grounds featured gardens and statues as well as quarters for servants and aides. The spiritual highlight of this beautifully designed haven lay on the far side of the lake where I constructed a mausoleum for Carin. Anti-Nazis had desecrated her grave in Sweden, and I could not permit anyone to hurt the man she loved.

Carin was removed from her tomb in Sweden and taken with full ceremonial honors to a ferry for the trip south to Germany. Here she was placed on a train decorated with flowers and wreaths, and everywhere the train passed people gathered to watch and mourn on this special holiday. At the train station I waited, quaking inside, as Carin was placed onto an open wagon, and soon church bells rhapsodized us during our final journey, to her new home, to Karinhall.

The Fuehrer came for the great ceremony, along with many other Nazi dignitaries, and Carin's soul and spirit were palpable to everyone as the soft and solemn beat of Wagnerian drums signaled her final descent into a mausoleum with thick walls. Inside, there awaited a custom casket easily large enough for me to someday join Carin in eternal intimacy. About all of this, Emmy was very gracious and concerned, and I then knew we would marry. Everything was eventually set for April tenth, and on this extraordinary day all of Berlin, it seemed, had been groomed and decorated. Thousands of citizens came to see not only me but the woman the Fuehrer now called the First Lady of Germany. Our troops marched a timely tribute, and hundreds of planes from my burgeoning Luftwaffe carved a salute in the sky.

After the wedding Emmy and I cuddled and kissed as we were driven back to Karinhall. I told her our honeymoon on the Adriatic Sea would be the most romantic thing in the world. Emmy felt so good to touch. I kept kissing her. When we got to Karinhall, I told Emmy to go inside and rest awhile, and I went around the lake and sat with Carin awhile and thought about many things.

THROAT
By Adolf Hitler

This had to be it. I'd always known. I'd get it somewhere. And I'd get it before destiny. It was horrible. My throat hurt all the time and my voice squeaked. My great voice was going to be stilled even before my body. I was going to be devoured.

"Herr Professor, tell me the truth," I said. "Is it cancerous?"

"I don't know. I'll have to operate in the hospital."

"No, not there. Do it here. I was in too many hospitals during the war. I'll never go back. If this is the end, I have only to start looking for a successor."

The polyp was removed and tested. This time it was benign. But that wasn't really it. There'd be trouble somewhere.

CONCILIATION
By Adolf Hitler

I could not have been more shocked, hurt and deeply alarmed. Despite my honorable and publicly stated intentions, the French, British and Italians huddled in Stresa in April and complained, in effect, that Germany wanted the same right and capability they possessed, namely that of self-protection. The ominous tone of their condemnation was soon greatly exacerbated by France signing a nonaggression pact with Russia, and Russia doing the same with Czechoslovakia. These nations were clearly trying to weave a noose around my neck.

Compelled to respond, I meticulously prepared a speech to deliver to the Reichstag and the world. Between final practice sessions I signed into being the Reich Defense Law. This confidential decree, certainly not one that concerned those already hostile, expanded the duties of Dr. Hjalmar Schacht and harnessed his economic genius as Plenipotentiary-General for the War Economy. We definitely needed a war economy. I also ordered our armed forces to reorganize, and assigned a new and inspiring name: The Wehrmacht. I loved those words and said them a lot.

Never had I felt more tranquil, friendly and authoritative than when I stepped tall and straight to the podium on the evening of May twenty-first. As an experienced international statesman, recently grown even more in stature due to discourse with aristocratic English diplomats, I began by explaining: "Wars and the rivers of blood shed therein have not in any way brought about results comparable to the horrific sacrifices. Nations have always retained their intrinsic characteristics despite hostilities that were prompted by dynastic egotism, political passion and patriotic blindness. There are many better and more lasting benefits than any conceivably gained by war. War can only destroy the flower of a nation."

I proceeded to give recent examples of Germany's goodwill, then stated: "I solemnly recognize and guarantee France her frontiers. For Poland I guarantee our commitment to national integrity, as demonstrated by our nonaggression pact with that great nation. Our intentions toward Austria are equally benign. We have no wish to interfere in Austria's internal affairs nor do we desire to absorb Austria through an Anschluss. I likewise promise to keep the Rhineland demilitarized, even though it is undeniably our territory.

"What Germany wants most of all is a series of bilateral nonaggression pacts with key European nations. Germany is willing to agree to any limitation which leads to abolition of the heaviest arms that are especially suited for aggression. I also offer to take part in a process that might someday abolish submarines. And I reiterate my offer to the British to limit our navy to a mere thirty-five percent of theirs. For Germany, this demand is final and abiding."

Then I concluded: "The flames of war, if ignited in Europe, will cause only chaos. We Germans, however, are resolved to bring about not a decline in the West but a renaissance. This is our proud hope and unshakable belief."

NEVER
By Eva Braun

I could not understand. We had been having a fantastic time, just us alone, and he told me it was fine if I went to Munich's ball later that night, at midnight. I had been invited a long time before by the wife of a party official, and it would have been rude not to go. He promised I could see him the following day, Sunday, but he did not call and ignored all my calls and messages. When I heard he was leaving, I rushed to the station but was too late, and could only stand near the tracks and watch lights at the rear of the train fade into darkness.

He just stopped seeing me. He stopped calling. He stopped sending notes and presents. It was as if I no longer existed. I bought more sleeping pills but still couldn't stop thinking. He must have found someone else. All the times he had told me how madly in love he was, it just meant at that instant for certain purposes. I couldn't help but think he might really be ashamed of me. He always arranged to have it look like I was just his photographer's salesgirl. We never went out, just the two of us. To see him I always had to sneak in alone someplace late at night.

He wasn't at all secretive about being seen and photographed with other women. Often I picked up the newspaper and saw some perfect actress grinning as she sat next to him at the opera or somewhere else very public. And the humiliations grew much worse. Now when he came to Munich, I had to find out where he was going to be, then stand in a crowd and watch. One time I waited three hours while he ate lunch in a hotel with actress Anny Ondra, who was married to the famous boxer Max Schmeling. Everyone in the street kept talking about what Adolf and Anny must have been doing.

After weeks of being alone nights and not hearing from him, I was so happy he invited me to the Four Seasons Hotel. Just before dinner he had me brought into a private room, and I thought he was going to hug me. Instead, he just leaned over and whispered, "I'm going to let you sit next to me during dinner, but I don't want you to talk to me, not a word. It wouldn't look right if we talked."

So I sat there while everyone else talked to him, and afterward, without even a word, he gave me an envelope of money. I wish he could have said something nice.

Sometimes I tried to talk with my parents and oldest sister, Ilse, but they told me I was a fool to be involved with a man like him, and even more foolish to stay involved after being treated like that. They did not understand. I could never stop loving him. By late May I knew I had to get a response, or else. I mailed a letter telling him just how I felt. I hoped he would care and get in touch. If he didn't by ten o'clock tonight, I was going to relieve myself forever. Please let him call me, even if he's angry, I prayed. Please let him show me he's thinking. Nothing happened by ten, or later, or in the morning, so I took all my sleeping pills and lay on my bed. Soon I stopped crying and did not hurt anymore, and things were already changing, and I never wanted to wake up as darkness came. Slowly the haze did begin to wear away, though, and there was Ilse, sitting beside the bed, stroking my hair.

"I'm so glad I work for a doctor," she said.

Soon the Jewish doctor was there, and my parents, too. "Eva just had an accident," Ilse said. "She's emotionally exhausted. That's all it is."

The next day I got a call.

"My sweet little one, I'm so sorry to hear you're so tired."

"I've been very tired lately, and very lonely."

"I've been so very busy lately, I haven't taken good enough care of you."

"I think even when busy you need some time for pleasure," I said.

"I do. Of course I do."

"I need to see you more."

"Are you sure you were just tired? You didn't try anything foolish, did you?"

"For six years all I've been trying to do is make you happy."

"I know, and you've made me very happy."

"I'm so unhappy when you ignore me."

"I won't do that again. I promise. I love you too much."

"I'm so unhappy living with my parents. I have no privacy."

"I told you I'd someday get you a house, and now's the perfect time. One of your sisters can live with you. I can't have you alone. I'd be too worried."

"I'd still like a dog to keep me company."

"I'll get you a dog, and I'll spend all the time with you I can, little one. I don't think I can live without you. You must promise me you'll take care of yourself."

"I promise. You know I'll do anything you want."

DIPLOMATIC ASSERTIVENESS
By Joachim von Ribbentrop

Jealous Nazi slobs often said I was an unqualified newcomer, but in fact I had long been a sophisticated man of the world. Raised in the family of an officer, I received a very sound education and studied languages in France as well as Germany. At age seventeen I moved to Canada and worked as a merchant and learned much about that country, and America, and became quite fluent in English. In 1914, as a patriotic German, I'd immediately returned home to volunteer for duty, and served with such distinction I was awarded the Iron Cross First Class. Some insecure detractors claimed I didn't deserve the award because I had to petition for it. That is nonsense because the Fatherland only awards the distinguished.

After the war I had resumed an international lifestyle through my new business of exporting wine and champagne. My primary customers were the French and English. I gained additional experience by writing a newsletter that explained Germany's need for strength and a healthy antagonism toward the Soviet Union. My social prominence also grew after a relative legally allowed me to add the noble and prestigious von to my name. Joachim von Ribbentrop. That sounded very good. I also looked good. I was handsome and sophisticated, and Anneliese Henckel was happy to marry me. I loved her, and hated the slander, spread by ugly Nazis, that I had married her because her father was the most successful champagne manufacturer in Germany.

The Fuehrer understood what I really was, and often asked me to interpret foreign documents and assess international developments. My expertise at once began to prove manifestly helpful. And now, in June 1935, I reigned in London as a special envoy at the naval conference pivotal to our future. All Germany really wanted was security. But Germany demanded security, and I saw no reason to play silly diplomatic games. The instant talks began, I boldly told British Foreign Secretary John Simon: "Germany must insist upon an immediate agreement that allows us to build a fleet with a mere thirty-five percent of Great Britain's tonnage. I refuse to even discuss other issues, technical ones like what kinds of ships would be allowed, until the British acknowledge our fundamental and entirely reasonable requirement for naval tonnage."

"This most difficult issue of the summit should be saved for later," said Simon.

"The essential issue has to be dealt with immediately," I insisted.

Simon because flustered and walked out. His assistants tried throughout the morning to persuade me, and continued later that day.

"Germany's position is simply not going to change," I said.

The British eventually offered to meet again tomorrow. In the board room of the Admiralty, as all of us sat high on plush red chairs around a long table, I was told Germany could have its thirty-five percent. Foreign Secretary Simon returned the following day and was very nice when we discussed specifics. The specifics did not really matter. Germany had permission, from the world's most powerful maritime nation, to build a fine navy.

With potent symbolism, we signed this agreement on June eighteenth, the one hundred twentieth anniversary of joint British and Prussian action that defeated Napoleon at Waterloo. This naval agreement was an extraordinary success for Germany, and for me. The French did not like it, of course, but the Fuehrer did, and when I got home he proclaimed I was greater than Bismarck.

CULTURE
By Adolf Hitler

"Germans have always been the procreators of all true creative art," I stated at the 1935 Party Rally in Nuremberg. "All other art is inferior. The art of the Jews is particularly worthless, especially since they are so fulsomely praised for their artistic ability. The Jews have in fact never created an original work of art because they are fundamentally incapable of originality."

As I had explained in *Mein Kampf,* but not in this September speech, the parasitic Jews derive everything they have from superior races. The Jews undermine financial institutions, then suck in rivers of money. The Jews undermine political institutions, then usurp power. The Jews

— and this is the real basis of their danger because it sets up all other machinations — undermine better races through bastardization.

Determined to safeguard the Aryan race, I established the Law For The Protection of German Blood and Honor. This critical legislation made it illegal for Germans to marry Jews and also banned Jews from having intercourse with, and thus bastardizing and diluting, the German people. To clarify this law, I drafted another that decreed only a German or someone of like blood can be a citizen. Obviously, Jews were not citizens. They had always been aliens in fact, and now they were by law.

Two days later, still in Nuremberg, I spoke to a special gathering of the Reichstag and pronounced: "These laws are good for Jews since they lessen the dangers presented by them and therefore could create tolerable relations between Germans and Jews. If, however, the omnipresent Jewish agitation cannot be lessened, then these measures — the Nuremberg Laws — will have to be reconsidered. Perhaps my leniency will be betrayed."

CONQUEROR
By Benito Mussolini

I ordered the marble maps huge. They had to be huge to show the tremendous scope of the Roman Empire. I loved to look at the maps. The maps proved we Romans were the greatest people ever and Caesar was the greatest man ever. I was as great as Caesar. I knew I could be. My animal instincts were always right. I knew that for men war has every bit the natural importance that maternity has for women. Women were always having babies. Now it was time for men to go to war. I knew I was greater than Napoleon. He was a cuckold. I was more qualified to lead men. There definitely was no doubt I was brave, but I was so lacking in vanity I admitted to myself that I had to prove it.

I showed subordinates how capable I was. They were not allowed to contradict me. That would have impeded my innate correctness. I alone made decisions, and no one could be permitted to fill my head with absurdities. I was, after all, the Duce. The Duce knew war was paramount. We had to expand. The dynamism of fascism was at stake.

So was my prestige. I ordered massive preparations. Ethiopia contained untold prizes, extraordinary natural resources — oil, coal, diamonds, gold. By conquest we could solidify the colonies we already had, Somalia and Eritrea, and establish an Italian juggernaut in Africa poised to dominate in many directions.

I could do what I wanted. Italy, rapidly approaching preeminence, was less troubled than other European nations. I knew Germany had problems because I discussed with France the possibility of defending Austrian independence, and if necessary even smashing the Nazis. I also reminded the French about something that already worried them: England's growing closeness to the Nazis. England and France were, at any rate, declining and pacifistic nations, and afraid of me.

By contrast, I was absolutely fearless. Every time I announced another of the dozens of flagrant atrocities committed by the Ethiopians against us, atrocities that demanded we respond aggressively, I told my staff and implied to the world that I was ready for much fighting. I was ready to fight England and destroy its fleet in the Mediterranean. I might therefore need to capture Suez, Gibraltar and Malta. If necessary, I could also destroy France, perhaps with Germany's help. It did not matter. War did not frighten me. I had too many urgent plans. Egypt would probably need to be conquered, and the Sudan and Kenya and British Somaliland. I knew I could mobilize ten million soldiers in one day if needed. These plans were realistic. They simply required courage.

Thousands of sirens and bells galvanized the nation on October second and called some thirty million Italians into the streets and plazas to hear my declaration of war. The following day I attacked, with appropriate moral justification, the Ethiopian town of Adowa. It was there, in 1896, that black savages castrated several thousand virile Italian soldiers. Now my planes bombed and machine-gunned the savages and destroyed their worthless homes. Soon, I announced to the world: "The Ethiopians are ecstatic about their opportunity to be uplifted by superior Western civilization."

In order to save valuable Italian lives, it became necessary to employ mustard gas, a very effective and legitimate secret act of war. The League of Nations condemned my attack but Italians were aroused by such hypocrisy. While England and France, and even the United States, decadent democracies all, complained and used ineffectual sanctions, the Fuehrer sold us arms and natural resources. He wanted to be on the winning side.

RHINELAND
By Adolf Hitler

I was tired a lot and sleepy but could not sleep, and I kept worrying everyone might forget about me. There were signs. That would be it. I told followers: "I'll kill myself if I can't do what Germany needs."

Inevitably, I began to be alerted to possibilities. Now might really be the time, I realized. Political and psychological opportunities, which only I could perceive and which might never reappear, had to be taken advantage of right away. I could not forever permit French forces uncontested access into Germany. That's what they had — a Rhineland long demilitarized by foreign decree.

I tried to be friendly to the French. I told them German aggression was not possible. Instead of publicizing that, the sneaky French voted to ratify the previously-signed mutual defense pact with the Soviet Union, and only afterward did they acknowledge my peaceful position.

French treachery facilitated my decision and fortified my resolve. Germany definitely had to remilitarize the Rhineland in 1936. I gave orders to ready the operation. It was set for March seventh, a Saturday. The generals, including Blomberg, responded with timidity. They said French troops, if they attacked, would have overwhelming superiority against our small force of occupation. The generals, unlike me, did not understand the French were politically torn, spiritually decayed, and lacked essential determination.

Only to be creative did I determine how long I would have the option to cancel the operation. After all, in twenty-four hours I might need to improvise. I did not think so. But I thought all night. It was possible the French would attack when we entered the Rhineland. I could not be certain, not alone in the dark. Actually, the French response was quite unpredictable. But I was sure I knew. I had to know. I kept thinking about it, concentrating, rolling on my right shoulder and wrenching onto my left, wresting sheets from the mattress, forever assuming the ultimate responsibilities of command.

At sunrise on Saturday my troops tromped in straight columns west

241

across the Rhine and were bestowed German cheers of liberation and bouquets of gratitude. Later that morning I addressed the Reichstag, and the response was hysterical as I revealed: "German soldiers are at this moment marching into the Rhineland."

France's agreement with Russia had nullified our previous commitment to keep the Rhineland demilitarized. That was no longer compatible with our security. Now we needed only peace. We certainly had no territorial demands to make in Europe. In diplomatic communiqués delivered today, I offered to sign a twenty-five year nonaggression pact with France, and similar pacts with other countries, and additionally I offered to rejoin the League of Nations.

France could not deny the Rhineland was German. I knew the British understood. All my sources indicated they would not fight over this. But I was not positive about the French. I thought they would not. But what if they did? In the whole Rhineland we had only twenty thousand troops. The French could attack with ten times that. On Sunday, when the French started to reinforce their bastion of defense — the Maginot Line — General von Blomberg panicked and urged me to retreat, at least partially.

I was not going to retreat. The next day I toured the Rhineland and gave an oration in Cologne. My confidence inspired Germans and discouraged foreigners, especially the French. I was very stern. The French would not attack. We really could not stand that. My twenty years of sacrifice for the German nation could be destroyed if they attacked. I had to bet they would not. But I kept thinking — if I were the French, I definitely would. I would attack hard and right away. I would already have attacked. What if the French attacked? That burned my nerves. But my nerves were born of steel, and I withstood the fire.

The League of Nations met on March twelfth and condemned Germany. Again the generals panicked and wanted to retreat. Blomberg, in particular, played the weak-kneed coward. I was not going to retreat now. The French might not attack. If they did not, there would be no compulsion to retreat. I told my staff that the world belongs to the brave. A hero cannot retreat when he is not attacked. The French might not attack. They in fact did not. I fooled the French and showed my generals they were Prussian baboons. Ninety-nine percent of Germans voted to approve my move. Now we had to fortify the West.

MY WAY
By Adolf Hitler

I did not really want to get up but usually I did. I got up when I wanted. Creative forces determined the time. I therefore arose quite late. When I got up, everything had to be right, no matter where I was. The quilts were folded just so, and a night table stood on my right, and nearby there was always a picture of my mother. I gained strength from that.

I arose very slowly. There was no reason to rush. Even slowly it did not feel good, and always I strained up and sat on the edge of the bed. I needed to lean forward and put my face in my hands to try to feel better. After awhile I stood in a daze, then walked to the door and unlocked it. I did not want anyone nearby as I reached out and felt around for newspapers and dispatches on the table next to the door. Only after I had shaved, bathed and dressed did I permit anyone to see the Fuehrer.

My breakfast was sweet and eaten rapidly so I could be in my office most days by noon or so. I did not like going to the office since there I had to meet many boring officials. They stacked "urgent reports" on my desk dealing with economics and other crappy domestic matters, and I just could not read those things more than ten seconds.

"This will keep," I reminded my officials.

If they persisted with a presentation, I got a little sleepy and did not hear much, and would have to stop their blabbering and ignite energy by telling them about my dreams of building cities on an unprecedented scale and with incomparable skill. I also reminded these simpletons about the imperatives of my foreign policy.

If anyone tried to bore me again, I pounced on the nearest newspaper and started reading. As soon as I put the newspaper down, I left. I could go anywhere, and often I went on picnics. I liked long slow drives, and troublesome officials certainly could not come. I liked my picnics far too much for that.

At night I was tired and wanted a relaxed and happy atmosphere. My servants and secretaries were nice company, and we gathered almost every night for movies. I watched many movies and saw the good ones lots of times and did not allow bad ones to run more than a few minutes. I liked many foreign films but most could not be seen by Germans. Greta Garbo might have been all right but a lot would not.

Afterward, while everyone sat around a fire, I discoursed about many stimulating things. At four in the morning I was still articulating my dreams, and fascinated followers listened until they fell asleep.

SPAIN
By Adolf Hitler

After coming down from the theater on the hill, buoyed as always by a night at the Wagner Festival, I received a letter from a General Franco of Spain. He desperately needed my help to battle the communists. Italy's aid was not enough.

Goering was also in Bayreuth, and I ordered him to come over right away.

"Yes, Mein Fuehrer, I also received a letter."

"I've already made the decision. Franco must have our help."

"You're right."

"It would be catastrophic if the communists took over in Spain and allied with leftists already in France, and thereby created a vise with the Bolsheviks to crush us."

I pressed my palms hard against each other.

"The strategic implications are very grave, indeed. I hope you'll let me unleash my Luftwaffe."

"The Luftwaffe will certainly be represented in Spain," I said. "We'll send planes and pilots as well as advisers."

"We can smash the communists right away."

"There'll be plenty of smashing, all right. But we must be restrained."

OLYMPIAN
By Adolf Hitler

The 1936 Summer Olympics in Berlin proved Germany's greatness in every sphere, and showed that negro-jungle-runner Jesse Owens' primitive speed was irrelevant. The real story, ignored by cowardly foreign journalists, was a white racial delight. National Socialist Germany won far more medals than any other nation. The United States was a very distant runner-up. Germany beat the Americans thirty-three to twenty-four in the race for gold medals, twenty-six to twenty for silver, and thirty to twelve for bronze. That makes you think.

NEW HOME
By Eva Braun

The Fuehrer's half-sister, Angela, who should have stuck to keeping house, often blistered me in front of lots of important wives. Once was so bad. I wanted to scream I was glad her daughter, Geli, had died. But I just boiled inside. Eventually, the Fuehrer heard something. And he asked.

I turned away.

"I can't tell you," I said.

"I want to know what my sister said."

"I just cannot tell you." I walked away when he tried to put his hands on my shoulders.

"You must tell me, my little sweet."

I sobbed, a little at first, then broke down and put my face into knuckles.

"I have to know what she said."

I took the tissue I had been squeezing and dabbed tears on my face, then blew my nose. He came to me and put his soft warm hands around my cheeks.

"Please, I need to know."

"Your sister said, 'You're just a stupid blond preying on my brother like a streetwalker.'"

"She'll never drag my private life in front of everyone again."

The Fuehrer got a new housekeeper on the Obsersalzberg. He also decided to really expand the house. He drew all the plans himself and called the place the Berghof, and everything became quite beautiful. In the Berghof we had a huge living room with a fireplace and a gigantic window that gave us a fabulous view of the ancient and famous

Untersberg Peak. There was a large deck outside to lounge and sunbathe on, and inside we had a huge dining room with the largest oak table I'd ever seen.

My private quarters were fantastic. I had a living room, and a bedroom with walls of silk I loved to rub against, and sumptuous furniture that made me feel good. My bathroom had a big marble bathtub, a gift from the Duce, and I always felt so nice as I lay in the tub and tickled myself with soap. This room attached my bedroom to the Fuehrer's, and I loved it when he wanted me to come.

"I saw you looking at those paintings this evening," I said.

Adolf smiled.

"The women have beautiful bodies and very big bosoms, much bigger than mine."

"Your figure is much nicer than theirs."

"Is my body nicer than the women's in all those books."

"Of course it is."

I undressed, smiling as I did so, and then lay on his bed, looking up and running my hands up and down my warm smooth body.

"I love you very much," I whispered.

"I love you, too."

"Please come here. I need you. That's right, darling. Oh, that feels so good. Come down on me. That feels so incredibly good. I love you on me. But darling, please, take off your clothes."

"Not now, sweet one, I don't feel like that just yet."

EMINENT GUEST
By Adolf Hitler

In dark stinking foxholes, I had thought about him a lot. I thought about how I'd like to kill David Lloyd George, Britain's wartime prime minister and our greatest enemy. He called us barbarians and said he wanted to hang the Kaiser. Down in the dark holes, I had feared this powerful man. But now it was he coming to me.

At the Berghof, Lloyd George and I got on well. We shared the dream of lasting peace between Germany and England, and I emphasized our common race and culture. I also stated: "The danger to Germany lies not across the English Channel but primarily to the

East, the den of Bolshevism. If Bolshevism is unchecked, it would quickly spread across the continent. That we will not tolerate."

The handsome, gray-maned Lloyd George was clearly fascinated by me. And as he traveled across Germany in September and saw our swift rise in employment, unlike in his own country, and heard the cheers for me and felt our dynamism, he understood how far Germany had come, and how far she could go. Soon after leaving he wrote an article that declared I was a great and fearless leader lionized by all.

CLOSER FRIENDSHIP
By Adolf Hitler

I was so happy to meet the Duce's son-in-law, Count Galeazzo Ciano, a dashing fellow barely in his thirties. He came to the Berghof in October 1936 to represent his father-in-law, and his country, as foreign minister.

"Count Ciano, I want you to know that for many years I've felt the Duce is the world's preeminent statesman, and in fact no one now living has the remotest right to even be compared to him. It was perhaps the greatest honor of my life to have met him, and I thank God my friendship with the Duce, and your country, is continuing to grow.

"As nations, Count Ciano, we couldn't possibly be more complementary. Our ideologies, our dynamism, our burgeoning might — all make us the most natural of allies. I know a coalition between us would be absolutely invincible."

"I couldn't be more in accordance with your views," Ciano said. "It's important that Italy be a reliable friend of Germany because both us have had so few worthy allies."

"That is true, tragically."

"It was particularly galling to the Duce, and to me, when we saw this telegram from Britain's ambassador in Berlin to his superiors in London."

Ciano handed me the message and watched me read.

"So here we have more British treachery," I said, and Ciano nodded. "Those effete snobs think they're the only ones entitled to pursue vital interests. They call me dangerous. They call me an adventurer. They

247

say I'm upsetting the balance of things in Europe. They say the same about Italy. This is nothing more than garbage, hypocritical garbage. The current leaders of England, Stanley Baldwin and the rest of those moles, are merely jealous of the Duce and me because we have the verve and talent that England's leaders used to have.

"I assure you, Count Ciano, England is a listing battleship. Her military programs are lagging in every way. German rearmament is way ahead. And so is Italy's. I hope to make an accommodation with England. It would certainly be in her self-interest. But if necessary, England can be crushed. We can crush her. We can form an invincible coalition to defend ourselves against Bolshevism and the democracies."

"That is reasonable," Ciano replied.

Three days later Ciano and Foreign Minister Constantin von Neurath signed a secret document that committed Germany and Italy to a common and mutually beneficial future in foreign affairs.

The Duce was so enthused he soon publicly called the Berlin-Rome relationship an Axis around which the rest of Europe would revolve while collaborating for peace.

NEW ALLY
By Joachim von Ribbentrop

I should have been made Foreign Minister so I could use my international experience to Germany's advantage. But I also knew there were many opportunities as ambassador to Great Britain. I spoke English so well, and understood the British better than they understood themselves, and was still close enough to hop back across the Channel to be involved in strategic planning and not worry about old Nazi slobs ruining the grand diplomatic process I often discussed with the Fuehrer.

In England I met and was courted by many royal personages who had heard so much about my performance at the naval conference last year. Many of England's important politicians and military men also cultivated me. Despite these contacts, and in spite of the growing communist menace in Spain, the British government had yet to heed my calls to ally itself with Germany.

In the meantime, in November, I again stunned the world with a diplomatic tour de force, the Anti-Comitern Pact with Japan. This powerful and dynamic nation of brown-skinned pygmies shared with us an intense hatred and distrust of Bolshevik Russia. Our agreement, in addition to symbolic unity, contained secret protocols that guaranteed, in event of a Soviet attack, we would hold discussions about shared interests and would not in any way aid the Russians. We additionally vowed not to sign any agreements with the Soviet Union that violated the essence of our growing concern about, and unity against, international Bolshevism.

In December Germany lost its most influential friend in England when King Edward abdicated so he could marry his divorced girlfriend. The Fuehrer was thunderstruck. I too was displeased but still confident I could help the British comprehend their vital interests.

HITLER YOUTH
By Baldur von Schirach

The Fuehrer decreed the Hitler Youth Law, and on the first day of December 1936 I pronounced that every thought, act and goal of every youth must be forged by the party into one dynamic and unified will. This enormous task required that training start at age six, when boys joined the Pimpf and began careers as committed and ideologically sound citizens. At age ten, qualified boys were promoted to the Young Folk to serve four years until ready for the main body of the Hitler Youth. The best boys later progressed into the Labor Service and the Wehrmacht. German girls became Young Maidens at age ten and progressed to the League of German Maidens at the pubescent age of fourteen.

We trained our youths to march and parachute and keep their bodies strong. And in communal settings, we inculcated values essential to defending our nation: courage, self-sacrifice, and the ability to bear pain. Teachers in regular schools were notified that the leading children in the Hitler Youth should not be admonished for lackluster class work since they spent so much energy on more important tasks. Parents also had to understand our unequivocal position: "The rearing of young people is an inalienable sovereign right of the state." Those failing to promptly enroll their children in the Hitler Youth might well go to prison. As the organization grew to more than six million, my job became so crucial that I often preceded the Fuehrer at the podium and spoke to cheering youths all over Germany.

Less prestigious Nazis sometimes claimed that I had a soft face and effeminate tastes in the bedroom. That was slanderous. I had a wife, and she was Heinrich Hoffmann's daughter, and I did not decorate our bedroom and was not effeminate. Some simply could not accept that I was tough despite having had an aristocratic father. I did not need to grow up in an alley to be rough. I also tried to ignore jokes about my American-born mother having two ancestors who signed the Declaration of Independence. None of those things threatened me because I surely was man enough to be the one Adolf Hitler trusted to make sure all German youths were focused and tough.

THE CURE
By Doctor Theodore Morell

This was going to be a special Christmas season. My wife and I were going to be the guests of Heinrich Hoffmann, who sent his private plane to fly us to Munich. Hoffmann was grateful to me since my revolutionary ministrations had recently cured him of alcoholism and homosexual tendencies. No matter what the ailment, I could usually cure it. That's why my elite practice in Berlin included lots of actors and actresses.

On Christmas day Hoffmann drove us down to the Berghof. The Fuehrer really wanted to meet me. He needed a special doctor. All of his others had failed. And he was miserable. His stomach and digestive track were pulverizing him, and he suffered from severe gas. In addition, he had not been sleeping much, and his legs were covered with eczema so bad he couldn't even get his boots on.

The Fuehrer asked to speak to me privately, then offered to make me his personal physician. I agreed, and soon examined him as thoroughly as he'd let me.

"Don't worry," I said, "I'll have you healthy again in less than a year."

I suspected the Fuehrer's intestinal track contained many bad kinds of coli bacilli. They disrupted his digestion. A laboratory examination of the Fuehrer's stool soon confirmed my diagnosis. I immediately prescribed Mutaflor capsules, which contained the good coli bacilli. I also gave him lots of anti-gas pills and vitamins and heart-extract and liver-extract, and before long he was eating well and feeling good and his eczema had gone away. The Fuehrer was so grateful he bragged about me to other doctors and all his friends.

MODEL NATION
By Adolf Hitler

From all over the world came this request: let us come and study Germany. I was thrilled by the interest and planned to be a gracious host. I wanted foreigners to come and experience our economic revival. I wanted them to see the contented faces of people who had good jobs. I wanted them to feel our national camaraderie. I wanted foreigners to behold our proliferating autobahns and our beautiful buildings. I wanted them to come and share my vision of immaculate cities, cities so brilliantly conceived and structured that everyone would have plenty of room to walk, drive, work and play, cities on our drawing boards soon to be real. These were things everyone should see.

NECKTIE
By A Valet

"Hurry. You've only got ten seconds," the Fuehrer urged as he handed me his necktie.

I put the necktie around my neck and worked fast. The Fuehrer was holding his breath, nose clamped with thumb and finger, cheeks puffed way out, and he nodded as each second ticked off. Helped greatly by all the practice I'd had, I wrapped one side twice around the other, pushed the big long end through the loop, and pulled a loose knot just after the ninth second.

The Fuehrer exhaled, greatly relieved, and smiled very big as I handed him his tie, ready to go.

STRENGTH THROUGH JOY
By Robert Ley

I knew a real man needed a woman, and any man who did not get one by his mid-twenties, at the latest, was a diffident lump of questionable masculinity and one not likely to procreate for the good of the state, which was everyone's duty. I loved to procreate, especially after I had my drinks. I did not like back talk after drinking, or before, either, so I often had an extra woman, a wife on my left arm and a girlfriend on my right.

The Fuehrer knew what I could do. A few years back, he had put me in charge of the German Labor Front. Now, with twenty-five million members in my organization, I must have been the second most popular man in the Reich, and always made sure agitators did not misrepresent the workers' true best interests. Fortunately, the Fuehrer had long ago banned trade unions, strikes and the like. Now no one could be fired without our permission. The workers, and everyone else, also benefited tremendously from Strength Through Joy, an organization that controlled all aspects of leisure and fun and made sure everyone got enough relaxation to be happy and productive. There was really no reason for any club to remain independent, not when the party could do things so much better. Even poor provincial people now got to attend operas and plays, which we arranged and sent to every corner of Germany. All sporting activities were also much more fun now that people had communal recreation and at the same time prepared their bodies for military service.

The most impressive part of Strength Through Joy was the Travel and Tourism Bureau. This provided an opportunity for countless simple Germans, who otherwise never could have, to take luxury cruises. We built a dozen beautiful white ships, including the Robert Ley, and for extremely reasonable rates took tens of thousands on dream cruises in the North Sea and on the Mediterranean. In the morning everyone did calisthenics together, and in the evening everyone sang, and everything was very organized and fun, and everyone talked about what a great deal it was.

PROPER EDUCATION
By Bernhard Rust

I was awarded the Iron Cross First Class during the Great War and did not let it bother me long when I was shot in the head. I think many non-Nazis resented that I had been shot, and some accused me of being not quite right. That was absurd. I was the Reich Minister of Science, Education and Popular Culture, and very capable of giving the proper shape and emphasis to German education.

I made sure we had the right kind of teachers. Every teacher had to belong to the National Socialist Teachers' League, and those who would not join or who we did not want were run off. Maybe a quarter of the university professors were dismissed. The rest were enthusiastic about National Socialism and wanted a strong and resolute Germany. We established training camps for professors to ensure ideological soundness and provide an opportunity for them to throw away their pseudo-intellectual training and embrace the new unmuddled vigor already enjoyed by the masses.

We did not want, and in fact could not tolerate, a nation of skinny, squinty-eyed intellectuals. We had to teach the real values and most essential facts. Racial biology therefore became a compulsory course for students of all ages. They learned about the importance of good Nordic genes and the degeneracy of mixing with inferior races. This lesson was linked with studies in geography, which underscored our urgent need for living space.

To emphasize our shift away from decadent intellectual pursuits, we instituted several hours of daily physical education. Students were taught to run and tumble, box and fence, and glide and sail and row. I was proud every time I toured a school and saw all our smiling, muscular youths learning so much and becoming so motivated. Any wimps were unlikely to be permitted to go to college. A well-trained body was definitely a prerequisite for a worthwhile mind.

DER STUERMER
By Julius Streicher

Slimy scum suckers were graphically portrayed in my paper, Der Stuermer. I didn't withhold any crap for anyone. Cartoons, photos, gross god-damn sex organs — Der Stuermer had everything, and a huge circulation, a half million. Sure, people knew me as a district leader and the most powerful man in Nuremberg. I was also a hell of a speaker. All that helped. But my paper was most important and the favorite of so many. That included the Fuehrer, who often bragged he read every page.

There was a lot to show and tell. Stinking Jewish doctors with grimy, vagina-rubbing hands had to be publicized. Avoid those bastards, my paper blared. Ten thousand Germans wrote in every week agreeing. They also learned to beware child-molesting Jews. It was O.K., though, for me to screw some kid. If he complained, there might be plenty of trouble.

Jews weren't the only problems. Some goddamn Nazis were bad, too. A lot of them were perverts, effeminate as hell. Goering, for example. That fat-ass must have had his balls cut off. I could tell he was impotent. He wasn't the only one. I hated the bastards. I'd like to have horsewhipped their asses and screwed their screaming wives. The Jews deserved much worse. Der Stuermer preached that.

TRUE ART
By Adolf Hitler

I assigned my art jury to pick the very best Germanic paintings for the spectacular House of German Art in Munich. When the process of selection was well underway, I stopped by to see. Most of the chosen paintings were fine. But some were not.

"This one," I said. "You can't possibly think this one is good. What's it doing here? This is garbage. That's right, don't answer. Are you idiots? This is manure plastered on canvas. It shouldn't be here. It certainly won't be in the exhibition. And that one, over there. Yes, that one. Stand aside. That's worse. It looks worse the closer I get. I made my standards clear. What's this garbage doing here? And over there. That's right. There. Get the hell out of my way. Don't try to stand in front of it. Move. This is horrible, too. I can't stand this. You must be idiots. I told you what I wanted, what the House of German Art had to have. Oh, shit. And over there, too. There's another one. Move. Move."

Grabbing the perverted expression of the human soul, a hand on each side of the frame near the top, I grunted and lunged and kicked my right boot hard right through the canvas and yanked back, ripping even more. I flung that frame down, breaking it, and stomped to another bad painting, the jury clearing wide in my wake, and grabbed that one and jack-booted it, too, and threw it down hard and stormed around and kicked everything obscene.

By July 1937 my requirements had been realized, and people all over Munich celebrated the great opening of the House of German Art. On the walls hung several hundred of the purest expressions of healthy creativity. In my revolutionary speech I said: "We're creating a new human type, a strong joyful healthy creature, and I can't tolerate depictions of malformed cretins and cripples that bespeak a highly defective vision. If the cultural Neanderthals responsible for such abominations don't desist, then I'll certainly have them hospitalized if they're crazy, or jerked into jail if the criminal acts are intentional."

While Germans enjoyed this opportunity to see the best in art, I provided an enlightening contrast, the Exhibition of Degenerate Art, also in Munich. Thousands of perverse paintings, by lunatics like Kirchner, Kandinsky and Chagall, had been purged from our museums, and several hundred of the worst comprised a display so appalling that I ordered it taken around Germany. Almost three million paid to see what degeneracy really was, and many wrote urging us to tie up the artists next to their paintings so everyone could spit in their faces.

AGGRESSIVE ECONOMICS
By Hjalmar Schacht

If I had had a thimble, any thimble, it would have been far more than capacious enough to accommodate the collective economic knowledge of Hitler and Goering. I cannot fathom why those two charlatans dared disagree with me in the first place. My financial accomplishments were internationally acknowledged, and more than anyone I was responsible for Germany's declining unemployment and burgeoning public works programs. Our government did not have much money, but well-oiled presses printed piles of Mefo bills, which represented the promise to someday pay. I kept shuffling economic instruments like a grand card sharp, and by restrained bookkeeping was able to disguise the magnitude of our industrial surge.

But by 1936 I had warned Hitler that everything had gone far enough too fast, and we would have to slow down or face bankruptcy. I explained matters even an economic imbecile should have understood: "Our import prices are rising. Our export prices are decreasing. Our harvests have been poor two years in a row. We have shortages of many key raw materials, including fuel. We cannot forever depend on Mefo bills."

Nevertheless, in the fall of 1936, Hitler had astounded me, and everyone else who knew economics, by placing Goering in charge of the Four Year Plan for economic development and giving him unbridled backing. That made the fat one even more arrogant when I tried to explain two plus two. As the top economist in the land, and perhaps the world, I was not going to subordinate myself to a nincompoop.

In August 1937 I went to the Berghof. The Fuehrer and I sat down.

"You're too important to quit," he said.

"I must."

"But you're too important to Germany."

"If I'm so important, then why is Goering, a fine military man but no economist, given control over a program that cannot work and that could, I think will, break the country?"

"The Four Year Plan will work."

"Germany simply does not have the wherewithal to sustain itself.

We don't have the natural resources."

"Herr Reichminister, you know I'm not talking about, and have never talked about, Germany sustaining itself within its current restricted borders. That's why the war economy is so important."

"The war economy is overheated and in danger of fizzling, and I must remind you, Mein Fuehrer, that the borders of Germany cannot become unrestricted without adequate resources."

"It's always been my understanding that you don't like Germany's current borders."

"That's true. I don't."

"Then I need you to sustain an economic revival that'll expand our borders."

"I'm no longer, it seems, in a position to carry on in a way commensurate with my abilities."

"Your abilities are paramount to our needs."

"I believe, Mein Fuehrer, that Goering's abilities have been deemed paramount."

"Goering is a great man."

"Indeed."

"And so are you."

"Thank you, Mein Fuehrer. I believe in you and have served you enthusiastically. But I must now resign."

"You can't resign."

"I must."

"It would look bad."

"I believe I've more than adequately stated my reasons."

"A complete withdrawal from my administration would be most damaging."

"I simply cannot continue as Plenipotentiary-General for the War Economy. That is my position."

The Fuehrer got up and turned away, clasping his hands in back. He bounced them tautly while he looked out the window. Then he turned around.

"All right, Herr Reichminister. You can resign that post. But I can't announce it for a couple of months."

"That's fine."

"Good. You'll still retain your position as President of the Reichsbank. Compared to your massive duties to date, that shouldn't be uncongenial."

"I can do that, yes."

"And it will be necessary, though of course no burden on you, to retain you in the cabinet as a Minister without Portfolio. We need your prestige, and your counsel, if you choose to give it."

"That, too, is fine."

"Herr Reichminister, thank you for helping to keep things looking good."

GERMAN WELCOME
By Benito Mussolini

I ordered specially tailored uniforms. I was not taking civilian clothes on something like this. I tried on many uniforms in front of the mirror and stood tall straight and big-chested as I studied myself. Only the best fitting uniforms were chosen for this September 1937 tour, which began in Munich with throngs at the train station shouting "Duce, Duce." Hitler stepped up to greet me warm two-handed on a long red carpet, and on the drive to his apartment we rolled between busts of the great Roman emperors, my predecessors. The Fuehrer provided an interpreter I did not need.

"Duce, millions of Germans are anxious to greet you. There's so much we want you to see."

Hitler still seemed a little strange, his eyes glowing like those of a crazed cat. But he was more of a man now.

"I'm sick of the English," I told him. "They're a nation of feeble old people who utterly lack the resolve to defend themselves. Their women are even afraid to bear children. They can't withstand pain. Their whole nation is in decline. Their navy is absolutely abominable compared to Italy's. The Italian Navy can destroy Britain in the Mediterranean."

"The Mediterranean is certainly your bailiwick, Duce. You should dominate the region. We want you to. And I know you understand we have our vital regions, Germanic regions like Austria."

"I grant that Austria is very important to you."

"I'm delighted you understand."

"Certainly I understand. I'm appalled by the same things you are. The Bolsheviks, for instance, are a horrendous threat in the East, and elsewhere. If it weren't for my commitment in Spain, the Bolsheviks might take over there, too."

"Bolshevism absolutely must be stopped, Duce. Thank God for your efforts in Spain."

"We're doing quite well in Spain, Fuehrer, despite what the British newspapers have been saying. They're making the most scandalous statements about the Italian military because they're jealous. We're performing much better than the democracies want to believe. You were wise to get away from them and withdraw from the League of Nations. We'll soon withdraw, too. I want no association with any of them. France is obviously everything that is despicable."

"It is, Duce, it is," the Fuehrer said. "France could be our greatest enemy. It's as Jewified as anywhere."

"I want you to understand, Fuehrer, that I'm aware of the Jews. Italy is prepared to publicize the Jewish problem with increasing commitment. And in accordance with our overall common thrust in foreign policy, we're also ready, as you've done, to expand ties with Japan."

"Those are marvelous ideas, Duce, marvelous."

For the next few September days, the Fuehrer and I toured massive factories where big furnaces generated endless lines of products taken immediately to warehouses bulging with energy. Germany was red hot. I could feel it and told the Fuehrer so. He was very proud, especially as we arrived at Mecklenburg to watch Wehrmacht maneuvers.

"In our entire history, Duce, these are the biggest military maneuvers, the very biggest military maneuvers by far."

German artillery covered the horizon with exploding shells, and the panzers, more than I could count, almost more than I could estimate, drove forth fast and mobile and struck me as powerful steel instruments of conquest, leading infantrymen with rifles in strong hands. Overhead, the Luftwaffe provided coordinated support with bombs and machine gun bursts.

"We're developing a new kind of warfare, Duce."

I nodded, my strong jaw still firm and impassive. My military experts had assured me Germany was still not as strong as Italy.

A few days later I was en route to the German capital. As my train got close, I undid my wide belt and put it back on, tighter, and straightened it, and made sure my fascisti hat was straight on my shaved Roman head. Then I looked out the window and saw that

Hitler's train, unannounced, had appeared alongside mine chugging in unison as if we were on one train, one axis, moving toward Berlin. The Fuehrer's train eventually eased ahead, and on the station platform he was waiting to welcome me for our ride into the heart of the city. Next to each other we stood in an open car that moved very slowly. One million Germans overwhelmed the streets, and all of them roared into me like thunder as their hearts beat so hard and fast my feet melted the floor of the car. The Fuehrer insisted I step out first. I hesitated. I wanted him to go first. I motioned with my hands. This was his country. This was all his. No, no, his friendly sweep told me, you go first, Duce, this Germany is for you, our most special guest. On the reception stand I smiled and pointed at the Fuehrer and nodded.

The next night, before a huge throng in Olympic Stadium, bright spotlights ignited the sky and ten thousand torches, flowing in unison, formed a river of fire. In his speech the Fuehrer proclaimed: "The Duce's genius alone is responsible for the resurgence of Italy. He is one of those lonely men of the ages on whom history is not tested, but who themselves are the makers of history."

In my speech, delivered in loud, energetic German, I boomed that our two nations had to be reckoned with because we were resolute and unified and comprised one hundred fifteen million people. Gesturing with a clinched fist, I promised: "I have at last found a friend I'm prepared to march with to the very end."

The uproar lifted me, and I smiled and soft pounded my chest once, a pat for everyone there, a hand of friendship. When I stepped off stage, tired and happy, I did not notice for some time it was pouring rain.

NEW QUARTERS
By A Veteran

"Didn't you hear me?"

Two men in black shirts looked like idiots.

"I said, 'I served the Fatherland during the Great War.'"

"Who'd you bribe to stay out of action," one said.

"Don't talk to me like that. You were a child. I was fighting at the front. I was decorated. Here. Look at this."

"How much did that cost?"

"Wretch. What have you ever fought for?"

"I'm fighting to clean you off the streets."

The men each took one of my arms and led me straight there. I arrived at an especially bad time. The guards were ranting: "You've brought this on yourselves. The foreign papers are attacking us again. You instigated this. You keep doing it. Try it now."

They nailed the windows shut and confined us to the barracks all the time, except for roll call and quickly eaten bad meals.

"You assholes get back in bed," a guard shouted.

"We've been in bed five weeks," I said.

"You want to be in the ground?"

"I served the Fatherland," I said. "I'm not going to live like this."

"Shut up," said another prisoner.

"Are you just going to take this?" I said.

"Shut your mouth. I'm sick of you."

"You're all sick," I said.

The prisoner lunged at me. I grabbed his greasy shirt and jerked him down and punched the back of his neck and would have continued but he stunk so bad I had to get up and some way out of Dachau.

DO I?
By A Valet

"Do I? Do I look like the Fuehrer?" he said. "I have to. I absolutely do. I really do. Of course I do. I look just like the Fuehrer."

The Fuehrer saluted into the mirror before turning and marching toward his people.

PREPARATION
1937-1939

HOSSBACH CONFERENCE
By Colonel Friedrich Hossbach

"But, Mein Fuehrer, I'm not a stenographer," I said.

"You can do it, Colonel Hossbach. Just get my general principles and aims. You can organize the memorandum later. This is quite important, Colonel, so you must take good notes."

"Jawohl."

I made sure I had plenty of paper. The Fuehrer was preparing to address the five most powerful military and diplomatic leaders in the country. A little after four p.m. on November fifth, 1937, these elite men were seated and the Fuehrer waited a moment, engrossed, then began to speak and I began to write. We had, of course, assumed this meeting would be confidential. Still, the Fuehrer riveted us by saying, "You must all vow absolute secrecy. My following statements are so vital they should be regarded as my final testament, a blueprint for action in event of my death."

We all swore secrecy, I wrote, and I hoped the Fuehrer would not start speaking too fast.

He then told us, "In order to survive, Germany has to preserve the racial community and obtain more resources. I'm not particularly interested in distant colonies in strange environments. Those things are burdens. What we must have, what we Germans have every right to have, is more living space right here on the European continent in areas contiguous with our current borders as well as places contiguous with those areas."

I glanced up. Everyone was staring at the Fuehrer.

"All space has always had a master, and an aggressor in need has eternally had to confront a possessor unwilling to relinquish his space," he said. "Therefore, Germany ultimately has to use force in order to survive. The Romans and the British expanded their empires through force, and to do so they had to take great risks. Germany, too, must now take risks. The risks are worth what we can gain, what we absolutely have to obtain. Since we know what we have to do, that reduces the equation to three simple and fundamental questions: where and when and how?"

During the brief times when Hitler was not speaking, when he was drawing a few breaths or pacing, all I could hear was the fast scratching of my pen on paper. No one else seemed to be breathing. Certainly no one else was talking as the Fuehrer stated: "Germany must begin to secure her borders by absorbing Austria and Czechoslovakia no later than six to eight years from now. We have to act by then, or our two hate-filled adversaries, Britain and France, will close the gap that has developed due to our rigorous rearmament programs. Time is also imperative because there's no guarantee how long I'll live and be able to contribute my unique talents. Fortunately, I believe that events will compel us to act much sooner than anyone can imagine. An internal crisis in France, always a possibility, would constrain the French Army and present us with a relatively unimpeded opportunity to strike Czechoslovakia. We might very soon have an even better opportunity. If Britain and France both become embroiled in a war with Italy in the Mediterranean, we could simultaneously strike Czechoslovakia and Austria. We do, at any rate, have to have Czechoslovakia and Austria in order to lay the strategic groundwork for further action then deemed necessary."

My military colleagues did not look happy but were certainly silent as Hitler enumerated our advantages: "Britain and France have probably already tacitly written off Czechoslovakia. Britain's too preoccupied with Italian aggression and its own extended and tottering empire to make a major military commitment in central Europe against Germany. The French would have to act without Britain — a risk they'd unlikely accept — and even if they did act, they couldn't be potent without help from England.

"In the East, Poland is a concern, but with Russia a constant threat, it's unlikely the Poles will expose themselves by attacking us. Russia, too, would probably be reluctant to act because of threats to its east, from Japan, which defeated Russia three decades ago and would likely be able, and willing, to do so again. All of these scenarios favor us, especially if we strike with lightening rapidity and thereby present our adversaries with faits accomplis."

The Fuehrer thus completed his statements after about three hours, and I looked up at him and put my pen down to flex tired fingers. When the Fuehrer told his commanders to respond, he sat down and I picked up my pen.

"Mein Fuehrer, we're not at all prepared for the risks you're asking the Wehrmacht to assume," said General von Blomberg, Commander in Chief of the Wehrmacht.

Hitler gazed at him.

Blomberg continued: "I think we need to take into account, for example, that the frontier fortifications in Czechoslovakia are very strong, comparable, I believe, to the Maginot Line. We could be delayed quite some time there, and losses could be heavy. That would leave us extremely vulnerable to a French attack. I believe the French would still have the wherewithal to strike us even if they were involved in a war with Italy."

"It's extremely important to keep in mind," interjected Foreign Minister von Neurath, "that France isn't at war with Italy, and I don't see the prospect that they will be engaged in hostilities. We certainly can't count on France being engaged with Italy. What indications do we have? None, really."

General von Fritsch, Commander in Chief of the Army, was very stern as he said: "This plan is much too risky. The French could easily attack the Ruhr."

"The Fuehrer has already said that great nations must take risks," Hermann Goering, Commander in Chief of the Luftwaffe, fired at Fritsch.

"There's a great difference between taking risks and committing suicide."

"I'm not sure the Commander in Chief of the Army has the heart for battle."

"I'm not sure you have the necessities to understand battle," Fritsch said. "I won't have my spirit impugned, especially by someone with an insufficient grasp of military matters."

"What the general is trying to explain," Blomberg intervened, "is that the Army is simply not ready for the dangerous tasks being discussed."

"And why is the Army not ready?" Goering asked. "Could it be the people who're supposed to be making the Army ready aren't doing so?"

"I'm building up the Army at the appropriate pace," Fritsch stated.

"Let me remind you, General von Fritsch, and General von Blomberg, that the Fuehrer determines what pace and action are appropriate."

"The Fuehrer has asked for our reaction," Fritsch said. "I must add that neither the Luftwaffe nor the Navy are ready for major conflict."

All voices were harsh, and being closeted with so much authority unnerved me. Admiral Raeder, too, must have been overwhelmed. The German Navy did not have the status of the Army. Raeder was silent. I was writing, hurriedly, but also looking up when I could. The Fuehrer was studying the debaters. When he started getting grim, I expected him to take over. But he did not. After about thirty minutes of querulous discussion, the meeting ended and Hitler left. Then Fritsch stormed out.

"Don't worry," Blomberg told Raeder. "The Fuehrer was merely trying to motivate Fritsch to strengthen the Army more rapidly."

I think Raeder felt better. He did not want to be smashed at sea.

A frantic Fritsch soon met with Hitler at Berchtesgaden, and confidential Army sources indicated the general had not persuaded the Fuehrer. Neurath also tried to get a meeting, but the Fuehrer refused to see him. Then Neurath had a heart attack. I really did not know if everyone should have been so upset because I could not be sure the Fuehrer had been speaking literally.

SHOCKING EVIDENCE
By Heinrich Himmler

A couple of years ago I'd warned the Fuehrer that an unassailable eyewitness had seen General von Fritsch engage in vile activities in a dim alley, and I also provided numerous documents in corroboration. The Fuehrer, however, had said to burn everything. In early January 1938, Goering and I met about this disgraceful matter.

"Evidence is mounting," I said. "The Fuehrer should be apprised again."

"I agree."

"When?"

"Soon," Goering said.

"I don't want to wait long. The general's a threat to the SS, physically a threat."

LOVE
General Werner von Blomberg

My life had been rather painful since 1932 when my wife of almost thirty years passed away. With my children grown and gone, I was really alone, and as my emptiness persisted I realized there probably would never be any relief. I did not want to hope too much when Erna Gruehn started working in my office a few months ago. I tried to ignore her. I never said anything more than hello, but every time I passed her desk my face got hot and the whole world changed. I really did not want to feel this way. I knew she could not be interested in me. I was almost sixty, and she was so pretty and younger even than most of my children. I thought she might like me rather like a father, or an uncle, but never all the way.

I liked Erna Gruehn more every day. She always smiled when she walked near me. I was almost certain. She was smiling at me. And the way she walked. Could she really be walking like that for me? Maybe I did have a chance. I was, after all, Germany's highest-ranking soldier, and many friends had always told me I was handsome and distinguished. I had been good with my wife, and maybe Erna would think I could be good with her, too. But maybe she would think I was much too old. Every time she looked at me, I died to find out. I really had to. One day I did.

"Fraulein Gruehn, would you care to dine with me this evening?"

She was delighted. I could tell. She was absolutely delighted. And we had a great time. What a lovely and charming girl. We saw each other a lot away from work, and I began to feel things I had not in a very long time, and was simply happy, and soon I told Erna I loved her and that, despite our difference in years, I wanted us to marry but would understand if she did not. But she did. She said she loved me and wanted to be my wife.

This was a most delicate matter. A man of my station was supposed to marry a certain kind of woman, and Erna was not from an aristocratic family. My status-obsessed colleagues on the General Staff would certainly be outraged. I decided to confide in Goering.

"General, I think it's absolutely marvelous you're getting married," he said. "I know how happy you'll be and how much this means to you. I know too well how terrible it is to lose a beloved wife and think there'll never again be any happiness, and then, by extraordinary luck, find someone else to love."

"Do you think the Fuehrer will object to her modest background?"

"I'm sure the Fuehrer will be as happy about her as I am. In our National Socialist state, everyone is equal. We don't care about old aristocratic customs. I'll call the Fuehrer right now."

Goering went into the next room and picked up the phone. I tightened as I listened to words I could not decipher. Goering reentered, grinning big, arms outspread, and said, "The Fuehrer is very happy for you and wants both of us to attend the wedding of his finest general."

This was wonderful, and on January twelfth Erna and I got married in the War Ministry. We then departed for a honeymoon in the Mediterranean. Occasionally, during this revitalizing trip, I thought how lucky I was. A lot of other men had wanted Erna. She had been seeing one young officer in particular, and I was afraid she might change her mind and choose him. When I told Goering about my concern, he said, "Don't worry. I'll ship the bastard to South America."

And he did.

UNPLEASANT DUTY
By Hermann Goering

The police handed me appalling evidence, and it was my unpleasant duty to inform the Fuehrer. I was very nervous going to the Chancellery on January twenty-fourth. I knew how the Fuehrer would feel. The pictures shook in his hands as he grimaced and looked away, then studied the pictures again. There she was, the new Frau General von Blomberg in the nude, doing all kinds of things, sometimes with several people at once. Dreadful.

While I stood silently to the side, the Fuehrer threw the pictures on the desk and said: "I absolutely could not have believed a General Staff officer would do this. This is beyond everything."

"I'm as stunned as you are, Mein Fuehrer."

"He must be removed, obviously. I want you to go and tell him right away, tomorrow. Tell him we'll spare him the humiliation of publicity. We'll spare all of us that."

DISGRACE
By General Werner von Fritsch

This was the most disgusting and immoral thing that had ever befallen the German General Staff. I lost all respect for the man. So did the other officers. Many of us did not approve of him, anyway, since he had long been a Nazi lackey. Now he had disgraced us, and many generals were already getting calls from low class women who giggled how honored they were to have one of their colleagues on the General Staff. This whole thing was intolerable. I called the Fuehrer and told him how the General Staff felt.

BENEFIT OF DOUBT
By Colonel Friedrich Hossbach

Documents quaked in the Fuehrer's hands as he studied them. At times, too upset to continue reading, he turned and walked away, muttering, "They're degenerates, absolute degenerates."

"Mein Fuehrer, I don't believe these charges," I said.

"The evidence is undeniable," said Hitler, pointing at the papers scattered on his desk.

"I still don't believe it."

"I'd like not to believe it, but I have to be responsible when overwhelming evidence is presented to me."

"I ask your permission to go at once and speak to the general. He has a right to know about and answer these serious charges."

"Absolutely not. I forbid you to go."

GRIEVOUS ASSAULTS
By General Werner von Fritsch

Colonel Hossbach alarmed me coming to my apartment late at night in the early morning of January twenty-sixth.

"Herr General, I must ask you, I must tell you, I must, with all respect, ask you about something. I don't believe it, but I must tell you that the Fuehrer has been given documents that accuse you of... that accuse you of being a homosexual and of bribing the witness."

I glared at Hossbach as the most horrible shock shot through me. This was shattering, humiliating.

"It's, it's a goddamn stinking lie. It's all a lie."

"Herr General, I knew they had to be lies."

"If the Fuehrer wants to be rid of me, why doesn't he just ask for my resignation? I'll give it to him in two seconds. But these charges are outrageous."

"I'm going to the Fuehrer and demand that you be given a chance to clear yourself."

Devastated and confused, I sat dead in my chair for hours. Later, the faithful Hossbach called and told me the Fuehrer would see me that evening in the Chancellery.

As I entered the library, Hitler acknowledged me with a grimacing nod. Goering and Himmler stood together to one side, looking at the Fuehrer and me. Hitler told me what the charges were and picked up some documents and gestured with them as he expounded.

"These charges are absolutely untrue," I stated. "They're lies. I give you my solemn word as a German officer."

Hitler glanced at Himmler. He left briefly and returned with a filthy miscreant who, when Himmler pointed at me, exclaimed, "That's him. That's him. He's been paying me bribes for years."

I looked at Hitler, and with as much dignity as I could summon, I said, "The gentleman is mistaken. We have never met."

"That's definitely him," said the man Himmler soon identified as Otto Schmidt.

I did not deign to look again at Schmidt, Himmler or Goering. To the Fuehrer I said, "Are you going to take the word of a German officer, or this..."

Hitler motioned with his head for Himmler to take Schmidt out. Then the Fuehrer stated, "Himmler and Heydrich and their staffs have investigated this thoroughly, and they know Otto Schmidt is telling the truth."

I could not believe that. But I was really too stunned to speak. I had not done anything wrong. I had said so. I wondered what else a German officer should have to say to refute the accusation of some slime. The Fuehrer kept waiting. I did not want to say anything about my private life, which was entirely proper, though embarrassing. Whether or not the Fuehrer believed the charges, I knew what he was also thinking. People often commented about it. "Fritsch never has any women," they'd say. "Fritsch doesn't like women." The inference was that maybe I liked men. I liked men, but only as comrades. I liked women, too, but did not feel comfortable around them. They only talked about frivolous things. Sometimes I tried, too, but the women always subtly grimaced and excused themselves. To hell with that. I did not really need a woman. I was more worried what others thought about me not having one.

"Mein Fuehrer, if any of this has to do with the two boys from the Hitler Youth," I said. "If any of this has to do with them, I can certainly clear this up. On several occasions I've invited the two boys to my apartment for dinner. I gave them lessons on military tactics, and if they weren't attentive, I tapped their rears with a ruler. But they were just taps. The boys were just there for dinner. That's all. I hope this isn't part of the problem."

"Two boys in your apartment, General. That obviously compounds things."

"There's nothing here to be compounded."

"I'm afraid I must ask you to resign immediately."

"I will not."

"I demand your resignation."

"I insist upon a military court of honor to settle this. As an officer, I'm entitled to it. My innocence will be proved."

"I won't have this scandal dragged through a military court of honor."

"I demand a military court of honor."

"You can't have it, and you must resign."

"I won't resign."

"I assign you to indefinite leave immediately."

TEMPORARY FAREWELL
By General Werner von Blomberg

Erna and I talked, and made a decision. We knew what mattered. So, to the unforgiving officers, my colleagues for so long, I said, "I'd sooner shoot myself than divorce the woman I love."

The Fuehrer and I met on January twenty-seventh.

"I'm so sorry this happened," he said. "You'll be virtually impossible to replace."

"Thank you, Mein Fuehrer."

"I would, of course, be very interested in hearing your recommendation for a successor. It's too bad about Fritsch. He might have made a good one."

"I don't think the General Staff embodies the National Socialist spirit you need, Mein Fuehrer. I couldn't recommend anyone from the Army. I think Hermann Goering would be a fine Commander in Chief of the Wehrmacht."

Hitler shook his head. "No, I'm afraid Goering lacks discipline and wants this job too much to understand his deficiencies."

"In that case, Mein Fuehrer, there can be only one man for the post, and that's you."

The Fuehrer did not comment on that.

"General von Blomberg, I want you to remember that when Germany's time of crisis inevitably comes, nothing in the past will matter. I hope you'll return and lead my forces in our battle for survival."

"Absolutely, Mein Fuehrer. I'll be there for you."

ENEMIES OF THE PARTY
By Reinhard Heydrich

Maybe we should not have. At first we should have because Otto Schmidt convinced us. But then we discovered Schmidt had been lying. Instead of revealing that, we marched into Army barracks and interrogated everyone who might know. The generals protested vehemently and started their own investigation. I ordered my agents to counter-investigate, and learned the generals had found out everything and begun privately cursing Himmler and me. They also demanded that General von Fritsch be exonerated with maximum publicity to discredit the SS. My agents then told me the generals wanted to decapitate us. They had infantry and panzers and probably could. I loaded my pistol and worried the generals would do to us what we had done to Roehm.

REORGANIZATION
By Adolf Hitler

I called a cabinet meeting on February fourth to obtain a rubber stamp decree for things I needed. One thing I would not need again was a cabinet meeting, which only wasted my time.

The most important changes were announced to the nation. Blomberg and Fritsch had retired. Sixteen other generals had retired, too, and forty-four were transferred. I took over as Commander in Chief of the Wehrmacht and disbanded the War Ministry and replaced it with the Oberkommando der Wehrmacht, the OKW, which I would also head in order to better coordinate the Army, Navy and Luftwaffe. I named General Wilhelm Keitel, Blomberg's former aide, as my OKW Chief of Staff. Blomberg had jealously told me that Keitel was not qualified for the post. I appointed General Walther von Brauchitsch as my Commander in Chief of the Army. Several diplomats also had to be replaced, especially Foreign Minister von Neurath. His key role I entrusted to the shrewd and experienced Joachim von Ribbentrop.

These vital improvements in command structure would surely facilitate future decisive actions.

AUSTRIAN GUEST
By Adolf Hitler

I wanted them there. I wanted them standing uniformed and earnest behind me on the steps of the Berghof. When Austrian Chancellor

Kurt von Schuschnigg arrived on February twelfth, 1938, I shook his hand and introduced him to General Keitel and two Army and Luftwaffe generals who commanded forces near Austria.

Schuschnigg and I went directly to my big study. I wanted to be alone with this bespectacled pseudo-intellectual prig. He had become chancellor of a rotting country a few years earlier, in his mid-thirties, and I knew he was proud of that, but he should have been ashamed.

"Herr Reichkanzler, this is a magnificent view," he said. "The snow makes the mountains even more beautiful."

"We're not here to discuss the view or the weather, Herr Schuschnigg. You were invited here, as a favor, so I'd have the opportunity to warn you, for the last time, that Austria's vile and outrageous behavior will no longer be tolerated."

Schuschnigg feigned surprise.

"Austria's entire history has been one uninterrupted lecherous act against the Aryan race," I shouted. "That has always been a grave problem, and you've done nothing to improve things. I'm not going to permit this historical perversity to continue. I'm resolutely determined to rectify things. A solution is long overdue. Germany has always been patient with Austria, and Austria has never caused anything but chaos for Germany."

"We have no problems with your country, Herr Reichkanzler. Austria's role in German history has been very helpful and significant."

"Absolutely zero," I stated. "Every German attempt at national unity has been sabotaged by the Hapsburgs and the Catholic church."

"Austrian contributions to German culture really cannot be ignored, Herr Reichkanzler. Beethoven is an excellent example."

"Beethoven was from the Rhineland."

"But he chose to live in Austria, like so many others."

Outraged by this bigmouth, I thrust my finger at him and proclaimed: "I am the greatest German in history and all of my unprecedented accomplishments have so far been achieved without force. I've been compelled solely by the love of my people."

"I'm quite prepared to believe that, Herr Reichkanzler."

"Providence has selected me for a special mission, and I'll use any means necessary to resolve the intolerable situation with Austria. I'm sure you know I'm more popular in Austria than you. And I'll prove so with a plebiscite."

"That would be constitutionally impossible."

"It is mandatory, Herr Schuschnigg. I'm not going to permit Austria to continue fortifying our border."

"Herr Reichkanzler, we have no such fortifications."

"You're a fool to think I don't immediately learn about everything that happens in Austria. I'll blow your absurd and meager defensive measures into a billion pieces and storm in if you don't respond to Germany's grievances. Not even I could prevent bloodshed in such an event."

"Other nations might help Austria," he whined.

"Italy and the Duce are now my closest allies. And France — look what happened in the Rhineland. The French won't help you. And England, maritime England. Forget it. You have to decide by this afternoon. I won't wait any longer."

"Herr Reichkanzler, if you could just tell me what your specific demands are, I'm sure something reasonable can be worked out."

"The details can be discussed later," I said.

SMOKE
By Chancellor Kurt von Schuschnigg

I wanted some during lunch. I had to have at least one. But I had been ordered not to because Hitler detested smoke. I did not say much. This was not a very good lunch. At least Hitler sounded friendly saying how Germany was building the biggest and best buildings in the world. I was glad to hear that and nodded while I chewed.

In a little while Hitler said he had to meet with Foreign Minister Ribbentrop, and I was taken with my aide to a small room. He anxiously asked what Hitler had said. I inhaled several times and blew out stale smoke before I answered. Then I lit another cigarette and smoked very hard.

"Hitler surely isn't going to abrogate the Austro-German agreement," I said after a silence. "He promised to honor our sovereignty and not meddle in internal matters. Surely he won't go back on something he said less than two years ago."

After two grim hours, I was taken to Ribbentrop, with Ambassador Franz von Papen also present, and given two typewritten pages. As I began to look at the top of the first page, Ribbentrop said in razor tone, "The Fuehrer isn't willing to discuss any of these points because they're his final demands. He insists you sign the agreement right away."

After peering up at Ribbentrop, who stared haughtily at me, I began to read sentences that exploded. Hitler demanded the ban on the Nazi party in Austria be lifted and that all Nazi prisoners, including those who had murdered my predecessor, Chancellor Dollfuss, be amnestied within three days. The Fuehrer further insisted we relinquish our ministries of war, finance and the interior. Though not in type with the rest of the tripe, Hitler was clearly demanding: give me Austria.

In a gentlemanly way, I told Ribbentrop, "This is completely unacceptable."

"You must sign this agreement right away."

"Before agreeing to come here, I was assured by the Fuehrer, through Herr von Papen, that our existing agreement with Austria would not only be upheld but reaffirmed. I'm not prepared to be confronted with these assaults on Austria's independence."

When I glanced at Papen, he avoided my eyes.

"I must know if you're prepared to sign," Ribbentrop persisted.

I went over the document point by point and explained why each was completely unfair. I had not expected anything nearly this bad. I could not believe it, yet I had to.

I was taken back to Hitler's study. The Fuehrer marched back and forth across the room before he stopped and glowered at me.

"Herr Schuschnigg, we have nothing to discuss."

He huffed toward me and slapped another copy of his agreement into my hands.

"I won't change a single point. You must sign now, or I'll decide what action to take. I can't be responsible for what happens if you don't sign."

"Herr Reichkanzler," I said, trying to be composed, "the Austrian constitution doesn't permit me such authority. Only President Miklas can sign something like this. My signature would mean nothing."

"You must guarantee it."

"I simply cannot, Herr Reichkanzler, as I've tried to explain."

Hitler stormed to the door, ripped it open and roared, "General Keitel, General Keitel."

Jerking his hand toward the door, Hitler said, "You'll be summoned later."

Keitel hustled past me in the hall. The generals must have been ready to move into Austria at any hour, at any minute. Maybe Hitler was already ordering an attack on my defenseless country. Everything inside me burned before I was brought back.

"Herr Schuschnigg, I've decided to change my mind for the first time in my life," Hitler said.

That was an extraordinary relief.

"But this is your last chance. If you sign now, I'll grant three days before the agreement goes into effect."

I thought about risks both incalculable and imminent, then I said, "All right."

The Fuehrer became quite friendly and started calling me Herr Bundeskanzler and assured me everything was now fine between us, and our Germanic peoples could live in full cooperation. I thought maybe the world picture was indeed getting better.

"I think it would be a good idea if we publicly reaffirmed our July 1936 agreement, when news of this meeting is released," I said.

"Absolutely not. Austria must first prove its trustworthiness by adhering to the terms of this agreement. The only thing going to the press now is the fact that we met here today."

I really did not feel like staying for dinner, as Hitler requested. That was one term I could decline. Back to Austria I rushed through a cold and foggy night.

SIGN
By President Wilhelm Miklas

"Absolutely not," I told Schuschnigg and other key Austrians during our private sessions. "I'm not going to hand over the police. I'll amnesty the Nazis, but I won't give them control. I won't sign."

We continued to argue while reports arrived: "The Germans are coming, the Germans are coming." My cabinet panicked. I suppose I did have to sign. But this was all the Nazis were going to get. They got that, and Austria was saved.

RACIAL BROTHERS
By Adolf Hitler

On February twentieth I ignited my Reichstag audience with what had to be said: "Two states adjoining our frontiers are systematically subjugating ten million Germans within their borders and denying them the inalienable right of self-determination. It is excruciating and intolerable for us to think about these crimes being further visited upon our sympathetic brothers. We have a sacred obligation to protect those neighboring Germans who are not able to secure their own spiritual and political freedom."

PROVOCATION
By An Austrian Nazi

In the town square of Graz, loudspeakers were mounted high all around twenty thousand of us waiting for Schuschnigg to speak. We knew he was going to spew garbage. Then he began, and we bridled as he said, "Austria has gone to the very limit of concessions. We must call a halt and say, 'thus far and no further.'"

"We'll go further than he ever dreamed," someone yelled, and our fists shook as one.

Then Schuschnigg sneered, "Neither Nationalism nor Socialism are the watchwords in Austria. Our rallying cry is patriotism."

"Patriotism is his way of saying: 'Down with the Nazis,'" shouted a big man. "The real rallying cry in Austria today is 'Heil Hitler.'"

"Heil Hitler, Heil Hitler..." enveloped the square.

Schuschnigg concluded his assault by asserting Austria would always be independent, and he invoked the anachronistic flag, and all it represented, with the insult: "Red-White-Red until we're dead." His audience roared. Ours stampeded like a long-confined herd and grabbed the hateful loudspeakers and ripped them down, and then yanked the Red-White-Reds off walls and soiled the ground with them, and a quick-moving comrade scaled town hall and planted high the swastika.

"Sieg Heil, Sieg Heil, Heil Hitler," we erupted.

278

Now Graz was National Socialist. Schuschnigg quickly sent in troops and planes and armored trains to prevent us from holding an even larger demonstration. He might have cooled Graz briefly, but Artur Seyss-Inquart, the new Minister of the Interior, prompted friendly police to protect Nazis and clobber non-Nazis. All over Austria our comrades were on the march, pounding the country into chaos. Schuschnigg became so desperate that he freed from jail and otherwise unfettered his (and our) long-time enemies, the Social Democrats, espousers of democracy and trade unionism. Only a few years ago, just before my Nazi comrades killed him, Chancellor Dollfuss had at least done one good thing, suppressing the Social Democrats, who comprised more than forty percent of voters. Now Schuschnigg's friendly overtures were well received, and simple computation indicated our enemies, as a coalition, might be able to destroy National Socialism in Austria.

On March ninth Schuschnigg stood on a stage in Innsbruck, and several comrades and I huddled around a radio. The chancellor proclaimed there would be a plebiscite on Sunday, a mere four days hence, and the issue was singular: "Are you in favor of a free and independent, a Christian and united Austria?"

His crowd cheered and grew even louder when he exhorted, "Say 'Yes' to Austria. 'Men, the time has come.'"

We sat looking at the radio and did not move.

DECISION
By Adolf Hitler

I was worried about the Duce. Actually, I was concerned about the Duce's feelings. I wanted him to know ahead of time. Otherwise, he might not understand. He might still in some way be friendly to and supportive of Austria. I did not think so. There was no reason for me to think so. But to make sure, I drafted a letter that fully explained the critical situation: "Austria and Czechoslovakia are scheming to restore the Hapsburg dynasty and then hurl twenty million hostile men against the German Reich. I cannot permit Austria to prevail over Germany again. Now that I'm able, I have to intervene to restore law and order and ensure that Austrians can decide their future in a clear and open manner. As a man of character you, Duce, would act the same way if the fate of Italians were at stake. As a man of character, I can do no less. I have been your only comrade during your critical hour in Ethiopia, and you can forever count on my sympathy."

To an aide I said, "I want this letter flown to the Duce immediately, and make sure he's encouraged to respond as rapidly as possible."

Thursday afternoon I met with General Ludwig Beck, Chief of the General Staff, and General Erich von Manstein. They told me we had no existing plans for the invasion of Austria, only theoretical exercises.

"We must be ready to march into Austria Saturday morning," I stated.

"That's probably not possible," General Beck said. "We couldn't prepare such an operation in less than forty-eight hours. We'd have to issue orders to our units by six o'clock tonight."

"Fine," I said, "that gives you more than five hours to draw up plans. I want my orders implemented immediately without complaints or excuses."

General von Manstein finished his plans around six, and the order to mobilize was transmitted. Very early on Friday March eleventh, I completed my tactical directive: "We must prevent further outrages against our Austrian brothers. German troops are to march peacefully and avoid provocation, but, if necessary, be ready to ruthlessly break any resistance by force of arms. Furthermore, any Czech troops encountered in Austria are to be regarded as hostile, and Italians are everywhere to be treated as friends."

ENCOURAGEMENT
By Chancellor Kurt von Schuschnigg

I had everywhere been hearing the chant Ja, Ja, and Ja, again, as patriotic Austrians waved placards and banners, and marched through the streets in far greater numbers than Nazi poltroons. Artur Seyss-Inquart also enhanced our cause by deciding to back the plebiscite and say so on the radio. I went to bed very hopeful and rested quite well until several sharp rings startled me awake to fumble for a phone that blared: German troops are moving to seal us off. I sprang from bed and got dressed and rushed to the Chancellery Friday morning to tell the police chief to station men around key government buildings. Then I looked for Seyss. He might know a lot. But I could not find him. The cabinet began to confer in confusion. Finally, at ten a.m., Seyss arrived from the airport where he had received orders flown in from Berlin. The Fuehrer demanded we postpone the plebiscite. That incensed President Miklas, and we all sat stunned as the Germans closed in. Even if we tried futile resistance, German peoples would be slaughtering each other. To me that was unthinkable. The plebiscite had to be postponed. I notified Seyss at two p.m. He said he would let Hitler know right away. Now I expected something in return for our many concessions.

ON THE PHONE
By Hermann Goering

Every time I talked to him from the phone in my office, the Fuehrer's voice pitched high like a shriek, and he was just too overwrought and concerned to say exactly what he wanted. Fortunately, I knew.

When Seyss-Inquart called, I told him I'd have to talk to Hitler. But in fifteen minutes, a little after three p.m., I decided to enforce Hitler's will. I called Seyss and said, "Tell Schuschnigg we're ordering him and his cabinet to resign and for you to replace him. I also want you to transmit a telegram that declares you're asking for German intervention to quell Austrian chaos. You've got two hours."

ACKNOWLEDGEMENT
By Chancellor Kurt von Schuschnigg

I had urgently cabled Italy and England for assistance, or at least advice, and Italy said it could render no advice, and England said it could not advise us since it could not protect us if its advice proved dangerous.

Austria was alone, and while thugs with scarred faces prowled the Chancellery, mobs right outside were shouting, "Sieg Heil, Heil Hitler, hang Schuschnigg." I told President Miklas I better relinquish my post. He said I could but that Seyss-Inquart was certainly not going to replace me. I resigned around four p.m.

President Miklas started asking people, but no one wanted to take my place. The old man protested everyone was deserting him. I assured him I would stay until he found someone.

AT THE OPERA
By Hermann Goering

I did not have much time. I needed to be on the phone. But I also needed to go. I had to change into a nice big uniform. It was fancy like all my others, and I stumbled a little, only one leg on the ground, as I tried to fast force my big other one through. I got my pants on, then the whole uniform, and was so excited and in such a hurry I felt my heart pounding my medals like a medley of drums.

I rushed to the State Opera for a gala I was hosting for one thousand diplomats, who I greeted with conviviality. They obviously loved having me there. But I could not stay too long. I just needed to find the Czech diplomat. There he was. I ushered him to one side, and following warm amenities I said, "We're having a little family affair with Austria, and I give you my word this has absolutely nothing to do with Czechoslovakia. Germany wants — the Fuehrer desires this expressly — to establish a close and lasting friendship with Czechoslovakia."

"I'm delighted by your friendly intentions," the diplomat said.

"Germany needs to know in this important hour if Czechoslovakia also has friendly intentions. We hope, and assume, that Czechoslovakia isn't planning to intervene in Austria."

"I've heard of no such plans. I can't imagine that we'd become involved. Let me verify this for you. I'll call Prague."

I mingled while I waited. Everyone wanted to talk to me. I obliged as many as possible until the Czech returned.

"Herr Reichminister, the government of Czechoslovakia gives you official assurance it is not mobilizing and is in no way planning to intervene in Austria."

"Thank you very much, sir. This news will make Germany feel

much better. And we'll continue to appreciate your understanding. We want very much to be close to Czechoslovakia. Please tell Prague that I'm speaking for the Fuehrer."

FAREWELL
By Chancellor Kurt von Schuschnigg

President Miklas would not surrender. He said he detested coercion. I did too. But I knew that appointing Seyss-Inquart was the only way to save Austria. Miklas still refused, so I had to take responsibility. A little before eight o'clock Friday night, I solemnly walked to a microphone in the Chancellery, a few feet from the spot where my friend, Chancellor Dollfuss, had slowly bled to death a few years ago.

"The German government has delivered an ultimatum to President Miklas ordering him to name as chancellor a person designated by the German government," I told the nation. "If we do not accede, German troops will invade.

"I today declare before the world that German accusations about Austrian threats and atrocities are lies from A to Z. Since we are not prepared even at this terrible hour to shed blood, we have yielded to force and will offer no resistance.

"So I take leave of the Austrian people and offer my most fervent hope: God protect Austria."

ON AGAIN
By Hermann Goering

I was walking with the Fuehrer now, and he was most agitated as he said, "What's the matter with Seyss-Inquart? Why hasn't that cowardly bastard asked us for help that he and Austria have to have?"

"We really shouldn't delay any longer," I said.

"All right. Move in. Move in. Hurry up."

I grabbed a phone and told an aide in Vienna to write down exactly what I said. Then I dictated a very good telegram from Seyss-Inquart urging us to send German troops right away so peace and order could be established in Austria and bloodshed prevented.

"Seyss doesn't actually have to send the telegram," I said. "All he has to do is agree."

A long hour later, during which the Fuehrer was very upset, Seyss finally complied.

WAITING
By Adolf Hitler

I could not imagine why the Duce had not responded. He knew we were great friends. I definitely knew we were. I admired the Duce more than anyone. He had always known that. He also knew how much I had done for him and how much more that was than Austria could ever do. Surely he would have let me know immediately if he agreed. He must still be friendly with Austria. Maybe all those horrible things he said about me a few years ago still stood. Maybe he did not really like me. Maybe he was going to help Austria. Maybe the Duce was going to desert me.

Pumping hot inside, I walked fast to the phone when my contact with the Duce called. I pressed the receiver hard on my ear and heard that the Duce accepted everything in a very friendly way. He said everything was fine, and he sent me his warmest regards. The Duce did not care about Austria. He cared about Germany.

"Please tell the Duce I'll never, never forget him for this. Please thank him from the bottom of my heart. I'll make any agreement he needs. No matter what danger he faces, I'll always help him. Even if the whole world is against him, I'll never, never forget."

BAD NIGHT
By General Wilhelm Keitel

The generals continued to call and screech that I had to convince the Fuehrer to halt. Seyss-Inquart wanted German troops restrained on our side of the border. The Fuehrer was alerted about two-thirty Saturday morning. He groggily said to proceed, and fell back in bed.

The generals would not stop harping at me to intervene. I explained that shortly before midnight President Miklas had finally done what we would have regardless — installed Seyss-Inquart as chancellor. That should have settled things. The generals still insisted I reawaken the Fuehrer. But I knew better.

PLACE OF MY BIRTH
By Adolf Hitler

The road was jammed with people, and swastikas wafted from the sky, and everyone swarmed toward my Mercedes, trying to touch me, yearning to be near as I crossed the River Inn into Brannau. After so many years I was overwhelmed passing Pommer Inn, the place of my birth and now a sacred historical shrine. I stood tall, my right arm stretched straight out, and everyone cheered.

Jubilation continued, and in fact intensified, as my caravan eased through the land of my birth, and I could not help but become more excited. My people were not merely ecstatic: they clearly yearned for an absolute commitment. Having long suffered the degradations of Hapsburg incompetence and racial bastardization, they knew they were weak, and now wanted officially to be what they had always been. They wanted to be Germans. They were Germans.

They were hysterical everywhere throughout the clotted roads on the way, and it took hours to get to Linz. The sky was dark when I arrived, but in fact everything was alight as a hundred thousand souls embraced me in the town square. Even in a career rife with delirious expressions of love, this was overwhelming. Here in the town where I had first formulated my grand ideas, here in the very place where I'd really begun to become me, they were thanking me for my greatness. That night I could not sleep because crowds below the hotel were singing "Deutschland Uber Alles." I loved the song and what everyone meant, but I had to send word to please stop. Soon there would be so much to do.

In the morning I crossed the Danube, rolling toward Leonding. And as I arrived at my old family home and the grave of my parents, which I had not visited in thirty years, my heart was beating in my head. I asked to be alone, then laid a wreath upon the grave. With my head bowed, I looked at the soil that covered my dearest mother, and was so sorry she could not really feel what I was going to do.

Before midday I ordered the document drawn up. The "Law Concerning the Reunion of Austria with the German Reich" had to be sent to Vienna immediately so the new Austrian government could vote. I guaranteed a plebiscite would soon follow to allow free and open expression regarding the reunion. Then I relaxed a little. Old friends came to see me at the hotel, and their faces showed special excitement as I recounted numerous details of our youthful experiences.

Late that night, Sunday March thirteenth, the date Schuschnigg thought he was going to let Austria rape Germany, again, I shook the hand of Seyss-Inquart, who had just flown in from Vienna. Then I signed the "Law Concerning the Reunion of Austria With the German Reich." Staring down at the document, I could not talk or think of anything else. Now there was only a free and healthy Germany, ready to flourish, my homeland. Tears poured hot down my cheeks onto the table, and I dared not move.

VIENNA THE MAGNIFICENT
By Adolf Hitler

The road to Vienna, like all others, overflowed with worshipers, and the slow advance sharpened my desire to see the city where a quarter of a century ago I had painted so much and studied beautiful architecture and learned about race and politics, and where I had become a man and now absolutely had to be.

Then I was there, standing straight up in a magnificent city swathed in swastikas and lined with crowds that cheered and chanted the name of their favorite native son. I was further gratified to be the ultimate in honored guests at Hotel Imperial, an elite establishment that during my youth had seemed so rarefied and unapproachable I was always unnerved when I walked by and even imagined what it would be like if I entered.

On Tuesday a quarter of a million Viennese jammed the Heldenplatz where I had so often strolled, and longingly they looked up at me on the balcony of Hofburg, the esteemed former imperial home of the Hapsburgs. Those who could not find standing space in the huge Heldenplatz climbed the tall statue there and clung to it as I pronounced: "As Fuehrer and Chancellor of the German Nation and Reich, I hereupon report to history the entrance of my homeland into the German Reich."

Befitting this grand development, a new name was needed. The name was East Mark. Now the word Austria existed no more, and neither did the country. From the province I that afternoon flew to Berlin.

WITNESS FOR THE PROSECUTION
By Otto Schmidt

The Gestapo had definitely been interested, excited even, when I told them about the man in the picture they showed me, and they promised I wouldn't have to worry about the generals. I thanked them for that. Often I had been quite scared by a lot less powerful men. You can get killed watching people do things.

After awhile the Gestapo quit being friendly and started asking questions I had already answered. They demanded to know if I was sure I'd seen General Werner von Fritsch engage in vile activities. I kept saying yes until an officer slapped my face and yelled, "You're a liar." Then he slapped me again.

"All right, all right," I said. "Please quit hitting me. Absolutely everything was just like I said. The place, the details. Except the individual I blackmailed was named Captain von Frisch. There's no 't' in his name."

"You're a dog."

"I'm sorry. I promise I'll admit I'm a terrible liar in court. I'll admit everything."

"You'll stick to your original story," he told me, and stuck a long finger in front of my nose.

At the trial before the military court of honor, I tried to stick to what I said to convince the generals. But Hermann Goering began to confuse me with his vicious cross-examination, and I felt like an overwhelming idiot in front of those stern generals, friends of Fritsch.

"I must tell the court I wanted to tell the truth," I blurted. "I'm sorry. I'm so very sorry."

General von Fritsch was cleared, and I wanted to leave. I could not see any reason to detain me. But the Gestapo took me back to some dark room where they had been keeping me for my "safety."

"You're going to let me go, aren't you?" I asked several times the following week.

All they did was frown. I didn't dare say much. Then one morning a guard came with a pistol and, without saying anything, shot me several times.

ANSCHLUSS
By August Kubizek

When we were boys in Linz, and later almost men in Vienna, I had often listened with fascination to Adolf's extraordinary plans, and now here he was, doing exactly what he always said. This was so exciting. I really wanted to see him. Even though he had disappeared thirty years ago without telling me, and I still wondered what I'd done, I decided to go to Hotel Weizinger and leave a message. I knew Adolf might be too busy. Six hundred thousand were unemployed, and he was going everywhere to explain how he could help and that Schuschnigg had lied and tried to turn everyone against him.

Despite his overwhelming concerns, Adolf sent word he'd be delighted to see me. On April ninth, the day before the plebiscite, I went to Hotel Weizinger, and the instant Adolf walked in he yelled, "Gustl," with youthful gusto and shook my hand hard and held it as he looked warmly into my eyes. That feeling really was great again, and Adolf was as enthusiastic as ever. He pointed out the window and said, "There's got to be another bridge across the Danube, and Linz certainly needs a new concert hall and a symphony orchestra to play in it, and naturally the streets and neighborhoods and the city's center all need modification, if not outright demolition."

Stopping at once, Adolf earnestly asked, "And you, Gustl, what have you become?"

"I'm afraid I'm only the town clerk of Eferding."

"But your music, Gustl. What happened?"

"After the war I started a family and had to forget my dreams. But we have three sons, and each has a lot of musical talent."

"Gustl, I don't want them to have to struggle as we did in Vienna," the Fuehrer said, and just like that he beckoned an aide and instructed him to take care of my boys' musical instruction. Then we had a great time looking at some letters and drawings he had sent me, and that I cherished long before anyone knew what he was going to do.

"Gustl, these are important historical artifacts, and you're the only one in the world who understands what I had to endure in Vienna. I think you should write a book about me."

That was a great idea, and so was Adolf's suggestion we see each other more often. I would certainly love that.

The next day I cast my ballot for the Anschluss, and almost one hundred percent of Austria agreed.

THE RAG
By Kurt von Schuschnigg

It was a rag. The Gestapo called it my towel, but now it was a rag I used to scrub bathrooms at Gestapo headquarters. Many times I vomited when I had the wretched rag in my hand but soon I was fed so little my gnarled stomach heaved only aches as I retched in filth on the floor I scrubbed with the rag.

MIME
By Adolf Hitler

"Here, here, watch this," I'd say. Then I'd walk and talk just like him as I lampooned the fat, lambasted the arrogant, and parodied the lame, every anybody idiot with bleeding Achilles heels. I also did lots of weapons, too. Bombs, planes, machine guns. Boom, zoom, tat tat tat tat.

George Thomas Clark

EARLY MAY
By Adolf Hitler

The country was not a country. I at all times refused to even vaguely think of it as such. It was stolen land maliciously formed into a cauldron of racial mongrels. It was an outrage of an entity that savaged and oppressed its most sacred people, the Sudeten Germans. It was a jagged sword plunged already deep into our strategic waist. It was a moral scourge and a mortal threat. It was Czechoslovakia.

I had to do something. I resolved it would be decisive. I knew France, England and Russia, countries that always benefited from German vulnerability and grief, would oppose me if they could. But I had a plan. I knew it would work, but I still had to be careful and shrewd. What might the Duce do, I continued to brood? I'm afraid my sources did readily prove that my closest foreign friend vacillated on occasion and threatened to abandon our cause.

I did not think the Duce would do that, but I had to be sure. In early May 1938, I accepted an invitation and arrived by train in Rome. I was greeted — and hosted at many festivities — not by the Duce but by the monarch, King Emmanuel. I referred to this pipsqueak bastard as King Nutcracker and was outraged by his pompous behavior, which might diminish my stature with the Italians. Maybe some of the Duce's alleged insults were hurting as well. But I did not actually think so. The Italians were trying hard to impress me, and I was aroused by their showmanship and stimulated by their beautiful cities but quite concerned about their modest martial might.

The key to the trip turned on my superb speech that proffered the South Tyrol to an Italian nation nervous about Austria. I know the Duce was pleased. Upon our farewell, he gripped my hand and vowed: "No force will be able to separate us."

LUNCH AT LADY ASTOR'S
By Prime Minister Neville Chamberlain

My world picture was comprehensive and painted clear and vivid by careful historical analysis that revealed to me, rather more clearly than anyone else, the delicate steps that had to be taken in order to preserve peace and ensure Britain would never again become embroiled in a general and devastating war on the European continent. In that regard, I had willingly stated the hard fact that nothing could have stopped what actually happened in Austria unless several countries, and especially England, were prepared and willing to fight. Furthermore, I foresaw it would have been a severe and repetitious mistake to try to counter an at least strategically valid German action by agreeing to confer with Russia and France and others in a way that could only disturb Germany. My peaceful intentions had been established even before I became prime minister, for example at the time of the Rhineland crisis, when I, like a majority of my countrymen, indicated our understanding of Germany's remilitarization. Additionally, I had stated I would not for a moment hesitate to transfer ownership of Tanganyika to Germany, if that would promote European peace.

Czechoslovakia, of course, was much more important than anything in Africa, but, as a mere collection of scraps and patches, it could not reasonably be called a state. Czechoslovakia was, quite frankly, a potential powder keg, and on May fourteenth, at a luncheon at Lady Astor's, I explained my views in a private discussion with American and Canadian journalists: "The German districts of Czechoslovakia should be removed and annexed with Germany. That is indisputably fair since there is no justification for a non-state, a haphazard stitch work of Eastern races we know nothing about, to dominate ethnic Germans who are clearly expressing their desire to be part of Germany. The current Czech state, such as it is, cannot at any rate continue, and England and others certainly should not be expected to spill a generation of blood in order to protect something that in itself is not vital to us but is important to Germany."

When my "off the record" remarks were published around the world, I was aggravated. But the aggravations of a strident and probing House of Commons I could surely withstand during my careful and comprehensive course toward peace.

MAY CRISIS
By Adolf Hitler

There the map was, hideous and obscene. I could not look at it long before pacing away to the big Berghof window where I gazed far out at mountains beautiful and mystic and mine. After several minutes of contemplation, I demanded vital information that arrived rapidly by wire: I had twelve divisions near Czechoslovakia that could be mobilized within twelve hours. The next day, while looking out the window, I thought about the Sudeten mountains filled with danger. How many and what kinds of fortifications do they have, I ordered by wire? The answer screamed I had to soon act or Germany would forever be open to unwanted entry.

Naturally, I was very anxious when my plans arrived on May twentieth. The Wehrmacht had been drafting them for the fall, and here they were, Case Green, spread portentously on my table. I studied my plans and became so aroused I had to stop reading while I thought. Then I continued and saw this: "It is not my intention to smash Czechoslovakia by military action in the immediate future without provocation..." I had to wait for the Czechs to commit some atrocity so horrible that the world could not deny it. Then I'd take lightning action. That was my plan, Case Green, top secret.

I loved it. Then I was suddenly slapped in the face by a wire from our embassy in Prague. The Czechs were wailing about an imminent attack. That was absurd. The next day I stormed around my room upon hearing they had also reinforced fortifications and called up reserves and screamed lies, all dirty Czech lies concocted by President Benes and others.

In Paris, the effete Prime Minister Daladier threatened my ambassador, pointing at a mobilization order on his table. Again the French imperiled a new generation of Germans. That is why they had signed a defense pact with the Czechs in the first place. The opportunistic English also menaced us. Their twisted message was that if their co-conspirator, France, decided to make war on us because France's co-conspiratorial Czech criminals were lying about us, then his majesty's government "could not guarantee that they would not be forced by circumstances to become involved also."

Beyond dispute, these filthy cowards conspired our end. And before they destroyed us, they wanted to humiliate me personally. I roasted a couple of days before announcing what should have been obvious: Germany is not prepared to attack.

The foreign press gloated. They said I backed down. They said I was afraid to invade. They were liars. They were all liars and scum. I hated their putrid lying guts. I hated what all of them were doing to Germany and to me. They would not be able to do this with impunity, not to my Germany, not this time. Now things were different.

I explained the new circumstances a few days later at the Chancellery. All my top generals were there and needed to know the new emphasis for Case Green, which I insisted be ready by October first. To eager and attentive faces I announced: "It is my unshakable will to wipe Czechoslovakia off the map."

AUSTRIA NO MORE
By Sigmund Freud

Though my palate had for more than a decade been consumed by cancer — and I needed an awkward prosthesis to talk — I still smoked cigars because at this very late stage they provided more comfort than any more harm they could inflict. I was too ill to work and really could do nothing except grieve that depraved souls were arresting countless thousands of Viennese Jews and forcing many others to their knees to scrub the streets.

I knew the danger would increase but did not want to leave Austria. In my eighties, I was too old to uproot. Also, by staying, I would in important ways be fighting. But others in my family, especially my daughter Anna, had every reason to leave. Numerous people in Austria and abroad were trying to obtain my release. Still, I did not think I should go and did not know if I would. Then the Nazis detained Anna, and my fear became more painful than the cancer. When they released her, I agreed we would leave if possible. At the same time, I was horrified that my sisters would have to stay.

On June second, after endless paperwork, it was finally arranged. I would take my final leave of Austria on the morrow. The Gestapo insisted I sign a document certifying I had been treated appropriately. I signed, and at the bottom I appended: "I can heartily recommend the Gestapo to anyone."

ORCHESTRATION
By Joseph Goebbels

My ideas formed so rapidly four secretaries at once took dictation. To one I'd turn to pronounce policy and strategy for publicly dealing with racial problems but before completing that an irrepressible nugget about the theater would manifest and I'd get a new secretary started then spin to another for a creative fusillade about the foreign press but before finishing I'd be overwhelmed with a stunning idea about the nation's youth and with a whirl I'd expound on that then back to this one and over to that one all around back and forth get this down be right back now hear this a whirlwind I am.

Many times, more often now than ever, I had guests coming and wanted to finish fast so I could be ready. I am not referring to political guests, bores like that. I mean actresses. A lot of actresses came to see me, and after dismissing my secretaries with orders to type and disseminate, I liked to dash into my private quarters, adjacent to my office in the Propaganda Ministry, and make sure I looked good. Sometimes, I'd turn back the covers. But not always. It depended on the actress. Did I know her? Had she visited me before, and with good results? If so, it wasn't necessary to talk much. I was polite, of course, and very charming before I took her hand and felt it heat in mine, and kissed her exquisite face and neck while guiding her to a bed soon aflame.

I never needed much rest until I started again, and they loved it, all these unbelievable actresses, and they weren't the only ones. Sometimes I entertained my secretaries, or friends of the family, or wives of so and so. I was as eclectic as I was prolific, and each time my spirit was renewed. If a business appointment had to wait, so what? I didn't care. And I wasn't worried about being interrupted. I had a system of bells for employees to alert me. Afterward, I drank lots of coffee and inhaled a few dozen cigarettes as I arranged for waves of newspaper reports and radio broadcasts to alert the nation about our Sudeten German brothers being arrested, beaten and killed by the ruthless Czech government.

FREEDOM
By Konrad Heinlein

Before the Fuehrer came to power, we had not been able to sustain effective opposition to the arrogant Social Democratic Czech regime. It bragged about being the only democracy in the history of central Europe but was in fact an anti-German juggernaut. Only National Socialism could save the Sudeten German Party and help us gain autonomy.

The British and French knew our aspirations were reasonable. I got every indication of that during a visit to London, and I told the Fuehrer so after my return. He said I would soon have a great future, along with all Sudeten Germans, and to start making demands and keep making them and to make sure they could not be met.

GROWING CONCERN
By General Ludwig Beck

After reading the Fuehrer's initial plans for Czechoslovakia, I had sat quiet and composed and scared as I considered inexorable consequences that had to culminate in Germany's destruction. My duty as Chief of the General Staff demanded I articulate my concerns. In a memorandum to General von Brauhitsch, Commander in Chief of the Army, I stressed that Germany was encircled by nations that would surely fight if we tried to further expand. England had always been unwilling to concede primacy to one continental power and had formed many pragmatic alliances with the weaker to check the stronger. It was, after all, the Prussians and the English who combined to defeat Napoleon at Waterloo. Hitler's Napoleonic stripe now strengthened the alliance between Britain and France, and those nations, wracked with alarm, were resolute in their drive to rearm. We also had to be wary of a Russia looking west because to its east Japan was less a threat due to adventures elsewhere in Asia. Additionally, the

Wehrmacht lagged years from its peak, and we at any rate were incapable of keeping our forces adequately fed or supplied.

Soon, Brauhitsch told me that Hitler had called me a pessimist. Then the Fuehrer's staggering pronouncement to us in late May 1938 had spurred me to write a second memorandum. When I arrived with it, Brauhitsch was morose.

"General, please listen carefully," I said. "I don't think the Fuehrer is receiving realistic advice and we must make him understand. I want to read this to you: 'Hitler is correct in stressing our need for more living space and for decrying the existence of Czechoslovakia in its current form, which we can't permit forever. But he's absolutely wrong in his assessment that Germany is relatively stronger than in 1914. We are, in fact, in an even worse position regarding raw materials than the Germany of 1917-18, which had been enervated by years of war. We simply don't have the wherewithal of our adversaries. They could, if necessary, draw men and strategic resources from an essentially limitless reserve of land and colonies and bases, and probably from the United States.'"

Brauhitsch nodded but did not speak.

A few days later, after Hitler had put his words into an official directive, I stirred again and wrote that the General Staff had not formulated the plan, believed it disastrous, rejected it and refused to take any responsibility. To demonstrate these points, I conducted an indoor war game based on Germany attacking Czechoslovakia, and France intervening (as it had pledged to do). The results of this exercise were rationally undeniable: we overran the Czechs, but the French in the meantime penetrated us deeply and ensured our defeat. In an after dinner address to consummate the conference, I emphasized that our political goals must be shaped by military and economic capabilities. Most of the generals concurred. But some stood and sharply accused me of not grasping the way panzers would revolutionize warfare.

"The French have armor, too," I replied.

Hitler still made feverish military preparations. A half million men scurried to strengthen the West Wall defense along the French border. Unique exercises were conducted in seizing fortified positions. Annual autumn maneuvers were accelerated into summer. And the Sudetenland roared with unrest.

Through my mind I repeatedly ground the lessons of history,

alliances, soldiers and resources, and my conclusions always emerged like bloody meat. Finally, I picked up my pen and slashed paper with words difficult to countenance but impossible to ignore: "The risks are far too great and our means much too meager. Our proposed provocation would mean a life and death war against Germany waged by England and France, and we would lose with consequences far greater than after the Great War. Therefore, with full knowledge of the significance of the following, compelled by the responsibility vested in me, I insist that ranking members of the General Staff confront Hitler at the appropriate time and tell him we are opposed to war. We have not merely a military obligation but a moral one. Vital decisions for the future of the nation are at stake, and history will indict commanders of blood guilt if, in light of their professional and political knowledge, they do not obey the dictates of their conscience."

After presenting this to Brauhitsch on July sixteenth, I said, "If Hitler resists, we as a group must resign at once and thereby deprive him of the means of waging war. Exceptional times demand exceptional measures."

Brauhitsch seemed impressed and like he might want to act. But he was noncommittal. I was not. My mind stormed with ideas quickly articulated. Three days later I went to see Brauhitsch again.

"This action will bring internal upheaval," I told him, glancing at notes. "But we must act, and I do mean for the Fuehrer. Our oath to him is sacred and there mustn't be the slightest hint of a plot. What we must do is rescue Hitler, and the nation, from the criminal and repressive clutches of the SS and other powerful Nazis. The scoundrels have got to be physically confronted and neutralized. The Fuehrer definitely would be more amenable without the SS. Then we could unite against war and for a return to the role of law in the Reich. This is for the Fuehrer. This is for Germany."

Numerous reports continued to distress me. Hitler wanted Czechoslovakia now, no matter what, and as the picture of his truculence vivified, my determination to go still further intensified. I still had one more moderate idea, though, and wrote a speech for Brauhitsch. It was strong, included all the key points, and urged that we be our best.

"General," I said. "It's exceedingly important that you read this speech to the generals when we meet August fourth. We have to stop Hitler right away. I need your unequivocal backing."

"We'll have the meeting August fourth, just as you say," said Brauhitsch.

Many high-ranking generals attended. I read my memorandum from July sixteenth. Brauhitsch then solemnly walked to the front of the assemblage. I sat down, nervous but confident. What would the men think? I moved my head slightly up and to the left. That wasn't enough, so I lifted a little off the chair and saw Brauhitsch's hands. They were empty, and instead of my speech he offered his own (more timid) assessment. Almost everyone agreed. We were unprepared. After the meeting I silently approached Brauhitsch.

"I'll give Hitler your memorandum," he said. "I'll show it to him and explain."

A few days later Brauhitsch told me that Hitler said to tell me politics were his province, exclusively. I really could not do anything more, in a vacuum. I knew what was coming, and was not going to be responsible. I resigned and asked to meet with Hitler. He refused but sent word: "It's vital for national security that your retirement not be publicized."

I complied and wondered why.

A JOKE
By Ewald Klesit-Schwenzin

Right after the amenities in meeting Sir Robert Vansittart, a British diplomatic adviser, I said, "Solely because of Hitler — not his party cronies — there isn't merely a threat but a certainty of war unless Britain publicly and unequivocally makes it clear that he'll face unified military opposition if he attacks Czechoslovakia. That could topple him because of opposition at home."

"When is he planning to attack?"

I laughed hard at that one.

"I really don't know," he said.

My jaw must have dropped. Our people had been briefing key British politicians and diplomats for a good long while.

"Late September," I said. "It'll be too late after the twenty-seventh."

WEST WALL
By Adolf Hitler

On this wonderful late August day happy crowds greeted me in the Rhineland, and I loved seeing everywhere the hectic implementation of my plans. This was my most important one yet, West Wall, our bastion against the French. We toured West Wall. We might need it soon. I did not think so. But we might. Maybe the French would attack, though probably not. But if they did attack, we had West Wall. Though not complete, it was very impressive. I toured West Wall with my entourage and was happy dreaming, thinking, that is, about Czechoslovakia. A strong West was the key to my new East.

"Mein Fuehrer, I must speak to you privately," said General Wilhelm Adam.

Grim-lipped and disgusted, I nodded for Himmler and other comrades to leave my railroad car.

"Mein Fuehrer, in the event of a French attack, we couldn't possibly hold West Wall."

"You will hold it," I said.

"We simply don't have enough troops. It's a matter of numbers. Our defeat would be inevitable."

"I'm sick of your goddamned defeatism and I'm sick of your pacifism. That applies to all you generals. You understand nothing outside the narrow boundaries of your duties. Well, let me tell you, Herr General, I understand everything, and the French would be annihilated if they tried to fight us."

"I'm afraid it's we who would be destroyed. I again emphasize that we don't have enough troops in the West to withstand the French. In some areas we'd be outnumbered as much as ten to one."

I jumped straight up and began to speak even louder: "You generals obviously don't understand. I've rebuilt Germany to such a degree that the whole world is terrified. We're now much stronger than France, and stronger even than France and England combined. I won't tolerate having my plans questioned by those who don't have sufficient information. I order you to hold West Wall, and any man who doesn't hold it is a wretched dog who'll be garbage in German history."

CRITICAL DECISION
By Prime Minister Neville Chamberlain

I was most disheartened. It seemed everything I had done to maintain peace might be for naught. Hitler apparently was determined to act irrationally, even with rational alternatives favorable to him.

We British, of course, could do nothing militarily to save Czechoslovakia. We simply were not strong enough. I had long favored rearmament — and we were rearming — but not at a pace beyond prudent fiscal policy. We clearly could not fight the Germans in central Europe, and I was against warning them since that might give Hitler a berserk reaction. I had always stated that "no democratic state ought to make a threat of war unless it was both ready and prepared to carry it out."

I had anyway decided on something even bolder: Plan Z.

NEW TASK
By General Franz Halder

I understood the circumstances. General Beck had kept me informed. Now, as the new Chief of the General Staff, I contemplated many things while trying to be ready. I had to be. I knew that. Everything just had to be right.

I agreed with Beck and others that Hitler would be a disaster. He was a bloodsucking criminal who should be done away with. But many generals did not understand Hitler's nature and real desires. They were convinced he did not really want war and had some kind of understanding with the West. The rank and file of the Army also worried me. They were ill-informed and had no reason to support a coup against Hitler. The same applied to the masses.

Instead of risking a civil war, we might have to wait until Germany actually invaded Czechoslovakia. But even then we could not be sure when England or France would declare war on Germany. Our adversaries had to show strength in order to prove Hitler's course meant certain war. If we acted against Hitler too soon, we could be accused of breaking the law and betraying our oath. If we waited until the outbreak of hostilities, then perhaps we could bomb Hitler's train in a way that would involve other countries and absolve the Wehrmacht. I knew this whole thing had to be handled properly, and in early September 1938 it was most unclear exactly what that meant. But I did tell Hans Oster, of Abwehr intelligence, that plans did have to be made.

COMPROMISE
By President Edvard Benes

As President of Czechoslovakia I now bargained with Sudeten Germans the same way I had always conducted negotiations as foreign minister. I proceeded with the belief that the best way to make a person keep a promise is to trust him and deal with him on that basis.

The Sudeten Germans, represented in the main by the Sudeten German Party, repeatedly assured me they were not seeking to secede from Czechoslovakia and join Germany. They said they simply wanted more autonomy. We worked to accommodate them, and in the previous year agreement was reached, and implemented, to increase German administrative involvement — which had never been insignificant — in the Czech government. In education also, the Sudeten Germans enjoyed fine benefits, even better than Czechs and Slovaks.

I well knew that it was in many ways better to be a German in Czechoslovakia than most people in many places, and probably better, for instance, than being a German in Germany. But these things did not matter. The Sudeten Germans intensified their agitation. Finally, on September fifth, I said, "All right, write down your demands and I'll agree to them. Yes, that is precisely what I said."

Evidently that was not good enough.

PLAN Z
By Prime Minister Neville Chamberlain

Many opponents I long ago proved lacking had been harassing me with opinions I neither desired nor needed. They simply did not understand. I had a plan. On September tenth I discussed it with an entirely more amenable group, Lord Halifax and my other top aides. We, naturally, were on edge about the current Nazi rally in Nuremberg. What was Hitler going to say and what would he actually do? The Germans were taut, angry and excited, reported Sir Nevile Henderson, our ambassador in Germany. He quite rigorously urged us not to insist that he officially warn Ribbentrop about our obligation to France, if France became involved in a war with Germany, in the event France decided to fulfill its obligation to Czechoslovakia. Henderson had already made our inevitable involvement in a general conflict clear, and it would be unwise and quite dangerous to risk nudging an agitated Hitler over the edge of sanity he seemed always to totter on. There were more important considerations than Czechoslovakia. I had simply to wait for the propitious moment to implement Plan Z.

FAIR WARNING
By Adolf Hitler

Solemnly, with the eyes and ears of the world fixed on me, I strode head straight to the rostrum, my right hand a salute en route. It was my duty to consummate the Party Rally in Nuremberg this evening, September twelfth, and I thoroughly recapitulated our long struggle, which catapulted me into saying: "In no way am I going to tolerate a second Palestine in the heart of Germany. Though the poor Arabs are defenseless and deserted, the Germans in Czechoslovakia are not. I won't permit a blackmailing and terroristic Czech regime to forever perpetuate itself. Nor am I going to tolerate further humiliations as in May. I insist that the Sudeten Germans receive justice. The blame certainly won't lie with us if, by making these entirely reasonable and duty-bound demands, our relations with other European nations are damaged."

IMPLEMENTATION
By Prime Minister Neville Chamberlain

Again the world staggered toward mindless bloody war, and panic was almost everywhere thick. The French in particular were in a fix, trying to decide whether or not to intervene if Czechoslovakia were attacked, which seemed inevitable. If the French did intervene, that would involve the British Empire in another brutal conflict. Prime Minister Daladier cabled me on the night of September thirteenth. I replied that I had a resolution but could not tell him about it just yet. Plan Z had to be implemented when entirely unexpected and when conditions seemed utterly hopeless. That time had come. I was determined not to allow a repetition of mistakes that precipitated the Great War. Now there had to be a frank face to face discussion. I cabled Herr Hitler and offered to come at once. The next day he invited me to Berchtesgaden for the fifteenth. That morning I arose quite early and stimulated and was manifestly reinforced, as I left Ten Downing Street, by the hearty and hopeful applause from a great many countrymen gathered outside. My mandate was clear, and after embarking on my first flight of any consequence, I periodically looked out the window, not so much to see what it was like so high in the sky, but to contemplate what my mission meant to those on the ground below, on both sides of the English Channel. This journey, if I shaped it as planned, would surely herald a new and comprehensive era of European peace and diplomacy.

A bit after noon I landed in Munich, and during my car ride all the way to the train station, friendly Germans greeted me with salutes I well knew beckoned peace. The confidence of these Germans had been earned by their Fuehrer, and I resolved to cooperate with him completely. Hitler's domestic enemies, and they seemed so few, struck me as a most unsavory lot who desired something repugnant: a reprise of the monarchy and Prussian militarism that prior to and during the Great War almost demolished Western civilization. No, this was not a group that represented the future of Europe.

On the train, as I was planning how to deal with Hitler, I saw, rolling relentlessly on the opposite track, car after car filled with soldiers. These were mere boys who, like the sweet-faced boys at home, had not yet had a chance to live. That they must have. I was gambling my entire political career for them. I knew if I should be wrong, and the worst ensued, I would be pilloried and blamed. I could not let that happen now.

Tired but still vigorous after seven hours journey, I climbed the Berghof steps and clasped Hitler's hand and smiled. We had tea and talked informally before adjourning to his study for a private discussion, accompanied only by the German translator, Paul Schmidt. I was open and attentive as the Fuehrer, in a rather subdued way, enumerated his ideas and contributions in world and Anglo-German affairs, and, finally, his complaints about Czechoslovakia.

"I'm prepared to discuss redressing your concerns as long as it's understood that force not be used," I said.

That agitated Hitler, and the ruthless peasant in him surfaced as he said, "President Benes is the one using force. Three hundred Sudeten Germans have been murdered, and I'm absolutely not going to tolerate any second-rate country abusing Germans. I'm in my prime and ready to do whatever has to be done, including starting a war, in order to settle the crisis."

Cutting the rascal short, I told him, "If you were determined to go to war without even discussing and negotiating your grievances, then why have you wasted my time by letting me make such a long trip? It is, in this case, best that I return to England at once."

When Schmidt completed the translation, Hitler seemed shaken back into reasonableness. Before long, and I commended him for it, he got down to the crux of the matter: "Is England willing to agree to a secession of the Sudeten German region based on the right of people to self-determination?"

I agreed to the principle. It was immaterial to me, and England, to whom the Sudeten Germans were attached as long as they were attached where they wanted. That was self-determination, and implied a majority would agree without force. I explained to Hitler that I would have to consult my cabinet and the French. In the meantime, I got him to promise not to take military action until I met with him again.

I had a very good feeling when I left the Berghof. My personal intervention alone prevented an invasion of Czechoslovakia. And I established a relationship with Hitler. Despite his uncouth qualities, I definitely got the impression that here was a man who could be trusted when he gave his word.

BUT
By General Franz Halder

I was almost decided. Actually, I was decided. I simply knew my decision should not be final, ahead of time, if England and France were going to give the Fuehrer what he wanted anyway. I hoped they would. Then I wouldn't have to decide.

"But I've already decided," I told fellow conspirators. "Furthermore, a day or two before final orders to march are issued, I'll know. Then I'd be willing to act."

I wanted to know what would happen after Hitler. I needed to foresee the fate of the nation. Agreement evolved there would be a brief military dictatorship followed by a Weimar-like democracy. That's what some said. But the aftermath wasn't really clear. I hoped for a better picture.

I certainly was part of the plot, though, and said we had to occupy the Chancellery and important Berlin agencies as well as communications and other important facilities. Things had to be done quickly and with a limited number of men. I believed key Army group and corps commanders would be supportive, including General Beck, who had recently been recalled. But to maintain secrecy, I did not tell any of these generals yet.

PERSUASION
By Prime Minister Neville Chamberlain

Upon my return to England I met with the cabinet and explained that, based on Herr Hitler's attitude and demands, we had but two choices: either accept the principle of self-determination for Sudeten Germans or face and endure certain devastating war. There was no doubt which alternative was infinitely more desirable, and the cabinet was appropriately impressed when I asserted, "It had never entered my head that I should go to Germany and say to Herr Hitler that he could have self-determination on any terms he wanted."

The French came to London on September eighteenth, and to Prime Minister Daladier I also explained our contrasting choices. He was concerned Germany would take advantage of Polish and Hungarian territorial disputes with Czechoslovakia, and demand more plebiscites, and continue to gobble up the country. I overcame French worries by suggesting outright cession of the Sudetenland, and offering to guarantee the boundaries and existence of a new Czech state, thereby limiting self-determination to the Sudetenland. Daladier heartily assented.

The following day I conferred with cabinet colleagues who agreed with what they perhaps thought was Daladier's idea for cession. A joint Anglo-French communiqué was soon sent to the Czechs, explaining our recognition of how great their sacrifice must be in order to maintain peace. They would have to turn over to Germany all areas with a majority of Sudeten Germans. In return, we would protect them against unprovoked aggression. This was also a very great sacrifice and concession on our part: by promising to defend the proposed and essential new Czech state, we would potentially be relinquishing the decision of whether or not we went to war.

FRIENDS
By President Edvard Benes

I had just finished lunch when our friends, the British and French ambassadors, came and kicked me in the stomach. I almost passed out, that is my head went blank, and I stung too much to reply. Then I told them I was too angry to say anything. Their shame was palpable but, alas, so was the urgency of their cowardice.

"You have abandoned us," I finally stated. "Your promises and commitments are evidently without worth. France is beyond debate obligated by treaty to help us defend ourselves against aggression. Isn't France prepared to keep its word? Aren't France and England at least prepared to act in what is obviously their self-interest? Do not believe, gentlemen, that German encroachment will end in the Sudetenland."

The ambassadors slithered out of my office, and I sat in painful confusion about how to save a country with friends intent on peeling its hide. Perhaps Russia can help, I thought. Who else? I contacted the Soviet minister in Prague and requested urgent answers to two questions: "Would the Soviet Union honor its obligation to render immediate and effective assistance if France also did so, and would the Soviet Union help, even if France did not?"

The next day, September twentieth, we received two affirmative replies. There might be hope. Our Sudeten fortifications were strong. We had thirty-five trained and determined divisions. The Soviets were showing resolve so egregiously absent elsewhere. There really might be a chance. If so, we had to resist. That night we sent the British and French this message: "Agreeing to your proposal would ensure eventual absolute domination of our country by Germany and would also severely damage France's prestige in Europe as well as her strategic position."

Quite late that night I retired, nervous and tired, and lay in bed hoping I was asleep and that what I was thinking was really just a dream, a nightmare, and none of this would be real in the morning. But a new day did not come. At about two a.m. I was torn from semi-slumber and bludgeoned by this British and French ultimatum: "Unless you agree to cede the Sudetenland to Germany forthwith, we will renounce all responsibility for your security."

But Czechoslovakia still might have Russia. That's what I talked about for hours later that day. The Russians had been urging collective resistance to German expansion. Today they again affirmed they would help. But what kind of help? How much help? If we don't get enough, we'll be crushed, I kept thinking. We can resist a few weeks, probably, but unless there's massive intervention in our behalf... So what will the Russians do? What can they do? We pounded hard questions against softening brains. I felt Russia would fight if France did, but France had already shamed itself. If Russia came, it would be alone, alone with us against Germany. But does Russia, despite its anti-German rhetoric, really want to fight the Wehrmacht now? I hoped so. I prayed so. But I could not convince myself. The Russians had said they would feel "authorized" to come to Czechoslovakia's aid. That did not mean obligated. And even if they decided to try to help, how would they get here? They would have to move troops through either Poland or Romania. And neither country would allow that. The Russians really could not intervene in force, even if they wanted. At most they could airlift supplies in a sincere but inconsequential effort.

We also had to analyze what might happen if the Soviets actually fought the Wehrmacht. My military experts said the Germans were superior. I didn't doubt that. The cringing democracies would watch with delight while fascists and Bolsheviks destroyed each other. And after Germany won, Czechoslovakia would be forever entombed. I knew we were alone and had to accept Franco-British cession of our soil and their soul.

FOR THE FUEHRER
By Hans Oster

General von Witzleben and other patriots met at my house and discussed the plan. At the advantageous moment our raiding party would forcefully enter the Chancellery. I had no intention of letting Hitler continue being Hitler. He'd already had that chance. I therefore hoped he and his guards would resist. If they did, he would be shot. If, however, they surprised us and did not resist, then we would provoke them and shoot Hitler. If for some reason we could not provoke them, we would shoot Hitler anyway. Simultaneously, General von Witzleben's Army Corps in the Berlin district would overwhelm key installations and, in particular, get a stranglehold on the SS, criminal fanatics almost certain to resist.

Quietly gathering men and weapons in Berlin apartments, we planned and waited. Everything was ready for the Fuehrer.

MISERABLE WEAKLING
By Adolf Hitler

I wanted the prissy bastard to have a very big German panorama, high over the Rhine in a castle hotel. Then he would feel what he should when he came steep down to be ferried across the wide Rhine to meet me in Bad Godesberg. I waited for him at Hotel Dreesen where I had always been very relaxed and comfortable.

The old man emerged from the car he rode up from the Rhine, and

I shook his hand and said, "I hope you're comfortable and satisfied with your lodging."

His oily manner nauseated me, but I knew I had to endure our critical meeting. I later listened politely while he gave an enthusiastic explanation about what a thoroughly good fellow he had been to influence his cabinet and the French. Then he said, "And I have convinced Czechoslovakia to relinquish the Sudetenland — and without a plebiscite."

That absolutely stunned me.

"Do I understand that the British, French and Czech governments have agreed to the transfer of the Sudetenland from Czechoslovakia to Germany?"

"Yes," the wizened fool said, grinning big dumb and effete as he leaned back in his seat.

"I am exceedingly sorry, Herr Chamberlain," I said, "but I can no longer discuss these matters. Your plan, after developments the last few days, is no longer practicable."

Chamberlain jerked straight up in his seat and declared: "I can rightly say I've obtained everything you asked for without a drop of German blood lost, and I risked my political career in so doing. I'm puzzled and disappointed by your attitude, and want to know what has changed?"

"We have a sincere and empathetic concern about the aspirations of Polish and Hungarian nationalists who, like the Sudeten Germans, are being subjugated on land that is really theirs but has been artificially ripped away by the Czech pseudo state."

"What proposal do you have to settle matters peacefully?"

"The Czechs would have to leave the Sudetenland right away and the Wehrmacht would move right in. All Czech military, police, and governmental entities have to be removed. And, of course, the Czechs wouldn't be compensated for losses. Plebiscites could then follow."

Chamberlain argued acquiescently until a telegram from the Sudetenland arrived. After reading the message, I stared at the prime minister while thrusting the paper at my translator.

"Read this."

Twelve more Germans had been murdered.

"We won't tolerate these atrocities much longer," I stated. "If I wait, Prague will be Bolshevized. That will not happen, Herr Chamberlain. This I certainly will not permit."

CONFUSION
By Prime Minister Neville Chamberlain

Back in my hotel I kept trying to determine what lurked in that man's morbid mind. I could not comprehend anyone going to war now to get something he had already been granted and would quite soon receive. No rational explanations emerged during an interminable night. I was simply overwhelmed by the imminence of senseless slaughter.

In the morning I did have to agree, in part, with alarmed members of government who insisted we withdraw our objection to Czechoslovakia mobilizing. A message was sent apprising the Czechs that we could no longer take responsibility for advising them not to mobilize. But far more importantly, I wrote Hitler a letter and offered to submit his needs to the Czechs for their examination. I assured him my problem with his position was not in Germany acquiring the Sudetenland, but by doing so immediately and by force. That would not be acceptable to Britain and France, or to Czechoslovakia, which would likely resist. Instead, I suggested Hitler let the Sudeten Germans maintain peace in their areas until an orderly transfer could be arranged.

I waited many hours for a reply. When it arrived, I was standing composed and ready on my balcony aerie, watching the German translator open a large brown envelope. Hitler's message then splattered me with complaints and demands. I responded with a crisp note telling him to write out his terms along with a map and that I would submit them to the Czechs. I indicated I would return to England, upon reading his memorandum, since it was apparent I could perform no further service in Godesberg.

As it had at Berchtesgaden, my resolve to at once terminate worthless talks prompted Hitler. He invited me to see him that evening. The meeting began late, past ten o'clock, and Ribbentrop and other Germans were present with a few members of my staff. I sat near Hitler, and he examined me as I listened to the translator read his memorandum. Gradually I hardened my expression toward this most outrageous man who demanded the Czechs begin evacuation in a little more than two days, on September twenty-sixth, and be completely out by the twenty-eighth.

"But this is an ultimatum," I admonished him.

"It is not."

"It certainly is."

Hitler pointed to the top of the page and said, "Look at the heading. It says 'Memorandum.' Memorandum, not ultimatum."

"It's an ultimatum, and one I refuse to send to Czechoslovakia because it's absurd, arbitrary and unfair, and could not possibly be carried out in such short time. The Czechs would refuse, and many other countries would concur, and my country would too."

The Fuehrer argued. My advisers vigorously buttressed my point of view. Our stake in this grim exchange was the ultimate one of preventing war.

Discussion stalled as an adjutant entered and gave Hitler a message. The Fuehrer said something in German that included my name and handed the paper to the translator, who read: "Benes has just announced over the radio a general mobilization of Czechoslovakian armed forces."

Silent and still, everyone stared at a human powder keg before he said, "Despite this unheard of provocation, I'll still keep my promise not to start hostilities while the prime minister remains on German soil. But this does settle everything. The Czechs are preparing to fight and go back on their word."

"Herr Hitler," I said, "this maneuver by the Czechs is in no way offensive in nature or threatening to Germany. They're merely taking a precaution. They've agreed to self-determination in the Sudetenland."

"Then why did they mobilize?"

"They had to. Germany mobilized first."

"Ridiculous. Germany hasn't mobilized. Czechoslovakia has. I must tell you, Herr Chamberlain, that I've been patient, much too patient. We have a saying, a philosophy forged long ago by our nation's suffering: 'An end, even with terror, is better than terror without end.' I say that to you, Herr Chamberlain. I say that to the world."

Despite my continued efforts to reassure Hitler that his aims could be peacefully attained, he remained belligerent. So I asked him, "Is the memorandum absolutely your last word on this matter?"

"It is my last word," he replied.

"In that case, there's no point in continuing these discussions. I'll go home with a heavy heart because you've shattered the last hope for peace in Europe. I've made every effort, and my conscience is clear. Unfortunately, Herr Hitler, you haven't responded with equal sincerity."

"Herr Chamberlain, especially for you, I'll make a very rare concession and postpone the date of the Czech evacuation until October first. I hope that will facilitate your task."

"I fully appreciate the Fuehrer's consideration on this point."

"I certainly appreciate your efforts to preserve peace, Herr Chamberlain. Your being here is especially noteworthy since the Sudetenland is my final territorial concern in Europe. I promise you that."

Now I felt considerably better, and told Hitler I would transmit his proposals. Then, just before leaving, I smiled and said: "Auf Wiedersehen."

Later that day, refreshed and encouraged after sleeping, I flew home fully resolved to maintain peace. As my plane approached London, humming high over the Thames, I surveyed countless thousands of houses beneath me, and thought about the mothers inside with their children.

"We cannot protect our citizens," I told my cabinet. "Hitler will fight if his terms aren't accepted. Since the Czechs have already agreed to the transfer of the Sudetenland, then the sooner the better. I feel encouraged by this. Hitler wouldn't deliberately deceive a man with whom he had been in negotiations."

Dissension stirred during a rousing debate.

"Ultimately," I said, "the proposals aren't ours to accept or reject. That's up to the Czechs."

The French, including Prime Minister Daladier, came to London on Sunday, the twenty-fifth. Daladier said his country could not approve of Germany invading the Sudetenland.

"Then are you willing to go to war?" I asked him.

No precise answer emerged.

The French worried me by not asking if we would go to war with Germany if they did. At any rate, the French would not accept Hitler's demands outright. Neither would many cabinet members. We've conceded enough, they said.

War was the one thing I would not concede.

READY TO SPEAK
By Adolf Hitler

I had had enough and was going to get more. The situation had to be made exactly clear. We Germans were not going to take it anymore. I was going to say that tonight at the Sportpalast. I had to speak strong and very well, so I paced passionately as I pined and prepared.

I did not want to be interrupted, not ever, and especially not now, but I had to meet with an insipid emissary, Horace Wilson, and a couple of others coming to me at the Chancellery. These idiots brought a letter, and I shifted and frowned as I listened, then heard: "The British public doesn't like your proposal."

I shot up and stomped toward the office door.

"That's it. That's it. There's no use talking any more."

Looking back at the meek and silent buffoons, I decided to continue back in my seat. The translation resumed, and I periodically jerked my hands in disgust. Then the translator said: "The Czechs regard your proposals as wholly unacceptable."

"This is ridiculous," I said, "and not worth further discussion. The Germans are being treated like niggers. I tell you, I'm not going to take it. We're not a bunch of niggers, and Czechoslovakia's going to be where I want her by October first, and I don't care a pfennig if France and England decide to strike."

"Please negotiate with the Czechs," said Wilson. "The principle of cession has already been agreed upon."

That night at the Sportpalast I burst onto the stage and exclaimed: "Now before us stands the last problem that must be solved and will be solved. It is the last territorial claim which I have to make in Europe, but it is the claim from which I will not recede and which, God willing, I will make good. You must understand. We are confronted by an evil criminal government that has perpetrated the most appalling and horrendous crimes of the twentieth century, and President Benes is the cold architect. While he kills and maims Germans, Mr. Benes is able to sit in Prague, convinced: 'Nothing can happen to me. In the end, England and France stand behind me.'

"So now, my fellow countrymen, the time has come when I can no longer mince matters. Mr. Benes will have to hand over our territory on October first. Peace or war, the choice is his.

"I have made every effort, every concession imaginable, and I do so now by expressing my complete disinterest in annexing Czechoslovakia as a whole. I tell you: I want no Czechs. I merely want our German brothers no longer mired in pain.

"So I now step before you as the nation's first soldier, and I ask you, my German people, to take your stand behind me, man by man, and woman by woman. Let the world know: my will is the will of the people, and behind me there now marches a people of overwhelming determination.

"Is there to be peace or war? Mr. Benes must decide."

This roar in a life of uproar was memorable and intense, and I sat electrified in my chair, delighted and exhausted as images of thousands stretched arms entered my glowing eyes.

The brave and clever Goebbels then leaped to his feet and proclaimed: "One thing is sure: 1918 will never be repeated."

Pouncing tall from my seat, I exploded: "Ja."

GOOD NEWS
By Horace Wilson

Soon after Hitler marched in, and we were seated, I smiled and conveyed the news: "Early this morning Prime Minister Chamberlain announced that the British government 'feels morally responsible' to ensure that the Czechs keep their promise to cede the Sudetenland. He stressed this should be carried out with 'all reasonable promptitude, providing the German government will agree to the settlement of terms and conditions of transfer by discussion and not by force.' I hope the chancellor appreciates and can accept this proposal."

Everything is up to the Czechs," Hitler said. "I'll destroy them if they defy me. This I will do right away."

Shouldering a great burden, I slowly arose and read this official statement: "If France, in fulfillment of her treaty obligations, should become actively engaged in hostilities against Germany, the United Kingdom would feel obliged to support France."

"That's a matter of complete indifference to me. We'll probably be at war within a week."

I still tried to negotiate, but Ambassador Nevile Henderson

indicated we should leave. Before getting to the door, I managed to evade Henderson and tell Hitler up close: "I shall try to make these Czechs sensible."

MILITARY PARADE
By Adolf Hitler

I did not have to wait any longer and was not going to. Waiting was for cowards. Secretly I issued orders for assault units to advance to forward positions athwart Czechoslovakia. I was absolutely prepared, and Germans almost were, and would soon be much more so. One of my motorized divisions was rolling through Berlin for all to see. I stood at the Chancellery window, reviewing mechanized might and men of steel. I knew crowds were going to dash into the streets like I had in 1914, like the whole nation had. Some spectators began to emerge. But only a few. Certainly more would soon appear. They had to. Where were they? What was the matter? I waited quite awhile, then stepped away from the window.

Maybe now was not the divine instant. Only I would know. I reminded myself of that. Maybe some were worried about one million Czechs mobilized in mountain fortifications. Perhaps some were concerned about French numerical advantages in the West. Others might be aggrieved by perceived British advantages at sea. The timid probably worried what Russia might do. My generals cried about the preponderance arrayed against us. These things should not have been concerns, but for the spineless, they obviously were.

PLEA
By Prime Minister Neville Chamberlain

On September twenty-seventh, 1938, as I was ordering preparations for the inconceivable, I sent a message warning President Benes that unless his government accepted Germany's conditions by tomorrow at two p.m., his country would be attacked, and England could do nothing to prevent that. Furthermore, I pointed out Czechoslovakia could not be reconstituted in her current form no matter what the result of a wider war might be.

A little after eight that evening, I was dazed and aggrieved as I walked to microphones to deliver perhaps the most critical words ever uttered: "How horrible, fantastic, incredible it is that we should be digging trenches and trying on gas masks here because of a quarrel in a far-away country between people of whom we know nothing. It seems still more impossible that a quarrel which has already been settled in principle should be the subject of war.

"However much we may sympathize with a small nation confronted by a big and powerful neighbor, we cannot in all circumstances undertake to involve the whole British Empire in war simply on her account. If we have to fight, it must be on larger issues than that."

After my speech, the cabinet indicated its unwillingness to submit to immediate German occupation of the Sudetenland. If that was their position, then at this late hour we would leave it for the time being. I was very tired and my stomach hurt. Every possibility for peace seemed exhausted. I did stir, however, when a message arrived. Hitler said he regretted the idea of any attack on Czechoslovak territory and was even prepared to give a formal guarantee for the remainder of Czechoslovakia. He was also ready to work out details with the Czechs. He asked me to help bring the Prague government to reason and prevent it from implementing its plan of dragging England and France into world war.

Though it was now well past midnight on the twenty-eighth, little more than twelve hours from the expiration of Germany's ultimatum, I wrote with hope and told Hitler, "I feel certain that you can get all the essentials without war and without delay."

THE MOMENT
By General Erwin von Witzleben

We called Hitler the bird and Berlin the cage, and the bird had been in our cage a few days, just where he had to be. We could strike anytime now. We had been thinking about it a lot, anxious, waiting for the exact moment. We already would have struck if everything had been ideal. And now, finally, it was. Word just arrived that Hitler irrevocably planned to go to war. I hurried through heavy morning air to tell General Halder, whose rage brought him to tears. He rushed to inform General von Brauhitsch. When Halder returned, he said Brauhitsch was almost ready. But Brauhitsch wanted to wait, needing more proof, which was ridiculous. Hitler's deadline lurked two hours away.

"We have to do it now," I said.

"We should," General Halder said.

"Everything is ready."

"Then I think we can."

There was a knock at the door — a message for General Halder. He read with concentration and care. Then he looked at me.

"Now we can't do anything," he said. "Chamberlain, Daladier and Mussolini are going to meet Hitler tomorrow in Munich."

IN CHAMBERLAIN'S HAND
By A British Diplomat

Clear and clean and white as canvas the paper flew over the English Channel with Prime Minister Chamberlain. Though a mere medium for considered thought and communication, lacking all vital animalistic organs, it was still taut as everyone else, and quite more privy than most to the real currents around. The prime minister, in whose special service it was, carried a heart fraught with fatal obligation, and his words and thoughts always, inevitably focused with force on no war, no war and, again, no war. This especially pronounced disinclination was forged to a significant degree by Chamberlain's much younger and beloved cousin, Norman, who he had looked up to with a special admiration for the latter's sensitivity and devotion. During the Great War, Norman had written Neville that "nothing but immeasurable improvements will ever justify all the damnable waste and unfairness of this war," and that truth, combined soon with Norman's death, reinforced the future prime minister's will that never, almost absolutely never again will something like this happen, not with him now in charge, which he certainly was, and to a most thorough and unusual degree.

In Munich, there wasn't much bickering since those most aggrieved were not permitted in the special conference room walled in leather. After midnight on September thirteenth, following a dozen hours of discussion, the most important leaders signed some other paper that stated Germany would occupy the Sudetenland in stages between October first and tenth. Later, Chamberlain yawned as he and Daladier and others explained terms to the Czechs, who had been waiting somewhere in the huge stone convention and were most anxious to find out. What they heard displeased them but could not be helped, and the prime minister certainly needed sleep to be ready for Hitler in a few hours.

When the meeting started, the paper had just been adorned with portentous black type that pledged England and Germany would never go to war with one another, and would as well cooperate in many places and in many disciplines. Hitler's soft hands touched it but an instant before he signed. And soon we were off, back across the Channel. After landing, Chamberlain held the paper nicely while reading the news then lifted it high and happy in his smiling hot hand, and that ignited joy and celebration in England and throughout the world.

BASTARD
By Magda Goebbels

I didn't like looking in the mirror anymore, but sometimes I had to see. My face was widening as wrinkles encroached and my blond hair faded. Many things change after bearing five children in six years. I had thought it was all right. It wasn't really bad. It just was not the same.

It was horrible. I had chosen to be unaware but could not remain so after receiving so many scurrilous letters. The letters were unsigned, but foreign press reports were well documented. I tried to be stoic. I think I was. But my pride chewed me up. Not only was my husband behaving like a libidinous tramp, a male whore, he often coerced women into bed with threats of professional exile. He was heartless, a devil. And the whole world knew.

I confronted him and said, "You are?"

He smiled.

"You are," I said, louder.

"Yes."

"You must not do this anymore. Please don't do it so much."

"I hope you haven't forgotten the agreement we made before marriage."

"I didn't think it would be like this."

"You know my creative needs."

Often I reminded myself that Joseph was indeed an extraordinary man, and the sheer number of his whores in a sense diluted my humiliation. At least he was married to me. At least he still loved me. I hoped he did, until Lida Baarova. I tried to ignore her, but everyone was talking. Eventually, my husband brought her to our weekend home, Schwanenwerder. Lida was wearing the smallest bathing suit, just two thin pieces, and she and Joseph cuddled while our guests cut me with glances.

"I want a divorce," I told Joseph afterward. "And I plan to talk to the Fuehrer about this."

"Don't do that. And don't worry. I'll stop seeing Lida."

I trusted my husband. He had a lot in this marriage, too. I hoped he needed me. I thought we might be happy again. Then a close associate of Joseph's, Karl Hanke, showed me photocopies of letters Joseph had recently written to Lida. Shortly thereafter, I went with friends to see a play. When I entered my box, there, in the next, sat Joseph with Lida. As everyone in the audience looked up, I solemnly turned and marched out of the theater.

The following day I demanded Joseph come out to Schwanenwerder, where I now lived most of the time, and told him I must have a divorce. He attempted further deceit, but I insisted this was the end.

"I'm going to shoot myself," he declared.

"I hope you do. And soon."

He grabbed a revolver and said: "Goodbye."

I became frantic. I still cared about the father of my children. I couldn't stop that. I called everywhere. Where was he? Was he even alive? Finally I reached his adjutant at the Propaganda Ministry. Joseph was taking a bath and whistling.

A few weeks later Karl Hanke provided more incriminating letters from Joseph to Lida, and I confronted him again.

"You're a liar, and I'm sick of all this."

He denied everything.

"Then swear to me on the lives of our children that you haven't been seeing Lida and never will again."

He walked, that is he limped like a misfit, to our children's pictures, clasped his hand on one, and made the vow.

"Now do you believe me?"

"No," I cried, and ran from the room.

In a few days, after we reviewed our pile of lamentable documents, Karl arranged for me to see the Fuehrer, who had always admired me as the most cultured of Nazi wives. I told him the whole sordid story and showed him copies of the letters. He seemed to understand and said he would talk to Joseph. During that discussion, Hitler more or less sided with my husband. Karl interceded to explain everything again, and this time he convinced him. The Fuehrer banned Joseph from all social activities in his presence. That was the ultimate deprivation.

I had a second meeting with the Fuehrer and told him I had to have a divorce.

"I'm sorry, but I can't grant you that," he said.

"But my husband said he wants a divorce, too. He wants to marry Baarova. He'll give up all his power for her."

"Yes, he wants to, but I'll be needing him."

"I've got to have some assurances, some protection. I want you to ban Baarova from the Reich. Surely you can do that for me."

"All right. She'll be expelled and never allowed to return. I'll do that just for you."

URGENT MATTER
By Hirschel Grynspan

Years ago my parents had fled Poland for Germany. They thought everything would be better there. I don't know why. All they did was have children. At home there was never anything for me. I was so sick of that. I ran away. Nobody really cared. The only thing I could do as a teenager in Paris was go to clubs. At one I met Ernst vom Rath, and we became very friendly.

"Hirschel, this is too much," he said.

I embraced him and eased my head on his shoulder. He pushed my chest but I held tight.

"Ernst."

"This is too too much, Hirschel."

"Please, Ernst."

"I'm sorry, Hirschel, but you're just going to have to go."

"I can't..."

"No more, Hirschel. You certainly aren't my only friend."

He ripped my arms from his body and lifted me off the couch and handed me my shirt, shoving it into my chest, and put his hands on my shoulders and pushed me to his front door.

"I'm sorry, Hirschel, but you can't come back."

I hardly survived, and everything became unbearable when my family wrote. The Nazis had just torn them and thousands of others from their homes, jammed them into boxcars and pushed them back into Poland. The Poles did not want them, either, but Nazi machine guns faced anyone who turned around.

Perspiring in the cold, I went to a cafe to think, and decided to go to the German Embassy to see Ernst. I told him I had to talk to the ambassador.

"You'll have to get out of here immediately."

"No. This is too important."

"I cannot help you."

"You've got to. Someone has to."

Ernst moved toward me with irritation, and I grabbed a pistol from my coat and shot him a few times. I wanted to shoot the ambassador, too, but guards rushed in and disarmed me.

"I'm not a dog," I yelled as they twisted me away. "You always chase me like a dog."

NIGHT OF BROKEN GLASS
By A Rabbi

From high my eyes saw them marching with flames shining on wrenched and stupid faces. They would be coming for me, I had feared, but was convinced it could never really happen. Yet outside they stood, cursing before they kicked in my door and shattered around inside, forever applying more fire, and I saw through smoke the waning image of pews as fire climbed my walls and blackened everything, and soon flames smoked the ceiling and enveloped my neck, while throughout Germany shops were sacked and windows broken and people yanked from homes then kicked and beaten before being dragged away, and as fire engulfed my head all was alight, and I saw jagged glass in the street glowing like crystal before my frame collapsed in a charred heap on the ground next to shining glass in flames.

BRIEFING
By Joseph Goebbels

Reporters always waited for me because I told them to. I was in total charge of information, and no one could discredit that. I ordered all prevaricating bastards thrown out right away. Sometimes they were taken to the nearest border and shoved across, along with their vicious lies. Any disagreeable journalist not expelled was at least warned his health might decline if his reports didn't improve.

Now I was going to the Propaganda Ministry to brief the foreign press. I made sure I was very calm and smooth when I walked in and summoned everyone around me, and announced: "Anything you have heard about looting and destruction of Jewish property is a stinking lie. Not a hair of a Jew was disturbed."

They didn't say a word. I waited at least two seconds, and they still didn't say anything. So I left, walking calm and smooth and fast.

REMEMBERED
By Doctor Bloch

I felt better when the Gestapo removed the yellow paper from my house and office. And when all Jews were ordered out of Linz to Vienna within forty-eight hours, the Gestapo told me I was an exception, and I realized the Fuehrer had remembered my efforts to save his dying mother. But someone broke in and stole all the postcards he had painted and sent me years ago from Vienna, and I knew I better leave, too. I only asked if I might be allowed to take my life savings, since I was an old man. The Gestapo refused, and I doubt he would have approved.

INVESTIGATION
By Heinrich Himmler

"Jawohl, Mein Fuehrer.
"Jawohl.
"Jawohl.
"Jawohl, Mein Fuehrer."
I clutched the phone pressed extremely tight to my head, and my heels were click click, clicking hard as I talked to the Fuehrer, who several times had ordered me to investigate his father's background and find out why he'd so long been known as Alois Shicklgruber, the surname of the Fuehrer's grandmother.

"I must know who my grandfather was," said the Fuehrer.

"We haven't been able to find a thing, Mein Fuehrer, and we've certainly made extraordinary efforts."

"This is for history. Try harder."

"Jawohl."

We still could not find a thing, and there was nothing to worry about anyway. The newest racial laws decreed a German was still a German even if he had a Jewish grandparent, so long as he wasn't married to a Jew or didn't worship like one.

WITH THE FUEHRER
By Renate Mueller

Being around him in public had not been enough. This time he wanted me alone. I was so excited entering his private apartment. He kissed my hand and told me I was a beautiful actress. Then his servant closed the doors and left. Bowing slightly the Fuehrer said to please sit down on a big soft sofa. He offered me some tea and asked about my career. I could tell he was going to take his time. He didn't have to.

What a gentleman. In front of me he walked back and forth, very crisp with excellent posture. His soft hands joined behind his back.

"It is extraordinary everything has been happening," he said. "It is extraordinary and unbelievable everything I have done."

"It really is fantastic," I said.

I wanted him to come sit next to me. But he continued to pace.

"I've done things no German has done. My accomplishments have never been approached. Frederick the Great and Bismarck were children compared to me. All future leaders will also fail in comparison. Sometimes I fear my legacy may be too great. But that's all right, because it must be. The really extraordinary thing, what even I can't fathom sometimes, is that I started with such a weak and degraded Germany, and now, in so little time, I have built this great nation and my genius just keeps getting stronger and everyone is so terrified. I guarantee you Germany will never be degraded again and I'll do things beyond comprehension and the whole world is going to..."

Exhaling hard, I lunged from my seat and embraced the Fuehrer. He started kissing me, his hot hands caressing my cheeks, and I stuck my tongue in his mouth and used two wild hands to stroke all over his back.

"Make love to me," I said.

Stepping back I kicked off my shoes and jumped out of my dress and said, "Get undressed," and he started, and I tore off my bra and stepped out of my panties and ran to the Fuehrer and helped him pull off his shirt then his pants and grabbed his underwear and pulled but he pushed away so I moved quick to the sofa and said, "Come here right now."

"No. You come here."

He lay on his back on the floor. I loved that. As I smiled, preparing to go down, he said, "Stop. Wait. You don't understand. You can't. But you've got to."

"What?"

"Kick me."

"No, I, ah..."

I started to back away but the Fuehrer grabbed one of my legs.

"You've got to... now."

I put my hands over my eyes but that didn't work and I didn't know what to do. There was the Fuehrer, squirming on the floor. I had to, I think. I couldn't think. I just suddenly kicked him a little.

"Harder."

I did it again.

"Harder."

I kicked him hard with a cold foot, my eyes getting hot as I screamed, "No more, I can't," kicking, kicking hard until tears jarred onto his belly. Then he held my ankles and pulled one over the other side, forcing me over him, and jerked my feet toward his armpits before he grabbed my hips and pulled me squatting down over his face, which felt like a sword, and I said, "For God's sake."

"Please, understand."

"I can't."

He kept me there, pinned, my hands shaking over my face, and I had to get out, but he kept pulling, and I had to stop, I had to, somehow, I shot little puddles of horror on his face. Chest heaving from the floor, he released me, and I tore on my clothes and ran out the door, wishing I was dead.

REASONING WITH A FRIEND
By Adolf Hitler

Certainly there were problems. There had long been problems. But these things could be overcome peacefully by a statesman like me. After all, I was friendly with Poland. We were outstanding friends. It was I who had signed a twenty-year nonaggression pact with Poland in 1934. The spirit of that pact was very much alive and needed to be discussed. In January 1939 I invited Jozef Beck, the Polish foreign minister, to the Berghof.

I wanted to be friendly. So I asked Beck if there was anything special on his mind. After all, his concerns were my concerns. Well, Danzig was on the foreign minister's mind. That was not a surprise. Danzig pervaded many people's thoughts and emotions. Danzig certainly pervaded mine. And I wanted my friend to understand. We Germans daily suffered the ignominy of having to travel through a "Corridor," a hall of shame astride the Baltic, so we could get to Danzig and East Prussia. This Corridor was intrinsically ours and had been earned in battle long ago and, without giving Beck a history lesson, I did politely tell him: "Danzig is German, will always remain German, and at some point will be reunited with the Reich. I can assure you, Colonel Beck, that no machinations are brewing, but certainly you realize that long-suppressed and inexorable forces are becoming manifest.

"Germany needs Danzig, and control of the Corridor. We'll modernize it, for everyone's benefit. We also need a big new autobahn through the Corridor, and a major train throughway."

"I'm afraid, Herr Reichkansler, that I don't see how Poland could possibly benefit from such a change. I do understand, of course, that Danzig is a very difficult problem."

"I must assure the minister that this would create a great advantage for Poland. Your boundaries would be secure and guaranteed by the Reich, and our countries could forge a treaty that would endure for decades."

"Naturally, I'll consider carefully everything you've said. But I must have time."

Ribbentrop met with Beck the following day, and the Pole said he had come away from our talks feeling pessimistic, and saw no way at all to reach agreement over Danzig. I had been afraid of that. In fact, I had always known the Poles would want to subjugate Germans.

MISSION OF MERCY
By President Emil Hacha

They were coming. They certainly could. I was sure they would. Nothing could stop them. The Germans were in fact already occupying one of our towns. As I left Prague I knew I had to placate Hitler, or the city would not be there when I returned. The train ride to Germany was long and rough, and bad for my heart, and I did not want any of this.

In Berlin the Germans received me, as well as my daughter and the foreign secretary, and took us to a very nice hotel to wait. It was a very long wait, all afternoon and evening on March fourteenth, and I felt quite ill as I kept thinking and talking about the Germans' ability to blast us. Finally, they summoned me. At one a.m. I staggered into the Fuehrer's cavernous office, which was so gloomy I could barely see.

"I've wanted to meet you for a long time," I said. "Your wonderful ideas and actions have been a great help to everyone. I, myself, have never mixed in politics. Until very recently, as perhaps you know, my career has been confined to law, and I was just a supreme court judge. I've always been suspicious of the politicos. I saw very little of Benes and the others, and when I did, it was unpleasant. The Benes regime was a bad regime, one absolutely alien to me, and last fall when it became my task to be head of state, I was determined to silence the Benes supporters, but, as you know, there were still too many of them. We're trying everything possible."

After listening attentively, Hitler pounced: "The Benes spirit is still poisoning Czechoslovakia. Your country has far too long been a barbaric, uncivilized state. You Czechs have tortured and maimed the German minority, who by accident and Versailles treachery were caught within your absurd borders."

Stark silent, I stared at the Fuehrer.

"Of course, President Hacha, I don't at all mean to imply any distrust of you personally. I do trust you, and that's why I agreed to see you. I wanted to extend this final kindness to the Czech people, if they're deserving. If so, there could be dawning a great opportunity for peace among our peoples."

Perhaps there is a little hope, I thought.

"Whether there will be peace or war is entirely up to you, President Hacha. This morning at six, the German Army will move into Czechoslovakia from all sides, and the Luftwaffe will occupy all airfields. If there's any resistance, Czechoslovakia will be destroyed. I would've exterminated your country last fall if it hadn't at least pretended to acquiesce. But I'm in no position to extend any more favors. The situation is intolerable. You do have a choice. If, in a few hours, German soldiers are peacefully received, then I'll be inclined to be generous with Czechoslovakia."

"I understand absolutely what must be done," I said. "But how can I possibly convince my whole country in such a short time in the middle of the night?"

"I suggest you and the foreign secretary contact Prague at once. It's embarrassing to have to remind you how devastatingly outnumbered you are."

Goering and Ribbentrop accompanied us to the next room and gave me some documents. After reading, I put them down and said, "I can't sign these. My people would forever curse me."

"You have to sign," Goering said.

Ribbentrop snatched the documents from the table and jammed them into my retreating hands.

"You must do as he says."

"I can't do this," I insisted, placing the papers back on the table and walking away from two Germans who chased me like hungry dogs.

Goering shoved a pen at me and said, "I would naturally hate for my Luftwaffe to have to destroy a beautiful city like Prague. That would be a tragedy. But I'll do it if I have to. The Czechs aren't the only consideration, you know. I want the British and French to see what can happen. This could be a great opportunity to show them. But Prague is so..."

That's all I heard until opening my eyes in a haze. I think I was on a sofa. Above me stood a man with a syringe. He must have been a doctor. The Germans gave me a phone, a direct line to Prague. I explained what we had to do. There was no major argument. Soon I signed documents that said we unanimously agreed about everything: Czechoslovakia wanted to be pacified and have its fate placed in the Fuehrer's protecting hands.

PRAGUE
By Adolf Hitler

Exhausted but elated, I boarded my big bulletproof train and slept several hours before I arose and opened the shades to study with amazement a Czechoslovakian landscape now mine. The final part of the journey I made in a caravan of cars, and even snow and ice could not cool me as I moved toward the heart, to Prague. Cruising in after dark, I was taken to the pinnacle, Hradshin Palace, high on cliffs overlooking the city. That night at our celebration I grabbed a beer and chugged some before drumming my chest with a few fistic strikes.

The morning emerged icy and overcast but clear enough still to see from my throne a grand city of ornate towers and buildings obviously designed by German architects, who alone were capable of such feats. Bismarck and Moltke had stayed here as statesman and warrior, and now I reigned here as both, though during my journey of expansion scarcely a shot had been fired. I certainly wanted to maintain peace. Everything was getting very nice and tidy. This former abscess of continuous disturbance was pacified and incorporated in keeping with our law, the universal law of self-preservation. Naturally, my maps would now need delightful revision, for in fact Czechoslovakia had ceased to exist.

FAKERS
By Joseph Stalin

"The democracies are a sham," I told the Eighteenth Party Congress in Moscow. "They're obviously trying to push Germany to the East in promise of easy prey, hoping the Nazis will eventually, inevitably clash with us. That isn't going to work because we will pursue a policy of peace and expanded economic relations with all countries. Weak-kneed Western warmongers aren't going to get me to pull their asses out of the fire."

GUARANTEE
By Prime Minister Neville Chamberlain

Clearly, we had not been obligated to try to save a Czechoslovakia that had really stopped being a state. What was there to save then? Certainly, though, there were grave concerns. My Foreign Office people were outraged. And so was I. I in fact was the most aggrieved since it was I who had risked so much to try to build a special diplomatic relationship with Herr Hitler. By deceiving me, the wretched little dog had put all of us in peril.

I responded on March thirty-first, walking taut and numb into the House of Commons to deliver these urgent words: "In the event of any action which clearly threatened Polish independence and which the Polish government accordingly considered it vital to resist with their national forces, His Majesty's government would feel themselves bound at once to lend the Polish Government all support in their power."

TERROR
By Adolf Hitler

When the news arrived I screamed and kept smashing the table until my hands were bruised. British hypocrites, after centuries of colonizing the world, were still telling me I couldn't even pursue territory that had long been German prior to its theft by Versailles bandits. The British did not understand fairness. Neither did the Poles. I prepared a lesson for them. It was called Case White and designed to forever remove the Polish threat. Danzig would be declared part of the Reich at the first shot, if not before, and the Polish military would be annihilated. If possible, the war would be confined to Poland. England and France, at most, would make a passive declaration of war to save face. Defensive measures could at any rate protect our Western Front. My only serious worry was the moaning of timid generals.

DIVIDING GIANTS
By Colonel Josef Beck

As the paramount and otherwise craftiest of ruling Polish colonels, I designed foreign policy maneuvers to confound and hamstring the two giant savages menacing us one on each side. To make sure the Russians would not feel compelled to attack, I was unreceptive to German overtures to align against the communists. In the same spirit, I told the British and French that Poland could not possibly include Russia in an alliance against Germany.

Chamberlain's offer of support was in harmony with a safe — and soon to be burgeoning — Poland, and I was pleased to go to London and sign the agreement on April sixth, 1939. The prime minister agreed it was better to exclude the Russians because, though overtly anxious to be aligned with England and France, they were militarily quite weak and inept, and could not be trusted.

TODAY
By A German Woman

I got to come to Berlin for the celebration on April twentieth, and everyone was so proud and excited. Big planes ignited the sky in perfect formations, and the road roared beneath rolling panzers and marching troops and horses. Banners, bright and German, festooned the horizon, and I kept jumping to see everything I could, and was so excited I could hardly stand it as he came at us, standing high with a riveting salute, looking right over at me, looking near me, at least, the Fuehrer, fifty today, surrounded by so many troops and citizens and important people from all over the world, all there to celebrate the birthday of our incredible Fuehrer.

MY ANSWER, MR. ROOSEVELT
By Adolf Hitler

I was absolutely delighted to receive such a concerned and urgent message from President Roosevelt. He raised essential issues, and by inference invoked others, and, by God, this esteemed man deserved answers, and those I was prepared to provide on April twenty-eighth as I glided in, a sleek and eloquent panther-statesman, to address the Reichstag, and the whole world, which had been unprecedentedly wired, primed and prepared for this tour de force.

"England and Poland, as proved by their recent treaty of treachery, are clearly conspiring to encircle and destroy Germany," I stated. "As a result, there is now obviously no basis for a continuance of the Anglo-German naval treaty nor the generous nonaggression pact I gave Poland a few years before. Not only have the Poles unilaterally abrogated our agreement, they have, I reveal now for the first time publicly, declined my one and only magnanimous offer regarding Danzig and the Corridor. The Polish attitude and actions are most regrettable and incomprehensible, yet an international press campaign of lies still insinuates, and sometimes baldly accuses, that it is I who have aggressive intentions toward Poland. This is outright invention by our enemies. In truth, it was the Poles who mobilized while not a single German soldier did so. The situation is obviously outrageous, but still I remain the most eager of all to maintain peace. I would in fact welcome new treaties to ensure tranquility."

And, of course, there were the issues in Mr. Roosevelt's noble telegram, the translation of which I held soft in my hand, high on the stand overlooking the Reichstag. Most obligated I was to address each and every one of Mr. Roosevelt's concerns. First, it seems that Mr. Roosevelt believed all international problems can be solved by negotiation.

"Answer," I solemnly said.

Then I explained: "If this is so, it is most ironic that the United States itself was the first to forsake the greatest conference of them all, the League of Nations. Years later I myself, after much frustration, saw the wisdom of their move and followed the American example. Certainly, it is essential to also note that the subjugation of the North American continent was not achieved at the conference table nor was the resolution of conflict between North and South.

"Mr. Roosevelt, your view is doubtless honorable, but it finds no confirmation in world history nor in the annals of your own country."

I knew Mr. Roosevelt would understand also the following point: "We Germans at Versailles were inflicted even greater degradations than those imposed on the chieftains of Sioux tribes."

Mr. Roosevelt's most essential concern was that I offer assurances to thirty-one nations that I would not attack.

"Answer," I said.

Then, one by one, I read the many names on the list and was not in the least unnerved by raucous laughter in the Reichstag. Now, now gentlemen, I motioned with a quieting wave of my hand. This is quite really serious.

"I took the trouble to find out which, if any, nations listed in Mr. Roosevelt's curious telegram felt threatened, and the reply was uniformly negative. I must point out that not every nation on the list was free to respond since some — Syria, for instance — are at this moment being subjugated by the military agents of democratic states.

"To me it is stunning, indeed, that Mr. Roosevelt would ask for my guarantee not to attack Ireland and Palestine. Never have I heard Ireland say so much as a single plaintive word about Germany; but daily I read that Ireland is aggrieved by England's repression.

"Evidently it has further escaped Mr. Roosevelt's notice that it is English troops, not German, who currently occupy Palestine and brutally restrict liberty."

Clearly, there were threats abound, and none were German, but still, as a favor to Mr. Roosevelt, I announced my eagerness to offer each of the states on his list just the assurance he asked for. And, with pause and great earnestness, I said, "I cannot let this opportunity pass without, above all, giving assurance to Mr. Roosevelt that I will not attack the territories that must surely concern him most: the United States and the American continent. Any rumors that we have plans to the contrary are rank frauds and gross untruths."

In schoolmaster style I again waved my hands to quiet the laughter. This was absolutely serious, and I wanted to let Mr. Roosevelt know: "I appreciate the burden of responsibility you bear for the history of the entire world and for the history of all nations, such is the enormity of wealth and size of the great nation you lead. My task in a small, formerly chaos-ridden nation is much more modest, yet fundamentally more difficult. Time and space are urgent and compressed in my world, and I do not have the opportunity and leisure of the esteemed American president to ponder universal problems. Providence has dictated to me the task of working for my small nation, and at the same time being of some service to our common pursuit of justice and progress and peace."

RUSSIAN DOUBT
By Count Friedrich von der Schulenburg

Perhaps it was a good sign that Stalin had recently replaced Maxim Litvinov, who was a bloody Anglophile. The new foreign minister, Vyacheslav Molotov, might be better. He beckoned me to the Kremlin for a chat in mid-May 1939. Molotov was concerned that our countries didn't have a better economic relationship, and the cooperative political activities that go with it. He wanted something new between our countries, but when I, as ambassador, undertook to find out what that meant, he was evasive and noncommittal. What specifically, or even more generally, did he and Stalin want?

PACT OF STEEL
By Benito Mussolini

I really did not trust the Germans. They were uncouth and barbaric and treacherous. Maybe they would dump me and align with France for the impending feast. I could not fathom the Huns being so stupid since I had already proved myself a prodigious conqueror by blasting Ethiopia, and exerting a great victory in Spain, and recently overrunning Albania. What the impotent democracies said about this, I did not care. They were terrified of me. They knew I would do what I wanted. And I wanted war.

I was not always precisely sure when I wanted war, so I told Count Ciano to inform Ribbentrop that the Duce did not want war for three years. When Ribbentrop said Germany also wanted to wait that long, I was ecstatic and instantly offered to sign a pact with Germany. The Fuehrer agreed right away. I wanted to name it the Pact of Blood. Instead, however, the Germans insisted we call it the Pact of Steel. I did not care. The Germans could write it up, and I'd sign. Any hostility involving one of us would require the other to promptly come to aid. Even if the Germans did start something earlier than planned, that would leave the Balkans vulnerable to me.

FRANK STATEMENT
By Adolf Hitler

My top military leaders were ordered to the Chancellery on May twenty-third. This eminent group of fourteen uniformed and decorated employees sat somber and eager before me in my study. Without temporizing, I told them: "It would be dangerous to anticipate more gains without violence. The life and death task before us now is to acquire more living space. First, we must isolate Poland to ensure that we aren't besieged by a second front in the West. If England and France aren't kept out of things, then we can't be successful in crushing Poland. I definitely won't make the same strategic errors of the Great War. But, if we attack Poland and the West attacks us, then we will crush Poland and the West simultaneously. I don't think Russia will help Poland, but if she does, we will devastate England and France before dealing with the East.

"All of this has to remain secret. Italy and Japan must not know. Even the General Staff must not know."

The generals understood and did not burden me with the timidity and defeatism of Blomberg and Fritsch.

RUSSIAN REASONING
By Count Friedrich von der Schulenburg

When we tried to trade with the Russians, they were wary of everything and suspected us of primarily trying to distance them from England and France. That was not at all the case. I believed it vital to improve Russo-German relations in all spheres, and I endeavored to convey that to Molotov in June. The talk on the whole proceeded rather well, though Molotov contested numerous points before he said, "I have strong doubts about the durability of treaties signed with Germany, based on recent history."

Small countries really weren't the point, though, and Molotov, despite his caution, managed to acknowledge that relations with Germany should and could be normalized.

COUNTRY FOLK
By Prime Minister Neville Chamberlain

The Russians were such simple country folk, I could neither understand nor trust them. They probably wanted to detach themselves while the capitalist countries destroyed each other. I suppose in that regard the Russians did display some primitive insight. Their armed forces, after all, were strategically insignificant and altogether undependable. It was, nonetheless, politically mandatory for me to attempt to work out a military agreement with them.

BLATHER
By Pravda

Instead of sending Foreign Secretary Halifax or anyone else of stature, the British assigned some very junior gnome to supposedly important talks in Moscow, and nothing got done. Therefore, on June twenty-eighth, my otherwise routine pages featured one that blared: "The British and French are just grandstanding and pretending to want an agreement with us. Their real purpose is to paint us as hostile and unreceptive, and thereby facilitate an agreement with our enemies."

FUN
By Eva Braun

Eyes closed tight and my head bouncing back, I just could not stop laughing as all these handsome SS guys and other friends tickled my feet and ribs, and lifted me — oh no you don't — and carried me kicking happily from the beach and tossed me splashing into the pretty blue Bavarian lake. I jumped up and splashed them hard with fast scoops from both hands, and we howled as we wrestled and tugged and splashed, and it felt so good to be wet and hugged and shining hot, with a pretty tan coming as well.

I ran over and climbed the diving platform, pausing erect with feet together before dashing straight to the tip of the board where I jumped high, floating up like a bird before I pointed two-handed diving down and eased in deep, kicking to propel myself under before smooth kicking up fast to break the surface where I shouted and waved to friends.

I loved swimming and did so every day near the Berghof, and after swimming, or before, I exercised on gymnastic bars and often dismounted with a flying flip, turning in mid-air, before landing in good form on my feet, arms styled toward the sky. My favorite feat was bending backwards, absolutely straight back, and pushing my palms onto the ground as a brace as I arched my back and then raised one of my legs high and straight as the other held me bent over backwards and very much in place.

I also loved the feel of new clothes and shopped everywhere I went, moving fast through stores taking this and that, telling clerks to send the bills to the Chancellery as I dashed out and jumped into my chauffeured Mercedes. I was often going to the hairdresser. My hair had to be just right, and that meant many changes in style and color, from natural blond to blondish brown to brown and back. But I had to be careful. Sometimes the Fuehrer said he hardly knew me.

I wanted everything to be perfect when he got off work, and whenever it was I rushed right to him. He really depended on me now, and in many ways I was his hostess. After dinner I got to sit nearest him when everyone gathered to listen to him talk, and only I could snap candid photos. But he still would not let me attend state dinners and formal affairs. I had to stay in my room then.

RUSSIAN COOLNESS
By Count Friedrich von der Schulenburg

My instructions direct from Foreign Minister Ribbentrop stressed our new and resolute desire to forge a fundamentally different and really comprehensive relationship with the Soviet Union. Substantive conversations must therefore be arranged. In Moscow I explained this seminal development to Molotov on the night of August third, 1939.

"I regret, Mr. Ambassador, that we still don't have any proof that a 'new' German attitude exists. What we do have, however, is an extended pattern of German hostility toward the Soviet Union. The Nazis, I must point out, created the Anti-Comintern Pact. That was, and remains, blatantly anti-Soviet. Your relations with Japan are designed solely to threaten Russia. And Munich. Where were we at Munich? The Soviet Union will need far more than rhetoric, Mr. Ambassador, before concluding that Germany really has changed."

Late that night I telegraphed Berlin my impression the Soviets desired, and were progressing toward, an important pact with Britain and France. We would need to exert great effort to reverse Soviet policy and avoid facing a powerful alliance.

PEACE MISSION
By Count Galeazzo Ciano

I loved going to Germany. After important political discussions I generally had the option to host a variety of beautiful German women. Naturally, I also adored Italian women, not just the Duce's daughter, but women in the North were new and different, and the same, too. This time, though, there wouldn't be any fun. The Duce had sent me urgently because he sensed the Germans were again on the precipice.

The first night there I met with Ribbentrop. It was always painful dealing with this dim and utterly reckless man. Though I was entirely frank during our discussion, I did not want to waste much energy or logic until tomorrow, August twelfth, when I'd meet with Hitler.

White-uniformed and determined I bounced up the Berghof steps and soon was listening to Hitler lecture about military and political issues as he periodically referred to expansive maps on a huge table in his study. He had all the answers. Poland was weak. The British and French were weak and timid. His West Wall was impregnable.

"We, your trusted ally, have not been consulted, and feel we're being misled," I said. "This is especially disconcerting since an attack on Poland would lead to a general war."

"No, Count Ciano. No, it will not."

"You must understand how weak Italy is. I don't want you to have any illusions. Our army, navy and air force are all quite ill prepared."

I elaborated. I reasoned. I entreated.

"We don't need you," Ribbentrop sneered.

"History will tell," I said.

"You need also to keep in mind, Count Ciano," Hitler said, "that the Russians must in the future be a part of all discussions."

Now he introduces them into an already overcrowded equation. Well, my dear Fuehrer, when might hostilities with Poland begin?

"It has to be before the end of August, or fall rains will muddy the dirt roads my panzers need. But I might strike much sooner if Poland keeps provoking me. Within forty-eight hours, if necessary. I might strike at any time."

That was enough for one day. Hitler had worn me out, devastated me, really. Then he dragged me to his aerie teahouse and explained what a great view I had.

The next day I did not have much rhetorical fight left. The deal with death had been cemented.

"Let's at least not say a word to the public about this," I said.

"I agree," said the Fuehrer.

Two hours after I left, the Germans issued a communiqué saying Italy and Germany were in complete agreement about Danzig and everything else.

RUSSIAN OVERTURE
By Count Friedrich von der Schulenburg

My diplomatic instincts were warning me in strident tones that the pace of negotiation with the Russians should not be rushed. This feeling I wired to Berlin, but much too soon, on August fifteenth, I received a "most urgent" and frenzied telegram from Ribbentrop. Events now had reached nothing less compelling than a "historic turning point." And this very communiqué was so critical I was instructed to present it to Molotov at once.

That evening I read what Ribbentrop wrote: "English policy has subverted Polish-German relations to a crisis level and a speedy clarification of German-Russian relations is necessary. Rapidly developing events might prevent restoration of German-Russian friendship, and that would prevent us from clarifying jointly territorial questions in Eastern Europe.

"Given the urgency of issues, and the too slow pace of normal diplomatic procedure, I propose to come to Moscow for a short visit to set forth the Fuehrer's views to Stalin. Only in this way will it be possible to lay the foundations for a final settlement of German-Russian relations."

"That's encouraging," said Molotov. "I think such a meeting could generate results, but only if preceded by thorough preparation."

"What results are of interest to the Soviet Union?"

"The Soviet Union would like to find out, for example, if Germany is interested in a nonaggression pact."

I believe I did not permit my arousal to become evident.

"We also want to lessen tension in our relations with Japan.

Germany could certainly help us in that regard. I wonder if Germany would be willing. Any substantive assistance from your country would be most well received here since many Russians have already died in Manchuria.

"Also, the Baltic States. Germany and Russia need to reach an accommodation in the Baltic. I wonder how Germany would feel about that."

"Foreign Minister Ribbentrop is ready to come right away to discuss these matters," I said.

"These discussions must be of a concrete nature," Molotov emphasized. "We're not interested in a mere exchange of opinions. Decisions must be made."

I dispatched Molotov's quite stunning proposals early on the sixteenth, and very late that night I received unequivocal acceptance as well as emphasis that Ribbentrop wanted to come to Moscow in two days or so. This message, too, had to be conveyed directly to Molotov.

After I complied, the Soviet foreign minister unleashed his customary torrent of complaints about Germany's behavior. I sat and listened and became entirely pessimistic until he stated: "I welcome a change in Germany's Soviet policy and am ready for improvement by serious and practical steps. These steps are historically significant, so they can't be rushed."

URGENCY
By Adolf Hitler

My submarines and pocket battleships were rammed in short of where they had to be and so were hundreds of thousands of soldiers. I knew the Russians were responsible, probably with British and French connivance, all of them ganging up to trick me. The hell they would. I wrote Stalin and told the eminent heathen: "It is urgently necessary to clarify matters as soon as possible... because things have to be clarified in the shortest possible time... since intolerable tensions exist... and therefore we should not lose any time... and please receive Ribbentrop in two or three days... I should be glad to receive your early answer."

The rest of the day was miserable. So was the night. I did not bother trying to sleep. Quite late I called Goering, but that didn't do any good, and neither did anything all next day as I paced and inquired and waited and grimaced and squirmed and thought I would pop until the Russians' reply came during a dinner not eaten, and I banged the table and shouted, "I have them. I have them."

DEPENDENCE
By Adolf Hitler

Despite my generals' ignorance of politics, I deigned to favor them with my clear and ruthless picture of the situation. On August twenty-second at the Berghof, I proclaimed: "The most essential fact is that everything depends on me, on my existence. My political talents and the overwhelming fanatical support I enjoy will probably never recur, so we must take advantage of my existence now. It is certainly a perfect time to do so. All our enemies are in decline, and the men who rule them are just blind little worms who groped at the idiotic illusion that Russia would not perceive their real intentions.

"Our life and death task demands iron determination and no shrinking back from anything. There really should be no obstacles. We have the better men. I have unshakable faith in the German soldier. We have to destroy and eliminate Poland quickly. The attack will begin early Saturday, the twenty-sixth. Close your hearts to pity and act brutally."

FINAL WARNING
By Prime Minister Neville Chamberlain

Reports of military movements in Germany were most disturbing and so was news, just released like a bomb, of a possible Soviet-German agreement. Resolving to send an unequivocal message, I wrote Herr Hitler: "His Majesty's Government are determined, as stated in public repeatedly and plainly, to fulfill their obligation to Poland. No greater mistake could be made than to assume recent developments meant intervention by Great Britain on behalf of Poland is no longer a contingency that need be reckoned with. If war once starts, it would be dangerous delusion to think there would be a quick ending, even if German successes were secured on any of the several fronts that would doubtless become embroiled."

SUPREME DIPLOMACY
By Joachim von Ribbentrop

Before reaching the top step to the plane, I turned to pose a Nazi salute and smile very white-toothed, and was delighted to soon be attempting this most stunning diplomatic feat. In the plane I peered happily out the window into cameras, and then we took off. That night, August twenty-second, we landed in East Prussia, and I studied hard in my quarters to prepare for history.

In Moscow the next afternoon I was greeted with top honors and taken to special accommodations that had once been the Austrian embassy. I was very comfortable in this fine place, readying to go to the Kremlin. I arrived there at six p.m., and right away I moved into the key points of Europe's future, and so did Stalin, and our concentration was so incredible we did it all in three hours.

TOASTS
By Joseph Stalin

No one could be trusted, not for long, but right now that did not matter. This deal was really quite a deal, and the best part was a strictly secret protocol. In it the Germans granted us Latvia, Estonia, Finland, Bessarabia and a lot of Eastern Europe and a nice slice of Poland. We gave Germany Lithuania and a free hand in its part of Poland, and we simply divided up Europe in a hell of a feast.

The vodka tasted great, and I posed grinning with Ribbentrop, and we seemed to agree on so many things, including England, that I did not care the Germans for years had been heaping pails of manure in our faces.

"I know how much the German nation loves its Fuehrer," I said. "I should therefore like to drink to his health."

I also toasted Germans in general, and I toasted our pact, and so did Molotov, and Ribbentrop toasted me, and Russia, and I toasted Ribbentrop, and this was damned great.

Feeling very good and sincere as the festivities ended, I took Ribbentrop's arm and told him, "We take the new pact very seriously and will never betray our new partner."

MAGNANIMITY
By Adolf Hitler

Despite Ambassador Nevile Henderson throwing Chamberlain's grenade of a letter in my face on August twenty-third, I responded that I was still anxious to negotiate Danzig and the Corridor with Poland in a spirit of unparalleled magnanimity. My attitude was remarkable since England's unconditional guarantee had emboldened the Poles to commit even more terroristic acts, including several atrocious castrations, against a million and a half Germans in their phony nation.

My good will continued early afternoon the twenty-fifth as I summoned Henderson to the Chancellery and told him: "I am guaranteeing the existence of the British Empire. Yes, I want to assist in her defense should that ever become necessary. Furthermore, I regard Germany's western border as already permanent.

"I'm an artist. That's my nature. I want to spend the rest of my life in creative pursuits, not in war and politics. I am, however, a man of determined and decisive action. If this final offer is not accepted, there will be war. But that hardly seems necessary. I'm prepared to offer England so much just as soon as I settle the German-Polish crisis."

"I must continue to remind you, Herr Chancellor, that Britain cannot consider your proposal unless you proceed peacefully with Poland."

"In that case, don't bother sending my offer at all," I bellowed. "It's clear what you're trying to do. All of you. But I'm a man of exceptional resolve. I still want to maintain peace. Please take my offer to London. You will do that, won't you?"

TO THE FUEHRER
By Benito Mussolini

I was delighted to receive a letter from the Fuehrer, and assured the German ambassador that the Fuehrer had my support all the way. The Duce had long loved and prepared for war. Now it was time. I told my advisers, "I think the democracies will fight, but maybe not. They're quite weak. I don't want to anger the Fuehrer. I'll support him at any cost. If I did less, the whole world would call me a coward."

"Hitler's treating you like a servant," said Count Ciano. "He didn't even tell you about his negotiations with Russia. Tear up the Pact of Steel and throw it in his face."

I really did not want to do that, but I did write the Fuehrer: "It is my duty as a loyal friend to tell the whole truth and inform you beforehand about the real situation. My armed forces are not quite ready. They will be, of course. I am in total charge of preparation. But the Pact of Steel envisaged war in 1942. I will be ready then. I just am not ready now. Therefore, I have to tell you that if the Polish conflict remains localized, Italy will provide political and economic assistance. If, however, Poland's allies counterattack Germany, I will not initiate military action due to our state of war preparation, about which you, Fuehrer, have been clearly and repeatedly informed. But I do want war and will fight right away if Germany can deliver the necessary thousands of trainloads of military supplies and raw materials."

STOP
By Adolf Hitler

With disbelief I received news that Poland and England ratified their treachery and were now mutual defense partners. I could only sit and stew until being struck by the Duce's cannonade of cowardice.

"Stop it, stop everything for now," I ordered. "I'll have to pull a diplomatic coup with the British."

344

BARBARISM
By Joseph Goebbels

All Germans realized the extreme threat. Polish troops were attacking our border and shooting at passenger planes. German civilians in Poland were either being killed or forced to flee, and German property was torched. As an enflamed Poland continued to mobilize, war fever begot chaos. All my newspapers spread the news, and everywhere I went Germans told me they were very upset.

AWAKENED
By Birger Dahlreus

Above all Nazis, my friend Hermann Goering appreciated the possibilities for peace, and he joined me to rush to the Chancellery just after midnight on August twenty-seventh. I had a letter from Lord Halifax. The British emphasized that only a few days would be necessary for negotiations.

Glaring at me upon introduction, Hitler launched a lecture without reading the letter. Finally, I was able to interject, "I'm not a professional diplomat. I'm a businessman from Sweden. But after years of dealings I know and understand the British. Their resolve should never be underestimated. Furthermore, Britain and France are strong and..."

Wild-eyed and gesticulating, Hitler began to rant, "I'll build U-boats if there's a war. U-boats to strangle the enemy. I'll build airplanes, too. Airplanes. I'll build airplanes to annihilate the enemy..."

Goering just watched the outburst.

After expending himself, Hitler said, "Since you know England so well, Herr Dahlreus, can you tell me why my many efforts at reaching agreement have been rejected?"

"I believe the British government lacks confidence in you."

"Idiots'" he shouted, and hammered his heart with a fist. "Have I ever in my life told a lie?"

REASONING
By Prime Minister Edouard Daladier

Under great duress, I had informed Hitler: "Unless you believe French honor and sincerity less sacred than what I myself recognize in the German people, you cannot doubt France will uphold her solemn promises to other nations, such as Poland."

On August twenty-seventh Hitler replied: "As a fellow old front-line soldier, you surely understand my patriotic duty. Imagine what you would do if a French city was, like Danzig, separated from your country? Would the French not be aggrieved if their countrymen were persecuted and murdered? Germany would never fight France for trying to redress such injustices. As an old soldier, I believe you surely see that a nation of honor cannot ignore the cries of countrymen in need of reunification and safety."

Hitler always had an explanation, even when there wasn't one.

AMATEUR ASSISTANCE
By Nevile Henderson

Dahlreus, the irksome amateur, stumbled around with such determined energy he actually fell upon a chord that rang a concession: Germany would agree at once to negotiate with Poland. Dahlreus informed Chamberlain on August twenty-seventh, and by late the next night I carried our reply into the Chancellery. To the Fuehrer I read in German: "No matter what advantage Great Britain might gain by so doing, His Majesty's government will not acquiesce in a settlement that jeopardizes the independence of a state given their guarantee. This position, at the same time, should be considered with Poland's definite assurance that it is prepared to enter into negotiations on a basis that safeguards Poland's interests and secures them by international guarantee. Failure to reach a just settlement might well plunge the whole world into war. Such an outcome would be a calamity without parallel in history."

"We're quite willing to negotiate with the Poles in a just and comprehensive way," Hitler said. "But they, by their relentless assaults on Germans, have shown no inclination to be fair. And you, and your government, have not indicated any concern about German suffering."

Blistered by this boor for the thousandth time, I burst: "I've done everything possible to prevent suffering wherever it may occur and as well to forestall this war you seem intent on provoking. England's word is her honor as it once was with Germany. You must decide whether it's more important for you to subjugate Poland than have peace with Britain."

"We're not bluffing and anyone who thinks so is mistaken."

"And we, sir, are not bluffing either."

At this impasse, having at least precluded one of his harangues, I stressed in parting the need to find out if he was willing to negotiate with the Poles. The German answer would come tomorrow, he promised.

The flower of my life may have been wilting from the ravages of cancer, but I still held hope that the life of Europe would bloom. For that reason I again wore a carnation into the Chancellery early evening on the twenty-ninth. Hitler and Ribbentrop were present and attentive as I received and began to read their reply. Despite its doubts, Germany is willing to negotiate directly with Poland, solely to please England and promote Anglo-German friendship. Good. The German government has never had any intention of threatening the vital interests or existence of an independent Poland. Well, very fine, indeed. The German government agrees to accept our offer to secure the dispatch to Berlin of a fully empowered Polish emissary. All right, I suppose. The emissary is expected to arrive tomorrow...

"This sounds like an ultimatum," I said. "Poland can't be expected to prepare on such short notice."

"When two armies are nose to nose, time is urgent and imperative," Hitler said.

"Can Poland expect to be received on a basis of complete equality?"

"Of course."

"This arrangement sounds very much like ones you've already extended to other unfortunate guests."

"You obviously don't care a whit about how many Germans are butchered in Poland."

"I'm not going to listen to such insults from you or anyone else," I shouted. "If you want war, by God you can have it. You'll find Britain has more resolve and endurance even than Germany."

"I have great admiration for England," Hitler said. "My eternal desire has been to earn your friendship and approval."

I nevertheless departed with the sense that I would never again wear a carnation in Germany.

TOO LATE
By Joachim von Ribbentrop

On my feet I was railing at Nevile Henderson that this was unreasonable and that was out of the question and much was absolutely unheard of. Too much had happened for us to allow more delay. The Poles had to come here by our midnight deadline on August thirtieth, and midnight just passed, so I refused to give a copy of our generous proposals to Henderson. He acted like a criminal, jumping crudely so close to my face. I almost belted the bastard.

SHORT INTERVIEW
By Josef Lipski

Some strange Swede named Dahlreus romped into our Berlin embassy, bringing a British diplomat and sixteen German proposals. After contacting Warsaw, I was ordered to request an immediate interview with Ribbentrop to tell him Poland was favorably considering the proposals.

I arrived at the Foreign Ministry at one p.m., and there I sat one, two, three, four, five hours and more before Ribbentrop received me. I indicated our amenability and my personal regret at being delayed.

"Have you come fully empowered to negotiate?" he said.

I had not.

"I expected you'd come with full authority."

"My government is ready to negotiate very soon."

"There's really no point in our continuing this conversation."

When I got back to the embassy to telephone Warsaw, my line was dead.

GOODS
By A German

"What are you doing? What kind of shot is this?" the prisoner had protested.

He still got injected, and so did about a dozen others, and their bodies were put in Polish military uniforms. The SS called the bodies canned goods. They looked quite real, but then there had been a delay, and the bodies got too stiff and would not look good.

I was kept fresh in reserve for tonight, August thirty-first, 1939.

"Put that uniform on," a guard ordered.

"No," I said.

He shot me a few times, ripped off my stinking prison clothes, and made the switch.

Still breathing, my body was laid at the gate to the radio station at Gleiwitz, not far from the Polish border. SS men, also dressed as Poles, stormed the station, breaching the broadcast room, and fired shots while shouting in Polish. One polished speaker of Polish broadcast threats about how much Poles hated Germans and how imminent war was. A few additional shots were fired inside. When leaving, an SS shot me a few more times to make sure I missed the national broadcast that explained to the German people each of the quite generous sixteen points the Poles had rejected.

George Thomas Clark

THE NEW WAR
1939-1941

PREPARATIONS
By A Polish General

An alarmed and resolute Poland prepared to meet the enemy. We had defeated the Russians in 1920 and knew we could at least delay the Germans for a long time now. By then France could launch an offensive to relieve us. Maybe then we could even counterattack and expand. The Germans sure as hell weren't going to get back the Corridor to Danzig. Into this area we deployed about a third of our thirty-five divisions. The French and others had advised us to dig in further back, behind the Vistula and Sun Rivers. But we could not concede so much industrial territory, vital if we were to sustain war.

WAR
By A German Officer

A little before five on the cool first morning in September 1939, our modest yet formidable cruiser guns began firing on Danzig. The honor to initiate this fusillade enlivened everything from the bowels of the magazine to the tips of guns that hurled shells onto the city, where smoke erupted, and I knew far distant on our Polish frontier other German guns were also firing, and the roar here linked other martial thunder, and the blitz on Poland had begun.

SELF DEFENSE
By Adolf Hitler

I moved with bounce into Kroll Opera House and announced: "The Poles began firing on us early this morning, and we returned fire and will answer bombs with bombs. This treachery has come despite my modest and loyal proposals, and my patience and love of peace. England has also rejected me. The only alternative is therefore to once again put on my dear and sacred uniform, and I will not take it off until victory, or I will perish before the end."

ONLY ALTERNATIVE
By Prime Minister Neville Chamberlain

Everything I had worked for and believed in crashed on this saddest day of my life. Germany did not respond to our ultimatum to at once remove all its troops from recently occupied territory. Consequently, England declared war on Germany a little after eleven on the bleak morning of September third. A somewhat reluctant France had to be stiffened by us and convinced to do likewise later in the day. Though disturbed by the French delay, I did empathize since their forces alone in the West would have to thwart German aggression, as none of ours had yet arrived.

CHARGE
By A Polish Officer

Fearless and determined, we were braced on the ground for their panzers when from above the Stukas began diving — with unimaginable shrieks — to bomb and machine gun us. As soon as possible I ordered my cavalry to ready rifles and swords, and charge. The gruesome green panzers were rolling fast among us now and firing everywhere accurately as more Stukas hurtled in and the panzers stormed by, leaving us entirely naked and confused. After very much fighting in an eternal short while, I buried my face in my sleeve, never wanting again to see so many comrades lying next to slaughtered horses.

PANZERS
By General Heinz Guderian

Following the Great War, I had seen the future of warfare. It lay in movement, and panzers were the key. I immersed myself in training and tactics, and battled many hidebound generals who felt infantry and artillery were still paramount. I knew that would never be again and refused to compromise essential principles. The Fuehrer had eventually supported my ideas, and now he was visiting the front within sight of Kulm, my birthplace and German territory for generations before Poland stole it. Surveying the battlefield, the Fuehrer was as emotional as I, and he smiled and swept his hand and said: "My Luftwaffe did this?"

"No, Mein Fuehrer. The panzers."

PRUDENCE
By General Maurice Gamelin

France wanted to relieve Poland, but there were problems. I had thought the Poles could hold out six months. A lot depended on that. Contrary developments provoked great concern about what France should do. We had promised to partially engage the Germans right after any attack on Poland, then launch a full-scale offensive as soon as we could, perhaps in a little more than two weeks after hostilities began.

We certainly stuck to the first part by attacking Germany in the Saar and claiming about seven miles of enemy territory. But everything bogged down. We were confined to a narrow front of attack since we could not invade through neutral Belgium and Holland, and in Germany the enemy had sown tens of thousands of mines. That was troublesome because we had no mine detectors. Also, most of my artillery was still in storage or en route to the front and would not be ready in time for a great offensive. We, at any rate, were not focused on attacking. France had bled its youth into the battlefields of the Great War and did not want to do so again. And we wondered what

353

would be the use of launching a real offensive to relieve the Poles since they were by now pretty well beyond relief.

JOINING HANDS
By Vyacheslav Molotov

Soon after attacking Poland, the Germans began pestering us to do likewise. At first I replied we would do so at a suitable time that had not yet arrived. On September fifteenth Ribbentrop wired that Warsaw would be captured within a few days and that he expected prompt Soviet military action. The next day I summoned Ambassador Schulenburg, assured him of an imminent Soviet attack, and stated our pretext: we would be preventing a third power from exploiting the chaos to hurt our Ukrainian and White Russian blood brothers.

The following afternoon Schulenburg complained to Stalin about our unpleasant allusion to Germany. Stalin promptly deleted offensive sections so our explanation now stated that since Poland had ceased to exist, the 1932 Polish-Soviet nonaggression pact also ceased to exist, and the Soviet Union was moving in to forestall dangerous developments and protect its minorities. On the eighteenth our troops joined hands with the Germans at Brest-Litovsk, a place of anti-Russian perfidy but a generation ago.

WARSAW
By Hermann Goering

Around Warsaw the Army had placed a noose of artillery, but that was not enough. I told the Fuehrer the Army was incapable of the highest tasks. The Luftwaffe would have to crush the final pockets of Warsaw resistance delaying the Fuehrer's celebration. I ordered four hundred planes to attack, and Stukas began dive-bombing a city soon in flames. Next I employed Junker transport planes with loads of incendiaries. Since my men had to wrestle the bombs out side doors of the unsleek transports, accuracy was not perfect, and some of our troops were hit. The Army demanded we cease bombing, but the

Fuehrer wouldn't hear of it. Wave after wave of planes continued to attack, and my pilots said they could not see much except smoke and debris.

ADJUSTMENTS
By Joseph Stalin

Our friends fought so well and so fast that I offered to stick to our original agreement or, far better for both of us, make a few adjustments. If Germany would give me Lithuania, I would grant it the provinces of Warsaw and Lublin. The Germans already had those areas but were honor bound to give them to us. I invited Ribbentrop to Moscow to discuss these matters. He came on September twenty-eighth, and by early next morning we had carefully redrawn maps and agreed on everything, with Hitler's approval, of course, and now Germany had most of the Polish people under its control, which was a big advantage, and I still had a nice chunk of Poland as well as the Baltic States, and we agreed not to tolerate any Polish agitation against either partner.

OPERATION REINHARD
By Reinhard Heydrich

I had many lists. They were quite long and contained the names of undesirable Poles. Most of them were aristocrats, doctors, teachers, priests and businessmen. My specially-trained Einsatz Commandos hunted these dangerous criminals, and by late September had shot all but three percent of the Polish upper class.

This territory now was an ideal place to transport the Jews. We should not have had to bother. They should already have left Europe, but no one else wanted them either. The United States and England had turned away shiploads of Jews. So they were still our problem, and my particular responsibility and burden.

WHY WAR?
By Adolf Hitler

There did not have to be war, and there should not be war. That I explained October sixth in Kroll Opera House. Everyone had to understand: "I always offered Poland the utmost friendship and every time was spurned. Just as a fine English diplomat wrote in 1598, the most glaring characteristics of Poles are 'cruelty and a lack of moral restraint.' Obviously nothing has changed in three hundred fifty years. Despite my repeated offers to permit civilians to leave Warsaw, the Poles rejected me and forced continued conflict that exposed a great city to destruction. Ten thousand Germans have died because of Polish treachery, and a few thousand missing are no doubt being tortured.

"German suffering at the hands of Poles has long been too great to ever permit a restoration of the Poland of the Versailles Treaty. That Poland will never rise again, though Russia and Germany are willing to consider the formation of a reasonable Polish state. That, however, is exclusively our business and certainly cannot be solved by a war with the West.

"So why should there be war? Why should millions die and property in the billions be destroyed in order to save a state that from its artificial inception was an abomination and a fake? Is there some other reason? Should millions die in what would be a vain sacrifice to try to remove Germany's current regime?

"How could there possibly be a need for war? I have forever endeavored to create harmonious and tolerable relations with France. We have no claims against France. I have always expressed to France my desire to bury our ancient enmity and bring our two glorious nations together.

"My relations with England have been characterized by the same devotion and sincerity. At no time and in no place have I ever acted contrary to British interests. There can only be real peace in Europe and throughout the world if Germany and England come to an understanding.

"We need a great conference among leading European nations to work out the issues of the day. Peace can be unconditionally guaranteed. Weapons of all kinds should be regulated and reduced. The problem of Jewish resettlement can be resolved. International trade agreements need to be forged. These are just tasks of great urgency. History proves that in war there can never be two victors, and that everyone loses. Let those who want peace accept my outstretched hand. But if those who want war to prevail, men like Churchill and his followers, then there will be war. With profound hope, I await a response that compassion and foresight will prevail."

WHAT NOW?
By General Walther von Brauhitsch

The Fuehrer ordered top military chiefs to his new Chancellery late morning October tenth, 1939. We were worried what he was thinking might be dangerous. We didn't want that and were going to tell him. He needed to listen. But right after we arrived he began lecturing and soon pronounced: "For three hundred years Germany has suffered from Western hostility. Our imperative task, therefore, is to destroy forever the capacity of the West to threaten German growth and security. For that we need time, but time is against us and for the enemy. We must strike quickly and ruthlessly because Germany cannot wait for a long war. Our supplies of food and raw materials are limited, and our industrial base is vulnerable and could be shattered, and that would destroy our war economy and the capacity to resist. We shall overcome vulnerability by waging our new methods of warfare.

"The attack can only be launched through Belgium, Holland and Luxembourg. There we will destroy enemy forces, including the British and French, and obtain bases on the Channel and North Sea from which we can brutally employ the Luftwaffe against England. This historical mission requires novel tactics. You must improvise, and you must do so right away because the time for this attack cannot come too soon."

All of this dumbfounded our increasingly troubled group, and we left without argument. But indignation and outrage soon festered within the General Staff. Complaints and pressure increased when England rejected Hitler's peace proposal, and General von Leeb sent this strong memorandum: "The enemy possesses as many tanks and anti-tank guns as Germany, and even if we aren't overrun, we can do no better than exhaust ourselves in positional warfare. Furthermore, Germany would place itself clearly in the wrong by violating Belgium, leaving us friendless, isolated and encircled by enemies. The German people, having already regained far more than Versailles took, want peace, not military adventurism, and will not support offensives.

"We must also note the array of advantages if we restrain ourselves. First, the German Army in the West is unassailable in its current defensive position. An enemy attack would cost it severely and still not destroy German forces. Industrial production would continue unabated if we stay on the defensive, and enormous political advantage would accrue if warmonger England presses hostilities against peace-seeking Germany. Poland also remains in Germany's hands as a tool of negotiation. If we do not attack, the West will eventually accept a rump Polish state as well as a reestablished Czech state, minus the Sudetenland and anyway under German influence. All of this presents Hitler a magnificent opportunity to appear a prince of peace."

Leeb stressed that the fate of Germany might depend on me, the Commander in Chief of the Army. I agreed, and twice in mid-October I implored the Fuehrer not to attack. He dismissed every point without consideration. I then talked to General Halder and others who had urged me to eliminate Hitler a year ago, and they again pressed me to take action. Many of them could have shot Hitler themselves. Some thought about it. They said they wanted to, but as officers they had to refrain. I certainly could not shoot Hitler, either. Many still reminded me I was the only one empowered to order the Army to strike. I did not think I should, but I agreed to consider it.

This conspiracy, fomented by others, began to take form. Hitler, Goering, Goebbels, Himmler and Heydrich were to be arrested. Goering would be charged with stealing millions of marks from taxes paid by workers. Plenty of proof existed for that, as well as for charges that Himmler had jailed, tortured, and killed thousands of innocent people. The Fuehrer would be charged with plotting to wage an illegal and immoral war doomed to bury Germany.

Erich Kordt and other conspirators fortified our commitment with this incisive memorandum: "Hitler should not be preserved based on the premise that he has achieved numerous stunning successes. These are illusory since Germany, even without him, would have achieved military autonomy as well as an Austrian Anschluss and hegemony over Czechoslovakia. The invasion of Czechoslovakia provoked France and England into backing Poland against us. Hitler has blundered us into world war.

"Failure to strike the warmonger cannot be justified on grounds that a debacle has not yet occurred. History proves that a debacle is obvious only once it has happened, when it is too late. A coup therefore has to be founded on courage gained from moral rectitude. Officers are also freed from a fallacious personal oath to a man who has broken countless oaths for insane purposes."

I couldn't sleep or stop thinking about coups and wars and Hitler, and on October twenty-seventh I again urged him to call off invasion plans. Instead, he set a date: November twelfth. I told relevant people about my doubts. Most of our troops and many young officers were rabid Nazis. They wouldn't help overthrow Hitler. And how could we weaken and disrupt the country with an armed enemy poised in our faces? Still, I agreed to seriously consider a Putsch if Hitler did not respond on November fifth when our troops were scheduled to move to forward positions.

On that date, in the Chancellery, I told the Fuehrer: "I've talked to all the field commanders and they're unanimous in their conviction that we're unprepared for war in the West."

Hitler stood with arms locked across his chest and grimaced that I could continue.

"Our artillery units are very poorly trained and more a menace to us than the enemy. And the enemy is probably better trained than we are, and he has the advantage of the defensive. Also, the poor weather is bound to hamper our offensive."

"The enemy faces the same weather we do."

"All the same, Mein Fuehrer, the enemy would be in a covered and fortified position. I don't think our troops are up to it. They lack discipline, and they don't have the same fighting spirit our troops had at the start of the Great War. Now they're more like those in 1918. In Poland there were many lamentable examples of defeatism, even cowardice."

"I don't believe it," Hitler shouted.

"Well, Mein Fuehrer, the reports..."

"In what units was there defeatism and cowardice?"

"The exact units, I can find out which ones..."

"I want to know what happened. Where? Specifically. I'll fly there tonight. You say there was cowardice? How many death sentences were carried out? Who were the commanders? I'm asking you questions, General, and I don't hear any answers.

"Well, I'll tell you a few answers. There's plenty of cowardice in the Army, but it's not on the front lines. It's right in front of me. The truth is, the generals don't want to fight. You generals stink of defeatism. You lack even the will to fight. What the hell do you think your job is? Do you expect to spend your entire career on your ass. Your job is to fight. That's why you exist. Your job is also to do what the hell I tell you to do. I'm tired of constant avalanches of cowardly, defeatist General Staff shit about why we can't fight and win. My judgment has proved infallible and will continue so.

"I obviously need to remind you, General, and this applies to Halder and all the others, that in my career I've always struck my enemies with brutal force. And if necessary I'll annihilate the General Staff. You all make me sick."

Hitler spun hard and stomped out the room.

Sick feeling and empty, I returned to military headquarters outside Berlin. We had a lot of documents to burn, fast.

BOOM
By Georg Elser

"Elser, come with me."

"Where?"

"Come on. Now."

The guard took me to an office. I could not figure out why. Two strangers in suits were sitting with the commandant. He got up and looked sternly at me before leaving us alone in a small windowless room.

"You want to get out of Dachau?" the oldest one, maybe mid-thirties, my age, said.

I hesitated, then replied: "Of course."

"We can arrange it," the same one continued.

I nodded.

"We have a job for you. A secret mission. You have to swear absolute secrecy, Elser."

"I can do that."

They explained the mission and its importance. Secrecy was essential. They would help with all the details.

I knew they chose me because my clever hands could make cabinets and all kinds of mechanical devices, and my communist convictions, which had gotten me into prison, ensured loyalty to the mission.

I obtained tools and materials at places they told me about, and I learned all about the guards at the Burgerbrau in Munich. Many times at night I sneaked in, and into a wood-paneled pillar I cut a hole and covered it with identical wood, a door on hinges. Later I lined the door with an inch-thick plate to protect the cavity. There, on November fifth, I placed a bomb, made by me, attached to two clocks, and set the mechanism to go off at 9:20 p.m. on November eighth. I prayed no one had seen me. I wish I could have stayed and watched from a safe distance, but of course I had to get away, and my friends helped me with forged papers and dropped me off near the Swiss border. My luck ran out when I tried to cross and was arrested. The Gestapo caught me carrying a Burgerbrau postcard and some detonating devices that I guess I'd forgotten I put in my big coat.

Before long, Heinrich Himmler was interrogating me.

"Who helped you do it?" he screamed.

"Like I said, sir, I did it myself."

The Fuehrer and top Nazis unfortunately had left their annual celebration of the Beer Hall Putsch just before the bomb went off, and only several nobodies were killed.

"You sleazy bastard, you better tell me who else is involved in this plot."

"I acted alone."

Himmler kicked me in the stomach, knocking me out of the chair onto the floor, and stood over me, grinding his boots into my stomach and face. When he left, others worked on me until he returned.

"We have two British agents in custody," Himmler said. "They're behind this, aren't they."

"No Englishman helped me. I did it alone."

Himmler kicked me again and shouted: "You repulsive dog. You better tell me the British helped you. The Fuehrer demands to know."

I was in bad shape but still assured him no one had helped. Himmler jerked his head toward me as he left. His subordinates beat, drugged, and hypnotized me, and warned that at my trial I better say it was the British. But there was no trial, and they returned me to a concentration camp where I was treated fairly well.

PEP TALK
By Adolf Hitler

The cowardly and diabolical attempt against my life aroused the nation, and me as well, and fortified all for requisite tasks. Scores of determined generals came to the Chancellery on November twenty-third and were very attentive as I said, "In all modesty, I must tell you that I'm irreplaceable, but not even my genius can at this point circumvent the single mandatory solution of the sword. A nation must either fight or go under. My decision to strike is therefore unchangeable. I shall attack France and England at the most favorable and earliest moment. No one will question our violation of Belgian and Dutch neutrality after we've won the war. Recent cancellations due to weather and technicalities are merely brief reprieves. Fate demands that we annihilate the enemy. Only then can we oppose the Soviet Union."

ALMOST PERFECT
By Eva Braun

Every one of my six suitcases was always crammed with clothes and things, and I also took three dozen pairs of shoes. Usually I vacationed with my mom or a girlfriend or one of my sisters, and we flew, trained and cruised all around, everything first class. Italy was my favorite spot, warm and beautiful with great places to shop and lots of handsome guys. During most vacations I did things I couldn't when the Fuehrer was around. I smoked and drank and had a great time dancing for hours. Lots of guys loved to twirl on the floor with me. Some knew who I was and some didn't. This was all innocent, of course. About ten o'clock every night the Fuehrer called to see how I was and always told me to be very careful. He made everything safe and easy by arranging special transportation and occasionally sending SS officers to make sure I didn't have any problems at customs. I always had a good time but often lay in my hotel bed, wishing the Fuehrer could do more fun things with me.

CHOIR
By A Jew

After the German Army took over our Polish town of Turck, we were all very worried. The soldiers were not so bad at first, but the SS came, wearing black uniforms, and they were different. The second day here they beat and prodded scores of Jews, including my wife and me, into our synagogue. A few resisted and were hit in the head with rifles and left out front. Inside, the black shirts ordered us to crawl back and forth beside the pews.

"Now, start singing or you'll die right now," they hollered.

We could not believe this, and did not say anything.

One guard shot the man next to me in the head then kicked another in the ribs and yelled: "I told you rotten pigs to start sing."

THE GRAF SPEE
By Captain Hans Langsdorff

A little before the war, before the British fleet could cap our inherently bottled up ports, I secretly eased the *Graf Spee* out and cruised south and made it into the Atlantic and Indian Oceans. My task of destroying enemy shipping required speed and power, and my sleek pocket battleship moved pretty well at twenty-six knots and had strong guns with six big ones at eleven inches. The British fleet floated more ships than Germany's, and many were heavier with larger guns. But, loose on the seas, I engaged numerous vessels not so big, some without guns, and in three months my big ones blasted fifty thousand tons of enemy shipping into the salty murk. News of my deeds thrilled Germany and appalled Britain. Now I too would be the hunted, and that was fine since I knew how to strike and quickly steer into disappearance then feint here in the Indian Ocean and at once steer back into the Atlantic, befuddling British predators.

I sank two ships on December second and another on the seventh before heading toward the River Plate in Uruguay. Early on the thirteenth we spotted smoke on the sea, and I declared the three enemy ships a light cruiser and two tiny destroyers. Full speed ahead, I ordered, and everywhere felt the hot, scrambling feet of alarmed and excited men. Only then did I discover we faced cruisers three, a malignant threat. Some officers expected me to turn away but I said straight ahead, and nailed their largest ship, the *Exeter,* with big blasts that destroyed a turret and the communications bridge and everyone on it. The *Exeter* nevertheless rocked us with eight-inch shells. And I was also occupied by the smaller ships, *Ajax* and *Achilles,* which from the start had detached from the *Exeter* and circled to fire at my flank. After they stunned us several times, I turned and bombarded them with my elevens, and all three adversaries continued to trade salvos with us until I let out a smoke screen and tried to disengage. This maneuver put the *Exeter* again in my sights, and I knocked it into a severely damaged state. The *Ajax* and *Achilles* pressed the chase, and we pounded each other without mercy in a battle now eighty minutes old. The two feisty little ships then withdrew under cover of smoke, allowing me to plow away and stagger about midnight into port at Montevideo.

Repairs immediately began on the *Graf Spee's* wailing and battered frame. The *Exeter* had escaped toward the Falkland Islands and no longer menaced me, but up from there would surely come, probably already had come, a convoy of reinforcement, compelling me to ask the Uruguayans for a stay beyond the three-day limit of international law. They insisted we leave. While so doing some comrades wanted to fire all our guns, but I said a breakthrough was hopeless. My men were accordingly transferred to a merchant ship.

Thousands of Uruguayans leered at my ship's doomed hulk as a tugboat lugged it out of the harbor. And soon, in the ignominious style of naval capitulation, the *Graf Spee's* insides were ripped by explosions that opened it to a sea soon entered. A few days later I wrote that I bore full responsibility for the scuttling, expressed firm faith in the future of Fuehrer and Fatherland, wrapped myself in our naval flag on the bed in a hotel room, fired a bullet into my brain, and joined my ship.

MERCY
By A Doctor

We had a lot of very bad cases. They were all hopeless, really. The children were deformed, retarded, or grievously diseased in some other way, and the law required all of them to be registered. Right after birth was best but not always possible. Many times the children were registered retroactively. Reporting this information was the responsibility of every participant from midwives to attending physicians to district medical officers.

Each case was thoroughly examined before being decided. If an expert concluded the "life was unworthy of life," he marked a plus by the name. After a couple of weeks, the deformed child was given a sedative. This regimen was repeated several times over two or three days, whatever was necessary to save the child and the state from more pain and degradation.

SITZKRIEG
By Joseph Goebbels

Not many guns were firing but that did not matter for I provided fusillades aplenty. Every time the British lied and distorted, and they did so in ways beneath contempt, I bashed them with the real story. In particular, it was outrageous for the cruel but clever Churchill to blame Germany for the sad sinking of the passenger liner, Athenia. More than a hundred civilians were killed, including some Americans. No German U-boat did that. The Fuehrer had already threatened the death sentence for any commander who sank a civilian ship. The culprit had to be someone who wanted to blow a hole in German-American relations. That could only be Churchill. On the radio I reported to the whole world he was a murderer. To ensure our people heard only the truth, I convinced the Fuehrer to prohibit Germans from listening to foreign radio broadcasts. Some violators were severely penalized for exposing themselves to shameless lies.

Our enemies continued to pile all responsibility for war upon us, and as a war aim demanded the Reich be dismembered. That absolved the Fuehrer of any future moral qualms. Despite enemy treachery, we still wanted peace. German hearts beat in tune with Gallic comrades who listened to the warm French songs we broadcast across the front. After playing music for our friends, we reminded them again of peace and asked why war should be since we did not want it. Only the British wanted war. We published captured British diaries to prove that. And from the sky I showered leaflets with drawings of the poor French soldier: cold and deprived at the front while some grubby Englishman rolled in bed with his wife.

ASSESSMENTS
By General Maurice Gamelin

In late 1939 we had a supreme defense, and in no way felt offensive. We'd learned where offensives led. No more. France had been right to ignore its potential in 1936 for a seven to one advantage in the Rhineland. We had no reason to attack and squash Germans as they remilitarized their own territory. In September 1938 many said we had a great opportunity. The Czechs could bog the Germans down, and we could breech West Wall. That, however, would have killed many French and brought no lasting military security since we would have had to leave Germany in a while anyway. I suppose there'd been another opportunity in September 1939. Most German soldiers and panzers were in the East fighting Poland, and we could have been aggressive. But that would have led to a real war.

MY CHOICE
By Benito Mussolini

They laughed at me and derided me. I should have shot the bastards. No Italian should ever make fun of the Duce. But some did. Not many, of course, but some. I blamed Hitler. The Teutonic pervert, arrogant beyond comprehension since his recent incredible luck, felt he could lie to me and dictate what Italy would do. Italians hated Hitler and showed it. I still might decide to destroy him. He deserved it. Secretly I warned the Belgians and Dutch that Hitler planned to attack. They were most grateful. I had plenty of allies against Hitler if I wanted them.

Maybe Hitler would be my ally against others, however. The Duce had many choices. I contemplated them primarily alone. The possibility of contradiction was devastating. Not really devastating. Not for me. I was still tough despite whispers and catcalls. My prime lay still in the future. I ignored rumors that my face and frame were bloated. I was not fat, I wouldn't be for long. Maybe it was syphilis. Something had gotten me down a bit, but only temporarily. I felt great. Everything generally seemed clear. My options were unlimited. Everyone wanted me as an ally.

I decided to give Hitler another chance, to provide him with insight that could save him. In early January 1940 I wrote a letter explaining he could never conquer Britain and France. That was a delusion. He should not risk his already substantial empire and unassailable regime to try to destroy decadent democratic fruit that was anyway doomed to tumble rotten to the ground. Germany was much too good for that.

I also explained he had to quit betraying our revolutionary ideals by consorting with the Soviets. All Italians hated the Bolsheviks. Germany's pact with the Russians outraged everyone and so did the ongoing Soviet invasion of Finland. Catastrophic repercussions would occur in Italy if the Fuehrer took one further step toward the Bolsheviks. He needed to be a resolute fascist like me.

HARD BARGAINS
By Julius Schnurre

I want this, I need that, I demand these, we've got to have those. That's how Stalin behaved during economic negotiations he seized from his economists. He wanted everything and asserted Germany owed him for rendering great services that had gotten him into plenty of trouble elsewhere.

"Germany should not take advantage of the Soviet Union's good nature by charging unsuitable prices," he warned.

After exhaustive negotiations we finally signed a deal on February eleventh. Among other wonders of German ingenuity, Russia received thirty of our most modern warplanes, a cruiser and other ships, heavy naval guns, tons of explosives, industrial machinery, and all sorts of other tools and equipment.

In return, mother Russia opened her fertile maw and gave us hundreds of thousands of tons of wheat, cereal, oil and cotton, and many raw materials essential to making war. This wide-open gate from the East flooded the British blockade.

NEW PLAN
By General Erich von Manstein

A few weeks ago a German officer was flying over Belgium when engine trouble necessitated an emergency landing. With absolutely unjustifiable carelessness, this officer had somehow been authorized to carry most of our battle plan for the West in his briefcase. He tried to burn the documents and claimed he substantially did so, but Belgian authorities rushed in and seized at least something. How much the Belgians and their friends now knew, we did not know.

Our plan would have to be changed, and that heartened me since for months I had been writing memorandums about why the plan would not work and what we really should do. I feared the Army High Command, the OKH, might be pigeonholing my proposals. General Halder and I certainly disliked each other, with only too little subtlety, and the OKH, besieged by Hitler, was not receptive to innovative ideas.

I still continued my efforts but eventually provoked the OKH, and it removed me as General von Rundstedt's chief of staff and made me commander of a divisional corps. No matter what the opposition, I could not embrace the old plan, which fell far short in scope of even the old Schlieffen Plan that almost worked during the Great War. Instead of also driving south toward Paris and trying to destroy all French forces, current thinking called only for a drive through Belgium and Holland to the Channel ports. Substantial, and perhaps decisive, French forces could then counterattack our southern flanks. Only one solution existed: the new plan I had been outlining and trying to get accepted, or at least properly examined.

I tried to get word to Hitler, though this approach certainly didn't adhere to German military doctrine that only the Commander in Chief of the Army and the Chief of the General Staff were competent to make such recommendations. Brauhitsch and Halder were solid General Staff officers but could not be counted on for daring and imagination. I asked Hitler's adjutant, Rudolf Schmundt, to help, and he agreed to try to arrange a meeting when Hitler gave a luncheon for corps commanders in Berlin on February seventeenth, 1940.

The Fuehrer insisted on dominating the conversation with us, but I found him fascinating as he poured out figures of technical innovations by our enemies as well as by us. After lunch, as I had hoped, he invited me into his study.

"Herr General, I understand you have some novel views on attacking the West. I want to hear them."

"The offensive must be aimed at achieving decisive results on land, Mein Fuehrer. The huge military and political risks cannot be justified by the current limited objectives. We must not permit ourselves to become mired in static warfare while the West inevitably reduces our current significant advantages in training, leadership and equipment. Germany also cannot wait indefinitely to attack because the aforementioned disadvantages would still accrue. The Soviets would, additionally, become more a threat the less they needed us and the more vulnerable we became. The operation must therefore be directed toward winning a final decision in France and destroying France's resistance."

"Absolutely, yes, Herr General. How?"

"We must unequivocally place the main point of attack not in the north with Army Group B, but in the South with Army Group A. The decision of emphasis cannot be decided as hostilities unfold. We must now resolve to make our main thrust through southern Belgium and the Forest of Ardennes. We can then move across the Meuse River near Sedan as our panzers pour into France. Since our main attack is probably anticipated much further north, we should achieve surprise."

"Most generals tell me the Ardennes is much too hilly and wooded for panzers to penetrate."

"I don't agree, Mein Fuehrer. And neither does General Guderian. His experience during the Great War, combined with our detailed studies of maps and terrain, indicated that panzers can indeed roll through the Ardennes."

Hitler nodded and said, "What then?"

"A frontal assault by Army Group B in the north would set up the enemy to be cut off and destroyed if Army Group A drives swiftly through to the Channel ports. That must be the first phase of the campaign. The second will be the envelopment of the whole French army with a powerful right hook.

"This scenario is the only one ambitious enough and bold enough to justify the risks and quickly eliminate the enemy."

The Fuehrer asked relevant and insightful questions, then stated: "I'm very impressed, General. I believe this shall be our plan."

Three days later it officially was.

NORWAY
By Admiral Erich Raeder

After we lost the Graf Spee, the Fuehrer talked worse to me than anyone ever had. Despite that, I continued to advocate what I knew: we needed Norwegian ports. This was not due to malice on the part of Norway. It was, rather, because of our Great War experience when the Royal Navy had erected a blockade from the Shetland Islands, northeast of Britain, strong east to the Norwegian coast. Our warships and merchant fleet were thereby imprisoned at home.

"This must not under any circumstances be allowed to recur," I warned Hitler.

"I believe it best for Norway to remain neutral," he said. "As long as we can ship iron from Sweden down the Norwegian coast during winter, I don't want to take risks in Scandinavia."

"Norwegian neutrality will be impossible to maintain," I said. "I've been consulting someone who also fears the British. He's been gaining fascist support and thinks he can lead a coup if Germany helps. It's vital you talk to him right away. His name is Quisling."

RUSSO-FINNISH WAR
By A Finnish Officer

Late last year that troubled giant to the south had started making demands, the principle of which was that we surrender some islands in, and a port on, the Gulf of Finland. We said we might agree to cede a few islands, but giving away the port would damage national pride as well as undercut our desire for neutrality. The Russians then became increasingly bellicose and attacked us last November. Lurching into this icy land of dark forests and sharp winds, they often linked arms and sang while minefields and bombardments chewed them up. Our network of railways and communications also gave us superior mobility and intelligence, and our troops, clad in camouflage white, merged with nature, gliding fast on skis to out-flank and destroy the cold and starving enemies. We stacked their corpses high and were not at all bothered looking into so many frozen-open eyes.

Staggered and humiliated, the Russians summoned vast reserves and attacked us with improved coordination and sufficient blunt force to knock us back. The English and French urged us to hold out and said direct military aid was a good possibility. We were far from certain they'd come, and the Russians were already here, so we had to accept harsher terms, on March thirteenth, 1940, that displaced a half million Finns.

As a matter of soldierly discourse, we officers argued whether our soldiers were that great or Russian soldiers that bad. Or, did winter and unfamiliar terrain account for such an abysmal showing by a giant?

AT THE PASS
By Benito Mussolini

Emerging from his train in the mountains at Brenner Pass, the Fuehrer trudged high-booted through snow to my train where I hosted him. As usual, I did not need an interpreter. I listened carefully, except when he blathered, and understood everything he said. For the most part, his dynamism rivaled my own. This man deserved to be my equal.

371

That also meant I equaled him, and he therefore did not need to remind me: "Italy has to become involved in the war in order to avoid becoming a second rate power."

"Italy shall become involved. I know it's impossible to remain neutral, and I have no desire to do so. We just need more time to prepare, perhaps three or four months. I hope Germany can delay its invasion plans."

"No, Duce, I'm sorry. We cannot. There have been too many delays already. Our offensive will soon begin."

"Italy is in no position to wage a protracted war, Fuehrer. That's why my date of entry is so critical."

"I can certainly help you, Duce. German forces can combine with Italian and move into southern France through the Alps. Such a move would naturally come after German forces have smashed the main part of the enemy in northern France. And once France capitulates, Italy will obviously be mistress of the Mediterranean, and England will be forced to sue for peace."

"When Germany has so shaken the West that it needs only one more blow for a knockout, I shall intervene and deliver that blow."

"How soon after our attack would you intervene, Duce?"

"If the German advance is not decisive, then I should have to wait for the propitious moment. I cannot now state precisely when that would be."

PASTORAL INTERVENTION
By A Norwegian

Long and narrow Norway stretched peaceful and cold from the Arctic Ocean south a thousand miles to the North Sea. Our land was rich and mountainous with coasts carved stunning into fjords bright green and blue, peaceful havens in a nation already tranquil with fishers and farmers and traders. Faraway in time, and more distant still in deed, had lived vicious Viking forefathers who sailed wide and wielded swords of conquest. Our mere three million souls wanted now only peace, and accordingly strove to placate powers all around. Contemporary warriors still schemed and studied Norway as if it were a prize inherently their own. I sensed and really knew and actually felt their unholy acts. Along our coast, long a neutral sanctuary, German ships sailed north not empty back to Sweden but laden low-in-the-water with guns and ammunition. The British, too, had poisonous plans, and poured mines so near our tranquil shores.

I knew they were coming, all of them, though not exactly when, and at dawn on April ninth, by fate a shade ahead of the British, Germans pounced from planes and ships at five strategic ports and other places spanning our land, and by mid-morning or so had clenched Narvik, Trondheim and Bergen, and spread also fast en route to Oslo. Our people, otherwise so unprepared, readied huge guns in old Fortress Oskarborg and blew one invading ship to the bottom of Oslo Fjord and bashed another into a meek and smoking retreat. Nazi aggression elsewhere also began to encounter aroused resistance, but it was a brief and futile fight. The Germans had sprung rapid audacious upon us, sneaking smart and bold by superior but somewhat timid British naval forces, and by the end of April the king and all British visitors were boating beaten back to Britain. Our peaceful land lay now in the German hand.

THE MAGINOT LINE
By General Maurice Gamelin

The Maginot Line dotted big hot concrete spots into the ground south of Belgium and ran on that way and buttoned the Germans in, in Germany, over the border, out of France, and this we felt very good about.

THE FOREST OF ARDENNES
By General Heinz Guderian

It was shadowy and green on the mountain floor in southern Belgium, and you could not see far. Here I had been walking peaceful dirt roads, studying maps and terrain, thinking what I had from conception: mass the panzers and strike hard. Strike hard and keep moving. The French had lots of armor, too, as much as we had, and some of it bigger. I also knew they had as many men, counting Belgians and Dutch and the British Expeditionary Force. But numerical equality really shouldn't matter. The panzers were already rolling into columns that stretched a hundred miles to the rear, and we readied to move softly through where we hoped we could. Other people had said it was impossible. No one could. But we had to believe: the impenetrable Ardennes isn't really impenetrable.

PARTY RIDE
By A Secretary

We were on the Fuehrer's armored train and trying to guess what was up.

"No, it's not a picnic," he said. "And it's not a ride to a speech. It's much more than that."

Early in the dark morning of May tenth, 1940 we arrived at Felsennest, a new headquarters camouflaged into a mountain near our Belgian border. Soon we heard distant rumbling, and as it grew louder everything became a big surprise.

VINCINNES
By A French Messenger

The chateau was crafted massive in stone, rising with walls and towers like those of a castle, and had a presence at once so elegant and imposing we were all delighted. General Gamelin, especially, loved it here, and preserved tranquility by banning radios and telephones. Communication was instead maintained by men on motorcycles cruising to this beautiful place so far away.

WATER
By General Kurt Student

Canals, rivers and flood areas crisscrossed the horizon, so we could not be slow. From the sky we jumped behind the hazards onto Rotterdam, The Hague and other cities. And on the ground, from the east, our troops hammered against Holland.

IMPREGNABLE FORTRESS
By A German Soldier

For weeks we practiced on a replica of Fort Eben Emael. Everyone said it was better than anything in the Maginot Line and even better than any part of West Wall and certainly the greatest fort in the world. Steel and concrete bunkers boasted giant armored guns, and more than a thousand troops manned a fort embedded on high ground. I worried we only had five hundred airborne troops for all of Belgium and but eighty for the menacing fort.

Military aircraft towed nine gliders over Aachen, Germany twenty miles away, and the gliders and we were released. I hoped our training had been precise, and I prayed they wouldn't see us coming. It was a long twenty-mile glide. The descent was slow and beautiful. But what if the defenders see us? We were getting close. If they see us, that will be it. Then I felt it. Clip clop. I felt my feet land one-two on top of the fort. We were on top of the greatest fort in the world.

Pouncing, we threw new explosives into the bunkers below. Behind the fort Belgian soldiers counterattacked us. Ducking bullets, we shot flames through the fort's vantage points and gun portals, and now the Luftwaffe dived at the Belgians, and we kept shooting flames inside, and by next day the greatest fort in the world surrendered.

PLAN D
By General Maurice Gamelin

Just as I had insisted, the Germans were again using the Schlieffen Plan from the Great War and attacking to their northwest. My strategy, embodied in Plan D, called for a counterattack northeast into Belgium and Holland. These countries, in order to protect their neutrality, had declined to coordinate defenses with us, but that was not insurmountable. They had defensive assets. And now we had great momentum. In we charged to repulse the Germans.

ACHTUNG
By General Heinz Guderian

In astounding silence we had already slithered through the Ardennes, and now only the Meuse River lay in my way. We were on its bank at Sedan where we quickly got some artillery and anti-aircraft guns into place, on May twelfth, and panzer infantry began to cross in rubber boats. Then ferries chugged over bearing light vehicles.

While our guns, aided by the Luftwaffe, started to smash still unfinished enemy emplacements, our engineers moved in to build pontoon bridges aimed at the heart of France. Scores of brave French and British pilots soon attacked the bridges, but our anti-aircraft gunners shot half of them into flames. Meanwhile, our Stukas continued to pound French defenses, and we kept expanding the bridgehead and knocking out pillboxes and blowing up planes, and now the panzers flowed across the Meuse, and I crossed too.

Jubilant troops greeted me as Hurrying Heinz, and I smiled because they were right. Forward fast our panzers went on May thirteenth, fourteenth and fifteenth, rolling ever further into France. General Ewald von Kleist, leader of our panzer group, did not understand. He had once been an impediment to panzer development, and now by phone he groaned, "We're stretching thin and exposing our northern and southern flanks. Wait for the infantry to catch up."

"To hell with what's going on behind. We've got to keep moving."

Kleist agreed to let me proceed for twenty-four hours. Two days later my panzers were penetrating still deeper into France. Now was no time to hesitate, much less halt. Panzers need the green light.

Early on the seventeenth I reported to an airstrip, as ordered.

"Good morning," I said.

"You're insubordinate," Kleist yelled. "You know what your orders were. You've disobeyed every damn one you've received. I won't tolerate these outrages. Your wildness and your arrogance are imperiling the whole campaign, the whole Fatherland."

"In that case, Herr General, I'd like to be relieved of my command."

Kleist was startled but he nodded and said, "Hand over your command to the most senior general in your corps."

From Army Group A headquarters, General von Rundstedt sent word I could not resign my command and that the order to halt had come not from Kleist but the OKH. I was told my corps headquarters must remain in place, but a "reconnaissance in force" could proceed.

I interpreted that my way, and by the nineteenth we were at the Somme battlefield of the Great War, our open left flank protected by the river as well as anti-tank units and combat engineers. And we kept moving, now two hundred miles into France. When officers in the field told me they had to stop because of fuel shortages, I ordered them to keep going. I'd noticed that tired officers generally lacked energy, not fuel.

Our high command had thought that by now, nine days into the attack, we would just be crossing the Meuse, having brought the bulk of our artillery and infantry into the region. The French must have thought the same. Too many high commanders, pigeonholed in offices far to the rear, kept a Great War clock in their heads. My clock ran much faster. So did my panzers, which had repeatedly sped through positions the French later tried to counterattack, and on May twentieth they charged up to the English Channel, and three French armies and the British Expeditionary Force were sealed.

DUNKIRK
By Hermann Goering

Without my Luftwaffe our victories could not have been so extraordinary. Holland certainly wouldn't have surrendered after only four days if bombers hadn't pounded Rotterdam into rubble. The Luftwaffe had also been the key in Belgium.

The Army, craving most of the credit for the way things were going in France, wanted to downplay the overwhelming air superiority that made their advances easy. The Army must also have realized my power in the skies forced the French to fire General Gamelin and the British to sack Chamberlain and rush in Churchill. The whole world was terrified of my Luftwaffe, and our enemies were too shattered to think.

"The Army would just be in the way, Mein Fuehrer," I said. "Let me destroy the British at Dunkirk. I'll blow them to bits. They won't get away unless they can swim."

"I have not yet decided the best course," Hitler said. "I shall soon make the correct decision."

"Don't forget what the generals are like, Mein Fuehrer. If they get all the glory, you know how hard it'll be to handle them."

HALT
By Adolf Hitler

I was very happy and calm. Everything was proceeding wonderfully. I knew this would be a good meeting with General von Rundstedt on May twenty-fourth at his Army Group A headquarters. He was a master of maneuver and the most senior general in the Army.

"This is all a decided miracle," I told the general and his staff. "We should have the French on their knees in six weeks, and at that point I shall be quite generous. All I want is a reasonable peace with France, and with England. In particular I shall be magnanimous with the British. They've done so much to civilize the world. Their empire, in fact, provides great international stability. I want them to have their colonies. We don't want them. Germans don't want to live in the tropics. Let the British civilize the savages. That's their contribution, one of many. It's certainly in our interest for the British Empire to survive. I'm even prepared to provide troops to help wherever they might have difficulties. All I want is their acknowledgment of our dominant place on the continent.

"Of course, they'll have to be taught a lesson at Dunkirk. And I'm leaving that task to the Luftwaffe. Please apprise your commanders of this right now."

UNBELIEVABLE
By General Walther von Brauhitsch

"Mein Fuehrer, please, listen," I urged during a meeting at OKH headquarters. "I'm sorry, but I must speak. I cannot not speak. I must tell you this is wrong. We cannot halt the panzers now. Guderian is within twenty miles of Dunkirk. Resistance at this time is light. We can destroy the whole British Expeditionary Force."

"That is precisely what I'm going to do — with the Luftwaffe."

"The Luftwaffe won't be sufficient."

"The Luftwaffe will be more than sufficient."

"That is wrong, Mein Fuehrer, absolutely wrong. We've got to press our advantage with the panzers."

"You obviously don't comprehend these matters. I should have expected that from you, and you, too, General Halder. None of you generals has ever understood my thinking. You were all timid about the Anschluss and Czechoslovakia and Poland, and especially about France. Only my genius and determination have made our great victories possible."

"Mein Fuehrer, right now we have an essentially uncontested opportunity for our greatest victory," I said.

"I'll explain the reasons for my decision. Then perhaps you'll understand. First, the Flanders marshes covering the approaches to Dunkirk aren't suitable for ideal panzer maneuver. Second, due to the rapid and unprecedented surge by the panzers, which would not have been possible without my plan, there have been numerous mechanical breakdowns. We ..."

"Mein Fuehrer, we've already brought in many new panzers to replace them," I said.

"Don't interrupt. We need to make repairs and give the troops time to recuperate. And, I should think it would be obvious, we need to preserve our armor for the main attack south into the heart of France. The bulk of the French army, perhaps you're aware, has yet to be destroyed."

"I must vigorously endorse General von Brauhitsch's assessments, Mein Fuehrer," Halder said.

"Neither of you comprehends even the most rudimentary concepts."

"Mein Fuehrer, this really is unbelievable," I said.

"Both of you get to work implementing my orders."

THE BEACH
By A British Officer

Where was the Royal Air Force? At Dunkirk, diving Stukas had shredded us with bombs and bullets, and smoke from burning oil clogged the air and darkening the sand. Didn't our pilots understand? Corpses were starting to rot. When the Germans attacked again, I dived under a demolished truck and hit my head, landing next to a man with brains on his face. I panted. I cried. Get me the hell off this stinking beach.

BOATS
By A German Pilot

I had never seen so many boats. Big small new and old they converged on Dunkirk, and in my Stuka I dived after them. We all did. We bombed the boats, blasting debris and water high and thick. When no boats were in range, we strafed the men who had been in the boats.

Circling to strike again, I saw it. Another Stuka was riddled, by a plane I couldn't identify, and hurtled into the ocean not far from a boat. The plane was faster than their others and equal, maybe, to our best fighter. We started seeing more — Spitfires, we learned — and shot down a lot of them, but they downed more of us, I think. Anti-aircraft fire from the beach targeted all planes and hit some of theirs, too. As much as possible we concentrated on bombing and strafing boats, which kept coming and going, the ones we didn't sink.

RIDICULOUS
By General Franz Halder

By the time the Fuehrer allowed our panzers to attack again, late on May twenty-sixth, French and British defenses had been strengthened markedly, and our progress was slow. Two-and-a-half days earlier, we could readily have tightened the noose. Now we engaged in inconsequential ground clashes.

CROSSING
By A Fisherman

Even though they told me German artillery was so close we couldn't evacuate during the day anymore, I said sure, I'd do it. At night on June second I took on a load of French lads. They were tired and covered with soot and such, but they talked with so much excitement I understood a lot they said even though I didn't speak a word of French.

We got back to England alive, and the lads jumped out and just lay on the land. We were lucky, all right. The Germans had sunk about two hundred fifty ships and boats. But that sure wasn't good enough for bloody Jerry because six hundred of our motley crafts stayed afloat and evacuated more than three-hundred thousand men, including sixty thousand French. Unfortunately, thousands of other French were still pinned on land, holding off the Germans.

VICTORY
By Benito Mussolini

I always knew I would lead Italy into a great battle. There had never been any question of my not attacking. I wanted booty, and I wanted casualties. The only reason I had not attacked was I could not decide who to attack. I would have attacked Yugoslavia and Greece in the spring, but, as a personal favor to the Fuehrer, I did not. I realized I would get those areas without fighting anyway. But I did want war, and I continued my build-up in Libya. My plans there would doubtless become clear at the right time in the future.

Right now I needed to strike France a mortal blow. On June tenth I declared war and even sent many civilian ministers to the front. All Italians needed war, though not with full mobilization or inconvenience in daily life.

DEFEAT
By A French Officer

Our big guns in the Maginot Line had been aimed at them, but the Germans were far behind us, attacking south on a four hundred mile front into the soul of France, and we did not have an opportunity to defend anything. Our steel and concrete forts nevertheless stood as formidable testaments to determination and readiness.

Below ground in the forts, our men rumbled when news arrived: the Germans were in Paris. Millions of refugees, carting a few stark belongings, were struggling west through clogged roads. I understood that retreat was mandatory and prudent. And on June seventeenth, I understood it when Marshal Petain, the new prime minister, and his cronies asked Hitler for an armistice. Only then did the Italians, who south of us outnumbered French troops five to one, start to do a little more than scowl in place. They did not get far. But they tried. And that I could never understand.

COMPIEGNE
By Adolf Hitler

This was my most important document, and I spent much of the evening writing and revising it, and periodically I handed some of the papers to General Keitel and ordered him to hurry across the street to the church in Bruly-de-Peche, a Belgian village recently cleared to serve as my latest headquarters. In the church, working by flickering lights of candles, my secretaries were typing and retyping the armistice. Sometimes I walked over and leaned down, looking over their shoulders, and this quite excited the ladies.

Everyone was as impressed as I by my generosity. I was granting the French an unoccupied southern slice of the country to govern. And I would only hold my million and a half French prisoners until the end of the war, which everyone knew would come soon. Other key terms were equally reasonable. German traitors living in France would be handed over to us, and renegade French in other countries would be subject to spontaneous justice if caught betraying this document of peace. And the French navy, now dispersed in various North African and English ports, would be spared. That I solemnly vowed. The navy would be brought back to France and demobilized. All this surely was much better than what we got in 1918.

With the armistice ready, I was driven the next day — June twenty-first, 1940 — to Compiegne and its pretty clearing in the lush forest northeast of Paris. I had never been happier. This is where I had always dreamed of someday being, the ultimate place for a German, and now I was here. My legs and everything else felt especially strong as I saluted and strode toward the very historical railroad car that had recently been removed through the flattened walls of a museum. Now it was clear in the middle of the pretty forest. The French must have about dropped when they saw that.

I sat on the same historical chair Marshal Foch had sat on for France in 1918. And when the French delegation entered I stood and saluted them, and we all sat down, and the preamble to the armistice was read, and I got up and saluted again, looking at each of the defeated but very brave Frenchmen, and I left so they could be told about the generous terms. Afterward I ordered this site blown up and the railroad car brought to Germany.

TOUR
By Adolf Hitler

I had always been very anxious to see the city. If not for the Great War, I probably would have been an artist there. Now I was landing in Paris with young Albert Speer and another architect and a sculptor and a few aides, and right away I told the driver to go to the Opera. This magnificent building, so huge and ornate, was just like I'd always read, absolutely stunning. But something was missing.

"I know there should be a room right here," I said, through an interpreter, to the French guide. "Where is it?"

"It was taken out during a reconstruction," he said.

"Hah, you see. I told you how well I knew the grandest theater in Europe."

It was still early, a little past daybreak, and not many people were on the streets. Those who noticed me were very surprised. I was in such a hurry to see the sights. I was driven by the Arc de Triomphe, and I stopped at the Eiffel Tower, peering high at this inspiring structure. Then I went to Napoleon's tomb and from a balcony looked down where the eminent man lay. I was very somber with the sense that now even the French knew I was undeniably greater.

"I'm so happy how things worked out," I told my artists. "Before the war I was worried I might have to destroy the city."

PEACE IMMINENT
By Adolf Hitler

I did not think the British would listen to the drunken leader of a tottering regime. Why should a great people subject themselves to "blood, toil, sweat and tears"? Why should they believe German victory means "the whole world will sink into the abyss of a new Dark Age"? I, in fact, planned an empire of light stretching from occupied France to the Urals, a colossal empire abetted by hundreds of millions of specially bred new Aryans who could prevail in the inevitable struggle for survival against two billion Asian savages.

I continued to wait and hope my compassion would prompt the British to join the future. And I ignored Goering, an extraordinary man but one too hungry for glory, when he panted for all out air strikes. They were unnecessary. The British were beaten and knew it. But they kept failing to acknowledge it, and as there are limits even to my patience, I ordered immediate and thorough preparations to invade the island. This would begin at an undetermined date, and I stressed the "invasion is still only a plan and has not yet been decided on."

I didn't want to proceed, but on July third the British ignored my generous guarantee to demobilize the French fleet. Instead, they seized French warships in English ports, and in the Mediterranean they treacherously bombarded and sank French ships, killing French sailors.

This aggression did not damage my great victory parade. On July sixth two million Germans celebrated as I rode standing high through the streets of Berlin. Faces that had always been excited and reverential were now way beyond that. And I knew they wanted more and expected more. I could not stop now, not with all of this.

SEA LION
By Admiral Erich Raeder

The Army had dutifully responded to the Fuehrer's wishes with a Sea Lion plan that called for a massive assault on southern England along a two hundred fifty-mile front. Unfortunately, this action would be sensible only if the English Channel were a river — the Meuse, perhaps — instead of an often wicked and unpredictable open sea. I decided it would be edifying to put Army commanders in a boat, preferably a small one, and let them rise and fall with the tides, and rock and reel on harsh whipping waters, and be lashed in the face by salty winds, and in general learn that it is manifestly more difficult and dangerous to travel by sea than by land.

I was accordingly uneasy about meeting with other military chiefs and Hitler at the Berghof on July thirty-first. After Generals Brauhitsch and Halder explained how Sea Lion would bludgeon England into submission, the Fuehrer responded, "There's no doubt our Army would have scant difficulty dealing with theirs, what's left of it, once we're on land. We therefore must surmount the critical task of crossing the Channel in sufficient force. Would you please address this, Admiral Raeder?"

The generals looked at me. They looked down on me, on all naval officers, whom they considered military bumpkins. I looked squarely at the Fuehrer.

"This is an exceptionally difficult undertaking," I said. "The logistical difficulties, quite frankly, might be insurmountable. The very wide front would disperse our transports to such a degree that I couldn't guarantee the Navy would be able to protect them. Given the Royal Navy's vast numerical superiority, I would even have to warn that our Navy could under no circumstances protect that many ships. We really must shorten our front. The Navy might be able to protect fifty miles. Anything more is too risky. Since the majority of resources has always been given to other services, the Navy needs time to build its fighting strength as well as gather the multitude of transports, tugs, barges and motor boats required to move all the men and material. All things considered, the best time for this operation would be next year."

"We can't wait that long," the Fuehrer said. "British defenses are already strong and would become more so. I want preparations to continue. We must be ready by September fifteenth. I shall make a final decision after the Luftwaffe has launched massive attacks against southern England."

EAGLE DAY
By Hermann Goering

This morning as usual I took a bunch of codeine pills. Some I poured down with water, then several more with coffee, and I popped a few just before I took off my silk robe. Wanting to feel just right for the critical meeting, I put on my new sky blue uniform of the Reich Marshal. I was the only Reich Marshal in Germany, and in my uniform I bounced like a big ball of excitement, and everything seemed even better when I looked out ornate windows at my forest sparkling in summer sun.

"Here, gentlemen, look at all my masterpieces," I said to four of my commanders. "There's a Renoir, and a Degas. And look at those tapestries. Have you ever seen anything like them in someone's home? What I really have is a museum. Come this way. Here. Isn't this statue magnificent. I can't find room for all these prizes.

"Have some more brandy. And take all the cigars you want. These are the best you've ever had. Here, look at this. I know you'll like this chandelier. It's from France, a little different than the others. You really can't have too many chandeliers. How's the brandy? Come on, I want to show you my cinema. I've remodeled it. The bowling alley, too. There's always so much to worry about at Karinhall."

After a while we gathered over big detailed maps on a table. Here were the dispositions of my three great air armadas, the Luftflotten, which surrounded Great Britain all the way from the south to the northeast. Kesselring and Sperrle commanded Luftflotten 2 and 3 in Belgium, Holland and northern France, and Stumpff led Luftflotten 5 in Norway. Milch was my operations chief.

"Gentlemen, we've bombed British shipping and the Channel ports enough," I said. "That's just been a slap, a little aggressive reconnaissance. Now it's time for our onslaught — Eagle Day. We're going to destroy their radar stations along the coast and take out all their forward bases. In four days we'll wipe out the Royal Air Force, the part that counts. Anything else can be handled very shortly thereafter."

"Since the British are totally dependent on shipping, I think we should target all their key ports," said Sperrle.

"No, we must destroy the RAF."

"Perhaps, Herr Reich Marshal, a massive attack on London would better serve us," said Kesselring. "Or maybe we could attack Gibraltar, and avoid fighting the RAF over England."

"Gentlemen, why are you worried? We have almost three thousand planes operational. At most, the British have a quarter of that. And we'll wipe those out on Eagle Day — August tenth. You have four more days. Prepare your Luftflotten for the mightiest aerial assault in history."

ATTACK OF THE EAGLES
By A German Pilot

I flew the ultimate weapon, a Stuka dive-bomber that shrieked at victims before they died and intimidated survivors about the next attack. Now it was England's turn, and with other bombers escorted by fighters, absent many who missed the in-air rendezvous, we swarmed toward southern England. I was anxious to strike. No doubt I would be accurate. I could hit anything on the ground, and land loomed now in sight. I wanted to hurtle straight nose-down and feel gravity burst in my head. I wanted to hear my engine wail. I wanted powerful air brakes to grab me in the seat and position the plane. When the British fighters came after us, I was unafraid. Let them swarm around me. I was prepared — to dive. But below me still lay only sea. Maybe I should dive anyway. I decided to. I started, but before I could: bop-bop-bop-bop bullets shattered my arm, my dive-operating arm, and fire sprang into the cockpit where I shrieked as the plane spewed smoke and shot into the sea.

HOME DEFENSE
By A British Officer

Our silver radar towers ringed the island in every key spot, rising three hundred fifty feet and peering out a hundred miles. On the screens we saw how many German planes were coming, and how high they were, and when and where they might arrive. This information we continuously relayed to expert teams, at sector stations, that quickly determined which fighters were fueled and ready, and at what altitude and in which direction they should be sent for the projected moment of interdiction. How much of this the Germans knew, we had no idea until they bombed us hard in several places on August thirteenth, knocking some of our radar stations out of order for hours. From emergency transmitters we could only send signals that imitated real detection activity.

NORTHERN ENGLAND
By A German Pilot

The Reich Marshal had been telling everyone: "The Messerschmitt-109's are adequate, but they're only fighters. My new Destroyer is almost twice as large, and it's a fighter and a bomber. It can do everything."

I did not know what to think, especially when they took away my rear gunners so extra fuel tanks could be added. Certainly I would need the fuel for the long round trip from Norway to northern England. The quick and battle-tested Me-109 did not have the range for this operation. So today I escorted bombers from Luftflotten 5.

The Luftwaffe had pounded southern England so heavily two days ago that most enemy fighters must be down there. Just to make sure we'd have no interference in the north, a group of seaplanes feinted away from our real objectives. I'll bet the British detected them and sent out fighters. They must have. But now the damn seaplanes were way off course, entangled with us in the midst of Spitfires. One dived at my rear, and I jerked hard to maneuver my big wings. I was turning as well as I could. I tried to go faster. I wanted to stop going down with lots of other Destroyers, and pure bombers, too.

ONSLAUGHT
By A British Officer

All day and into the evening our radar screens lit up at least fifteen hundred times. The Germans were coming here and faking there, it looked like. Actually, they were going there and faking here. They were all over, pounding, pounding, pounding airfields and blowing up lots of other things, though with relief I realized they weren't attacking our radar.

ENGLISH ADMINISTRATION
By Reinhard Heydrich

I controlled many parts of the SS, and right now I was defining the duties of the Reich Central Security Office. We would soon have many new responsibilities. All healthy young Englishmen, and some not so young, were going to be brought to the Reich as laborers. At the same time, we would confiscate all valuables, personal and industrial, and exploit them for our enrichment. Many political and social organizations would also have to be eradicated, especially the majority that had been anti-German.

As in Poland, I organized Einsatz Commandos to arrest or eliminate everyone on our Special Search List. Many politicians were on the list, topped by Churchill, and so were writers and intellectuals, certified troublemakers all.

FARMERS
By A German Pilot

I hadn't done it. Not me. I didn't like it, and I said so: "Leave those guys alone. That's not what we need to do."

After a British pilot bailed out of his shot-up plane, he'd often be gliding down, vulnerable, and he'd look right at one of our planes and into the eyes of the pilot. He'd look with hope then horror as the plane dived right at him and riddled him limp in his harness gliding still toward ground or sea.

I hadn't done it, and I really didn't like bombing, either. But in order to defeat the British, we needed to destroy the RAF. Since August twenty-fourth we had been attacking aircraft factories and inland fighter bases. We kept hammering every day, and our intelligence kept telling us we had almost won. The British were down to their last three hundred fighters. These reports were naturally quite heartening. I'm afraid disenchantment did creep in when RAF fighter opposition remained, so far as we could tell under siege in the sky, as deadly and well-coordinated as ever. Why, if the enemy was defeated, did our esteemed Reich Marshal, svelte as ever, feel compelled to berate our pilots and deny leaves and insist upon constant effort and constant risk while offering so little encouragement?

Why, if the enemy was defeated, were my three crew members entombed in our crashing Heinkel as I parachuted toward British soil? It was quite beautiful, really, the scene on the ground. The meadows were lush and green, glowing under a nice summer sun, and the sheep were so peaceful and unthreatening. I felt great landing. When farmers approached, I nodded respectfully, and in my best English I said, "Good afternoon, gentlemen. To you I surrender."

"You bloody beast," a farmer screamed, and all four charged. Right away they knocked me down, and one of them started hitting my head with a shovel, and the others kicked and stomped my head until it broke flat into the ground, not far from the sheep.

PRESSURE
By A British Officer

Every time I saw a plane, I cringed. This I had been doing more often as German bombs hurtled in and blew big craters in our runway and destroyed vital facilities. Several other airfields in the southeast were knocked out for days, and our pilots were also being pummeled. A quarter of them were dead or wounded, and raw replacements lunged out of abbreviated flight schools into hot cockpits. The veteran pilots, once so vigorous and assured, now often seemed lost in the holes of sleepless eyes. The Germans simply had more to sacrifice in this clash of attrition. And grind us they did with a thousand planes a day in late August and early September. Under this continual hammering, all of us shuddered on the brink.

NURSES
By Adolf Hitler

The Sportpalast was full of nurses, and they were very happy. They had just found out I was going to speak to them this afternoon, September fourth.

"In England," I said, "they're filled with curiosity and keep asking 'why doesn't he come?' Be calm. Be calm. He's coming. He's coming.

"Mr. Churchill, by his behavior, is in fact hastening my arrival. The noted war correspondent has been demonstrating his latest brainchild, the night air raid. He is carrying out these raids not because they promise to be highly effective, but because his air force cannot fly over Germany in daylight. Our planes, by contrast, fly over English soil every day. It seems that British pilots, like their prime minister, are nervous old hens who drop bombs whenever they see lights. In particular, they fancy bombing residential areas, farms and villages.

"Soon I must teach the British that our forbearance to date has not been weakness, as they had hoped. If they drop a few thousand kilograms of bombs on us, we will at once respond by dropping a thousand times more kilograms than they ever fathomed. If they declare they will increase their attacks on our cities, then we will raze their hideous cities to the ground. The hour approaches when one of us will break — and it will not be National Socialist Germany."

Jumping and panting, the ladies roared: "Never. Never."

LONDON BOMBS
By General Walther Wever

My plane had zoomed down the runway and left the earth, and my heart kept rising with the plane, and I surely felt I was going to heaven until the engine weakened and sputtered. It sputtered and stopped. The engine stopped and my heart dropped, and I grabbed and pulled every relevant instrument, and others, but the engine was just out, and the plane was turning down, and my heart fell through my stomach and did not stop until my plane smashed.

That was in June of 1936, when I was Chief of Staff of the Luftwaffe. In that vital office I had stressed: "Bombers will be decisive in aerial warfare, and only a nation with strong bomber forces should expect decisive action by its air force." I had therefore spearheaded a program to build big four-engine bombers, strategic bombers, and they were almost ready to be tested when I crashed. But my successors did not understand strategic aerial warfare. They wanted dive-bombers and medium bombers, and they built them and canceled my big bombers.

So now, on September seventh, 1940, they were sending tactical weapons to fill a strategic roll, expecting boys to do a man's job; and the boys did all right. The British clearly weren't expecting three hundred bombers and six hundred fighters to attack London this afternoon. Our bombs rocked docks, arsenals, oil and gas works, and other military targets, and the flames provided targets for another attack that night. A lot of damage was inflicted, but not enough.

CROMWELL
By A British Officer

This summer there hadn't been any tourists on this sandy southern beach, and I missed the children running about and into the water, and their parents telling them to settle down, so they, the parents, could nuzzle a bit. Now the only activity occurred when men put all the mines and barbed wire in front of the beach and tank obstacles behind. It was rather noisy then. But mostly I heard the eternal symphony of the sea, wave by wave, until church bells rang. That signaled Cromwell:

invasion imminent.

It had been a thousand years since foreign enemies trod over our land, and now they might again, any time, today, perhaps, or tomorrow. It had to be soon, if they were coming this year.

INVASION PORTS
By A German Officer

They were all there, thousands of barges and other invasion crafts along the ports of northern France, waiting to be boarded. I hoped they could be moved soon, but no troops were in sight. This was a hell of a bad place to just float. The British continued attacking by sea and air. Lots of crafts were going down, shattered by guns and bombs. This didn't make sense. Why the hell were we really there?

LONDON SLAUGHTER
By A German Pilot

Listen, I flew the best fighter plane in the world, the Messerschmitt 109, a fast and dangerous wonder armed with four machine guns and four cannons, and I went wherever I was told. I'd been flying sorties over London in daylight for about a week, and, as ordered, I flew close to the bombers. But didn't anyone understand? I was a goddamn fighter pilot, not a wart on someone's slow-moving ass.

This was crazy. Those final fifty Spitfires the British had must have really been something. We were supposed to lure them out. And we did, swarms of them, and there I was flying way under top speed. To hell with that. I broke away from the bomber. He was being shot to shit anyway. I was sick of seeing my red light snap on to signal very low fuel. Last week I had to ditch in the Channel and soak several hours before being rescued by a seaplane. And today, after flying through Spitfires all the way to London, I could only stay ten minutes. Longer, and I'd have been back in the Channel.

THE BIG PICTURE
By Admiral Erich Raeder

This military conference did not matter much, not to me, and I wanted it to be over. The generals, as always, were trying to turn the Fuehrer's vision their way, inward, and away from the horizon, my way. So I waited for the blabber-fest to end.

"Mein Fuehrer," I said, then walked to him as he prepared to leave. "I must talk to you, privately."

He nodded.

"It's time we attacked the British somewhere else. We can't continue to subordinate the Mediterranean theater, which they've always viewed as the pivot of their empire. We can hurt them more there than anywhere else, and we really must. Italy's weak and certain to be under increasing attack from British power in the region. The Italians don't understand how vulnerable they are or the danger in refusing our help. We must act soon.

"If we don't take control in the Mediterranean, the British and the Americans might be able to capture areas in northwest Africa for use against us in a prolonged war. They'll certainly try to do so. But we can eliminate the British right now. We just have to act promptly and strike with all our forces."

"I understand your reasoning, Admiral. Before I can take any action, however, I need to discuss this with Mussolini and Franco, and probably Petain, too."

WOLF PACK
By Otto Kretschmer

On the surface of the dark Atlantic, our seven U-boats crept like wolves toward three dozen merchant ships and a few escorts. This was our first attack as a pack. The British, I hoped, would not see us either directly or on radar. They also might not be sure if they heard us. Whatever groans their equipment picked up could be their own engines. And while their sonar was looking down, searching underwater, there we were, unseen, unheard, creeping on the surface, now among the big ships.

I had one right in my sights. But it wasn't big enough. I needed some of the really good ones tonight, and searched carefully before spotting a tanker. Get ready. Fire one. Direct hit. The ship erupted. I assumed the British still had not seen us. They must not have. With casual malevolence I continued to ease between their ships. During the night only their best ones were torpedoed, and by morning half the convoy was gone, and we seven wolves crept away, small on the huge Atlantic surface.

ASSHOLES
By Adolf Hitler

The little brown bastard was late, and I wanted to boot his fat belly when he got off his train and kept pumping my hand and grinning fulsomely like some Latin buffoon. I had not come all the way to the Spanish border for nonsense. At once I motioned for us to move to my train.

"The British are beaten, and beaten badly," I told General Franco. "They're not admitting it now, of course, but soon they'll have no choice. Once I take Gibraltar, the British won't be able to operate in the Mediterranean or reach northern Africa. I'm therefore in the historically unprecedented position to invite you to join our military alliance. In return for your joining the war, it would be my honor to hand over Gibraltar to you. Also, Caudillo, I would add to your empire various African colonies that will be determined soon, at the end of the war."

"We in Spain have long been spiritually united with the Axis and are loyal in every way," Franco said. "Your great achievements are to me an inspiration. I certainly want to join forces with you. That obviously would be my great goal. I want to do so as soon as we can."

"Thank you so much for offering to take Gibraltar for us. Our honor demands that we capture it ourselves, however. And we intend to do just that. We do have to be very particular about when we enter the war. As you know, our poor country is being pressured by your enemies. We would really need a lot of aid. At least several hundred thousand tons of wheat. Could you provide that? And we'd certainly have to have thousands of big guns, shore batteries, to protect ourselves against inevitable attacks by the British.

"I must respectfully tell the Fuehrer that the British aren't beaten yet. Aided by the Americans, they could continue the war a long time. And one shouldn't underestimate the hardships of war in the desert. The British might be pushed back there, but not all the way out. The sand around a fortress provides just as much protection as the seas surrounding Great Britain. As an old African campaigner, I'm quite sure about that."

Ramming to my feet, I shouted: "There's no point in continuing this conversation."

That chastened the transparent Franco. He knew he owed his dictatorship to my support during his civil war, and realized only I could deliver the colonies he craved in Africa.

"Will you sign a treaty?" I said.

"Yes. I would be honored. But we must have sufficient wheat and guns, and the independence to attack at the moment we know is best. Our position now in that regard is very similar to Italy's last fall."

For nine tortuous hours I dealt with this greasy little sausage. He reminded me of an incompetent major, at best. In Germany he would have been lucky to make corporal.

The next day I met with Marshal Petain in Montaire. This eighty-four year old antique, a hero from the Great War, now played my French puppet as head of state.

"Someone obviously has to pay for the lost war," I told him. "England is certainly going to lose its empire. France can receive compensation if it now agrees to take an active part in eliminating the British."

"My country has already suffered too much to engage in another conflict."

"In that case, if you're sympathetic to England, you'll lose all your colonies and be subjected to terms similar to those I plan for England."

"No peace of reprisal has ever endured."

"I'm not seeking a peace of reprisal. In fact, I want to guarantee the peace of Europe for centuries, and this can be very favorable to France if it helps me beat the British."

"We must know the fate of the two million French prisoners you hold."

"The prisoners are hostages. Your collaboration would bring leniency."

Petain agreed that France would not make trouble. And though the old man didn't say it, I felt he, like Franco, might come around and join the fight. Surely even these assholes could see what was developing.

SURPRISE
By Benito Mussolini

I did not need advice or help, certainly not from Hitler. He just wanted a slice of my glory in the Mediterranean and North Africa. I was not going to let him get involved. When he stepped off his train this October 1940 morning in Florence, I announced: "Fuehrer, we're on the march. Victorious Italian troops attacked Greece today."

The Fuehrer could not complain about Italian inactivity now. I was doing so many things even while partially demobilizing for winter. As we stood on the balcony of Palazzo Pitti, I knew cheering Italians could see I was as successful as Hitler and a much finer specimen.

STEPS
By Adolf Hitler

No one could come. There was too much to contemplate. Alone I strolled paths around the Berghof, surrounded by horrors. The Russians in particular were conspiring to snare us. While we Germans battled for survival in the West, Stalin was devouring Baltic States right up to the Reich. He also grabbed part of Rumania and was waiting to pounce on Hungary. My consternation only grew as England tried to jump in bed with Stalin. I knew he was planning to attack me. He would have ravaged my scant forces in Poland during the French campaign if he hadn't been occupied with easier prey. I tried to delay catastrophe by rushing troops to Poland now.

Despite this beast lurking in the East, I instructed my diplomats to sincerely explain that the recently signed Tripartite Pact was anything but a threat to Russia. Germany and Italy had pledged that Asia was for Japan, and Japan pledged that Europe was for Germany and Italy, and we all promised to in every way support each other if one of us "is attacked by a power at present not involved in the European war or in the Sino-Japanese conflict." Surely even the paranoid Russians could see this was actually a tacit warning to the United States to stay out of Europe.

OGRE
By Adolf Hitler

Not only had I, the greatest conqueror in history, just received Molotov with full honors, I generously told him: "If your country can resolve its disagreements with us, then you can gain vast territories that include warm water ports in the Persian Gulf."

"Why are German troops fortifying Finland's border with our country?" he said.

"We certainly are not. I've heard of no such thing. But of course there must not be a war in the Baltic."

"I'm talking about Finland."

"No war with Finland."

"Then you're going back on our agreement. And our government is also displeased about your defense guarantee to Rumania. We'd like to know if this is aimed against our interests."

"Our guarantee applies to anyone who violates Rumanian territory."

"We want you to revoke that guarantee."

"That's impossible."

"Our government would also like to know if the Tripartite Pact is designed to undermine Soviet security. And what do you mean by the New World Order?"

"You would benefit manifestly by the dissolution of the British Empire."

"We're interested in developments in Europe. What would Germany think if we gave Bulgaria a guarantee identical to Germany's guarantee to Rumania. We have permanent interests in Bulgaria as well as Turkey and the Bosporus and the Dardanelles."

What did I think about all that?

"As it is getting late, we should adjourn now," I said.

TO YOU
By Vyacheslav Molotov

I was toasting Ribbentrop at a party in the Russian Embassy when sirens intruded. Our delegations moved to a bomb shelter under the Foreign Ministry where Ribbentrop urged us to join the Tripartite Powers and feast on the British Empire.

"Your assumption the British are defeated is premature," I said.

"The British have already lost the will and the capacity to fight us," Ribbentrop insisted.

"Then why are we in this shelter, and whose bombs are those I hear exploding?"

INADEQUACIES
By Admiral Erich Raeder

Most anxious to see Hitler and pound home vital points in a memorandum from the Naval War staff, I went to the Chancellery on November fourteenth, the day Molotov left town. After handing the paper to the Fuehrer, I watched as he read.

"The Italians are being routed in Greece, Mein Fuehrer," I said when he finished. "They're retreating faster than they ever attacked. And the British strike at the Italian naval base in Taranto two days ago was devastating. Small numbers of carrier-based aircraft severely damaged three warships, at little cost to the attackers. All of this immeasurably strengthens the British in the Mediterranean and increases their prestige everywhere.

"We ought, perhaps, to look at the Italians more as a burden than an ally. They have no chance of sustaining an offensive in Egypt. Their leadership is abysmal, by far the worst of any major power. Their whole effort — and it's a tentative effort — is disorganized and incompetent.

"Clearly, Mein Fuehrer, it's up to us to concentrate our forces in the vital Mediterranean and African theaters. Our current measures there are just not adequate."

"They're certainly adequate, especially in the relative sense. Remember, our main enemy must first be eliminated."

OPERATION BARBAROSSA
By Adolf Hitler

"Whenever they ask, no matter how many times they ask, tell them their proposals are under study," I said.

Stalin's terms for joining the Tripartite Pact were way beyond reason, beyond blackmail, even, and certainly far beyond consideration. He demanded my troops be promptly removed from Finland, and that I acquiesce to a Russo-Bulgarian mutual defense pact and to Soviet bases being established nearby, and that the oil-rich Persian Gulf be designated as a Soviet prize, and that Japan renounce its territorial claim in eastern Russia.

I ordered accelerated planning and often emphasized these points: "If the new Reich is to acquire desirable land in Europe, it can only come at the expense of Russia, which is no ally in our fight for freedom. Let no one argue that an alliance with Russia precludes war. On the contrary, an alliance whose aim does not embrace a plan for war is senseless and worthless. Present-day Russian rulers are, after all, nothing more than common bloodstained criminals. Don't forget that they belong to a race that combines, in a rare mixture, bestial cruelty and an inconceivable gift for lying. Yes, in Russian Bolshevism we must see the attempt by Jews to achieve world domination."

Thus, I had originally articulated my concerns fifteen years ago in *Mein Kampf*, and now waited for the remedy, which arrived on December seventeenth. My plan was easily the most important in human history and deserved an appropriate name: Barbarossa, the great Holy Roman Emperor who had crusaded and fought with élan Germans always revered. And still they await his return from a cave near the Berghof. In Barbarossa they await a massive and lightning attack by armored wedges that will cut off and destroy Russian armies and establish an impenetrable wall up to the Urals to seal off Asiatic hordes.

"But this means a two-front war," a few complained. "You always said you wouldn't make the mistake of the Great War, the same mistake Napoleon made."

"We really don't have a front in the West, not on land," I explained. "And England won't admit it's defeated until we eliminate its illusion that Russia might someday provide a lifeline. We must never forget that time is against us and for Russia. We can't allow the enemy to grow stronger, then strike us first. We'll annihilate Russia much faster than Napoleon ever fathomed."

ORANGE NIGHT
By An Englishman

Our windows and doors were blown out, and part of our roof, but we still had family and neighbors and lots of singing and fun. That made this all special, together like never before, in shelters, too, for seventy-six straight nights the Germans bombed us. Then they switched to Coventry and Birmingham and various ports, and only occasionally bothered us, and Christmas 1940 was nice, and everything seemed like it might stay peaceful until sirens seared about seven p.m. on December twenty-ninth. It was dark and very windy, and soon the Germans were back over London, pouring bombs over there and behind us and across town, even right here, and fires soon started and I ran and reported to my unit and activated the hose. Water came fast but flames got so hot they obliterated it in midair. Then the water main broke here and apparently lots of other places, and I couldn't see anything but flames on broken buildings that lighted a dark night orange.

UNIVERSAL CONSIDERATIONS
By Adolf Hitler

I had to think very far ahead. Russia was certainly going to be beaten very soon after our attack in May 1941, three months hence. What would I do then? Guided by unequaled strategic insight, I ordered plans for giant pincers to sweep east across North Africa, and south from the Caucasus, and to converge in the Middle East for a drive down into India, the heart of the British Empire.

That would certainly doom the British, even if America entered the war. But America probably would not want to bear primary responsibility, which it would have to with Russia annihilated and England almost so. Furthermore, our friends the Japanese, spurred by the shattered Russian threat, could invade south and hurt American interests in the Pacific. The Americans were, of course, already weakened by Jewish elements that controlled Roosevelt and the economy and war cabinet. Otherwise, this nation of immense size and wealth, founded on virgin territory and long energized by many healthy and dynamic Germanic peoples, would have been unassailable.

Last year I had thought America could not become a factor in Europe until 1960 or 1970. But if I did not act swiftly and brutally elsewhere, America could become involved next year. In fact, American supplies to Britain already concerned me. Nevertheless, in all modesty, I did acknowledge that we could not, at least at this time, directly threaten the North American continent.

UGLY
By A Yugoslav Officer

I was sick of it. But it was getting harder to avoid. In neighboring Hungary and Rumania, hundreds of thousands of his troops marched in. Then Bulgaria signed the Tripartite Pact. We in the Yugoslav air force did not want to see it here. But our government soon enraged us by also signing the Tripartite Pact. The next day we overthrew the government. Crowds roared in the streets, and I saw one man tear up his picture, throw it down and spit on it.

LESSON
By Adolf Hitler

The adjutant entered and handed me a telegram.

"I don't believe it," I shouted. "This must be a prank. I can't believe this. Surely they wouldn't. If they did...

"This better be a prank. They better not wire me this morning that they're delighted, then do this.

"You're sure? Outrageous. This is an unprecedented betrayal. They've personally insulted me. Get Ribbentrop over here. And call Goering. Tell him I want him here now."

Right away they arrived and sat with General Jodl and General Keitel.

"This mess in the Balkans endangers my most important plans," I said. "I'm going to sweep the whole goddamn mess into the sea. Yugoslavia, for its treachery, is going to be smashed militarily as a state.

"Don't tell me we can't do it. We can easily do it. So what if you've got to delay Barbarossa? Start these plans the minute I'm finished here. I want them carried out with merciless harshness, in Blitzkrieg style.

"Hungary and Bulgaria will go along. This afternoon I'll offer them some Yugoslav territory. Italy'll get something, too, a little."

BALKANS
By A Historian

The countries, states, territories, and territorial concoctions on our troubled Balkan Peninsula had for centuries been like a deck of cards clumsily shuffled by "great" powers too inept to keep their own cards in order but presumptuous enough to meddle with ours. The most outrageous incursion yet began on April sixth, 1941 when the Germans pounced on Yugoslavia from Rumania and Bulgaria — as well as from non-Balkan Austria and Hungary — and they did the same to Greece from Bulgaria and soon also entered Greece through Yugoslavia.

Though on April fifth the Russians had inserted a joker into our

Yugoslav deck, and pledged to defend it, they did nothing about the assaults, which were most horrific in Belgrade. There the German planes dive-bombed with precision, blowing holes in the city and massacring thousands. Enemy panzers and troops were also destructive, and Yugoslavia surrendered on April seventeenth and soon so did Greece, from which more hustlers — the British — were trying to evacuate, Dunkirk style.

FLIGHT OF PEACE
By Rudolf Hess

Those the Fuehrer had been turning to would only poison him. He needed extraordinary help now, a miracle, and only I had a chance. As the Fuehrer's deputy and third most powerful man in the Reich, I was able to convince Willi Messerschmitt himself to loan me a Messerschmitt 110 and add extra fuel tanks. Then I took a couple dozen training flights, improving my already fine flying skills, and without explaining why, I obtained a special map, radio, and an official leather flying suit.

"I'll be home in a couple of days, at the latest," I told my wife on May tenth.

"You won't be back that soon."

"I promise I will."

All morning I had been looking at my son in the nursery, and I looked again, for a long time, maybe the last time. Then I left and took off.

I felt they would probably get me. They'd spot me and shoot me down. They were already trying to. I dived almost to the ground and sped just above houses and trees, slicing through night to elude the Spitfire. Now I was near my destination and had to bail out, so I climbed to several thousand feet and... I could not get out, pinned in upside down flying fast, and I saw only bright colors. Grimacing before the crash, I blacked out but awoke and finally fell out and opened the parachute, gliding now toward destiny, toward the Duke of Hamilton, friend of Churchill, confidant of kings, and the first man to fly over Mt. Everest.

At first I did not tell my captors who I really was. When I did, they were shocked. Then I got to see the Duke of Hamilton and others, and warned them: "You must surrender or you'll be destroyed. The Fuehrer doesn't want that. He wants the British Empire to survive. All he wants is freedom on the continent. You'd still have almost everything else.

"Of course, Churchill would have to leave office. He tried to start this war long before he actually did, and everything is his fault. The Fuehrer would never negotiate with him or his government."

The British did not seem to realize how important I was. They made me a prisoner, me, the Fuehrer's deputy. I should have been treated as an envoy. They did not know what I knew. I would never tell. I hope the Fuehrer understood. I'm sure he did. I had left a letter for him. That must have comforted him. I had conceded I'd probably die, but if I didn't and failed, I'd take the blame. And if I didn't die, and I succeeded, I'd give the Fuehrer all the credit. I prayed the Fuehrer would forgive me.

It was hard to tell about anything in captivity. I could not see the stars or consult those who understood the signs as I always had in Germany. Now my life was restricted and horrible and getting worse. I knew the British were planning to kill me. At first I thought they'd shoot. But then I saw what they were putting in my food — gas, stinking fish, and dung. If they kept this up I was going to kill myself.

RECREATION
By A German Maiden

I thought about him all the time. He still had not come back from Poland, and they said he was missing. But by now I guessed it was more than that and our child would never know his father.

So I lived with my parents on their farm, and I cooked for them and the Polish prisoners who worked on the farm. My parents told me not to get too friendly, but the guys were very nice and much different than I expected. They taught me some Polish and I taught them some German, and this was a nice treat in a dreary life not at all like the League of German Maidens had told me I'd have.

I liked Jozef the best. He was really cute, and it just felt right and finally we started seeing each other in the barn as often as possible and in the house, too, when my parents were gone. That's when it was best. And nobody actually caught us. But I got pregnant.

"You slut," my father said. "You stinking slut. How could you?"

A bunch of men came and got Jozef and later made all his friends stand right by his feet and look up. They didn't make me do that, but they cut off all my hair, mounted me backward on a mule, and paraded me through the village. The authorities then sent me to a camp for fifteen months labor.

TROUBLEMAKERS
By Joseph Stalin

I hugged Ambassador von der Schulenburg in public, and I even embraced another German. I didn't know who the hell he was, but I hugged him and told him we were all great friends. Then I kicked out several diplomats from countries unfriendly to Germany.

Violations of our air space by German planes did concern me, and I complained. Those planes should not have been there. But I was much more worried by the British attempt to use Hess to make a deal with Hitler. Those scheming islanders wanted to save themselves by making peace and encouraging Germany to attack us. This abject plot was no more effective than the capitalist press barking in June 1941 about German troops concentrating on our border.

INQUIRY
By Count Friedrich von der Schulenburg

I knew why Molotov was calling me on June twenty-first. I was getting worried, too. I hadn't been unduly alarmed in late April when I met with Hitler in Berlin and told him: "I can't believe Russia will ever attack us. Stalin wouldn't risk war even when France and England were still strong. I'm convinced that he's ready to grant us even more concessions."

I had since been repeatedly embarrassed by rumors in Moscow that Germany was going to attack Russia. My discomfort intensified as I learned the talk emanated from Germany and was buttressed by reliable observations. I still denied an attack was possible. It couldn't be. Molotov and Stalin agreed.

Now, at 9:30p.m. in the Kremlin, Molotov was most concerned and eager as he said: "There are a number of indications your government is dissatisfied with our government. Germany did not even respond, publicly or privately, when we denounced the rumormongers. We can't understand why Germany is dissatisfied. The most important issues have been resolved, particularly in the Balkans. I would appreciate it if you could tell me specifically why Germany is so dissatisfied."

I had no idea.

George Thomas Clark

WAR IN THE EAST
1941-1943

BARBAROSSA
By Adolf Hitler

Horrified that the Russians were about to attack, I before dawn this morning unleashed three million grim warriors and several thousand panzers and planes. In three great waves they pounded toward Leningrad and Moscow and the Ukraine, and had already doomed the heathens, whose aged planes were being crushed on the ground while inept soldiers died or surrendered even faster than I'd imagined. The only things working for the Russians were their trains, which were loaded with supplies for us and running on time.

RESPONSIBILITY
By General Dimitry Pavlov

I was as good as most Russian generals late in June 1941. So I don't think I was primarily to blame. Stalin just claimed I was. Then he sent some of his people.

"How do you explain your failure?" shouted a commissar who had no combat experience.

"I prepared very strong defensive positions, and everything was done according to procedure," I said.

"But you were annihilated."

"I don't think static defenses are going to work anymore."

"Then why didn't you strike first?"

"Stalin wouldn't let us."

"Watch what you say."

"He insisted the Germans weren't going to attack us, and that we not attack them."

"You were there to fight."

"We did. But the panzers rapidly closed the circle and chopped us up."

"That's unforgivable."

"That's precisely what happened in lots of other regions."

"The others will also have a chance to explain. Come with us."

"I've already explained."

"There must be a thorough inquiry, General Pavlov."

They took me somewhere and asked more questions, but they weren't interested in answers. What they wanted was me in front of a wall.

RUSSIAN ROADS
By A German Soldier

Our Army continued to conquer territory more rapidly than anyone ever had and already engulfed an area the size of Germany. That was amazing since the roads were often very bad and never good and always so dusty they dirtied our faces and made our equipment sputter and choke. Next to the roads stood many troublesome signs. They had been switched by the hardening folk fighting us as we went. Our maps also were a problem. They showed roads that were not there and omitted some that were, and our logistical precision, so decisive earlier, was sometimes askew. We needed to rest a little and service and reorganize the panzers. Then, in groups, they churned right onto roads that dirtied our faces and made moving and breathing gritty and unpleasant on the hot and dusty roads toward Moscow.

DIVERTED
By General Heinz Guderian

This was outrageous. There was only one war-winning target. That's what I needed to tell Hitler. On August twenty-third I arrived at his dreary Wolf's Lair headquarters in a hot, mosquito-infested forest in East Prussia. The timid Commander in Chief of the Army, Brauhitsch, greeted me with the lament: "I forbid you to mention the question of Moscow to the Fuehrer. Discussion is pointless."

"In that case, Herr Field Marshal, I'd like permission to return at once to my panzer group. I don't want to waste time with a meaningless discussion."

"You must talk to Hitler. But don't mention Moscow."

Neither Brauhitsch nor General Halder nor anyone else from the Army High Command, the OKH, attended. Only those from the Wehrmacht High Command, the OKW, were present along with Hitler's staff.

"Are your troops capable of making another great effort?" Hitler said.

"If the troops are given a major objective apparent to everyone."

"You mean Moscow, of course."

"Since you've broached the subject, let me tell you why it's so vital," I said. "From a military point of view, the ultimate objective, the only objective, must now be the destruction of the enemy's main forces in front of Moscow. We've already battered them. Now we must eliminate them.

"Furthermore, Mein Fuehrer, we must consider that Moscow is essential to the Russians maintaining their ability to resist. It's by far the most important capital in Europe. It is, for instance, the center of roads, railroads and communications. It's also a key industrial zone as well as the political solar plexus of the entire country. Losing Moscow would be a devastating psychological blow not only to the Russian people but the rest of the world. Our soldiers know this. They've prepared for this with the greatest enthusiasm.

"After the fall of Moscow, the Ukraine would be easy to take. But if we turn toward the Ukraine now, from our advanced position in the center, we would be heading southwest. That is away from Moscow, Mein Fuehrer, and back toward Germany. We would lose too much time to strike a fatal blow to Moscow before winter."

"In the Ukraine, and elsewhere in the south, there are vast reserves of raw materials and agriculture," Hitler said. "By taking the Ukraine, which I've already given strict orders to do, we will be starving the enemy while ensuring permanent supplies for our troops and our nation. My generals simply know nothing of the economic aspects of the war."

All the OKW officers, I noted with alarm, had been nodding every time Hitler completed a sentence.

LIBERATION
By A Ukrainian

These great Christian warriors were here, trying to replace the godless Stalin, and our women rushed forward with food and wine, and lots of us walked right up and stroked, and sometimes even kissed, the beautiful black crosses the German soldiers wore around their necks.

DUCKS
By A German Soldier

While our inner ring of forces began to strangle seven hundred thousand soldiers trapped in the Ukraine, our outer wall, facing East, loaded its guns and aimed at the Russians marching toward us. They had locked arms and were singing. We thought they must be drunk or drugged. They were all in the open. They were all in range. They were all doomed and rotting in great heaps by the time more of them appeared and began to walk over the corpses of their comrades. The new soldiers died like the old ones. And as others continued to attack, I wondered where they got so many men and so much courage.

MOPPING UP
By An Einsatz Commando

I was a lawyer, and most of the other men were also college educated. It was essential to have so many intellectuals in the SS. Our training had been very complex, and Reinhard Heydrich warned us: "You have heavy tasks. You must perform them with skill and unparalleled hardness."

Our Einsatz Group moved into the Ukraine right with, or right behind, the regular soldiers. We tried to stay away from them as much as possible. They would not have approved. And they started to complain. Many of us did not approve, either. And I said so. So did some others. But our orders came from the highest authority. The orders were therefore legal and had to be carried out.

We were too busy to worry much about ethics. We had our guns pointed at a column of naked people, and I told them to stand by the pit. Shooting the first one was hard. I didn't want to pull the trigger. The way blood spurted from her little head made me sick. This was not what I wanted to do. I had volunteered, but not for this.

This was our job. I hated all the blood and screaming, so I started shooting faster and did not stand there thinking about it. Thinking did not do any good. Those people in the pit had thought our posters were correct, and that they were coming to be re-settled. I was glad to put away my gun and start counting. It was difficult to count accurately with so many people on top of each other. I think I got the right number, though. One hundred seventy-three. That was important. I wrote the number in my report. A few days later they took me to the hospital for some rest. I'd been so tired I'd been screaming all night and not sleeping at all.

MUD
By A German Soldier

Christ, it was bad. Everyone's face was blackened by dust churned up by machines, and my teeth ground on hard little rocks every time I moved my mouth. I was so thankful the rains came. I stood looking into the sky and let water splash onto my face and wash away the dust. We were all happy and started to feel refreshed and almost clean.

The rain continued for three hours, and we rested the whole time. We'd come a long way fast. From north to south our three Army Groups had now captured an area maybe twice as large as Germany. That's what the officers said. We deserved to rest. I put an empty rations can out and let the water hammer in, and then I drank it. It was the best thing I ever tasted.

Now it was time to move toward Moscow again. The road was a little soft, but I could walk and the panzers rolled on their tracks. Vehicles on wheels could also move. They did for a few minutes. We pushed the ones that got stuck. They were pretty heavy. So was the mud on my boots. While slapping at bugs biting my face, I scraped one boot against the side of a truck. Then I raised my other boot and scraped it before putting it back in the mud.

Soon the goddamn vehicles started sinking so badly we hooked up horses. While pulling, the horses' skinny legs sliced way down in the mud and lots of them broke their legs and others pulled so hard they just whined and fell over, covered by mud.

That's where I heard the first sounds, right there in the mud. Thuuup. Thuuup. Thuuup. Then the bullets started hitting steel and horses and men. We couldn't drive away, and we couldn't run. I dived behind the truck and watched everything get shot, including my empty boots.

T-34

By A Russian Soldier

I wanted to be in the new tank as much as I wanted out of the old one. This T-34 was a beauty. The old one and all other tanks, as far as I'm concerned, were ugly. The T-34 must have been designed by a great artist. Its armor was sloped everywhere possible, and it was sleek. I loved this new tank, and in it we were rolling toward the Germans. I told my three crewmen to get ready. Get ready. Fire. Our biggest gun erupted. And a panzer exploded. It could not have reached us this far even if it had fired. Another panzer was moving toward us at about twenty-five miles an hour. We rushed it at thirty-two miles an hour, firing and missing, and its return fire hit us right in the thick, sloped armor. And the shell bounced off. In a calm frenzy we aimed again and fired a shell that tore into a steel oven of five Germans. Over to my right, a panzer was not moving well in the mush. Our much wider tracks eased around, and another panzer ignited.

MOSCOW NOW
By Adolf Hitler

Frankly, my genius was confounding even me. How could I be so great? How could I continually be so correct when so many others disagreed and proved themselves inferior? The answer is both elementary and profound: I was simply born of a different genus. I inspired when others despaired. I persevered when others quit. I foresaw when others were blinded. And before me now I conceived it all so clearly: a vast reservoir. That's what Moscow was going to be.

There was no way to disrupt my inexorable vision. Moving toward Moscow during the first half of October, my forces in Army Group Center crushed the Russians around Bryansk and Vyasma and snared six hundred thousand more prisoners. They were lucky we accepted their surrender at all. We certainly would not be accepting any surrenders in Moscow. Everyone there was going to be at the bottom of the reservoir.

GOOD PICTURE
By General Georgi Zhukov

"Congratulations," some people said. "You're the first commander to have his picture in the armed forces newspaper. Stalin obviously has unqualified confidence that you can defend Moscow."

"Don't be an ass," I said. "Stalin is afraid Moscow can't be held. Now he's got someone to blame if there's disaster."

SNOW
By A German Soldier

It started getting very cold in October, and I could not imagine that. We did not have winter clothing and were not permitted to mention the subject. I knew our commanders must have a good reason. I didn't want to have dodged all those bullets and seen so many comrades die and killed so many Russians, and then freeze to death.

That was not going to happen. We were going to be in Moscow soon. That's why the snow was probably going to be good. The roads froze harder than a rock, and now our panzers and vehicles with wheels and horses could move again. Through the snow we headed toward Moscow.

Walking was good for my feet. It did not keep them warm enough, but it seemed to help. I hoped that it would. I maintained a good pace. That had to help. I was convinced, walking on feet I could no longer feel. Eventually, beside a fire, I took off my boots and socks to see if my toes were still there. I put my hands on them but still couldn't feel them. I couldn't feel my hands, either, or my face. My nose hurt so bad I thought it was gone. I asked a guy if it was still there. He did not laugh. His feet were really bad, frostbitten dark and dead looking, like about a quarter of the guys' feet in our battalion.

RED SQUARE
By Joseph Stalin

My coat was thick and warm, and every time I breathed I heated the freezing air in Red Square. Hundreds of thousands of soldiers stood below me, and all of them could see. There was Stalin. Stalin was here. And the Germans were still at least forty miles away.

Every word I shot into the microphone heated the air and heartened the men. Two million citizens had already fled. Many government officials also ran. The Germans were moving toward Moscow. But Stalin was here.

Every Russian needed to know. No one had ever conquered Moscow. Our brave men had thrashed every invader. Our great earth mauled every intruder. All this I shot into the microphone in Red Square, and as planes riveted the gray sky above, hundreds of thousands of soldiers stood straight up in thick warm coats and furry caps. They stood shoulder to shoulder, and then they roared, and their long roar heated the air in Red Square.

DOMES
By A German Soldier

The others were way behind our advance party. They were resting and re-grouping or being buried. There weren't many of us, but there didn't need to be. We were only supposed to look. We were going to if we could. We didn't doubt we'd be able to. We trudged through snow while wind sliced our faces. Sometimes we hid from Russian patrols. Our troops would destroy them later. Right now we only wanted to get there. We had come so far. We had to see. We kept moving long after we felt it was impossible. We were going to do it. We were going to get there. We were going to...

"Look," I shouted. "The domes. We're in Moscow. We're really almost there."

MOSCOW
By General Georgi Zhukov

Comrade Stalin had not looked like the man of steel today. His face was as gray as his rapidly graying hair, and his voice was weak as he said, "Are you sure we can hold Moscow?"

"We can definitely hold Moscow," I said. "But you must give me the reserves I need. And the tanks. If you want me to hold the city, let me do so. Vital preparations must not be disrupted."

"I shall oversee everything."

"Fine. And I shall ensure that our sacred capital survives."

"Why are you so sure?"

"The Germans are exhausted. They've suffered heavy losses and their units are far under strength. They have no reserves left, none that can be brought into action here if we strike soon. Their morale has already been severely damaged. Now we must shatter it."

The great citizens of Moscow were committed to help. With shovels, with sticks, often with their strong hands, they were digging trenches and anti-tank ditches and building barbed wire entanglements. These obstacles were our last line. The Germans were here, and everyone knew what they wanted to do.

To the East I looked across a frozen white expanse. Japan might be a menace there, but nothing like the Germans here. The Japanese could not use armor very well. I'd learned that two years ago when I crushed them in Mongolia. They would be reluctant to ever fight me again. And Germany's predicament now was not going to embolden the Japanese. Our divisions in the Far East weren't really threatened anymore. We ordered them onto big trains heading West toward Moscow, our final place. These half million new troops, white-clad and winter hard, were massed with our other troops, now a million and more all getting ready for the Germans in front of frozen Moscow.

I had always been a big guy who smacked a lot of faces, and now I was the toughest general in charge of the ultimate defense. For this I demanded we constantly prepare. Trains and trucks by the thousands chugged in on frozen tracks and roads, and we hoarded tanks and guns and ammunition for our men. This time we were ready.

The counterstroke I initiated with artillery. It was loud and brutal pounding the long and cold German front on December sixth, and the barrage continued through a frigid night. Now the Germans were frozen in and blown out, and it was time. We counterattacked. Never had there been one so massive and so determined, and we quickly battered the enemy into retreat and in many places cut him off and ground him up. Pressing the onslaught, we clawed further west and recovered pieces of our country where we saw the most appalling things.

AMERICAN CRIMES
By Adolf Hitler

What great news. At Pearl Harbor the Japanese just proved what I had often asserted: "The Americans have no future. They've become so Jewified and Negrified that their best Germanic elements, once dominant, have been all but negated. Now the Americans can only grope at each other's throats for dollars in the most crass and commercial way. This undignified and absolutely fruitless effort underscores the abject failure of the New Deal. President Roosevelt knows, just as his numerous influential domestic enemies have discovered, that he can survive politically only if he diverts attention from his inadequacies at home. This he has done by trying to start conflicts elsewhere and destroy one nation after another."

For my part I had always conscientiously adhered to the principles of international law. I did this despite a series of cruel and deceptive acts by Roosevelt, the ultimate agent of international Jewry. His most serious crimes had begun with the Lend-Lease program that provided ships and weapons to the belligerent British. Despite this provocation, I restrained myself and demanded other Germans do so as well.

My forbearance had continued even as "neutral" American vessels followed and hounded my U-boats, which were engaged in legitimate and legal acts of war against that worldwide scourge, the faltering British Empire. My extraordinary restraint still endured when American ships dropped depth charges on my U-boats. Even after American forces replaced the British in Iceland in June, I had insisted that my Navy avoid conflict. Though American protection of enemy shipping in the western Atlantic was an unequivocal act of war by the dim-witted and ruthless Roosevelt, I remained a man of peace dedicated solely to the reasonable protection of my country. Inevitably, my compassion was rebuffed. In September Roosevelt had declared he would "shoot on sight" any German vessel he wanted. I, by contrast, ordered my naval commanders not to shoot at a ship unless it could be identified as belonging to a nation with which we were at war. This humane policy was indisputably not the work of a "gangster" or a "rattlesnake," as the American president had often called me.

The Japanese had also long been mocked and harassed by Roosevelt, who negotiated with them fallaciously while always planning, as he did, to deny essential raw materials as well as Japan's right to seek them in its natural spheres of influence, Indo-China and the western Pacific.

I was relieved to learn that at Pearl Harbor the Japanese had so quickly and brilliantly destroyed much of America's navy in the Pacific, and would soon obliterate the rest. That was an immense help to me since it would weaken Russia, which had been receiving American supplies. The United States could not even theoretically compete with Japan in the Pacific unless it concentrated all its naval forces there against the world's finest navy. That would weaken America in the Atlantic, and thus weaken Britain, which would manifestly strengthen me.

From my Wolf's Lair headquarters in East Prussia, I rushed back to Berlin, and for two days after arriving I polished and practiced my speech. Then — on December eleventh, 1941 — I announced to the world that Germany was at war with the United States.

And I certainly expected that the Japanese, as I had been urging, would also soon be at war with Russia. My allies needed the same incomparable struggles in order to prove their superiority and worthiness.

RUSSIAN WINTER
By A German Soldier

I hoped the new goggles would help. I needed to see the enemies when they came again. We had not even detected them, much less imagined so many, until the instant their guns began scattering trees. We didn't care then what our orders were, not entirely. There had to be a better defensive line than one besieged by howling snowmen. We hurriedly built fires under our engines and pulled back.

Now, in a place not being bombarded, we made new homes in holes in the frozen ground. Our small rifle-oil lamps gave us a little light and quite a bit of smoke. The smoke stunk and so did the tobacco and especially all the men stunk. Their clothes and their bodies stunk and so did their wounds from war and their wounds from frostbite. Everything in the holes was stinking and rotten, but these were the best places in a world of malicious ice.

I had put on every piece of clothing I had, three shirts, two pairs of pants, three pairs of underwear, one rag, three pairs of socks and two overcoats, one of which I'd taken off my friend's body. I prayed the new goggles would help, too. Now it was my turn for sentry duty. We all hated that because we had to leave our stinking holes. I stepped out into a blizzard. It seemed there was always a blizzard. It came from the East and ripped into my face like a million pieces of glass.

I kept looking to the East. That's where Ivan was still gathering. We knew that now. The hotshots in OKH headquarters had insisted he wasn't there. They could stick those intelligence reports up their asses. Ivan was certainly there, and coming here, and through my goggles I looked into ice.

Sentry duty used to be an hour, then thirty minutes and now was only fifteen minutes. It seemed like fifteen hours. It was long enough to about kill you. I was relieved. I had been dreading that, in a way. Now I knew I'd have to empty my system. I had not done so in days. Everything was frozen inside, too. But now I had to go. I went behind a jeep and, with frozen hands in frozen gloves, pried off layer after layer of clothes, and unwrapped the thick dirty rag around my penis, which was frozen down the size of a fingertip, and I tried. I had to eventually. The icy wind whipped my flesh so hard I whimpered. God, please let me. This was taking longer than sentry duty. And it was much worse. Inside me a jagged mass ripped my intestines all the raw and frozen way out. I put my clothes back on, the rag and layer after layer, and went back home to my stinking hole and took off my goggles and looked at the flesh from my cheeks stuck to the goggles.

INCOMPETENCE
By Adolf Hitler

The generals were a disgrace. Their incompetence and cowardice had deprived me of the greatest victories in history. Those victories would certainly come, but not until I made changes. Brauhitsch was out. He said his heart was sick. I was sick of his weak heart. And Guderian absolutely had to be replaced. He'd claimed his position was indefensible. The only thing that could not be defended was his loss of fire and courage. He withdrew without permission.

Defeatism had to be stamped out everywhere. Field Marshal von Leeb, leader of Army Group North, was certainly not going to continue. I'd told him to bomb and shell Leningrad without cease and ignore all surrenders and plow the whole goddamn city into the ground and sow it with salt. All he could do was keep the city under siege. He lacked the will to seize absolute victory. So did the commander of Army Group Center, Field Marshal von Bock. He was supposed to take Moscow. He'd promised me he could do it. But he didn't. He wasn't good enough. Neither was Field Marshal von Rundstedt, leader of Army Group South. Despite victories in the Ukraine and Rostov, he had grown weak. I ordered him to dig in at Rostov. Instead, he retreated and wanted to keep running while he complained about not

being able to hold his positions. I was glad to be rid of him.
Only one man could command this Army.

HAND TO HAND
By A German Soldier

The Russians never stopped attacking me. Even before they actually came, they had destroyed my sleep and ruined my food, which turned to ice right after leaving the field kitchen hot. I knew they wanted to kill me now, or take me prisoner so they could watch me die. I'd never permit that. I was shooting fast and watching Russians stagger and fall, but they kept coming and were howling and almost here, and I could not pull the trigger fast enough. It was frozen. So was my finger. Maybe my finger was gone. Something was wrong. I think I was still pulling the trigger. But no more Russians fell. My firing pin had snapped. That did not matter now. They were too close to shoot. I clawed out of a shallow hole and struggled to my feet. As a Russian charged, I screamed and stabbed him with the bayonet at the end of my frozen rifle. He grabbed his stomach and collapsed. Another Russian attacked. I jammed my bayonet into his eye. And I pulled back for the next guy. But my bayonet was still in the eye. Then some guy from my blind side lunged — he had to have lunged — and I heard him only as he fell and rammed his bayonet in low of target into my thigh. He was face down in the ice, trying to get up when I whacked the back of his head with my rifle butt. I heard breathing, or at least sensed it, and I whacked him again, and again, and again I whacked the back of his frozen head.

MOSCOW SOON
By Adolf Hitler

Of course I was not going to panic. The generals panicked. They panicked all the time. They were panicking right now.

"No, shut up," I said. "We're not retreating. We're not going to fall back to winter positions. We don't have winter positions. You idiots.

Don't you know the whole line will fall apart if we retreat? Don't you understand what happened to Napoleon when he ran?

"We've got to stay. Not an inch is to be yielded. Do you understand? Not an inch.

"What the hell — the winter cold. We'll stand and take it. We can take it, and we will. We're ready. We're not retreating. We can't give this up. Not an inch."

VACATION
By A German Soldier

In the train I was so happy I was going home, and on the way I sat up and looked out the window. Most of the other guys on board had to lie down in the back. I sat by myself looking out at cow-dung huts and dead terrain. This was what Germany had to have. We certainly had a lot of it. I just could not imagine what we were going to do with it.

It was not going to be easy to keep. My wounded thigh broke open after the glass hit me in the face and I crashed to the floor. The partisans were attacking us again behind the front lines. We rarely knew who the enemy was. All the peasants looked the same. One might give you his hand and the other a knife in the ribs. I stayed on the floor. It was very cold there and everywhere else in the unheated train. I hoped the train would keep going. I prayed the partisans had not been able to blow a hole in this stretch of tracks yet. I dreamed about returning to the warm snow of Germany. I stayed on the floor and listened to a winter symphony of clashing glass and steel. Curled up tight I thought this must be the worst work of some tortured Russian composer. I did not want any more pain or confusion. Right now I needed balance. I wanted Mozart. In a few days I was ready for Beethoven, too. They were waiting for me here in Berlin. I lumbered up on my crutches and went back to say goodbye to the guys who had not been able to look out the window.

"Don't go in there," the nurse said.

"Why not?"

"They're dead."

"They can't be," I said. "They weren't that bad."

"It wasn't their wounds."

That was terrible luck. Here we were in the warm snow of Germany, and those guys were like that. They did not get that way in Germany. I know damn well that happened somewhere out in the East. Here in Berlin I put on my nice warm Russian fur cap, lurched out of the train, and smiled at all the Germans pointing at me.

VANS
By Adolf Eichmann

Even though the SS had sent me to Poland to see, I wasn't going to look through that peephole. No sir. I told the doctor in the white coat. I'd already had it. When they started emptying the first big van, it was the most horrible sight I've ever seen. Not all the people were dead, and some were groaning, and, dead or not, their faces were wrenched into the most grotesque expressions, and many people had defecated.

The men unloading the van suffered severely. They could not keep from gagging, and sometimes even weeping. I understood. This was frightful. The exhaust piped into the rear compartment was supposed to put the people to sleep fairly soon and kill them within fifteen minutes. Hell, even an hour wasn't enough.

This inefficiency appalled me. We needed much better vans right away. And from now on only Jews were going to unload them.

FINAL SOLUTION
By Reinhard Heydrich

Several months earlier Goering had commissioned me to as soon as possible draft measures for the "final solution of the Jewish question" in Europe. Only now, on January twentieth, 1942, did I have time for an official meeting. I had been busy with my new job as Reich's Protektor of Czechoslovakia. Stationed in Prague, I was controlling many essential projects and still outdoing the wretches from the Navy who years before had so often belittled me. They, along with Admiral Raeder, destroyed my naval career simply because a lady who was infatuated with me had a nervous breakdown.

I would like to have taken care of them. Someday I'd have a chance. My power was already extraordinary, and it was proliferating. Someday I was going to take over for the Fuehrer. I knew it. I think the old man did, too. He better not screw things up. If he did, I wouldn't hesitate to eliminate him.

Those considerations were not for today. This morning I was in my international police headquarters, a villa in Wannsee, outside Berlin. Important civilian ministers were present along with Adolf Eichmann and Heinrich Mueller, head of my Gestapo. I needed widespread cooperation and coordination for this massive project.

Pointer in hand, I stood in front of a large map and said, "The specks on the map illustrate the density of the Jewish problem. Our measures to date, though promising, have not been sufficient. We must shift our efforts from the casual to the precise. There are still eleven million Jews in Europe. They are all going to end up here in the East, the asshole of the world."

Everyone laughed and pounded the table with a fist.

"We'll comb Europe from West to East and send the Jews to their proper destiny."

"But that'll clog the railroads that supply our troops in the East," a minister said.

"This war is no less important. The survival of our people is at stake.

"Eichmann. Please report the steps we're taking in the Reich. Be brief."

Eichmann rose and earnestly stated, "The Jews must first be detected. Second, they are to be registered and segregated. Third, they will be arrested. Fourth, they will hand over their house keys and sign over their possessions to the Reich."

"That's illegal," said another minister. "We don't need the Jews to sign over anything. They automatically forfeit their property when they leave the country."

"This is entirely legal and necessary," I said. "Please proceed."

"Next," said Eichmann, "the Jews will be allowed to take one suitcase and fifty marks each to a remote railroad junction. Then they will be placed in freight cars for transit to ghettos, work camps or direct operations."

"Don't worry about appearances," I said. "In many cases, Jews will take passenger trains up to the Reich border. After arriving at the necessary destinations, they'll form a supervised labor pool and be marched to locations to build roads. They'll also break rocks and dry swamps. Many will be eliminated by natural causes. The strongest of them will survive. And these we must deal with appropriately. The history of natural selection proves survivors would otherwise be the germ-cell of a new Jewish resurgence."

Lots of fists pounded the table.

AMERICAN HISTORY
By Adolf Hitler

Roosevelt and the Americans were the biggest bluffers in the world. They didn't want war, not a real war. All the Americans could do militarily was destroy overmatched Indians. In this respect, at least, I did admire and carefully emulate the American masters of population control. They called their key facilities reservations. We called ours concentration camps. The Americans created policies that resulted in the starvation of Indians. We likewise had no interest in taxing ourselves to feed our enemies. We simply wanted to be as good at eliminating undesirables as the Americans.

RESPONSIBILITY
By Albert Speer

I wanted to help more with the war effort and often urged the Fuehrer to let me build bridges and widen roads and contribute in ways of immediate and critical importance. He assured me I was already irreplaceable as his special architect of vast projects for eternity. And he insisted I continue planning and designing Adolf Hitler Platz and the great buildings surrounding it.

I did manage to do some work for the war. Using prefabricated concrete parts for the first time, I organized the construction in only eight months of three vital bomber factories, each even more massive than the Volkswagen plant. Also I repaired bomb damage in Berlin and built air-raid shelters. Then I was able to assist Dr. Fritz Todt, who had built the autobahns, in armaments construction and repairing railroads and other facilities the Russians had damaged or destroyed while retreating. Dr. Todt soon placed me in charge of related operations in the Ukraine, where I was flown for an inspection tour.

After a week there I decided I must report directly to the Fuehrer and arranged to fly to the Wolf's Lair in East Prussia on February seventh, 1942. When I arrived, the Fuehrer was in a private conference with Todt. They had many things to discuss about the East. The conference lasted a long time. Todt was very tired coming out.

"I'm flying to Berlin tomorrow morning," he told me. "There's a seat for you if you want it."

"Yes, I do. Thank you."

"Eight o'clock," said Todt.

The Fuehrer received me after one a.m. He was exhausted. So was I. But I needed to apprise him of the severe technical problems in the East.

"And the men on the construction crews, Mein Fuehrer. They're singing some very sad songs."

"What were the words? Do you have them?"

"Here they are."

He read the lyrics to a couple of new songs about life in the East.

"These are traitorous, the words of an oppositionist. But I've had enough worries for today. Tell me about your plans for Berlin and Nuremberg."

"After the war those cities are going to be better than any city ever."

"Not after the war. Maybe very soon."

"That's right," I said.

Now the Fuehrer and I began talking like artists again. I forgot all about the snow and destruction, and I know he did too. We had a great time and did not stop until three a.m.

"In the morning please tell Dr. Todt I'm too tired to join him," I told a young officer.

I needed a good rest and wanted to enjoy it. This was my time to imagine. I could resume my extraordinary projects and again be Germany's greatest architect. And, if I were disciplined enough, and humble, and if the war improved, then I might be one of the greatest architects ever. I thought about that, lying in a warm bed surrounded by ice, and when I stopped thinking I started dreaming and did not stop until the phone erupted.

"Ah, yes, hello."

"Dr. Todt has just been killed in a plane crash," someone said.

That horror shook me completely awake. Germany had just lost a brilliant and decent man. I was only an irreplaceable architect. Todt was an irreplaceable force in charge of building all roads and improving all navigable waterways and constructing West Wall and all power plants and U-boat shelters and, most of all, he was Minister of Armaments. Only several exceptional men working together might have a chance to replace Dr. Fritz Todt.

Another call announced the Fuehrer wanted to see me at one p.m. He greeted me formally.

"Mein Fuehrer, I'm so sorry about Dr. Todt. I can't imagine this. He was a great man."

"Yes, he was. For that reason I must do something decisive. I've already decided, Herr Speer, to appoint you successor to Minister Todt in all his capacities."

The Fuehrer stepped up and shook my hand.

"Yes, I certainly will do everything possible to replace Dr. Todt in his construction assignments."

"No, Herr Speer. I said 'in all his capacities.' That means you're also Minister of Armaments."

"But I don't have any experience in armaments. I ..."

"You'll manage it. I'm confident of that. Contact the ministry at once and take over."

"I can't vouch for my ability in this assignment."

"I order you to take the assignment."

My chest tightened as I departed. Not only was I untrained for this job, I was temperamentally unsuited, being somewhat shy, and did not feel comfortable asserting myself at meetings. I preferred a more private and creative approach. That would not work in speeches, and I was anyway a poor public speaker. This whole thing was overwhelming. What would the generals and scientists say to me when I gave them orders? That concerned me so much. At least I soon received a guarantee from the Fuehrer that I would still be his personal architect once the war got better.

REHABILITATION
By An SS Officer

The Reichsfuehrer SS, Heinrich Himmler, had often explained his policies on the matter, and I was honored to be one of those selected for a special task. Certain criminals were going to be reeducated in the most rigorous manner. After being separated from normal people, they would be worked hard for the first time in their lives and watched very closely. They would also be indoctrinated about the cowardice of refusing to procreate for the state and the danger of believing their own lies. In time, these criminals would inevitably heal and mature into normal healthy Germans and be allowed to take off their pink triangles.

I believed reeducation so essential that I talked to these people compassionately. I explained that if they reformed they would not be castrated or executed. They said they appreciated my help. I think I was beginning to understand. They were not so bad. Once in a while we forgot reeducation and talked about other things. They told me about their lives and places they went. Once, to learn more, I joined them but the SS broke in and arrested everyone, including me. The Reichsfuehrer found out right away.

"You should be shot," he said.

"I was only investigating."

"If you tell another lie, you will be shot. Do you realize how this embarrasses me, and the SS?"

"I've always been a loyal officer, one of the best."

"If not for that, you'd already be dead."

"I swear I'll change. I was never like that. Being with them infected me. You've said that's how they work."

"You can't be like them. Nobody can."

"I won't be."

"You'll be demoted."

"Thank you."

"You're going to the front."

"I belong there. I can fight."

"That should help."

"It'll cure me."

"It better."

"I know it will."

"If it doesn't, you know what."

SPRING
By A Russian Soldier

Most days on the march we had not been fed, and we never had shelter, and by the time we got here our columns were not nearly as long. At first I mourned those who were gone, then I cried for not having died. I figured that would come right here. We weren't even in a prisoner of war camp. We were in a field, an open field where we made little huts of earth and huddled inside and cooked when we could. But cooking was not necessary. It was often stupid. Your slop might be stolen if you waited. We ate what we could raw. But that was not enough. We had taken too much. This was near the end. Otherwise, I would not have done it even though he was already dead. Someone else had cut him open, and I grabbed his liver and ate it. I didn't do that often. Sometimes I was just cold enough not to care. Three-quarters of us were dead. I could not imagine why I wasn't. I was certain I would be. Maybe now I would not have to die in the cold. I could leave in the spring. Things were growing in the fields and this would be a good place to be buried. I loved the pretty green fields, especially now that the Germans told us we could graze.

NEW PROJECT
By Rudolf Hoess

Last year when Heinrich Himmler had visited here he was ruthless, even for him, in insisting that construction be pushed beyond full speed and that all problems be ignored. Logistical difficulties did not matter. The concerns of other authorities were irrelevant. Only the relentless expansion of this new camp in the backwoods of Poland counted. I figured there must be something suspicious going on. But I had not asked even though I was the commandant. I only followed all orders without question. My father had taught me that. Unfortunately, my good intentions to build a useful camp were constantly undermined by the stubborn, ignorant and malicious group of officers and common criminals assigned to me. I just could not convert them to my way of thinking. Consequently, I had to take care of everything myself, even the pettiest of matters, like getting two kettles for the kitchen. Obtaining vital materials should have been routine, but it was unbearably difficult. I had needed barbed wire, for example. There were mountains of it on our original eastern border, and I tried to get a little. Just finding out who had responsibility was troublesome. Then I learned the Engineering Headquarters in Berlin would not give me any without a release. I eventually had to steal barbed wire out of abandoned battlefield trenches.

Most people clearly had not understood the importance of this assignment, whatever it was. Himmler must have understood. He wrapped a never-ending chain of new assignments around my neck. I had always been absorbed in my work. Now I'd become obsessed. I did everything with unprecedented energy but no longer assumed people were good. They had to prove it. My so-called coworkers were cheating and disappointing me every day. I buried myself in work to avoid them and everyone else. My wife and children suffered the most. The only way I could be happy again was by drinking. I handled it well and never missed any duty and was always refreshed. I insisted my officers maintain the same standard. Naturally, they resented that.

They were all going to have to improve. A major task was imminent. Himmler had ordered me to deport all Polish peasants in villages surrounding our camp. Then, in June last year, he'd summoned me to Berlin and explained the Final Solution. My camp would be the primary site because of ideal railway transportation. Adolf Eichmann soon arrived for consultation.

"Shooting isn't adequate for a project this size," he'd said. "It's also a terrible strain on our men. The gas vans won't be enough, either. We need something bigger."

We'd driven around the camp, and near the railroad we saw an old red farmhouse that impressed us. We designated this installation Bunker I and ordered that it be remodeled. Eichmann told me to find the right gas. It turned out we already had many canisters of Zyklon B, an insect and rodent control we often used. But would it work for the new job? To find out, we removed the beds from the basement of a barracks and jammed in two hundred fifty useless people from the hospital and an additional six hundred Russian communists. The Zyklon B capsules were broken open and dumped into the basement. Most people had died in a reasonable time, but some were alive the next day and needed more Zyklon B. This operation definitely required an airtight facility. Until the completion of Bunker I, we hoped the morgue of our only crematory might be efficient. More Russian communists were placed there for rodent and pest control. The process was so effective our crematory could not incinerate all the bodies, and many had to be buried down the road.

In January 1942, Bunker I had been completed. Eichmann and I had calculated correctly. Eight hundred Jews could be accommodated at one time. Their bodies were buried in the nearby meadows. Within months so many trains had begun arriving that I was forced to find another facility. A large white farmhouse looked appropriate. I designated it Bunker II and calculated it could accommodate twelve hundred Jews at a time. Again my assessment proved correct.

Himmler came to watch the entire process. He did not say much, so I assumed he was pleased. A couple of weeks after his visit, he sent orders that all the rotting corpses in mass graves were a danger to ground water and might cause epidemics, and they must be dug up and cremated. This was a laborious process. Two thousand bodies at a time were heaped onto piles of wood. We determined it would be more efficient to open the graves and burn the new corpses on top, then dump waste oil or methanol into the pits and keep the fires burning day and night. The smell was quite bad until you got used to it, but by then everyone in the region was gossiping. The anti-aircraft crews were also complaining about the visibility of fires at night. We still had to keep burning all the time. The only alternative would have been to refuse more transports to Auschwitz.

THE IDEAL PLAN
By Adolf Hitler

Some generals said I should not attack anywhere in 1942. A few even urged me to withdraw all the way to the Polish frontier. They were idiots who lacked strength of will. Of course I was going to attack. I could not stand still deep inside Russia along a thousand-mile front, and I could not continue without what I needed. That dictated everything. I would strike to the south and grab all the oil in the Caucasus.

PRAGUE SYMPHONY
By Reinhard Heydrich

What a great concert last night. I can hear the music so well. I feel it. I can always feel the music. It is forever within me. I really must play more often. Time is so short. Today I can only imagine as I roll toward the airport in back of my open Mercedes.

I can feel my hands on the violin. My hands are tender as can be. They cradle and caress. The violin is alive and delicate and precise in my hands. I stroke and massage the strings, making music so wonderful. I weep. I always weep after playing the violin.

I am such a different man. Today I must be. I am going to fly. I am going into the skies over Czechoslovakia to survey what I rule, and then I am going to forget. I have so many responsibilities. I need to ride horses and fence and shoot and drink more often. I do all those things so well. I do them better than other men.

I am not one of them. I am such a different man. The Fuehrer recognizes that. He made me the Protektor of Czechoslovakia at a critical time last year. Factory production had been dropping while sabotage increased. In a nation that produced many German panzers and provided railways vital to the East, that was intolerable. The day I took over I declared a state of emergency and announced that our economic goals would be realized and interference would cease.

Not many doubted my word. Several thousand who did were arrested and their weapons confiscated. I also arrested any German involved in black market crimes. Germans had to maintain the same standards as Czechs, who appreciated a fair man. I wanted them to be happy. I distributed shoes when they were hard to get and made nice hotels available to workers on holidays and I routinely received union leaders at Hradshin Castle, the most exalted place in the land. Production soon rose while sabotage plummeted.

The Fuehrer now wants me to achieve the same things in the West — in France and Belgium. Naturally, he also needs me to continue to run my vast security service in all territories and to oversee many special operations in the East. I will take care of everything. I know I can. So many people are learning now. I can do anything. I can fly today. I am tired of the walls around my villa. I am sick of my offices at Hradshin Castle. I am happy in my open Mercedes moving toward the sky.

BRANDED
By Jan Kubis

My God, what a wait. I'd been waiting for years. In exile I trained in England, and with my friend I parachuted back into Czechoslovakia last year. For months we'd looked for a way. There had to be one. But security was so heavy. We could not attack his villa or assault Hradshin Castle. And there was always a convoy between those two points, as well as to the train station. We waited and kept asking questions. Not everyone in the underground was dead. Some said to take a look at the road to the airport. The routine there was certainly different. We examined the road carefully and found a hairpin turn before the road entered a bridge. My friend Joseph Gabchik was stationed at the start of the turn. Back up the straightaway another guy was ready with a mirror. I stood a little beyond Gabchik, around the turn. We had been waiting all morning on May twenty-seventh, 1942. Maybe he wasn't coming today. The information we received might have been wrong. Or maybe he had changed plans. Maybe he was going to get me again. Every time I thought about my burning flesh, I thought about him. Before my exile the Nazis had ripped my pants down and branded my rear with seven swastikas. He had not even come to Czechoslovakia yet. But that was him.

I was still waiting. Then the guy down the road signaled. The Mercedes was coming. It was bringing the butcher. Gabchik grabbed the sten gun under his coat and ran up the sidewalk and jumped into the street and he aimed and ... He was aiming. He was aiming and pulling the trigger. But nothing was happening.

Heydrich sprang up firing his revolver at Gabchik.

"Shoot, shoot," I yelled and ran toward the car now stopped and hurled the grenade. It hit the rear of the car and exploded. Heydrich jumped out and started chasing me. He was screaming and shooting, and as I looked back I saw the bastard was outrunning me. I pumped my arms hard sprinting toward an oncoming train, and barely got across the tracks and onto a bicycle I'd hidden.

FULL MOON
By Air Marshal Arthur T. Harris

This new kind of warfare was so fundamental I expected everyone to understand, yet so revolutionary I also feared many would oppose. The strategy was brutally unequivocal: mass unprecedented numbers of bombers and send them wave after wave after the same target. Saturate the enemy's war-making facilities. Start with incendiary bombs to make target fires and then bomb the fires and keep bombing them with your whole fleet. Bomb them with a thousand bombers in a night.

Only a profound outcome could justify such expenditure and risk. The House of Commons was not convinced. Our vigorous Prime Minister Churchill was. He authorized me to proceed. I began to assemble bombers and crews from my four operational groups and even from training groups. Planes out of commission were repaired. We needed as many bombers as possible. New crews were trained in extreme haste, not knowing why.

A full moon of illumination was essential. And the sky had to be reasonably clear. Only visible targets could be hit. I conferred several times a day with my meteorologist. While crews waited at fifty-three airfields, we postponed the operation once, twice, then a third time.

This was the last night of the full moon. I supposed we could wait until the next one, but I really did not want to. Everything had been painstakingly calculated and planned. If we aimed at three adjoining areas instead of one central target, we would substantially lower the risk of collisions. In that regard, we also staggered the altitudes of our bombers. Some of them would still be susceptible to flak from hundreds of anti-aircraft guns. Night fighters would threaten many others. Regardless of the forecast, who knew what the skies would really be like when the bombers arrived. If our pilots didn't hurry, they'd later be trying to return to foggy airfields in England.

This operation could be contemplated forever. We had prepared an air force twice the size and with four times the weight in bombs as any that had ever concentrated on a single objective. I was overwhelmed by worry and exhausted by delay. When the meteorologist told me the skies would probably clear after midnight on May thirty-first, I ground a holder between my teeth, inhaled a hot cigarette, and, to my air vice-marshal, I said: "Thousand Plan tonight. Target Cologne."

OPEN HAND
By Hermann Goering

I had certainly heard. I didn't need one of my generals to call me with news that the Fuehrer was raging about an inferno. I was equally concerned. Of course I'd come right away. I hope the Fuehrer understood. He certainly should have. More than half my Luftwaffe was in the East and another quarter in North Africa. We were spread pretty thin over Germany and the West. I know I'd made promises about keeping our skies free of enemy aircraft. That was before the dispersal. I hope the Fuehrer understood.

I hurried to his headquarters and entered the situation conference. I was very concerned about everything. Walking right up to the Fuehrer, I held out my hand. He ignored it and said, "Well, Herr Goering, I hope I haven't awakened you. I know you were sleeping all night. You and your Luftwaffe. But I was awake. Unlike you, I can't sleep when one of my cities is under fire."

MASK
By Heinrich Himmler

This was a beautiful mask. It was our traditional SS mask, and it looked just like him. The long sharp nose was perfect. This was our wonderful blond Nordic beast. How terrible it was that we had to make his mask. How unfortunate that leather and steel springs from the car's upholstery had been blown between his ribs and stomach into his spleen. Everything possible was done. The Fuehrer sent his medical squad. Everyone tried heroically for a week. Nothing worked.

After the ceremony in Berlin, Hitler thrust his finger onto a map and dug into a village not far from Prague. Lots of Czechs were going to pay for Heydrich. On June ninth a team of security police entered Lidice. Every man there was shot. Every woman and child was sent to a concentration camp. Then the village was blown up and left in rubble.

CHASE
By Adolf Hitler

My enemies were fleeing, and I was after them. By mid-July 1942 I had already routed the Russians in the Crimea, and charged southeast between the Donets River and the Don River, snaring several hundred thousand more prisoners, and as I continued to attack I resolved not to limit myself.

WEREWOLF
By General Franz Halder

Hitler built his newest headquarters in the Ukraine, ensured that it was unbearably ugly, and called it Werewolf. The trees existing over the huts there provided no relief from the swelter that always worsened when a grandiose Hitler began waving his hands over big maps on a table in the conference room.

"The Russians are about finished," he stated. "They have no strategic reserves."

"They're much stronger than that, Mein Fuehrer," I said.

"We captured four million of them last year."

"We haven't gotten as many this time. They've slipped away to the East."

"There aren't many more to capture. The Luftwaffe's flights behind enemy lines haven't detected significant troop formations."

"We have a very objective report right here, Mein Fuehrer. The Russians can amass at least a million new troops to defend Stalingrad and the Volga, and about a half million fresh men for the Caucasus."

"That's idiotic. I won't tolerate such absurdities."

"It's my duty to tell you that we're the ones who lack strategic reserves, Mein Fuehrer. This year a quarter of our front line forces aren't even Germans. We really must question the battle worthiness of our Rumanian, Italian and Hungarian allies."

"All they have to do is hold territory while Germans attack. They're adequate."

"Mein Fuehrer, I must also apprise you that the Russians are currently producing more than a thousand tanks a month and are likely to increase their output."

Hammering the table, Hitler said, "That's ridiculous and simply underscores the General Staff's passion for making excuses. I understand the real situation. We must capture the Caucasus and all its oil right away. And at the same time, we've got to seal off the approach there by taking Stalingrad."

"We don't have the men and material necessary to simultaneously undertake two such major objectives."

"We can certainly do both. Army Group B will continue east toward Stalingrad. Since resistance is stronger further south, I'm transferring the Fourth Panzer Army to Army Group A."

"We might be able to take Stalingrad in a short time if Army Group B retains its armor."

"Armor needs oil, General Halder."

"I must encourage you to reconsider dividing our forces, Mein Fuehrer. We need to concentrate on one major objective at a time."

"I've already responded to some of your advice, General Halder. Don't forget. I let you talk me out of driving all the way to the Indian Ocean and linking up with the Japanese. That objective I'm quite willing to defer."

EXHAUST
By Christian Wirth

Some unscrupulous bastards were always trying to ruin my work as an SS Criminal Police Inspector. Not long ago Protestant and Catholic zealots had joined other whiners and finally convinced the Party to stop its euthanasia program, which eliminated more than a hundred thousand lunatics from the asylums. The program had worked so well only because the SS loaned me to the Party to design special chambers and the big engines that fed carbon monoxide into the chambers.

I did not have any more real tasks until Himmler had put me back to work in Poland. There I designed installations much better than anything in the euthanasia program. And they were far from the reach of fanatics. Belsec had opened in March 1942 with six chambers and enough engines to feed hundreds of enemies a day. I topped that at Sobibor, and in July I finished Treblinka, an even better place. I also added some chambers to the facility at Maidanek. Now the Reich had six special installations, all in Poland, and only two, Auschwitz and Chelmno, did not have my designs.

A lot of people were jealous. Two high-ranking SS bureaucrats showed up at Belsec in August. They demanded a demonstration and watched guards whip herds of people out of stinking boxcars. A loudspeaker ordered the people to undress. Then they went to the barber for a quick shave before entering the chamber.

"Pack em tight as you can," I said.

After nodding to start the diesel engine, I looked at the bureaucrats. They were waiting. The big engine groaned.

"I said start the damn thing."

The engine still groaned.

"This is the first time it hasn't started immediately," I said.

One of the bureaucrats took out a stopwatch and started it.

"What the hell's wrong with the engine?" I yelled at the Ukrainian mechanic. He was using both hands to tug on things.

The bureaucrat made a big deal of staring at his stopwatch. Five minutes. Ten minutes. How could the engine not work today? It had to work.

"Come here," I said to the mechanic. "What the hell's wrong?"

"I don't know."

Snapping his face with my whip, I yelled: "Find out."

As he only covered up I lashed him several more times.

Thirty minutes. For God's sake. Fifty minutes. One hour. The people inside were really carrying on. That made waiting worse. For one hour and twenty minutes. One hour and a half.

"This really is unbelievable, gentlemen."

The bureaucrat looked back at his stopwatch.

Two hours. Two hours and a half. Two hours and forty-nine minutes.

"There it is," I said.

Twenty-five minutes later the bureaucrats looked through the peephole.

"Not all of them are dead," said the one not holding the watch.

"They will be. Don't worry."

In only seven more minutes everyone inside was still as slabs at the butcher.

"This has been very inefficient," said the stopwatch. "You'll have to do better."

EAST
By A German Soldier

I had been glad to get back to the guys at the front, and that amazed me. My time in Germany should have been better. I should have wanted to stay, and I should have loved my girlfriend. But she was not really my girlfriend anymore. She was just a girl. She had a nice hairstyle and pretty dresses and so did all of her friends. They were all very happy and did not understand where I had been and did not want to talk about it. I did not want to talk about it, either. Not with them. I wanted to be with the guys. We understood and loved each other. Together we had a great cause in the East, and as we moved fast in hot weather the sweat on our faces covered memories of the cold.

THE GLOBE
By Adolf Hitler

I was almost king of the world. That was my destiny. I had always known it. Now the realization was everywhere. In North Africa General Rommel had recently taken Tobruk and was only a short drive from the heart of Egypt. The British and Americans definitely could not get near there. I had filled the Atlantic with ship-eating sharks, my incomparable U-boats that hunted in packs and were sinking several hundred thousand tons of enemy supplies a month.

After conquering Egypt, Rommel's small but incredibly powerful

Africa Korps would move through the Middle East, around the eastern end of the Mediterranean, and hook up with my forces in the Caucasus, which had just grabbed the Maikop oil fields and would soon scoot south over the Caucasus mountains and take more oil all the way to the Caspian Sea. Then the Russian war machine would sputter while mine refueled. I already controlled everything from the Spanish border to the Eastern Front, and did not have to wait much longer until I ruled the world, only until Stalingrad fell.

TWO STRIKES
By General Franz Halder

Like a forlorn bird, I had been ruffling my wings in exasperation and fear. The tension of this was unbearable. Today, things had to change. I had to use my wings. Today I was going to soar.

"Our left flank along the Don River is overextended," I told Hitler on August twenty-third, pointing at his big map. "This invites a counterattack. We need to withdraw and shorten our lines."

"If the men have sufficient will, that won't be necessary."

"The men have quite extraordinary will and determination, Mein Fuehrer."

"That we shall soon determine. Right now, I'm not convinced."

"Mein Fuehrer, thousands of brave young men and officers are being cut down because their commanders aren't permitted to make the only reasonable decisions. Their hands are tied behind their backs."

"What do you know about fighting at the front? Where were you during the Great War? You know where I was."

"I'm brave enough, Mein Fuehrer."

"Are you sure? I expect my commanders to be as tough as the troops. I don't think a brave commander would constantly come to me with pleas to retreat."

"We've already suffered more than a million casualties in Russia. Many of those men would still be alive and fighting for Germany if they'd been handled in a professional military manner."

"How dare you speak to me like that. That's outrageous. I have more first hand knowledge of war and suffering than you can imagine. Furthermore, I'm the ultimate commander and have delivered unprecedented victories, unimaginable victories, and I'll continue to do so and won't allow those with insufficient courage to stop me."

MEDICAL DOCUMENTATION
By Heinrich Himmler

Naturally, I was extremely flattered. But I wasn't surprised. Many very important foreign diplomats were contacting me through my agents about a compromise. They knew I had both influence and an understanding of people. But I could not fathom betraying the Fuehrer. As Reichsfuehrer, I had often proclaimed: "My honor is loyalty."

Forging peace with the West was not necessarily disloyal. Anything that strengthened us against Bolshevik hordes was thoroughly loyal. But I knew the Fuehrer would not understand since all my foreign contacts insisted he be removed. I certainly had no plan to harm him. I simply ordered preparation of a twenty-six page document certifying he suffered from advancing syphilis that threatened to paralyze him.

If matters did not proceed well in the East, then maybe it would be best if I, who alone was acceptable, established world peace. First, though, I had to see what happened and resisted pressure from those disloyal to the Fuehrer. I could not imagine betraying my oath to the greatest brain of all time.

URGENT CALL
By Nikita Khrushchev

Despite our fanatical resistance, the Germans were grinding toward the mighty Volga, north and south of Stalingrad, and threatening to strangle the river. They also continued battering us from the West, forcing us back as shells bellowed in our heads. At headquarters, officers scurried inside to talk about things they'd already discussed by radio. Everyone was grim and agitated, especially when this message arrived: "Large groups of German bombers are approaching Stalingrad from the west and southwest."

442

The bombers came all day, and the fires burned all night. In the morning hundreds of blackened chimneys mourned over the ashes of wooden homes. Many of the sturdier buildings in the city center were standing still but their insides had been incinerated. Numerous oil storage tanks had also blown up and spit fiery fluids onto the Volga, where burning continued in a terrible flow. Our factories north of the city had not been destroyed, but many of the brave women operating anti-aircraft guns in the region were overrun by German infantry. Thousands of citizens were dead, and most of the others wanted to leave.

Stalin then called.

"What's this about you ordering Stalingrad evacuated?" he said.

"Comrade Stalin, I have done no such thing."

"The political leader of the Stalingrad Front must not panic."

"I haven't panicked. I assure you."

"You better not."

"I won't."

"You haven't ordered evacuation?"

"No. Who said so?"

"I keep hearing it."

"It's a lie."

"If it's true, you know the consequences."

"It isn't true, Comrade Stalin, I promise."

"Stalingrad must not be abandoned."

"It won't be."

"Our troops won't defend a dead city."

"The city's alive, Comrade Stalin. It's very alive."

THE DON
By General Georgi Zhukov

On the map Stalin put his finger on the Don River northwest of Stalingrad, where our troops still held some strong defensive positions. Then he ran his finger southeast, as the river runs, before turning south fifty miles in front of Stalingrad. The Germans were way past the Don there. They were pinching in toward the city.

"Get down to the front," Stalin said. "Talk to the commanders. Talk to the troops. Examine our bridgeheads over the Don."

"I'll find out everything," I said.

"We need to be sure."

"I'll explain."

"Don't explain anything."

"Not even to the generals?"

"They have other concerns," he said.

STALINGRAD
By General Vasily Chuikov

Some cowards were running. They might have called it retreating, but to me it was treason. I'd take care of that now. On September twelfth, 1942 I was named commander of the army in Stalingrad. Enemies dominated our right and our left and our front, and almost had us shoved back into the Volga, our lifeline for supplies. German planes and artillery crunched the city during the day, and at night they attacked barges on a river lit by flares. The Germans could not keep the wind from blowing some flares off target, though. And they could not hit everything even when it was lit.

There was plenty the Germans could not do. Their panzers weren't so effective unless attacking positions already hammered by planes. And their foot soldiers weren't overpowering unless preceded by panzers. In open spaces the Germans had everything coordinated. In Stalingrad I demanded everything be different.

DOWNTOWN
By A German Soldier

Rolling into the city on troop lorries, we jumped off and prepared to assault the railroad station. The Russians were firing at us from over there and the other side. From both sides. And the rear. Which side now? The front? Wait. That's right. There. Somewhere. They were firing. Some of us were falling. But many of them were already dead.

We charged in and captured the railroad station. It was vital. The

Russians realized that, and regrouped and rushed right back in shooting to knock us out. But we counterattacked. Now they retreated. We had the railroad station and were positioning our men. So many dead ones had to be cleared out or they'd be stinking soon. I picked up one of my friends. He was heavy on my shoulder, and I was tired and moving slowly as a bullet ripped into him, knocking us both down. The Russians were coming again and soon started to encircle us. We got out.

The next day we attacked and recaptured the railroad station. Then we were forced to leave. We seized the station again the following day before being driven out. A day later we went back in but were swept away. Once more we counterattacked and grabbed the station. Then they ground us out. Again we counterattacked and took over until they kicked us out. On the fifth day, we captured the railroad station and knew we wouldn't lose it again because there weren't any new Russians coming. But there were still some old Russians to deal with. A few were shooting at us from a basement. They were disruptive as hell. So were the fanatics firing at us from behind platforms and the suicidal ones shooting from under railroad cars. This was crazy. And barbaric. We had the station. They could not possibly take it back, not this time, not with so few. They did not understand. Actually, they must have understood. They simply did not care. They were dying for nothing. The railroad station was definitely ours.

THE STREET
By A Russian Soldier

In this area we didn't have any tanks, none that moved. None of the others even fired. Mine was the only one that could still shoot. Thankfully I'd been disabled in the middle of the street. This was a very important street, one that led right down to the main landing area on the Volga. I sat in the street and fired all day until I was hit.

MYSELF
By Adolf Hitler

I wasn't going to eat with the officers anymore. They were cowards and liars and always ruined everything. Halder certainly had to go. I should have axed him long ago. What a weakling. He cried when I told him he was out. His professional pessimism was worthless. Only fanatical National Socialism mattered now.

I dined alone. That was so much better. It gave me time to decide what to do. My decisions were everything. I only needed someone who could implement my plans. General Kurt Zeitzler could do that as new Chief of the General Staff. He had deftly organized long supply lines in France in 1940. We certainly needed more supplies now. The siege of Stalingrad had to be maintained. And down in the Caucasus I needed more material, especially human material. The leader of Army Group A, General List, absolutely had to go. He was already gone. All he ever did was complain about the difficulties of advancing through well-defended mountain passes. The passes led to more oil and had to be taken. The next move was obvious. I took command of Army Group A.

THE BUILDING
By A Russian Soldier

There was a nice view from the window on the second floor, and we peered down gripping our machine guns. They covered the street. Last night from the other side the Germans had yelled: "Hey Russ, tomorrow, bang bang." When those guys came for their victory parade, our machine guns played a funeral march. Lots of confident Germans lay in the street, and two panzers rolled right over them to attack the building. Anti-tank guns on the ground floor shattered the steel intruders. A few men struggling out were shredded by machine guns from our floor and the one above.

Within hours the Germans formed some larger assault groups and began darting from building to wall to rubble pile, ducking and firing, moving in, some dropping, some still advancing, surrounding us, getting close, inside somewhere, until Luftwaffe bombers dived and pounded the building and everything around.

Now I was on the ground floor, my face covered by rocks and dirt. After a while I staggered up and looked for my machine gun. It was gone, buried with a lot of guys. I took a German's gun right out of his dirty hands and, below a clear and vivid sky, propped the weapon on a pile of rubble and started to fire.

AMMUNITION
By General Vasily Chuikov

The telephone lines to my command post had burned down, so I was using the radio.

"Get me some more men, now" I said. "I've got to have... That's not enough. No. You're insane. You can't reduce our ammunition. That's criminal.

"Be patient? Get your ass in here. We're getting killed. You be patient. What the hell are you doing? You can't tell me. Figure it out. O.K. I'm figuring."

THE FACTORY
By A German Soldier

I didn't know which factory this was, and what did it matter? I didn't even know the guys next to me anymore. My friends were in gutters leading to the factory and behind pillars in front and under machines and shelves inside. They were stiff on the factory ground with the Russians. And as smoke bellowed thick and high all over Stalingrad, I got word the city was now definitely ours, all but a sliver next to the Volga and a few corners in some other factory.

George Thomas Clark

BEER HALL SPEECH
By Adolf Hitler

The Russians were terrified to try to send many reinforcements to Stalingrad. I saw that. They had been introducing divisions to action elsewhere, in central Russia, then pulling them back in reserve for the next battle of Moscow. That would soon come.

My judgment had again proven preeminent. And I needed to ensure that none of the idiots around me undermined my genius. Their incompetence was astounding. In late October I had composed an inspirational "triumph or die" message for Field Marshal Rommel in Egypt. I hadn't told anyone to send it. But when the Afrika Korps began to be knocked out of El Alemain by much larger British forces, and Rommel radioed that he was withdrawing, some fool major sent the message without my knowledge. Rommel halted his retreat, and the British inflicted severe losses. When I got up and learned about that, I almost shot the major.

Who was I to trust? Certainly not the panicky intelligence officers who reported in early November that an enemy fleet in the Mediterranean was churning toward North Africa. How did they know? Odds are the ships were headed to reinforce Malta, which enemy naval forces used as a base to attack our supply ships for the Afrika Korps.

Right now I was not going to speculate. I did not want to be bothered. I had an immense spiritual obligation. I was writing my speech for the anniversary of the Beer Hall Putsch. The people needed that.

Before leaving the Wolf's Lair on November seventh, I received more thorough, and ominous, information about enemy naval activity in the Mediterranean. All right. It did look like North Africa was going to be attacked. I would counteract that in a variety of ways. Immediately I ordered preparations to occupy the rest of France. Then I got on my special train.

The next afternoon I arrived in Munich and received reports that our French allies in Morocco and Algeria were resisting the Anglo-Saxons and slaughtering them on the beaches. Buoyed by this, I stepped with aplomb to tell my old comrades-in-arms that for us Stalingrad was victory.

AFRICAN RESCUE
By Adolf Hitler

Surprisingly, the British and Americans were gaining strongholds in Morocco and Algeria to the west of Field Marshal Rommel. On the other side, General Montgomery also threatened, and Rommel was complaining that North Africa could no longer be held. He was tired, his liver infected, and his throat was constantly red and hot. He simply needed to regain his strength and understand that as he retreated west a powerful bridgehead was being built by the German-Italian forces I ordered flown into Tunisia. After linking, he and the rescue troops would repulse the Anglo-Saxons from North Africa.

With equal clarity I determined that the French really would not fight for us. Why should they? Their leaders were as treacherous and senile as their people were passive. That made occupying the rest of the country, Vichy France, very fast and easy.

We also needed to grab the French fleet in Toulon. Those ships would help us. Certainly they would no longer be dormant. They were coming into play. I knew some French might want to escape and sail to the Anglo-Americans. That was not going to happen. I was going to get the fleet. I was after it. I would have had it, too, but a traitorous French admiral and his sly bunch scuttled numerous ships before I got there.

FOREIGN ARMIES EAST
By General Reinhard Gehlen

I compiled, filed, assessed, asked and ruminated. Then I articulated what the enemy probably had, was thinking, and would do. That was my duty as head of Foreign Armies East. Young General Gehlen I was, a thorough and voracious researcher, a strategic thinker and planner.

I had much pertinent data. The Soviet colossus was about forty percent occupied, from besieged Leningrad in the north to the Caucasus in the south. We had killed or captured seven and a half million soldiers and captured or destroyed much of their original equipment. We had, additionally, been able to disrupt or eliminate some of their production.

My reports emphasized, however, that the Russians had still been able to send seven and a half million new men into the field. Many of them were not optimally trained, true, but they were good enough to fight. In the meantime the resourceful Russians had also kept arms production high by establishing numerous factories way to the East out of our reach.

Much of my concentration was on the Don River northwest of Stalingrad. Two weeks ago, at least, I had begun urging "intensive observation." The Russians were concentrating troops and equipment, more every day, on their two big bridgeheads over the Don opposite the Rumanian Third Army. The Rumanians, who wondered why they were so far into the Soviet Union, did not want to attack or be attacked, and were abysmally short of tanks, anti-tank weapons and artillery.

As enemy activity increased, so did my worries I conveyed to General Zeitzler. In my report November twelfth, I "warned emphatically that... we must expect an attack on the Rumanian Third Army. The objective is to interrupt our railroad to Stalingrad, endanger all our soldiers to the east of the two points of attack, compel those now in Stalingrad to withdraw, and regain control of the Volga." On the eighteenth I concluded an attack was probably also forming south of Stalingrad opposite the Rumanian Fourth Army.

ARTILLERY
By General Georgi Zhukov

Every truck was a warrior and every train a savior relentlessly bringing in cargo that was stacked along miles of front to await final delivery. At four a.m. on November nineteenth, my hand swung down and our big guns began to hurl death through the frosty dark, and four thunderous hours later our soldiers began to penetrate.

HEADQUARTERS
By General Friedrich von Paulus

I had three headquarters. Surely everyone understood. As commander of the Sixth Army, I might reasonably be at any of them. I'd been trying to explain that through a series of messages.

"You aren't in Stalingrad," the Fuehrer said.

"I'm right here, Mein Fuehrer."

"Outside the battle."

"Studying the battle."

"Get back into the battle. Move immediately."

"I'm prepared to. Also, I must be ready to break out. It's a contingency."

"You're not to worry about that one. Get back, then stay put. I'm doing everything to assist and relieve you."

NOTIFICATION
By General Kurt Zeitzler

Right away I discussed the crisis with the Fuehrer. He was at ease and confident. I did not know why. He felt we would handle this easily. Still, by November twenty-third, in just four days, I had to tell him: "Soviet forces have closed the circle around Stalingrad."

AIR LIFTS
By Hermann Goering

"That's cowardly," Hitler told the generals. "We can't withdraw from Stalingrad. Of course we can hold on. If we don't, we'll never get it back. There's only one way. That's right. Supplies. I know they need at least six hundred tons a day. What do we need to deliver that, Herr Reich Marshal?"

"We'd need at least three hundred Junker-52 transports," I said.

"How many do we have?"

"Four hundred fifty."

"You see," Hitler told the generals. "We already have quite enough."

"Mein Fuehrer," I said, "all of them would have to operate every day. With no breakdowns. No losses to antiaircraft fire. Or to Russian fighters. And no losses because of weather. That's not possible. Also, Mein Fuehrer, we're already using at least a hundred of the transports to supply Rommel in North Africa."

"What about bombers? They could deliver supplies, couldn't they."

"They could. But I don't recommend it."

"So you recommend we simply let our men in Stalingrad be butchered."

"Of course not."

"I know you have a wing of Heinkel 177s."

"Those are our new strategic bombers, Mein Fuehrer. The crews are being prepared for offensives in the spring."

"Tell them spring is here. Gather all bombers with transport capabilities. Gather all our transport planes. Get every available civilian airliner, too. Tell Lufthansa I said so. Get everything. Do you understand?"

"Of course, Mein Fuehrer."

"With all that, we should have no trouble keeping our fighting men supplied until spring. You can do it, can't you?"

"Of course, Mein Fuehrer. I guarantee I can do it."

TWO NOOSES
By General Georgi Zhukov

Propelled by thousands of big guns and nine hundred tanks, my million new attackers strengthened the noose around Stalingrad, and also charged as far south and west and northwest as possible, creating another noose. I did not want anyone breaking in since eighty-five thousand Germans would soon be trying to break out.

HEDGEHOG
By Adolf Hitler

The Russians didn't realize Stalingrad was our hedgehog, our secured and tightly concentrated defense. Each building was an obstacle, every street a corridor of death. Yes, two hundred fifty thousand Germans were inside. That made our hedgehog stronger. The longer we held out, the worse it was for the enemy.

CONFIDENTIALITY
By Doctor Theodore Morell

Those young, slim doctors in SS uniforms made me miserable with their insults. In so many ways they said, or implied, that I was a fat, bald, middle-aged slug. They never invited me to any of their gatherings or excursions, and were careful in concealing those plans from me. This was envy of a very obvious and unsavory sort. After all, I was the one the Fuehrer depended on for essential medical advice and an array of scientific ministrations. Only I was informed enough to respond when the Fuehrer said, "I want you to tell me the whole truth."

"You have coronary sclerosis, Mein Fuehrer."

"Hah. I've always said I was going to die soon."

"Not necessarily. The prognosis is unclear."

"Your medications are helping me?"

"Absolutely. But your condition can be worsened by hard work and worry."

"My burden for Germany."

"More exercise might help."

"That's impossible now. You should've told me."

"I proceeded with treatment so I wouldn't bother you."

"When did you find out?"

"A year and a half ago."

"Morell, listen to me. If things ever look really black, you must tell me. I'll have to quickly make some vital decisions for Germany."

RESCUE
By Field Marshal Erich von Manstein

I sent Hitler my thorough assessments regarding the new objectives. Army Group Don, which was now being formed, must try to forge a corridor to the Sixth Army in Stalingrad. Then we needed to supply it with food, fuel and ammunition. That would restore its mobility. At that point the Sixth Army must charge right out of the only hole in the encirclement. I emphasized it would be strategically impossible, and certainly fatal, to continue to confine our forces to a constricted area, a single city at the tip of an exposed point, while the enemy capitalized on hundreds of miles of space in which to maneuver. Maneuverability had been the key to German victories. Static warfare by the Russians had ensured many of their defeats. Now they were emulating us in victory as we aped them in defeat.

Hitler's response indicated he agreed on the main points. I was quite relieved since heretofore he had clung to every patch of land like a dog to its favorite bone. My main concerns now were how to approach Stalingrad and with what forces. The former issue I settled with alacrity. Soviet forces to the west of Stalingrad were roughly three times stronger than those southwest of the city. Though we were closer in the west, we would attack from the southwest. It remained unclear how I could marshal sufficient forces. Since several of the divisions theoretically under my command had already been routed or were besieged, I demanded more men. We got two Luftwaffe divisions, which had limited hitting power, and some divisions from the West, Poland, and the Caucasus, but only three were panzer divisions. Two of our infantry divisions could not even be assigned to the rescue. They had to be shipped north to stiffen the Rumanians, who in many cases were running away.

Despite these problems our attack had to begin. On December twelfth we struck toward Stalingrad seventy miles to the northeast. Maneuvering adroitly, our panzer crews struggled through tough enemies and after three days had plowed twenty bloody miles. I hoped we could get there. The men were extraordinarily determined, battling now twenty-five miles from the starting point. This progress was encouraging but not fast enough. Russian forces from outside Stalingrad were rushing down to counterattack and harass us as we hammered to thirty miles out — a mere forty miles from the city.

We could get there. We could save the surrounded Sixth Army, especially if it broke out toward us. The instant for that would soon come. Air supplies to Stalingrad were significant, though less than half the required daily minimum. The supplies would still be good enough to fuel the panzers and other vehicles and load the guns and feed the weakening men. They would be good enough to soon enable a surrounded and static army to roll.

We kept punching toward Stalingrad. Then, on December sixteenth, another Russian hammer dropped, clobbering Italian forces on the Don River, northwest of the already routed Rumanians. Now the Russians were rumbling hard to the south at a point to the west of us. They therefore threatened not only to encircle us but also drive further south and cut off Army Group A in the Caucasus.

My Army Group Don still continued to gnaw a corridor, almost surrounded by enemies, toward a city that was thoroughly surrounded. By December eighteenth, it was time. I radioed General von Paulus in Stalingrad.

"You must break out now," I said.

"The Fuehrer has forbidden it."

"Either break out now or die where you are."

"You break in."

"We can't. We just don't have enough forces. But you've got more than two hundred thousand men."

"Not anymore," Paulus said.

"You've still got plenty."

"They're exhausted."

"They're alive," I said. "This is absolutely going to be your last chance."

"You know the Fuehrer."

"Don't you understand your situation? We aren't going to have any more reinforcements. They're being diverted north to shore up the Italians."

"My chief of staff says we'll still be in position at Easter. You just need to provide more supplies."

"The weather's been horrendous. Also, because of the Italian collapse, our supply airfields might very soon be under siege, or captured. You can't count on staying in Stalingrad. Break out. Break out now. We're only thirty miles away. Together we can smash the enemy forces separating us."

"The logistical difficulties of a sector by sector withdrawal are enormous. That's an extremely dangerous operation."

"Nothing is as dangerous as staying where you are. You'll be dead in Stalingrad by Easter."

I was not going to accept that. On December nineteenth I officially ordered the Sixth Army to "to commence breaking through to the southwest forthwith." Hitler interceded and stated that the Sixth Army could break out as long as it also held the city. That it might be able to do both was imbecilic. I contacted Hitler and explained everything to him several times.

"I fail to see what you're driving at," he said. "At most Paulus only has enough fuel for 15 to 20 miles. He himself says he can't break out."

WHITE CHRISTMAS
By A German Soldier

We heard it. We'd been hearing it for days, the greatest sound ever, German guns roaring louder as they closed in to save us. We huddled in horrible cold when we weren't fighting. We were tired of fighting and tired of freezing, and those guns were everything. They were almost here. I knew they were.

"Listen," my new friend said. "They're not as loud."

"Of course they are. They're louder."

"Just listen," he said.

"They must be reloading."

"They were reloading before, too."

We listened when we weren't fighting, for three days, and by Christmas 1942 we did not hear anything at all.

SUPPLY DROP
By A German Pilot

This was the worst damn flight. I felt like a big bird during hunting season. Flak was ripping near my head and my tail and my wings, and I could not imagine what I'd do if Russian fighters came after me. I was looking for them. Everything was a terrible sight. The worst was fractured remains of so many planes like mine rotting in the snow below. I was so sick of this flight. I'd already made it twenty-six times during the last month. I knew the supplies were vital. I lumbered on and eventually down onto a snowy runway where I spun and slid sideways before stopping. While artillery shells whistled and exploded nearby, the ground crews unloaded me with haste. Then movement control officers started loading stretchers of wounded men. I wanted to get them back right away. We were ready to go. An officer almost had my door shut. Then he yanked it open and pointed at a soldier.

"Take that bandage off your head," he said.

"Certainly not. It'll bleed."

"I don't think it's bled yet. Get off the plane."

"The hell I will."

The officer pointed his pistol at the soldier.

"Get off the plane."

I wanted to get away, too. Down the runway I struggled through snow and barely got off the ground into icy air. There, just a couple of minutes later, I was hit, like a wounded bird, and knew this was the last damn flight I'd have to make.

RATIONS
By General Kurt Zeitzler

At the Wolf's Lair I sat down to dinner with my closest staff members.

"Don't complain," I said. "We're not the ones outside. This is pretty good, isn't it? I'm getting to like it. How about you? Uummm. We can be thankful. Six ounces of horse meat a day isn't bad. I've read about men surviving on less. We're all doing fine. Pass the bread, please. It's damn good, too. Three ounces a day. We aren't getting fat. I hope our men realize that."

ULTIMATUM
By General Friedrich von Paulus

On January eighth, 1943 the Russians sent me a typewritten ultimatum stating many facts: "You have been completely surrounded for several weeks. You have no hope of rescue since we have already routed the forces assigned that impossible task. Your transport air force continues to have its bases overrun and has to fly your starvation rations from further and further out. Any hopes of receiving meaningful aid are now an illusion. Your sick, starving and freezing men are doomed to suffer immeasurably more as the Russian winter is only beginning. Your hopeless situation makes further resistance completely pointless.

"In order to avoid senseless bloodshed, we propose that all the encircled German forces cease to resist. We guarantee to all officers and men their lives and safety, and, after the end of the war, return to Germany or any other country to which the prisoner desires. All personnel who surrender may retain their uniform and medals and personal effects, and in the case of senior officers, their swords. Normal rations will be instituted and medical aid will be given.

"Your reply is expected tomorrow. If you refuse our proposal for capitulation, we warn you that your forces will be annihilated, and their destruction will be your responsibility."

OPERATION RING
By General Georgi Zhukov

We had prepared by placing four thousand guns and mortars around the ring. Since the Germans were still inside on January tenth, the operation was bound to begin. At five after eight in the morning Stalingrad again became the most dangerous place on earth, especially for Germans. We pulverized them with shells and bombs, then chewed them up on the ground. Within a week we devoured more than half of their defensive perimeter. By January twenty-first we had repositioned our big guns. They continued the slaughter, erupting every six yards for fourteen miles, and within three days the Germans were constricted and split up in a mass grave.

NO
By Adolf Hitler

From inside Stalingrad, and even inside my own headquarters, I was being harangued by small men who did not understand our historical duty. On January twenty-fourth I pronounced: "Surrender is forbidden. Can't you see. Every day enemy forces fight at Stalingrad they can't strike us anywhere else. Furthermore, it is irrelevant that our forces no longer have a continuous front. They can fight in small groups, like guerrillas, and they can do that for a long time. That's so much better than capitulation. The Russians wouldn't let them live anyway. Now they can fight to the last man and the last round in defense of Western civilization."

PROMOTION
By Field Marshal Friedrich von Paulus

The Fuehrer yesterday promoted me to field marshal. What an extraordinary honor that was. All of my officers were very proud. This was the pinnacle of any military career. But today, January thirty-first, I really did not feel like a field marshal. I had, in fact, never felt so bad. In the basement of a department store, my new headquarters, we were being shelled, and the walls and roof rattled and threatened to collapse.

"You tell them," I said to my officers. "Yes. Now. Go right on up there and tell them."

I lay down, shivering on a cot, inhaling cigarettes to keep warm and stay calm. My officers brought some Russians down into the next room to negotiate. There was not much of substance to say. I let my officers take care of that. I lay smoking on the cot. When the details had been arranged, I agreed to talk to the Russians. They told me I had one hour to pack up and accompany them to the headquarters of General Shumilov, who commanded one of the seven armies that converged on Stalingrad.

"Good afternoon," I said.

"Your identification, please," said General Shumilov.

I groped my pockets and came out with my service book. Shumilov examined it and said, "I need a document verifying you're commander of the Sixth Army."

I gave him that.

"Is it true you've been promoted to field marshal?"

"Yes sir."

"Then I may report to my high command that Field Marshal Paulus has been taken prisoner by my army?"

"Yes sir."

"We have many questions for you."

The questions were entirely relevant and professional, and I knew I was dealing with high caliber men.

During lunch with my officers, I poured vodka for everyone. Then I rose and raised my glass and said, "To those who defeated us, the Russian army and its leaders."

RELIEF
By A German Soldier

This was the longest line I'd ever seen and certainly the most unusual I'd ever been in. I hadn't realized there were so many of us still alive, some said maybe ninety thousand. It was a hell of a cold line, but we no longer had to worry about getting shot or shelled. You can't imagine the relief.

The line was getting colder, though. There weren't any crumbling walls to block the bitter winds. We were in the open, marching, marching in a howling winter, somewhere, we were definitely marching.

"Where are we going?" I asked a Russian.

He gave me the meanest look. God, how a mean look can hurt. That made the march so much worse. Lots of guys couldn't take it.

There was plenty they couldn't take. And I wondered if they were in a better place when they fell and whipping snow covered them up.

SALVATION
By Adolf Hitler

I accepted responsibility for Stalingrad. I accepted every bit of it and was proud to do so. My resolve in holding Stalingrad so long was all that saved Army Group A from being trapped in the Caucasus. Those soldiers escaped to their northwest and would fight again. On the Eastern Front, the initiative would once again be ours.

Despite my manifest encouragement about the future, I did have some fundamental worries about my commanders, especially Paulus.

"What an incomprehensible coward," I said at a conference on February first, 1943. "I can't fathom an Army commander, a man I'd just made a field marshal, just meekly giving up after so many of his men had died so heroically. I would like to believe that Paulus had been severely wounded before surrender, but I can't. I was naive to believe there would be a heroic ending.

"That's what's so disgusting. I have no respect for a soldier who's afraid to do what a woman I once knew did. She was really a very beautiful young woman. Yet when someone close to her made a few insulting remarks, she locked herself in a room and shot herself. Over a triviality, really. She had so much pride. A weakling of a woman.

"And, now, look at Paulus. Twenty thousand people a year in Germany commit suicide, and they haven't seen thousands of their comrades bravely die. His cowardice cancels out the heroism of everyone else. And for what? So he can be tortured and put on the radio to denounce me. He should simply have shot himself, like a beautiful young woman. He doesn't understand what life is. It is the nation. The individual must die anyway. It is the nation which lives on after the individual. How can anyone be afraid of the moment that sets him free from this vale of misery?"

TOTAL WAR
1943-1944

TOTAL WAR
By Joseph Goebbels

For many days I had refined every vital word of my speech, and now, on a chill February 1943 night at the Sportpalast, thousands of eager Germans rose from their seats and cheered as I marched onto a stage backed by a gigantic banner promising: "Total War — Shortest War."

"Every one of you must know that Stalingrad has purified us to the depths of our being," I said. "We have stared into the hard and pitiless face of the enemy and now feel the cruel truth. Two thousand years of achievement by Western humanity is being threatened by hordes of savages from the East. It is better, and in fact mandatory, that we take this unvarnished look at matters because a danger acknowledged today becomes a danger averted.

"We must not in any way underestimate what is necessary. The most radical measures are just radical enough. The most total sacrifices are just total enough. It is time to take off the kid gloves and bind our fists and strike our enemies with unprecedented force. German men, to your weapons. German women, to work."

The crowd jumped up in a roar, and I demanded: "Do you want total war? Do you want total war? Do you want it if necessary to be more total and more radical than anyone today can imagine? Do you accept that anyone who undermines the war effort will lose his head? Is your faith in the Fuehrer even greater and more unshakable than it has ever been?"

"Ja, Ja, Ja, Ja ..."

"All right, people. Total war is yours. Rise and storm break."

AFRIKA KORPS
By Field Marshal Erwin Rommel

At night I lay with open eyes burning up through the dark, and I could not see a good end to any of this. Hitler had never allotted adequate troops, supplies or attention to North Africa, yet last

November he refused to permit our men to evacuate when it would have been feasible. Instead, he'd begun throwing in troops. I told him they could not be adequately supplied. He insisted otherwise. Those under his spell provided the optimistic reports he craved.

Now no one could dismiss General Montgomery's British Eighth Army closing in from the east or the American and British troops approaching from the west. Since our enemies possessed far more troops, weapons and planes, I resolved not to sit like a fool in a nutcracker. I struck hard to my west, trying to knock out the Americans. We outmaneuvered and outfought those amateurs, and hammered in an inferiority complex so deep they needlessly set fire to some of their supply depots.

I wanted the Afrika Corps to continue attacking and force the Anglo-Americans out of Tunisia and back into Algeria. To be successful, I needed independence of maneuver, and that should have been automatic. No one else had my experience or success in the region. Hitler, nevertheless, had demanded that the Italians be in charge. And they wallowed in customary confusion before finally permitting me to advance, not where resistance was light, but where I'm sure we were expected, right into enemy strength. This appalling shortsightedness limited our advances, and in two days we were halted by heavy American artillery fire as well as grave reconnaissance that large Anglo-American reinforcements had already arrived and more were coming. Now the least gruesome alternative would be to wheel around, rush east and clobber Montgomery.

I was, of course, immensely gratified on February twenty-third when the Italians, at Hitler's behest, named me to head Army Group Afrika. Within the strategic framework of someone's high orders, I would have freedom of action, but not until the end of an ill-conceived offensive launched to my north. It never had the requisite force. It was, however, a marvelous reprieve for Montgomery, who probably only had one division all the way up to his front.

By March sixth, rather than striking Montgomery with a slightly superior force, I was confronted by a two to one disadvantage in men and six to one in armor. Heavy and thoroughly-prepared British fire promptly destroyed one-third of our panzers. That made me sick. On March ninth I was ordered to leave Africa for a cure. In Rome I talked to Mussolini. His delusions aggravated me. Then I visited Hitler.

"You're a pessimist," he said. "We can certainly hang on to Tunisia. We'll get Libya and Egypt back, too. Then we'll take Algeria and Morocco. Make sure you get well in time to command our operations against Casablanca."

TWO POCKETS
By Colonel Rudolf-Christoph Gersdorff

Hitler was lured to the Eastern Front for meetings in March 1943, and two bombs in a package said to contain liquor were placed on his plane. The fuse had been set for thirty minutes and an explosion somewhere over Russia. We waited for news the horror could start to end. That should have already happened. Then the message came. Hitler had just landed back at his headquarters.

After calling the Wolf's Lair to explain someone sent the wrong package, General von Treschkow from Army Group Center dispatched an officer, with real liquor, to retrieve the bombs. Treschkow determined the fuse and the striker had worked, and that even the detonator cap had probably worked. Cold weather must have ruined things. We needed to try again with these bombs British agents had given us.

"You understand," said Treschkow.

"Yes," I said.

"It will be your life."

"That's the only way."

It was hard to get to Hitler. His security arrangements had always been extensive. Now they were maniacal. His adjutant, Rudolf Schmundt, did not want to reveal even what time the ceremony in Berlin would take place. That was pried loose by an unsuspecting General Model, commander of Army Group Center.

"Colonel Gersdorff won't be allowed in the exhibit of captured Russian weapons," said Schmundt.

"My intelligence officer has to be there," Model said. "I won't be embarrassed in front of the Fuehrer if I can't answer all his questions."

"All right. But remember. Anyone releasing vital information will be subject to death."

I already had my death sentence. I merely needed the right fuse. A very short fuse, one lasting about ten seconds, would have been best. But that would not work with these bombs, and other bombs and fuses were difficult to get. How do you explain the need for personal explosives? We had only the two British bombs and ten-minute fuses.

I put on a big coat with a bomb in each pocket. The bombs were rather heavy, and I was nervous watching Hitler arrive at Unter den Linden in his open Mercedes. He greeted numerous dignitaries from the military before going inside the hall. I moved near the entrance to the exhibition of captured weapons. The orchestra played Bruckner's Seventh Symphony, but only the first movement. Thank God. Hitler started speaking about how he had overcome the crisis and ensured victory not only over the Bolsheviks but capitalists, warmongers and Asiatic barbarians. How long was this going to take? Hitler often spoke forever. I put my hands in my pockets. The speech went on, but only twelve minutes.

Now Hitler was coming to see the weapons. As he moved by I saluted him with my right hand and used my left to activate the bomb in that pocket. Ten minutes. That's all Adolf Hitler and I had. In the meantime, there were lots of weapons to look at. Hitler and his entourage entered the exhibition. I followed the group closely. That was my duty. There might be questions. I had answers. I wanted Hitler to talk to me.

I needed to talk. My pockets were getting heavier. It was hard to keep up. Hitler wasn't looking at anything in the exhibition. He was moving so fast, almost running. Wait, I thought. I can explain. But I need more than two minutes. In that time he was gone, heading to talk to the war wounded. I tried to follow but wasn't permitted. Now he was much too far away. I walked in two or three directions before turning down a hall.

"Where are you going so fast?" shouted a guard.

"To the bathroom. Do you mind?"

FRIENDS
By A German

The young SS officer was wearing a very black uniform.

"What did you tell them?" he said.

"Who?

"Your friends."

"Which ones?"

"What did you tell them?"

"Nothing."

"You know the law."

"They're so many laws. More all the time."

"You understand me."

"No, actually, I don't. I'm accustomed to rather higher discourse. You're confusing me."

"I'll make it clear. I'll shove it right up your blue nose. At least seven of your Jewish friends can't be found. All of them have been seen with you recently. Where are they?"

"I don't know. Berlin's a cosmopolitan city. They're probably enjoying themselves at some of the centers of culture."

"We're going to clean up Berlin entirely."

"That's delightful. Things are increasingly messy around here."

"One more chance. What did you tell them?"

"Perhaps I said Wagner's overrated."

"All right, get up. You'll be there when they arrive."

AT NIGHT
By Adolf Hitler

I'm exhausted. I have to sleep. But I almost never do, not for long. I hate to sleep. It's not real sleep. It seems I can't get any even when I'm so tired. I have to get away. Sometimes I do. I escape for awhile. I think this is sleep. It must be. Surely I sleep sometimes. I am right now. This is the greatest relief. I'm no longer the most worried man in the world. I'm away in some dark place. They can't get me. I'm too relaxed. I'm going to rest forever. That's all I want. Let me be. Keep your hands off. I can't breathe. Let me up. You horrid bastard. I'll scream until you stop. I'll cut your goddamn head off.

BONFIRES
By Nikita Khrushchev

Our men were really working hard. They knew how necessary it was to work fast now that the snows were melting. If we didn't clean up this mess right away there might be an epidemic. It was extremely difficult work. The ground was still frozen and each German had to be dug out. Many of them clung to Stalingrad as doggedly as they had before. We got all of them out, though, all of them we could find, and we stacked thousands of them in layers separated by railway ties. The stacks burned very hot and slowly, and some guys said they enjoyed the scent of burning enemy corpses. I didn't like it much and wasn't going to watch anymore.

HOME
By Eva Braun

I was so happy to have the Fuehrer back at the Berghof where he could relax. He really needed to. He was getting so gray and serious. I knew I could help him and was always ready the moment he left his military conferences. Usually I was the first person he went to, and in front of all the others he'd lean over and kiss my hand. Then the guests got to shake his hand. The Fuehrer was charming with everyone. I know how relieved he was to be away from the military people. They did not get to socialize with us. The Fuehrer wanted everything organized just right, and he always escorted a lucky lady to the dinner table. I did not mind. His chief deputy, Martin Bormann, escorted me.

"Gnadiges Fraulein, you're especially pretty this evening," said Bormann.

"Thank you. You're very kind."

"Is that a new dress?"

"Yes."

"Of course it is. And I'll take care of it. Right away."

"The Fuehrer'll be delighted. He trusts you so much. He tells me all the time, 'I just couldn't get by without Herr Bormann.'"

"We're both indispensable, indeed."

"How is your wife?"

"Pregnant."

"Again? How many is that?"

"By my wife? Ten."

"That's extraordinary. Great for the Fatherland."

"I hope, Gnadiges Fraulein, that someday you too can be a mother."

Bormann pulled out my chair and seated me at the table. I was concerned about him. He was getting fat and jowly. He must have been eating and drinking too much. I was glad the Fuehrer never drank. An occasional drink might have been good for him, but having me there was all he really needed.

"You're not eating very much," the Fuehrer said to me. "You must be trying to make the other women jealous. You don't have to do this for me, you know. I liked you as well when you were pleasingly plump. The only thing I ever ordered Fraulein Braun to do was quit smoking. Either that or give up me. I can't tolerate the smell, and I know very well smoking shortens life and lowers resistance to illness.

"I'm quite worried about all of you, really, eating those animal corpses. They're nothing but blood and fat. Have you seen how they're prepared? You should. Not long ago I toured a slaughterhouse in the Ukraine. Those big peasant women with dirty hands were hacking away at the corpses and slogging through blood ankle-high on their rubber boots. They often dropped the flesh into the blood and just picked it right back up. I tell you, I'd never eat meat."

After dinner the Fuehrer had another military conference but said he'd hurry through. While the secretaries, aides, and adjutants concentrated on the war, the guests and I went to the basement to look for a good movie. I missed not having American movies very often. They were the best. Tonight, though, we had to watch something German. It was pretty good and getting better when the call came around midnight. Right away we freshened up and gathered in front of a fire in the living room. We loved listening to the Fuehrer, and everyone had a very good time until four a.m. Then the Fuehrer went off to his bedroom, and in a few minutes I went off to mine, and even though everyone knew our bedrooms were connected by a beautiful marble bathroom, that's all they knew.

George Thomas Clark

PALM SUNDAY
By An American Pilot

This was a fine Sunday. Back home I would have been at church, standing out front enjoying the pretty mid-April sun. I loved to talk to everyone and get nice and fresh before I went in. That's what I wanted to do as soon as I could. I had been working just about every Sunday, though. Today I was over the Mediterranean, and it was as pretty a blue as I've ever seen.

We were all flying high and knew very well the Germans would have to bring in supplies somewhere through here. Without help in North Africa, Rommel would soon be cornered and exhausted. That made this operation special. I was hunting the ultimate fox and soaring so high I could see it all. To be sure, I stared through binoculars. There. Right down there. At least a hundred big three-engine Junker transports were cruising about a hundred feet above the water. They were in three V formations, flying steady and low and beautiful like big birds happy on Sunday morning.

We called our P-40's the Warhawks, and about forty of us swooped on the Junkers. They were so slow. Every time I squeezed my guns I ripped into something. The Junkers jerked and staggered; they smoked and flamed; they spilled and crashed. That's all they could do, that or keep flying big and dumb like slow birds in shattered formations.

Some of our other Warhawks joined a dozen British Spitfires to deal with the escort Messerschmitt fighters. They weren't supposed to act like big dumb transports, but they did. They couldn't figure anything out. Our planes dived a lot faster than theirs climbed, and within ten minutes we'd massacred them, more than half the transports and more than half the fighters. It was easy to see. There'd be a party tonight.

INITIATIVE
By Adolf Hitler

People all over the world were doubting the invincibility of German arms, and that I could not allow. I did not have to. I already saw victory again. It was right on the map in front of Kursk. The Russians

470

occupied a massive fist shoved a hundred miles into our line and about that wide. We in turn held large bulges on each side of the Kursk salient. I did not dare wait for the Russians to attack. From their fist they could strike and link with forces driving from opposite directions and envelop us in two places, which would destroy the whole southern half of our Eastern Front and doom the civilized world.

My dedication was too profound and my sense of history too acute to ever permit such a catastrophe. Instead, I vowed to strike first, from north and south, and hammer massive armored wedges into the Kursk salient to encircle and destroy the enemy, then tear open the front so I could roar back into the heart of Russia and not only regain the initiative but wheel north and charge the mere four hundred miles up to Moscow and win the war. I certainly had the means to do so. I would in a few months. That's why I warned the generals in April 1943 that we probably couldn't attack right away.

This operation was going to wait for the greatest weapons in history. Our new Tigers were thundering panzers of fifty-five tons, twice as large as the Russians' vaunted T-34. Next to the Tigers in the armored wedge would be the massive new Elefant self-propelled guns. I squeezed my hands when I saw them tested. They were far too much for the enemy. So were the Panthers, our new medium panzers, which also dwarfed the T-34. The Russians simply would not be able to stop us once we got a little more production and training. We had to hurry, though. The world urgently required another beacon of German victory in the East.

ARMORED FORCES
By General Heinz Guderian

I had told Hitler I wouldn't leave retirement to become Inspector General of Armored Troops unless my authority was both extensive and clearly defined. I was much too sick for any nonsense, having just recovered from a heart attack that rendered me unconscious several days. I think Hitler understood he needed me. He must have been ashamed. Despite my unprecedented panzer victories, he had dismissed me late in 1941 for withdrawing to save my troops from slaughter. Now a much older Hitler placed his trembling left hand on a document, signed with his right, and thereby guaranteed me the opportunity to forge armored troops into a decisive weapon for winning the war.

For a few months I had been conferring with generals and armaments experts, and became quite worried by our meager panzer production, which certainly trailed that of the Russians. I was further troubled to learn that most panzer divisions now had at most two hundred panzers, only half as many as I had originally designed. My anxiety increased at the military conference on May fourth, 1943 as Hitler himself outlined the views of General Model, who would lead the northern pincer in the proposed assault on the Kursk salient. Model had written to Hitler that extensive air photography proved the Russians were preparing powerful defenses in precisely the places where our two assaults were aimed. Furthermore, even if we did penetrate, it would not be possible to destroy much Russian armor since it had already been withdrawn well behind the areas we planned to envelop.

Hitler asked everyone to comment. Some strongly supported the plan. Others backed it only if it took place right away, before the Russian defenses got any stronger. I vigorously opposed the plan for the reasons Model articulated as well as my conviction that new armor should be deployed on the Western Front, where the Anglo-Americans would certainly land sometime next year. It was not possible to determine how the Fuehrer felt.

After the conference ended and most had left, I took his warm hand and said, "Mein Fuehrer, may I please speak to you frankly?"

"Yes. Certainly."

"You've thoroughly detailed the difficulties our offensive would face. It's certain our losses would be far beyond any equivalent benefits we might achieve. Why do you want to attack in the East at all this year?"

"We must attack for political reasons," said Field Marshal Keitel, the OKW chief whose primary duty was to pant when Hitler spoke.

"How many people even know where Kursk is?" I said. "No one cares whether we attack it or not. I repeat my question: why do you want to attack in the East at all this year?"

"You're quite right. Whenever I think of this attack, my stomach turns over."

"Your response is the correct one. Leave it alone."

"I haven't made any decision. Nothing is committed. Don't worry about that."

SPLENDID DAY
By Adolf Hitler

I was very concerned about propaganda. That's what I explained to Rommel in May. I didn't want the German people to blame him for losing North Africa. It was essential to tell everyone, for the first time, that he had left there more than two months ago and not returned. I know Rommel was pleased by my determination to protect his good name. I'd soon be needing him, and he, and all Germans, would be extraordinarily well prepared because, by battling to the climax in North Africa, I had delayed any Anglo-American assault on Europe by at least six months. That was manifestly more important than the two hundred thousand prisoners taken. Only half of them were Germans, anyway.

ATLANTIC SPRING
By Admiral Karl Doenitz

Hunting had been superb. Last year we'd sunk at least eleven hundred merchant ships, yet we lost only eighty-seven U-boats. The enemy could not continue replacing losses like that. He'd tried to survive in the Atlantic by launching support groups to protect merchant convoys and chase U-boats. He'd also deployed new land- and carrier-based aircraft and improved his radar. We'd countered with radar receivers that detected enemy transmissions and enabled us to strike fast and escape. Recently, in March 1943, we'd demolished a hundred more ships. Now victory was so near I felt it warming my chest. I also confirmed it in our production figures. Despite beginning the war with only fifty-six U-boats, we now had almost four hundred, more than half operational, and were producing seventeen a month.

We were ready to sever England from the New World. We were looking for convoys. In the North Atlantic, we found plenty. Right away we sank a ship, but the enemy bombed a U-boat. After we torpedoed another ship, enemy guns shredded a U-boat trying to submerge. Another U-boat nearby did slide underwater just before the enemy scattered hedgehog explosives that blew it up. We lost seven in three days. Maybe traitors were giving away our codes. Maybe the enemy was breaking our codes. For certain the enemy knew more than he had known. I told Hitler this was our greatest crisis. Revolutionary location devices must have caused us to lose forty-one U-boats in May. We could not replace losses at this rate. I ordered all U-boats out of the North Atlantic until we improved technology.

SNAKES
By A Russian

We liked living in the woods. The Germans rarely went in there. When they did, they usually didn't come out. The woods belonged to us. What the Germans did not understand was that most of the rest of the country was also ours. They held a lot of cities and transport centers and supply depots, but they did not hold the woods, and they did not hold the country. All they really had was a bunch of targets.

I told my leader which ones I wanted now. I was tired of sniping. Like that I could only shoot one German at a time. Fine. That was important. So was poisoning enemy water supplies. But I'd never gotten to do any big jobs like blowing up those snakes that by the thousands crawled into our homeland and spit out poison.

I asked all our best guys about explosives. At first we could only get regular mines. They blew up locomotives that ran over them, but they did not destroy the rest of the snake. Then we learned to sow tracks with mines that detonated by remote control. That killed the whole snake and everything inside it. But the Germans started setting off mines with a massive flatbed car the locomotive pushed way in front. Fine. We developed mines that were activated by the flatbed but didn't blow up until the real snake crawled over them.

As vulnerable as they were out in our open country, the snakes were even better targets bunched in railroad yards. We had quite a few people in there and gave them magnetic mines with delayed fuses. I smuggled a good strong one to our guy at a big station. He put the

474

mine on the cold belly of a gas car in a long line of panzers. At detonation an inferno burst from the gas, which also exploded, and the whole fiery mess tore apart and ate up the other cars. On adjacent tracks the efficient Germans had placed an ammunition snake, which soon erupted onto a food snake that ignited, too, and there were so many fires and explosions and so much smoke and panic and confusion that the Germans probably didn't notice, and definitely could not have cared, that a fourth snake was also ablaze.

LUCY
By General Georgi Zhukov

There was only one responsible plan, and I told everyone, including Stalin, to quit worrying about Moscow and send troops from that front, and others, to the point that counted. Our well-placed spy high in the German command — code named Lucy — had provided information that was daily being verified by reconnaissance.

"We really know?" said Stalin.

"Yes," I said. "We even have details."

"Then we attack right away."

"Attacking is pointless. It's much better for us to wait. Let the enemy attack. After we smash his panzers and exhaust him, then we'll strike and destroy him forever."

Stalin was sometimes a nervous old hen, but after much indecision he proved tough enough to order three hundred thousand civilians to help carve several thousand miles of tank traps and trenches into the Kursk salient. More than a million mines were also being sown. For the Germans, that would be a problem. They couldn't attack minefields like Russian soldiers, who moved through them as if they weren't there. Our losses were no heavier than if the Germans had instead used troops to defend the area.

Mines were not going to be the Germans' primary obstacles. One million three hundred thousand tough men were moving in along with twenty thousand artillery pieces and three thousand attack planes. The three thousand five hundred tanks en route guaranteed a new standard of violence.

SECRET DIPLOMACY
By Joachim von Ribbentrop

There could be no consideration of my being the visitor. Why should I? We still occupied very much enemy territory. Molotov would have to come to me. In June 1943 we met in Kirovograd, two hundred miles behind our front lines in the Ukraine.

"The war has turned against you," Molotov said.

"Where are we now," I said.

"You can't stay."

"For two years we've proved we can."

"We've thrown you back three hundred miles the last six months," Molotov said.

"We've recovered, and we're stronger than ever."

"I don't think you are. The Soviet Union is the nation growing in strength."

"You've sustained horrendous losses," I said.

"We can make up the losses. I know Germany cannot."

"The Fatherland can make any sacrifice."

"You have too many enemies to continue like this."

"Neither of us has to bleed for the democracies."

"That's why I'm here."

"We can stop the bloodshed," I said.

"Get off our land."

"In that regard, I have an extraordinary concession."

"What is it?"

"We'll withdraw two hundred miles more and establish our frontier along the Dnieper River through Kiev, then extend the line north up to the Baltic Sea."

"So you expect to keep the Ukraine, Belorussia and the Baltic States."

"Naturally."

"They're ours."

"I'm offering you two hundred miles that you don't have."

"The only frontier acceptable to us is the one you violated two years ago."

"We've sacrificed too much to withdraw."

"Give it back or we'll take it back."

"Nonsense. It's ours now."
"I see Nazi diplomacy hasn't changed."
"We'll never change."

NORTHERN PINCER
By A German Soldier

What a weapon the Elefant was, a fortress on tracks, an outright war winner. This self-propelled gun would, in fact, be the biggest thing that had ever really moved on a battlefield. Mounted on the chassis of a Tiger panzer and equipped with a deadly big gun, it weighed an astonishing seventy tons and was protected in front by unprecedented eight-inch armor. To our crews every Elefant represented power and victory early on July fifth as our artillery began pounding the Kursk salient. One hour later we attacked.

The spearhead of our wedge was formed by Tigers and Elefants. Medium panzers followed along with armored personnel carriers. My crew and I were lucky. All five of us had survived duty in smaller armored vehicles destroyed in action. Now, in our Elefant, we charged into heavy fire. A big anti-tank shell hit us and bounced off. That would have devoured anything else I'd been in. Machine gun bullets sounded like rain at home, ridiculous, no threat at all. We ran over a mine. We heard it, felt it a little. That's all. We rolled on. Planes strafed us. More anti-tank shells hit us. We crushed more mines. None of them mattered.

"We're in the Elefant," I shouted.

Now we had penetrated to the great T-34 tanks, scourge of so many German attacks. The first shot from our big gun tore open a T-34's sloped armor and left it in flames.

"There's another," I said.

We shredded that T-34. Then another. Then another was crumpled and smoking. And we continued to smash the dense Russian defenses, rampaging in an Elefant, pounding southeast in the direction of Kursk. We were going to stampede the Russians. We were going to envelop them. We were going to destroy their front. We were going to ...

"Get out, get out," I screamed.

Opening the hatch I groped out on top of the Elefant and was shot several times before I collapsed and rolled off onto the hot Russian earth. Some bastard with a cheap flamethrower had jumped out of a trench and fired the thing through a ventilation slit.

"Stupid Elefant," he said. "Thinks he can survive out here by himself."

SOUTHERN PINCER
By A Russian Soldier

A week of attacking the Kursk salient from the south had gotten the Germans thirty miles and more misery than they could afford. We knew they had to do something decisive. For them that meant massing armor at a critical point and trying to break through. Our reconnaissance and logic both pointed to the same wretched place, a sloped and ravine-ravaged strip of land between a river and a railway embankment. We planned to be there first with eight hundred fifty tanks and self-propelled guns.

By the morning of July twelfth our columns of steel were fast chewing up dry soil that choked the sky. To the south we knew our planes were already hammering German lines. Maybe not that many panzers would get through, and we wouldn't have to face those big guns on the Tigers. They were deadly. From far away they could penetrate our tanks before we could penetrate theirs. We planned to be ready, though. We'd studied this area. We knew which orchards and gullies would help. We were headed for the right places when word came. The Germans were almost here and fast chewing up dry soil on a day getting hotter.

From our position on slightly higher ground, the order was immediate: Attack. Attack full speed right now. Down the slope our tanks roared to bushwhack the Germans diagonally, surging right into their columns, in some cases through them, right among them, under their big guns, all over the Tigers and Panthers. The Germans tried to get away and set up for battle, but we charged after them. Fire, I said. Fire. We nailed a Panther. Its engine was burning. Then I saw we'd blown up a tree behind it. No one had even hit the flaming Panther. Get that Tiger, I said. Turn. Turn. Fire. Up close our shell cut right through the side, where its armor was thinner.

The Germans were struggling to break free. Some did and ripped us. But most of us clung to them, attacking and smothering them like agile fighters going after clumsy giants. The Tigers couldn't really move. Not like a T-34. Kill the Tigers, I said. Kill the Tigers. Fire. Fire. Fire. All day we chased the beasts over a satanic, dust-strangled stretch of thundering land, and at sundown, when everyone was either dead or too tired to fight, and the Germans who could had left, I crawled out of my T-34, wiped my face with a sweaty hand, and shouted: "Look. Everywhere. The Tigers are burning."

MY ALLY
By Adolf Hitler

Surely the Russians had learned that German iron was poised again. Now the Anglo-Americans needed the same lesson. They had attacked Sicily, off the toe of Italy, with a large force. I therefore decided to halt the Kursk offensive and redeploy some of my forces. This move required personal consultation with the Duce, who I agreed to meet on July nineteenth at an old villa in northern Italy.

Surrounded by our staffs, the Duce and I sat in two huge chairs in a great hall. I looked sympathetically at my friend. His face was gray as winter sky, and he must have lost forty pounds.

"Duce," I said, "I'm going to speak to you frankly because I know that's what you want. You'd be insulted by anything less than the truth. I must tell you that Italy's contribution in this war is nil. It is appalling. Your officers, your soldiers, your entire nation are riddled with defeatism. Your men don't want to fight. They're just giving up in Sicily. We have a grave crisis that can only be overcome if Italians start fighting with the fanaticism of Germans. We've got to defend everything to the last man and the last bullet."

The Duce uncrossed his legs and rubbed his back and sighed. Then he crossed the other leg on top.

"Every German," I said, "has the will to conquer. And I'm not merely speaking of adults. Even our fifteen-year olds, Duce. Fifteen-year old boys are operating many of our antiaircraft batteries. We must have total mobilization. We can't leave this task for another generation.

This is the generation of giants, you and I, Duce. It is your responsibility to resurrect the glory of ancient Rome."

Pulling a handkerchief out of his pocket, the Duce wiped his face. One of his aides gave him a message he read and handed to me. Rome had just been bombed.

"The British can't continue much longer," I said. "If they do, I'll flatten London with my new weapons. They're almost ready. The British are going to suffer a Stalingrad."

STAMINA
By Benito Mussolini

I didn't need any sleep. After last night's ten-hour meeting with the Fascist Grand Council in Rome, I was at my desk at the regular time. There were many stacks of reports to consume. Right now I was studying the phone intercepts, a pile of them. I'd been doing this for years. The Duce always had to be aware of what was said.

Last night those traitors had been impudent before voting to establish a constitutional monarchy with the king in charge of the armed forces. I was probably going to punish the traitors. But I had agreed the war might be lost. This afternoon I went to explain everything to the king. He told me nothing was good anymore and I had to resign. Maybe retirement would be all right. I did not berate the kindly little king.

"I'm the only friend you've got left," he said.

I think he was right. I had overestimated Italians. Most of them descended not from the great Romans but from slaves of Romans. Modern Italians were a trivial, superficial people preoccupied with chatter and bourgeois comforts. I should not have expected heroism or loyalty. Just after walking out the palace door I was arrested and driven away in an ambulance.

HAMBURG
By Karl Kaufmann

"What the hell happened?" I said. "Our fighters and antiaircraft guns were hardly involved."

"The British were playing tricks, District Leader Kaufmann," the officer said. "Here. Look at this."

He handed me a piece of tinfoil and explained that bundles of it were dropped last night, igniting our radar screens with thousands of false readings. Then at least eight hundred big bombers flew in and unleashed high explosive and incendiary bombs that broke many water pipes and burned like hell. The next two days American bombers attacked our docks before another massive British air fleet approached on the night of July twenty-seventh. The fires of Hamburg were still glowing and must have made easy targets despite the suffocating shroud of smoke. Every bomb the enemy dropped multiplied the flames, and unending avalanches from the sky transformed fires into thousand-degree infernos that sucked in oxygen and stormed through the city like typhoons ablaze. Those who ran were incinerated on streets of boiling asphalt. Those in bomb shelters were either cremated alive or asphyxiated.

The British attacked two more nights within a week, and many of us wondered why. Half the city was destroyed. Fifty thousand were dead and eight hundred thousand dazed survivors roamed the wreckage.

I sent the Fuehrer messages to please visit right away. He could not imagine how much his people needed him. He had to see. I was devastated he refused to come.

COMMITMENT
By Hermann Goering

The meeting with Luftwaffe generals in my office at the Wolf's Lair had been extraordinary. We fervently agreed about everything, and I rushed to tell him: "Mein Fuehrer. Don't worry. This will never happen again. It must not. And it won't. We've decided how to change everything. Everything has got to be committed to defense. Our air offensives have been devastating, of course. But right now we need defense in the skies. That's the only way our enemies have been able to strike the Reich. We have to stop them. I know we can."

"I certainly can't depend on the Luftwaffe. You've ruined things so many times. You're incompetent. Any idiot should realize the only way to stop terror is by dealing out more terror than the enemy."

Walking out I passed my generals and went into a room. It seemed like an asylum. I sat down and curled my arms on a table and put my head in my arms. After awhile, without looking up, I called for two of the generals to come in. I could feel them looking at me. And I was definitely going to look at them as soon as possible. When I did, I wiped my eyes and said, "The Fuehrer has made me realize my mistake."

FIRST
By General Georgi Zhukov

For two years the Germans had determined where and when and how hard to punch. I grimaced after every blow and constantly bore down on everyone, and especially myself, vowing to change everything. Then the long dormant and trod upon Russian colossus would be forever aroused and ready to obliterate the spirit of Napoleon and the flesh of Hitler.

Massive preparations had been completed in mid-July 1943, and we punched first with the Bryansk Front. Then the West front. Then the Central Front. Then the Voronezh Front. Then the Southwest Front. Then the Steppe Front. By early August we'd struck so hard the Germans were knocked behind where they'd started their attack on the Kursk salient, and we kept punching their head and solar plexus, then their neck and groin, hammering up and down, fifty days of thunder forcing them ever back and reversing many debacles.

MY DARLINGS
By Rudolf Hoess

The party was in my beautifully decorated villa. A Polish artist had spent three days helping me select and display my best paintings. The guests were very complimentary about the art, and they talked and laughed while drinking plenty. I joined them in a very good time.

After the party my wife and I were in the bedroom. I began to undress.

"Stop," she said."

"What?"

"Don't."

"I'm tired."

"I thought your dedication never stopped."

I unzipped my pants.

"No," she said.

"What's the matter?"

"What were you and that man talking about?"

"What man?"

"The bigmouth."

"Who?"

"Answer me."

"Business," I said.

I started to pull my pants down.

"Keep those on," she said.

"I do what I want."

"You're in charge inside the fence over there, not here."

"Darling, tell me what's the matter."

"Who are the children and I living with?"

I looked at my dear good wife.

"You talked about four new crematories, and how big they are. Why do you need them?"

"That's the order."

"That's insane."

"Stay out of this."

"The smell, Rudolf, good god, what are you doing?"

"I have to."

"You don't have to."

"I do."

"Get out of here."

I reached to embrace her.

"Don't touch me."

I got dressed and went down to my stable. I often went riding when I was upset, but it was much too late now. That did not matter. My horses were still there, and I visited them. It had been that way as a child, too. I hadn't needed playmates. Instead, I talked to my horses and brushed them and gave them sweets. That's how I relaxed. With horses and books. When I'd been a political prisoner after the Great War, I avoided the insanity around me by reading. I developed a very sensitive inner life but suffered so much from the psychological abuse of guards. They lacked the depth to understand a man struggling to remake his life. My coworkers now were the same kind of heathens. The only way I got any peace at Auschwitz was to visit my darlings.

FOREIGN PRESTIGE
By Heinrich Himmler

Johannes Popitz, the Prussian Minister of Finance, wanted to talk to me. Since his business probably pertained to the latest in my line of duties, as Minister of the Interior, I agreed to see him.

"Herr Reichsfuehrer, we need order," Popitz said.

"I'm more committed to that than anyone."

"Indeed. Only you are qualified to be guardian of the Holy Grail of Nazism."

"Thank you."

"The nation needs someone to wipe out corruption."

"I won't tolerate corruption."

"Many influential foreigners agree. They think you can save Germany, and at the same time save the rest of Europe from the Russians."

"The Wehrmacht must do that."

"No, Reichsfuehrer, the war is lost if it continues its current course. It cannot, at any rate, be won. You can only save Germany by reaching accommodation in the West."

"The Fuehrer wouldn't have that."

"That's why you're so highly regarded abroad."

"Many don't think much of me."

"They admire your power. And they know you're so much more pragmatic than Hitler."

"The Fuehrer will never surrender."

"That, perhaps, doesn't have to be his burden. He could be transferred to a less burdensome position — say, honorary president."

"You know the Fuehrer would never consider that."

"Herr Reichsfuehrer, the people of the world want to know. Are you going to allow terror to continue or are you going to establish order?"

"These issues we can discuss again very soon."

I considered telling the Fuehrer right away but decided to first get more information. In little more than a week the Gestapo broke a code and, without telling me, sent information straight to the Fuehrer's headquarters. That resulted in the arrest of an associate of Popitz. If asked, I was ever ready to provide plenty of facts about Popitz, too.

COMEBACK
By Joseph Goebbels

While a malicious sky dumped buckets of rain on Berlin, I thanked God it wasn't raining bombs on my way to the airport to fly to the Wolf's Lair. The Fuehrer wanted to see me. I definitely had to talk to him. He would likely listen to me more than anyone else. It was imperative I convince him to speak to the German people. They were desperate to hear from their Fuehrer. They could not understand why so great an orator, once so active and visible, had not addressed them a single time during six months of increasing horror.

Despite the criminal bombing attacks on our cities, our morale had not been broken. All the same, there was no point pretending in private that our predicament was less than appalling. Russian hordes fell like animals before our guns, but there were so many of them they often overwhelmed our men. Our retreats were still orderly. All foreign reports of routs were outright lies.

We Germans were being undermined by countless contemptible liars. The Italians were the worst. Two days ago, on September eighth,

1943, they announced their unconditional surrender to the enemy. The treacherous swine, Marshal Badoglio and the king in particular, did this despite repeatedly promising us they were committed to the war and to the Axis. Now the Axis was broken. And Anglo-American troops, after capturing Sicily, had just invaded southern Italy. Because of this our other allies — the Hungarians, Rumanians and Finns — might also give up.

Waiting at the Wolf's Lair, I ached about all our problems and feared they must have pounded the Fuehrer into very bad shape. But right after he summoned me I declared with surprise: "You look like you just got back from a vacation."

"I've been walking Blondi every day. Out here, that dog's my only companion."

"I can come any time you want."

"I hope you will. A real National Socialist might understand my thinking."

"What is our biggest concern right now, Mein Fuehrer?"

"I've been especially preoccupied about the Duce. We've got to rescue him. He's the only one who can get Italy back in the war."

"Where is he?"

"We don't know. They've been moving him around."

"The Italians won't fight us," I said. "The cowards lay down their arms against far less formidable soldiers than ours."

"I don't know. Italian soldiers near Rome outnumber us at least four to one. I think the city's lost. We'll have to establish our defensive line to the north, along the Apennine Mountains. If we don't hold there, the enemy could rush right into Germany as well as the Balkans. They'd be behind our troops on the Eastern Front. Still, we're going to have to move some troops from the East to the West. I expect the Anglo-Americans to strike very soon."

"I think, Mein Fuehrer, it's getting to be a question as to which side we should turn to first. Germany really can't fight a war on two fronts for long. What about approaching Stalin? He's a practical politician."

"I prefer Churchill."

"He's fanatically anti-fascist, Mein Fuehrer. He's also an adventurer."

"We'll take advantage of that aspect of his character. It's a British colonial trait, really. We'll let them have Sicily and southern Italy. I don't mind them dominating the Mediterranean. They can also have

Sardinia and Corsica. Once their lust for land has been satiated, they might be amenable to some kind of accommodation.

"We'll certainly compel them in other ways. We're resuming submarine warfare in the North Atlantic with incredible new equipment. We've got new acoustic homing torpedoes that go right after the propellers. They'll sink every enemy ship around and we'll starve Britain. By then her cities will be devastated far beyond what ours are. The world can't fathom anything like V-1 flying bombs or V-2 rocket bombs. The British'll be helpless. They'll have to make peace."

"How much did the strike at Peenemunde last month delay our programs?"

"We're almost back in gear. The German people will soon be astounded by our miracle weapons."

"No doubt, Mein Fuehrer. But they need something right now. They're waiting to hear from you."

"I'm preparing the speech."

"Give it tonight, please."

"I should wait until matters are clearer in Italy. Then I can say more."

"Mein Fuehrer, the people have been suffering. They deserve a word from you."

He finally agreed. And that evening I put him in front of a microphone that sent his words, so wonderfully read, to Berlin for recording. Then the speech was broadcast several times. The Fuehrer emphasized his commitment to the Duce, the greatest son of Italy since antiquity, and warned the world, and any traitorous Germans, that it was fantasy to think he could be dismantled in the Italian style. The Fuehrer also spoke encouragingly about our problems with the Russians and the British and the Americans.

Upon returning to Berlin in a couple of days, I was engulfed by the extraordinary spirit of our people. The Fuehrer's voice had soothed everyone like fine champagne, and we sensed that misfortune had turned into good fortune. Our resurgence was manifestly heightened by news the Italians had just surrendered Rome to us. This felt almost like taking Paris in 1940.

George Thomas Clark

TOP OF THE MOUNTAIN
By Benito Mussolini

The real nature of people, which I had always instinctively understood, was still becoming intellectually clearer by increments that ravaged me. The idol, I realized, would always be torn down. It happened to Christ. Now it had happened to me. The similarities were astonishing. Someday people would realize that.

I might have to die for the mistakes of traitors. I might well kill myself. I'd recently slashed my wrists. That didn't work. Perhaps destiny saved me. I was still needed, but I suffered so much. My stomach was a horror I often described to the hotel workers. They were astounded by my remedy. Daily I drank a gallon of milk and ate several pounds of grapes. I loved to chew on the grapes one at a time, or, if necessary, shove a whole handful into my mouth.

Maybe I felt so bad because the traitors were poisoning me. They couldn't look the Duce in the eye and shoot him. So they put him on top of the highest mountain in the Apennines and made him prisoner in an isolated hotel. My window on the second floor was open. I liked looking out. I saw everything, and I saw nothing. Today, I definitely noticed something. A glider? Yes. A glider. Then more gliders. And parachutes, too. All were landing in the rocky meadow below, and men began dashing toward the hotel. Who were they? More traitors? No. Germans? Maybe. They set up a machine gun. My captors ran toward the meadow.

"Don't shoot, don't shoot," I shouted down to everyone. "No bloodshed."

A tall man dashed into the hotel and soon into my room.

"Duce," he said. "The Fuehrer has sent me. You're free."

I embraced him, and we hustled downstairs and toward a plane my rescuers had landed in the meadow. I helped clear some rocks so we might take off. This was a very small plane. I'd never flown one like this. The big man, Otto Skorzeny, and I squeezed in with the pilot. Our plane didn't build much speed, scraping along the sloping meadow, and just after barely getting off the ground, one wheel hit a rock and we dived into a gully, and instantly I braced for the end. The traitors were going to win. Twenty years of fascism were about to be shattered until the pilot jerked hard, almost ripping out the steering column, and we were airborne on our way to Rome, the crucible of my power, where a German transport waited to fly us to Vienna. There I slept at liberty for the first time in almost two months. The next day I visited my wife and family in Munich, and the next I was flown to the Wolf's Lair.

The Fuehrer awaited me at the airstrip, and we clutched each other's hands. What an extraordinary feeling emanated from this friend. Only he had always understood me. I knew he always would. In a short while we were sitting together.

"Retirement. That's best for me, Fuehrer," I said.

"What sort of fascism melts like snow before the sun."

"I've been betrayed."

"We've both been betrayed. Nevertheless, I'm still willing to be generous and treat Italy like an ally. I don't want to be Italy's enemy. I can't imagine that I'll have to be, not now that you're free, Duce. You're the only man who can restore fascism in Italy. And it must be restored. The war must be won. We won't surrender, Duce. We're men of iron."

The next day I pronounced to Italy and the world that I was determined to cleanse with bloodshed the shame that traitors had brought upon the nation. I would do so from my new, that is my traditional, position as head of government. I planned to take over in Rome, but the Germans were so worried they insisted on keeping me safely guarded in northern Italy. Right away I began scouring newspapers and telephone intercepts from my period of captivity, and I reunited with my love, Clara Petacci, and rejoiced that I was again very much on top of things and indisputably the Duce.

REAL ESTATE
By A German Woman

I was only independent a little while. I understood the need for state control. Those who did not were sent away. I had agreed to all regulations in writing. Now everything was much better. I got my own room, and business really improved. Already I had bought one tenement back in my hometown and soon planned to buy a couple more. That motivated me to work harder. It certainly wasn't easy.

Some days I entertained thirty or forty soldiers. I tried to think about property while I was working and hoped when all this was over I'd never need to work again.

PROPRIETY
By Heinrich Himmler

Gathered before me was a large and stoic group of political leaders who deserved more than hearsay. I told them what they needed to know, but stressed that the sensibilities of the German people had to be protected. All of us now in influence must remain silent about my men of the SS, who were setting an unequaled example of perseverance and restraint as they shouldered the painful responsibility of eliminating those who wanted to exterminate us. The SS did not, however, have the right to enrich themselves with so much as a watch or a cigarette. I emphasized that. Two larcenous camp commandants had, in fact, been executed for bringing dishonor to the SS.

FORTRESS EUROPA
By Adolf Hitler

In the East we held tracts of land so vast that we could, in an emergency, temporarily relinquish some of them and still have plenty of room left for strategic maneuver. This was not at all the situation in the West, where an enemy breakthrough would immediately put his foul breath on our vital areas. I consequently ordered that we stop siphoning troops from the West and concentrate instead on strengthening the Atlantic Wall, from which we would soon launch our flying bombs and rocket bombs against the enemy, and which he would have to attack. I also decreed that we prepare mobile forces to counterattack and destroy anyone who might penetrate the Atlantic Wall. That operation would be spearheaded by Rommel, the ultimate armored warrior.

FESTIVITY
By Joseph Goebbels

The British really were the cowards who had started the murderous attacks on innocent civilians. Now they were committing their crimes with many more bombers. Hundreds had just executed two massive raids on Berlin that left flames lashing at our throats. Much of the Reich Chancellery was devoured, including the Fuehrer's private apartments where many of us had so often been inspired. The Kaiserhof Hotel was also hit, and it hurt particularly to see destroyed the historical site the Fuehrer had returned to right after being named chancellor.

Conditions looked hopeless all over the place. At least four hundred thousand Berliners were homeless, and many slept in the subway. I would have provided shelter in my house on Hermann Goering Street, but bombs had scorched the top floor and knocked out heat and running water. All telephone lines in the city were down, and modern living had ceased. Supply trucks couldn't help much because debris clogged the streets.

My city needed immediate action. I ordered that each Berliner's weekly ration of meat be increased by almost two ounces. I also demanded that we not refute the hugely exaggerated British boast that one-quarter of Berlin no longer existed. Let them believe we'd been destroyed. They might leave us alone.

In a couple of days I went out to see the people of Berlin, and they engulfed my car. When I got out they tried to hoist me onto their shoulders, and I barely convinced them not to, and instead let them put me on a box. From there I cursed the British bastards and urged everyone to endure. That way we'd win. Men and women patted my back and embraced me and called me Joseph and asked for autographs. I signed many papers and gave them cigarettes and smoked one with them and, under Berlin's bloody red sky, spirits were high as at a carnival.

TEHRAN
By Adolf Hitler

I knew exactly what Stalin, Churchill and Roosevelt were secretly doing in Tehran in December 1943. They were blabbering how easy it would be to invade Germany after grinding our cities from the air. Stalin no doubt hoped to fool the others about that. But the two democrats were horrified about getting what we'd been giving the Russians. These three heathens really desired something entirely different than Germany's unconditional surrender. Our interrogations of prisoners of war proved that. The British and the Americans wanted to join Germany against Russia. And the Russians wanted to unite with Germany to crush the democracies.

PRIVACY
By Gerhard Palitzsch

I can't imagine why Rudolf Hoess and other big asses didn't realize I was the most influential person at Auschwitz. As duty officer I worked far more hours than assigned, and performed all tasks with efficiency and skill. Charges that I tortured prisoners and stole from them were not proved. The bureaucrats should have left me alone. My time off was private. With my wife more than a year dead, I needed lots of drinks and plenty of action. Women guards often came to my quarters. But you know how they are. There were lots of better women to choose from. I started bringing a beauty to my room. Here it didn't matter what she was. I certainly didn't care. She was happy enough. This wasn't torture for her.

I wish I'd known who was spying on me. He'd have gotten real sick. Then I'd have had my privacy. Instead, I was arrested. At my trial the authorities grunted: "We've executed people for this."

I pointed out my record. I was far too influential and dedicated to die. Even my enemies agreed. I deserved to live, even if only at the Eastern Front.

HOLIDAY SEASON
By Eva Braun

Snow had forever been falling into big walls around the Berghof. That made everything so difficult. The Fuehrer hated snow.

"I want to go skiing," I said.

"It's not safe."

"I need to go somewhere."

"You can't. Look. We can barely get out the door."

"It's going to stop someday."

"It still won't be safe."

"I really should get out."

"You have everything right here."

"I'm bored. You're always working."

"You have me afterward."

"I need something when you are working."

"Your mother'll be here soon."

"Please let me ski."

"I can't. You might fall."

My mother came just before Christmas. She appreciated the Fuehrer excusing her from his late night talks so she could go to bed early.

"The Fuehrer's such a nice man," she said. "I'm worried about him. He's so bent over and feeble, not at all like he was."

"It's the strain of the war."

"What about that fat Dr. Morell?"

"I don't trust him," I said.

"He gives the Fuehrer so many shots."

"Anytime he has a complaint."

"He seems worse than ever when the injections wear off."

"He is," I said.

"Why does he let the doctor do it?"

"He thinks his pains are unbearable without Dr. Morell."

"Is the Fuehrer being treated for the trembling in his left arm and leg?"

"Of course."

"How many medications do you think he's taking?"

"Dozens."

493

MIDNIGHT
By A German Man

When I checked her bedroom she was gone. This being New Year's Eve was no excuse. She'd sneaked out many times. I wasn't going to tolerate any more. Those guys were ruining my daughter. I knew who they were, the swine from the Luftwaffe airfield near here. They listened to negro music and did not respect anybody. There was no respect in Germany anymore and there was no order. I'd change that.

I got on my bicycle and rode out to the old house not far from the airfield. No music was playing and the lights were out. I put my bicycle down easy and went to the front door. It was unlocked. As I stepped inside smoke and liquor blasted my face. That's how those bastards got thirteen year old girls. Now they'd be dealing with a veteran. My wounded shoulder had almost healed. I was a soldier again, stalking the enemy. When I heard moaning down the hall, I prayed don't let that be my daughter. I couldn't take that. She was so loud. There was no doubt. I charged into the room and screamed: "God, I'll kill you. I'll kill you."

COMMAND
By Field Marshal Erich von Manstein

I envied the Russians. Not only did they possess seemingly unlimited manpower and production capabilities, they also had an extraordinarily high-placed conspiratorial ally. His name was Adolf Hitler. No one, not even Stalin or Zhukov, was capable of abetting enemy efforts so effectively as the Fuehrer.

To every rational military man it was indisputable the Russians had planned to advance to the Dnieper River in the Ukraine, and were brandishing forces powerful enough to do so. The Fuehrer, in concert with Soviet grand strategy, forbade us to withdraw to the Dnieper. Furthermore, he had earlier forbidden us to fortify the Dnieper Line because he said rear-guard defenses encourage retreat.

When, inevitably, the Russians had advanced and taken Kiev and many other places in the region, Hitler droned that we must hold on.

Hold on at all costs. That was his essential vision. Meanwhile, growing Russian forces were advancing with blunt brutality and improved operational skill.

This trend was enough. It was too much. On January fourth, 1944 I flew to the Wolf's Lair. Along with numerous staff officers, we met at the daily conference.

"Mein Fuehrer," I said, "we must radically shorten our front in the south. If it collapses, so will the entire Eastern Front."

"Shorten our front? Say what you mean."

"Yes, Mein Fuehrer. Withdraw."

"Withdraw, no. You mean retreat."

"As you wish."

"I can't. That would provoke Bulgaria and Rumania. They'll only stay with a strong ally. Retreating from economically essential areas would also be devastating to our war machine. As I've told you, you lack overall perspective."

"Mein Fuehrer, may I please meet with you privately."

"About what? All right. All right."

The aides, emissaries, two stenographers and Goering left. Only General Zeitzler remained.

"May I speak openly?" I said.

"Please do."

"We need to acknowledge, Mein Fuehrer, that the extremely critical situation we now face cannot be attributed alone to the enemy's superiority. Our problems are also due to the way in which we're led."

Hitler drilled his eyes into me. He had silenced many people that way. I kept talking.

"We can't go on with the present type of leadership. We need to establish a Chief of the General Staff who is thoroughly responsible for all military policy. Then we can appoint an Army commander for the Eastern Front. We need professional military leadership, and it must be cooperative and no longer divided, as it is now, between the Army High Command in the East and the Wehrmacht High Command everywhere else."

"I'm the only one aware of what forces are available, and where they're needed, and what our strategy and tactics should be. Furthermore, no one else has my authority. And even I can't get the field marshals to obey me. Do you think they'd follow your orders any more readily?"

"Mein Fuehrer, my orders are always carried out."

"I'm glad you appreciate the rules of command. This meeting is dismissed."

On January eighth the Russians captured another city. They grabbed another the next day and another on the thirteenth and on the twentieth they overwhelmed one more. Our situation maps were graphic horrors of pierced defensive lines, encircled troops, and German notations revised westward if not altogether obliterated.

The Fuehrer evidently had a solution. He ordered dozens of generals to leave their commands on the Eastern Front and come to the Wolf's Lair on January twenty-seventh.

"You must understand the reasons for this war," he said. "This is a battle not merely of survival but of ideologies. The side with the strongest ideology will win. All of you must unequivocally support National Socialist principles. You must do this with inner conviction. If you have enough faith that we can win, we will win. If, however, Providence does deny us victory and catastrophe falls on the German people, then it should really be the field marshals and generals who stand by the flags to the last."

"And so they shall, Mein Fuehrer," I pronounced.

FOR THE FUTURE
By Martin Bormann

I didn't care that others got so much publicity. I didn't want any. I already had what everyone else craved — permanent access to the Fuehrer. I earned that by protecting him. Only those deserving got to see the Fuehrer. If someone caused me trouble, he not only didn't get in, I made sure his enemies did.

The Fuehrer knew my only ambition was to help him, and Germany. Even in private I always contributed, especially by fathering many children. My wife was so often unavailable. She understood my needs and was very proud I wrote her about seducing an actress who could not resist my willpower. My wife realized marital arrangements such as ours would be mandatory after the war when only one man would be available to service two or three women.

496

GENIALITY
By A Stenographer

My old boss was an ass. Every day his crudeness and inconsideration made me so sick I could've killed him or myself. I was relieved beyond gratitude to get this exciting opportunity at the center of everything. And the new boss was incredible, the smartest man I've ever met, and the most dynamic. I loved being in a room with him. He did so much for everyone. Despite extraordinary pressure, he often told me, "I know you have to sort out all these voices. It must be extremely difficult to get them down. I couldn't do it, but you're doing so well."

COMBAT
By Marshal Ion Antonescu

For three hours the Fuehrer had been ranting.

"Rumania must do better."

"Rumania has done its best," I said.

"Horrible. No. No help at all."

"Then why do you oppose us leaving the war?"

"You have an obligation."

"We can't do it."

"You must. You signed the Axis Pact, Marshal Antonescu."

"Circumstances were quite different then."

"You're not going to pull out on me. You wanted the spoils when I was handing them to you. Now you've got to sacrifice."

"Sacrifice?"

"Yes. Do something heroic for the Axis."

"Two hundred fifty thousand Rumanians have been killed."

"Germany's lost far more than that."

"We have a much smaller country. Our losses are devastating."

"You're not fighting with fanaticism."

"Don't you understand? Three of my generals recently died in hand to hand combat."

DEPRIVATION
By A Soldier's Wife

"You're aware what happens to offenders," said the official.

"Well, I've heard things, but they can't apply to me, under these circumstances."

"What circumstances?"

"My husband's been away three years," I said.

"He visits you, doesn't he?"

"Not very often."

"He's defending the Fatherland, like millions of others."

"I understand that. I love him."

"You have to enjoy his visits."

"I do everything possible."

"Then how do you justify your behavior?"

"The visits aren't enough."

"They have to be."

"I just don't know him as well."

"So you know some stinking French prisoner better than your husband."

"That man forced me."

"He raped you?"

"He took advantage of me."

"Evidently he did about every night."

"He said he'd beat me if I told."

"We'll make sure he never does that."

"I promise to avoid foreign men. They're beasts."

"Really? One of your friends said you told her Frenchmen were better lovers than Germans."

LEFT RIGHT
By Adolf Hitler

The enemy is coming, I told the generals in March 1944. He is surely coming somewhere soon in the West. When he does, we will annihilate his forces and destroy his morale with such unparalleled ferocity that he will never again try to set foot on the European continent. Thereby free in the West, we will hurl all our forces East and settle matters there. This we can do if every man in the West understands he is personally struggling to ensure the survival of Germany.

PRIVATE PRACTICE
By A Doctor

"Why did you do it?"

"I haven't done anything," I said.

"We have a witness."

"To what?"

"Murder."

"That's ridiculous. What witness?"

"The woman."

"Which woman?"

"Frau Strang."

"I don't know her."

"Here are some records from your office. Do you see the name, Herr Doktor."

"Yes, I see it. I treated her for a stomach ailment."

"So you lied about not knowing her."

"I can't remember all my patients."

"Can you remember what you cut out of them."

"I'm not a surgeon, sir."

"You're a butcher."

"That's not true."

"Our doctors have examined Frau Strang. There's no doubt what you did."

"She asked me to."

"You're despicable."

"She already has four she can't take care of."

"Our enemies are killing our men, and you destroy the future."

"I helped a troubled woman."

"You got her two years of labor."

"This's outrageous."

"Indeed, Herr Doktor. And you're going to get the same thing you gave."

LOGISTICS
By A German Staff Officer

In the unrivaled tradition of General Staff efficiency, I had been trained to compile and maintain precise information about which supplies were needed, and where, and how to get them there. Improvisation was a skill I both respected and nurtured. Creativity was a gift I doubtless possessed. Despite all of this, I was thoroughly perplexed about how to support our troops at and near the Atlantic Wall. Most railways and bridges between there and the rest of France, as well as between France and Germany, had already been destroyed along with most of the Luftwaffe fighters that tried to stop enemy bombers.

SPECIAL TREATMENT
By Doctor Theodore Morell

We tried not to notice. Instead, we looked at the Fuehrer's face. We never stared at his left arm or leg, not if he could see us. Even when he was turned, we had to be careful. The Fuehrer wouldn't want anyone watching him rattle every paper he touched.

"Morell," he said, "what can you do?"

"I've been injecting my multi-vitamin cocktails for two months."

"What do you think's wrong?"

"I'm not sure."

"Should I see a specialist?"

"No, Mein Fuehrer. Another doctor might botch things."

"I'm getting worse."

"At critical times, Mein Fuehrer."

"For too long I've known the Anglo-Americans are going to invade in May. I hate the waiting. All I can do now is strengthen our Atlantic Wall while enemy ships roll into England. I must tell you they have more ships than I ever imagined. The U-boats can't stop them, can't really even try to anymore."

"Please, roll up your sleeve, Mein Fuehrer. I've got something new for you."

The Fuehrer had so many scars and punctures. It was hard to get a good vein. But I found one. To combat his tremor I pumped in my special compound of glucose, iodine, and extracts from bull testicles. I knew that would help. He always needed more male hormones.

SONDERKOMMANDO
By A Jew

Right here, I wave to the SS. Yes sir. I'm ready right now. Certainly I'll follow you. I'll do everything you say. I'm fine. I can do the job. My family? I swear. I won't let that interfere. I'm sure. But perhaps you could find out how they are. Yes sir. I won't mention them again. Of course I'm sure. Where do I go?

This crematory looks fine. There's a job right now. About a hundred and eighty guys from the previous Sonderkommando have been shot in the back of the neck. They're all over the floor and need to be cleaned up. The ovens are already roaring. There are five big ones, each with three doors. The other volunteers and I pick up the bodies. They're a little heavier than most inmates. Better fed. We shove them into the oven. Those guys had about four months. No Sonderkommando gets more. That's better than the oven right now.

After climbing to the second story of the crematory, we see our new room and clean up after the old Sonderkommando. Now we have a place so much nicer than the other barracks, which are just long rows of filthy shelves stacked with skeletons that move. I haven't gotten like that yet. That's why I qualify for the Sonderkommando. What a break.

Right away we get to take a good shower. There is tile in the shower. Afterward we have a fine meal. My stomach feels good. Then we get rum. I've never been a drinker until today. I drink plenty of great rum, and we tell some stories and laugh. Then we get to sleep on bunks with silk coverlets and embroidered pillows. This is the best rest I've had in a long time. We need it. Tomorrow our new Sonderkommando starts regular shifts.

ON THE RAMP
By Dr. Joseph Mengele

Let's see. Which cologne shall I wear today? That one. No. This one I haven't used in a while. It smells great as I open the bottle and even better patting it on my cheeks and neck. I'm almost ready now. I'm already perfectly shaved. In the mirror I examine the little gap between my front teeth. It looks so cute when I smile. Ladies often tell me that. Today the new ladies will feel the same even though I won't smile. I'm going to be sure. I pin my Iron Cross First Class on my uniform. I'm not just a doctor. I'm a wounded warrior from the Eastern Front. But I look like an actor. I look like a star. My boots shine so bright they light up my face.

When I stand on the ramp, everyone is going to notice. I love my job. It's always so exciting when the trains arrive. But the smells are unbelievable. I have to step back as the doors open. Then I whistle while I wait for unloading. I start with Wagner. Something majestic. Then I whistle a little Strauss, the waltz king, while the SS line everyone up in two groups, women and children in one, men in the other. I step in with vigor. Come along now, I motion with my riding crop. You're old. Left, I say. You're sick. Left. You look strong enough. Right, I say. Not too bad. Right. You're ugly. Left, I point with my thumb. Oh God, covered with rashes. Left. A beautiful woman and her beautiful daughter. Right, I say. They certainly are a painting, I tell my assistants. Oh God, scars on that one. Left. Definitely left. A lot of weaklings. Left. Too many children. Left. A few more strong ones. Right. Out of three thousand, about five hundred qualify.

"Where are we going?" says an old man on the left.

"You're going to be clean," I say. "All of you. No more lice. Then you'll rejoin your families."

"I can't walk far."

"Don't worry. The Red Cross truck will take everyone who needs help. There it is. Please be careful getting in. The rest can walk. It's not far."

The ones on the left are marched away.

"Now, listen," I say. "All doctors out. All twins out."

That's good. Two more sets of twins for my research. And a couple of dozen doctors.

"Who studied at German universities?" I say. "Who is expert at pathology and forensic medicine?"

One man steps toward me.

"Who were your pathology professors? When were you in his class? I know him. What did you study? What did the professor think of your work? Who else evaluated you? Where? You're sure? I can check. What's your name? Nyiszli? Dr. Miklos Nyiszli. What have you done to develop a thorough knowledge of forensic medicine? How long did you practice? Are you respected?

"Your responses are adequate. But remember. You must be proficient at all procedures I assign. If not..."

IN THE ROOM
By A Jew

I don't know why I'm in a line being marched down stairs into a huge and very bright underground room.

"Everyone is to get undressed," the SS order.

Old men and women look at each other and wince. Teenage girls cringe. Mothers embrace their children. Young men like me stare at the SS.

"Don't stand there," they shout. "Every one of you must be undressed in ten minutes."

Thank God, I think. There he is. One of us. A man from my town. Dressed like a regular person. I wave. He comes over.

"Don't worry," he says. "You can all relax. Just put your clothes on the hangers. And don't forget your numbers. Tie your shoes together, too. You don't want them separated. Everything'll be here when you're finished."

I get undressed right away. I understand the reluctance of many others, especially the women. But they can do it. They're all right in a few minutes. We're all better now, brothers and sisters united in this state, waiting to be clean.

The SS tug open two big swing doors, and by the hundreds we trudge into another huge and very bright room. There are showers in the room and, every so often, square pipes from floor to ceiling.

"SS and Sonderkommando leave the room," an SS orders.

I see them counting each other. After that, they leave and shut the doors. I look around. There are holes in the pipes. I'm wondering why as the lights go off and shrieks rip the darkness.

"Quiet," I say.

I think I hear something. I'm pretty sure I do. Yes, I do. It's hissing. It's hissing like a big snake. I can smell it. I try to talk, but I gag. I need to get away from this spot. I start pushing. Someone grabs me. I throw her off but feel so many people in my way. The idiots are hitting me. I strike back and struggle to move. Get your filthy hands off me. I pound more heathens. They're desperate. They're trying to kill me. I grind into the farthest wall. That doesn't help. Gas is everywhere. I'm gasping and choking. I need a way out. There. I can feel a mountain. It's in my hands. It's under my feet. I start climbing. I'm getting out of here.

THE DAY SHIFT
By A Jew

Everyone can see I'm strong enough to be in the Sonderkommando. But there are many who are stronger. They're the ones who, after the room is ventilated, go in with big hoses to blast away the messes. Then they do all the heavy lifting. I've always been a barber, anyway. I wait for the bodies to come up on the elevator. There's so much hair to cut today. Every day. It really is quite a job. After my group finishes, the bodies go to the guys who pull teeth. Lots of them are dentists and they're fast prying jaws open with levers and using pliers to yank out anything that might have gold. Extractions are tossed into buckets of acid that devours everything but the gold. Other members of the Sonderkommando make sure rings, earrings, necklaces and the like are removed and dropped into a strongbox.

More strong guys load pushcarts with three bodies, or more, and haul them to the ovens. It only takes about twenty minutes to burn the couple of dozen bodies that'll fit into each oven. Ashes falling through grates in the ovens are crushed and removed right away so incineration won't be interrupted. On busiest days I know a couple of thousand come through this crematory. Three others are about as busy. Big trucks are needed to haul the ashes to the Vistula River. What a wretched river. I hope I never go there.

ON THE TABLE
By Dr. Miklos Nyiszli

There is no other table like this around here. I haven't even had one like it before. It is made of polished marble, and to clean my instruments all I have to do is turn to three porcelain sinks. Afterward, I often go into the next room, which has paintings and stylish armchairs, and look through microscopes before I study many fine books in the medical library. Our facilities are quite impressive and every bit the equal of a large city's institute of pathology.

Dr. Mengele is passionate about research, and he orders many experiments. His favorites involve twins. By weighing, measuring, comparing and thoroughly studying every part of twins, he believes the secrets of advantageous, and adverse, heredity can be discovered. He is determined to understand thoroughly the relationship between disease and racial types, and especially the key to multiple births, which surely can soon be induced throughout Germany and Germanic territories.

Dr. Mengele treats his twins very well, and they like him so much they often call him Uncle Mengele. Sometimes, after finishing anatomical examinations, he demands absolute confirmation of his diagnosis. The only way for there to be a scientifically accurate comparison, of course, is for the twins to die at the same time, and to be dissected right away. I very much disapprove of Dr. Mengele injecting or shooting the twins, many of whom are his personal favorites. If I say anything, however, he'll no doubt have me shot. He might even do it himself.

I perform my dissections in a very systematic and professional manner, and I note and duly record many extremely interesting anomalies such as glandular dysfunction, hereditary syphilis and spina bifida. Sometimes I have deep discussions with Dr. Mengele about my work. In the dissection room I am no longer a Hungarian Jew in Auschwitz, I am an expert in my field. I articulate and defend my observations as if we are at a medical conference, and several times I contradict Dr. Mengele, who has but a fraction of my experience at dissection.

DANCING
By Eva Braun

I hated looking at the sky but could not help it. Munich was burning, and maybe my family and my villa were, too. I tried calling all the time. It was hard to get through from the Berghof. I hung up and stared at a glow so red.

"I've got to go," I said.

"No. I can't have you in the middle of an air raid."

"I've got to know."

"We'll find out. They're all right."

"What can we do?"

"I'll punish the British. I'm getting the weapons I need."

The skies were soon hot again, and the next day someone drove up to tell me one of my best friends was dead. I didn't ask the Fuehrer about this one. I just went. The funeral was really for the whole city.

"You can't imagine," I said.

"Don't ever go again."

"You need to see the suffering."

"I know about it."

"They need to see you."

"I work all the time for their suffering."

It was so hard to find happiness. We were all delighted when my sister Gretl said she was going to marry Hermann Fegelein, a suave SS officer. Ordinarily, I might not have wanted him for my sister. Too many women were talking. But that did not really matter now.

I called a fashion salon and ordered them to send everyone up right away to create the finest wedding dresses. Everything was going to be perfect. I told the Berghof staff it better be. The Fuehrer knew he had to cooperate this time. Even though he couldn't stay long, he let us use the Eagle's Nest high over the Berghof for the reception on June third, 1944. During a night of laughter and kisses, the band played beautifully for people relieved to dance here the first time since the war. I spun around this happy world until dawn, wishing things could always be this way.

George Thomas Clark

SACRED LAND
1944-1945

ATLANTIC WALL
By Field Marshal Erwin Rommel

The enemy was soon going to strike, probably somewhere on the Atlantic coast of France. Maybe that place would be Pas de Calais, the shortest point across the Channel from England. The Fuehrer had been urging me to also pay attention to Normandy. I was worried about many areas and demanded that millions of mines and obstacles be deployed. Overlooking all approaches, men with sharp eyes aligned our formidable guns of the Atlantic Wall.

The enemy had to be punished where most vulnerable. If he established a strong beachhead, he could overwhelm us. I told the Fuehrer we must position our main panzer forces near the beach, back ten miles or so, just out of range of the enemy's big naval guns. The Fuehrer, Guderian, and Rundstedt, who was in overall command in the West, clamored for a strategic reserve of panzers. For what? Those panzers would never get near any beach. The enemy held a thirty to one advantage in the air. That superiority made all our movement by land no better than perilous. I'd learned that in North Africa against odds far less overwhelming. Those with brains frozen in the East, where air to ground interdiction had not been decisive, still overruled me. I got only three of the seven panzer divisions available.

All that could be set aside a little while. Our reports of bad weather and dangerous tides indicated an invasion would not be possible for at least two weeks. On June fifth, 1944 I left by car for Germany to celebrate my wife's fiftieth birthday. Before that I planned to stop at the Berghof and urge the Fuehrer to send two more panzer divisions to the coast. I also had an even greater duty.

D-DAY
By An American Soldier

We're ready to go. Again. Get on the boats, they say. This is it. Be ready for fire. Out into the night we ride. We're always in the dark, going somewhere, trying to attack. This time I pray we really will. No more false starts, they say. We're riding toward a fight. That's what we've got to have. Don't say that. Not tonight. It's never tonight. Make up your minds. When? Tomorrow, maybe. Or in two weeks. It better be soon. Otherwise, this is going to kill us. Where are we going now? Is this really the night? The weather isn't so bad. This time we might. Maybe we can. I know we should. We're too far out not to. Everyone feels the same. No more nonsense. On June sixth we scramble into the assault boat. I'm scared as hell. But my pants aren't wet. Maybe it wouldn't have mattered. Nobody's saying much. I think I'm going to die. I pray I won't. I hope nobody dies. But the officers have said there'll be casualties. Of course there will. How could there not be? I wonder if I'll be one. That's how it is on the boat.

I want off. The beach horrifies me, but I know waves of bombers have pounded heavy German gun emplacements. Our naval guns have also bombarded the defenders for hours. That might have helped. It better have. I hear some boats around me get hit. Naturally they are. Right out in the open. That's where we are now, running toward the beach. This is insane. No one can survive. There's so much fire. I'm running like hell. Into an explosion I fall dead on the beach, waiting for God.

"Get the hell up," some guy screams.

I stagger onto feet I can't feel and run hard and low, one hand on top of my helmet, until I fall again. I haven't fallen. Another explosion has knocked me down on the beach. There's so much fire. All of it at us. The Germans are behind several feet of steel and cement. I wish I were a German.

"Get the hell up and move forward," someone screams.

DELIGHT
By Adolf Hitler

Hah. There it was: the landing right there at Normandy, just as I'd said. This was great news. No longer would I have to worry about the build-up in England. No more would I have to wait for the attack. Now the enemy was here.

My generals at the Berghof had been right not to wake me during the night. There was plenty of time to talk today. What a beautiful day.

I was being driven to Klessheim Castle in Austria to fortify the nerves of some timid Hungarians. On the way I explained our good fortune: "The Anglo-Americans can't fight us here. We'll bloody them on the beaches. Those few who survive will quit. They can't imagine what they're in for. They certainly aren't as tough as the Russians. I can hold out as long as I like."

At the castle I marched into the midday military conference and announced: "So, we're off." What an extraordinary relief this was. What a great day. The drive back was wonderful. So was my afternoon meal at the Berghof. Everyone was emboldened by me. It was a splendid march up to my teahouse. I always saw everything from there. What an incredible view. The enemy couldn't fool me. I wasn't going to commit too many reserves to Normandy. That had probably been a feint. Next he would launch his main assault. At Calais. Or perhaps in the Mediterranean, at Italy, because he had just taken Rome. I couldn't rule out the Balkans, either. I was looking everywhere.

BEACHHEAD
By General Max Pemsel

I understood Field Marshal Rommel's being away. He needed the rest. And he certainly hadn't known the attack was coming June sixth. When he found out early this morning, he started right back. It was a shame he couldn't fly, but that was much too dangerous for commanders and forbidden by the Fuehrer. The field marshal had to be driven. He got back to his headquarters by four p.m., and within an hour he called our Seventh Army headquarters near the front.

"Order the panzers to attack immediately, whether or not reinforcements arrive," he said.

"The Twenty-First Panzer Division has already attacked," I said.

"The Fuehrer wants the beachhead destroyed tonight, at the latest."

"That would be impossible," I said.

ALTERNATIVE
By Field Marshal Erwin Rommel

Hitler either didn't believe what was happening, or he didn't understand the implications. I was determined to explain matters face to face. So was Field Marshal Rundstedt. We repeatedly urged Hitler to meet us. Eventually, he agreed. I was not informed until three a.m. on June seventeenth. At nine o'clock that morning I arrived at headquarters northwest of Paris, near Soissons, where a cold man waited for us. After shaking hands Hitler sat on a stool. Pallid and bent, he looked like a cadaver.

"Mein Fuehrer," I said. "The enemy has poured several hundred thousand men into his beachhead the last ten days."

"That's outrageous," he said. "You generals have undermined me again. You've ruined everything. The Atlantic Wall should have been impenetrable. I need better commanders."

"You need to acknowledge the situation," I said, standing over the stool. Rundstedt was nearby. "The enemy has overwhelming superiority in the air."

"I'll soon wipe his planes from the skies with my new jets, the only operational jets in the history of the world."

"Even if this is possible, it won't diminish the enemy's vast superiority in manpower and ships and supplies. Our capabilities, by comparison, are very modest and completely inadequate."

"My V-1's are ready. Attacks have already started. London's going to be annihilated by flying bombs. Then Britain will beg for peace."

"If these flying bombs really are revolutionary, then they must be turned against the invasion beaches," I said. "If it's technically impossible to send them such a short distance, then they must be fired at the invasion ports in England."

"I expect that kind of small-mindedness from the military. Obviously, a miracle weapon can only be used for political purposes. That means attacking London."

At this moment, as usual, it was we who were being attacked, so we descended deep into Hitler's bombproof bunker. He spent far too much time inside, too well protected from the outside.

"Mein Fuehrer," I said, "Field Marshal Rundstedt supports me fully."

Rundstedt sternly nodded.

"I have the professional responsibility to tell you that our defenses in the West are certain to collapse," I said. "Furthermore, the Russians are continuing to advance in the East. Our defenses in Italy are also in trouble. And our cities and factories are every day hammered from the air. We're being destroyed, Mein Fuehrer. You must make peace."

"Don't concern yourself with the future of the war. Take care of your own invasion front."

After this Rundstedt and I were invited to dine with the Fuehrer. While he gobbled a horde of medications deployed around his plate, two SS officers tasted his food. When he saw they weren't going to die, the Fuehrer began to eat.

FLYING BOMBS
By Colonel Max Wachtel

I had been told the British knew who I was and what I was doing and that they were trying to kill me. Immediately I'd changed my name and started growing a beard. Then I changed my name again as my beard filled in. The British must have been too confused to find me. Unfortunately, they had figured out the precise locations of the one hundred V-1 launch sites I helped organize and build, and their bombs destroyed all but twenty. The British also blasted railways and roads leading to the launching areas. My superiors charged that I was slow and careless and threatened to court-martial me.

I had still been manifestly encouraged, a couple of weeks ago, as the first ten flying bombs were launched. My relief could not remain absolute, however, as three of them exploded immediately and one thudded nearby. Six flew off toward London. None of them got there, but a few did hit British soil and killed several people.

We rapidly improved our launching capabilities and within four days fired five hundred flying bombs. By late June the total shot to two thousand. Now we were getting much better results and killing people by the score and more. Results would get even better unless enemy advances forced us to abandon our launch pads.

FATE
By General George S. Patton

I can't believe those bastards. They'd kept me out of battle almost a year just because I tried to slap some fight into two goddamn yellow cowards who were crying about their nerves in the same hospital tents as brave soldiers with bad wounds. I suppose Eisenhower was glad to have me pigeonholed. Ike didn't understand warriors. He didn't have the stuff. Neither did General Omar Bradley. In Sicily he'd bolted in fear. All he could really do was wear glasses and talk profoundly while saying little. I guess Ike liked that. He'd put Bradley in charge of our forces that attacked Normandy.

I had to keep waiting. That was worse than a wound. What would I do if the damn war ended before I got there? My whole life had been lived for this. No one could lead men in battle like I could. I'd already proven that. I swore I would again as soon as my new Third Army was activated. I was training my men to kill every German they encountered. That required discipline and teamwork. The overpowering shine on my boots was a message. So was the pearl-handle pistol on my hip. I was ready to lead the best goddamn army in the history of warfare. I knew all about that. I hadn't used my wealth or my wife's to loaf. I only sailed and played polo when there was no one to fight. Most of the time I had studied great generals and prepared for war.

Now I was almost released to return to battle. I was going to France. Thank God for that. I was about dead in England. Maybe this adversity would help. Damn right it would. I was a fool and a coward to have doubted it. I knew my fate, and made final preparations in bed with a few society women. I wasn't kidding when I told my boys: "A man who does not screw will not fight."

THE ENEMY
By Colonel Claus von Stauffenberg

This was the opportunity for which I had prayed and striven. At last I was going to be able to get to him directly. The generals definitely weren't going to do anything. It was up to the colonels. It was up to me, the new chief of staff to General Fromm, who commanded the Replacement Army. This collection of the too old, the too young, and the feeble was the source our great Fuehrer now called on to stop the bleeding where his Wehrmacht was being ripped apart. Hitler, you see, was not merely the enemy of Germany's victims. He was the enemy of Germany. He was the enemy of the world.

I had not realized how wrong everything was until I traveled in occupied territories. The unimaginable developments there were not at all what those of us from aristocratic families had really desired. We had simply wanted the destruction of Versailles, and we'd wanted the Anschluss, and the Sudetenland if it had been absorbed in a proper way, and we'd been delighted by the quick conquests of our enemy neighbors, Poland and France. But we had not wanted Russia. We hadn't wanted anything in the East after a while. Nor did we want to keep fighting England and the United States and be bombed into a primitive state. We did not want anyone to suffer anymore.

We wanted to kill the man responsible. I was the only one who could do it, the only one with access. On July sixth at the Berghof I carried a bomb in my briefcase. Himmler was there, too. That was essential. I had to get them both. I was going to. I merely had to activate the bomb. But I could not do so in front of everyone. Where would I do it? And after I did it, where would Hitler be?

TRANSPORTS
By A German Soldier

"You're late," the officer said. "You're always late. All of you. We can't stop the Russians unless we get to critical points before they do."

"We can't do that, sir."

"Don't be defeatist."

"You should know, sir."
"I order you to speed things up."
"That's what we've been telling these horses to do."

THE ONLY ONE
By Colonel Claus von Stauffenberg

I was back at the Berghof on July eleventh and better prepared to activate the bomb. My practice had been decisive. It's not easy working without a right hand. The two outside fingers on my left hand were also gone, somewhere on the infernal terrain in North Africa. With my right eye, the only one remaining, I saw that Himmler was not present. General Beck and other high-ranking philosophers had insisted I get Hitler and Himmler at the same time. That seemed ridiculous now. Hitler was the only one who really mattered.

CHOICES
By Field Marshal Erwin Rommel

I had been meeting with my commanders at the front in France. Their assessments corresponded with my own. We could not prevent a major enemy breakthrough within two or three weeks. I also talked to my troops. These brave and determined men understood more directly than anyone what was developing, and many asked if new and decisive action could be expected. I felt them looking to me for something extraordinary. My commanders offered the same faith.

Now I was confident almost everyone would understand and follow me when I ordered our troops to withdraw from France and dig in behind our West Wall in Germany. After this great relief from bloodshed, the Anglo-Americans would surely stop bombing us and allow their new ally to gain strength before joining us to attack our most dangerous foe, the Soviet Union. The centerpiece of this plan was the arrest of Hitler. He should not be assassinated. That would get him eternal sympathy. Instead, he needed to be put on trial in Germany and tried and convicted by Germans.

OPERATION VALKYRIE
By Colonel Claus von Stauffenberg

At the Wolf's Lair on July fifteenth, I was ready. This time I was going to use the bomb. It was in my briefcase on the ground. I was waiting for Hitler in front of the briefing hut. I would have preferred his bunker. It was strong and deep and assured total destruction from an internal blast. But the briefing hut, covered with concrete except for some windows, would be an adequate coffin.

I needed to activate the bomb. I already would have but hadn't known when Hitler was coming. My briefcase was still on the ground when he arrived and shook my left hand. Numerous officers accompanied us inside. The conference lasted about a half-hour. There were going to be more conferences. I didn't know when. I called Berlin. The generals wanted to talk. This was the longest conversation I'd ever had. They still wanted to get Himmler, too. Well, he wasn't here, and I didn't care about him anymore and was tired of talking. I knew General Olbricht, second in command of the Replacement Army, had already ordered troops to march in Berlin. They'd follow us once Hitler was dead. He was close to that. I simply had to activate the bomb less than ten minutes before we met again. I just did not know when that would be.

FALLEN WARRIOR
By Adolf Hitler

This was devastating. My greatest soldier had just been severely injured by fire from a diving enemy plane, and he might not live. He certainly couldn't command for me anymore. In addition to bullet wounds, he suffered a fractured skull. Thank God I had no longer been depending primarily on Rommel in the West. I already had a fresh new commander there, Field Marshal von Kluge. He had been inspired by spending a couple of weeks at my headquarters and was completely unburdened by the pessimism of Rommel and old man

Rundstedt, who Kluge had replaced a couple of weeks ago.

THE NEXT TIME
By Colonel Claus von Stauffenberg

Some of the philosophers insinuated I hadn't really wanted to activate the bomb. The implication is they would have. That was a comfortable position since they could never get near the flash point. I knew my convictions. They were stronger than anyone else's. I was destined. After I killed Hitler in two days, on July twentieth, I'd need to get out of the Wolf's Lair and back to Berlin to orchestrate the coup. We had a lot of support. But not all of it could be activated as early as on July fifteenth. Fromm and Keitel had roared at General Olbricht for marching the troops. He saved us by explaining it had just been an exercise. Valkyrie, after all, was the official code for mobilizing to protect the Reich from enemies within.

RECLAMATION
By General Georgi Zhukov

The corps and division commanders claimed their offensive was continuing very well. Fine. I'd take a look. Climbing toward the observation post in a tree, I placed my foot on a board that collapsed. From the ground I scrambled up and said, "You incompetent bastards. I'm relieving you of this corps. And you. You'll spend the rest of the war in a penal unit."

Later, when I visited General Batov, head of the Sixty-Fifth Army, he urged me to simply reprimand the officers.

"For the corps commander, all right," I said. "But that other idiot is never going to run another division. Too much is at stake. Don't you realize that? No. You're busy shaving and using cologne. Why the hell haven't you taken your objectives? Get out of here and forget about luxuries until you've done what I ordered."

I booted the stool next to Batov and stormed out, slamming the door. My commanders had to be tough, and they had to be fast. I knew what Stalin would think if other generals took their objectives before I did. All of us had to keep driving and destroying German armies and grabbing prisoners and taking now land the Germans had held before the war.

VALKYRIE AGAIN
By Colonel Claus von Stauffenberg

My adjutant was scrambling through his briefcase as I dug in mine. Gripping special pliers with my thumb and two fingers, I squeezed and broke the acid capsule. That activated the bomb in my briefcase.

"I need more room," I told Lieutenant von Haeften. "Help me get these papers out. Wait. Not all of them. I might need some. That's right. Now, get that one out of yours."

The door to the anteroom opened, and a major intruded: "Hurry up, please. Marshal Keitel doesn't want to be late for the Fuehrer."

"I'll be there soon enough."

The officious bastard insisted on gawking.

"Fine, Lieutenant von Haeften," I said. "I've got all the pertinent documents. You keep the rest."

The bomb in my briefcase was going to explode in less than ten minutes. The one in Haeften's briefcase should have been in mine, too. I prayed one would be enough and walked outside.

"Marshal Keitel," I said, "I'm sure the Fuehrer will be encouraged by the troops the Replacement Army can provide for the front."

"Please make sure he is. And, as I said, be brief. The Fuehrer needs time to prepare for Mussolini this afternoon."

Entering the briefing hut I walked to the telephone room and said to the sergeant: "I'm expecting an urgent call from Berlin. Please summon me immediately."

Keitel led me into the conference room. Hitler's back was to the door. He sat on a stool, slouching over a large wooden table covered with maps.

"Mein Fuehrer, this is Colonel von Stauffenberg, here to report on the Replacement Army," said Keitel.

Hitler turned and saluted me, then said, "We'll do that later. First I'll hear the rest of Heusinger's report."

I asked an officer, who had carried my briefcase the final steps, to please make a place for me near the Fuehrer so I could hear everything. News from the Eastern Front was devastating, and General Heusinger explained the details honestly. He was an empathetic man, but we had not been able to warn him about today.

I tried to pry through everyone right up to the table. It was too crowded, so I picked up my briefcase and reached between Heusinger, who was immediately to Hitler's right, and another officer, and placed it near the end of the table about six feet from Hitler. There couldn't be more then five minutes left. On such a hot day, maybe less.

"I must make a call," I told an officer. "It's urgent."

I eased out to the telephone room and put a phone to my ear. That was enough. I put the phone down and left the briefing hut and walked about two hundred yards over to the communications building where General Fellgiebel met me.

"You can do it?"

"As thoroughly as it can be," he said.

"Completely?"

"No. There're too many backups."

We looked at the briefing hut. That's where the problem was. It needed to be eliminated. Very soon now. Maybe in a minute. That's all we needed. The whole world would benefit. I tried not to stare. I imagined the sound, a thunderous call for liberation. That it was, so loud it blew the building apart, so strong it exhilarated me. The enemy was dead.

Alarms roared into barking dogs and yelling men, and smoke curled into the sky. I got in the back seat of my car with Haeften and ordered the driver to get going. At the first checkpoint they'd already lowered the barrier. I bounced out and demanded to use the phone. After a quick conversation I hung up and announced: "Herr Lieutenant, I am allowed to pass."

He raised the barrier. I had to get back. By now General Fellgiebel must have called our comrades in Berlin and started to isolate the Wolf's Lair. Operation Valkyrie had begun. Freedom was imminent. The barrier at the next checkpoint was already raised. Only one more barrier now. It was down.

"Raise this at once," I said.

"No," said the sergeant major. "There's a general alarm. No one is allowed to leave."

I shot out the back seat into the guard hut. On the phone to the camp commandant's aide I said, "General Fromm is waiting for me at the airfield. I must be allowed to pass."

He agreed.

"There, Sergeant Major. You heard. Let me through."

"I didn't hear anything, Colonel."

He made the call himself. Of course the result would be the same. The aide couldn't have changed his mind so rapidly. He couldn't have known anything yet. How could he? He told the sergeant major to let me go.

On the winding road we drove fast through a hot forest laden with mines and mosquitoes. By a quarter after one we were in our plane, flying to Berlin. I worried what was happening. There was no radio. I strained to feel the words of our broadcast. Hitler was dead. A new government was being proclaimed. The horrors were ending. All that I'd have to hear later. It was a long flight back to Berlin. We landed about a quarter after three. I phoned General Olbricht at the War Ministry.

"Everything is underway, General."

"Not yet," he said.

"General, you can't have wasted almost three hours."

"We're not sure."

"What?"

"Hitler might be alive."

"I guarantee he's dead. He can't be alive. Start Operation Valkyrie at once."

THE OTHER HAND
By Benito Mussolini

I was delighted to be visiting and wanted the train to get there right away. The Fuehrer needed to see me as much as I needed him. I remembered that. This was still a partnership. I was still the Duce. Hitler still respected me. Italians would learn. I too craved victory. I had sacrificed. The Fuehrer appreciated that I'd agreed to execute my traitorous son-in-law, Count Ciano. The Fuehrer and I always agreed, even about his need for Italian labor in Germany. Anything that helped

Germany was bound to help me.

Happily I stepped onto the platform. There the Fuehrer was, in a cape, smiling for me. But he only offered a limp left hand. Maybe that was a slight. I still smiled and moved to greet others. Soon I learned. I shouldn't have doubted the Fuehrer. His right hand was in a sling. He told me why. Then we drove to the briefing hut. It was destroyed.

"The bomb went off right in front of my feet," said the Fuehrer. "Many of my colleagues were severely injured. One poor officer was blown through the window. He's dead. A few others are dying. And here. Look at the pants I was wearing. They're shredded. Who else could have survived? But I'm virtually unhurt. This has been another miraculous escape. I've had so many in my career. Today is a climax. Now I'm more than ever convinced that Providence will bring my great cause to a good end."

"No one looking at this room can deny that heaven is holding its protective hand over you," I said. "Our position may be bad, almost desperate, but today gives me courage to believe it's inconceivable our cause will suffer from misfortune."

In a little while Hitler and I were gathered with his principal advisers.

"The Army is infested with cowards and traitors, Mein Fuehrer," said Admiral Doenitz.

"Absolutely, it is," said Goering.

"It's outrageous for you to talk about traitors," Doenitz said. "The Luftwaffe's failures are as bad as treason."

Ribbentrop smirked.

Goering brandished his baton and said, "Shut your mouth, you wretched champagne salesman. Or else."

"My name is von Ribbentrop, and I'm still the Foreign Minister."

I was rather embarrassed. I would never have tolerated such insolence in front of a visiting chief of state. If he hadn't been so tired, the Fuehrer wouldn't have, either.

"This treachery is worse than Roehm's in 1934," someone said.

The Fuehrer pounced up and shouted, "It absolutely is. In war it's much worse. I'll destroy the traitors. I'll exterminate every one of them in the most ignominious ways. I'll put their wives and children in concentration camps."

The Fuehrer continued until he exhausted himself and slumped back into his seat. Reaching over, I put my hand on his arm and smiled.

ACTION BERLIN
By Colonel Claus von Stauffenberg

At the War Ministry I talked to General Olbricht and his chief of staff, Colonel von Merz. Then Olbricht and I marched into General Fromm's office.

"Stauffenberg is positive Hitler's dead," said Olbricht.

"That's impossible. Keitel assured me the Fuehrer is fine."

"Keitel's lying, as usual," I said. "I saw Hitler's body being carried out."

"What matters now is we've already issued orders for Operation Valkyrie," Olbricht said.

"What do you mean 'We?'" said Fromm, erupting to his feet. "That's insubordination. That's treason. The penalty for that is death."

"General," I said, "you've always been ready to join the right side. Now that's us. This coup is Germany's greatest chance."

"I recommend you shoot yourself at once," said Fromm.

"Don't betray your people," I said.

"Both of you are under arrest."

"You're deceiving yourself," said Olbricht. "We're arresting you."

VERIFICATION
By Joseph Goebbels

What appalling ineptitude. These idiots hadn't even cut off my phone or occupied radio transmission facilities. They must have made other critical errors. Not many people would consider joining this group. Fewer still would actually do so. I also doubted the resolve of troops now marching on Berlin from several directions.

"My orders are to cordon off government buildings," said Major Otto Remer, pistol in hand. "The SS is staging a Putsch."

"You've taken a sacred oath to the Fuehrer."

"The Fuehrer's dead."

"Nonsense. I just spoke to him."

The young man didn't believe that. Staring at him, I gripped the phone and pulled it to my ear and ordered a most urgent call.

"Mein Fuehrer, I'm here with Major Remer, commander of the guard battalion."

I handed the phone to Remer.

"Jawohl, Mein Fuehrer, of course I recognize your voice."

Remer clicked his heels and shot to attention.

"Jawohl, Mein Fuehrer.

"Jawohl.

"Jawohl.

"Jawohl, Mein Fuehrer."

Remer hung up.

"The Fuehrer's made me a colonel and ordered me to use brutal force to secure the government."

SACRED LAND
By Colonel Claus von Stauffenberg

My wounded left arm, bleeding dark through the sleeve of my uniform, did not really hurt. The real pain was much worse as I stared at General Fromm. He had been freed by gun-firing colonels who just determined they better remain Nazis.

"In the name of the Fuehrer," said Fromm, "a court martial convened by me has pronounced sentence: Colonel von Merz, General Olbricht, the colonel whose name I won't mention, and Lieutenant von Haeften are condemned to death."

"General, I'm the only one responsible," I said. "I was the commanding officer. These soldiers obeyed my orders."

Fromm stepped from the doorway that led to the courtyard. Moving in silence I thought about General Beck, who shot himself a few minutes ago. As Chief of the General Staff in the late 1930's, he had been the highest ranking and most eloquent foe of Hitler. Now it was much too late for everyone but the enemy. Somehow it never seemed to be too late for him.

Several cars in the courtyard aimed their headlights at a pile of dirt. I was thankful my wife could not see this. She and our three children and the one to come would learn soon enough. Just before the salvo I shouted: "Long live our sacred Germany."

THE RADIO
By A German Boy

This was a special night. My parents said it was really morning since it was past midnight. I didn't get to stay up so late unless we were being bombed. And I never got to listen to the radio. My parents said it was dangerous. But tonight it was different. The Fuehrer had an incredible message. The worst criminals in history had planted a bomb to try to kill him. I'm not surprised it didn't work. Nothing could hurt the Fuehrer. He was working all the time to make sure we weren't stabbed in the back again, like in 1918. Now the Fuehrer was really angry and going to take care of these miserable creatures who tried to stop his work for Germany.

THE EAR
By Dr. Theodore Morell

Blood had been oozing from his right ear — the one that faced the blast — and he hurt so much I felt obligated to summon a specialist, Dr. Erwin Giesing, who told me the Fuehrer's eardrum was broken and he had some deafness. I already knew that. He couldn't hear much of what was said.

"I think the Fuehrer's also showing signs of senility," said the specialist.

"That's absurd. He's in marvelous shape. My ministrations help him work incredibly hard."

"Too hard, I think. Look at his bloodshot eyes. His skin's also much too pale. He can't even stand up straight."

"He'll be better soon."

"At least his ear will. I'm going to cauterize it."

"That's not the treatment I recommended."

"The Fuehrer's already agreed to it."

"Don't ever examine the Fuehrer without reporting to me first."

"I'm an officer. I report to my superior, not civilians."

"You better not do anything to undermine the Fuehrer's health," I said.

MY ONLY
By Adolf Hitler

While so many were making me miserable, here was my sweet little one, Eva, far away in body but so very close in soul. Whether she was sobbing through the phone or writing with passion, her message was always sublime: "I'm half dead because my whole life is loving you."

COURT OF HONOR
By General Heinz Guderian

I did not want to serve on the Court of Honor. As the new Chief of the General Staff, I did not have time. I needed every moment to concentrate on stopping enemies grinding in from the East. Not only that, I considered it repulsive to decide whether brother officers should be expelled from the Wehrmacht, and thus made immediately available for civilian justice through the People's Court. I tried to altogether avoid this painful duty, but Hitler demanded I occasionally attend.

There was no doubt, of course, that a relatively small group of officers were traitors of the most outrageous sort. They had tried to kill the commander in chief, who enjoyed the full faith and confidence of his people, at the time of greatest danger in the nation's history. That is treason. Those responsible had to be punished. The Fuehrer wanted this done quickly. We listened to and examined the Gestapo's reports. The accused could not comment. There would not have been much point anyway. Documentation was overwhelming against most of those we removed from the Wehrmacht and sent to the People's Court. These men, I should add, were not merely traitors. They were bunglers who never had much support. Most troops marching on July twentieth hadn't known why, or they wouldn't have.

My duty was to protect the Fatherland from more disloyalty and danger. To that effect I ordered all General Staff officers to not merely behave as ardent National Socialists but also to vigorously indoctrinate young commanders in accordance with the political tenets of the Fuehrer. Anyone unable to comply was told to apply for removal from the General Staff. I received no such applications.

HARD QUESTIONS
By A Conspirator

"I suppose you know," said the interrogator. "Oh, how could you, in here? So I'll tell you. I'm sure you'll want to know. We've arrested your wife. And your mother. We tried to arrest your father, too, but he's long dead. Lucky man. Not your brother. We got him. We had to take three of your uncles, too. And their wives. Bad people. All of you. Too many loudmouths. Too many traitors. It's in your blood. Your children would be just the same. We've got them, too. We're going to terminate this bloodline entirely, if necessary.

"How are you feeling? The bread's all right, I hope. Here, have some more water."

He threw it in my face, along with the cup.

"You look tired. What's the matter? The bed too hard? You should still be able to sleep. You certainly can't gripe about too much light. You'll sleep well tonight. Stand up."

I barely could.

"Don't move. At all. I'll be back after awhile."

In minutes, hours, an eternity, my knees buckled. A guard raced in and began beating my back with a bamboo cane.

"Stop," said the interrogator. "You didn't hit him twenty times, did you? You know regulations require a doctor for that many or more."

"I only hit him seventeen times."

"Good. I think he's almost ready. Tie his hands behind his back. And make sure the spikes go into each fingertip.

"There. How's that? Feel like identifying some traitors? Who helped you?"

"I worked alone."

"Turn the screw. Dig those spikes in.

"Who helped you?"

I didn't respond. I only whimpered. I couldn't help that.

They pushed me back onto something like a bed frame and put my legs in tubes with spikes. Then they shoved my head into a metal hood and threw a towel over my face.

"We know you had help. Who was it?"

"Tighten the spikes in his legs.

"Who helped you?"

He lifted the towel

"Stop this, God, please, stop this," I said.

He put the towel back over my face.

"Hit him with the bamboo cane. No. Harder. Here, give me that."

As spikes stabbed further into my legs, the interrogator ripped the cane into my torso. Inside the metal hood I barely heard my screams. Under the heavy towel I could hardly breathe.

"Who helped you?"

He removed the towel.

"Throw some water on him. He looks a little weak. Better get him up. Put that truss on him. Make sure he's bent over. Tighten it up. I don't want him moving."

Every time he clubbed me from behind I fell straight onto my face. That's the last I knew until I awoke in my cell, having a heart attack.

"Make sure you save him, Herr Doktor," said the interrogator, "he's going to help us a lot."

PEOPLE'S COURT
By A Spectator

Like many in the audience at the People's Court, I was wearing my uniform. It was important we look good. We'd heard the first trial was being filmed. I'll bet the People's Judge, Roland Freisler, was enthused about that. He had incredible authority and looked stunning up there in his bright red robe.

The eight traitors couldn't wear their uniforms or even their civilian clothes. Instead, tattered garments hung from them, and they looked pathetic tugging to hold up belt-less pants.

"Why didn't you support National Socialism and the Fuehrer?" Freisler asked one of the traitors.

"Well, there were the murders in Poland…"

"Murders," Freisler screamed, "you filthy swine are the killers. You're the vilest, most despicable garbage in history."

That silenced the traitor. Freisler later asked another: "Didn't you care about your crimes endangering the Fatherland?"

"That was the point. We were determined to stop the Fuehrer from hurting Germany anymore. In world history, he's the great perpetrator of evil. There are…"

"Shut your shit-infested mouth. The Fuehrer is the greatest German in history, perhaps the greatest man ever. You'll soon be in hell."

Field Marshal von Witzleben, slated to be the traitors' new commander of the Wehrmacht, was a wretched, toothless old man who didn't deserve to have his false teeth. Freisler shook his fists at him and yelled, "You, as a field marshal, owed everything to the Fuehrer, who promoted you, and to the country depending on you. You're an absolute stinking piece of slime. You'll rot the rope that hangs you."

"You can hand us over to the executioners," Witzleben said, "but in three months this outraged and suffering people will call you to account and drag you alive through the mud of the streets."

"Your death is going to be brutal," said Freisler.

"That's right," proclaimed Witzleben's defense attorney, standing up. "My client is a murderer, completely guilty, and deserves the worst punishment."

On the second day of the trial, August eighth, Freisler sentenced all eight traitors to die immediately. Speed was important because there were going to be a lot more trials.

ON THE SCREEN
By Adolf Hitler

The film was rushed to the Wolf's Lair the day it was shot. I knew it was going to be good. Everything had been specified by me. A girder was erected across the room a little below the ceiling. Eight meat hooks hung from the girder. The hooks definitely weren't going to be filled all at once. I wanted to savor this film.

There it was. The first traitor was led out and stood on a chair, and piano wire from the hook was wound around his neck. Then, as I insisted, he was lowered very slowly so he wouldn't drop and break his neck. No reprieves. The traitor grimaced and gagged and clawed at his neck and kicked his feet like a hooked fish jerking its tail. It took him a long time to quit writhing. Fine. Draw the curtain around that one and bring out the next. Then do the same thing. Be careful letting him down. That's it. Well done. All eight died just right, slowly and wiggling so hard their pants fell off, leaving naked fish hanging hot and then cold in the special room where justice was done.

SEAL IT
By General George S. Patton

West and south and east my men moved through France, ripping the guts out of the Germans, who could not have understood. I loved danger. It sharpened my intuition and revealed the most essential opportunities. I did not need a damn Ultra decoder supposedly intercepting enemy communications. Still, I agreed to talk to my worried adviser. His Ultra intercepts said the Germans were preparing to counterattack. That seemed ridiculous. I assumed they were retreating. In case they were not, I decided to redeploy a division. When the Germans did counterattack, they gained a little but we smashed their faces and forced them back into a pocket on fire. The only opening was between Argentan in the south, where we were coming from, and Falaise in the north, where the British were moving slowly. General Montgomery was so cautious he should have been sacked. What an insipid bastard. Thousands of Germans were being captured, but thousands were getting away. I demanded to charge up there and seal the goddamn pocket.

"You can't," said my order. "You might collide with the British."

"Let me go on to Falaise and we'll drive the British back into the sea for another Dunkirk."

ACCOMMODATION
By A Frenchman

You must imagine. Next to us had been a beast long determined to devour us. In 1940 he did that as much as he pleased. Anyone who resisted was killed. We did not want countless dead heroes under cities destroyed. Instead, we cooperated enough to survive. Now, while Paris stood, the beast was staggering, and we were hitting him, too. Some of us always had.

STIMULATION
By Adolf Hitler

Sinus pain cut through my head during August 1944 nightmares. In the East, Russian barbarians were chewing closer. Polish partisans attacked our garrison in Warsaw and behaved like heathens. Turkey broke off diplomatic relations. Bulgaria also turned on us. So did Finland. And Rumania declared war. In the West, Paris was captured. And that fat ass in charge of the Luftwaffe claimed he was too sick to come to conferences.

"If you can't get me some relief, I won't be able to resolve matters," I told my ear, nose and throat specialist.

"All right," said Dr. Giesing. "But we must be extremely careful. The mucous membrane absorbs this medication very rapidly. Overdosing is always a danger."

There were far greater dangers aplenty. I was not afraid. Dr. Giesing daubed my nose every other day. After the second treatment I said, "Herr Doktor, perhaps we should do this daily, or even twice a day. I don't even care about my stomach pains from last night. Or the insomnia. I don't think I'm trembling as much, either. I've never been so light headed and happy. It's as though I'm not ill at all anymore. I'm thinking so clearly. The Reich has a great future. Our architecture's going to be extraordinary, I guarantee you. It'll be entirely unapproached, even by the ancient Egyptians. Our art will also be incomparable. Everything's going to be magnificent. I simply need to survive another two or three years so I can pass on my work to someone else. You aren't making me into a coke addict, are you, Herr Doktor?"

NEW JOB
By A Russian Prisoner

To a man who could have sliced his hands on protruding bones, they offered more food. And I accepted. The new job did not make me feel comfortable. Believe that. The guns were pointed straight up at the sky, and I would like to have pulled them down and aimed at Germans. But that was impossible. We were guarded by very suspicious armed men who demanded quite specific prompt actions, or no more food.

We fired at the sky when the planes came. Lots of the guards thought this was very funny. They were especially amused whenever we actually hit our Russian planes.

PRODUCTION
By Albert Speer

No one should have suspected me. Conspiratorial documents that slated me to continue as Armaments Minister in the new regime were irrelevant. I had not been asked. The documents made it clear. I knew nothing. And I certainly would not have approved of killing the Fuehrer.

I was committed to production. Without it we would be overrun. I worked all the time. Despite being mercilessly bombed, our factories increased their output. We repaired damage as rapidly and creatively as possible, and we dispersed industry and recruited hundreds of thousands of foreign workers. I requested they be fed and housed humanely. I had also wanted a couple of million women working in our factories, but the Fuehrer only allowed a small part of that.

More vigorous measures were urgent. The Fuehrer decided to draft males as young as fifteen and as old as sixty. He also decreed: "Not a stalk of German wheat is to feed the enemy, not a German mouth to give him information, not a German hand to offer him help. He is to find every footbridge destroyed, every road blocked — nothing but death, annihilation and hatred will meet him."

Demolition of industry fell under my authority as Armaments Minister. The Fuehrer's order to destroy everything of economic significance was perhaps not what he really meant. In my orders, which went through supreme headquarters, I insisted that our evacuations in the West must not be preceded by the thorough destruction of factories. We would soon need them again. I emphasized that the Fuehrer himself had declared: "We will soon recapture territories now lost."

I was delighted my directive was approved, and only slightly amended to read: "Recapture of a part of the territories now lost in the West is by no means out of the question."

PETROL
By General George S. Patton

Oh Christ, that little bastard fucked things up. My Third Army was a hundred miles ahead of everyone else and ready to blow through the Siegfried Line. But Montgomery whined so loudly for the bulk of supplies that I had to slow down. I didn't have enough gas. Monty called it petrol. He liked prissy names. He needed a kick in the ass to get moving.

By now the Hun had time to recover all along his Western Front, and we became defensive. I took care of my men and made sure they had hot showers, clean clothes and good food. This lull was still a horror for me. My stomach always killed me when I wasn't killing Germans.

SCIENTIFIC CARE
By Dr. Theodore Morell

The Fuehrer, long working very hard and barely sleeping, was too groggy to concentrate but too angry to sleep.

"Morell, do something right now," he said.

I responded with a shot that made him very awake and happy as he grasped my hands and said, "I'm amazed, Morell. From desperation to this."

He was so thankful to have me forever on call. At headquarters he often bragged about my novel treatments and emphasized I was a pioneer whose research in bacteria he'd be delighted to finance.

Most of my colleagues were jealous. The unscrupulous Dr. Giesing stole some of the Fuehrer's anti-gas pills and sent them to a laboratory. Then Giesing and two other doctors tried to convince the Fuehrer that I was intentionally poisoning him with strychnine, or at least was incompetent in prescribing the medication, on which they blamed all of his ills. Those charges were ridiculous. First, many of the Fuehrer's digestive problems predated by years the beginning of my care of him in 1936. Second, I had not even prescribed those pills. The Fuehrer was taking them on his own, in far less-than-toxic amounts.

"What is this stupid bunch after?" the Fuehrer said.

"They want my job."

"I've told them you're my doctor. And I'll tell them again when I dismiss them."

"Will you please state your confidence in writing, Mein Fuehrer, in case anything happens?"

THE FINAL SHIFT
By A Sonderkommando

I hate that chimney. It is huge and square and the most hideous thing in the world. It is worse than a nightmare. It is real day and night, blowing out smoke that destroys every breath. No one gets it like the men of the Sonderkommando. That is why they call us the living dead. We're dying even as we live and work, and we all know doom is certain and almost here. It is October. We've been serving the devil since June. That's all he allows. Every one of the previous eleven Sonderkommandos has perished at this point, and without a fight.

This Sonderkommando is not going to wait. In the haunted rooms where people undress, in the unspeakable chambers of death, in the hellish holes by the ovens, we have been thinking. We have been planning. We're going to attack. Partisans have recently slipped in several machine guns and twenty grenades and some boxes of explosives. We must strike tonight because we get word they plan to eliminate us tomorrow or the next day, at the latest.

It is hard to think about work today. We're concentrating on details. Each of the four crematories is to relay the signal by flashlight. Then all seven hundred of us will attack. We have a good chance. There is already a hole in the electrified fence. If we get through we can make it to the Vistula River a mile away and get across its low water and then run only five more miles to the dense forests where they won't find us and we can be free. We just have to execute the plan. We need to take some SS hostage. We can eliminate them after they've served us. On the outside we might also meet some partisans. All possibilities are promising early in the afternoon of the long wait for tonight.

Suddenly our walls tremble. We've heard an explosion. It is so loud I feel one of the three other crematories must be destroyed. Machine gun fire erupts. Our comrades are fighting. We stop working and gather to discuss.

An SS guard marches in and says, "No one told you to quit. Get back to the ovens. Who's responsible for this?"

"You're responsible," says our work boss.

With his official cane the guard smashes the boss' head. He staggers, splattering blood, but snaps down to grab a knife from his boot, and lunges to drive it into a Nazi heart. A comrade and I pounce on the collapsing guard, pick him up and ram him head first into an oven. As the door is closing, another SS rushes in.

"Whose boot is that, whose boot is that?" he shouts.

A fist from the crowd busts his chin. Two comrades pick the guard up and shove him into the same oven, and we dash to grab our crematory's hidden share of guns and explosives. Lots of SS are coming now. We hurl some bottle bombs and grenades. Several SS go down. But most are firing at us. We take cover and watch them gather. Then, screaming and shooting, they attack. We try to repel them. We fire everything we have. But bullets are coming at us from so many places. We don't have any cover. We don't have anything.

IMMEDIATE DUTY
By A Jew

Yes sir. I volunteer. Of course I do. I'm ready. Lots of us are. We gather bodies from three crematories and haul them to a fourth. There we are told how to make sure the ovens are very hot, and after that we start heavy lifting. It is unpleasant work but much better than the fire right now.

THE DESERT FOX
By General Wilhelm Burgdorf

Naturally, all lines of communication had been cut between Rommel's home in East Prussia and his troops in the West. Furthermore, SS units and armored cars surrounded his estate on October fourteenth. That day General Ernst Maisel and I were driven out to talk to the field marshal. He invited us into his study.

"I'm not in condition to command, if that's really why you're here," he said.

"Your injuries are severe, indeed, Marshal Rommel," said Maisel. "The fractures in your skull could still be fatal. We don't want you to be foolish."

"Please look at this," I said.

Rommel read the document. It provided information obtained during interrogations.

"You're thoroughly implicated," I said.

"I didn't do anything. I was in the hospital at the time."

"You can't deny what you were planning," I said.

"I'm prepared to explain."

"That would be foolish," said Maisel.

"I'm not afraid of the People's Court, despite its methods."

"You aren't the only consideration, Marshal Rommel," I said.

"There's your family. And your place in history. If you cooperate, you'll receive a state funeral, and your wife'll get a pension. The Fuehrer guarantees that."

Rommel stood frozen a long time. Then he said, "All right. Let me talk to my wife and son."

In a few minutes the great field marshal and I were riding in the back seat. Maisel rode in front with the driver. Down the road a bit I said to pull over. Maisel and the driver went for a walk.

"Here it is, Marshal Rommel."

Clutching his field marshal's baton, staring straight ahead, he put the vial in his mouth and bit. Very soon he slumped.

I got out and shouted, "Hurry, we've got to get to the hospital."

THE SPOKEN WORD
By Adolf Hitler

This new crisis was unbearably grim and by far my most dangerous. If it could not be successfully resolved, we would be defenseless, and our enslavement assured. Everything hinged on the survival of my voice. It had been hoarse and was getting worse. With this polyp I could only whisper. That was especially troublesome in regard to my commanders in the West. I had to speak to them in the usual way, and I had to do so in person, or my new plan could not succeed.

I did not want to leave the Wolf's Lair. I knew I'd be back, though, and ordered all improvements completed. The Russians would not be approaching here after my stroke in the West freed troops to hurl back to the East. I was going West to get ready. We boarded my special train. All the blinds were down and stayed that way. I did not want to be upset. My secretaries were very friendly as I relaxed with them on the train. I just could not talk much. Gazing down at the white tablecloth, I was engrossed in the survival of the world.

We arrived in Berlin while it was still dark. I'd made sure of that. The next day I had surgery. Dr. von Eicken removed the polyp, then sent it for tests. That night I coughed up blood. There was plenty of medication to help. In a day or two I felt pretty good. I visited my secretaries and walked a bit. But no matter where I went, the polyp was there. It might be malignant. Under this pressure it probably was. Four days after surgery an aide told me: "Dr. von Eicken called."

"I want to know exactly what he said."

"He said to tell you everything is satisfactory. All you have is a singer's nodule."

My appetite increased immediately. I'd never eaten so much. Everything was great. Already I was stronger. I started walking about an hour a day. People began looking at me properly again. By December 1944 I wasn't a sick old man. I was the Fuehrer ready to charge West and turn everything around.

FAITH
By Heinrich Himmler

I had started believing in miracles again. The Fuehrer was the greatest genius of all time and the only one who could lead us to victory. I was overwhelmed when he told me I was the second most essential person in the Reich and that he had huge expectations for my new Army Group Upper Rhine in the West. I rapidly recruited a half million men and inspired fanaticism to compensate for lack of training. Everyone must believe in victory. Anyone who deserted was hung from a tree with a sign around his neck. That was only part of my big plan to transform every German house into a fortress and every person into a deadly partisan.

ROCKET BOMBS
By Hans Kammler

My urgent order straight from the Fuehrer had been to start firing his V-2 rocket bombs. They soared fifty miles high before searing down in supersonic booms on London, for revenge, and on the Belgian port of Antwerp, to disrupt the buildup against us. When Belgian civilians died during air raids on our launch sites in The Hague, that was too bad. The Belgians needed to appreciate the camouflage a city provides. Did they really expect me to make our launch pads easy to see? We were visible enough anyway, carting the big rockets other places in convoys of seven trucks. We set up quickly and fired. Then we packed up and moved. We had lots of launch sites. I'd gotten V-2 production increased. That was essential. In recent months we'd hurled four hundred rockets at London and twice that at Antwerp. I knew they were hitting something. Otherwise the enemy wouldn't have intensified attempts to bomb us.

SITTING
By General George S. Patton

I hated sitting so much I'd thanked God a few weeks ago for the order to attack. Steady rain screwed up everything, though, and the mud got so bad it was like four inches of liquid shit. We couldn't operate as mobile warriors in that. Instead, slopping around in misery, we got about thirty-five miles and lots of casualties. In my Third Army sector the Rhine still lay at least sixty miles to the east. To my north a corps of the First Army was static, and helping train new soldiers and rest old ones. That disturbed me. Sitting on your ass near the front invites getting hit.

CARE
By Eva Braun

I was so happy to see the Fuehrer again but very worried how he looked. Whenever he was away bad things happened. I tried to help him understand. We should always be together. In the Chancellery we could. The private quarters survived in the center of destruction. Lots of furnishings were gone, and many things didn't work, but this was his home, our home, in Berlin.

"You mustn't go back to the front," I told him.

"I have to."

"You can command just as well from here."

"My generals won't follow orders anymore unless they see me."

"I don't care. Your health is more important."

"You're the only one who'd say that. You're the only one who cares."

BUS RIDE
By A German General

All of us were generals. Most commanded divisions in the West. Somewhere on a snowy night in December 1944 we were riding a bus.

"The guy's taking us in circles," I said.

"We haven't been going anywhere for weeks," said the general next to me.

"We must be headed somewhere soon."

When we got there it was colder and darker. Two lines of SS were waiting.

"You must give us your pistols at this time," one said.

"Don't be insolent," said a general.

"Herr General, your pistol must be relinquished now. And your briefcase. No pistols or briefcases are allowed."

We surrendered our professional tools then descended into a bunker. This compound was familiar. I was almost sure it was Hitler's old headquarters in western Germany, near Belgium. The bunker was new.

"The Fuehrer will see you shortly," said an SS. "Please sit down."

We sat at tables, higher-ranking officers closest to where Hitler would be. I was near the back. A grim SS stood behind each of us. I wondered what was up. For weeks our radio traffic had been confusing. Maybe the enemy couldn't figure it out either. I was anxious for the Fuehrer to clarify everything. As he entered, we sprang to attention, and the SS on the other side tensed. I assume the man behind me reacted the same. We generals sat down. The Fuehrer glanced at notes held in trembling hands.

"You will soon undertake the most important and decisive military campaign in history," he said. "It is therefore vital to force our enemies to understand they cannot continue to coexist as a fighting force. Never has there been a coalition of such conflicted and mutually hostile nations. The communists seek to dominate the Balkans, the Mediterranean and the Persian Gulf. Those aims can only bring them into a collision with the capitalist British, who want to maintain their empire. The colonials from the other side of the Atlantic are greedily waiting for all European powers to destroy each other so they can consume the British Empire."

I needed to blow my nose and reached for my pants pockets. The SS opposite me tensed. I stopped my hand and put it back on the table.

"This alliance must collapse, and it will if Germany never shows any weakness. Then we will see a repeat of what happened to Frederick the Great in his fifth year of war, the time of greatest despair. His generals and ministers, even his brother, were begging him to end a war that could not be won. But he would not quit. The steadfastness of that one man sustained everyone two years until the alliance against him collapsed. Gentlemen, it is now our historical duty to force a similar dissolution.

"As in 1940, we will tear a hole where no one anticipates — through the Ardennes. Then our fast moving panzers will charge over initially light opposition and move on to Liege, then to a key Channel port, in this case Antwerp. By doing so we will encircle four enemy armies, divide the American and British forces, and throw them into irrevocable discord. With that opposition weakened, we will rapidly redeploy forces in the East to crush the Russians. All of our enemies must be beaten now or never. Thus lives Germany."

Sniffling after the Fuehrer left, I confidently reached for my pants pocket.

MALMEDY
By An American Soldier

I felt like kicking some commanders in the ass. They'd been telling us this couldn't happen. The Germans didn't have enough troops or weapons to attack. Then who the hell were those waves of men shooting us and whose massive Tigers and Panthers were storming by? Idiots. Let them get in here and tell me why we're so lightly defended in this part of Belgium. The Germans had us at least five to one. So what if they didn't have many planes? Our air power couldn't be delivered through stifling clouds and fog.

The Germans overran and captured us near Malmedy. They were in a hurry. That was certain. They ordered us into a field frozen white. Then they — "No, we're unarmed," I yelled.

Machine guns ripped us into the snow, and Germans began squashing around in big boots. I heard a buddy groaning, then a shot, silence, more boots in the snow, some talk, probably about who was breathing, then another shot, and a groan over there, whack, a rifle butt to the head, like a bat to a melon. My blood was crawling along snow from my chest to nose. I tried to stay quiet. It was cold as hell. I tried to hold still. I tightened my arms and held my breath. I had to stop shivering. It was out of control. Whack.

FLUENCY
By A German Soldier

My mother spent her childhood in the United States. That was very helpful. I hadn't needed the English school as much as the other guys. They spoke English very well, though, and did not sound like the British. That was essential since we, and about forty other squads, were in American uniforms riding in American jeeps. We reviewed some of our American cultural lessons as we searched for assignments. There were plenty. We turned almost every sign we saw and cut lots of telephone lines. The Americans were terrified by our offensive and retreating in a disorganized way that clogged roads with vehicles. We were waiting to move again.

"What's the capital of Washington?" asked an American soldier.

"D.C.," I said.

"You guys get out."

"Don't slow us down," I said.

"Get out or I'll blow you out."

"You'll answer to General Eisenhower for this."

My two buddies said: "That's right."

He pointed his rifle. We scrambled out.

"How many home runs did Babe Ruth hit in 1927?" he said.

"What's the population of New York?" I countered.

"O.K., wise guy. This is the last question. What's the password?"

"Password."

"That ain't it. One more thing. You guys ever been blindfolded and tied to a stake?"

LEFT TURN
By General George S. Patton

The Germans were advancing so well they'd battered a bulge into our lines. That horrified some of the generals. It shouldn't have. The Germans could advance as far as they wanted. We should let the bastards go all the way to Paris then cut them off and chew them into another Stalingrad. Eisenhower, at least, liked my attitude. He said the German offensive was an opportunity for us and not a disaster.

"When can you attack?" Ike asked.

"In three days, with three divisions," I said.

I felt shudders in the room. These mediocre generals just assumed my army, south of the action facing east, could not be turned north and maneuvered sixty miles over unknown roads covered with winter treachery. The doubters didn't understand my men. I ordered them to get moving. We were heading toward the bulge and our surrounded comrades in Bastogne, where five main roads had to be held to slow the Germans.

This was what God had saved me for. For two days I pounced on the phones. Get those tanks rolling, I said. The tank destroyers need to be there too. I want that artillery started over there. Do it. We've also got to have the infantry. Wait until the roads clear a little. Then more artillery's got to be transported. Be careful with that stuff. Time it right. Just like that. Get our logistical people going. We need ammunition, engineers, medical people. Don't worry about the snow. Plow it away. Fill those roads. Time it right. Get up there. Drive like hell.

As promised, on December twenty-second, three divisions attacked toward Bastogne. My Christmas Day cards to the troops urged that we march in our might to complete victory and that God grant us better weather for battle. He did. And our planes began pulverizing Germans, big and visible on pretty white roads, and by the twenty-sixth some of my men reached Bastogne and forged a small corridor.

WILL
By Field Marshal Gerd von Rundstedt

I hadn't wanted to come back and command anymore. I hadn't wanted this offensive. And especially I hadn't wanted another meeting with him.

"Mein Fuehrer, we don't have enough reinforcements to sustain the attack," I said.

"We will sustain it."

"We lack ammunition."

"That's a lie. Who told you that?"

"Every commander is alarmed by his lack of ammunition, and of manpower. We also don't have enough fuel."

"More fuel is coming."

"We'll need it to withdraw, not attack."

"We shall continue to attack in the Ardennes, and north and south of there as well."

"Mein Fuehrer, that really is quite impossible."

"For a General Staff officer, evidently it is. That's why Himmler is leading Army Group Upper Rhine."

"He isn't trained in military operations."

"He has political training. He has the will. You don't understand the vital role of a man's will. Here. Look at this. I found this letter written by Frederick the Great during the Seven Years War. Right here he says: 'My generals are incompetent, my officers cannot lead, and my troops are wretched. All I have now is a pile of manure.'

"Yet Frederick won the war."

A DIFFERENT PLACE
By An SS Guard

No matter what it was, I drank it. All the guys were doing the same. There wasn't much else to do. I couldn't just sit and think. Our officers had already ordered one crematory destroyed. We all knew what that meant. On this New Year's Eve at Auschwitz, I rolled around smearing snow on my face.

CARDS
By General Heinz Guderian

Rebuffed twice in one week by Hitler, I left Belgium to tour key sites in the East. On January ninth, 1945 I returned to headquarters.

"The threat is critical," I said.

"We still have a chance to decisively weaken the enemy in the West," said Hitler.

"That opportunity has passed. The enemy holds too many vital positions. But the situation in the East is quite different. Industry there is working at full capacity. We have many productive areas the Russians are preparing to attack."

"The Russians are bluffing."

"Mein Fuehrer, General Gehlen of Foreign Armies East has prepared a very thorough intelligence report. The Russians have at least a five to one advantage in manpower, seven to one in panzers, twenty to one in guns, and twenty to one in planes. We must move our men and equipment to what is now the decisive theater."

"That report is completely idiotic. The man who prepared it should be in a lunatic asylum."

"I wouldn't have shown you the report unless I agreed with it. General Gehlen's work is absolutely dependable. If you send him to a lunatic asylum, then you better certify me as well."

"I want that man dismissed."

"Absolutely not. He's too perceptive. Perhaps you remember, he forecast the Russian counterstroke at Stalingrad. We must learn from our succession of setbacks. Right now we need to pull back in the East to shorten our lines of defense and avoid being cut off."

"It seems that for you generals operations mean nothing but a retreat to the next rearward position."

"If you'd like a new Chief of the General Staff, Mein Fuehrer, please say so."

"General Guderian, you're doing a fine job. Our reserves on the Eastern Front have never been so strong. I'd like to thank you for that."

"The Eastern Front is a house of cards," I said.

BERLIN
By Eva Braun

Dying at my home in Munich, I jumped up as the maid said, "The Fuehrer is on the phone."

"My sweet one, I'm back in Berlin," he said.

"Don't leave. Only bad things happen at those other places."

"I won't leave."

"Please let me come."

"If you'll be careful."

Right away I packed what I hadn't already, and told my driver to hurry.

In Berlin the Chancellery still stood, and the Fuehrer was in his second-floor apartment when I arrived.

"You're going to stay with me this time," I said.

"Of course."

"I'll take care of you. We won't part again."

"That's right."

"Do you promise?"

"Yes, I do."

IN ANOTHER HOME
By A Russian Soldier

After waiting too long at the front with a couple of million men, I craved the artillery roar that started the offensive, and right away we began tearing through the enemy and moving so fast I couldn't estimate bodies or miles. Soon, I heard Warsaw had fallen. That didn't matter to me. There was only one real target, and I wasn't going to wait anymore. I advanced harder each stride, ignoring all pain, and ultimately I saw it, distant in the night, and broke out running, running hard until I had really arrived, right where I had to be. My feet were hot and my heart on fire. I was in a town with real Germans — the ones without uniforms. The enemy had so many times seen real Russians. He'd seen my mother, everything about her, and my sister, too. In a black German night, blowing smoke hot into frigid air, I wanted everything any German ever saw.

That house looked great. Get over here, I motioned to the guys. We ran up to the front. A big family inside saw us at the window, then watched as we shattered the door. There was food on the table. I stuck my hand in and ate some. That would keep. Where are your watches? Where is your jewelry?

The father had a pathetic look. I rammed my rifle butt in his face. Then I shot his head on the floor. Kill those three boys, you idiots. We don't need them. Now, we have a mother and two nice German daughters. One screamed as I grabbed her, and I belted her face and ripped her dress as she fell. Then I dropped my pants and jumped on her. She was jerking around and cursing — I knew she was cursing me — so I slugged her a few times and tore off the rest of her dress. She tried to keep her legs crossed. I yanked them apart. She put them back together. I ripped off her underwear and pulled her legs apart again and got down on her and thrust and thrust but couldn't get in. Fucking bitch. I pulled up to take a look. There. I pushed in, and she screamed as I pounded and grunted. This was the best, a hot real German whore.

I pushed my buddy away. You wait. I want more. He pulled me off. He was ready now. O.K. I'll be back. Where's the liquor? I chugged right out of the bottle. The other sister was screaming just like mine. Where's the mother? Her shriek told me that. Her hands were nailed to the wall in another room. My buddy was ramming her standing up. Hurry up, I said. I drank some more. When he finished I walked to the mother. Want some more, from a real Russian man. Well, I don't want you, whore. Let's kill them, I said.

Leave some for our next guys. They'll be here in an hour or two.

O.K., I said. Let's get some new Germans before the others.

George Thomas Clark

PHYSICS
By Adolf Hitler

My own miracle weapons were in action. That proved I had not needed the frizzy Einsteins, and the bearded others, and the hook-nosed ones. They were doing Jewish physics, a horrible and useless thing.

IN THE COLUMN
By A Jew

People are saying Dr. Mengele has run away with all his research materials. I believe that. He hasn't come to the hospital for at least a week. He'd been watching us, wanting to see the precise effects of work by his doctors. They've subjected me to very unpleasant temperatures, and I have a tendency to tremble. The man on my right is blind. His brown eyes were injected with blue dye. The man on my left has no testicles. Originally, only one was cut off. The other later became so infected its removal was in no way experimental.

All three of us, and everyone else, are emaciated. That's why we're still at Auschwitz. We aren't strong enough to go with the rest of the prisoners. A few days ago, surrounded by SS, they were forced to start marching toward Germany. I've never been there and have no desire to go. I don't think many will make it anyway.

Here things are getting tougher. The Russian air raid on a nearby power plant knocked us into darkness and cut off all food and water. German explosions even closer probably destroyed the rest of the crematories. Now the SS are prodding us into columns of frozen humanity. I guess we're going to get bullets. I decide that's fine. Why are they waiting? Why do they look so worried? For them this is an easy job. Just a few thousand victims, and all of us so weak and unarmed. They've handled bigger jobs many times. I wish they'd hurry up. I'm ready. Bring your bullets, swine. Don't turn away from me. Where the hell are you going? Get back here. I want to look at you one more time. I want to spit in your wretched face.

548

OUR CASTLE
By Helga Goebbels

For a long time my four sisters and my brother and I had been staying in Castle Lanke. That's what people called this place, but I've seen castles and ours really wasn't. It was two very nice houses, one on each side of a pretty lake. Big, sweet-smelling pines rose all around, and we often ran and played in the forest. Today everything was especially fun because we knew later Daddy would be here. Many times he couldn't return to this home because he worked so much in his office an hour away.

Tonight Daddy came to us with the greatest smile. He was so exciting. The others jumped on him, pulling hands and legs, but I didn't. I was almost thirteen. I just gave him a hug.

"Helga, you're already a lady," he said. "So are you, Hilde. Helmut, take care of these ladies. Ah, here's Holde, you're so pretty. All of your are. Look at Hedda. What a doll. And Heide, my baby. I can't imagine you're already four."

Dinner with Daddy was special. We had a big table and everyone talked as much as possible. Mommy smiled more and so did our governess. I was thankful but so concerned I said, "Daddy, who are all those people walking by? I see more every day."

"Don't worry," he said. "I'm going to take care of all of you."

ON THE RIVER
By Marshal Georgi Zhukov

We were there, on the ancient eastern border of the Huns, at the line they should never have crossed, on the long Oder River, only fifty miles from Berlin, but blocked now by quite a few Germans dug in ready to die.

Some generals wanted to rush on to Berlin. They thought taking the capital meant winning the war. That wouldn't definitely be so unless we first crushed those threatening us from other places. In particular, I was concerned about enemies against the Baltic Sea north of us.

"Don't ever tell me when," I said. "I only attack at the right time. We've stretched ourselves three hundred miles in three weeks. We need to build up supplies and transports in our immediate rear.

"You must be too stupid to see there's a thaw. We can't move in this mud. Look at the Oder. It's no longer frozen. Are you going to swim across? Don't tell me. I always know when."

OUR HERITAGE
By Wernher von Braun

As a child I'd often dreamed of making many long and sleek rockets that could soar away from earth and into the heavens. Driven by relentless energy, I rose by my late teens to be a leading researcher in those efforts, and at age twenty-five became director of our special weapons program. That was several years ago, when Hitler thought we were primarily eccentric if not thoroughly incompetent. Then he saw our film and heard me explain, and at once he too understood the future. It was there, in the sky.

"This will win the war," Hitler said.

My colleagues and I weren't convinced of that. Our big rockets four-stories high soared sixty miles into the sky but carried a modest explosive less than a ton. We needed many months of production to deliver the same amount of destruction as one Anglo-American bombing raid. To us it was more stimulating to think of sending men into space, and even to the moon and Mars. We could do anything and often drew our dreams on paper and encouraged journalists to do the same. After some of our ideas were published last year, Himmler arrested me and a few others. We were wasting time on peaceful pursuits, he said. That was a crime.

We got out pretty soon. Someone understood. We'd given adequate effort to killing. When that ended, we'd need to help. We took a vote. It was unanimous who would receive our heritage.

INADEQUACIES
By Benito Mussolini

I should never have trusted the Germans. Their generals were idiots who'd blundered in Africa, and in the Balkans, and especially in Russia because they hadn't understood politics. Neither had Hitler. And their incompetence cost me so much. If I'd run the war, the situation would be quite different now. Of course, I still could salvage things. Many Italians were impressed by the solidarity and power of the communists. I might make a deal with Russia and crush the democracies. If it were more expedient, then I'd come to an accommodation with Churchill. Only Hitler was preventing that. He was a bad ally and unworthy of the German people. He lacked my spiritual qualities and did not understand Italians. What a mistake he'd made last year by declaring Rome and Florence open cities. That made the conquest of Italy too easy. If I'd been in charge, we'd have fought in every street and every building until everything was destroyed, and there would have been no ridiculous worries about preserving works of art.

THIS DANCE
By A German Officer

I was delighted to be invited to the Chancellery on February fifth, 1945. I'd been there several times, but always for business. This time there was a party.

"Will you dance with me?" she said.

"Of course, Fraulein Braun. And happy birthday to you."

"This isn't my best birthday."

"I suppose not."

The record had a lot of scratches but still sounded great.

"You haven't danced in a while," she said.

"I haven't had a chance."

"Were you better before?"

"A little."

"I can't find a good man to dance with."

"Have you danced with the Fuehrer?"

"The Fuehrer doesn't do things like that."

I struggled to find the rhythm.

"You're a marvelous dancer, Fraulein Braun. Like so many ladies here."

"Look at her. She's too fat. I'd never let myself get like that. And that looks like a tramp. This party's full of bad dancers and tramps. I'll never have to see any of them again. The Fuehrer's making me go to the Berghof."

COMMAND DECISION
By General Heinz Guderian

We, a people brutally short of manpower, had twelve good divisions needlessly out of action, cut off in Courland next to the Baltic Sea. Furthermore, along the Oder River, the enemy salient was thrust at Berlin like a hungry head.

"The Russians are strengthening this vital area with three or four divisions a day," I told Hitler on February ninth. "We must attack there, and we must do so immediately. Your planned offensive in Hungary is completely out of the critical area of operations. We have a better opportunity now, we have an obligation, to decapitate the most threatening enemy forces. I must stress, again, that this opportunity won't last long."

"What would be required?" Hitler said.

"All forces must be withdrawn from Courland. They can still be evacuated by sea and air."

"That's out of the question. German forces fight where they are."

"They aren't fighting there. They're sitting."

"The Navy and Luftwaffe are otherwise engaged."

"Their contributions are limited. At least now they could evacuate fighting troops to help strike the Russians and, perhaps, gain us some time to negotiate with the West."

"I won't negotiate," Hitler said.

"That's not all. You must also withdraw our forces from Norway, and the Balkans, and Italy. Only by amassing these reserves would we have a chance to decisively beat the massive Russian spearhead. I assure you, Mein Fuehrer, that I'm acting solely in Germany's interest."

Straining to his feet, he said, "How dare you speak to me like that. My whole life has been a struggle for Germany. You've done nothing by comparison. You're unqualified to speak that way."

I shot up and replied, "I insist that our troops be evacuated from Courland at once."

Hitler stormed over and brandished fists in my face as he shouted. I grimaced at him until a staff officer grabbed the back of my jacket and pulled me away.

Unable to sustain the harangue, Hitler melted into his chair and said, "All right, you can have your counterattack. But it will be limited to those forces already available to Reichsfuehrer Himmler and his Army Group Vistula."

That was enough for my bad heart today. I rested a little and prepared for a showdown. On February thirteenth, after another tiring forty-minute drive from military headquarters, I was back at the Chancellery.

"Mein Fuehrer," said Himmler. "We must postpone our attack. Some of our gasoline and ammunition haven't been unloaded."

"We can't wait until the last bullet has been issued," I said. "The Russians will soon be too strong."

"Don't accuse me of wanting to wait," Hitler said.

"I'm not accusing you of anything. There's just no sense in waiting until another opportunity has been lost."

"I told you not to accuse me of wanting to wait."

"My principal adviser, General Wenck, must be attached to the Reichsfuehrer's staff and put in charge of the actual attack. Otherwise, there's no chance of succeeding."

"The Reichsfuehrer is man enough to lead this attack," Hitler said.

"The Reichsfuehrer isn't a soldier. He doesn't have the experience to command such a complex military operation. His staff, which includes many SS officers, is also lacking. General Wenck must therefore be in effective control."

"How dare you criticize the Reichsfuehrer?"

"How dare you foist the Reichsfuehrer on the Army, and the German people, who've suffered so much."

Hitler rumbled up. So did I.

"I told you not to criticize the Reichsfuehrer," he said.

Himmler watched like a servant. Hitler's face was flushed, his eyes bulging and bloodshot.

"I insist that General Wenck be placed in charge," I said.

"How dare you speak to me like that?"

Hitler turned and started to pace back and forth. When he stopped, we were nose to nose.

"I won't tolerate you insulting the Reichsfuehrer, or me."

"General Wenck must be in charge."

Hitler again jerked away into petty pacing before walking right up to me.

"The General Staff is a disgrace," he said. "I can only depend on the SS."

"The Reichsfuehrer's adversaries have been quite different than the ones now confronting him."

"You're insubordinate."

"I must insist that General Wenck be attached to the Reichsfuehrer's staff."

Hitler turned and paraded toward the fireplace. Rather than look at his hunched back, I gazed at Bismarck in a portrait hanging over the mantel. The Iron Chancellor had been a master of defining limitations and succeeding within them. Right now he seemed alive, glaring at me through dark light to demand: "What are you fools doing?"

Hitler walked back.

"I could replace you."

"You could. Or you could provide a qualified military man for this critical front."

Hitler moved to the Reichsfuehrer and said, "Well, Himmler, General Wenck will arrive at your headquarters tonight and take charge of the attack."

After sitting down Hitler gave me a crooked smiled and said, "The General Staff has won a battle this day."

YALTA
By Joseph Stalin

I liked President Roosevelt. He was a fine gentleman and statesman, and at our Yalta conference only his health concerned me. Churchill, by contrast, was a feisty dog, good as an ally but, I believe, anxious to someday have me as an enemy. If that were the case, Mr. Churchill, or anyone else, would first have to cross a big buffer zone. Much of central and Eastern Europe was, by agreement, going to remain under Soviet influence.

President Roosevelt understood the need for this and told me he was thankful that on D-Day four times more Germans had been in the East than the West. No one really tried to ignore our dominant role in the war. Accordingly, we would occupy the largest zone of a dismembered Germany. I agreed to let the French have one of the occupation zones. This I did out of kindness since the French hadn't done much fighting.

Generosity characterized most of my negotiations, and I promised to help my allies by declaring war on Japan two months after the war in Europe ended. For this sacrifice I obtained some quite modest territorial opportunities in the Far East. I also promised the British and the Americans that free elections would be held in Eastern Europe. I was determined to be just as helpful to these allies as I had tried to be with the Germans. They'd betrayed me, and committed vast atrocities, but I still announced that our dignity as Russian soldiers should compel us to start going easier on enemy civilians in that vanquished land.

FASCHING
By A German

Lots of Germans had brought their belongings and moved into public buildings and our wonderful park, Grosser Garten, making this by far the biggest of the grand Fasching celebrations we'd ever had in Dresden, and our first since 1939. We'd missed Fasching so much. It was the finest carnival in the world. I loved all the beautiful costumes, and many happy people were singing and plenty drinking very good beer and everyone was talking with a smile. This was Fasching in Dresden, a special place where ornate buildings blended with churches and museums to evoke the best in our forefathers and the best in us.

We were very happy all day on February thirteenth and not at all ready for bed that night. After swigging some more fine brown beer, I looked into a sky of brilliant red. The incredible color surely came from heaven and not from the enemy. Even in war it was understood no one could benefit by destroying a splendid opera house, or a great palace, or a famous castle. No, these monuments to the spirit had long stood and would stand forevermore under a night now redder still.

And loud. Very loud. It was so loud I soon couldn't hear. I only saw flames, and ran from them into more flames. This was part of the festival, I soon realized. Only during Fasching could things be this splendidly hot. I stopped and drank more beer. Oh, this was quite a sight, a sight you'll never see, so beautiful in flames taller than buildings, so compelling that everything around was fuel for celebration.

RETURN DRIVE
By General Walther Wenck

I couldn't stay awake, but I couldn't sleep. After briefing the Fuehrer, I had to return to the front. My driver was asleep in back. We'd been awake for three days of modest advances against Zhukov's forces. He had so many. I planned to keep driving, though. To get back to the front I had to stay awake. I put a cigarette in my mouth. I was too tired to smoke. I just chewed. That felt good in my mouth. I tried not to swallow. Then I tried to. The bitterness in my throat helped. I was getting comfortable now. I was sure I could get back. I knew I would. I was going so fast. I came to after they operated on my broken head.

UNDERSTANDING
By Heinrich Himmler

My stomach was in very bad pain. No one could imagine how I felt. I hadn't wanted my obligation any more than the Americans had wanted to exterminate the Indians. Cleansing simply must take place for a nation to grow, but it is a terrible burden.

I spent a lot of time at the sanitarium. Massages relieved me sometimes. The horrors still mounted. I did not have enough men to stop the Russians. The Fuehrer would be furious. I knew that. I needed someone to understand. I was trying to help. I was making many diplomatic overtures. People trusted me and wanted to talk. I told the vice president of the Swedish Red Cross that his organization could work in concentration camps, especially where Norwegians and Danes were interned. I also told the former president of Switzerland I would be happy to send twelve hundred Jews to his country every fortnight. The Swiss francs he offered for each one would not be for me. They would pay for transportation.

ANNIVERSARY
By Martin Bormann

This was a very special occasion — the twenty-fifth anniversary of the founding of the party — and important officials from all over the country were here in Berlin.

"Don't ask the Fuehrer any questions after the speech or during lunch," I told them.

"I must speak to him about Dresden," said a unit leader.

"He's already had ten days of reports."

"He still can't imagine the fires."

"Certainly he can. Look. Berlin's burning right now."

"Not like Dresden. They bombed us twice that night and again in the morning."

"Berlin's bombed all the time," I said.

"You haven't lost a hundred thousand people in one night, have you?"

"We're all suffering."

"Have you stacked arms and legs and watched them burn? I want to know what the Fuehrer's going to do."

"He's going to do plenty. He'll explain in his speech."

With great effort the Fuehrer told the officials that better jets were soon coming to destroy every enemy bomber and save us. Other miracles were also imminent.

At lunch the Fuehrer was informal and relaxed. He assured the men: "Certainly we're concerned about the architecture, I more than anyone. I was going to be an architect, you may know. Of course. Everyone knows. I love architecture and have done more for it than any man. Don't worry. Germany will be better than you can imagine. I guarantee that."

I pushed a note to the Fuehrer.

"Gentlemen, please excuse me, I must go," he said.

The Fuehrer got up and walked very well out the room.

"Oh my God," someone said.

"Gentlemen, we'll talk more in two weeks," I said, then turned and hurried toward the Fuehrer.

FORTRESS BERLIN
By Joseph Goebbels

Regular rations were enough for me. Usually I didn't even eat those. I sacrificed so much. Everyone was aware. I now served the Fuehrer as official Defender of Berlin. Every foot was going to be defended. Every street would be an aisle of enemy misery and death. The Russians were already in a terribly precarious situation, so overextended they threatened to snap. I reminded everyone. Many times people who seemed irretrievably doomed had reversed everything by superhuman effort. That is what Germany required. I made sure everyone understood. If I ever saw a white flag I'd blow up the whole street.

AT THE RHINE
By An American Soldier

I got sick hearing about some big goddamn river that was supposedly the last great natural barrier into the heart of Germany. Screw the Rhine. We'd cross it when we came to it, and for a hundred miles up and down our line that's where we were. But I didn't look at it much. I didn't care for rivers, and that includes the Mississippi. I was more interested in Cologne, on our side of the Rhine. You could tell it had once been a beautiful city. The buildings in a way still looked good. That big cathedral was the best. Even blasted and scorched, it was so pretty.

There was quite a bit to do in Cologne once we booted the

Germans back over the Rhine. I went to the zoo almost every day. This, too, had clearly been a very fine place, but now most of the animals were dead. Those lions had really been something. I hated seeing them like that. In a fair fight, imagine what they'd have done. Same for the elephants. I'd never seen those big old things on their sides. Hell of a shame. Thank goodness a hippo and two monkeys were alive. The monkeys were scared of me so I didn't get to know them. But that hippo was great. I fed him all the time and he got so he opened his mouth when he saw me coming. I even patted him once. Ordinarily, he probably wouldn't have let me do that.

DEMOLITION
By A German Engineer

My fellow Germans led me into the farmhouse. On a couch in the living room sat three judges. They had been rushed in for the Flying Special Tribunal West.

"You've betrayed your country," said the head judge.

"I've always served my country with absolute commitment," I said.

"How can you justify not blowing up the Ludendorff Bridge?"

"We tried. The key was turned."

"You were incompetent in preparing the bridge for demolition."

"No sir. I made sure at least sixty charges were placed at critical points on the bridge."

"Yet it didn't blow up," said the head judge.

"Evidently the circuit had been broken. The Americans were shelling the bridge."

"Why wasn't the bridge destroyed before the Americans got within range?"

"We wanted to blow the bridge a few days earlier. The only reason we didn't was because of the Fuehrer."

"Don't speak like that."

"He threatened to court-martial anyone who blew up a bridge over the Rhine too soon."

"It was your duty to know the precise moment."

"I did. The damn thing just wouldn't blow."

"And you were too spineless to do anything else."

"That's not true. Even though we were under heavy fire, we detonated the emergency charge. And it worked."

"It did not."

"It exploded. The bridge jumped up. I thought it was going to collapse."

"But you failed, and the Americans crossed the Rhine at Remagen."

"We tried one more time, with a hundred engineers bringing up a large explosive."

"You were too cowardly to use it."

"The Americans killed or captured most of us."

"I see you got away."

"I was very lucky."

"Not after betraying the Fatherland."

OUR CITY
By Eva Braun

Munich was still our home. Its ruins were very familiar and so much a part of where we had always lived. I loved my city and stared at it all the way to the house. In front I got out and hurried to the door, and after it opened I hugged Herta Schneider. She was my special friend. Years ago, before the Fuehrer had loved me, I could tell her how I felt. And whenever my parents were so mean I had to get out, she invited me to stay.

"Herta, this is still Munich," I said.

"It almost is," she said. "I hear it's better than Berlin."

"It's much better than Berlin."

Herta's children came in, and I kissed them. We talked and played all afternoon, and we were so happy.

"I could've been a good mother, Herta."

"You still can be."

"It might be too late."

"It's not that late."

"I better be going. The Fuehrer doesn't want me in a car at night."

"I'm glad you're going to the Berghof. It's much safer there. I'll come up in a few days and we'll go boating."

"We've had such lovely times together, Herta."

I kissed her and went back to the house the Fuehrer had given me so long ago. It was a wonderful place. I made sure it would be taken care of, and that my dogs would be, too, and put most of my jewelry and photo albums in very safe places. Everything was ready the afternoon I spent at my parents' apartment.

"You'll cheer up at the Berghof," said my mother.

"Yes, that always helps."

"You can take nice walks, and this summer you can go swimming all the time."

"Everything will be better by then."

"Be careful, Eva. And call us if you can."

I embraced my mother and did not want to let go.

Soon, on March fourteenth, I sat in back of my black Mercedes and thanked the young officer for agreeing to drive. Out on the road he told me to be alert. Our enemies had lots of planes, but I hoped they were somewhere else. This was a peaceful drive, and in a little while we had company, traveling behind an Army truck. I felt the rhythm of its gentle turns, swaying left and right in the back seat of a beautiful trip to Berlin. I was going home. I was getting closer to the Fuehrer and feeling happy, then cringing under a thunderous force and watching the truck shatter into flames, and jerking the door handle and dashing now with the driver to an air raid shelter. This was the first time I'd been in one in public. The people were very quiet and brave, and I tried to be that way, too. No one paid us special attention. They didn't know who I was. It didn't matter now. We were all in the shelter, listening to bombs. I knew they had to stop, and eventually they did.

We then drove the rest of the way to Berlin. Everything had changed. Craters and trees choked the streets, and the Chancellery now had big chunks blown from all its walls. I walked inside and straight to the Fuehrer's private study. He was sitting on the couch, talking to Magda Goebbels and some secretaries. Almost smiling, I watched him. When he noticed me, he was so surprised he just kept looking, unable to say a word. Then he got up and marched over.

"I told you to go to the Berghof," he said. "It's much too dangerous here. You shouldn't have..."

I wrapped my hands around his soft ones and knew I was looking at the happiest man in the world.

George Thomas Clark

THE NEW LINZ
By Adolf Hitler

The model of Linz was huge and very realistic, just as I'd sketched, and I so much enjoyed examining the city as it would soon be when I transformed it into the artistic capital of Europe. I was at the same time sad, however, since I knew I could never realize this — or any other — profound aspiration unless I at once acted in the most brutal and decisive manner, and destroyed all German industrial, transportation, and agricultural facilities along with every communications outlet and bridge. Only the enemy would benefit if these measures were not taken. But I was not even briefly conceding he would get here. I spoke rather of stopping the enemy in a wasteland dominated by fire and torment.

I had explained all this at conferences, and was now doing so again with even greater commitment. All Germans civilians in threatened areas would have to be evacuated. They were interfering with military operations and at times even begging, and convincing, German officers not to use their towns as fortresses. This was intolerable.

"But, Mein Fuehrer, there are no trains available," said a general.

"Then let them walk," I said.

"The people don't even have adequate shoes."

"We can no longer concern ourselves with the population."

That ended the conference.

"Mein Fuehrer, may I please speak to you?" said Albert Speer.

"Ah, Herr Speer, it's our sacrifice we can't be enjoying your beautiful architecture in the Chancellery. These days it's more expedient to carry out business in my bunker. That will pass.

"I'm delighted you're here. You've done so much for a man of only forty. Happy birthday. Here's your picture. I wanted to write something appropriate for a fellow artist. I hope you can read it. I've been having trouble writing."

"I can make it out. Thank you for the sentiments. Our collaboration has indeed been long and beneficial. I therefore hope you understand. It's my duty to give you this."

He handed me a memorandum.

"I've already been briefed about its contents."

"Have you read it?"

"Not yet."

"Will you, please?"

"I will respond in writing."

"Mein Fuehrer, it makes no sense for us to strike at the very life of our nation."

"It's others who are doing that."

"No one has the right to presume that the fate of the nation is tied to his personal fate."

"That's absurd. If the war is lost, the people will also be lost. It's unnecessary to worry about their needs for primitive survival. They will have proved to be weaker, and the future will belong exclusively to the stronger race in the East. You must remember. After this struggle only the inferior will remain. The good will have already been killed."

JETS
By A German Pilot

I saw those bastards looking big even so far away they should have looked small. They were American bombers coming to strike us again. I knew how terrified the runts inside were. Right at them my jet roared at five hundred forty miles an hour, searing straight into more than a thousand bombers, at least. That was ridiculous, and so goddamn obscene. Long ago our Messerschmitt 262's could have wiped the enemy from German skies. We would have if Hitler hadn't meddled.

"He should suffer for this," I told my commander.

"Don't speak like that."

"How many hundreds of jets have been lost? Only an idiot tries to turn a revolutionary fighter into a bomber."

"Quiet."

"Now that he's finally let a fighter be a fighter, we don't have any pilots."

"We have pilots."

"We have bodies," I said.

At least I had plenty of practice, and the big bastards were easy to hit. I felt one blow even before it did. I knew it. They didn't have a chance. And neither did our under-trained bodies being shot down right and left, flaming fast in the world's greatest fighter.

George Thomas Clark

OVER THE RHINE
By General George S. Patton

General Courtney Hodges was a hell of a soldier and his men from the First Army deserved to get lucky and find the one bridge over the Rhine the Germans failed to destroy. Courtney still hadn't expanded his bridgehead much — it was only a few miles deep — but that wasn't his fault. He didn't have enough men. Now General Bradley planned to give him nine divisions, with orders to wait until after March twenty-third to attack. A hundred miles to the south, I was supposed to wait, too.

This nonsense came from Eisenhower as a concession to Montgomery, who craved the glory of being the first to cross the Rhine in force. Ike failed to comprehend the real situation. He lacked command experience and had no feel for battle. Politics interested him more than fighting a war. I told several officers to just wait. They'd soon see Ike running for president. That's why he hadn't supported me when I slapped those two cowards in Sicily. He always wanted to appear proper, even if it cost American lives. I knew goddamn well that waiting now would mean burying more of our boys. I wasn't going to do it, not for Ike or a son of a bitch like Montgomery. If he got across first, the bulk of supplies would flow north to him, and he'd slow things down with weeks of unnecessary preparation.

We had to attack. The goddamn enemy was either already on the run or waiting to if we kicked him in the ass. I told my men from the Third Army, keep driving toward the Rhine. Drive hard and don't stop. You must trust me. I've been here. Two thousand years ago I was a Roman. I can smell the legions. God has ordained all of this. Drive on. To the Rhine. That's it. Keep moving. Don't ever stop. Before sundown on March twenty-second we reached the Rhine at Oppenheim. Monty was going to need artillery and airplanes and paratroopers. My men did not. That night they quietly began to cross the river in assault boats. By morning most of one division was over, and I charged to the phone.

"Brad, I'm across."

"The Rhine?" said General Bradley.

"Sure. Tell the world, for God's sake."

IN THE HOLE
By A Secretary

All right. I realized we could not work in the Chancellery anymore. No one imagined ever doing that again. So several of us on the clerical and other support staffs asked the Fuehrer directly: "Wouldn't it be better to move headquarters to the Berghof?"

"How can I ask my troops to defend Berlin unless I'm also here and prepared to accept their fate?"

Maybe I was also ready to sacrifice for the Fatherland, but did not want to do so in a tomb like the Fuehrer Bunker. To get there I had to climb down one flight of cold cement steps to the steel door entrance. Once the SS let me through, I descended another flight to a tight corridor stinking under a foot of water. Carefully I walked across boards to a door leading to more steps. They crawled down to the upper level, where we lived in twelve small rooms. To work I walked further into the hole until reaching the lower level. This was where the Fuehrer and Martin Bormann and Joseph Goebbels and a few others stayed.

The corridor here was at least fifty feet long and ten wide, and on the walls hung wonderful Italian paintings framed in gold. Looking at the paintings was a fine diversion and always fun except when I tripped on one of the fire hoses. Things had gotten bad before they'd been able to finish the plumbing.

BRAVE MEN
By General Heinz Guderian

Military reports from the East were alarming. We continued to launch futile counterattacks instead of withdrawing. This whole thing burned me on a long ride through destruction to the bunker.

"The commanders didn't fire enough artillery shells," said Hitler.

"They fired all they had," I said.

"Then you didn't send them enough."

"Here. Look at the figures. I sent all I was allotted. And every shell sent was fired."

"In that case the troops let me down."

"I must ask you not to make accusations against brave men."

"The men are unworthy of being German soldiers."

"They suffered unusually heavy casualties. Their self-sacrifice has been remarkable. I therefore insist that you not make accusations."

The old man got up and shouted: "I am the Fuehrer."

"Is the Fuehrer going to evacuate his surrounded troops?"

"Never."

I jumped up stomping toward him. Someone grabbed me around the waist.

"You have no right to belittle the brave men you've sent to their deaths," I yelled. "Your orders are without purpose. They're outrageous. Evidently I haven't said enough. I'm sick of this. I want those men evacuated. Does the Fuehrer understand? I said, 'Do you understand?' Do you understand anything?"

I was pulled further back and told I had a phone call. After that I returned to the conference. Hitler was sitting in a sulk.

"I must ask everyone to leave the room except General Guderian and Field Marshal Keitel," he said.

The officers solemnly walked out.

"General, your health requires that you immediately take six weeks convalescent leave."

I saluted the Fuehrer, my right arm tired but straight.

SPARE TIME
By Hermann Fegelein

"Hermann, no," Eva said. "You're my brother-in-law."

"That doesn't matter now," I said.

"Be sensible."

"You want to."

"Don't say that."

"I can tell."

"You certainly cannot."

HOPE
By Albert Speer

The Fuehrer did not shake hands or return my greeting.

"I have Bormann's report," he said. "You've been urging officials not to carry out demolitions or follow my orders. Are you aware of the consequences? If you weren't my architect, I'd take the ordinary measures."

"I ask for no consideration as an individual," I said.

"You're tired and ill. I've decided you're to go on leave immediately."

"I'm fine. I'm not going on leave."

"You have no choice. For political reasons, I can't dismiss you."

"I must continue my duty."

"Only if you can convince yourself the war is not lost."

"The war is lost."

"So many times I've been written off. After the Putsch in 1923. When we had election setbacks in the late twenties. Every time Hindenburg denied me the chancellorship. Before Munich. Almost everyone said I was doomed. Defeatism was even worse before I attacked France. And nothing was as bleak as our first winter in Russia. But I overcame everything. So did you. No one except I believed you'd be a worthy armaments minister."

"I don't want to be like those who tell you they believe in victory when they don't."

"You have twenty-four hours to at least hope the war can still be won."

The next day I went back. Hitler was on his feet.

"Well?" he said.

"Mein Fuehrer, I stand unreservedly behind you."

He firmly shook my hand and said, "Then all is well."

"Indeed. I must therefore again be entrusted with the implementation of your decree regarding demolitions."

"Draw up the document, and make sure it emphasizes the destruction of factories and bridges. Then I'll sign it."

George Thomas Clark

LAST REDOUBT
By Hans Kammler

I had flurried to push back our V-2 launch sites and test ranges, and as the enemy approached I'd ordered more evacuations. He'd bombed us en route but we soon got ready to fire and did. In a little while I'd retreated and set up again and last month fired two final rockets at London. By then I had also taken control of the V-1 flying bombs, and we'd quickly released a few more before the enemy forced us out of range.

I still had more underground factories, our last redoubts. Tunnels had been drilled and facilities expanded. Maybe the enemy didn't know about this one. He might simply have been advancing in the area. We left and hurried to another. Research was proceeding so well. We'd soon be firing rockets across the Atlantic. Right now we had to evacuate. In my private train I took several hundred V-2 scientists to the Bavarian Alps where I prepared an astounding offer for the Americans.

ALLIED ACTION
By Joseph Stalin

General Eisenhower was correct. Berlin had indeed lost its strategic significance. I sent him a personal message declaring the Soviet High Command would allot only secondary forces to the German capital. We too planned to concentrate in the areas south of Berlin and link up with our allies there.

568

SUPERPOWERS
By Adolf Hitler

The future was glorious and assured. Germany would always be essential. America and Russia were going to learn. The laws of history and geography doomed them to a monumental clash, if not militarily then certainly in economics and ideology. Neither side could prevail unless it had the support of the only great nation left in Europe. That applied now. That applied forever.

VOLKSSTURM
By A German Boy

I didn't have to go to bed early anymore. Neither did my friends. We were in the People's Militia and got to wear armbands and shoot rifles. Sometimes I got to shoot the grenade launcher too. Last night was best. I almost hit a Russian tank. It turned and fired at us incredibly hard. I can't believe some of us got away. I'd never run that fast, and my grandfather said he probably hadn't either.

INTERVENTION
By Adolf Hitler

Only the boldest stroke would suffice, and only I knew what it was. We would gather troops from places the pessimists claimed we had none, and we would arm them with weapons the defeatists said did not exist. These new forces would then liberate our three hundred thousand troops surrounded in the Ruhr, and together charge West with enough fanaticism to drive the Americans and British either into the sea or an armistice.

That was destiny, and destiny could not forsake me. Goebbels' call of congratulation proved that on April twelfth. Roosevelt was dead. The eternal supporter of Jewry had vanished. The coalition against us was doomed.

569

INSANITY
By General George S. Patton

Give me something to do. I can't stand visiting more concentration camps or watching broken people limp from shattered homes. The road to Berlin is open. Why are we stopping? This is insane. There is no glory in this. Everything is coming to an end. I must attack the communists before I die.

POISE
By Eva Braun

"You really are going to have to start controlling yourself," I said.
"They're incompetent. They're idiots. They're traitors."
"They're loyal and they're doing their best for you."
"It's not enough."
"It's difficult for everyone," I said.
"They need to understand."
"They do."
"They've got to be motivated."
"Your tantrums are demoralizing them. I can see it. You're losing respect."

THE RACE
By Marshal Georgi Zhukov

"The Germans are lying down in the West, inviting the Americans to take Berlin," said Stalin. "I know they won't advance to the south as they've said. Everyone has deceived us all along. When can you attack?"
"April sixteenth," I said.
"I want Berlin first. We can't tolerate the new enemy getting so close to our frontier. Are you sure you're ready?"
"I am, Comrade Stalin."
I never attacked before I was ready, and no commander in this war,

or any other, was ever so manifestly prepared. I had amassed more than two million men, sixteen thousand big guns and six thousand tanks. The Germans, my intelligence proved, could not counter with even half of that.

My massive blow came in the dark. It was for German treachery and millions of dead Russians. It was for Moscow and Leningrad and Stalingrad and a thousand other ravaged places. It was to end the past and start the future.

OUR LAKE
By Helga Goebbels

I loved Schwanenwerder most. The lake here was glowing now beside bushes green and flowers bright. This was such a pretty place. No tired and dirty people were walking by our houses here. The problem now was in the sky. Every day it grew more orange and loud, and my mother and grandmother were yelling more than ever.

"I want to know," I said.

"Just as I told you," my mother said.

"What would we do?"

"That's not going to happen."

"Where will we go?"

"We don't have to go anywhere. The Fuehrer's going to take care of our enemies, and I'm going to take care of you."

FREEDOM
By Adolf Hitler

Millions of soldiers were trying. But they weren't going to do it. No one ever had. Right now it was beyond imperative no one ever would. Otherwise, there was no doubt. They'd strip me and examine and torture me and laugh at everything they saw. They'd leer at me trembling in a cage. That's what they wanted. That's what they were dying for. They were dying for nothing.

IN THE GARDEN
By Martin Bormann

On this wonderful day the Fuehrer climbed out of the bunker to decorate some brave Hitler Youths in the Chancellery garden. The boys were thrilled to meet him, especially on April twentieth, 1945, his fifty-sixth birthday. Many people came to congratulate the Fuehrer. Goering and Goebbels and Himmler and Ribbentrop and Speer all shook his hand, and most offered the same good advice I had: get out of Berlin and lead our defenses from a better place.

CONVOY
By Hermann Goering

Even though he had stopped believing in me, I was happy to be at the conference in the bunker. It was my duty to be there.

"There isn't much time, Mein Fuehrer," I said. "Only one route south to Berchtesgaden is still open. It could be cut off anytime."

"I can't withdraw to safety at the very moment I order my troops into the decisive battle for Berlin. I demand the city be defended street by street, house by house."

"You're no doubt right, Mein Fuehrer. I shall give you full support from the south. To prepare for that, I must leave Berlin tonight."

"Very well then," the Fuehrer said, and shook my hand weakly.

I hurried to Karinhall. My exquisite paintings and tapestries and rugs had all been carefully packed and loaded onto a convoy of trucks. Nearby, members of my staff lined up. I shook their hands firmly and told them to get away. Charges had been placed throughout the estate. The Russians weren't going to desecrate my monument to Carin. They weren't going to desecrate her, either. Charges were in place at her mausoleum across the lake. I got in my staff car at the head of the convoy and did not look back.

BRIDGES
By Heinrich Himmler

Everyone was harassing me. What could I do? The Fuehrer would never resign. Yet peace was impossible as long as he lived. I didn't mean to say that. What if someone repeated it? I would be killed. Then kill him, I was urged. I couldn't do that. But maybe I'd be able to break through diplomatically after meeting someone from the World Jewish Congress. Late at night I went to a secret estate.

"Good morning, I'm delighted you could come," I told Norbert Masur. "Your being here is so important. I need to tell you, I'm in fact guaranteeing you, that I want to bury the hatchet between us and the Jews. It's time for that. Before we couldn't have. The Jews in our midst were a foreign element which had always caused friction. They were driven out of Germany several times but always returned. When we came into power we wanted to resolve this permanently, and in a humane way, through emigration. We negotiated with many countries that claimed to be friendly toward Jews. But they wouldn't let them in."

"It's against international law to force people from a country where their ancestors have lived for generations."

"Many countries have done so when necessary. We had grave problems after coming into contact with Jews from the East. They were infected by the most severe epidemics, particularly typhus fever. We lost thousands of our best men as a result. The only way to curtail the epidemics was to build crematories to burn the corpses of those who died of these diseases. And now our enemies are trying to get us simply for protecting ourselves.

"We did create part of the misunderstanding by referring to our places as concentration camps. We should have called them reformatories. There weren't only Jews in the camps. Criminals were also there. We were right not to release anyone. In 1941 our crime rate was the lowest in decades. Treatment in the camps was hard but just."

"You can't possibly deny that crimes were committed in the camps."

"It only happened occasionally. And I punished those responsible. I hope you know we executed the commandant of Buchenwald for ill-treatment of prisoners."

"There are many things which cannot be undone. The only way to

573

begin building a bridge between our peoples is for you to ensure that all Jews still in areas dominated by Germany remain alive."

"I'd like to help. I've tried to. I left four hundred thousand Jews in Hungary. But what thanks did I get? The Jews shot at our troops in Budapest."

"I'm afraid there are far fewer Jews in Hungary than that. But even if your figures are accurate, that still leaves four hundred thousand who've vanished."

"The press makes it so difficult to help. Every time I turn over a camp, the enemy photographs the guards with corpses. Then atrocity stories are spread. When I release more Jews, the enemy claims I'm only doing it for an alibi. I don't need an alibi. I take full responsibility for doing everything to fill the needs of my people."

"Jews weren't responsible for the newspaper stories."

"They controlled the press."

"They were in custody. And I'd like to emphasize that it isn't only Jews who are determined to rescue surviving Jews. Many other countries are interested. German cooperation would have a good effect. Right now is a particularly good time to help the women prisoners near here, in Ravensbruck."

"I can release a thousand women at once, but their arrival in Sweden must be kept secret. I suggest they be designated 'Polish' rather than 'Jewish.'"

MEDICATION
By Doctor Theodore Morell

As I filled my syringe to inject the Fuehrer, he seized my arm and pushed me away.

"I know exactly what you plan to give me," he yelled.

"Just a little caffeine."

"You're trying to inject me with morphine."

"No, Mein Fuehrer. Here, look, this is caffeine."

"You want me so drugged out you and the generals can kidnap me."

"Dear no, Mein Fuehrer."

"Do you think I'm crazy?"

"Of course not."

"I'll have you shot. I'll shoot you myself. Get out of that uniform. You're not my physician. Act as if you've never seen me."

Still weak from my recent stroke, I crumpled under the Fuehrer.

"Take that uniform off and get out. I don't need drugs to see me through."

CONFESSION
By Albert Speer

For more than fifty miles heading north out of Berlin the road was overflowing with machines: cars, trucks, motorcycles, even limousines and fire trucks. They all blocked my way to Hitler, the man I most wanted to see. I had not said enough on his birthday and was now compelled to risk two flights through enemy-dominated skies before my pilot landed on a wide avenue near Brandenberg Gate. Not far away, beneath the ground, lived the man who had given me the chance to organize spectacular rallies and be a key member of a great movement. There was the visionary who had entrusted me as his architect for eternity. There awaited the warrior who had insisted I invigorate a vast munitions industry to save the nation.

"The Fuehrer is ready to see you," an adjutant said.

I walked down stairs to face the most important man in everyone's life.

"What do you think?" he said. "Should I stay here or fly to Berchtesgaden?"

"Stay here as the Fuehrer. You couldn't do anything in Bertchtesgaden if Berlin falls."

"I, too, have decided to remain. At the right instant I'll liberate myself from this painful existence."

"I'm prepared to stay here with you," I said.

The Fuehrer did not reply.

"I feel I owe you. I must tell you. I haven't carried out the demolitions you ordered."

"Fraulein Braun is going to depart with me," he said.

"In many cases, Mein Fuehrer, I prevented others from carrying out demolitions."

"The critical concern is that my body be properly disposed of."

George Thomas Clark

TREASON
By Martin Bormann

In the radio room I received this explosive message: "Mein Fuehrer, since you are determined to remain in Fortress Berlin, do you agree, in accordance with your 1941 decree, that I as your deputy should assume total leadership of the Reich with complete freedom of action? If by ten p.m. no answer is forthcoming, I shall assume you have been deprived of your freedom of action. I will then consider the terms of your decree in force and will act accordingly for the good of the people and Fatherland."

I marched to the Fuehrer and gave him the message.

"This is unforgivable," I said.

"I see nothing to alarm me."

"Mein Fuehrer, this is a coup d' etat."

"Look at the end, Bormann. The Reich Marshal has blessed me and urged me to join him in Berchtesgaden as soon as possible."

At this moment the Fuehrer was too exhausted to understand. I did not know what to do. The treacherous Goering solved that, sending another telegram, this one to Ribbentrop, urging the Foreign Minister to fly to him at Berchtesgaden.

"Mein Fuehrer, this is treason," I stated. "He's already alerting members of government that he'll take your power as of midnight tonight."

"He won't do that. Send this message. Tell him the 1941 decree of succession is void. I'll exempt him from the normal punishment if he resigns all his offices for reasons of health.

"I've known all along that Goering's a traitor. He's also lazy and incompetent and a filthy drug addict. Our military situation today is in large measure due to the failures of his Luftwaffe."

In about an hour Goering sent his message of resignation.

"Of course, I still want Goering to negotiate with the enemy," said the Fuehrer. "He's better at things like that. If the war's lost, it doesn't matter who surrenders."

Along with the Fuehrer's message, I had privately sent my own demanding that Goering be kept under house arrest. I also ordered: "After our deaths, the traitor of April twenty-three is to be shot."

ENERGY
By Adolf Hitler

You can't imagine how much this helps. I can be so tired I can't think or even imagine an end to tiredness, and I grab a chocolate and another and another and right away I feel so much better. It's incredible. I barely need regular food anymore. I just need more cake. I've always loved it, but never nearly so much as now. I hope I don't run out of soldiers before I run out of cake.

LINK UP
By A Russian Soldier

The soldiers were paddling with rifle butts across the Elbe River. They were this far only because it had been easy. When it had been hard, they weren't even on the continent. They waited while most of the Germans fought us. Now these strange new soldiers were paddling across forbidden waters. One of them stood waving and yelled, "Amerikansky, Amerikansky."

"Amerikansky," I responded.

We helped them ashore and shook hands, and many of us embraced. They looked almost like fascists, but perhaps not as bad.

OUR FAVOR
By Adolf Hitler

This was the most encouraging development of the war and perhaps in all history. The Americans and Russians had met, and already there were reports of tension. Soon they'd be strangling each other.

"I've always said so," I told my generals. "But you didn't believe it. You couldn't understand. Now you'll see. Each side will be begging me to join it. I alone will determine who wins. But my participation will come at a very high price. How everything has changed. You've been telling me I had to negotiate, if not surrender. I tell you all history would revile me as a coward and a criminal if I gave up just when everything is turning in our favor."

THE SOFA
By A Secretary

I never had any idea what time it was unless I looked at my watch. We were working the craziest hours. After the final conference it felt like night but was really about six a.m. The Fuehrer was waiting in his living room. I didn't want to keep him up much longer or it might be too late. I hurried in to receive my orders. The Fuehrer was stretched on the sofa, gazing at the ceiling. He tried so hard to get up, and he made it.

"Really, Mein Fuehrer. You don't have to."

"I certainly do."

All his responsibilities had changed him. In front of a lady the real Fuehrer would never have stood with soup stains on his jacket. I wondered if he knew. His head was wobbling, and saliva dribbled from a corner of his mouth. Maybe he couldn't see himself. His eyes were bloodshot and he wasn't wearing his glasses. He only wore them while working. When he took them off they usually rattled the table until he put them down. Then he forgot where he'd put them.

Without glasses and almost at attention, the Fuehrer gave me my orders for the day.

"Good night, Mein Fuehrer," I said.

"Good night."

A NEW LIFE
By Magda Goebbels

"You must leave today," said the Fuehrer. "This is absolutely the last chance for a plane to fly out of here."

"I want to stay."

"Your children still have a future."

"What kind of future?"

"A good one. They're all smart and beautiful. They wouldn't be hurt."

"They already have been."

"They don't know. Look how happy they are."

"I can't leave them to a world I know would destroy them."

SIGNORA PETACCI
By Benito Mussolini

Wearing a German coat and a German helmet, I sat in the back of a German truck in a German convoy. We were being searched by Italian partisans. I did not acknowledge them. My collar was pulled up, and I simply rested my chin on the butt of a machine pistol squeezed between my knees. Through sunglasses I stared straight at nothing.

A partisan tapped my shoulder and in Italian said: "Comrade."

I did not twitch.

He tapped harder and said: "Excellency."

I ignored him.

"Cavaliere Benito Mussolini," he shouted.

Perhaps I moved a little.

The partisan removed my helmet, took off my sunglasses and deliberately, as a tailor, turned down my collar. Then he took my gun and helped me stand up.

"In the name of the Italian people, I arrest you," he said. "I give you my word that while you're in my custody no one will touch a hair on your head."

"Thank you," I said.

Most of the partisans were very young. At dinner that night I told them, "Youth is beautiful. Yes, I mean it. I love the young even when they bear arms against me."

In private the handsome commander promised to send my regards to a very good friend.

"What is her name?"

"That doesn't matter," I said.

"I'll find out eventually."

"All right. Signora Clara Petacci is her name."

The next day the partisans bandaged my head and started driving me north along Lake Como. At a bridge there was a parked car. After we stopped I stepped into the rain. Clara got out of the other car.

"Good evening, Excellency."

"Good evening, Signora."

"What's happened to you?"

"It's nothing. Merely a precaution."

We were taken to the house of a farmer. He and his wife had prepared a fire for unknown guests. When I took off my bandages, they must have known me. I could tell they suspected. Maybe they just didn't believe.

They were a wonderful couple. They showed us to a bedroom on the third floor. The bed was big and the sheets were clean. I pressed the bed with my hand and said, "It's nice. Thank you."

Two guards were outside but Clara and I were alone inside. She was such a beautiful woman. For twenty years she had loved me, the man, not the Duce, and for a long time I had loved her too. She was so much more than a mistress, she was my reason to survive. A mountain of problems dissolved as I embraced her. It was always this way with Clara. I should have been with her more. History had overwhelmed that. Not anymore. I was regaining my vigor. Where had it been? I'd thought it would never come back. Not without Clara. Now I was with her again, on the wonderful bed prepared by a farmer's wife.

The following afternoon hard footsteps hit the stairs and an older partisan stormed in.

"I've come to rescue you," he said.

"Really," I stated.

"Hurry up."

Stampeded down the stairs, across the yard, through a small town square, and into a car with two men on the running board, we were driven a short way.

"I heard a noise," the partisan said, easing out. "Be very quiet. I'll check ahead."

He did so and slipped back toward us.

"Hide near that gate," he whispered.

Clara and I followed his orders. The partisan looked down the road again, then turned and shouted: "By order of my comrades, I am required to render justice to the Italian people."

"He mustn't die," Clara screamed, and embraced me.

"Move away or you'll die too."

Clara let go.

He aimed a machine pistol and pulled the trigger. I felt my chest tear open, but the gun hadn't fired. He snatched his pistol and pulled the trigger. I winced, but this gun hadn't fired either.

"Bring me yours," he said to another partisan.

With the third weapon he finally hammered several bullets into my chest. Clara fell beside me.

FAITH
By Heinrich Himmler

I'd thought a lot but still couldn't decide: should I bow or shake hands when I meet Eisenhower? I knew he'd want to see me soon. And within an hour he'd realize Europe without me was doomed. My recent offer to surrender German forces in the West, which only I could do, would save thousands, perhaps millions, of lives on each side. Then I could lead the struggle against the Russians, and after vanquishing them, I would be prepared to establish a new government.

LIFE
By Helga Goebbels

"It's getting louder, Mommy" I said. "Do we really have to die soon?"

"Of course not. It only sounds so bad because brave German soldiers are getting closer to rescue us."

"Can't we get out of here?"

"Why should we? Don't you like being with your Uncle Fuehrer?"

All six of us did enjoy visiting Uncle Fuehrer every day. We also loved to pat his beautiful German shepherd, Blondi, and the little puppies she'd just had. The puppies were so happy with their mother. My younger sisters and brother were like those puppies. Not me.

"Mommy, I don't want to die. Why don't we run away?"

"Quit carrying on. I've already told you your future is better than you can imagine."

HIS GIFT
By Eva Braun

The Fuehrer said since everything else was over we could go ahead. I glided to my room and put on a black silk dress with pink shoulder straps. As I came to his side he told me how beautiful I was. The justice of the peace faced us, then made my dream real: I was Frau Hitler.

TESTAMENT
By Adolf Hitler

This was quite an occasion, unlike any I'd attended. I even drank some champagne. What a dedicated woman I had. Everyone appreciated that. I was very happy but forced to leave the reception to finish dictating my testament early on April twenty-ninth.

To a fine young secretary, and more importantly to history, I explained: "I made a modest contribution as a volunteer in the Great War that was forced upon us, and in the three decades since, all my thoughts and actions have been guided by but one thing — love for my people. For them I have given everything, even my health.

"It is absolutely untrue that I wanted war in 1939. War was desired and instigated solely by international statesmen of Jewish origin or those working for Jewish interests. My many offers to limit armaments, and preserve peace, as late as three days before the outbreak of war, cannot be explained away for all of eternity. Centuries may pass, but out of the ruins of our nation there will arise a new hatred for the people who alone are responsible for our suffering: international Jewry and its helpers.

"I had repeatedly left no doubt that if the people of Europe were again to be treated as mere packages of shares by these international money and finance conspirators, then the people who bear the real guilt for this murderous struggle would also have to answer for it. I also left no doubt that millions of Aryan children would not starve to death nor would millions of men and women be bombed and burned to death without the real culprit suffering his due punishment, though in a more humane way.

"After six years of the most glorious and courageous struggle in history, our forces are now too few to permit further resistance, and my personal resistance has been rendered useless by blinded and characterless scoundrels. I desire to share the fate of the good and brave millions who have chosen to stay with me in the capital. Here I am resolved to remain until my position can no longer be defended. Then I shall die with a joyful heart."

FAMILY MATTERS
By Eva Hitler

I knocked and entered.

"Please excuse me," I said.

"Not now."

"Aren't you finished?"

"I'm adding a second part, expelling Goering and Himmler from the party."

"It's about Fegelein."

"That's already decided."

"But why? Because he was wearing civilian clothes?"

"Because he'd deserted to his home. His pockets were jammed with money, and jewelry, some of it yours."

"He's my brother-in-law."

"He's close to Himmler. It's obvious what that means."

"My sister's pregnant."

"Family matters can't interfere with discipline."

THE DUCE
By An Italian

In Milan they were gathering by the pile of dead fascists.

"Look at them," a woman hissed.

She walked over and spit on the Duce, whose head rested on the bosom of Signora Petacci. A man lunged from the pack and kicked the Duce in the head. Then he kicked him again. Lots of people moved in to kick the bodies. Most wanted a few good swipes at the Duce's head. And I did too. I thought that prudent since I'd long been a fascist. I wondered how many fascists were kicking the Duce now. This passion reminded me of our great days of conquests and glory. And above all it reminded me of our incredible love for the Duce. He was the most popular man in Italy since Caesar. I kicked the Duce's head again. It was swelling to look like a bloody pumpkin. That was enough for me. I stepped back to let others in.

"Don't kick Signora Petacci in the face," a man shouted.

Not many did. When all the bodies were strung up by their feet, you could still tell Signora Petacci was a beautiful woman. You could tell that after a woman climbed on a box and grabbed the Signora's skirt, which dangled around her head, and tucked it between her legs.

BLONDI
By Adolf Hitler

Have you ever seen a dog climb a ladder? My dog can. She could. She's nursing her pups now. But she could do lots of tricks. She's really quite wonderful. Only Fraulein Braun is closer to me. That's why I don't want to look. I'm not going to. O.K. I have to. Otherwise, they might get me. That won't happen. I'll make sure. The poison works. There lies Blondi.

FORTRESS BERLIN
By A German Soldier

More vast than I'd ever imagined, Russia was now indisputably and forever a land of factories, endless factories producing mountains of artillery shells. No one could possibly do this as the Russians. For many days they had been firing a shell every second. At least. That is not the delusion of a broken soul. It is, rather, the entirely rational computation of an earnest soul who carefully noted the process of being broken. I guarantee you, in Berlin there were always shells. They'd just hit right here, a thousand of them shattering this small group of fortified houses. When they stopped here, I heard them elsewhere. Always. More shells. Far enough away they made a rhythmic sound. Dependable and strong they assured me I was still alive. Of course I was. Through choking dust I viewed a city destroyed.

TRUST
By An Adjutant

"Please come here," the Fuehrer said.

I marched right to him.

"I don't want to be an exhibition," he said. "You must make sure. Burn my body completely or they'll put me in a Russian wax museum."

I couldn't reply.

"I'm trusting you with this. Don't betray me like so many others. You'll need gas. Lots of gas. Can you get it?"

"I think so."

"You must be sure. Where is it?"

"There's some buried near here."

"Get it."

"The whole area is under fire."

"That'll let up. Get it then. I want my body drenched. Nothing is to remain. Do you understand?"

READY
By Eva Hitler

I had not been able to eat lunch with the Fuehrer. I was busy getting ready and took plenty of time in the shower. After stepping out I used a soft towel to carefully rub cold water off my skin. My body was firm and nice even though I had not exercised much lately. I massaged the sides of my waist. I wanted to feel good but you never really could in the bunker. I put on a pretty dress and elegant Italian shoes and slipped on a diamond-studded wristwatch the Fuehrer had given me. Then I rubbed on some wonderful perfume and combed my hair just right. It was so important to look good. The Fuehrer was back in his living room now. He had never seen me except when I knew he'd want to. I came in and hugged him and took his hand and eased him onto the sofa and lay my head on his shoulder. I stayed close to him long as I could.

"Are you ready?" he said.

I sat up and nodded. From the sofa we arose, and the Fuehrer opened the heavy iron door. The moment we stepped from our suite I smelled fumes. They almost made me faint. But I could not do that. I was walking arm in arm with the Fuehrer. Solemn people were waiting in a line. The Fuehrer went first and started shaking hands. He could not say anything. I know he wanted to, but that wasn't necessary now. I shook hands with all the men, and I embraced each of the ladies. Choking a little I said to one: "Please try to get out of here. Then tell everyone in Munich farewell."

The Fuehrer and I joined arms and walked back to our suite. I sat on the sofa. He bent over and put his hands on his desk. His back was toward me.

"Darling, please, come here," I said.

"Don't watch me, please don't watch."

"I'd never do that."

FIRE
By Adolf Hitler

Germany had betrayed me again and would suffer for all time. I made sure. My pain would soon end. I took a vial out of my pocket and turned. Eva was so serene on the sofa. She was sitting on her legs curled under, as she often does when relaxing, and she looked quite beautiful. I sat next to her and kissed her forehead and caressed her hair, and said: "This is going to be easy. I've never feared this." I was anxious for the vial. I could not imagine living. What unimaginable horror. No one really wanted to live. I wanted the vial. I bit it and ground my teeth and chewed everything up. This was the deliverance I had so craved. This was my essential act. My will had dominated again.

Everything was arranged. A servant came in and began to cry over me. He hesitated, then pressed my revolver to my skull. That's it. We're positive now. Hurry. Get my wife and me out of here. Take care of us. All of you. Carry us out of this grave. Take us into the sun. Let us feel the sweet air of spring. Let us escape. Pour that gas on. Don't stop. Drench us good. Don't worry about the wind. Strike another match. That's it. Throw it on us. Light this fire. Liberate us forever. Oh thank God. I can feel it. Fire. Glorious fire. Keep it going. Make it hotter. Be certain we're destroyed. Nothing must remain. Don't go away. Ignore those shells. This is for history. This is to save me. Get back here. I need more gas. I need more fire. Where have you been? We're still here. No, God, not in that shallow hole. Not there, under a little refuse. That's not enough. That's not nearly enough, you fools. I told you. The Russians are here. They're poking around. They've found something. They've got what everyone wanted. They've got a stinking corpse.

LIST OF REFERENCES

Bailey, George. *Germans*

Bailey, Thomas and Ryan, Paul B. *Hitler vs. Roosevelt*

Balfour, Michael. *The Kaiser and His Times*

Barnett, Cornelius. *The Swordbearers*

Bauer, Eddy. *World War II Encyclopedia*

Bezymenski, Lev. *The Death of Adolf Hitler*

Bleuel, Han Peter. *Sex and Society in Nazi Germany*

Bruce, George. *The Nazis*

Caidin, Martin. *The Tigers Are Burning*

Carell, Paul. *The Foxes of the Desert*

Carr, William; Cecil, Robert; Cooper, Matthew; Humble, Richard; Kennedy, Paul; Watt, Donald; Zeman, Z.A.B. *Hitler's War Machine*

Chant, Christopher; Holmes, Richard; Koenig, William; *Two Centuries of Warfare*

Chant, Christopher; Humble, Richard; Fowler, William; Shaw, Jenny. *Hitler's Generals and Their Battles*

Churchill, Randolph Spencer. *The Rise and Fall of Anthony Eden*

Churchill, Winston. *The Gathering Storm*

Churchill, Winston. *Their Finest Hour*

Churchill, Winston. *The Grand Alliance*

Collier, Richard. *Eagle Day*

Crookenden, Napier. *Dropzone Normandy*

Dear, I.C.B. *The Oxford Companion to World War II*

Dupuy, T.N. *A Genius For War*

Elstob, Peter. *Battle of the Reichswald*

Fest, Joachim. *Hitler*

Frank, Anne. *The Diary of Anne Frank*

Fuscher, Larry William. *Neville Chamberlain and Appeasement*

Galante, Pierre. *Operation Valkyrie*

Gallo, Max. *Mussolini's Italy*

Gallo, Max. *The Night of the Long Knives*

Garlinski, Jozef. *Hitler's Last Weapons*

Gehlen, Reinhard. *The Service*

Goebbels, Joseph. *The Goebbels Diaries 1939-1941*

Goebbels, Joseph. *The Goebbels Diaries 1942-1943*

Goebbels, Joseph. *The Diaries of Joseph Goebbels, Final Entries 1945*

Gordon, C.D. *The Age of Attila*

Graber, G.S. *The Life and Times of Reinhard Heydrich*

Guderian, Heinz. *Panzer Leader*

Hanser, Richard. *Putsch*

Hart, Liddell. *The German Generals Talk*

Hart, Liddell. *History of the Second World War*

Hastings, Max and Steven, George. *Victory in Europe*

Hegel, G.W.F. *Reason in History*

Hitler, Adolf. *Hitler's Secret Book*

Hitler, Adolf. *Mein Kampf*

Heiber, Helmut. *Goebbels*

Herridge, Charles. *Pictorial History of World War II*

Hoene, Heinz. *The Order of the SS Death's Head*

Hoess, Rudolf. *Death Dealer*

Hoffmann, Peter. *The History of the German Resistance: 1933-1945*

Infield, Glenn B. *Eva and Adolf*

Irving, David. *The Secret Diaries of Hitler's Doctor*

Jablonski, Edward. *Air War, Volume 1*

Jablonski, Edward. *Air War, Volume 2*

Jackson, W.G.F. *'Overlord': Normandy 1944*

Jetzinger, Franz. *Hitler's Youth*

Jones, J. Sydney; *Hitler in Vienna, 1907-1913*

Jukes, Jeffery. *Stalingrad, The Turning Point*

Keegan, John. *Six Armies in Normandy*

Kershaw, Andrew. *Tanks at War, 1939-1945*

Khrushchev, Nikita. *Khrushchev Remembers*

Kisch, Richard. *Bismarck*

Kubizek, August. *The Young Hitler I Knew*

Lang, Jochen von. *Hitler Close Up*

Lang, Jochen. *The Secretary*

Langer, Walter C. *The Mind of Adolf Hitler*

Levanthal, Albert. *War*

Lifton, Robert Jay. *The Nazi Doctors*

Lucas, James. *War on the Eastern Front, 1941-1945*

Macksey, Kenneth and Batchelor, *John H. Tank*

Mamatey, Victor S. and Luza, Radomir. *A History of the Czechoslovak Republic, 1918-1948*

Manchester, William. *The Arms of Krupp*

Manstein, Erich von. *Lost Victories*

Martin, Ralph. *The GI War*

Mastiiny, Vojtech. *The Czechs Under Nazi Rule*

Matanle, Ivor. Adolf Hitler — *A Photographic Documentary*

Morgan, Ted. FDR, *A Biography*

Mosely, Leonard. *The Reich Marshal*

Meissner, Hans-Otto. *Magda Goebbels*

Neumann, Robert and Koppel, Helga. *The Pictorial History of the Third Reich*

Nietzsche, Friedrich. *The Philosophy of Nietzsche*

Nyiszli, Miklos. *Auschwitz*

Payne, Robert. *The Life and Death of Adolf Hitler*

The Propaganda of the Third Reich. Authored by his Ministers of the Third Reich

Reid, W. Stanford. *The Reformation*

Riefenstahl, Leni. *Leni Riefenstahl, A Memoir*

Ritter, Gerhard. *Frederick the Great*

Rothberg, Abraham. *Eyewitness History of World War II: Blitzkrieg Vol. I, Siege Vol. II, Counterattack Vol. III, Victory Vol. IV*

Schuschnigg, Kurt von. *Austrian Requiem*

Schuschnigg, Kurt von. *My Austria*

Seaton, Albert. *The German Army 1933-1945*

Seaton, Albert. *The Russo-German War 1941-1945*

Shirer, William. *A Native's Return*

Shirer, William. *The Rise and Fall of the Third Reich*

Smith, Bradley F. Himmler: *A Nazi in the Making*

Smith, Bradley F. *Reaching Judgment at Nuremberg*

Smith, Dennis Mack. *Mussolini, A Biography*

Snyder, Louis L. *Hitler and Nazism*

Spahr, William J. *Zhukov*

Speer, Albert. *Infiltration*

Speer, Albert. *Inside the Third Reich*

Stierlin, Helm. *Adolf Hitler: A Family Perspective*

Taborsky, Edward. *President Edvard Benes, Between East and West 1938-1948*

Toland, John. *Adolf Hitler Vol. I and Vol. II*

Toland, John. *The Last 100 Days*

Trevor-Roper, H.R. *The Last Days of Hitler*

Vienna — *The Great Cities*
Waite, Robert G.L. *The Psychopathic God, Adolf Hitler*
Warlimont, Walter. *Inside Hitler's Headquarters, 1939-1945*
Winterbotham, F.W. *The Ultra Secret*
Wistrich, Robert. *Who's Who in Nazi Germany*
Young, Peter. *The World Almanac Book of World War II*
Zhukov, Georgi K. *From Moscow to Berlin*

DOCUMENTARIES

Hitler: Black Fox
Hitler: A Career
Hitler's Henchmen
The Secret Life of Adolf Hitler
Triumph of the Will
The Twisted Cross
The Wannsee Conference (docu-drama)
The World At War
Vol. 1 A New Germany
Vol. 2 Distant War
Vol. 3 France Falls
Vol. 4 Alone-Britain
Vol. 5 Barbarossa
Vol. 9 Stalingrad
Vol. 10 Wolfpack
Vol. 11 Red Star
Vol. 12 Whirlwind
Vol. 13 Tough Old Gut
Vol. 15 Home Fires
Vol. 16 Inside The Reich
Vol. 17 Morning
Vol. 18 Occupation
Vol. 19 Pincers
Vol. 20 Genocide
Vol. 21 Nemesis

About the Author

George Thomas Clark is also the author of *The Bold Investor*, *Paint it Blue*, *Death in the Ring*, *Obama on Edge*, and *Echoes from Saddam Hussein*. He has been an ESL teacher, material handler, salesman, newspaper correspondent, and the publisher of a monthly tabloid of features and columns.

www.ingramcontent.com/pod-product-compliance
Lightning Source LLC
Chambersburg PA
CBHW071330020726
47502CB00001B/48